D0212994

hummocks

hummocks

journeys and inquiries among the canadian inuit

JEAN MALAURIE

translated by Peter Feldstein

McGill-Queen's University Press
Montreal & Kingston · London · Ithaca

ISBN 978-0-7735-3200-7

Legal deposit second quarter 2007
Bibliothèque nationale du Québec

Printed in Canada on acid-free paper that is 100% ancient forest free (100% post-consumer recycled), processed chlorine free

This book has been published with the help of a grant from the Consulat Général de France à Québec and with the support of the Minister of Culture, Centre national du livre.

Ouvrage publié avec le concours du Ministère chargé de la culture – Centre national du livre.

McGill-Queen's University Press acknowledges the support of the Canada Council for the Arts for our publishing program. We also acknowledge the financial support of the Government of Canada through the Book Publishing Industry Development Program (BPIDP) for our publishing activities.

Library and Archives Canada Cataloguing in Publication

Malaurie, Jean
Hummocks : journeys and inquiries among the Canadian Inuit, 1960–1967 / Jean Malaurie ; translated by Peter Feldstein.
Translation of part of the ed. first published in French, in 2 vols.: Paris : Plon, 1999.
Includes bibliographical references and index.
ISBN 978-0-7735-3200-7
1. Malaurie, Jean – Travel – Canada, Northern. 2. Inuit. 3. Canada, Northern – Description and travel. 4. Canada, Northern – Discovery and exploration – French. 5. Ethnology – Canada. 6. Anthropologists – France – Biography. I. Feldstein, Peter, 1962– II. Title.
GN673.M3513 2007 305.897'12071 C2006-905923-3

Set in 10/12.5 Minion Pro with Frutiger
Book design/typesetting by Garet Markvoort/zijn digital

contents

THE SENATE OF CANADA

THE HONOURABLE CHARLIE WATT, O.Q.

Ottawa, Canada
K1A 0A4

LE SÉNAT DU CANADA

L'HONORABLE CHARLIE WATT, O.Q.

October 2006

I first met Jean Malaurie when he visited Fort Chimo, now Kuujjuaq, in 1969. As head of a France-Quebec joint mission, he and his colleagues published a report on the shocking conditions we faced in the early 1970s. I invited him to my house and we talked about how to find a remedy to fill the huge economic gap existing between Nunavik and Southern Quebec. We have made progress since the 1970s but we still have a lot to do for our future.

Malaurie was and remains a pioneer. I was delighted to have him applauded by all Senators when he visited Ottawa in 1980. This was the least I could do for our French friend.

Nakurmiik,

The Hon. Charlie Watt, O.Q.
Senator

preface

Nunavut and Nunavik: Guardians of the Canadian Confederation

Northwest Greenland, 16 June 1951. Three men are climbing a glacier with their dogsleds, bound for the legendary polar village of Thule. Two of them are Inuit: Sakaeunguak the shaman and Qaallasoq ("Navel"). The third is me. Our dress consists of animal-skin coats, bearskin pants, and triple-layered boots of seal and bearskin with an outer layer of caribou hide. We are returning from the great solitudes, the deserted lands of Ellesmere Island and Inglefield Land (North Greenland), where I have mapped uncharted coastline and plateaus at a scale of 1/100,000. Throughout my fourteen months of solitude among the Inuit, I have listened, mesmerized, to the mythic tales of a free and happy people.

Suddenly, Sakaeunguak draws the three of us to a halt. Visibility ahead is nil. With his knife, he beats out a rhythm on the cover of a metal can and raises his voice in an agonistic *ayayarpok*, a shamanic song. "A great tragedy looms before us. I sense it." As we continue along our route, Martians come into view in the sky.

Martians ... that would be the United States Air Force, which is here in utter secrecy building the largest offensive air base the Arctic has ever seen. The assignment involves the construction of a runway for bombers targeting Peking and Moscow. It is the height of the Korean War and Comrade Stalin has told Comrade Mao that the time has come to lay waste to capitalism. France and Britain are in no condition to fight, while the United States is disarming.

"We'll need to deploy five hundred thousand Chinese soldiers, Comrade Mao – no, many more than that – against the American divisions in Korea. The Red Army will follow them into battle." Mao declines, viscerally distrustful of Moscow, and peace is secured. For the time being.

On the peninsula, the American troops and their allies begin to fall back, losing Seoul. Soon they will be driven to the beach of Pusan, or to surrender. It is in this context that the Pentagon, in the winter of 1950, has decided that a secret weapon is called for. It has to be an aerial operation since the hundred ships dispatched the previous April are still iced in at Melville Bay to the south. I am the only foreign witness to this top-secret operation, carried out without deigning to consult the 302 Polar Inuit of Thule.

The three of us and our dogs approach the tent of the general heading the operation, who comes out to meet us.

"Who gave a Frenchman clearance to be on this base?" he snaps.

I have recently killed a polar bear, and my hair is long. I might as well be emerging from another age. I stare at him, then respond in kind:

"Who gave you 'clearance' to be on Inuit land, General?"

CHANGING TIMES AND CHALLENGES FOR THE INUIT

The US Air Force's invasion of Thule was followed by the crash, on 28 January 1968, of a B-52 carrying four H-bombs. Three of them exploded on impact, polluting virginal waters, while the fourth was lost and remains a threat to the Far North to this day. And so, in the infernal violence of a veritable invasion, the North American Arctic entered the strategic history books, while the Inuit were put on the front lines of our conflict with the East.

This book is dedicated to the Inuit of Canada. The current generation of Inuit has come through the greatest of perils and responded to them with extraordinary tenacity, thus earning the country's respect. To the east, the Inuit of Greenland have, since 1995, gradually expanded the scope of their self-government initiative. In this, they have built on the structures of "Greenland Home Rule" – a stable governmental apparatus – that the Danish state had gradually enacted over two centuries. Young Greenlanders have received business and administrative training through their involvement in the state agency Kongelige Gronlandske Handel (KGH).

By contrast, in the new, hastily founded territories of Nunavut and Nunavik, economic and social problems have proved particularly troublesome. An expanding economy (e.g., the rapid growth of the Makivik Corporation), a people striving for progress, cannot survive solely on tourism, sales of their artwork, or small-scale fishing. Thus the Inuit are having to face the future with steely determination. They are staring down the barrel of gradual assimilation as they try to regain the inspiration of their past, all the while demonstrating the forward-looking virtues of their civilization.

In the Far North, the clash of civilizations has been particularly brutal, and the West never more cynical. Today, the world's three largest fortunes represent more wealth than that of all the less-developed countries (LDC) with their combined population of 600 million. For the Inuit, the clash has been as dramatic as the military defeats suffered by the American Indians. To be sure, their adversary presents itself as a force of peace and goodwill, but the outcome looming – assimilation – is the same, and no one has any good solutions to propose. The northern peoples are not interested in a vast Navajo-style reserve or in the isolation of the Amish. Men and women of adventure, their goal is to devise a new form of government for their immense territory.

Realism will prove a major asset in this enterprise. All my life, I have maintained my principled resistance to the Thule base and to the symbol of dispossession and military imperialism that it represents. But astute statesmen understand that it is better to work around an obstacle of this size, or even turn it to profit, than to attack it head on. The urgent task facing the North is to forge an intelligentsia who understand the high economic and geostrategic stakes of the Arctic. In this regard, the creation of a centre of excellence in Thule represents an exceptional opportunity. I would venture to suggest to my American colleagues in the National Science Foundation (NSF), which has purchased the Thule radar facility, that it be turned into a first-class scientific and logistical headquarters for administration of rational and environmentally sensitive development in the High Arctic – self-administration that is, by the Inuit, for their own benefit. I hope that the NSF will give the Inughuit and the Inuit of Nunavut and Nunavik the chance to become these young scientists. The Inuit are strikingly gifted in mathematics, information technology, biology, and ecology. On the strength of these aptitudes, and working alongside US and European scientists, they have what it takes to be space engineers. In the medium term, this centre of excellence in Thule could serve as an international Inuit scientific academy. Unfortunately, no such decision has been made.

THE FOCAL ROLE OF MINORITIES

My own involvement in formal research on the Canadian Arctic dates back to 1960, when I was invited by Quebec ethnobotanist Jacques Rousseau, first francophone director of the Human History Division of the National Museum, to take part in a wide-ranging research program on the Canadian North. He felt that the research of the day was overly dominated by American concepts and sought the input of European researchers into the development of a new perspective on the difficult situation of the Northwest Territories Inuit. In 1964 Mr Rousseau and I co-edited the first comprehensive study of what was then called Nouveau Québec and is now called Nunavik, the immense northern portion of the Province of Quebec.* The publisher was the Centre d'Études Arctiques, which the great historian Fernand Braudel and I founded in 1957 in Paris under the auspices of the École des Hautes Études des Sciences Sociales (EHESS).† The involvement of France and the centre in Arctic affairs continued with the hosting of the first pan-Inuit conference, chaired by Professor René Cassin, a Nobel laureate, in November 1969. An outgrowth of this momentous event was the Inuit Circumpolar Conference (ICC), founded at Point Barrow, Alaska, in June 1977; I was honoured to participate. At Le Havre in May 1973, once again under the auspices of the centre, the historian Jacques Le Goff and James Wah-Shee, president of the Indian Brotherhood of the Northwest Territories, co-chaired the first conference on Arctic oil and gas. Inuit groups and the Canadian authorities were also represented.

For a Frenchman like me, coming from a nation with a venerable Jacobin tradition, it was not always easy to understand the uniqueness of such a complex, ambitious federation as Canada. And for a European who had witnessed the arduous unification of the "Old World," Canadian federalism's intricate framework of interaction among different orders of government provided much food for thought. The Inuit minorities being my main concern, I was inevitably struck by the value placed on cultural diversity and, in particular, by the lively yet conflict-ridden interplay between anglophones and francophones. To this day, this dynamic continues to protect Canada from being engulfed by continual US efforts to homogenize the continent, NAFTA being only the most recent example. As Ottawa works to defend the federation, it can look to what makes Canada unique, including its Inuit and Indian minorities. Throughout the intense debates raised by the aboriginal peoples (today, some one million strong, living on and off of reserves), Canada's national

* This work was recently reprinted with new matter under the title *Du Nouveau-Québec au Nunavik, 1964–2004: Une fragile autonomie.*

† It was later incorporated into the Centre National de la Recherche Scientifique (CNRS), while remaining associated with EHESS, its founding institution.

interest has nearly always won the day. Ottawa has demonstrated the confederal dimension of the problems posed and has often proved the best ally of aboriginal statesmen seeking to affirm their sovereignty.

The vastness of the Inuit lands (one-third of Canada's area, populated in the main by 40,000 hunters and fishers) has necessitated especially bold leadership. As of the 1970s the Inuit elites, with exceptional intelligence and skill as negotiators, began to assert their interests, and they have secured concessions far beyond what the less diplomatic and less assiduous Indians have achieved. The Inuit's strength has been their unity in the face of all obstacles. They have been astonishingly pragmatic and visionary vis-à-vis the Canadian authorities.

Now, in 2006, looking back on that bygone era, the self-government proposals put forward at the pan-Inuit conference of 1969 seem quite modest. What the attendees dimly perceived then is now clear to all: the minority question is one of the major issues of our time. If it is to find a satisfactory resolution, it can only be by giving the aboriginal peoples their due and empowering their leaders. But unfortunately, central governments, lacking the necessary high-mindedness, have too often improvised solutions in the sphere of "Indian affairs," where a host of intangible factors come into play. Likewise, the social sciences have refused to devote in-depth study to the first peoples' difficult transition to modernity and to the syncretisms that have characterized their mental evolution. Instead, many academics have doggedly cast their halcyon gaze on a past deemed to be pure, free of contamination. Nor is all research even that noble in its aims. For too long, study of the brute facts over the short, medium, and long term has been regarded as pointless, unaesthetic, even degrading. Academics have overlooked that in uncertain times, complex societal developments can lead to catastrophic breaks with the past, and from there to new births. We must, as necessary, exit the confines of the university and roll up our sleeves, and it is to that effort that this book testifies. The sociologist Jules Monnerot brilliantly reminds us, with the title of one of his works, that "social facts are not things." In stating this, he draws our attention to the unpredictability of human beings, who have a tendency to behave in ways that contradict our preconceived theories. And so it is for the oral traditions of North America's peoples; we now know that they can endure, even when many people assumed that they were gone forever.

I have stressed this point at length in my writings, and I am convinced of it: the first peoples are the leaven of tomorrow's humanity. And we cannot content ourselves with an aesthetic dialogue as we stand before the museums of the immaterial. This encounter can happen only if the groundwork for dialogue has been laid in advance. It can happen only if we make it happen, if we do our part to help them discover and nurture their own elites. One thinks of Jean-Marie Djibaou in New Caledonia, Amadou Hampaté Bâ in Mali, Nelson

Mandela in South Africa, Aimé Césaire in the French Caribbean, Mahatma Gandhi in India, and the humanists who supported them (famously, Albert Schweitzer in Lambaréné, Gabon). My friends Tagak Curley (who participated brilliantly in the Rouen conference of 1969), Canadian senator Charlie Watt, and "father of Nunavut" John Amagoalik would agree that "the mind does not conceive of minor nations; it only knows of fraternal nations and winners without losers."[1]

CANADA AS A MODEL

The great democratic nation of Canada, the world's second-largest country, has always scorned the variety of racism that stained Nazi Europe, the kind of racism that had such dire consequences for Jews and people of colour. In this, Canada has set itself apart from the United States, which, for example, only resolved the worst of the problems affecting its African American minority long after the Second World War. The relentless battle against Nazism will at least have had the merit of establishing the human truth that there is no superior people. All of us are equal, and each people is at a different stage of its history, its evolution, its genius. However, another sort of racism persists within each of us. It is a deep-rooted cultural racism, nurtured by our reverence for the revealed truths of Christianity and science. The rest is confusion, falsehood. Our educational curricula remain inspired by a philosophy of progress. If ethnology and history have succeeded in the monumental task of convincing Europeans and North Americans that so-called "primitive" peoples are just as important in the history of humanity as are we, it is thanks to the work of pioneering intellectuals such as the ethnologists Marius Barbeau and Diamond Jenness, the archaeologist Robert McGhee, and the historians Jonathan Dore and Robert Vaughan in Canada; the anthropologists Franz Boas, Alfred Kroeber, Bruce Jackson, Margaret Mead, and Clifford Geertz in the United States, and the historians Lucien Febvre and Fernand Braudel in France. But to proclaim, as some do, the received truth that "primitive peoples" are our equals while ignoring their troubling present-day situation is nonsense, pure demagogy. Consider the art world's enduring interest in Inuit painting and sculpture. If primitive art has carved out a place for itself, it is not because of its pantheistic message or the complex philosophy that inspires it but because of its aesthetic value, which determines its price. As a result, the Inuit co-ops and the metropolitan art galleries they deal with have been the incidental ambassadors of Inuit thought. Cultural racism, in the West? Some art observers found it revolutionary, even shocking, when a major museum such as the Louvre, by order of President Chirac, exhibited Inuit, African, and Oceanian masks alongside Italian *quattrocento* and French impressionist paintings. Likewise, it was no small matter for the anthropological collection *Terre Humaine** to publish writers such as Claude Lévi-Strauss, Emile Zola, and Victor Ségalen in the same series as the works of an Indian untouchable, a deaf mute, a member of the Amazonian Yanomami tribe, a Greenlandic Eskimo (Minik) deported to the United States, and a caribou rancher (Anta) in Lapland.

Like the Inuit, these and other minority peoples had been marginalized by the authorities. Their voices had been confiscated, and the white people were speaking for them. The historian Jules Michelet might have been lamenting this state of affairs when he wrote: "Barbarians, savages, children ... all have this common misery: their instinct is misunderstood, and they themselves do not know how to explain it to us. They are like those mutes who suffer and die in silence. And we hear nothing, we hardly know it ... Those weak and incapable ones, those miserable persons who can do nothing for themselves, can do much for us. They have in them a mystery of unknown power, a hidden creativity of living springs in the depths of their nature."[2]

Granted, the recent success at Cannes of the Inuit-made film *Atanarjuat* attests to the respectful, admiring public reception given to manifestations of the Inuit worldview in Paris, Ottawa, New York, and Rome. The Inuit have no greater ambassador than their arts – sculpture, painting, song, dance – whose beauty is that of an open book. Through them we can vicariously experience the epic lives of these ancient peoples, lives that I shared from 1960 to 1963 at Igloolik, Spence Bay, and Back River. Through them, we may be led to recall the legends of our own heroes. But once the first peoples' territories are occupied, the pattern is always the same: colonization (i.e., deculturation), Western-style education, evangelization, eradication of sacred customs as "pagan" or even satanic, and – with economic integration – decay and corruption. Black Africa is a deplorable example. In this connection, I would cite a sadly ignored text by Charles Péguy: "Because the bourgeoisie began to treat the work of man like a security on the stock exchange, the worker in his turn began to treat his own work as a security on the stock exchange ... Everywhere it is the same demagogy, the same widowhood ... Such poverty of thought may be unique in the history of the world."[3]

But, in Canada, in the last half-century, the wind has shifted. Prime Minister Louis Saint-Laurent, during a now-famous speech to the House of Commons on 8 December 1953, stated that "we have administered these vast territories of the North in an almost continuing state of absence of mind." And, as

* I founded *Terre Humaine* in Éditions Plon and continue to be its senior editor. The collection recently celebrated its fiftieth anniversary with an international symposium at the Bibliothèque Nationale de France under the aegis of the president of the Republic.

Areas studied on Jean Malaurie's thirty-one missions, 1948–97.

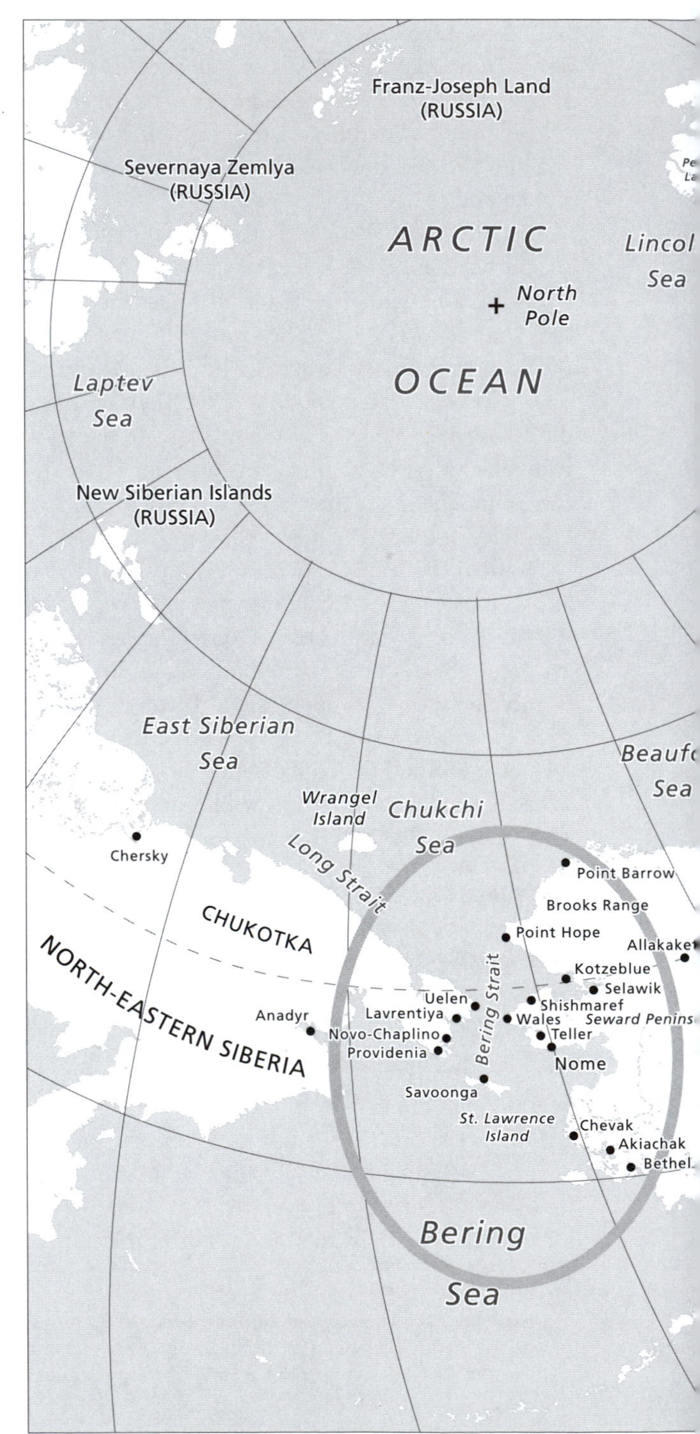

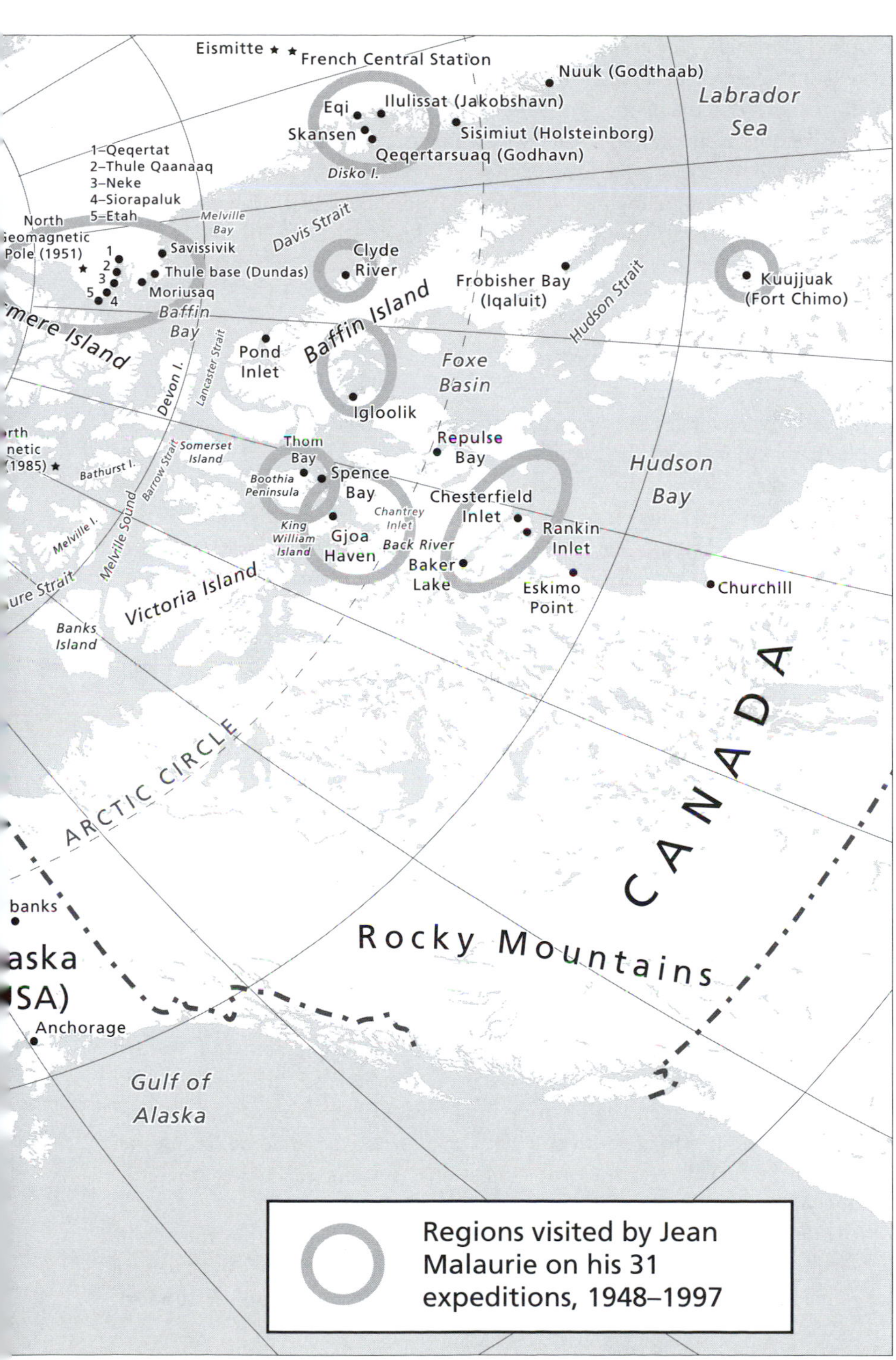
Eismitte
French Central Station
Nuuk (Godthaab)
Labrador Sea
Eqi
Ilulissat (Jakobshavn)
Skansen
Sisimiut (Holsteinborg)
Qeqertarsuaq (Godhavn)
Disko I.
1–Qeqertat
2–Thule Qaanaaq
3–Neke
4–Siorapaluk
5–Etah
Melville Bay
Davis Strait
Savissivik
Thule base (Dundas)
Moriusaq
Baffin Bay
Clyde River
Frobisher Bay (Iqaluit)
Hudson Strait
Kuujjuak (Fort Chimo)
Baffin Island
Pond Inlet
Lancaster Strait
Devon I.
Foxe Basin
Igloolik
Somerset Island
Thom Bay
Repulse Bay
Bathurst I.
Boothia Peninsula
Spence Bay
Chesterfield Inlet
Hudson Bay
Barrow Strait
Melville Sound
Chantrey Inlet
King William Island
Gjoa Haven
Back River
Rankin Inlet
Melville I.
Baker Lake
Eskimo Point
Churchill
Victoria Island
Banks Island
CANADA
ARCTIC CIRCLE
Rocky Mountains
Anchorage
Gulf of Alaska
Regions visited by Jean Malaurie on his 31 expeditions, 1948–1997

if by some miracle, this comment marked the beginning of a gradual process in which the requisite high-mindedness would be brought to the resolution of the many problems plaguing the North. Playing a role in this process were successive northern affairs ministers Jean Lesage, Jean Chrétien, and Arthur Laing, as well as senior officials such as Walter Rudnicki and Mark Malone (an official in former prime minister Pierre Trudeau's office), all of whom did me the honour of meeting with me. After decades of mistakes, the federal and provincial governments began to make improving relations with the Inuit a top priority.

THE CRUCIAL ROLE OF EDUCATION

Now, with the advent of self-government, the Inuit have everything they need to play a pivotal role within Confederation and in the province of Quebec. But education remains the crucial issue. Provide the typical colonial education, and you risk inculcating complacency in the elites, as has been seen in certain North American Indian communities. It has been my immense privilege to witness extraordinary changes and an acceleration of history in Greenland, the Canadian Central Arctic, Alaska, and Chukotka. In this, I was greatly assisted by the authorities, who gave me a relatively free hand to conduct my research as well as unrestricted access to confidential government and police archives. My recommendations were always received with interest. Is it even conceivable that the French prefect in New Caledonia, say, would grant a Canadian researcher similar privileges? No, of course not. Given the tensions between the natives (Kanaks), the European settlers (Caldoches), and the French Republic, such a thing would be almost unthinkable.

The recurrent conundrum that every Inuit premier will have to wrestle with is how to soften the blows of globalization. Can anyone legitimately protect a culture that young people seemingly want to shed through rapid "development"? It is unfortunate that some of these youths are afraid of learning English – or French – for fear of losing their own language. Many drop out of school at age twelve or fourteen and become unemployed; likewise, the lack of adequate housing leads to homelessness. The people's reaction to such bargain-basement democratization has been simple: they have rejected it. Their rejection has taken the form of alcoholism, drug abuse, violence, and an extremely high rate of youth suicide. The alternative would be to conduct an across-the-board reform of the educational system, as in the inner-city schools of Paris and New York. Reeducate the educators.

It is often counterargued, in a spirit of social Darwinism, that these self-governing territories should dissolve into a broader economic and cultural whole. No effort should be made to keep Inuit "authenticity" on life support.

To this I reply by stating what is for me a fundamental principle, namely that civilizations are of equal importance, even if not at equal levels of development. Cultural diversity is a major asset to any nation, and protecting it is vital to the future of humanity. Now, such diversity implies genuine self-government, not a simulacrum thereof. The Inuit elites need time if they are to achieve, through interactive dialogue, a salutary hybridization of their culture with the larger Canadian society. They must be given the opportunity to muster the resources necessary for a fairer confrontation. For this to happen, the Inuit and federal governments, as well as the Inuit and Canadian societies as a whole, must relate to each other on an equal footing.

But history turns upon timing; come too early or too late, and you are consigned to oblivion. Will the Inuit have enough time to complete this process? Pursuing the counterargument, some might say that it is pointless to focus on education and training of elites now that evening television is giving the Socratic spirit of school a formidable run for its money. Add to this the pornographic and violent videos available over the counter, whose images and plot lines do nothing to prepare northern minorities for their desired destiny, and what you have is mental miscegenation. The casualty of the process may well be the oral tradition.

Again, I reply: the people can and must be alerted to these perils. It is quite simply a matter of patriotism in its fleshly dimension. There is no people who, once aware that they are responsible for their own and their children's future, fail to take their destiny in hand. Thanks to the brilliant work of true statesmen, the Inuit now have the territorial basis for whatever policy they may choose to pursue; Nunavut is a vast, cohesive, self-governing territory. The next step is a critical one, truly a matter of life and death: Inuit leaders, after ensuring that the people, and especially youth, are fully informed of their options, must come to grips with what their constituents want for the future.

Obviously, this is not for me to prescribe, or even to foresee; I cannot get inside the secret thoughts and aspirations of an Inuit teenager. I did spend some time working as a volunteer teacher at Kangiqsugaapik on Baffin Island, but that was almost twenty years ago, in 1987. The children all told me, "We want a little job in the village; nothing too demanding." They did not want to shoulder heavy responsibilities nor – and on this point they were even more vehement – be cut off from their families. To leave the community would be to cut the umbilical cord, to divorce themselves from the spirits of their dead. A youth can sacrifice only so much to help his ancestral homeland – especially since, by discovering a world in which everything is foreign, he risks losing himself. Still, they might do well to keep in mind the exploits of historical heroes who could serve as role models. One thinks of Hans Hendrik, the legendary North Greenland explorer of the 1860s; Joe Ebierbing and Tookoolito, the Inuit-Canadian couple who accompanied Charles Francis Hall (d. 1871); and in our day, Ole Jørgen Hammeken of Uummannaq, Greenland (north of Disko Island), who travelled by sea for three years to meet his Inuit cousins from Alaska to Siberia.

I cannot recommend too strongly that the Inuit of 2006 who read these lines should beware of blindly following any such examples, or even suggestions from friends like me. They must rethink all recommendations. They will be Inuit only to the extent that they think for themselves, devising solutions equal to the immense problems that they face.

I have often written that the Inuit have a strong belief in the virtues of time, of waiting. Unfortunately, time is short and the stakes are considerable. The governing idea, the hidden agenda of the profit-driven West, is to reduce minorities – indeed, all of humanity – to a group of clients. Minorities are threatening and must be reduced to vassalage before they realize what is happening. The West has fought against them for too long to turn about and encourage them to take their place in the wide world. The purpose of neocolonialism is to nurture illusions now, only to take control later. Yes, the time is very, very short, and I am only moderately optimistic. We are all incurably colonialist in spirit. "Almost everywhere, two classes have wielded over the people a domination from which only instruction can preserve us: lawmakers and priests. The latter have usurped its conscience, the former, its affairs."[4]

THE COMING INVASION

My readers may find these considerations academic. They are mistaken, if only because of a major phenomenon currently weighing on the minds of every Inuk: planet warming and pollution. The average temperature measured at weather stations in Greenland has risen by 2–3°C. Recently, US Arctic Commission Chair George Newton, Jr, told delegates to the World Economic Forum in Davos, Switzerland, that Arctic temperatures could rise by 5°C within this century. Likewise, sea levels could rise by a dozen metres. Writing in *The Observer* for 22 February 2004, Mark Townsend and Paul Harris stated that catastrophic climate change could be upon us within twenty years. The polar ice has thinned dramatically. A short while ago, a Russian research vessel reached the North Pole during the summer without an icebreaker, indicating the extent of the melting.

One consequence will be the recession of the permanent ice cap. Partial early-season melting will open the famed Northwest Passage, the shortest northern sea route from the Atlantic to the Pacific. Similarly, ship traffic from western Europe to Chinese and Japanese ports through the so-called "Siberian route" is increasing. This is likely to lead to stepped-up exploitation of the vast oil, gas, and mineral resources of the North, some of which lie under the ice. Indeed, with the shrinkage of the ice cap, the Inuit should expect to see a "black gold rush" – a flood of whites looking for oil – in the coming years, probably within this generation. In fact, it is already underway. In Tuktoyaktuk, at the mouth of the Mackenzie River, a large Canadian tanker port is being built. The City of Churchill, on Hudson Bay, is growing. Each summer brings new expeditions by prospectors, geologists, cartographers. Spurred on by climate change, the conquest of northern North America and Siberia may result in the gradual dispossession of the first peoples and their ancestral land by virtue of an implacable ethnic calculus: whites versus Inuit. But this will happen only if nothing is done to strengthen the ethnic authority of the Inuit of Nunavut and Nunavik.

The gap between the forces of industrial development (white mining towns, ports, and so on) and traditionalist Inuit dispersed in their villages will continue to widen. I would like to persuade you, dear Inuit readers, that the colonization of the Arctic is not a long way off but right around the corner. Consider that when Alaska was purchased from the government of St Petersburg in 1867, its population was 99% Indian and Inuit. Today, they represent only 16%. In Chukotka, northeastern Siberia, the cradle of Inuit civilization, aboriginal peoples accounted for 90% of the population in 1926 and represent only 10% today. In the capital city of Anadyr, billionaire governor and industrialist Roman Abramovitch is pushing for stepped-up industrial development.

In Alaska the Indians and Inuit have already been shunted to the sidelines, as they have in western Siberia, the Yamal Nenets Autonomous Area, the Komi Republic, and Evenkia in Russia. The 300 Inuit villages of the Alaskan corporations can no longer hold their own against the powerful oil, mining, and financial forces concentrated in Anchorage, Fairbanks, and Juneau. Aboriginal homeless people are now living on the edges of these cities within sight of the most ostentatious luxury, a situation more typical of developing countries in, say, South America. It is not a situation that anyone wants to see repeated in Nunavut or Nunavik, but it may well be if urgent steps are not taken to prevent it.

The Arctic is under the sovereignty of eight countries: the United States, Canada, Russia, Norway, Denmark, Iceland, Sweden, and Finland. Maritime law is hotly disputed, and the Arctic Ocean is the subject of contentious international debate. Certain nations consider their sovereignty to extend 200 miles to the north of their continental shelf. Moscow, with legal arguments at the ready, has laid claim to half the Arctic Ocean, an expanse reaching all the way to the Pole. But maritime-law arguments can also be made for the rights of the aboriginal peoples who have lived in these high latitudes for millennia;

French map from 1800 indicating the state of knowledge of the Central Arctic before John Ross's expedition to North Greenland (1818), William Parry's to Lancaster Sound (1819–20), and John Franklin's to the Beaufort Sea and Victoria Island (1819–22, 1825–27).

Nunavut certainly has them in its favour. The Inuit of Canada, if they are to protect themselves from this predictable crisis, must work with jurists to establish bold new legislative provisions within Confederation.

PRESERVING TRADITIONAL VALUES IN MODERN TIMES

"What is the major problem of the third millennium?" I was asked by a journalist from *Le Monde.*

My answer: "The problem of minorities."

To prepare for this confrontation, it is essential for the Inuit to become aware that their history has been obscured. The Inuit public figures now emerging from the schools and universities must analyze their history, reflect on the modernity of their founding myths, and assess their pertinence to the future. Most such work to date has tended to take a rather utopian view of the past. Still, there is no doubt that the Inuit have remained strong throughout their history by being attentive to their elders and the wisdom of the group. There have always been strong personalities who carry the group forward and serve as the agents of its vital cohesion. In a recent interview with the Greenland newspaper *Atuagagdliutit/Grønlandsposten*, I was asked: "What wisdom and values should the Inuit retain from their past?" I answered without hesitation: "The courage to confront nature and its hazards, to fend off despair about the course of history, to transmit this history like a sacred torch from generation to generation."[5] I was also asked about my opinion of the contemporary controversy surrounding the proposal by certain elites to concentrate the population into two or three large cities, a prospect that only a minority favour. Proponents of this measure argue that it is a necessary response to the political and economic problems of independence. I have strongly opposed such projects ever since I co-chaired (with René Cassin) the first pan-Inuit conference in 1969, looking on as participants worked out strategies for negotiating with the colonial administrations. Yes, the time is very, very short. If I have one important goal in this preface, it is to echo the elders' concerns and awaken young Canadian Inuit to the realization that losing their traditional ways is a matter of one or two generations. The West has designs on the immense wealth of the Arctic. It has already polluted the air and water, and it will take control over the land if it can.

In short, it is to be hoped that the modern Inuit nation will not repeat the mistakes of the West. Urban concentration, the tragedy of Europe and North America, is the biggest of these, and the Inuit should avoid it at all costs. At present, Inuit communities and villages are still widely dispersed over the territory. Following John Amagoalik's advice, the people could use their considerable proficiency in information technology as a tool to preserve this spatial pattern. For example, they could use videoconferencing to stay in touch with their elders – a vital necessity.

My dear Inuit friends, the treasure of your world is your age-old relationship with the ice and the water, the wind and the game animals. It is more than an ecology, it is a religion, a philosophy. To herd the Inuit into a large city would be to denature them, to devitalize them; and do not be surprised if modernity, for the less robust youth, comes hand in hand with alcoholism and violence. I have always believed that the first peoples are the wellspring of humanity, provided that they do not turn their backs on their true nature.

With television and the Internet, the West has invented an extraordinary school of knowledge; yet paradoxically, these same technologies are spreading the virus of moral disintegration and cultural and national annihilation over the face of the globe.

THE SPIRITUAL DIMENSION

In the world's capitals, people are counting on the Inuit to preserve their clear-eyed awareness of the two faces of progress: one of them positive because it is liberating, the other negative – indeed, Satanic. The earth will wreak vengeance; in fact, it already is doing so with the ravages of pollution. If European, American, Canadian, Russian, and Japanese scientists and intellectuals are looking to the first peoples with such fellow feeling in the modern day, it is because these peoples have always lived in communion with the spirits of the earth, and they are the sentinels standing on guard for it.

"A civilization, then, is neither a given economy nor a given society, but something which can persist through a series of economies or societies, barely susceptible to gradual change."[6] When in extreme peril, a society either breaks apart or falls back upon what it sees as essential. History has shown that religion and respect for the dead are critical to a society. Only peoples who preserve their transcendence can persist. The Inuit are a people hungry for the sacred, possessed of an "implicit spiritual solidarity," to use the phrase of Michel de Certeau.

Defending against the various threats that I have described are a number of important institutions. Notwithstanding the grave crises washing over the Catholic and Anglican missionary churches, which have come in for strong criticism in the North following a series of scandalous sexual-abuse and paternity cases, the Inuit (with the contribution of the Pentecostal movement) are ardently attempting to "Inuitize" Jesus, to reinvent Christianity as a syncretic amalgam with their ancient pantheism. It is a process similar to the one followed by the Hopi and Mexican Indians. The neo-Christianity of these first peoples makes clear that the universal church is not behind us but ahead, still to be envisioned. It teaches us that the church of the future will be profoundly ecumenical, melding pantheism with all forms of Christianity and even Buddhism. The Assissi meeting of 24 January 2002 at the initiative of Pope John Paul II prefigures this evolving church.

In the academic sphere, the State Polar Academy in St Petersburg was founded in 1991 by my Russian colleagues and I with a mission to train young Siberian managers. Today, this unique institution consists of five faculties (including Arctic ecology) housed in 27,000 square metres of building space; it is attended by 1,600 students from forty-five ethnic groups. Its pedagogical mission is to help northern aboriginal peoples relearn the greatness of their history and become the agents of their own development. It is not perfect, but it is helping give new life to a traditional way of thinking.

CONCERNING THE FUTURE

The future is bright if such teaching and research institutions proliferate throughout Nunavut and Nunavik. Are there any precedents? Yes, Iceland, whose late-nineteenth-century population of less than 100,000 lived in dire poverty. Today, it has a network of research facilities and universities and is one of the richest European countries. The same is true for Finland. A century ago it was under Swedish domination in the South and czarist Russian domination in the North. Its mythic peasant worldview endured nonetheless and was consecrated with the milestone 1849 publication of the *Kalevala* (second edition), a compilation of Finnish folk poetry. In the twenty-first century, Finland has numerous first-class, forward-looking universities. It too is a rich country, one on which the European ideal is modelled. Costa Rica, on the strength of its highly educated population of four million, has propelled its economy into the digital age. It is a high-tech leader, attracting hundreds of millions of dollars in foreign investment from large North American corporations. On a per capita basis, Costa Rica is the Latin American leader in software exports.

A future for the Inuit?

LAST WORDS

2022. I float incorporeal, attempting in vain to dialogue empathically with a young Nunavut Inuk.

His home is an ultramodern hemispheric house, like an igloo, in a village of ten families linked by Internet to the rest of the world. On weekends he remains a fierce, happy hunter and fisherman. He has successfully built a unique, universalizable model of small-scale ecological development, a bubble protected from pollution that is the envy of the world. He speaks his own language, of course, which by now has produced several Nobel laureates in literature and the sciences. He is a political scientist, a mathematician, a biochemist, a computer scientist, a United Nations advisor, a doctor, an oceanographer, or an artist. Or perhaps he is an internationally renowned philosopher or an innovative theologian reinterpreting the gospel and the Buddhist texts. He is adept at choosing, from what the West offers, those things that are most propitious for his people. He has kept the spiritual flame alive and everywhere is recognized as a wise man standing on guard for the future of the world. He has finally regained the greatness and courage of his ancestors, something to which I was one of the last witnesses in 1960–63 at Igloolik and among the Netsilingmiut and the Utkuhikhalingmiut. Moreover, he has attained that serene wisdom to which this book bears witness.

Viewing him from afar, I am pleased at the small part I was able to play in his accomplishment.

Paris
30 March 2006
Jean Malaurie

author's acknowledgments

First and foremost, all my thanks go to my admirable Inuit companions at Igloolik (Piugatu, Awa, and Pacome Kolaut), among the Netsilik (Krokiarq and Arnaja) and the Utkuhikhalingmiut (Akretoq), at Clyde River on Baffin Island, and at Kuujjuak (Amoralik), as well as to the Hon. Charlie Watt.

For their various and inestimable contributions to my work, I would like to acknowledge the staff of the Northern Co-ordination and Research Centre (NCRC), Department of Northern Affairs, Ottawa; the RCMP; the Anglican and Catholic missions of the Canadian Arctic (in particular, Oblate fathers Fournier, Henry, Didier, and Lorson); John and Christina Roberts, founders of the Glenn Gould Foundation (Calgary); and Mark Malone (Ottawa/Paris).

Finally, I would like to express my gratitude to my excellent translator Peter Feldstein and to McGill-Queen's University Press for their fine work on the publication of this book.

above: On an Inuit whaleboat in Foxe Basin, where I conducted a micro-economic survey of the 494 Igluligmiut (99 families) living there in 1960. Photo: Jean Malaurie.

opposite, above: Awa, my companion, guide, and ambassador to the Igloolik families. Photo: Jean Malaurie, April 1961.

opposite, below: Awa unties the sled dogs' leashes on an intensely cold day during my survey of the Igluligmiut. Together we travelled from village to village and camp to camp over a 15,000 km^2 area of Foxe Basin. Photo: Jean Malaurie, May 1961.

above: Interior of a 15 m^2 one-room *q'angmat* in the Igloolik region in which I stayed for a week with its eight occupants. Soapstone oil lamp burning seal blubber. Photo: Jean Malaurie, October 1960.

opposite, above: At the RCMP post in Spence Bay. Photo: Jean Malaurie, August 1961.

opposite, below: Netsilik amulets. Photo: Jean Malaurie, August 1961.

DUTTON
THE LONELY SOUTH
COOPER
THE GHOST VOYAGE
NORTH

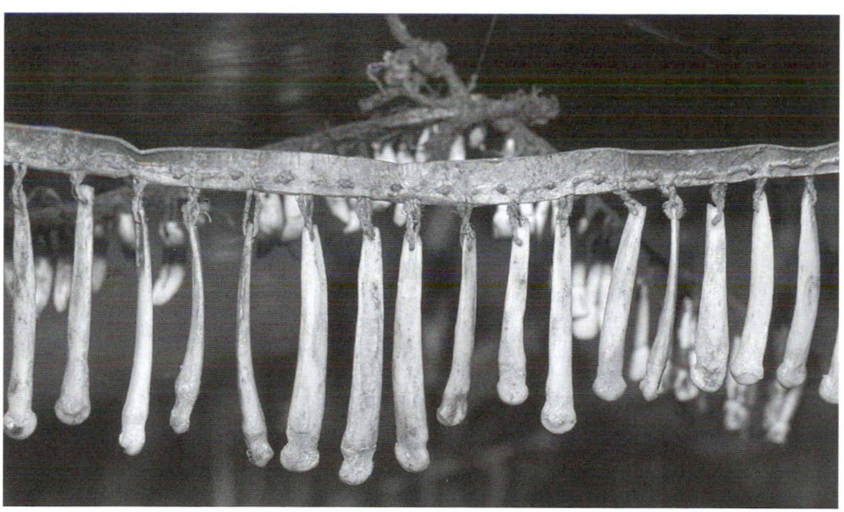

above: Krokiarq, who accompanied me on my trek across Boothia Peninsula from southwest to northeast. Photo: Jean Malaurie, August 1961.

opposite, above: At Cornwallis Island in the northeastern Canadian Arctic, ruins of a Dorset vaulted stone igloo that would have been covered with peat and snow. In the foreground, narrow entrance corridor; further back, floor made of 7 m^2 stone slabs and common sleeping platform. Photo: Jean Malaurie, August 1995.

opposite, below: Toy house at Thom Bay, built with stones by some Netsilik girls. Photo: Jean Malaurie, September 1961.

Thom Bay Netsilik, forty, who was my main respondent on shamanism.
Photo: Jean Malaurie, September 1961.

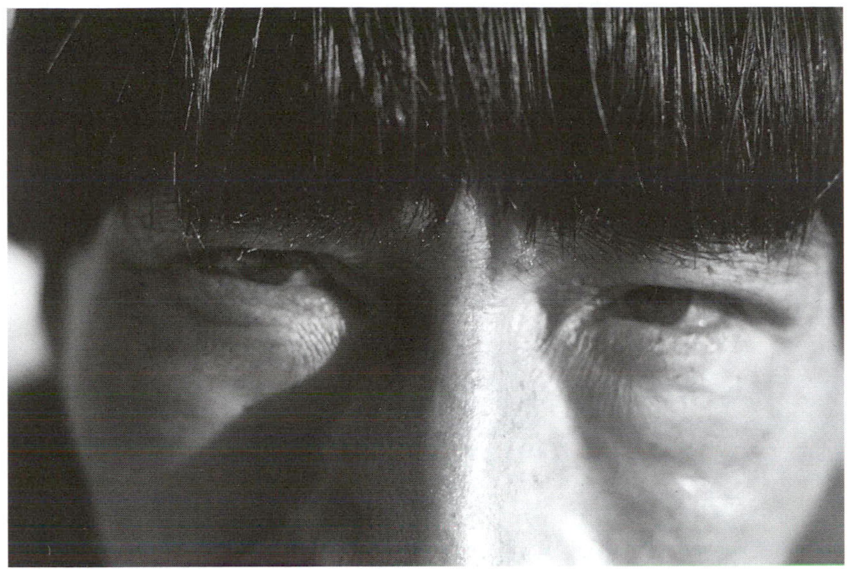

Netsilik hunter who accompanied me on my dogsled expedition from King William Island to the Back River estuary to meet the Utkuhikhalingmiut. Photo: Jean Malaurie.

above: At Back River, camp 1, our expedition has just arrived and we unload the sled into the double igloo that I will be sharing. Photo: Jean Malaurie, April 1963.

opposite, above: At Back River, camp 1, gathering of Utku in one cell of an igloo to prepare the next day's activities. This people of the tundra heated their homes very little and observed a draconian taboo on hunting or eating sea animals. Photo: Jean Malaurie, April 1963.

opposite, below: Back River Utku hunter recounting an inspired myth. Photo: Jean Malaurie, April 1963.

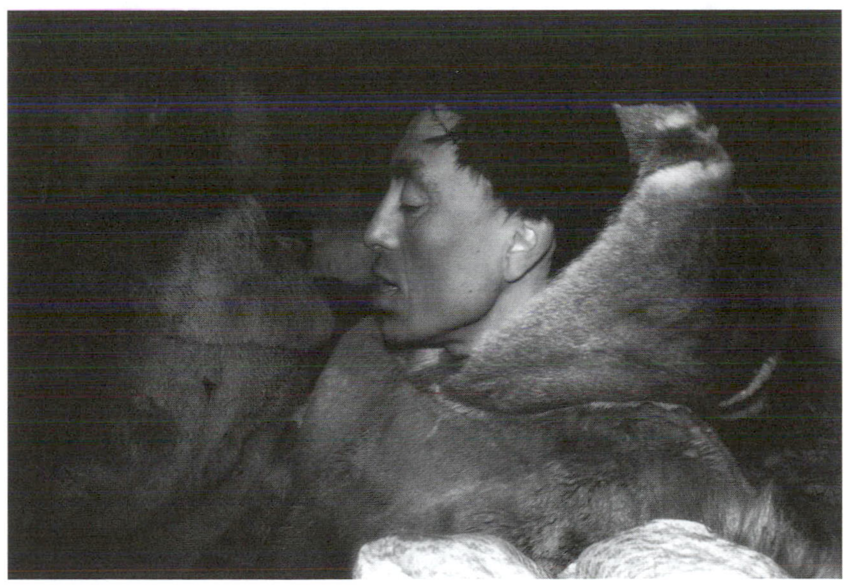

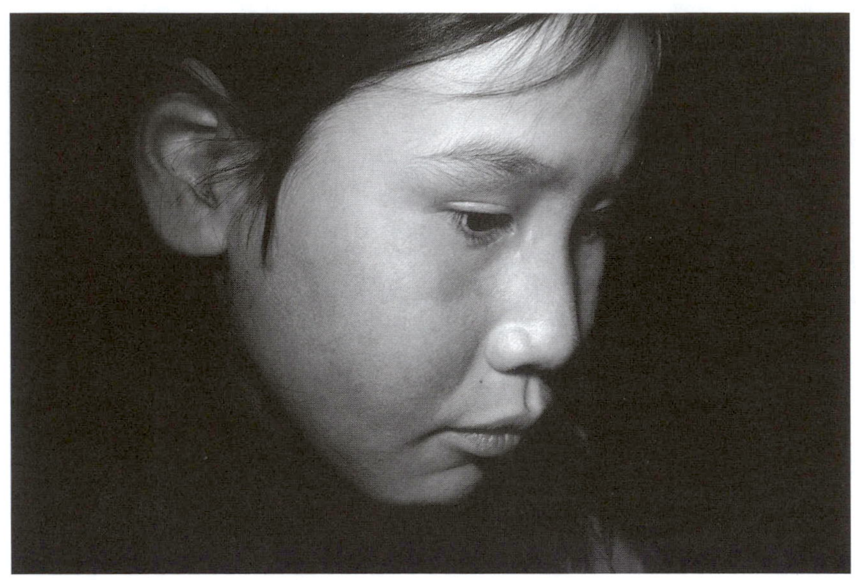

Teenage Netsilik girl whom I interviewed at Gjoa Haven on my return from the Back River expedition. Photo: Jean Malaurie, May 1963.

hummocks

1

In Foxe Basin

13 May 1961. The terrain is naked; the humidity amniotic. Sky and horizon merge into one. I am on the pack ice of Foxe Basin, an ice-water desert. A humble breeze lifts and swirls the snow, and my memory falters as I try to recall the words of the sacred text ... "and the earth was without form, and void, and the Spirit of God moved." Such an inhuman vastness, in which all notion of scale is annihilated. Awareness of my fragility, but also the irrepressible will that channels and constrains me as a man.

Raising my head, I see lines of perspective skating toward a distant, indistinct horizon the colour of the dried sprigs of lavender in our cupboards. The sled forges forward rapidly, past an ebony-black growler,* a piece of smaragdine ice like a bedsore, and now a shredded piece of animal skin. The dogs strain forward, tear it apart with their fangs, and resume their trot, their

* A chunk of ice jutting 1–3 metres above the pack ice, generally transparent but appearing green or black to the eye.

lacerated muzzles sniffing the wind. My ear harkens to a sustained note, the expression of subterranean energy in the ice, supplanting the familiar noise of sled on snow. This in turn is succeeded, closer to me, by the drawn out complaint of the frozen peat runner scraping over the rougher, older ice.*

On our left, a pale, diffuse sun rises in a veil of fine bluish haze. A profound sense of peace emanates from the frozen air. Eleven o'clock. The Inuit never set out before the first heat of the day, but it is –20°C, and the two of us, Awa and I, have been under way for five hours now, travelling together on a traditional *qaamutik*, a narrow sled ten metres long by forty centimetres high built of openwork boards and covered by a warm brown caribou hide mottled with faded patches of white. Our destination: the southernmost camp among the group of five hundred Igluligmiut whom I have been studying, family by family, for the last two field seasons. There is tongue-clacking, cries of encouragement for the dog team. Suddenly, a howl of pain: the black dog at the front right has sunk his fangs into his neighbour's ear and torn off a piece. The jolting of the sled causes my thoughts to undergo an anamorphosis, and I utter them aloud, trying to keep them ordered. The words couple and uncouple in a sequence that eludes my grasp. I set about exploring my territory like an animal, mentally pacing the square metre of caribou hide on which I am seated. If I stroke the fur, it comes off in handfuls. My thoughts float detached, an archipelago in my mind. Agitated, unable to concentrate, I stare fixedly into the distance, which is blanketed with new frontiers to discover. The sled is the centre of an imaginary circle whose circumference lies at infinity.

Awa's guttural voice intrudes with a word or two, as if speaking to himself. He does not turn his head; rather, the whole heavy mass of fur pivots slowly to the right and, without a glance at me, back toward the dogs. The ice man cracks the whip (*iperautaq*), which is made of broad leather strips from a bearded seal. An apposite few words, and we merge again into the frozen winter.

My thoughts flit to and fro and come to rest on Marshall Pétain. Why Pétain, here, in this remote country? Why does the mortal cold stamp upon my mind the recollection of May 1940, the disgrace of collaboration, when a few months were all it took for a bygone marshal to implicate all of France by breach of trust? Pétain, Bazaine, same intellectual lineage: a will to preserve the social order of the "good people" at all costs, coupled with a right-wing revanchist ambition. Result: an absurd "national revolution" that was immediately rendered moot by the Occupation. Frenchmen, notably the veterans

* Maniilrak: pack ice that did not melt in previous years and was incorporated into the next winter's freeze-up. Pressed by winds and currents, it becomes hummocked, impeding the passage of sled and dogs.

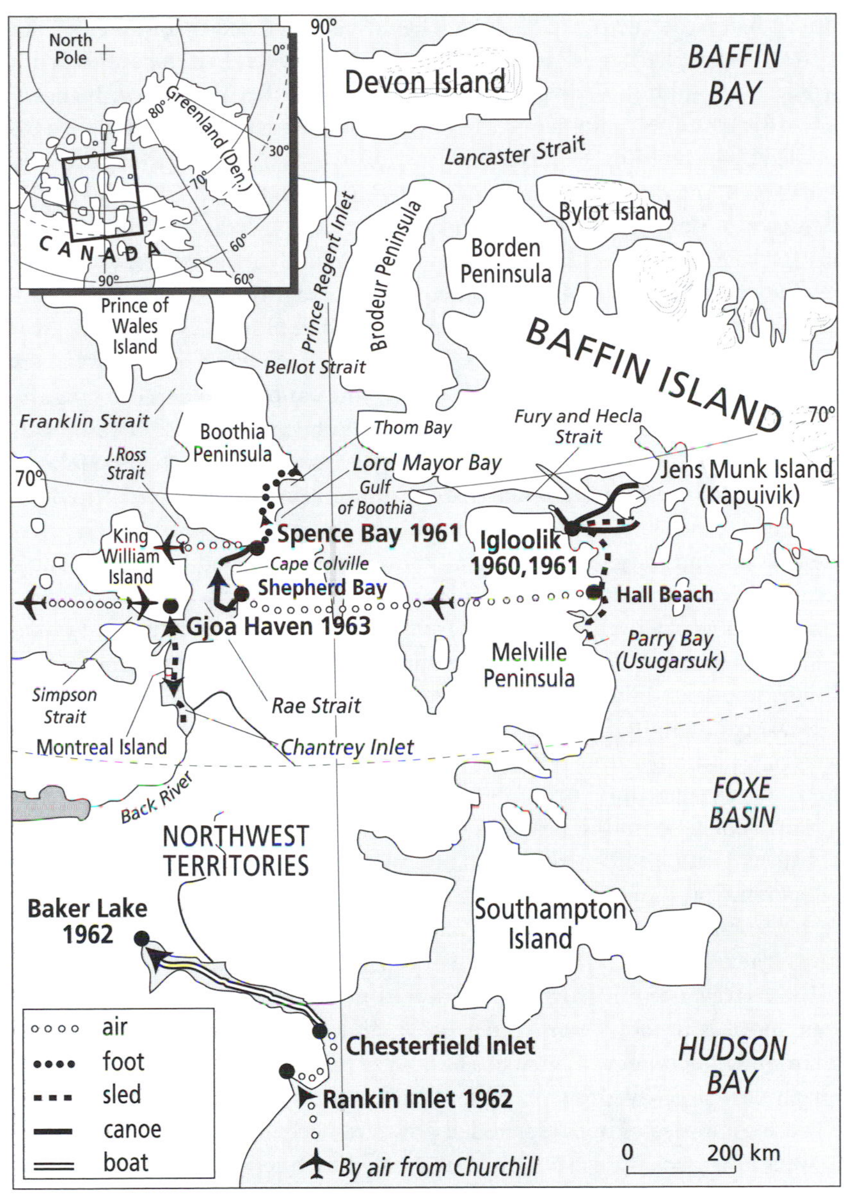

My expeditions to the Canadian Central Arctic: Igloolik, northern sector, 1960, southern sector, May 1961; Boothia Peninsula, July 1961; Rankin Inlet, Chesterfield Inlet, and Baker Lake, 1962; Back River, 1963.

of 1914, had respected the old soldier. They were convinced that the "Fox," the hero of Verdun, had a trick up his sleeve. My country has had the unfortunate privilege of building a nation in adversity. Every other generation brings a new calamity: Crécy, Azincourt, Pavie, Quebec, Trafalgar, Waterloo, Sedan, marked by resounding victories and revolts, by inventiveness and creativity. But in 1940, the insult of treason was added to the injury of arms, and under the cover of political correctness for good measure! Vichyism: the epitome of vassalage on the part of strategically and morally defeated generals who behaved like foot soldiers as they anticipated the wages of their felonious dealings. Duped by these cynical actions, and although ultimately redeemed by a bloody liberation, France will forever be ashamed. Now my memory warms to the flames of hope and courage ... one 18 June, another general risking his honour, his life when, flanked by a dozen rebels, he pronounces the immortal words: "The flame of the resistance will not be extinguished." The Republican French resistance is united: Gaullists, Communists, Freemasons, the deep strata of the French people, the downtrodden and stateless, Jews and Gypsies, the many groups targeted by Nazism, the 300,000 deported for political and racial motives, the thousands of fighters tortured and executed in the "Shadow War," and the 120,000 dead in the heroic, little-remembered Battle of France (May–June 1940). All these were the vanguard of the vast Allied campaign in which 55,000 more French soldiers died.

Hearing my muttering, Awa interjects: "Sumi?" – Where are we? We have been navigating by dead reckoning, orienting ourselves by the positions of the sun – or what could be descried of it – and the moon. *Unani*: east; *kannernark*: north. With the nearness of the magnetic pole, the compass is useless, its magnetic needle jerking and jumping and shuddering.[1] This evening I will plot my presumed trajectory on tracing paper laid over an old American 1/250,000 map and take note in my diary of the incidents that occurred along the journey. The Inuk will pay no attention: a Kablunak's affair.*

The conveyance on which we are seated may seem primitive, prehistoric even, but it is in fact sophisticated, solid, and robust, a perfect fit with the environment. It is not at all that of a backward people. The store-bought oaken uprights are supplely girded in place with sealskin straps, while the peat runners are composed of hand-sprinkled powdered lichen that is moistened and allowed to freeze. The glazed finish is created by filtering a stream of water through the lips and polishing with bearskin; *sermerpoq* is the verb designating this whole process. At two- to three-hour intervals, we inspect the surface

* Whites in the Hudson Bay region are called Kablunak, in North Greenland, Qaallunaa (for the Danes), and in northern Alaska, Naluagmiu or Tanik.

of the runners for damage caused by the rough ice. If necessary, we unload the sled and turn it over, melt snow with our urine, pat the peat layer back in place by hand, and glaze it with another stream of water. The Arctic demands a greater aptitude for patience. It is a place where human beings must synchronize their biological rhythms to the rhythms of nature.

Awa and I are both wearing wide caribou-skin trousers (*qaarlii*). Our ponchos (*qulitaq*) are topped with hoods (*nasak*) fringed with blue fox tail and they fit snugly at the neck. For protection from the blizzard, I face leeward, hunching deeply into the fur, letting my cheek be caressed by the downy fringe (*nuilak*) with its strong animal odour. My boots (*kamik*) are of caribou skin with the fur side out; the sole (*atungak*) is from the hide of a bearded seal (a large one, weighing some 100 kg), the fur having been removed by slow, natural fermentation. I am wearing an undergarment, a wool shirt, a thick wool sweater, and socks while my Inuk companion has only a shirt under his caribou-skin parka and is barefoot inside his double boots. We are both wearing lined mittens (*pualuk*), sealskin inside, caribou out. A modern item, added in the last ten years, is a pair of cotton long johns. Our weapons and tools are limited to an ice pick; a harpoon with a detachable head; a multi-pronged fish spear, or leister (*kakivak*), with a carved ivory fish for bait; two rather modern guns, a rifle and a shotgun; an axe; two knives; and a saw for cutting the icy snow if it becomes necessary to build an igloo.

ᑕᓇᓕ ᑲᓗᓇ ᑎᓕᔭᐅᒐᒥ ᐃᓯᒪᑕᓗᒍ ᒐᐸᒪᓄ ᑌᐃᒪᒍ
ᓄᓇᓗᑕᒥᒍ ᑲᐅᔨᒪᑎᐊᒪ ᐃᓄᐃ ᐃᓕᑯᓯᒥᓂ ᑲᓄ ᑭᓇᐅᔭᑕᒐᓯᐸᑐ
ᐃᓄᐃ ᐅᑭᐅᑯ ᐊᒪᓗ ᐊᒍᓇᓯᑎᑲᑎᐊᒥᒪᑕᓗᓂ ᐊᒪᓗ ᑭᓯᑲᒥᓗᐊᒃ
ᑭᓇᐅᔭᑕᒍᓇᒥᑐ ᑐᑭᓯᔭᐅᑎᐊᐸᑕᒍ ᐃᓄᐃ ᑕᓯᒍᒐ
ᐃᑲᔪᑕᐅᓂᓴᐊᓇᔭᑐ ᒐᐸᒪᓄ
****

1959ᐅᑎᓗᒍ ᑲᓯᓂ ᓂᑎᐱ ?..........
1960ᐅᑎᓗᒍ ᑲᓯᓂ ᓂᑎᐱ ?..........

1959ᐅᑎᓗᒍ ᑲᓯᓂ ᐅᔭᐱ ?..........
1960ᐅᑎᓗᒍ ᑲᓯᓂ ᐅᔭᐱ ?..........

1959ᐅᑎᓗᒍ ᑲᓯᓂ ᐊᐃᐸᐱ ?.........
1960ᐅᑎᓗᒍ ᑲᓯᓂ ᐊᐃᐸᐱ ?.........

1959ᐅᑎᓗᒍ ᑲᓯᓂ ᑎᑎᒐᓂᐊᐱ ?......
1960ᐅᑎᓗᒍ ᑲᓯᓂ ᑎᑎᒐᓂᐊᐱ ?......

1959ᐅᑎᓗᒍ ᑲᓯᓂ ᑭᓚᓗᒐᐱ ? NO....
1960ᐅᑎᓗᒍ ᑲᓯᓂ ᑭᓚᓗᒐᐱ? NO.......
1959ᐅᑎᓗᒍ ᑲᓯᓂ ᑐᑐᐱ
1960ᐅᑎᓗᒍ ᑲᓯᓂ ᑐᑐᐱ

Questionnaire in syllabic script that I administered to each of the hundred hunters in the group at Igloolik. Inventory (gun, sled, canoe). Detailed listing of the hunt and resources in 1959 and 1960. This script was invented and popularized by the Anglican missionaries John Horden, E.A. Watkins, and Edmund James Peck in the nineteenth century, following on earlier work by the Wesleyan James Evans. August 1960, Igloolik.

Nakahu and his wife Oomna at Igloolik. Sketch by Lyon, 1823.

Paul Valéry's "human far north": there I am. The sharp cold nips at my cheeks, and my brow is contracted with tension as if in response to a bout of sinusitis. I cover my cheeks briefly with my warm hands. If these grow numb with the cold, and if clasping them under my armpits doesn't thaw them, I curl my ten fingers and place them in my mouth. I am carrying no European food other than tea and sugar; my diet consists entirely of walrus meat, much of it from last winter, so it is very ripe. Freezing (*kruak*) renders the meat digestible. Some of it smells so bad that the strips of flesh are downright unpleasant to chew and swallow. Still, I remain in good health here, no longer afflicted by blood pressure drops heralded by sudden migraines, as I was in the fall of 1950 during my first exposure to the great Arctic cold of North Greenland (where the temperature with wind-chill can drop to −60°C). Every half hour, we ease off the sled in turns and run behind to stimulate the blood circulation, frequently turning our heads to keep the wind from freezing our faces and lungs. The sharp, aggressive bite of the frost on my cheekbones is not unpleasant. After five or ten minutes I speed up, draw alongside the front of the sled, pivot my upper body slightly, await my moment, and slide down into place behind the Inuk. Awa would not think of showing his passenger disrespect by slowing down to accommodate him. On the contrary, if he is feeling mischievous he whips the dogs just when I am about to sit down.

Suddenly, an event: On the horizon appear three black dots that grow rapidly larger. It is Angugatsiar, Malliki, and their wives, Kraernak and Erkraksak. The men advance like hidalgos in their *qulitaqs* and broad caribou pants, whips in hand, trailed by their panting dogs, while the women remain seated – a matter of protocol. Although sovereign in the igloo, here the women exaggerate their fatigue, and by keeping their hands retracted into their sleeves and adopting a submissive demeanour, they play up their men's strength.

They take their leave, headed west to Igloolik; we continue toward the southernmost camp in this group, Ugsugasuk (Cape Jermain), pausing every two hours or so. At rest stops Awa carves an ice arc out of the floe and hitches the team to it. The sled must be pushed ten metres away from the perpetually famished dogs, or else they will pounce on anything they consider edible: walrus meat, bags, skins, wood, my notebook ... Crouching upwind, I light the Primus* while Awa goes looking for a chunk of iceberg or, failing that, gathers some snow to make water. This is packed into the pot and stirred frequently to reduce the odour that it gives off; in a few minutes the inky black tea will be ready. While waiting, we untangle the dogs' reins, jumping and running in place to keep our feet from freezing. From time to time a friendly glance is exchanged, but Awa is no sentimentalist. He is on a mission and acts like a professional. We sip the tea noisily, as if the sibilance itself could warm us. Awa chews up and swallows the tea leaves. I spit out a few. The meal – slices of blood-red, dark-specked walrus meat chopped with an ax – is eaten standing up, our every movement followed by the twenty half-closed pupils of the prone dogs, their fur standing on end with the tension of hunger. Each receives two or three pieces of frozen meat, tossed out and caught on the fly. Our day at an end, we huddle together under a tent fly on the sled, our makeshift bed.

And so the hours go by. Distances are calculated by the height of the sun, while travel time is measured in *sinik*, "sleeps," the number of overnights that the trip requires. Low gray clouds veil the sky, the rents in them opening out onto an immaculate universe. Shades of whiteness whose every nuance I squintingly analyze: pallid, off-white, plaster, milky, alabaster, ceruse, shining crystal. We round a small iceberg uncannily shaped like a hunchbacked dwarf, its edges giving off a silvery glint. Far away to the west, on the horizon, a large dark stain rises like a vapour: the Melville Peninsula. My mind returns to idleness, wandering at the beck of a word, exploring a shred of an idea,

* A gas stove commonly used by Arctic travellers.

endeavouring to measure the small steam clouds exhaled from our mouths and compare them with those exhaled by the dogs. And once again comes the recurring question I have mused about over the years: why do I spend so much time out here on the white trail, enduring this discomfort and cold?

I have always liked discomfort, the good and familiar kinds. It builds my inner strength. How else to explain that I so quickly got used to living in fetid igloos, eating foul-smelling meat, casually spitting to the right, left, and centre like the Inuit, blowing my nose into my fingers, sleeping bare-chested, body to body, under animal skins, and cheerfully getting up each day to do it all again in this revolting *Umwelt*? *Ajortok!* I can't change my "prehistoric" nature. Be that as it may, my image as a white specialist has followed me here out of the hierarchical, status-obsessed world that I usually inhabit. I cringe from it, knowing too well that it can destroy what I sense to be my deep identity. Thankfully, to these communalist hunters it is a matter of indifference: I am a white man, a know-nothing, and that is that.

How else to explain my ability to adapt to such conditions if not in terms of my conviction that, by adapting, I get in touch with the most primitive layers of my being, the bedrock of my inspiration? Over years of research, this intuitive understanding has become overlain with depositions that have formed a fertile soil for my thinking, giving it the imprimatur of rationality in the process. From the study of ice crystals to rocks to human beings, my path in science has come with time to constitute a personal methodology, a guiding rule: anthropogeography, a discipline that seeks an understanding of the osmosis existing between human beings and the primordial elements since the early Quaternary. I am deeply convinced that discomfort is the great leveller, facilitating our empathic understanding of the Arctic world and the courageous societies inhabiting it.

Sealing in spring. The hunter walks cautiously in front of the sled carrying a white blind. Igloolik, 1961. Sketch by Q'ipsiga, a 30-year-old hunter. Ethnological notebook.

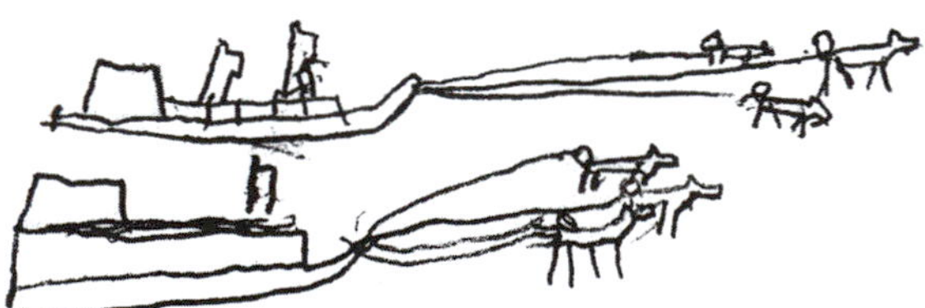

A COSMIC ORDER

Nature is the expression of order, not chaos, and the purpose of this order is the preservation of a whole.[2] Over the course of a ten-thousand-year process during which their social group has gradually become structured as a cohesive collection of families, the boreal hunters have assimilated this principle into their shamanistic expressions of space, time, and fate. It is evident in their sociologically egalitarian but functionally aristocratic social organization. Their anarcho-communalist societies are attempting to shake off the superstructure of a state and its subterranean wiles; put simply, they are antistatist societies, as Pierre Clastres brilliantly showed the Guayaki Indians to be.[3] I witnessed and described such a society while wintering among the 302 Inughuit (Polar Eskimos) of North Greenland in 1950–51.[4] The Inughuit have various subtle arrangements by which ritual redistribution of private wealth takes place amid festivities every two to three months. These ritual celebrations and anniversaries are a means of anticipating seasonal accumulation. Everything belongs to the group: soil, subsoil, water, fauna, flora, houses – even thoughts that one might wish to keep to oneself. The only private possessions are the men's homemade hunting equipment, including sleds and kayaks, and the women's domestic items, including round knife (*ulu*), bone thimble, needle, caribou tendon thread, and soapstone lamp and pot. Inheritance applies strictly to private possessions and is always father-to-son or mother-to-daughter. These hunters' worldview is underlain by the fear of violating the regulating principles of the natural order. Their civil code is a set of major taboos (*agliqtuq*) guiding each person's actions: do not mix food from the sea with food from the earth; temporarily but strictly isolate women who miscarry; eliminate malformed infants. These last two are seen as signs of having displeased the forces of nature. *Silarssuaq* is their word for the laws of equilibrium governing minerals, plants, and animals – what we Westerners call an ecosystem. By listening to this vital energy, the pulsing of air, earth, and sea, Native people have acquired extreme sensory acuity and remarkable powers of memory. No doubt they lack scientific knowledge of geodynamic problems as we understand them, but with their highly attuned neuronal dendrites, they have direct sensory experience of the man-nature dialectic that is the equal of, nay superior to, anyone else's. Using a cognitive approach different from the Western paradigm, the people of the circumpolar regions have come to enjoy an osmotic understanding of the natural order in which physiological memory becomes instinct.

In his last work – before being burned at the stake on the orders of John Calvin – Michael Servetus wrote: "God essentiates essences. From him is derived the lineage of the divine essences which, in turn, instill his essence into other beings ... It is a stone perceived as God. Is it a real stone? Yes, for God, in the wood is wood and in the stone is stone; and since he himself has the strength of stone, the substance of stone, I hold that this is tantamount to being stone, having its essence and form even though not being composed of its matter."[5]

Hunting fashioned palaeolithic human beings, breathed life into their social organization. I undertake to reflect, in the spirit of Gaston Bachelard and Jean Piaget, on the cognitive psychology of these boreal populations and the social logic that has emerged from it over 350 generations. Theirs is not a mechanistic worldview but an intelligence whereby humans, through decentring, have gradually constructed a code of nature, an ordering of the real. To apply Piaget's words on the subject of child psychology, "adaptation is a state of balance ... between two inseparable mechanisms: assimilation and accommodation"[6] – here, assimilation of the geographic environment by marking out the territory, and accommodation as necessary to construct a social life within that space.

Living among these hunters without special equipment or extra provisions, immersed in their conception of the world, I was gradually led to conceive of them as Ice Age atoms, human colluvia moving together, unit after unit, each group overlapping another like tiles on a roof. In such a constrained setting, anthropogeography describes the ongoing human-environment interaction as an increasingly complex series of dynamic innovations. My analysis traces such developments from the physical ecosystem to the contemporary social ecosystem, showing how it is elitist in practice even if egalitarian in intent. The Ariadne's thread of this research, the only excuse for such long journeys, is observation, participation, and from time to time, a brainstorm, a door unlocking. It is laboratory work of a sort: repeat the experiments with new parameters and watch what happens ... Time itself is creative. Anarcho-communalism: a concept I hold dear. I find myself analyzing it in depth, breaking it into its component roots and syllables, searching for their etymology, plumbing their multiple meanings.

And suddenly the shadow of Kropotkin is upon me, and that of Nestor Makhno (1889–1934), the anarchist leader of the peasant revolution in the Ukraine. I meditate on mutual incomprehension, ingrained barriers to communication, and on the peasant utopia built by the saturnine revolutionary of the steppe lands, who, at his only Kremlin audience, was misunderstood by Lenin the intellectual and ideologue. Like Marx and Engels, two other bourgeois men from the cities, Lenin never really grasped the nature of the Russian peasant soul, its decency and piety and heritage of mysticism. "There is a great distance between reality and the recording of reality ... The peasants speak to you seriously ... [B]ecause the bourgeoisie began to treat the work of man as a security on the stock exchange ... the worker in his turn began to treat his own work as a security on the stock exchange ... The capitalistic bourgeoisie ... has infected everything. It has infected itself and ... the people with the same infection."[7]

The people – and this applies to the mujiks and to the kolkhoz members in the Russian countryside as much as to the Inuit of Chukotka – lived their ideals but did not know how to express them. They did not possess the verbal and conceptual apparatus necessary to dialogue with power. Instead, they proudly cultivated their own heroes (heroes unknown to outsiders), knowing full well that they were misunderstood by the hierarchs of Russian society. What was truly needed was a people's university to teach them how to speak the language of the authorities; for what future could an egalitarian society look forward to without an intelligentsia? None. The soviets, cornerstone of Leninism ("all power to the soviets!") failed because the "big talkers" in the Communist Party immediately took away the peasants' and workers' right to speak. This was confirmed for me at Uelen, Chukotka, in September 1990 by the Siberian Inuit party members, who told me how the village, the Inuit "party cell," operated. The delegate from the Central Committee (a Russian, naturally) talked, guided – presided, to put it plainly – and the "Eskimo workers" were asked to state their reactions. The unhappy people would remain silent for what seemed an appropriate amount of time, whereupon one of them would speak everyone's thoughts: "You're right, comrade!" How could they have disagreed with the comrade-president? The KGB barracks, and its forty men, stood fifty metres away, dominated by a perimeter tower that spied on them day and night, there to remind them to observe "politically correct" speech.[8] Obviously, silence was their best option. But "option" is an inaccurate word since speaking in public, beyond sloganeering, was impossible for them in the Soviet Union. They lacked the concepts necessary to articulate a discourse.[9]

What is knowledge in a society of little means, one that has been isolated for millennia, if not the recounting of experience? How can one conceive of the progressive acquisition of knowledge by people of pre- and proto-history other than as an increasingly intimate connection of their being with the physical and animal world surrounding them? Goethe asked, "What is all intercourse with Nature, if we merely occupy ourselves with individual material parts, and do not feel the breath of the spirit which prescribes to every part its direction, and orders or sanctions every deviation by means of an inherent law!"[10]

What I say of the Inuit's toughness, their courage, their spirit of solidarity and equality, their vertical sense of the unity of the world (taking into account the filter of my intuitive and rational knowledge of their culture) is true – but it is only a minuscule part of their truth. Like every one of us, their complexity runs deeper, eludes categorization, and it is this hard core of their secret identity that I obstinately seek to discover. I increasingly sense that I cannot dissociate the people from the elements of their surroundings: the social group that is their backbone, the environment of ice and stone, the animals on which they live, the unreal beauty of the ice floes, and the icy, diaphanous air of which the Inuit are the spoken expression, the inseparable sons and daughters. Are they aware of the grandeur of the country that they inhabit and of being its children? A vain question. The place irrigates their unconscious, courses through their blood, and the same memory that inspires them also reassures them. Wrote Maeterlinck, "of what is this consciousness composed, whereof we are so proud? Of far more shadow than light, of far more acquired ignorance than knowledge; of far more things whose comprehension, we are well aware, must ever elude us, than of things that we actually know."[11]

A Kablunak's concerns. Doubts impel me this way and that on our sled from another age. A seeker of memory, I quest toward all horizons. So many hours in which the mind's gears slip, hours lost forever. Wouldn't it be wiser to sit at home ensconced in old books? A recurring objection that I dismiss at once: I must be *right here*, sitting kitty-corner at this peculiar outdoor office desk, jotting down notes or sketching a landscape. It is lived experience that provides the rusty key.

The dogs, their tails arched upward for ten hours at a stretch, offer the spasmodic contractions of their little pink sphincters to our view. After departure, the first hard turds are expelled, sometimes with a muted cry of pain and a burst of flatulence. Two of them have blackish stools: the "runs." Unforeseen copulation takes place at the slightest hint that we are slowing down for a break. In the early morning, during the first half hour, the dogs nibble one another's ears – a game? – jockeying for position next to the female according to a hierarchy determined by the male leader. Weak, muted cries of complicity, followed by lapping of snow to quench their thirst. And they're off, the wild wolves, for ten more hours of pulling.

This evening my observations will be elementary. Ever the dutiful naturalist, I will transfer the landform details to my notebook, adding pell-mell various ethnographic reflections emerging from my study of names and naming practices. These will be interspersed with more personal comments that vie for space with those devoted to the human-environment osmosis that I have been describing. I reread and carefully transcribe several nouns, Awa assisting me with the pronunciations.[12]

Night falls as we cross Parry Bay en route to the Amitioke Peninsula, progressing at three kilometres per hour along the route of William Edward Parry and his crew (1821–23). At Ignertoq Point we make camp. The ground is

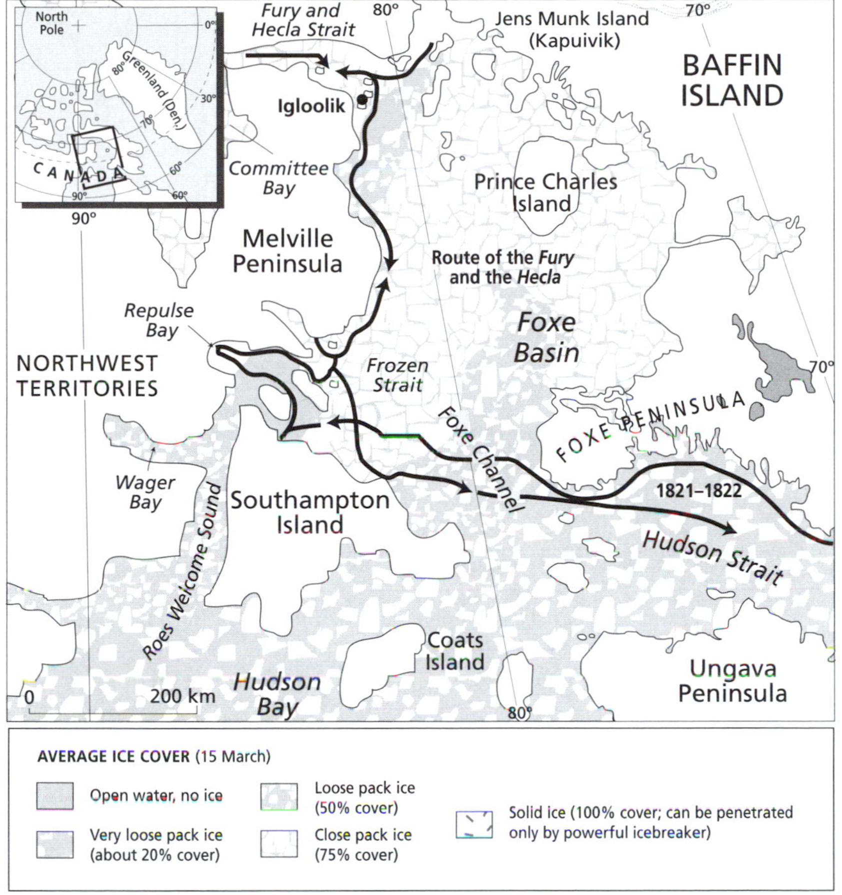

Route of the *Fury* and the *Hecla*, commanded by William Parry, 1821–23. (Ice conditions on 15 March.)

slushy in mid-May, so we travel at night when the sun is low on the horizon and the snow is harder packed. At long last the five overpopulated igloos of Ugsugasuk appear before us. Awa assures me that he has a cousin by marriage who will give us the thirty kilograms of fat and meat (seal and walrus) necessary for his powerful team. If not, he will have to go hunting himself, and this four-day journey will turn into eight. The Inuk's life is at the point of a harpoon or gun; he cannot live alone. He simply must have skins and furs for clothing, walrus and seal leather for whips and harnesses, meat and fat for food and for the dogs, oil for light and heat, but these vital resources are all in unreliable supply. Hence he needs alliances, the primary and surest of these being kinship.

My mission will come to a close in a few days, on 26 May when, at Foxmain, a wide runway with two hangars, I board a military aircraft connected with the DEW Line.* Awa's sled will lead me right up to the craft. Awa, my incomparable guide, diplomat, and friend, *tâwâutit* (adieu).

INSIDE THE Q'ANGMAT

Kapuivik, northeast of Igloolik on Jens Munk Island, northern Foxe Basin. 15 May 1961. Three families of walrus hunters, a subgroup of the Igluligmiut. Arriving late, at 11:00 P.M., we are greeted by two men standing in front of the house in absolute, motionless silence, as protocol requires. While we exchange stares at a distance of five metres, the dogs are kept at bay by slow, balanced movements of the whip. Then appropriate words are spoken and bare hands are shaken – a custom introduced by the nineteenth-century explorers.

Our backs bent, we traverse the low narrow three-metre-long hallway, or *turhuuk*,† scrapings of frost from the ceiling dripping unpleasantly onto our necks. Past this we enter a wide, fifteen-square-metre *q'angmat*, or composite igloo with walls of stone, peat, and wood; a snow roof over a tarp insulates the single bubble-like room. Eleven people are here. The visitor's first sensation is the acrid scent of rotting meat catching at the throat. The common platform is made of uneven boards lined up in a row, while the walls consist of layers of plywood as insulation between the inner and outer walls, of peat and snow respectively. Sealskins lie here and there, shreds of newspaper plug holes as a substitute for wood.

Three seal-oil lamps give off light and heat, two made of soapstone (35 cm long, 12 cm wide, 4 cm deep) and one of blackened metal. The yellow crest of flame (*ikkuma*) shudders, its verticality inhabited by a vital energy. On a shelf, in bohemian disorder, are rags, fake pearls, an empty tobacco can, a ketchup bottle, and some half-eaten seal ribs; on a chipped plate are some char bones and two greasy *ulu*. Also a hammer, a hatchet, and an old soot-encased pot containing walrus meat bathing in a broth. Fat is a way of life here.

* The Distant Early Warning Line was a radar system stretching from Greenland to Alaska and under the exclusive control of the American armed forces.

† The *turhuuk* is the entrance corridor to the traditional igloo. Approximately 85 cm high and 80 cm wide, it reminds the visitor of an umbilical cord leading into the womb. In North Greenland, *kataq* designates the inside of the *turhuuk*.

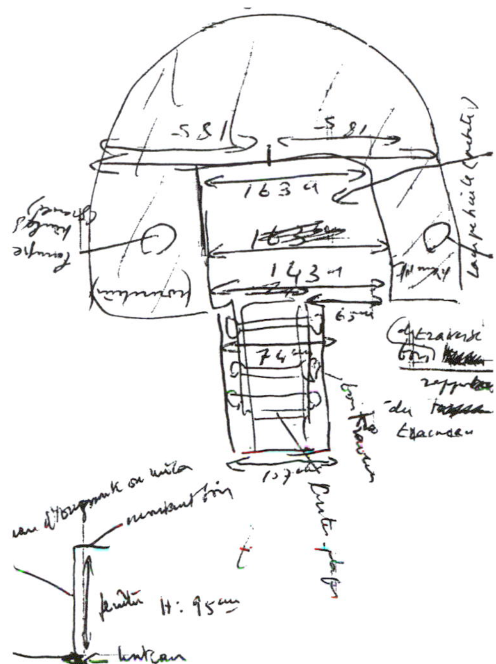

Q'angmat at Naujarolu. Peat walls 24 cm thick (snow-covered in winter), covered by a strong fabric tent and several layered seal or walrus skins: two or three on the sides, two on the apex. The dimensions of this structure are indicated for both the living quarters and the hallway, which measures 74 cm wide by 2 m long. The sole window is made of the bladder of a large seal, 95 cm high. My respondent and fellow canoeist was Pacome Kolaut (b. 1924). Igloolik expedition, August–September 1960. Ethnological notebook.

Yesterday, X, my guide for the evening (Awa being unavailable), had blithely assured me that he would be well received by our hosts. He was alone in this impression: he is treated with scorn, unwelcome, lucky to be allowed to lay down his caribou skin inside. X had hidden an old quarrel from me, believing that his status as guide to a Kablunak would smooth things over. In the silence, a slight curl of the lips serves as a reminder of the dispute. His back curved like a defeated Sarmatian, X acknowledges the awkwardness with a vassal's comportment all the more humiliating in that I am its witness.

The box of tea that I produce as a gift for my hosts is acknowledged as a matter of form, without effusiveness. My provisions will be explored without great interest and will be returned to only out of courtesy. In the centre, standing with torso erect, is the patriarch of the family, Piugatu ("the noble one, the one of good name"), with whom I have spent the previous summer visiting the camps in his sail canoe. His broad forehead and eyes regard the visitors benevolently, but this evening there is also something in the carriage of his head that evinces contempt. I sit to his right. By the wall stands a young woman like a vestal virgin – a *tiguak*, an adoptee, Piugatu tells me, his

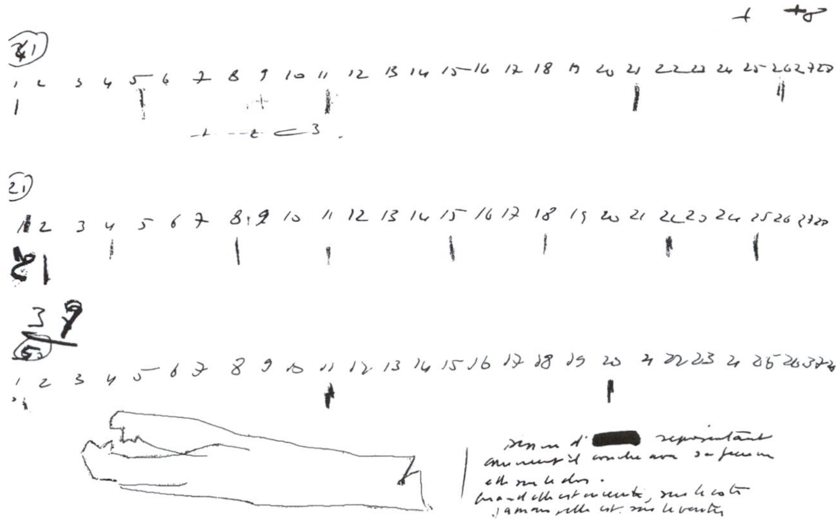

Sexual calendar of a 40-year-old hunter. Depiction of the couple's typical position; the woman lies on her back, while he is on top. When she is pregnant, he approaches her laterally; she does not sleep on her stomach during this period. Igloolik, May 1961. Ethnological notebook.

voice ever so distant. But not a true *tiguak*, the son-in-law, Kripsiga ("he who annoys"), later explains, for she was too old at adoption and the kinship is remote. Charged with keeping the seal-oil lamp lit during the night, she carries out her task with the habitual humility of those who owe a debt. Gestures and stances reflect rank, and I take care to respect the precise hierarchy of seated and prone places. This longstanding custom functions to guard against sexual promiscuity among adults of all ages.* To the left of the host sits his wife, who is keeping an eye on the fat in another oil lamp in case it should start to smoke. Her face is crumpled; her body bespeaks weariness of the daily routine.

Further back on the platform (*illerk*), an old toothless woman stricken with backache lies prone on a caribou skin pillow, gnawing away at her hardened pink gums. As soon as I enter she raises her head like a spring seal and emits

* Unions with sons-in-law, daughters-in-law, nieces, nephews, adopted children, first cousins, and namesakes are prohibited; keeping round-the-clock control of the violence inherent in Inuit culture is a necessity.

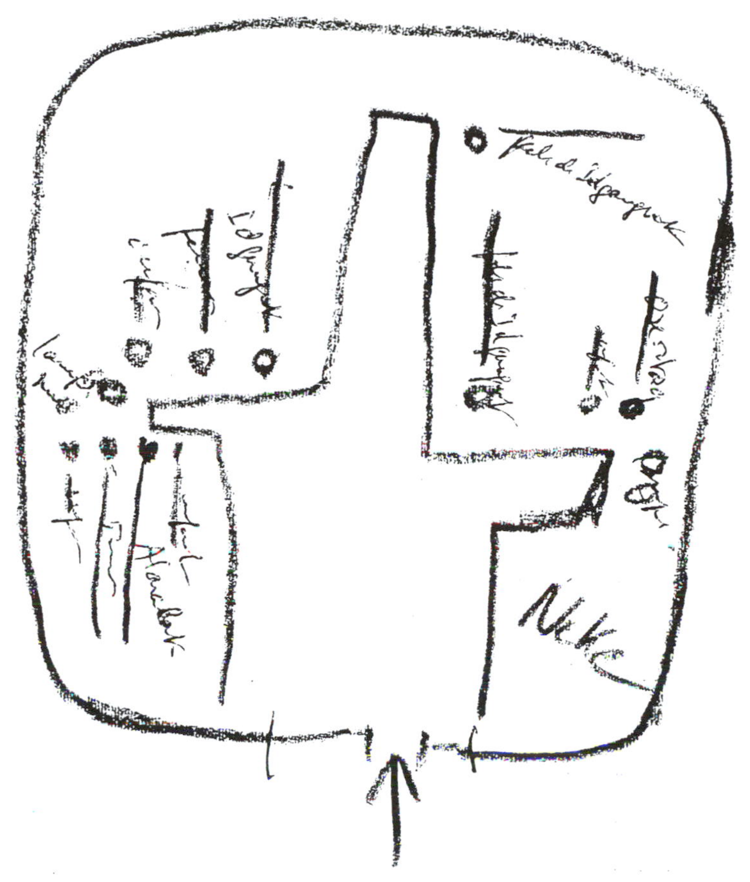

Q'angmat on Q'apuivik (Jens Munk Island) of my respondent Marc Idganguak (b. 1923), a 40-year-old walrus hunter. Winter 1960–61. The *q'angmat* is a 20 (5 x 4) m² winter house made of snow-covered stone, peat, and boards. No table or chairs. Eleven inhabitants. Idganguak sleeps at back left with his wife Keedlah (b. 1923) and one of their children. To the left on entering are three children and a woman, Alarak, who made this drawing. Back right, Idganguak's son and two young children. To the right on entering, frozen seal and walrus meat (*neke*). The *q'angmat* is heated and lit by two stone seal oil lamps at the far left and right; see my *Call of the North*, 159–79, for more photographs. My microeconomic study of the 110 families living in Igloolik in 1960–61 shows that although the area was richer in biological resources than Thule (North Greenland), living standards were much poorer. The reason was the difference in economic systems. While the Greenland economy was protected by socialistic price supports (the state-run Kongelige Grønlandske Handel, or Royal Greenland Trading Company, held a trade monopoly with the Inuit), precipitously declining fox pelt prices in the liberal economy of Hudson Bay ($60 in 1930 versus $5 in 1960) caused major social disruptions. Igloolik, August 1960 and May 1961. Ethnological notebook.

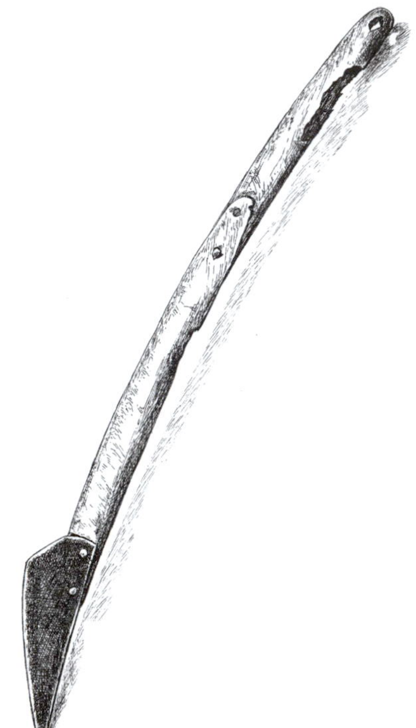

Cleaver, 30 cm in length, still in use among the Inuit for cutting up walrus meat. Given to me by Qayarssuak (b. 1917), one of my best respondents; it was his usual implement for this purpose. Imported iron blade riveted to two-piece bone handle with hole pierced for leather loop. Q'apuivik (southern end of Jens Munk Island), August 1960.

groans and hisses of loathing for the Kablunak, muttered oaths betraying ancient resentments. To her right is an old man whose brief, dry, incessant coughing leaves no doubt that he is tubercular. Hour after hour, he strokes a sealskin belt with scaly fingers. Sitting like buddhas when they can sit up at all, these ageless ones try to get up for a meal in a show of respect for the new arrivals. The meal consists of frozen caribou chopped with an ax on the ground and walrus meat boiled in a blood broth. Fragments of news are exchanged between bites. Two young girls, aged ten and twelve, stand inquisitively by the door, murmuring confidences and hugging each other. Small gifts – a ribbon, seal bones, multicoloured pearls – are passed from hand to hand and commented on in whispers. Childhood friends building an inner world out of such small joys.

A young mother who has just come in wears an *attili* (tailcoat) decorated with rows of white, blue, red, and black pearls and, on the front, at the level of the breasts, two embroidered flowers. Her one-year-old child is in the *amaut* (hood) of her wide *qulitaq*. She rocks from one foot to the other, trying to put him to sleep, but in vain. She sucks away her baby's mucus, turns him over and licks his behind, then slides an abrupt hand under his buttocks and takes him outside to pee, but returns immediately: he doesn't have to go. She feeds him caribou fat mouth to mouth.

A bad cold has swept through the camp; young people, adults, and elders cough open-mouthed, some taking real pleasure in the scraping of the throat.

Camp at Naujarolu, twenty-five kilometres north of Igloolik, summer 1960. Four fabric tents anchored with stones, plan view. At far left (before first tent), top (between second and third tents, left to right), and far right, sealskin drying lines stretched between wooden sawhorses, with pink salmon fillets and black seal intestines drying in the sun. Top left, small stone shelter for puppies; to its right, lake used for camp's fresh water supply, since there were no nearby streams or icebergs. Two boats on the coast; the circles represent barrels. Sketch by Martha, third of Awa's seven children (b. 3 March 1951), age 9 in 1960. Ethnological notebook.

Inside of a snow house at Igloolik, winter 1822. Parry's expedition with the *Hecla* and *Fury*.

They all blow their nose into their fingers and nonchalantly fling the snot onto the ground with a shake of the hand. Sleeping, talking, eating, or lovemaking take place according to whim. Two teenagers kiss nose to nose, something not uncommon now, although it was unknown in 1950 among the Inughuit of North Greenland. The men undress without shame, the women more prudishly. No one stares indiscreetly.

The clothing, mine included, is hung out on the rustic dryer above the lamps. Above our heads hang our spare boots and mitts. The heat rises ... it is imperative to have dry clothes tomorrow. Shreds of printed fabric dangle from the ceiling like hanged men, reminding me of the gypsy caravans or the miserable shacks of famished Irish labourers in London's Soho district. I glide bare-chested into the place assigned to me, under the caribou skins next to the adopted girl, one child away from the host.

Muffled words are whispered in the falling dark flecked with the calming glint of the two small flames. Harmonics of their guttural language, punctuated with "ndgl" and "qr" sounds. Rustlings. Brief words interpreted as secret appeals, submerged thoughts punctuated by furtive glances. Nocturnal citadels in which nuances of accent, or silence, fill the spaces between words. Hyperacousia: like cats, they hear everything. Bodies not touching. A foot away from my face on the blackish floor (*natiq*) are the contours of our prehistoric meal: walrus rib, sucked-dry bones, large axe, two knives red with drying blood. There is a vat of urine, with smaller pots for different people's needs. A few groans, then snores.

In the sticky dark, my lungs drink in the stench of frozen rotted meat, peat, and sweat, the acrid odours rising off the boots and *alirhiq* (socks lined with hare fur). If the foul smell is apparent to me, it must be even more noticeable to them; I am well aware that the Inuit have sharper senses than we do. White people's odours that we ignore – perfumes, toothpaste – are instantly perceived here, leaving most people indifferent but a few revolted. Their sensory acuity is on a par with that of Kaspar Hauser (1812–1833), the German "wild child" studied by Feuerbach who appeared in Nuremberg in 1828 dressed in peasant clothes and bearing a letter indicating that he had been kept in a small dark cell for sixteen years. He often claimed, after his release from captivity, that he preferred the odour of turds to our perfumes and soaps.

On 17 May I leave Kapuivik.[13] Protocol again: Piugatu accompanies me on my sled for several hundred metres. He knows that I will not be coming back. "Tâwâutit," goodbye, he says as he glides off the sled and slowly walks back to his people. He does not turn around.

2

Toward Inuit Self-Government in Canada

The "glorious thirty"* were the years of my prime.

Never had France been so rich. One might imagine that I had considerable resources at my disposal with which to carry out my expeditions. I never did. All my life I and most of my colleagues have suffered the political, scientific, and industrial establishment's neglect of the social or "soft" sciences in favour of the well-endowed, industry-backed "hard" sciences. During one period of austerity, French researchers were limited to one North American trip per year. A government agency oversaw these distant trips and would denounce violators to the Treasury! If I was able to carry on my work, it was thanks to officials of the Canadian government – indeed, I cannot thank them enough. France would have paid for my round-trip ticket to Ottawa, no more. The Far North? Too far, too expensive – and to what end? No sizeable budgets would

* The years 1945–75, corresponding to the rise of Europe as an economic power following the end of the Second World War.

ever be allotted for research in these icy lands over which France exercises no sovereignty. And so history will record that French polar research, especially in the social sciences, has always been a partially failed enterprise due to the absence of an encompassing vision, a spirit of continuity. "Most of the French explorers have been solitary men, left to their own resources; only very rarely has the Government or some company employed or assisted them. Englishmen, Americans, Germans, Spaniards and Portuguese have accomplished, with the support of the national will, what in our case impoverished individuals have begun in vain." The source of these bitter remarks? Chateaubriand, in his memoirs.[1] The problem is longstanding.

CONSULTANT TO OTTAWA

Starting in 1960 and continuing through 1963, fearing that I might be one of the last witnesses to traditional Inuit structures of civilization before they became irrevocably adulterated, I made a considerable number of study tours to the northeastern part of the Canadian Central Arctic,[2] working on contract to the Canadian government. During those years I observed the meanderings of a policy in search of itself. The government departments responsible for industry and the economy were encouraging major investments in the North, but university anthropology departments were sparse in this immense country, and bona fide specialists on Inuit and First Nation issues could literally be counted on the fingers of one hand. It was my great good fortune to meet Diamond Jenness, one of Canada's preeminent anthropologists, in Ottawa, where we had offices on the same floor of a government building. Since his retirement he had wisely been retained to produce a comparative circumpolar study of Arctic administration policy.[3] We both enjoyed free access to confidential departmental archives (reports of ministers, department administrators, the RCMP, etc.), giving us an ideal vantage from which to evaluate federal Inuit policy. I soon became acquainted with this cultivated francophile, Oxford graduate, and former director of the Anthropology Department of the National Museum of Natural Sciences, who had also accompanied Vilhjalmur Stefansson[4] on the ill-fated Canadian Arctic Expedition (1913–18).[5]

Our conversations would continue at lunch in the local pizzerias. Jenness was highly critical of Ottawa, and his verdict was damning: the government's policy for the Indians and Inuit was lacking in coherence.[6] Surveying and lamenting the muddle-headed activities of various departments and divisions, whose outcome had been to condemn several generations of Inuit to miserable lives in the slums of semi-reserves – "a deplorable apartheid," was his comment – he felt compelled to express a rueful desire to see aboriginal assimilation take place even more swiftly than it was. I agreed with his diagnosis – how could I not share the point of view of this eminent observer and renowned specialist on the Copper Inuit of the Mackenzie River delta? – but disagreed with his forecast. In fact, I was continually surprised by his abrupt shifts of opinion. In my view, time must be allowed to do its work, and I have confidence in today's generation of Inuit. The generation then in midlife had, of course, been delivered a knockout punch; the generation born around that time grew up stunted by the creeping, insidious workings of neocolonialism, which sought to buy off inexperienced aboriginal politicians at their people's expense – a rather successful venture, given the genius of certain Inuits for politicking. But the latest generation has brought forth a number of public figures with a vision all the more clear-eyed for their consciousness of their people's humiliation. In preparation for this auspicious development, however, they would have to be sought out and encouraged; and if they were to gain any decisive political influence, the demagogues would have to be kept at bay at all costs.

A RADICAL SCHOOL REFORM

I therefore considered it necessary for a profound pedagogical change to take place at the earliest levels of schooling. This, in my view, is the alpha and omega of any serious thinking about social development and self-government. Primary school is the crucible in which a class of intellectuals is forged. But because the government viewed schooling as mere literacy training, it attracted mediocre teachers from the South (many of whom could not have made a career of it there) by offering substantial isolation premiums. What was needed instead was an elite network of the kind of committed cooperants who are fluent in the local language and regard their mission as a priesthood. My experience of several years of work with Ottawa, and later Quebec, taught me that the emergence of an intelligentsia from a group of communalists takes a great deal of care and time. The Inuit youth of the 1960s did not understand where we were trying to take them and, out of prudence or laziness perhaps, turned in on themselves; the sacrifice of a generation was the result. All things considered – and this was the usual conclusion at which Jenness and I arrived – what was needed was a genuine, comprehensive, well-thought-out policy for the aboriginal minorities. But how could such a thing be implemented when the custodial government (i.e., the English and French speakers in Ottawa) had yet to assimilate the concept of a pluricultural, multinational federation, with all that this awareness entailed? Of course, in Canada there were plenty of physicists, engineers, natural scientists, jurists, bankers, businessmen, and managers, many of them of the highest calibre. But the humanist, the philosopher inspired by the Encyclopedists, the jurist open-minded enough to grasp the importance of customary law – in a word, the intellectual equivalent of a Braudel with knowledge of the Far North and its issues – was a rare individual in the 1960s. Ottawa operated with the paternalism characteristic of the welfare state.

Really, a visionary like Jenness should have been given full authority to act as early as 1945–50, when the first stirrings of modern aboriginal policy were being felt. "They would never have given it to me," he confided. "The political class here does not delegate. When Inuit society was still intact, your ideas of renewal spearheaded by an indigenous elite might have worked. Now it's too late. We've ruined our chances through an addled policy of 'relief.' That's the byword. I'm sorry to say it but our politicians are mediocre. In New Zealand where I come from, there was a policy – right or wrong – for the Maoris. Here, as you've seen, it's the reign of the slapdash. Who is at the helm in Canada? There aren't many true statesmen and policies fluctuate from one election to the next. But you're young: go ahead and form your own opinion!"

The Indian reserve policy had been a disappointment all around, decried by the government, the Indians, and the public alike. Some of the people with whom I spoke had given long thought to British, French, and Spanish colonial history. A group of them had become fascinated with the experience of the Jesuit "reductions" in Paraguay, and their reading had led them to some thoroughly predictable and unfortunate conclusions. The Inuit, with their obscure shamanistic philosophy, had to be sedentarized around the trading posts, "educated," "civilized"; new needs had to be awakened in their youth. The children would attend "residential schools," the adults, immersion programs. Their ethnic structures would be done away with. The indigenous authorities would eventually be "empowered" – but not before they were inculcated with the values of the British-inspired civil service. In a word, assimilation was just the thing.

Now, a people's survival is contingent upon some very specific conditions. First, they must have a genuinely autonomous territory. The Inuit did not.* Second, their language – the foundation of any system of thought, any civilization – must be protected. They did have a language, but the bureaucrats could not speak it. Meanwhile, the English language, through the combined, enduring effects of unilingual education, radio, television, and day-to-day governance, was steadily wiping away the indigenous culture, the culture of the small number of First Nations who coexist with empire, like a damp

* See below for discussion of the founding of Nunavut and Nunavik as self-governed territories – a matter of common sense that nonetheless took over one hundred years (dating from the birth of Dominion in 1867 or the passage of the *Indian Act* of 1876) to achieve.

Group walrus hunting at the edge of the ice floe at Igloolik. The four-metre-long animal, weighing a ton and a half, is harpooned and finished off with the spear; the hunter then drags it onto the ice. In foreground, man fishing alone. Parry's expedition, 1821–23.

sponge.* The third imperative is a self-sustaining economy, the basis of any modern society. To ignore this requisite would be to condemn their way of life to unerring destruction by the market economy. Any inclination to envision a different future would be sapped by a growing dependence on welfare. How could it be otherwise? Our neocolonial system corrupts, and its thrust destroys.

More is better: that is the credo of "development." In the shadow cast by its powerful neighbour to the south, Canada spent millions of dollars in the Arctic on English-language schools and museums, telecommunications, and industrial projects. Everything was a handout. The Inuit were steadily unlearning the very idea of working to survive, as an unpiloted administra-

* For example, the Inuvialuit (Mackenzie Inuit) saw their language driven to the brink of extinction in the twentieth century through contact with Anglo culture.

tion led them onto the slippery slope of relief. In the living laboratory that was the North, I vainly sought for the outlines of a policy, a science of man with its genealogy of ideas. All I found was humdrum bureaucracy.

Specifically, the North was administered by offices populated by bureaucrats, some of whom had no personal experience of an Inuit village, people whose careers were nurtured by intrigue, ambition, and patronage. However, the real power in those villages had long been – still was – the Hudson's Bay Company (HBC). From the promulgation of its charter in 1670 through the extension of its mandate to the entire North with the absorption of the North West Company in 1821 and onward, it had operated something close to an unregulated monopoly in the North.[7] As for policing and education of the Natives, the privileges of the RCMP and the churches in those areas rested on the *Indian Act* of 1876 and various subsequent interpretations of federal law, and were jealously guarded. The government, torn between divergent interests, hewed to its narrow course, while the ultimate arbiter of the situation – the voter – remained quite ignorant of what was happening.

Late spring, breakup of pack ice. The Inuit come and go on the ice, now intercut with channels, carrying their kayaks upside down on their heads to keep their hands free. Birdskin jacket, feathers turned out; bearskin trousers with dog- or musk-ox-skin knee pads; sealskin boots. Igloolik, 1823. Drawing by Lyon.

TO LEVEL UP OR TO LEVEL DOWN?

Yes, "development" was the governing idea of the years 1960–65 – but the unfortunate Inuit hunters, in thrall to their past, were not seen as its vehicle. Isolated as they were, how could they have had a ghost of an idea of our intentions? Amid a welter of projects, the status of Indians and Inuits was an issue to be moved to the back burner, left to be resolved at some later time.[8] Meanwhile, their traditional way of life was obviously, inevitably deteriorating, and I denounced the metastases of this cancer, which was bound to render the intended assimilation abortive. So many forces were aiding and abetting the deterioration: the mining companies, the school system, television, the job market, the government agencies, and substance abuse, among others. "They will assimilate," thought the bureaucrat. "Their history will meld with Canada's. The country will become one people from the Atlantic to the Pacific and from the Arctic to the Great Plains." In this benighted nationalist vision, then reigning supreme, Canada's interests dictated an ever-increasing degree of centralization. Meanwhile, the Winnipeg-based HBC managed the situation as best it could, although it had no such thing as a plurinational social policy. Obviously not: the Company wouldn't have tolerated that kind of an imposition by government. The trader is not an agent of the state. But equally germane, how could the Canadian federal government have imagined the necessity of such a policy? In two centuries of searching it had not succeeded in finding a solution to the problems posed by the coexistence of two founding peoples, French and English, from the Atlantic to the Pacific – let alone their coexistence with the Natives.

What about the Inuit, in their camps? Could they have resisted? They did not possess the means, nor did the white intellectuals and specialists who took an interest in their case. And Ottawa had a knack for keeping distant troublemakers in check. Any individuals with the tendency to be insubordinate were demoted. If they put up public resistance – as in the case of the governor of the Bank of Canada (a national debate that I witnessed) – a smear campaign was mounted and their careers were ruined. If they kept quiet, they might be offered other positions. I dare say that advocacy on behalf of the rights of the First Nations was a highly subversive notion in the early 1960s.

"Ethnology is an expiation," as Claude Lévi-Strauss reminds us. The West's colonization of the First Nations has completed its fifth century now. Starting with Columbus's arrival, a genocide swept over the native American empires, leaving at least fifty million dead. As we enter the third millennium, policymakers have all the proof they need that civilizations are mortal. The cemeteries are there before their eyes, to be visited with the family, allowing us to

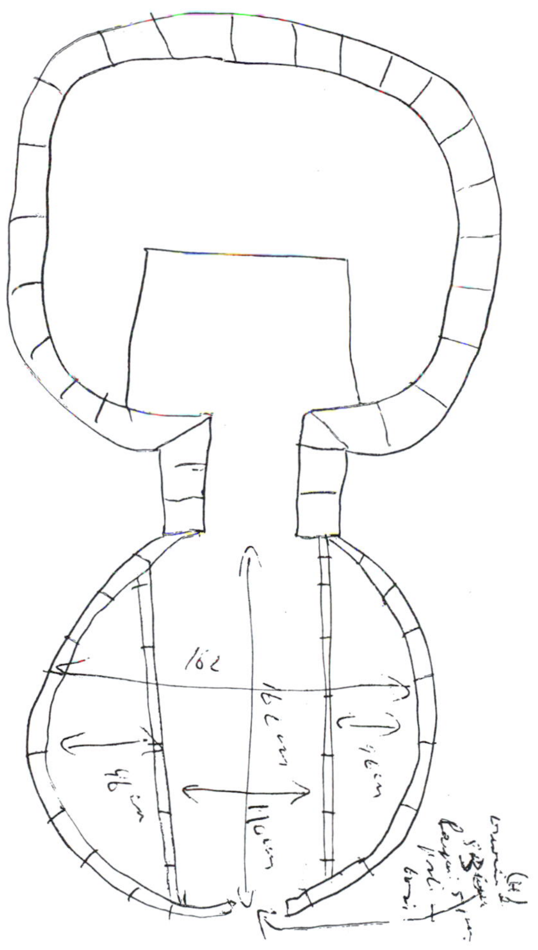

Sketch by Awa (b. 1921), my guide and respondent, of his snow house, Igloolik (Naujarolu); measurements indicated by the author. Plan and side views. Igloolik expedition, August 1960.

experience a twinge – a little twinge – of nostalgia for lost exoticism, mixed with pride in our conquering force. And if this is not enough, there are the "museums of civilization" in our imperial capitals – temples built in honour of the civilizations that we have reduced to extinction.

"A CONTINUING STATE OF ABSENCE OF MIND"

It would be unfair to imply that no Canadian public figures ever expressed concern about the situation. Some did – at the highest levels, in fact.

In a now-famous speech to the House of Commons on 8 December 1953, visionary prime minister Louis Saint-Laurent made this resounding admission: "Apparently we have administered these vast territories of the North in an almost continuing state of absence of mind."[9] 1867–1953: it had taken nearly a century for a great nation to become aware of its identity as an Arctic state and of its concomitant responsibilities toward its Indian and Inuit populations. *Puissance oblige.* Yet nearly half a century more would elapse before this same nation would take decisive action.*

The strategic issues were clear: the Northwest Territories and the Yukon made up 39.3 per cent of Canada's area while the aboriginal population of these four million square kilometres, Indians and Inuit combined (the former comprising a slight majority), was only 40,000. And so, under the *Indian Act* of 1876, the aboriginal nations were protectorates of sorts, their members wards of the state without full civil rights until much later, due to their small numbers and their stigma as an "uncivilized" people. They did not begin to receive family allowances, for example, until 14 August 1944, when an act of Parliament authorized an allowance of five or six dollars per child, depending on the age and size of the family; however, this allowance was often confounded with relief, and it is likely that the distinction was not always clear in subsequent years.[10]

In 1960 there was progress in the form of an international research program, an audit of sorts, undertaken with the guidance of American and European experts. The impetus for the program came from Jacques Rousseau, the eminent director of the Human History Division of the National Museum of Canada and former director of the Montreal Botanical Garden, who was to become a good friend. To inaugurate the cooperation program, the National

* Consider suffrage, for example; it was not granted to status Indians at the federal level until 1960, and a similar situation obtained with regard to provincial suffrage.

Museum invited me to coordinate an initial expedition (July–October 1960) to the Igloolik area of Foxe Basin (Inuit population: 494 individuals, 109 families, in August 1960) north of Hudson Bay. My mandate was to ascertain the current status of Inuit societies and to formulate policy recommendations. I was the only European in a wide-ranging program that should have been broader still. But unluckily, Rousseau was one of those strong personalities subjected to political pressures. Stupidly maligned by some of his colleagues, he was forced to resign, and his departure scuttled the program. My four subsequent expeditions (1961–63) took place under the aegis of the Northern Co-ordination and Research Centre (NCRC), a division of the Department of Northern Affairs and National Resources, to which I am greatly indebted (see figs 2.6, 2.7, and 2.8 showing route maps of these five expeditions).[11]

My solitary expeditions were sequenced so that I visited the sites from east to west, continuing in the direction that I had been following since 1950, the reverse direction of the great prehistoric Inuit migration. The important sites visited included three trading posts central to the history of the west coast of Hudson Bay – Rankin Inlet, Chesterfield, and Baker Lake.* I also went to Spence Bay (now Taloyoak) in the Canadian Central Arctic to study the seminomadic Netsilingmiut of the Boothia Peninsula (south of the Magnetic Pole) and to Gjoa Haven to study the enigmatic Utkuhikhalingmiut of Back River.

As I began this work, I was naturally curious about the nature and foundations of the government's policy. Unlike the Indians, the Inuits' relations with the authorities were not governed by the *Indian Act* of 1876 or other laws. Policy was decided pragmatically, by trial and error. Since the nineteenth century, the only new contributions to their way of life had been trading-post items such as firearms, metal traps, cloth fabrics, wood, nails and screws, domestic utensils (knives, hatchets, saws, files, gimlets, teapots, cooking pots), matches, certain staples (flour, molasses, sugar, tea), and tobacco. These purchases had been subtly encouraged by the HBC, a profit-making enterprise, and the Inuit had become financially dependent. Other than that, they continued to face their harsh lives with exceptional courage grounded in ancient traditions and rudimentary technologies.

As for government-sponsored medical care, it had been a sporadic, uncertain affair prior to 1921. In that year, O.S. Finnie became director of the Northwest Territories and Yukon Branch of the Department of the Interior and began to advocate a generous health and social assistance program. He

* Baker Lake is at the head of Chesterfield Inlet, 300 kilometres from the coast.

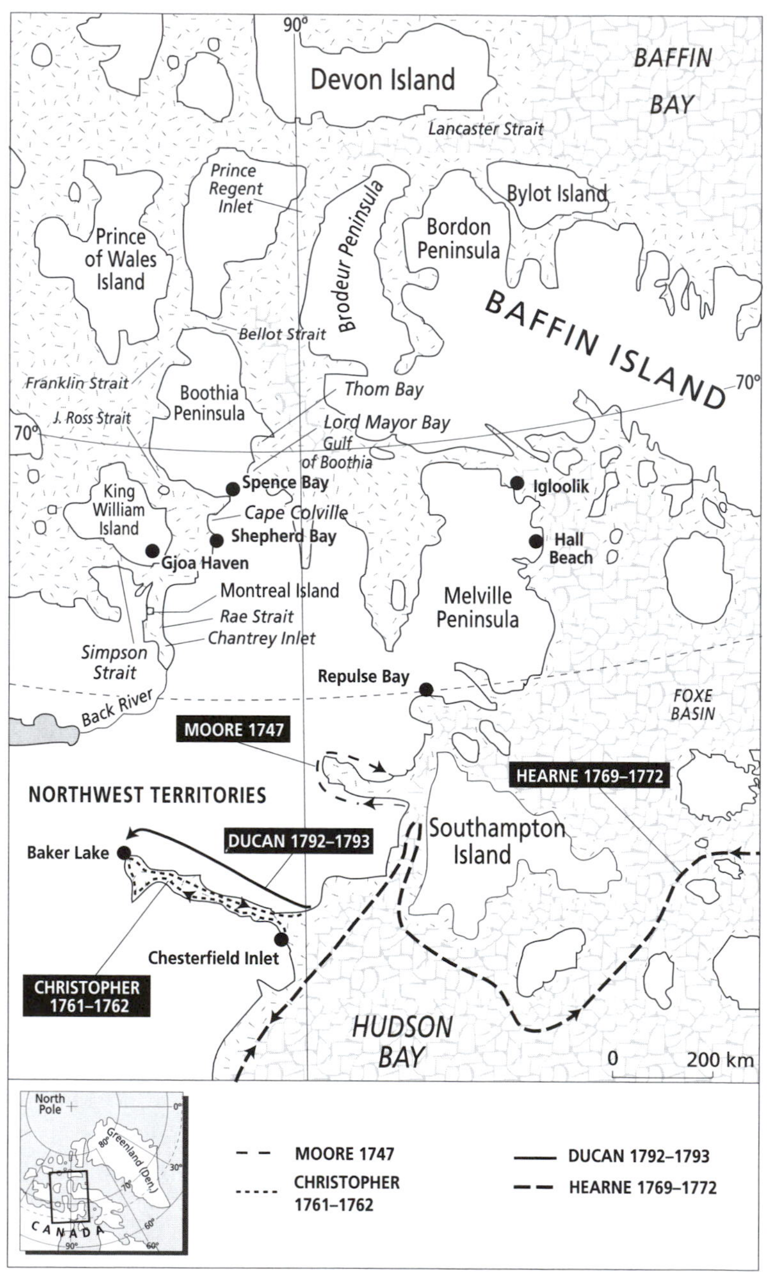

1747–1924: Routes of major expeditions to the Canadian Eastern Arctic, indicative of the many close contacts between Inuit and explorers during that time.

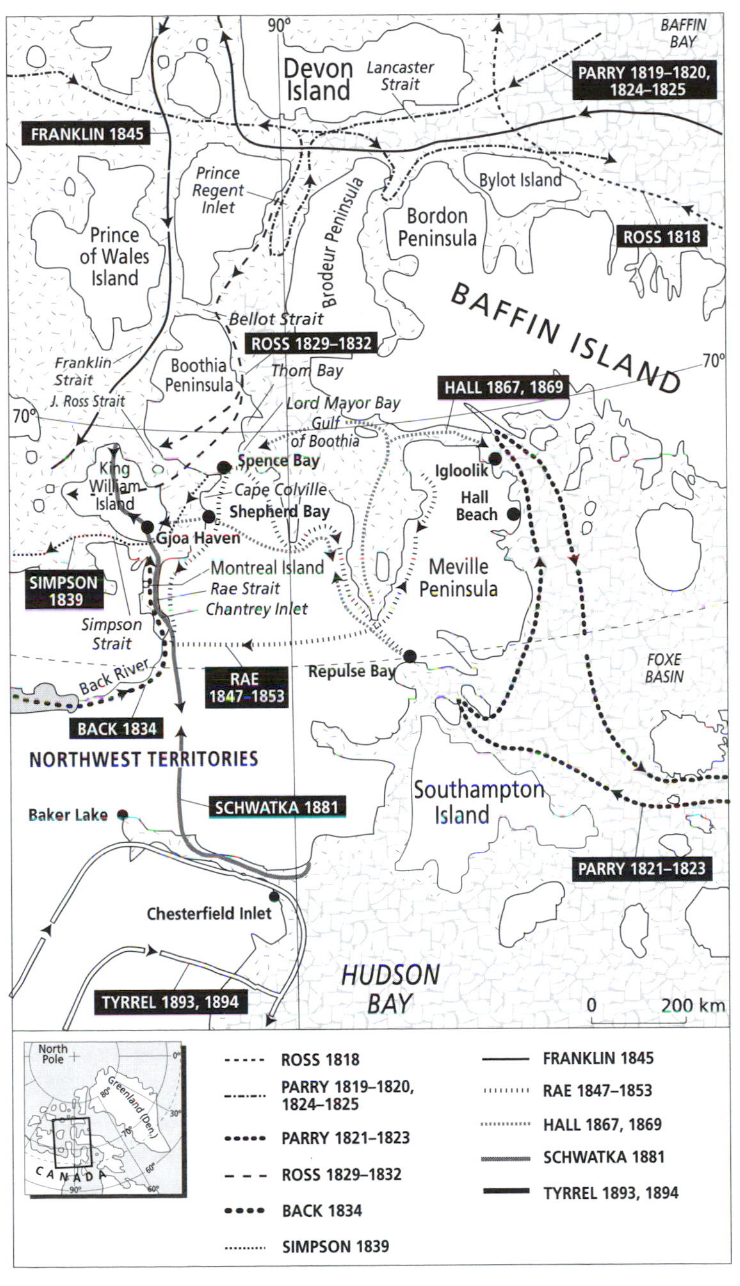
Devon Island
Lancaster Strait
BAFFIN BAY
PARRY 1819–1820, 1824–1825
FRANKLIN 1845
Prince Regent Inlet
Bylot Island
Bordon Peninsula
Brodeur Peninsula
ROSS 1818
Prince of Wales Island
BAFFIN ISLAND
Bellot Strait
ROSS 1829–1832
Franklin Strait
Boothia Peninsula
Thom Bay
HALL 1867, 1869
J. Ross Strait
Lord Mayor Bay
Gulf of Boothia
Spence Bay
Igloolik
King William Island
Cape Colville
Hall Beach
Shepherd Bay
Gjoa Haven
SIMPSON 1839
Montreal Island
Rae Strait
Chantrey Inlet
Meville Peninsula
Simpson Strait
Repulse Bay
FOXE BASIN
Back River
RAE 1847–1853
BACK 1834
NORTHWEST TERRITORIES
Southampton Island
SCHWATKA 1881
Baker Lake
PARRY 1821–1823
Chesterfield Inlet
HUDSON BAY
TYRREL 1893, 1894
0 200 km
North Pole
Greenland (Den.)
CANADA
ROSS 1818
PARRY 1819–1820, 1824–1825
PARRY 1821–1823
ROSS 1829–1832
BACK 1834
SIMPSON 1839
FRANKLIN 1845
RAE 1847–1853
HALL 1867, 1869
SCHWATKA 1881
TYRREL 1893, 1894

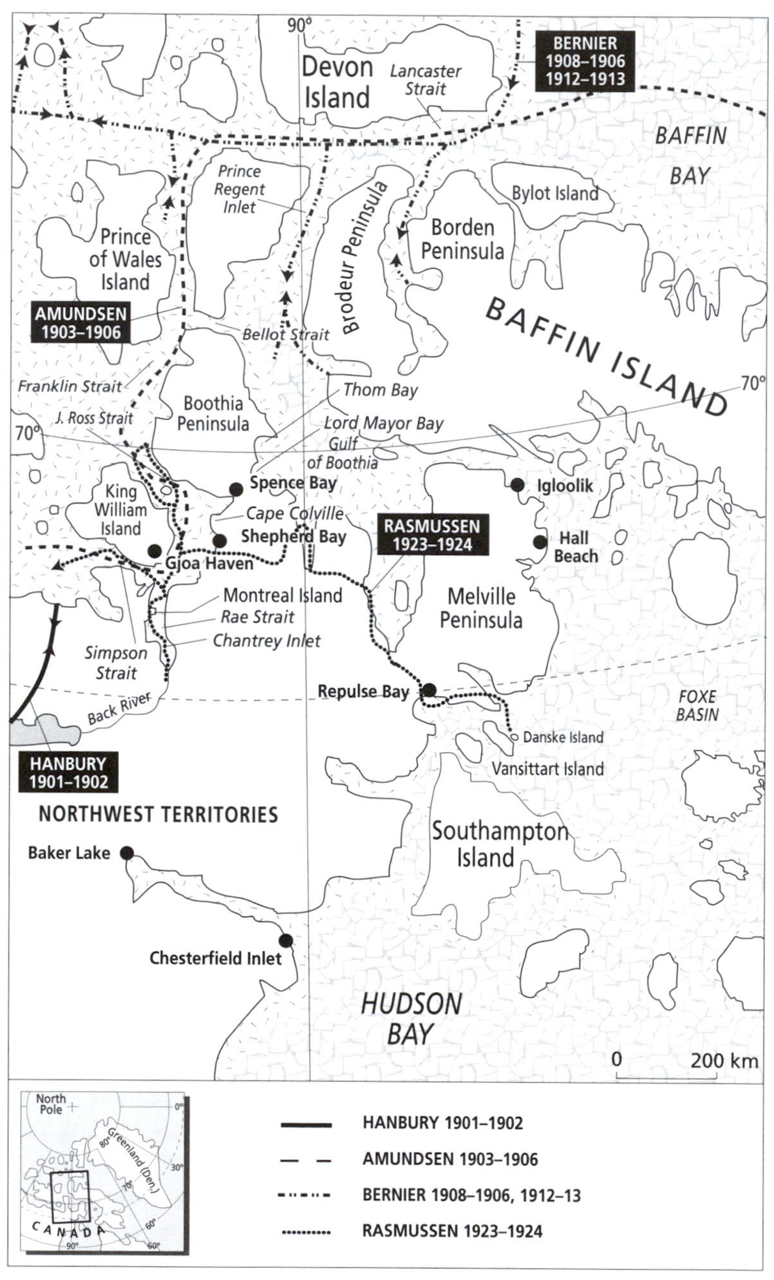

Devon Island
Lancaster Strait
BERNIER 1908–1906 1912–1913
BAFFIN BAY
Prince Regent Inlet
Bylot Island
Brodeur Peninsula
Borden Peninsula
Prince of Wales Island
AMUNDSEN 1903–1906
Bellot Strait
BAFFIN ISLAND
Franklin Strait
Thom Bay
Boothia Peninsula
J. Ross Strait
Lord Mayor Bay
Gulf of Boothia
Spence Bay
Igloolik
King William Island
Cape Colville
RASMUSSEN 1923–1924
Shepherd Bay
Hall Beach
Gjoa Haven
Montreal Island
Melville Peninsula
Rae Strait
Chantrey Inlet
Simpson Strait
Repulse Bay
FOXE BASIN
Back River
Danske Island
HANBURY 1901–1902
Vansittart Island
NORTHWEST TERRITORIES
Southampton Island
Baker Lake
Chesterfield Inlet
HUDSON BAY
0 200 km
North Pole
Greenland (Den.)
CANADA
HANBURY 1901–1902
AMUNDSEN 1903–1906
BERNIER 1908–1906, 1912–13
RASMUSSEN 1923–1924

was successful at first, appointing physicians to serve on the government's Eastern Arctic patrol ships and providing medical care to four coastal Arctic settlements. Unfortunately, his branch was abolished as a cost-cutting measure when the Conservative Bennett government came to power in 1930. The prevailing idea then was to push responsibility for health care provision off onto the churches and charities, an illusory delegation, as anyone can see: missionaries cannot take the place of medical doctors and nurses.[12]

Meanwhile, the realities remained stubborn. Infant mortality was high and the average life expectancy of twenty-five years as low as ever.[13] The federal government's provision for a police force was insufficient: two RCMP constables in each of only thirty posts distributed over an immense area, with powers circumscribed by law. And as I have stated, white authority in the North was in fact exercised by a triumvirate that also included the manager of the HBC post and one or two resident, constantly feuding Catholic or Anglican missionaries.[14] The schools, most of them, were denominational.

Scientific research on the Eastern Arctic Inuit had begun with the nineteenth-century British expeditions and continued at the impetus of other nations. Setting aside the forty expeditions in search of Sir John Franklin, the initiative to pursue the study of the Arctic after William Parry's pioneering work in the Igloolik area (1821–23) and John Ross's among the Netsilik (1829–33) had been European. The many European explorers included Franz Boas, the German American geographer and anthropologist, who travelled to Frobisher Bay/Iqaluit (1883–84); Knud Rasmussen of Denmark and his watershed Fifth Thule Expedition across the Canadian Arctic (1922–25);[15] and the Swiss Jean Gabus and the Frenchman Jean Michéa, who led expeditions to Eskimo Point (now Arviat) for geographic research (1938–39) and ethnographic research (1946–47), respectively. Later observers included the Dutch jurist Geert van den Steenhoven, who visited the Netsilik (1955, 1957); the Belgian Oblate Franz Van de Velde, who took meticulous notes about the communities of Pelly Bay starting in 1954; US ethnologist David Damas, who studied kinship issues (1967–70); US anthropologist James Van Stone; and myself (my microeconomic and ethnohistoric studies of 1960–63). There had been no follow-up to the debacle of Stefansson's Canadian Arctic Expedition. Due to the ensuing recriminations (several scientists had questioned Stefansson's competence) as well as the spectacular cost overrun, the government had become disenchanted with the idea of funding further research. The next major Canadian effort had to wait until 1959–65, when my colleague and friend Asen Balikci of the National Museum of Canada did extensive research on the Netsilik. However, only in the latter half of the 1960s did Canadian Arctic research in the social sciences come into its own with the creation of ambitious multidisciplinary research programs.

AN ALARMING SITUATION

On my arrival in 1960, the social and economic status of the Inuit was indeed stark. In the previous decade, an unprecedented economic crisis had struck the high latitudes with extreme severity. Plunging fur prices and steadily declining caribou numbers (this latter trend being of uncertain causation and beginning about 1930) had drastically impoverished the Inuit, especially the group of nomadic hunters known as the Caribou Inuit, even then one of the most destitute peoples on the planet. Decimated by endemic famine, their awful plight caused no outrage among Canadians; in fact, it was just about invisible. The people's misery, if noticed at all, was written off as natural and inevitable; two deaths here, five over there. Who in the world knew that rich Canada, with its powerful banks, busy universities, and wealthy churches was also home to starvation? Only the atrocious famines of Garry Lake (nineteen deaths) and Back River (5 per cent mortality) in the late 1950s attracted any attention.* Further, both miscarriage and infant mortality rates had risen in all the groups of the Central Arctic. In the first four decades of the twentieth century, the Inuit population of the Ungava Peninsula (then known as Nouveau-Québec, now Nunavik) had dropped by over 60 per cent.†

Precarity was nearly universal, indigence the norm, abject poverty the lot of many.[16] All the Inuit groups that I visited on the Boothia Peninsula and in the Central Arctic were living a life on the margins. My two expeditions to the Igloolik region confirmed the high infant mortality rate and the troubling incidence of morbidity (tuberculosis, polio). Lung diseases were, in many cases, fatal. In the 1960s, nearly 8 per cent of the Inuit population was hospitalized in the sanatoriums of southern Canada; in fact, after visiting Igloolik I carried on my research in a large sanatorium south of Toronto, conducting individual interviews with several patients from that region. To the Canadian government's credit, it ultimately succeeded in eradicating tuberculosis thanks to an assiduous effort started in 1955. Still, no economic alternative to hunting and fishing was ever envisioned. In short, I witnessed the beginning of the end of a suppressed history of ethnic and familial tragedies.

Following his expedition in 1925, Knud Rasmussen had deplored the Canadian government's sluggishness in addressing the problems that plagued the Inuit. He urged the authorities to take action, warning that the HBC, whose

* We return to this matter in the discussion of my own expedition to the region in 1963; see chapter 5.

† These latter Inuit groups were only – barely – saved by the arrival of American military bases in 1942–43.

considerable profits depended on trapping, stood to kill the goose that laid the golden eggs. Years later, continual appeals by the writer Farley Mowat, a man of great courage, also went unanswered. Worse, the HBC used a polemical style ("those are just stories") to conceal from the public the hardness of the dramas evoked in his generous books, which are rare in contemporaneous Canadian literature for their forceful expression of solidarity with the Inuit. The reality was truly awful, and only late in the day did the facts become impossible for all to ignore. At the time, no nongovernmental organization (NGO) or quasi-NGO – not the Red Cross, not even the Quakers – undertook the defence of these threatened peoples. The churches with their rich endowments and extensive networks of cathedrals, schools, colleges, universities, and hospitals held no special fundraising drives, deferring instead to the local missionaries, who were themselves (particularly the Oblates) impecunious.[17] Why this inertia on the part of an otherwise charitable Canadian public? I wonder. For one thing, the icy solitudes of the North were remote, separated from the country's major population centres by vast, impenetrable boreal forest; the collective memory of struggles with the Native peoples may have prevented the average Canadian, the man on the street, from even imagining that he could venture beyond it. Besides, all the trappings of a sovereign administration – police, trading posts, evangelical missions – were in place. Public opinion was ill-informed by a press that was delinquent in its duty, while the universities took no interest in the academic issues raised by these regions and remained mum. In short, Canadians had little idea of the dire poverty afflicting these societies. They simply assumed that if the Inuit needed help, then the government must be providing it, as the fraternal spirit of the great and generous Canadian democracy demanded.

1960–65: Ottawa dithered, adopting a most English "wait and see" position. But it was not indifference. As I reread the reports of the Department of Northern Affairs' Arctic Division, I am struck by the honesty exhibited by some senior officials, by their pragmatic, extremely cautious approach to decision making. To intervene, they argued, would be to shoulder the burden of across-the-board relief, while to do nothing would be to run the risk of a catastrophe. They were worried. They conferred at length. But they lacked encompassing vision, perspective, a guiding philosophical or geohistorical worldview. Their reports were inspired by "soft humanism": *someone*, they said, should be devising an innovative policy for this minority. Fine, but who? More than consultation, what was needed was decisive action. The police reports – in tones varying according to the constable's personality – talked of laziness, ingrained fatalism, or transitory difficulties. The missionaries lamented their inadequate means, while the accounts of other on-the-ground observers (prospectors, filmmakers, photographers) formed a chorus of con-

...aux Esquimaudes à conception différée

L'Université de Montréal, un carrefour mondial des études arctiques ? . . .

Un eskimologue français, encore jeune mais déjà internationalement connu, M. Jean Malaurie, le souhaite aussi vivement que ceux qui l'ont invité à donner une série de cours au nouveau Département d'Anthropologie de l'U. de M.

par Raymond GRENIER

Il considère même que la grande université montréalaise faillirait à une vocation naturelle qui est en même temps un "devoir", en ne profitant pas de sa position géographique et culturelle unique pour développer "de toute urgence" un foyer de recherche arctique s'inspirant à la fois des travaux français et américains dans ce domaine et s'enrichissant de ses propres études dans le Grand Nord canadien.

— Pourquoi un "devoir" pourquoi "de toute urgence"?

Interview with the author, *La Presse* (Montreal), July 1960.

tradictory clichés: "all is well"; "fish is abundant but they refuse to eat it"; "the trading posts have reduced a once-great people to laziness and begging."

No initiatives were taken to give the Inuit administrative responsibilities or, for instance, to equip them with radio transmitters in case of emergency. "Too primitive. They wouldn't understand," I was told in the spring of 1963 on my return from Back River, the remark betraying the prevailing official prejudice of the Inuit as underdeveloped and taboo-ridden rather than the heirs of a genuine philosophical worldview. In the grips of this confusion, the administrator in question sent a second team of investigators to interview just one of the between 40 and 100 Keewatin families, after which it was decided to do ... well, nothing in the way of a solution. This was typical; problems like these were left to be "solved" downstream instead of prevented with prompt action. An "in-depth review" would be undertaken. For good measure, the department's and the Royal Canadian Air Force's (RCAF) aerial operations were stepped up. Numerous pilots built their qualifications from these northern overflights, the costs of which ballooned to prohibitive, even scandalous levels compared with the human tragedy unfolding below them and the paltry amounts of relief distributed. All expenses considered, the disproportion was unbelievable.

In the late 1940s, discouraged by the administrators' perceived inability to help these intractable nomadic peoples, the government had come to favour deportation or villagization – "relocation," in official parlance – as a solution. It had no illusions about the value of this enterprise, and the inevitably disastrous outcome is well known – one thinks of the misbegotten 1953 attempt to colonize the islands of the Arctic archipelago by creating the towns of Resolute Bay and Grise Fiord and populating them with Inuit families from Ungava (see below). The failure of this typically short-sighted manoeuvre on the part of the responsible authorities was obvious by 1963. Nor were Canada's social sciences faculties equal to the challenges of administering Canada's North and northern peoples. They lacked the resources and a specific research interest in the Inuit minorities. In 1961, at the request of Fernand Braudel, the president of my home institution, I accepted a visiting professorship in the

Caribou hunting on the lake by Inuit hunters using a mixture of land-based and coastal techniques, at Igloolik. Parry's expedition, drawing by Lyon.

Anthropology Department at the Université de Montreal as part of his initiative to establish a professorial exchange program with Quebec. For my part I would have preferred a nonteaching assignment in the Department of Northern Affairs in Ottawa, which held authority over Inuit policy for the Northwest Territories. This would have enabled me to build closer ties with my English-speaking colleagues (although naturally, I did maintain my interactions with that department). Although I was warmly welcomed at the Université de Montréal, I had some difficulty at this time convincing my colleagues that Inuit civilization should be a larger and more prominent part of the research agenda.

That era is remote now. By the 1980s a vigourous reform was taking place, a sign of the gradual enlightenment of the governing classes in Ottawa and Québec City, leading to self-government for the Inuit with the imminent creation of the territories of Nunavut and Nunavik. Large, high-calibre northern studies units had made their appearance at both English-speaking and French-speaking universities. The future of aboriginal minorities was now clearly seen as pivotal to the future of the great Canadian nation.

"RELOCATION": RESOLUTE AND GRISE FIORD, 1953

But let us return for a moment to darker times; specifically, to the Inuit relocations of 1953. Strategic goal: to stake Ottawa's claim to sovereignty over the High Arctic deserts of Ellesmere Island by establishing an aboriginal presence there. The government was concerned, among other matters, that my Ellesmere sledge expedition of 1–6 June 1951 in the company of four Inuit hunters from North Greenland (the island was their traditional hunting grounds) had exposed a threat to Canadian sovereignty.

In August 1953 seven ill-informed volunteer families from the Inukjuak (Port Harrison) area in northern Quebec and three families from Pond Inlet on Baffin Island boarded the *C.D. Howe* with their belongings. They were taken to the existing military outpost and weather station at Resolute Bay on Cornwallis Island as well as to a new settlement called Grise Fiord at the southern end of Ellesmere Island.[18] Other families would join them over the years.

Much later, in 1991, stirred by rumours and goaded by justly alarmed public opinion, Parliament finally reexamined the episode as part of the newly appointed Royal Commission on Aboriginal Peoples. The inquiry revealed that the officials in charge had failed to provide the conditions necessary to bring sustainable Inuit hunting communities into being in this new, desolate land. The hunters' total dependence on the neighbouring military bases quickly became evident. Such "post Eskimos" had been described in demeaning terms by the authorities after a similar experience at Frobisher Bay; one RCMP constable had deemed them "unpredictable, unreliable, and unemployable."[19] Yet the relocation experience had been backed by the most modern equipment (icebreakers, helicopters, radio), qualified RCMP and HBC staff, and substantial budgets. What was missing was a guiding logic.

It came out that the officials in charge had possessed minimal sociological and ethnographic training and expertise, and that what they did possess was tainted with colonialism and paternalism. As for the Inuit, they were perfectly competent hunters and did not lack for competent, even charismatic leadership. At Resolute Bay, a man named Joseph Idlout played this role. However, he ultimately proved unable to cope with the difficult transition from Pond Inlet, succumbed to alcoholism, and died in an unexplained accident (possibly suicide) in 1968. If the Inuit had been employed on contract and allowed to return to their community of origin from time to time, the "experiment" might have been a resounding success – I say "might have," but it is doubtful, for the mistrustful authorities would probably have undermined it.

Media attention to what became an "affair" revealed that this modern state, lacking the appropriate civil servants, had every interest in delegating its powers. Power to the Eskimos! Indeed, and without delay. The Inuits' five-thousand-year history on this coastline has always stood as an eloquent demonstration of the capacity of these semi-nomadic bands for adaptation and innovation. And this was not the only significant affair: the first slums had made their appearance on the west coast of Hudson Bay at Eskimo Point and Rankin Inlet as well as at the far-inland settlement of Baker Lake, where the slow death of a land-based hunting culture was taking place. I had observed this in 1962 and heard the distressing grievances of the "relocatees." The Caribou Inuit despised hunting at sea and did not get along with their coastal cousins. Observing the scene at the time, various officials came to rather embittered conclusions.*

In fact, the government's internal audits revealed that the main concern of officials at the time was to "put out fires," to deal with problems that could not be put off while letting others slide. For a region representing one-third of Canada's land area, it would have been the prime minister's responsibility to define an overarching policy. But the North, from 1940 to 1970, was of no electoral consequence. Oil and ore were not yet being exploited due to the costs of extraction and shipping. The bureaucrats wavered, feeling quite alone in the face of the daunting realities. There was, as I have mentioned, an abor-

* My Rankin trip is described in chapter 4.

Group of Inuit women at Igloolik wearing caribou skin clothing, as drawn by Lyon during Parry's expedition. In 1961 roughly the same cut of clothing was in use, although it was narrower and had fewer decorative motifs. The women no longer wore double vests, nor were the younger ones (under age 60; i.e., born after 1900–10) tattooed.

tive attempt to institute a wide-ranging research program in 1960 (in which I participated as a consultant), but that was all.

Of course, when a crisis (famine, epidemic) occurred, the authorities were keen to make a show of their charitable intentions. The churches, characteristically prudent, contented themselves with acerbic but subtly couched jibes against the government in their parochial journals, while the academic and cultural authorities proved timorous. As for the members of Parliament and senators, it was all so far away, so complex. The North was the preserve of bureaucrats under the minister of "Indian affairs," and so much the better.

During the famines, not one significant voice was raised in a national forum or on the front page of a major newspaper. Not one Anglican or Catholic bishop expressed his concerns to the federal government. The churches, it should be recalled, were jealous of their extensive privileges in the area of "native" education and were careful not to displease the government by taking an official stand on aboriginal affairs. The HBC, for its part, continued to trade as usual, never considering that it might have any philanthropic role to play. Its lavish journal *Beaver* (Winnipeg), while excellent on historical matters, kept its distance from aboriginal policy debates. Absolute silence reigned over these topics, as if the peoples in question had no contemporary history.

Who was everyone afraid of? Himself, of course. That is, each was afraid of making a decision worthy of the ethical responsibilities that his position entailed.

DECENTRALIZATION

Into this context, Prime Minister Saint-Laurent's 1953 House of Commons speech fell like a bombshell, albeit one whose repercussions were long in making themselves felt. Jean Lesage, the first of the northern affairs ministers (1953–57) to pursue the policy of decentralization of federal powers that gave rise to the Northwest Territories, was fond of saying that "Canada's centre of gravity must shift to the North." One consequence of his policy was the integration of an increasing number of Native people into the department's administrative staff. Lesage also supported the founding of the Inuit cooperative movement in northern Quebec. This movement, modelled on the pioneering Desjardins cooperatives, was also given tremendous impetus by my friend Father André Steinmann, a noble, responsible, generous missionary and a man of action with little tolerance for hand wringing.

I met Lesage while he was minister of northern affairs in 1956.[20] We sat in his Ottawa office in the Langevin Building and had a lengthy discussion of his ideas for northern policy. He was anxious to see a leading role be played by the ethnologists working at the National Museum under the direction of Jacques Rousseau. I observed the strenuous efforts to implement this policy, which was clearly the product of resolute leadership. Unfortunately, the tangible results were poor. Ethnologists, sociologists, and geographers specializing in the North were still few and far between. Their academic interests were diverse and, as I have said, few were interested in devoting themselves to contemporary problems. An alliance between university research and public policy, pejoratively termed "political sociology" by its detractors, could not simply be willed into being. Canada lacked a worthy successor to someone like Hinrich Johannes Rink, the eminent late-nineteenth-century Danish administrator,[21] or Knud Rasmussen.[22] Young researchers were interested more in cultural anthropology, archeology, geology, biology, and zoology than in the degraded vestiges of a once-proud people. Further, the Achilles' heel of Lesage's policy was the HBC staff, who lacked the requisite training, authority, and charisma. Then there were the northern service officers (NSO), whom I generally found to be inferior to the indigenous affairs officers that I had admired in the Algerian and Moroccan Sahara in 1948–49.[23] The northeastern Inuit, for their part, were indifferent to directives emanating from Yellowknife, their "capital" far to the west. It had become a truism in the Arctic villages that Ottawa was unconcerned with their distress and too far away to do much about it anyway. Ottawa? An archipelago of words.

A serious reexamination began only when oil was discovered. During that period Lesage's post was filled in succession by the brilliant Alvin Hamilton, a native of rural Saskatchewan (1957–60), Walter Dinsdale (1960–63), the energetic Arthur Laing (1965–68), and Jean Chrétien (1968–74). Under the direction of these five men, the Arctic took a resolute turn toward industrialization. The banks were given incentives to join the program and in effect became the architects of the present-day Arctic. An entirely new development, presaged by Saint-Laurent's 1953 speech, was the initiation of dialogue with peoples hitherto considered "primitive and backward." Such an orientation would normally call for a "third worldist" ideology, but Canada, in those postwar years, exhibited a big conceptual lag with respect to other nations as regards its ethnic minorities. It was anxious and uncertain about what its postcolonial future should look like. If I can bear witness to this, it is because, as I have mentioned, I was a visiting professor of anthropology at the Université de Montreal in a young department in search of its identity. The few excellent sociologists and ethnologists whom I met (Vic Valentine, Franck Vallée, J.J. Honigman, Asen Balikci) received hardly any backing, and the recommendations in their reports went unanswered. Not until twenty-five years after the war, in the 1970s, did Canadian history, geography, and anthropology departments (at McGill, Université de Montréal, Windsor, Laval, Edmonton, and Vancouver), following the lead of European and American academics, finally give the young intelligentsia an opportunity to discover the reality of Canada's multiethnic patchwork, the Other, his ethnic uniqueness and philosophy. There was still opposition, of course, particularly among the general public. "Give the Eskimos rights and land? That's going too far," I was told by a young Montrealer, a bricklayer's daughter, in September 1973 during a "man-on-the-street" interview for a film in the *Inuit* series. "We built Canada. Not them. And it was hard work."[24] But this was rearguard resistance.

TOWARD A MULTINATIONAL CANADA

The protagonists of organizing efforts by northern ethnic groups were given impetus, in latter years, by the reports of the Carrothers Commission (October 1966)[25] and the Mackenzie Valley Pipeline Inquiry (1977) and their widely differing conclusions.[26] I was in Ottawa when the initial fact finding was done for the Carrothers report. As I mentioned, Diamond Jenness and I would meet to discuss these and other matters on my sporadic visits to the offices of the Department of Northern Affairs. Jenness was then working on the last of his celebrated works on the comparative administration of the Inuit peoples of Alaska, Canada, Labrador, and Greenland and would read me a few pages from time to time.[27] Meanwhile, I was working on a report on policy options for Nunavik in which I commented on a situation of de facto colonialism epitomized by an income disparity of 1 to 8 (or even 10) between the Inuit and the bureaucrats administering their territory.

The verdict of the Carrothers Commission was equally devastating for the custodial nation: Canada's lack of a clear-sighted policy for the Inuit had led to widespread poverty, inadequate housing, deplorable hygiene, rampant tuberculosis and polio, and high infant mortality – scandalous conditions in one of the richest countries on the planet. Further concerns of the report were inappropriate school curricula, demoralization and violence, and last but not least, nonexistent economic prospects. Academics like myself were no longer alone in calling for the urgent action that the situation demanded. What options were available to the increasing numbers of aboriginal youth for whom hunting offered no future due to lack of markets? What future could the Caribou Inuit look forward to if caribou populations continued their steady decline? Better medical care had certainly improved the demographic statistics, but no genuine alternatives were being explored by the administration in charge.

It was a courageous, lucid report, and it marked a turning point in the long history of Canada's antiquated colonialist approach to aboriginal relations, which was then modelled on that of the old colonial empire. In broad outline, the approach had been to negotiate agreements with moderate Indian chiefs or

The technocratic future in a remarkable depiction by an Inuit student in Kuujjuaq, Nunavik, in June 1987, on my visit to his school.

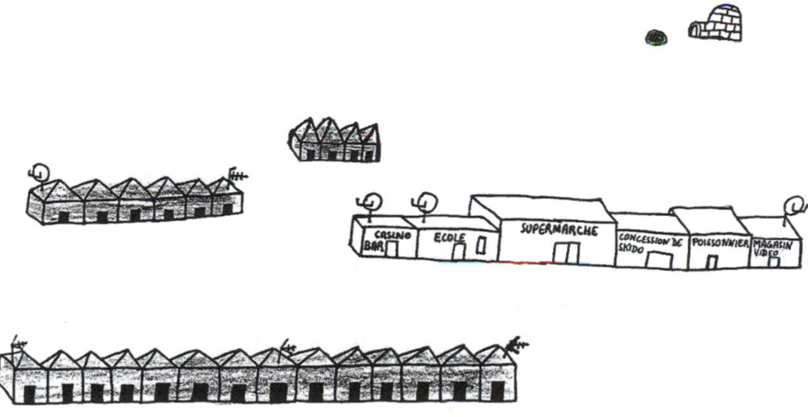

caciques, offer considerable subsidies in exchange for suppression of "tribal" rights, and thereby confine the Native peoples to shrinking territories. But although the anarcho-communalist Inuit had no officially declared leaders – the entire group played this role – their delegates were brilliant negotiators, generally possessing much greater political acumen and pragmatism than the Indians.

One of the most positive outcomes of the Carrothers Commission was to give rise, as of 1979, to full-fledged aboriginal assemblies – Inuit parliaments in embryo. It was here that the Inuit became versed in the rules of democracy and began to erode the powers of the commissioner for the Northwest Territories. Their self-government movement, driven forward by fierce resentment, was unstoppable. The commission's report was weaker on "education" – read integration – which it held to be fundamental in order to avert a situation of pervasive welfare dependency. The children would have to go to public schools and be exposed to some aspects of the white way of life. Inescapably, the aboriginal population would have to integrate into the white economy (development, trade, globalization). Here, it seems to me, the commission overlooked the key ingredient of teacher training.

As for the Mackenzie Valley Pipeline Inquiry, headed by Justice Thomas Berger, it took place a decade later when large-scale oil development was on the agenda in the Canadian Northwest. One proposal that emerged from the ongoing prospecting activity, particularly intense in the Beaufort Sea, was to build a pipeline through the Mackenzie region. The question put before the inquiry was whether this would be industrially feasible and economically rational and, if so, what the authorities' attitude toward the aboriginal populations should be. Berger's conclusions were a shock: yes, there is oil; yes, a pipeline is feasible; but no, industrial development in the Mackenzie must not take place until after the instatement of an autonomous aboriginal authority. Caught out, stupefied by a conclusion unprecedented in its history, the Government of Canada decided – displaying its usual attitude toward such complex, sensitive dossiers – to do nothing. Washington, with its Alaska interests, was disinclined to back such a pipeline. The Mackenzie project was abandoned.

My time as a consultant to the NCRC predated the positive effects of these commissions. The officials with whom I interacted in the early 1960s were torn by conflicting, confusing initiatives. Coffee-break debates were lively, and it was to a great extent at the rank-and-file level of the administration that ideas were exchanged and mentalities gradually shifted. This is a strength of democracies. A sample discussion might have begun as follows: "Decolonization, maybe ... but decentralization first. It makes no sense to govern the North from Ottawa and the Northeast from Yellowknife. The North needs an administration with local capitals, one for Mackenzie and one for Baffin Island." A traditionalist would respond: "We should solidify our centralized system. It's always been our strength. Decolonization is utopian and costly, and the results are unpredictable. Let the Natives live according to their rules. It hasn't worked out so badly since 1867, has it? They've never revolted. Strategically, we should hold the course and steer clear of triggering big changes. Primary schooling for the Inuit will do just fine." A conservative might then chime in, "It's going to get costly, increasingly so, and it will continue to be a thankless burden. Leave the Natives alone. Wherever you look in the colonies, the attempt to turn them into whites through modernization has never had anything but disastrous effects. Hunting holds out no economic future for them, and we ought to be cautious about what the North has to offer in terms of natural resources. Mines? Oil? Sure, there is plenty of that, but the cost of transport is prohibitive. Our priority should be to exploit the resources of southern Canada. Alberta has oil sitting right there under the surface. Twenty years from now, if northern mining revenues perk up, we can review our approach to indigenous problems. Besides, noninterference is sure to please all the hand wringers – anthropologists, human rights advocates, sensitive souls – and Ottawa can avoid being tarred with the brush of imperialism as the Americans have."

"And it isn't up to the government to offer social assistance in a market economy anyway," the conservative argument would continue. "That's the charities' job. Let's not hurry things along. Give it another century, and meanwhile we can solidify Canada in the South by exploiting the immense wealth of the Western provinces. Mr Diefenbaker's dream of developing the North? Utopian.[28] Canada's future is in the West, not in the North. The Inuit and the Indians will be history in twenty or fifty years anyway. Give them self-government now? An irresponsible, left-wing idea."

SELF-GOVERNMENT: AN IDEA BELOW THE SURFACE

In Ottawa I heard these lines of reasoning about Native self-government not only at high levels but also at the grassroots, from labourers, foremen, pilots, nurses, postal workers, and taxi drivers. Such skepticism was equally widespread at high levels of the Quebec government during the period of Franco-Quebec cooperation (1968–70) inaugurated by an agreement between President Charles de Gaulle and Quebec Premier Daniel Johnson (1966–68) (see p. 55). It was particularly evident in the Nouveau-Québec and Natural Resources Branch, headed by my friend Guy Poitras. "The Natives are costly regardless of whether the federal or the provincial government shoulders the financial burden," the bureaucrats would say. The Inuit were a federal responsibility, as the 1939 Supreme Court decision in *Re: Eskimos* had confirmed, and this was as it should be.

It would be untrue to say that European and Canadian research (by demographers, sociologists, ethnologists, physicians, and so on) amounted to nothing in the end. To be sure, we had a sense of our own insignificance as our reports piled up into mountains of paper. And when I had cordial conversations with civil servants (generally English-speaking, always professional) and meetings with the minister, the deputy minister, or various senior officials (R.A.J. Phillips, Ben Sivertz, Walter Rudnicki), their reactions were far from encouraging. My ideas of Inuit self-government provoked nodding of heads and condescending smiles from the mid-level bureaucrats: "Interesting, but unrealistic." I let them have their say. My life experience has shown me that history is driven by ideas. At first they dig underground chambers like termites, gradually destabilizing the complacency on the surface. Then, like beavers, they build. At times our reports and accounts were given some coverage in the press, on radio, or on television. They empowered officials who had never seen the North with their own eyes, then, by word of mouth, the entire administrative North, and finally public opinion, the third power in a democracy. Ultimately, it is public opinion that makes and unmakes governments. It may take time: ten years, twenty years, a hundred years ... but time will prove us right. These documents, as limited as they were, played their humble role in the birth of a new agenda. Once-impervious politicians saw their inertia disrupted by a leftward shift of public opinion on Native affairs. As we hammered away at a few essential points – the Inuit are heirs to a great civilization and exceptional works of art; the government's vision is myopic and ineffectual; the effects of its policies are not all positive; there is no leadership; Canada's future is in the North – the responsible agencies, the lower-level officials representative of mainstream Canadian opinion, became increasingly concerned. Their minds gradually opened to more modern approaches, and they started to listen to the Native peoples' demands. It seems clear that our modest writings, like those of hundreds of others, played their role in dismantling prejudice.

But if the whole truth be known, from our vantage point in the early 1960s, we anthropologists, sociologists, demographers, and geographers often felt terribly alone as we stared at our blank pages. Ottawa lacked the modern-day equivalent of a Sir George Grey (1812–98), the inspired British administrator who, with a Puritan's rigour and a gentleman's humanism, saved New Zealand from anarchy by associating the Maori people with development and enforcing strict respect for their rights. The absence of such an individual in Ottawa often left me with the impression that our notes and recommendations were disappearing into the void.

I was wrong, although it was not easy, in that context, to foresee how events would transpire in the long term. Both in the capital and in the field, I was a privileged witness to a difficult period of transition in which a new ideology was taking shape. Political thought, like water, sometimes enters a supercooled state, and as I stared at my reports, I did not perceive its subtle, silent transformation. I was too close to the problem and lacked perspective. Be that as it may, the authorities, with their thoroughly British prudence, were still hesitating to make a move, knowing that an ill-advised intervention in these small Inuit groups, each comprising a few hundred people and with a total population not exceeding 20,000, could have disastrous and irreversible effects.[29] They dreaded provoking the vicious spiral undergone by all "primitive" civilizations in prolonged contact with the West. History invited caution. As Captain James Cook incisively remarked on returning from his first voyage (1768–71), which took him to Tahiti, "what is still more to our Shame [as] civilized Christians, we debauch their Morals already too prone to vice and we interduce among them wants and perhaps diseases which they never before knew and which serves only to disturb that happy tranquility they and their fore Fathers had enjoy'd."[30] The Indian reserve policy had been too insubstantial, too ill-conceived not to leave the best intentioned of Canadians skeptical. A Sir George Grey would have brought the requisite high-mindedness to the initial decision making.

THE FIRST PROGRESSIVE DECISIONS

In 1965, 2,600 units of housing were built for the Inuit. Some observers wondered whether the necessary precaution was being observed, if these people were not being set up too rapidly in a state of dependency, and there was truth in this. Still, one must pay tribute to the ever-so-English spirit of pragmatism that stands in when vision is lacking. Those administrative years were dominated by ministers and department heads with strong personalities whom I knew only by their signatures. Three commissioners of the Northwest Territories are of particular note: Gordon Robertson (1953–63), a senior official from the rigourous civil-service tradition who signed the memoranda of concern to me; Ben Sivertz (1963–67), an old hand at northern administration whose primary concern was the rapid decentralization of the relevant powers from Ottawa to Yellowknife; and Stuart Hodgson (1967–79), a man from a trade-union background whom the Inuit called Umingmak (musk ox).[31] It was clear from the outset that Hodgson was a redoubtable mover and shaker. This is the impression that he left, on me in particular, at Le Havre in May 1973 when he attended the first Arctic Oil and Gas Conference, chaired by the eminent historian Jacques Le Goff under the auspices of the Centre d'Études Arctiques.[32]

Confronted with acerbic public criticism of his administration by the Inuit and Indian delegates, represented by the president of the Indian Brotherhood of the Northwest Territories, James Wah-Shee,[33] Hodgson responded witheringly: "In June 1944 I was on the beaches of Normandy and I came ashore to participate in the liberation of Europe, with canons firing. In May 1973, it is not with canons that I will respond; I will remain silent."[34]

The conference was taken aback by the tense standoff and by the long, glacial silence that followed. The Inuit and the Indians were certainly used to it. Two centuries of being bullied and abused in response to their attempts at dialogue and criticism had hardly encouraged them to show initiative. But fissures had appeared in the technocratic pack ice, and the Inuit leaders slipped between them, putting on a display of calm pragmatism before the international audience. And their forthrightness was not without recent precedent. At Rouen in 1969 at the historic first pan-Inuit conference (Greenland, Canada, Alaska, Siberia) held under the auspices of the Centre d'Études Arctiques,[35] Inuit delegates had gained a physical awareness of their internationality; united, they asserted their strength to the world. The proceedings of these two conferences are fascinating to reread, as I have often been told by my old friend Tagak Curley, chair of the Rouen and Le Havre conferences and cofounder of Inuit Tapirisat, Canada's national Inuit organization. Others who have expressed their thanks to me at having been thus distinguished, supported, and honoured in one of the birthplaces of human rights were John Amagoalik, Curley's successor to the presidency of Inuit Tapirisat, and my friend Senator Charlie Watt, regarded by many as the "fathers of Nunavut and Nunavik," respectively. Both were grateful to Paris, Rouen, and Le Havre for having catalyzed a necessary mental revolution leading to the break-up of the monolithic ice.

France is at its best when spreading around the world its principle of freedom for all peoples, but these are slow processes. The government in Ottawa held on to its prerogatives, moving ahead at a stately pace that was completely out of step with the increasing swiftness of events and their jumble of consequences. Well represented at the 1969 and 1973 conferences, Ottawa wanted to take its time and observe the repercussions of developments to the west (the *Alaska Land Claims Settlement Act* of December 1971, epitomizing the US government's stark vision for the North) and to the east (the social democratically inflected Greenland Home Rule process).[36]

Throughout these arduous negotiations, women were eloquent agents of the ongoing political revolution. It was they, I recall, who held de facto power in the villages and served as the catalysts of change – as was subsequently the case in northern Siberia (1992–95). Women such as Rhoda Inukshuk, Edna Elias, Rosemarie Kuptana, and others, some of them born in a tent or a snow

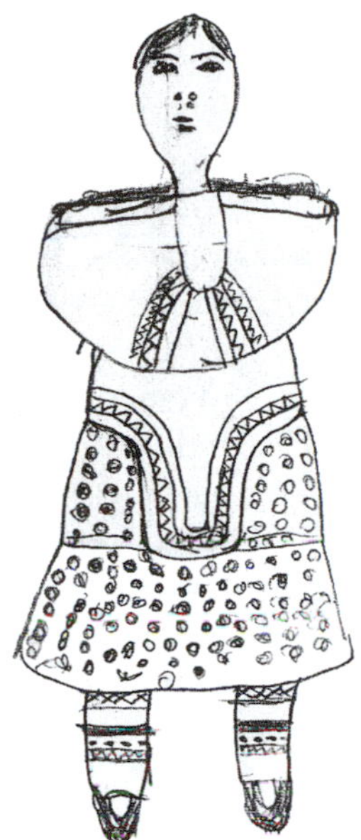

Summer costume. Self-portrait of woman from Rankin region, Hudson Bay. August 1962.

house, come to mind. Respectful of their heritage but open to the future and the prospect of self-government, the women saw that an essential condition was dialogue with the whites, the Occident. What the Inuit wanted from us was a dialogue between equals in which they could gain access to our knowledge while preserving their spiritual vision.

HISTORY IN HIGH GEAR

The catalyst for Inuit self-government came from Quebec, particularly its sovereignty movement of the late 1960s. The Québécois, a people of rural origins, were outraged by the arrogant comments (some of them truly despicable) of certain Canadian anglophones,[37] and the outrage spilled over into terrorism with the assassination of Pierre Laporte.[38] In the years that followed, and particularly after 1988, Canadian prime minister Pierre Elliot Trudeau and his successors forged ahead with a multicultural vision of Canada that trivialized Quebec's distinctness. That Quebec should have inspired the country's Native peoples in their striving for self-government was an irony of sorts, for the province's authorities had always been quite circumspect about granting additional powers to its Indian and Inuit minorities, but so it was. In the North, the pace of events picked up, and the Inuit understood that their moment had finally come. After the Meech Lake Agreement of 1987, Prime Minister Brian Mulroney signed a bold, historic agreement on 25 May 1993 that would give legal existence six years later (on 1 April 1999) to a self-governing Inuit territory – Nunavut – covering two million square kilometres of the Arctic archipelago and adjacent mainland, an area four times the size of France with a population of approximately 25,000 (80 per cent Inuit). John Amagoalik advised the federal government throughout the process, and Tagak Curley also played a crucial role in the negotiations. They showed tenacity and vision tempered with a dose of realism – the great political asset of the Inuit, one that made reaching agreement with the like-minded English-speaking senior officials a virtual certainty.

After forty years, just like the European empires in Africa, Ottawa had finally come to its senses ... and learned to keep its ulterior motives in check. This is an aptitude of the great democratic nations. Basic assumptions about governance were being revised. The aboriginal peoples would finally govern themselves. The nation of Canada had realized that its federalism binds together not just two but many founding peoples: the Cree, the Montagnais, the Athapaska, the Dene, the Inuit, and all the other First Nations. Symbolic of this realization was the location chosen for Mulroney's signing of the Nunavut agreement: Iqaluit, an emblematic Inuit settlement, today the capital of the territory. At the ceremony he presented John Amagoalik with a pro forma cheque for $70 million to cover the initial costs of instituting an aboriginal government. Canada had become multinational at last.

I had met Amagoalik in Kuujjuaq in the early 1970s, at a turning point in Inuit history, while shooting the *Inuit* series of seven circumpolar films. Nouveau-Québecers spoke to the camera with bitterness, decrying the housing discrimination that they had suffered in Kuujjuaq and elsewhere – nice houses for the Québécois, tenements for the Inuit. The situation had not changed since my report to the government of Quebec in 1970.[39] But now the wheel was spinning fast. In August 1995 on a First Air flight to Iqaluit, the English-speaking steward handed me a copy of the in-flight magazine, and I was pleased to find an interview with Amagoalik, in which he elaborates on the organizing principles of Inuit government:

> "The concept of self-government is not new," he insists. "Before Europeans arrived, there was a society up here and it had rules, it had leaders, it had politics ... Inuit politics will fit nicely with the type of government we're trying to put together: small, efficient and working on the principles of co-operation between people." One of the keys to making this lean and efficient government work, admits Amagoalik, is the use of new communications technologies. In other words, Nunavut – a land without roads

– is going to be built on the so-called information highway. According to the report of the Nunavut Implementation Commission, "[p]athways of the past were forged by dogsled and snowmobile … pathways of the future will be travelled electronically … The day may come when an elder in Baker Lake or Pond Inlet will … address the legislature sitting in some far-removed capital, via video-conferencing, so that the MLAs will benefit directly from elders' advice … We have to be realistic. I hope that people don't have sky-high expectations." The streets of Nunavut communities are not going to be paved with gold after 1999. In fact, says Amagoalik, it will just be a beginning. "The opportunity is there – people just have to take advantage of it," he says. "I really hope that the creation of Nunavut means that we're climbing out of a hole we've been in for a long time, a hole part of which we dug ourselves – suicide, alcoholism, family abuse, all this stuff. I think we're turning the corner."[40]

FROM GREAT DARKNESS TO NUNAVIK

Let us once again turn back the hands of history's clock to July 1963, when the Government of Quebec created an administrative branch responsible for Nouveau-Québec.[41] It had become pressing for "la belle province" to redefine its minority policy for this immense Arctic-Subarctic region covering one-third of the province's territory. The new policy had to make a clean break with that of Maurice Duplessis (premier from 1936 to 1939 and 1944 to 1959, a period known as the "Great Darkness"), in which the province essentially ignored its northern aboriginal peoples, leaving their administration to the federal government and seeing no need to fill the obvious gaps in Ottawa's policy. Quebec's leaders had always been quite content with the situation, its financial aspects in particular.* But now, they reasoned that if the province did not quickly assert its authority over this region vis-à-vis the federal government – something that would require a radical change of course – then its strivings for sovereignty, if not independence, would be severely constrained.

In 1967 General Charles de Gaulle and his good friend Quebec premier Daniel Johnson reached agreement on a wide-ranging bilateral cooperation program for the Ungava Peninsula.[42] I was appointed coordinator and rapporteur for the French contribution to the program. At the behest of the Quai d'Orsay, I quickly formed a team of French experts, and we departed for Fort Chimo (now Kuujjuaq), the administrative capital of the region. It was rough going for us at first. The town was in a dreadful state, with no coherent development program in sight for the Native people. Provincial and federal

* In the narrow defeat of the 1995 sovereignty referendum, the 95 per cent aboriginal "no" vote weighed heavily in the balance. A people once humiliated does not forget easily.

jurisdictions overlapped and acted at cross purposes. It was fast becoming – already was, in fact – a slum. Compounding this difficulty was the chilly reception we received from many Natives. Most were English-speaking Anglicans who were quite reserved, not to say hostile to the Quebec government and to French speakers of any description, all pejoratively known as "les oui-oui." The weight of history's defeats and betrayals, beginning with the Treaty of Paris in 1763, had never been forgotten. More recently, during a period of crisis in the 1920s and 1930s, the French trading posts that the Inuit patronized and to which they were indebted, including the Révillon post at Ivujivik, had been relinquished to the HBC.[43] The effects of this betrayal had been devastating. The churchmen, in typical Jesuitical style, advised me to keep a low profile.

The implementation of a solid, generous, inventive cooperation program was in order, and it had to go beyond what Ottawa was proposing. As the minority nation of Canada's founding pair (francophones made up 30 per cent of the population in 1960, down to 23 per cent by 1996 with declining birth rates), Quebec had a duty, a high calling it seemed to me, to point the way for all the other provincial governments on ethnic and cultural minority policy by adopting a progressive, forward-looking policy for its own minorities, beginning with the Nouveau-Québec Inuit population of 3,245 (1 January 1968). I felt that this complex problem could best be addressed with a simple guiding idea: empowerment of the interested parties, the Inuit, as equal partners in a collective endeavour to build the future. The Quebec authorities of the time were slow to embrace this principle, but the Inuit whom we consulted grasped it quickly and very much concurred. As Silassie Cookie told me at Whale Cove in 1970, "The Eskimo has to do his own thing in his own way, in his own land. This is not the land of the White Man. The Eskimo has to be the boss. You, white people, have your own bosses in your own land."

During the two years of our mandate, in Nouveau-Québec as well as Québec City, Ottawa, and Paris, we gamely and energetically worked on our common agenda with the open, unanimous support of the Inuit leaders. I met many distinguished Quebec public figures, some of whom became friends: the brilliant René Lévesque (1922–1987), founder of the Parti Québécois (PQ) and premier of Quebec from 1976 to 1985; Jacques Parizeau, professor at the École des Hautes Études Commerciales, successor to Lévesque at the head of the PQ, and premier of Quebec from 1994 to 1996; Jean Chrétien, federal minister of northern affairs, later prime minister of Canada (1993–2003), who provided me with constant support; Benoît Robitaille, the eminent Université Laval geographer; Gilles Lefebvre, a linguist working on a uniform Inuktitut language; and Jean Lacasse, the highly competent counsel to the aboriginal minorities in Québec City. I also renewed my acquaintance with Jean Lesage,

Hunting group at Igloolik, Parry's expedition (1822). Apart from the absence of coattails, the cut of the men's caribou-skin clothing remained the same in 1961.

whose term as premier of Quebec had recently ended. Above all I must acknowledge the warm, confiding cooperation of Guy Poitras, director of the Nouveau-Québec Branch, to whom our team reported.[44]

After a cursory exploration of the territory by my team in 1969 (joined by Arctic expert Paul-Émile Victor at his request),[45] I began to lay out the foundations of our research agenda, joined by several eminent French researchers as of September and October 1970. Our objective was to facilitate the advent of Inuit self-government in the years 1970–75, to empower the parties concerned by defining their respective obligations in a charter. Although this did not happen according to our schedule, we were pleased that our efforts were partially responsible for the emergence of several important Inuit leaders during those years. One of these was Charlie Watt, to whom I was introduced by others in his community and who was then living in a very modest dwelling and employed at menial work. Sensing what he was capable of, I was shocked by his inadequate circumstances and backed him energetically.

ᐊᕙᑎᑖᖅᑐᖅ!

The Makivik Corporation, founded by Charlie Watt under the aegis of the historic James Bay Agreement, celebrated its twentieth anniversary in December 1995. Its mission is to aid in the development of the autonomous territory of Nunavik.

Years passed. I had the pleasure of returning to "Fort Chimo" in 1998, by which time it had been officially rechristened with its Inuit name of Kuujjuaq, while "Nouveau-Québec" – the entire 660,000-square-kilometre territory of the Ungava Peninsula above the fifty-fifth parallel, including the offshore waters – was renamed Nunavik. In the interim, the Inuit population had grown to 8,600 people living in fifteen villages, with the under-thirty age bracket accounting for 60 per cent of the total. But the changes went much deeper. In the context of the James Bay and Northern Quebec Agreement (JBNQA) of 1975 – Canada's first Native self-government agreement – René Lévesque had made several remarkable, statesmanlike decisions whose effect was to assert Quebec's unity from south to north.[46] Under the agreement, Quebec and Canada paid compensation to the Makivik Corporation, a non-profit organization owned by the Inuit of Nunavik, which used the moneys to fund the region's supramunicipal structures. Preliminary negotiations were underway with the two higher orders of government to establish a bona fide self-government arrangement, which would lead in 2003 to the signing of the Negotiation Framework Agreement. A long process of negotiation was still to come, but Nunavik was on the way to becoming a self-governing territory.

The people's faith in themselves had been restored, and Kuujjuaq was now a fine example of ethnic awakening. The Makivik Corporation's operations were computerized and Internet-enabled; it had, in effect, leapt the Gutenberg galaxy into the electronic world. In conformity with communalist tradition (and to compete with imported tinned meat), cooperative Inuit squads were hunting fish and game and distributing the catch to the population free of charge.[47] The harvest obeyed guidelines dictated by the biogenic capacity of the environment. Another new feature was a top-drawer school, the equivalent, in fact, of a small university. At the lectures that I gave during this visit, I noticed that the audience was quite diversified, including both southern Canadians and Natives as well as, among the former, some European and Lebanese immigrants, bringing fresh ideas. A modest but effective airline, Air Inuit, served the region. In the area of justice, Judge Jean-Luc Dutil of the Court of Quebec was supervising the adaptation of the criminal code to accommodate the customary law tradition. Changes made to sentencing guidelines in 1990 allowed for less serious cases to be dealt with by public confession coupled with pardon by the entire community, instead of a prison term. However, drug dealers, Judge Dutil felt – and the elders shared his opinion – remained undeserving of pardon. May justice be served to these corrupters!

The Quebec government had taken up some of our recommendations. We "maudits français"* had not been altogether useless. We had blazed a trail that others had followed, and some of our ideas – the right ones – had made headway.

In February 1994 I was pleased to receive the following message from Senator Charlie Watt, president of Makivik Corporation and architect of the Nunavik process, acknowledging our role:[48]

> I wish to extend my best wishes to Jean Malaurie whose visit to Ungava twenty-five years ago I well remember.
>
> During a visit to Paris several years ago, I was in a position to observe the good work being accomplished by the Arctic Studies Centre. While my people are small in numbers, we live in a large territory the world is only beginning to recognize. This growing recognition is due in part to the Centre's focus on the Arctic and its nations, including the Inuit.

I took his gratitude to heart. And this was only the beginning, as the Inuit understood. They had no interest in the stultifying solution of a cultural ghetto. On the contrary, young, enterprising decision makers began to assert themselves as real statesmen, giving a new direction to their history. Inuit experts were increasingly present at conferences and symposia. Their energy was indomitable. No longer were they willing to sit on the sidelines of the ongoing Canadian constitutional reform process. And the Inuit nation as a whole was working toward structured international cooperation agreements among Nunavik, Nunavut, and Greenland.

* Such, unfortunately, is the typical slur heard in Quebec against my countrymen. Louis XV's betrayal has never been forgiven.

Colymbus grylle. Drawing by S. Koenig (1818).

I am glad that I have lived long enough to watch Canada grow into a federation of multiple nations and cultures as a result of these far-reaching developments so critical to the country's future. As a foreigner, I was perhaps freer than my North American colleagues to criticize the timidity, the overcautiousness, the myopia of the Canadian and Quebec constitutional politics of the time. I considered it my duty as an intellectual in 1960 to stand with these people in their distress. Doubtless, the results would have been even more favourable if regional self-government had been implemented while the Native people's traditions were thriving. But the Occident, with characteristic self-interest, always attempts to force those nations under its custody to relinquish political control in exchange for rights, helping the process along with relief and patronage.

History has shown the error of such ways.

3

The Netsilingmiut

July 1961. After my two expeditions to the Igloolik region (July–October 1960, May 1961),[1] the Canadian government retained me to conduct a summer expedition to the Netsilingmiut living on the Boothia Peninsula in the Central Arctic. The logistics of these expeditions were organized by the Northern Co-ordination and Research Centre (NCRC), which entailed negotiations with the US Air Force, the lofty keeper of the DEW Line. I departed 25 July for Hall Beach (Sanirajak).

BY CANOE THROUGH THE RAE STRAIT

Hall Beach: a landing strip, several prefab duralumin barracks, and a United States flag flapping in the wind.[2] As the plane's only passenger, I am greeted on the runway by the chief officer, a likeable man of French descent, who arranges my connecting east-west flight to the uninhabited eastern arm of the Rae Strait, composed of Shepherd Bay and Rasmussen Basin. It must be done quickly, as bad weather looms.

CN Telecommunications

local time · heure locale

MOA170

MO GA315 32=OTTAWA ONT 24 NFT= 1961 JUL 24 PM 3 47

PROF MALAURIE= DEPT ANTHROPOLOGY UNIVERSITY OF MTL
MTL

=PLEASE PROCEED FOXE MAIN VIA NORD AIR TUESDAY NIGHT STOP
FEDERAL ELECTRIC WILL ARRANGE ONWARD TRANSMISSION TO
SHEPHERD BAY STOP COPY ROWLEYS LETTER TO DEFENCE DEPARTMENT
ON WAY TO YOU SPECIAL DELIVERY=
SAVILLE NORTHERN COORDINATOR RESEARCH CENTRE.

J.R. White, general manager · directeur général Toronto 6122b

Telegram indicating expedition instructions: departure for Shepherd Bay on the Boothia Peninsula aboard a US DEW Line flight. Federal Electric was a code name for a unit of the US Air Force. July 1961.

From an altitude of five hundred metres I observe the deserted hematitic tundra of the Melville Peninsula: Cain's land in perspective. A waterlogged land dotted with craters and lakes. Successive bands of elevated beaches bearing witness to the powerful respiration of rock and sea. Seemingly deliberate geometric patterns indicative of the differential upthrust known as frost heaving; immense polygonal latticework, periglacial rock joints running for kilometres. But no life. None of the bands of caribou or musk oxen that were still numerous thirty-five years ago. The Caribou Eskimo, the most traditionalist of the Inuit, are exclusively inland hunters: how are they managing to survive? Entire groups of Quebec's Naskapi Indians disappeared around 1910 when the caribou herd declined.

We fly over a relay base of the DEW Line. This, the largest and most secretive radar program of the time (commissioned in June 1951), consists of main stations situated every 200 kilometres along the sixty-ninth parallel from Iceland to Alaska – a distance of over 20,000 kilometres – with smaller, higher-tech stations every fifty kilometres. A Babylonian project undertaken at the height of the Cold War. Object: to fend off a surprise attack by Moscow with a nuclear riposte from Thule or the submarine missile launchers housed in a secret base under the Arctic ice.

After flying over the Simpson Peninsula and Pelly Bay, where the ice is already encroaching, we land at little Base 3 (only a dozen or so permanent residents) on the shore of Shepherd Bay, where I am to be met by two men in a canoe. Formerly the land of the Kuungmiut ("river people"), the country is today uninhabited yet still harbours an abundant population of sea mammals. According to Knud Rasmussen, who visited the area in 1922–23, thirty-one Inuit (including twelve hunters) lived here during the winter, consuming one seal per day. Charles Francis Hall, the pioneering American explorer, bivouacked here on 30 April 1869 while searching for survivors of Sir John Franklin's expedition of 1845–49. It was here that he acquired Franklin relics from the Inuit, who produced a sketchy map indicating the explorers' fate (see map, p. 199; for a fuller account of Hall's remarkable expeditions, see pp. 195–6).[3]

No sooner have I landed than a strong northwest wind picks up, and it is impossible to continue the journey. In the early afternoon, rain mixed with snow beats down on the land. I wait, scanning the foggy horizon. Out of the storm, dripping wet, there suddenly emerge two short, stocky, animal-skin-clad men from another age. Coppery, pentagonal faces with imposing jaws. Triple skin pouches under fox eyes. Posture radiating coiled tension, necks hunched in to the shoulders as if poised to dodge. Like all the Netsilingmiut, they speak little and stare distantly; they are of that race of "men who never look at anything and remember everything."[4] As to their dialect, it is unfamiliar to me. I speak the North Greenland and Igloolik dialects – or rather, a pidgin version of the latter. Nevertheless, I quickly find myself making out similar word roots and groups.

What are they saying? "The north wind is too strong. Silaluktok! Bad weather! We have to wait." They will stay in their canoe, and I will go to meet them when the weather clears. As is often the case with such initial encounters, mutual timidity produces a show of boldness, making us act as if we understood each other. I pretend that I am in control of the situation.

The next day at dawn I depart by truck for their coastal bivouac. The driver, a Detroit native, earns a monthly wage of $800 the first year and $900 the second, all expenses paid. Not counting bonuses and gratuities. The least qualified base employee, he says, can save up to $20,000 in three years, provided he is unmarried and does not gamble away his salary at the nightly poker games. Putting this amount in perspective, these twangy-voiced white giants, indifferent to their surroundings, collect an Inuk's lifetime income in the space of a few months while hardly ever venturing beyond the hermetic fifty-square-metre enclosure of their barracks.[5] Blessed America! My head bobs to the rhythm of the track and the dollar figures. The Inuit? The North? He has no interest in these Ice Age primitives. The conversation shifts to the weekly airdropped cartoons and movies.

Scanning the shore of a black, menacing sea – the Rae Strait – through binoculars, I spot a grayish-white specked tarp mounted on two paddles. The driver spits out his chewing gum. He clearly thinks it insane that I would go to sea with paltry supplies, no radio or compass (but we are in a sector of intense magnetic activity), and a couple of "prehistorics" as companions. My plan is to proceed by dead reckoning and by scanning the coast for identifiable landmarks. He leaves the motor running, champing at the bit to be gone. "Come on, John!" We shake hands and I hastily jump out. With the window rolled down, assiduously ruminating his next piece of gum as if to help him think, he reiterates the imagined dangers: treacherous bottom, ever-present reefs, violent late-summer storms. "Too bad for you!" he says ruefully. "Take care!" And off he drives.

My two new Inuit acquaintances crouch beneath a modest five-metre-long open canvas canoe resting on the gunwales. They raise their heads with a trace of reluctance, stare at me for a moment, then set about doing what needs to be done. Our destination, as they know, is Spence Bay (Taloyoak), a 150-kilometre trip to the north. To get there, we will have to detour southwest into Rasmussen Basin to avoid dangerous Cape Colville, then turn around and make our way up the Rae and James Ross Straits.[6] We are alone. No craft shares these waters. My thoughts turn excitedly to John Rae (1813–93), Scotland's glory, the physician and explorer from the Orkney Islands who surveyed and mapped 2,300 kilometres of Arctic coastline (more than any other explorer) in what was truly an epic life. I can see his craggy face and penetrating stare in my mind. On his first expedition in 1846–47, travelling with a group of Inuit, he proved that "Boothia Felix"* was not an island but a peninsula, by the same token disproving the existence of a northwest passage in the vicinity. In 1851 Rae travelled more than 8,500 kilometres looking for Franklin, mapping more than 1,000 kilometres of unknown territory along the coast of Victoria Island. It was on yet another expedition in 1854 that he discovered the first solid evidence of the lost expedition. Truly, it was to exceptional overland explorers like Rae – HBC employees, trappers, *coureurs de bois* – whom the Admiralty should have turned in the search for Franklin, not to naval officers whose arrogant colonialist worldview, obsession with discovering the "Passage," and distaste for walking made them ill-suited to the adventure (see map, p. 67).[7]

* Named for London multimillionaire brewer Felix Booth (1775–1850).

Another person concerned about Franklin's fate was Captain John Ross, to whom the Admiralty responded with a learned, tragic "quite unnecessary" when, in early 1847, he urged that a relief expedition be organized and offered to lead it. This was, of course, the same man who, with his nephew Commander James Clark Ross,[8] had masterfully led an expedition to the Magnetic Pole on the Boothia Peninsula in 1829–33 (see maps, pp. 101, 193; for an account of John Ross's first and second expeditions, see pp. 100–5).[9] Unnecessary? Franklin's men were dying, his ships trapped in the ice. In the years that followed, some thirty-nine maritime search expeditions and four overland ones would be conducted, yet to this day no one has fully elucidated what happened to the 129 sailors and officers who lost their lives after a frightful ordeal to the west of King William Island (for further discussion of the enigma of Franklin's failure, see pp. 192–8).[10]

We embark. It is 8:30 A.M. The vastness is a hard reality, indifferent to men, like the dawn of history. The thin, supple wooden-lath ribs of the canoe, spaced twenty centimetres apart, seem fragile, so fragile – the whole conveyance does. It would take only a wayward growler, a pebble,[11] the touch of a rock to shear the flimsy canvas and turn us into an unceremonious shipwreck. Life expectancy in these frigid waters: three minutes at best. And these Inuit are no swimmers. The younger of the two is at the bow watching for black reefs and ice chunks jutting above the water like seal heads. The other is at the motor, a 7-HP Johnson. I am between them facing forward, legs extended, bailing water with two empty soup cans. Heading into the northwest wind, three hooded, mapless lunatics play at being old salts.

Why such an early departure? An enigma to the Inuit, surely, these high-powered white people's agendas. But they get caught up in our wake and dragged along willy-nilly. It will take time before my circadian rhythms are fully adjusted to their slow, hibernating pace, but for now I am a Westerner like any other. The two men must have thought – was it my size, a certain self-assurance, the behaviour of a government envoy? – that I was a highly proficient seaman, for they did not hesitate to set out on these hostile waters, convinced that I knew what I was doing. But I am not at all a sailor. My intention was to follow the coastline on the Canadian ICAO 1:1,000,000 topographic map, but after Cape Colville, surveyed and named by Rae in 1854, the bad weather frequently veils the coast. To make matters worse, I am absolutely clueless about mechanics. Meanwhile, I have placed my total trust in these two Inuks, assuming that they were in their element. In fact, throughout my voyages to Greenland, Alaska, and Siberia, I have never hesitated to place my life in the Inuit's hands and to travel, as they do, by dead reckoning. These two, however, turn out to be pitiful navigators, without the slightest experience of the sea: they are caribou hunters of the tundra, and their crude kayak is designed for lake travel. Our endeavour is founded on this misunderstanding. Very quickly discovering our mutual inexperience, we form a silent alliance to save our skins.

The sky darkens. Black, Brahmsian clouds skate along the horizon, their edges ablaze, as the sleety wind batters us. At the bow the lookout is watching so intensely, leaning over so far, that his nose practically grazes the water; only the small of his back is visible. The water flows past the boat in hesitant trickles that I imagine to be the lines of my fate. Signalling with gloved hand, he guides our tortuous path through the floating ice, while I keep my eyes riveted on the small nameless island to the west of Acland Point. Coming level with Cape Colville we move far off shore – but not far enough. The dry gusts of wind fight our progress, driving us toward Stanley Island and its three islets, then toward the jagged coast. The 7-HP Johnson is failing us as we are drawn into a maze of other islets. I gesture northwest toward safer open water. Between two immense waves I spy the sombre contours of King William Island, Qikiqtarmiut territory, but at the same time lose sight of the coast to the east. The height of the swell indicates that it must be coming from a considerable distance, from the wide James Ross Strait to the north and the narrower Rae Strait below it. Strong winds through that narrow passage must account for the relatively open water here in summer. Now the sleet turns into a full-fledged blizzard, and the makeshift canoe plunges into two-metre troughs. It will surely break in two at any moment, I think, yet it does not; something about its lightness allows it to withstand the shocks. The motor begins to knock. I withhold my prayers. We stay the course with our paddles while the Inuk at the stern fiddles with the motor, a detached smile on his face. I watch his plump, freckled fingers at work. The motor starts, and we are past the confounded cape at last. Resuming our northward route, we ply as close as possible to the coast, the waves lashing at us all the while, water trickling down our faces. Surprised at the fool's trap into which we have so readily fallen, we react determinedly, our bonds stronger now that we have overcome this initial hazard as a team. A softness comes over the gaze of the Netsilik at the motor.

With chattering teeth, we allow the boat to drift toward the coast, and after De La Guiche Point, in Balfour Bay – the northernmost point reached by Rae on 6 May 1854[12] – the canoe slumps down onto land in the falling dark. Oh, the joy of touching solid ground in the lee of the wind! We are on low, desolate tundra not far from where Francis Leopold McClintock's brave companions travelled by dogsled a little over a century ago.[13] We try to warm up around a dodgy fire built out of some roots, but it takes a good hour before the heart of the wood, stripped with a knife, ignites into timid, smoky, yellow-blue flames. We nurse them with damp shavings, laughing to keep up morale and jumping

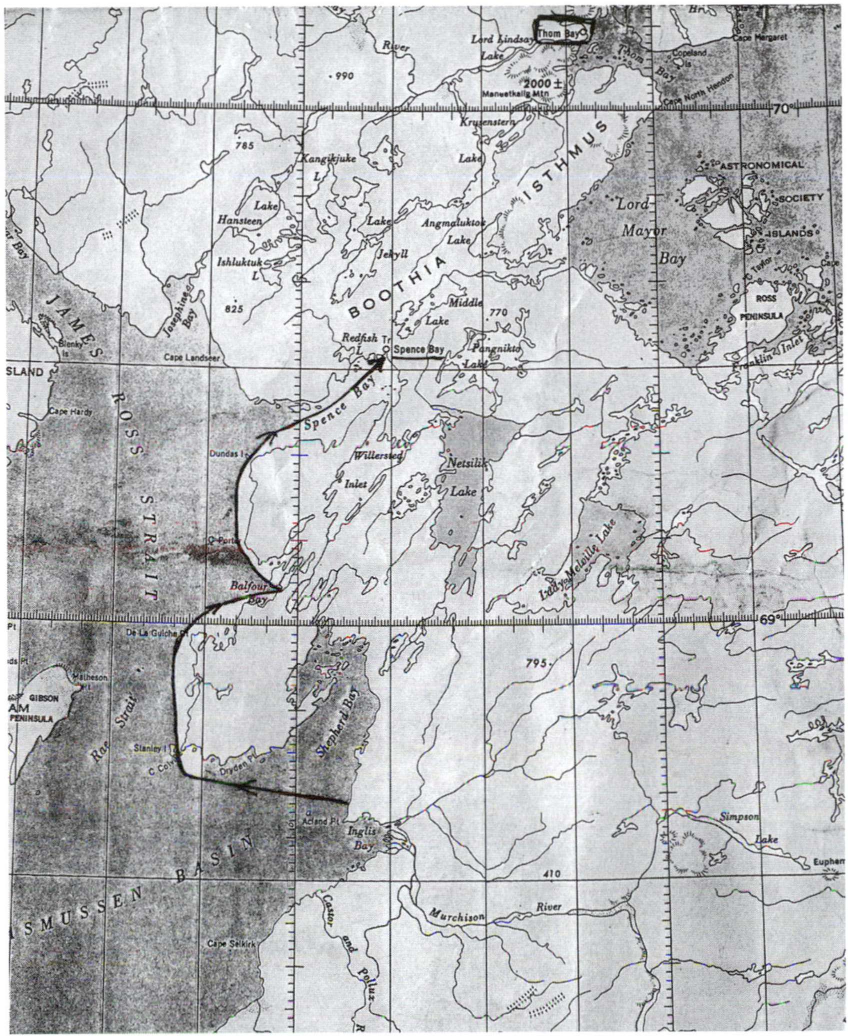

ICAO 1:1,000,000 map of Rasmussen Basin, Rae Strait, and James Ross Strait. The line indicates my northbound route starting in Shepherd Bay, north of Inglis Bay. We crossed Rasmussen Basin off Cape Colville, passing Stanley Island and De La Guiche Point before bivouacking on Balfour Bay. We hugged the coast all the way to Spence Bay, navigating the narrow channel created by Dundas Island. This last manoeuvre explains why the RCMP search party that set out at dusk was unable to find us.

Beluga hunting by motor canoe. Drawing by Q'ipsiga, Igloolik, August 1960.

in place for warmth. We drink our tea standing up. A bit of dried salmon is passed from hand to hand and, between them, from mouth to mouth.

11:00 P.M. The wind is down. Revived, we set out again on a calmer sea, no longer at the mercy of a squall. Toward midnight, gaping Josephine Bay is visible in the distance. I admire, to the north, the gray granite of Cape Isabella (152 m), discovered and named by James Clark Ross in April 1830.[14] We head due east, manoeuvring south of Dundas Island, then northeast. Spence Bay is right before us at the head of the fjord. Like medieval barons, we glide in at full power in a groove of crystalline foam.

THE RCMP AT WORK

Spence Bay, 3:00 A.M.[15] Nineteen white canvas tents, sixty Netsilingmiut and Kingarmiut, the Hudson's Bay store (founded 1949), two Christian missions (Catholic, 1950, and Anglican, 1956), and a police post (1949), whose door swings open when I push on it. Empty. Nothing is locked in the Arctic. Shivering in the white night, I lift a tent flap, slip in among the sleeping bodies, and warm myself against a stranger. A few grumbles and groans are audible before I sink into sleep.

Sudden shouts. Lifting the flap, I see a canoe arriving at speed – the RCMP, out in search of us since yesterday evening, certain that we had capsized. They have searched for hours, retracing our supposed itinerary, looking for a shred of clothing or tent fabric, a paddle, the slightest clue to our fate. They had navigated to the north – and we to the south – of Dundas Island.

I am given a cordial welcome by the two police constables, the HBC clerk Ernie Lyall (a Labradorian married to an Inuit woman),[16] and the Inuit interpreter Peter Adams, a.k.a. Tootalik, a robust, reliable man with whom I will collaborate subsequently. Mission accomplished, my two companions vanish; I will see them only once more, very briefly, two months hence. The policemen invite me to live with them, and the simple life we share gives me new strength in these places haunted by tragedy. I begin this expedition with a catechumen's curiosity.

The station, two rooms and a common area, is organized with military rigour, a far cry from the Inuit disorder so dear to me. Everything is clean and squared away, the papers filed, the famous, ceremonial khaki felt hats hung on nails above the cots, the everyday caps lying on a table. The men press their regulation pants with an antique iron. Seven o'clock "reveille": whistling country and western tunes, we take turns preparing the British breakfast of eggs and bacon (decidedly, I will never get used to that unpleasant fried-food odour). We eat around a small table, our eyes drifting from time to time to the Playboy pinup on the wall. Common language: English. Never a barrack-room joke. Dishes, a shared task. As the days go by, I get used to the discipline of a fixed schedule.

They allow me to accompany them on their ordinary rounds.[17] Their vast territory, encompassing the localities of Spence Bay, Thom Bay, Gjoa Haven, Pelly Bay, and Back River, is inhabited by 577 Inuit and non-Inuit, or, counting by families, sixty-two in the Spence Bay and Thom Bay districts and forty-five in the Gjoa Haven district (see maps, pp. 80, 86). They graciously open their files to me, explaining the method used in producing their socio-economic and demographic reports, an incomparable source of objective information. Reciprocally, I show them how I group and map data (equipment, work time, family-by-family and item-by-item revenues, purchases, etc.) using the method of graphic semiology to provide a visual portrait of a society. A year-over-year comparison of these charts across ethnic groups and subgroups yields valuable observations about the impasses that a group may be facing, the ways that it may have refused to evolve – what we, in our ignorance, think of as "taboos." The RCMP's superbly meticulous surveys of the Indian and Inuit societies, group by group, since 1867 could be even more useful if modern methods had been introduced in collaboration with historians, ethnologists, sociologists, economists, and statisticians. My hosts marvel that a scientist would consider their work vital, and I find that I have contracted the virus of communication.

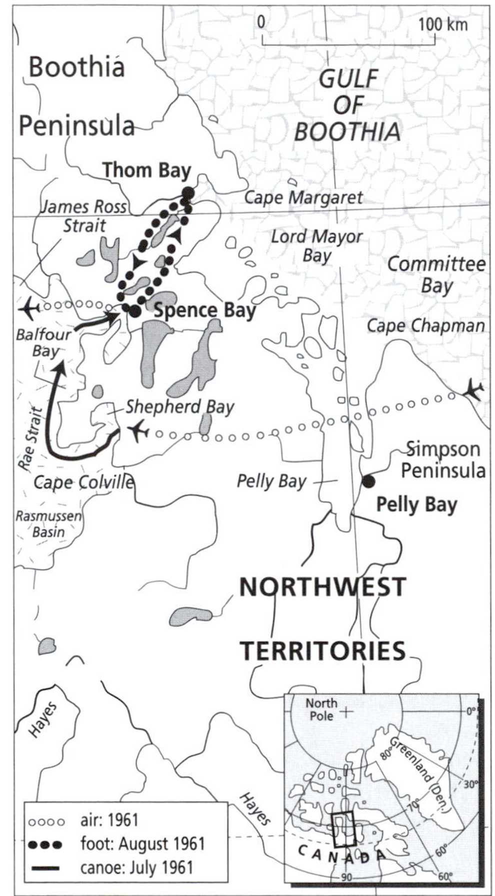

My routes in August–September 1961. Boothia Peninsula (Shepherd Bay, Spence Bay, Thom Bay). (Ice conditions on 16 July.)

ON DIFFERENCE

Over the course of our evenings together, the affable constables develop a fascination with anthropology. "Why don't we learn this at the academy? We would be excellent research assistants." They are keen to learn more about what I do, so each morning, while we eat our ritual bacon, I delve further into my plan for the day and explain my ethnohistorical research approach. For example, I explain to them that I am interested in the stoicism, the fatalism of the Netsilingmiut, their ubiquitous "Ayortok!" (impossible). In winter, at a rate of one to two pounds of meat and fat per person per day plus food for the dogs, they would need 60 to 100 seals or 70 caribou for heat and food. Yet they shiver in their tents from May to November, in snow houses from November to May, with no more than 10 seals annually, plus a few caribou and fish. How do they do it? By reducing their needs to a minimum. The weakest are eliminated through disease or suicide, while the least hardy survivors are always on the verge of pulmonary illness. The slightest infection, and the entire group coughs and spits, a truly pathetic sight in September. As Roald Amundsen wrote in 1905, "It has always been believed that the air in the Polar regions is absolutely pure and free from bacilli; this, however, is, to say the least, doubtful, in any case as far as the regions around King William Land are concerned, for here the Eskimo nearly every winter were visited with quite an epidemic of colds. Some of them had such violent attacks that I was even afraid of inflammation of the lungs."[18] During my trip, one out of three had a cough. In summer many Netsilingmiut were wearing fabric shirts, which, unlike the animal-skin *attili*, offer poor protection from the cold and humidity. As well, like the Back River Inuit, they rarely made a fire. Why not?

They could organize, collectively hunt seals in spring, and if none are to be found in Spence Bay – frequently the case – send hunters north to the Bellot Strait, east to Lord Mayor Bay, or south to Shepherd Bay and the deserted estuary of the rushing Murchison River, where the seal population density is high. They could put away provisions in natural refrigerators made by digging pits in the loose pebble beaches along the coast. Why this refusal to organize, this inability or unwillingness to accumulate? Is it that their anarcho-communalist system of sharing, their staunch egalitarianism, demands constant equalization among the most active and the least skilled? In other words, is it the law of the group? Or is it an inherited fascination with risk? Or the slow withering of the race? Whatever be the case, life for them must be – and this fact has always struck me – a daily peril. Security is unhappiness, the boredom of days that look alike. They live for challenge.

Borne along Celt-like by the satisfaction of reasoning aloud, I find myself rehearsing an explanation, listening to my own voice as if I were alone in the room. The constables, disciplined introverts in the Anglo-Saxon mould, observe my performance with shining eyes. Finally, displaying surprise at their own boldness, they join in, recounting their extensive experience and extraordinary stories. Their presentation is factual, their interpretations terse and to the point. The habit of reasoning is unfamiliar to them since they are used to leaving that task to the hierarchy. In their estimation, the Inuk is in constant rivalry, trying to be the best, at the risk of losing his life through an excess of daring. I concur that he is motivated by a desire for renown, that he is Cornelian; but, I persist (we three persist since they, too, are caught up in the dialogue), why are there enterprising societies like ours and other societies that seem to live from day to day? The answer, it appears, is that they are motivated more by ideology than by incapacity. Precarity in this society is a matter of volition, a consequence of willed risk and voluntary nondevelopment. Consequently, hoarding is considered unwholesome. Surely, some historical factor must account for this refusal to obey what one might suppose to be universal principles of societal evolution. Most germane to this issue, it seems that their life is governed by a set of taboos, the most hallowed being respect for the *Inutuqait*, the elders.

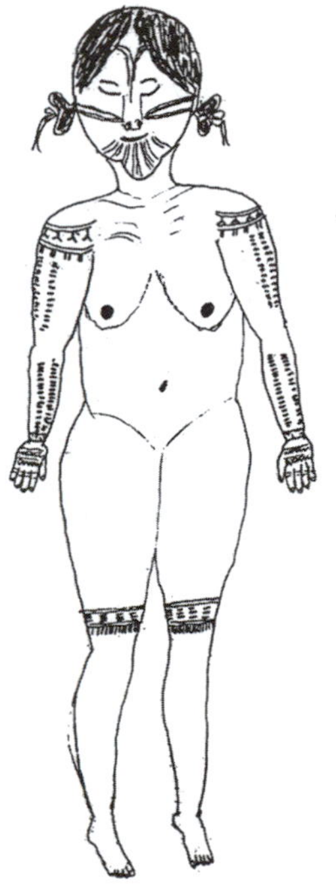

Tattooed woman (b. 1910), drawn by her son. The four triangles on each shoulder symbolize breaching whales. The number of lines is indicative of the powers with which certain numbers are invested. Spence Bay, 1961. Ethnological notebook.

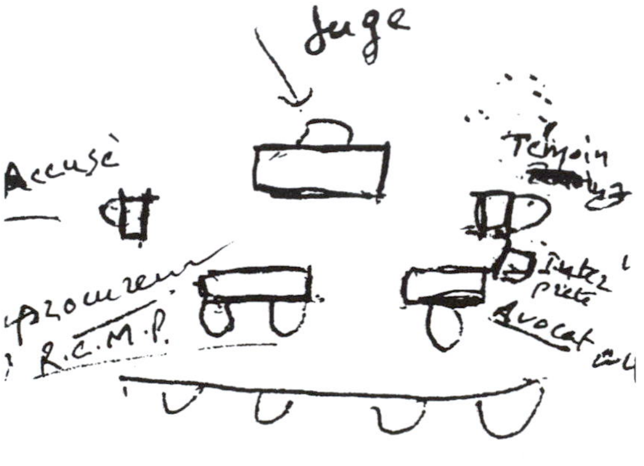

Trial held in a Spence Bay schoolroom, 1959. I produced this sketch from the account of Ernie Lyall. At top, judge's table. Diagonally to his right, the defendant; diagonally to his left, the witness, assisted by Lyall as the judge's official interpreter. Directly facing the judge are, at left, the Crown prosecutor assisted by an RCMP officer and, at right, the counsel for the defence. The public gallery is behind them. The charge was incest; the defendant was accused of having had a child with his own daughter. He was a recidivist. He had been reported by his elderly wife and the young mother. He was sentenced to eighteen months in prison at Fort Smith in the southern Northwest Territories. When the judgment was spoken, he laughed defiantly at this manifestation of white justice, an attitude that he had maintained throughout the trial. Spence Bay, August 1960.

The three of us are emboldened to take the reasoning further, and I wonder aloud: What is the reality behind the word "education" here in the North? The three of us agree: it means destruction of a "primitive" system followed by pell-mell integration into a new one – ours – through evangelization, schooling, and the labour market. Their choice is either self-driven development or hurried Canadianization through schooling, Christianization, and the economic straitjacket of trapping. Those are the alternatives. But whose land is this, anyway, theirs or ours? And who occupied it without treaty or agreement?

To overthrow a philosophy, I tell them, to destroy an ancient system, is to stifle the creativity that is born out of necessity. The people can see that the elites have been paralyzed by our actions; and so, lacking leadership, they wait ... for Godot. The constables volunteer relevant examples from their personal experience but stop short of drawing any "political" conclusions ("That's not for us to say"). Still, they are curious to hear the political viewpoint of a European anthropologist from a colonialist country.

Because of their role as census takers, they are also interested in demographic questions. For example, are conclusions about the population dynamics of such a small, isolated group meaningful if the statistics do not include accurate data about *all* sources of infant mortality (of which the rate here is high)? Certainly, miscarriages are excluded, and prenatal, neonatal, and postnatal deaths are lumped together. Netsilingmiut reproductive patterns can perhaps be elucidated by comparison with the Inughuit (Polar Inuit) of Thule, North Greenland. For example – and contrary to the typical pattern in Western democracies – the Inughuit displayed excess female mortality[19] and a high incidence of winter amenorrhoea in the years 1900–50. The birth interval in the absence of contraception was thirty-two months (1940–50), whereas ovulation in lactating European women may return on the thirty-fifth day after birth. Are any of these trends observable here?

Or consider the high incidence of sterility in both places (16 per cent of couples at Thule in 1950–51), as well as the relatively frequent cases of local epilepsy and nosebleeds, seemingly at the slightest show of emotion. Are these due to inbreeding? Is the prevalence of sterility due to the occasional induction of girls into sex at age ten to twelve, cases of which have come to my attention? Women are comparatively scarce, probably because of the infanticide commonly committed against infant girls.[20] Is wife swapping a means of expanding alliances and favouring maximum fecundity in an endogamous group? Or is it a method of cracking the hard kernel of the couple in order to realize the utopia of primitive communism?[21] Is adoption, the lot of one in four children (*tiguak*, "adoptee"), designed to equalize wealth among poor and rich families or to keep everyone conscious that one is more the child

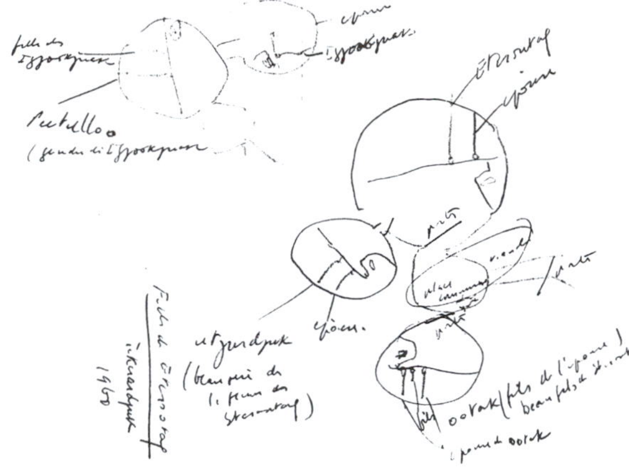

Snow houses at Thom Bay, winter 1960. Lower right, house of three related families, each in separate chambers. Leftmost occupied by Utjurdjuk (b. 1935, Anglican), head of household, and his wife, Oohooeektayuk (b. 1941). Larger central chamber occupied by Iterutaq (b. 1899) and his wife, Tagayogak (b. 1916), adjoining an entrance hallway common to this and the third chamber (bottom). Off of this hallway, a small recess for storage of frozen meat. Third chamber occupied by Utaq (b. 1929, related to Tagayogak); his wife, Angmadloq; and their daughter, Teegah (b. 1/8/1956). Top left of drawing, double house in which left chamber occupied by Putulloo (b. 1936) and his wife, Naloongeaak (b. 1/7/1940), and adjoining chamber occupied by her mother, Igjookjuak, a widow (b. 1916). Sketch by Igjookjuak in my ethnological notebook, 1961.

of the group than of his or her biological family? And given the frequency of adoption, what shall we make of the concept of orphan (*iliarhuk* in North Greenland, *iliappak* or *illiyardjuk* in northwestern Canada), the despised second-class Inuk whose status seems so incongruous in an egalitarian society – a person who is never truly accepted, even after marriage, or so I sensed? Is it a vestige of a functionally elitist system predating today's anarcho-communalism? Research into these and other questions would certainly be of the greatest interest.

Given their responsibility for administering family allowance and relief payments, taking the census, and conducting cursory socio-economic surveys, it is no doubt regrettable that the RCMP's men had no grounding in ethnography, demography, and the social sciences in general. Be that as it may, many of their reports and accounts are *much more valuable* than the papers of certain experienced researchers. Although these two refrained from speculating on issues within the domain of the specialist, their presentation of the raw facts was remarkably honest, accurate, and free of prejudice or ideological preconceptions.[22] Yet – and I find this frankly incredible – this readily available source is almost never cited in sociological and anthropological papers.

One of the files to which they gave me access for study and citation purposes – the one on Back River and Chantrey Inlet – was simply astonishing. *Could such an austere Inuit group still exist?* Every evening I perused the past decade's reports by constables Pringle, Fryer, Giesbrecht, and Sargent, finding myself riveted by one from 1957 that described the fatalism of the Back River people in the face of adversity, the vigour that they derived from their isolation, the pride that they had maintained in their traditional customs. The two constables echoed and commented on these characterizations with the utmost respect. As our conversation went on, I became increasingly determined to investigate the mythic place on which Franklin's exhausted men had once set their sights: Back River, the territory of the Utkuhikhalingmiut, the littlest-known, most traditional people in the Arctic.

If the RCMP are the honour of Canada, its backbone, then these two men were paragons of the force. I found myself noting the profound contrast between their respectful demeanour and the chauvinistic words of Joseph Chamberlain, colonial secretary in the Salisbury government (1895–1906) and apostle of unionist imperialism in the late nineteenth century. Who has never heard his credo, so revealing of the overweening arrogance of the British oligarchy: "no change of climate or condition can alter [the British race] ... which is infallibly destined to be the predominating force in the future history and civilization of the world ... I believe that the British race is the greatest of governing races that the world has ever seen."[23] Who is unaware of the Scottish philosopher Thomas Carlyle's doctrine of "mights and rights," elaborated on in his powerfully influential 1841 work *On Heroes, Hero-Worship and the Heroic in History*? It was an influence, unfortunately, that would extend beyond the British elites and across the centuries to shape, among other things, the devastating events beyond the Rhine in the Second World

Small hunting camp (seal and walrus) on the Melville Peninsula coast. The tents are secured with stones. Next to each tent, individual gas tank for canoe motors. Community tanks at right. Drawing by Naduk (b. 1920), Igloolik, September 1960.

War. In fact, it continues to permeate the thoughts of conquerors all the way to this desolate tundra.

Living day to day with these law enforcement officers, I discovered a very different, quintessentially Canadian ethos. The multicultural Canada of the North had been in gestation, in law if not always in fact, since the *Indian Act* of 1876, and their attempts to understand the Inuit were informed by this multicultural environment – their experience with the Indian reserves in particular. I can attest that if these two modest constables had heard Chamberlain's words, they would have found them perfectly ridiculous and out of place. Their Achilles' heel, however, as they distributed the meager allowances ($170 per family per year)[24] and methodically carried out the population census, was their ignorance of Inuktitut (or any language other than English). They could not keep the Inuit names straight, so they assigned each person a number engraved on an aluminum disc, which he or she was to wear on a necklace at all times. For example, Arnaja, an Anglican head of household born in 1913, wore number E4 293, the first two digits designating the district of Spence Bay. A practical system, if somewhat redolent of a penal colony. The policeman interviewed each person, checking his or her answers against the typed annual census as I followed along on another copy. Illiterate as they were, the Inuit could still catch the meaning of the questions – how many children? who has died? who is ill? where did you hunt? – and pick out their families on the page.

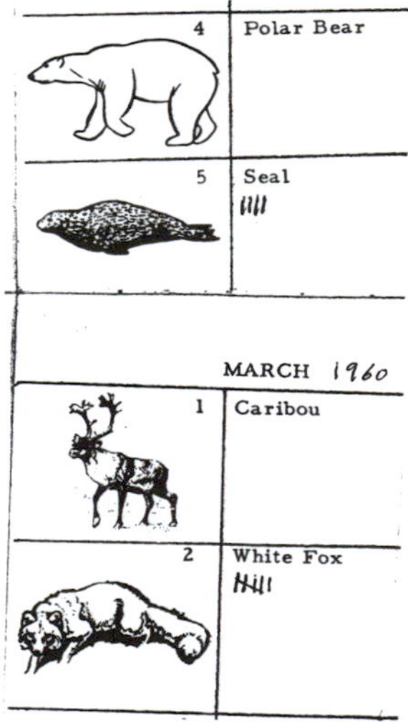
4 Polar Bear
5 Seal
MARCH 1960
1 Caribou
2 White Fox

Annual federal government form on faunal resources that Inuit hunters were required to fill out. Accuracy level uncertain since the hunters tended to be recalcitrant to this exercise. Vertical lines indicate catch. Spence Bay region, August 1962.

Friday, 4:00 P.M. A man and a woman from a distant coastal camp are standing in front of the table in the police station. Sweat rolls down brown-black faces burnished by sun and wind. Wrinkled foreheads, sharp eyes buried in epithelial pockets of fat. The man's gaze is doubly elliptical, at once cheerful, worried, and on constant alert – within seconds it can turn exceptionally harsh. Prognathic jaws, bitter mouth, hardly any chin, no beard. A few boar's whiskers for a moustache. All the energy is concentrated in his square hands: the curved thumb, the short plump fingers with prominent phalanges curled as if set to punch. His body bent as during seal hunting, his elbows held above the table – to rest them there would be too familiar – the man moves to within centimetres of the seated constable, watching the movement of the pencil, indifferent to the questions asked in a language that he does not comprehend. In an instant of understanding, his face brightens into a carnivorous smile: the constable is giving him his allowance. Better, in fact: it has been increased to account for one extra child. In some sense, the Inuk regards himself as the "trapper" in this encounter and the white man's random bonus, whose purpose he vaguely grasps, as the prey. The tundra remains his, and he reserves the right to hunt whatever he may be lacking.

"We are unilingual, that's true," the men tell me that evening, "but by miming and gesturing we manage to make ourselves understood." Their heartfelt respect for the Inuit shines through in their constant attempts to provide support without overly interfering with their customs. How far should they go?* It is not at all clear, and in that climate of doubt the authorities make sure that the minimum is covered, providing relief in times of crisis, elementary schooling, and medical checkups (in the last decade), with particular attention to tuberculosis and polio (now largely eradicated). As for the HBC post, it offers advances to the best hunters in times of economic hardship, a situation that condemns some of them to increasing dependence on trapping.† A class structure would develop were it not for the traditional celebrations in which surpluses are redistributed.

In typical English style, we give each other plenty of space. In the evenings, we sit reading magazines or books from their small collection of Arctic literature[25] or occasionally discussing their problems, with a civil servant's discretion. Protocol, their status as representatives of an elite body, dictates that they preserve a certain distance from their civilian guest, a foreigner at that. All things considered, I could spend an enjoyable fall and winter in their genial company.

* Family allowances for Spence Bay totalled $15,744 in 1947–48 and $73,952 in 1948–49.

† Trapping was, in fact, the crux of the market economy for over half a century.

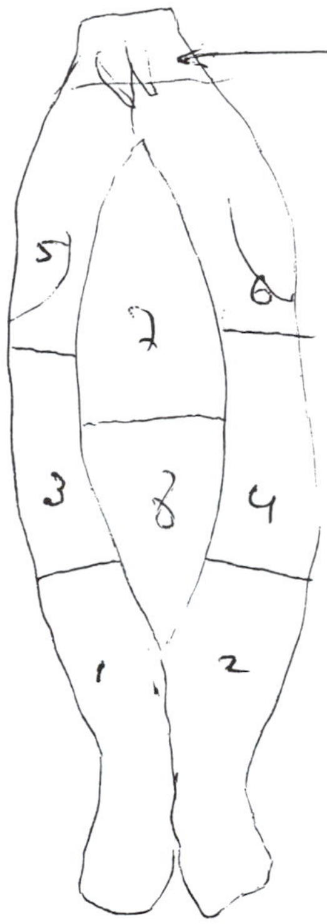

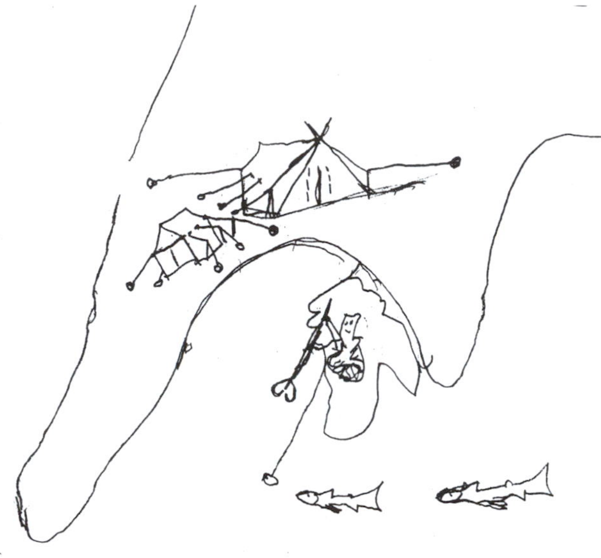

left: Carving a walrus into eight shares. The head and entrails belong to the hunter who fired the first shot. Share number 1 belongs to the boat owner, number 2 to the one who provided the gasoline. The other shares are distributed according to a hierarchy that corresponds to each person's role during the hunt. Igloolik expedition, May 1961. Ethnological notebook.

right: Salmon fishing at sea. The fisherman fishes from a drifting chunk of ice with a spear in the right hand and the lure in the left. Drawing by Ivaluk Iaarani. Spence Bay, August–September 1961.

"MAY CIVILIZATION NEVER REACH THEM!"

The more senior of the constables had been, in a previous assignment, responsible for policing an Indian group on a reserve near Vancouver. He quickly realized that a people without traditions is eaten away from within. Said the chief of the band to him, "I can't talk to them anymore. Take my power and act. You still have some authority." Here in Spence Bay, this man was troubled. He sensed that the Netsilingmiut were doomed if they did not return to their nomadic ways and disperse across the peninsula from Fort Ross (Bellot

Strait), where Arvertormiut territory begins, to Shepherd Bay in the south, a 400-kilometre range (see maps, pp. 70, 80, 86, 186).

Spence Bay was formerly known by hunters as an obligatory stopping point between lake and sea. The reason is the unique constricted topography of the area. The peninsula is pockmarked with lakes (Pangnikto, Willersted, Netsilik, Middle) at the same latitude that it narrows to a wasp-waist between the James Ross Strait and Lord Mayor Bay (Gulf of Boothia), making caribou easy prey when they move north into the Boothia Peninsula at winter's end. But caribou numbers had been declining steadily since 1930, leaving seals and fish as the major food source. Taloyoak was no longer a good place.* Still, its population was on the rise, from 47 Inuit (20 M, 27 F) in 1951 to 19 families (including 8 on welfare) in 1961. The attractions were the school, the Catholic and Anglican missions, and especially, the post. There was a future for their children, if a hazy one. Government jobs were there for the taking. It was in this artificial, deadly dull village that the government chose to build ten houses next to the tents and igloos, tempting the Inuit with a future of relief. I brought up the matter with the local authorities. All of them knew that Spence Bay was a bad place.

The police constables were right: the hunters had to disperse over the entire territory, from the northern tip of the peninsula to the south. It was repeated over and over, *sotto voce*. Their seal and fish supply (90 per cent of their diet) would be assured, as would their monetary income from trapping. If the government were to act decisively by guaranteeing fur prices, by making an exception to the sacrosanct rules of the liberal economy, it could induce the Inuit to resume the hunting life, to inhabit once-active camps such as Cape North Hendon, Avatootsiak, Cresswell Bay, Tasmania Island, Netsilik Lake, Fort Ross, Brentford Bay, Lord Mayor Bay, Thom Bay, and Josephine Bay, each continuously inhabited by two or three families until only a few years before. In this way, it would be possible to preserve the continuity and cultural vitality of a people whose average annual family income was only $200–300, half of this from family allowances or relief. They could be resupplied by air drops. A country as powerful as Canada not only had the means to do this; it had a duty to defend the culture and provide for the future of one of its first peoples, and their continued vitality was conditional upon a dispersed habitat. Eight thousand people inhabited a region comprising more than one-third of Canada's land area, and while their hunting culture was still intact, their presence was the only thing justifying Canada's authority over these vast northern lands. But the Canadian government pursued a bulldozer-style settlement

* The bay is navigable by ship for only about eight weeks a year since it begins to ice over in late September and only thaws in mid-July.

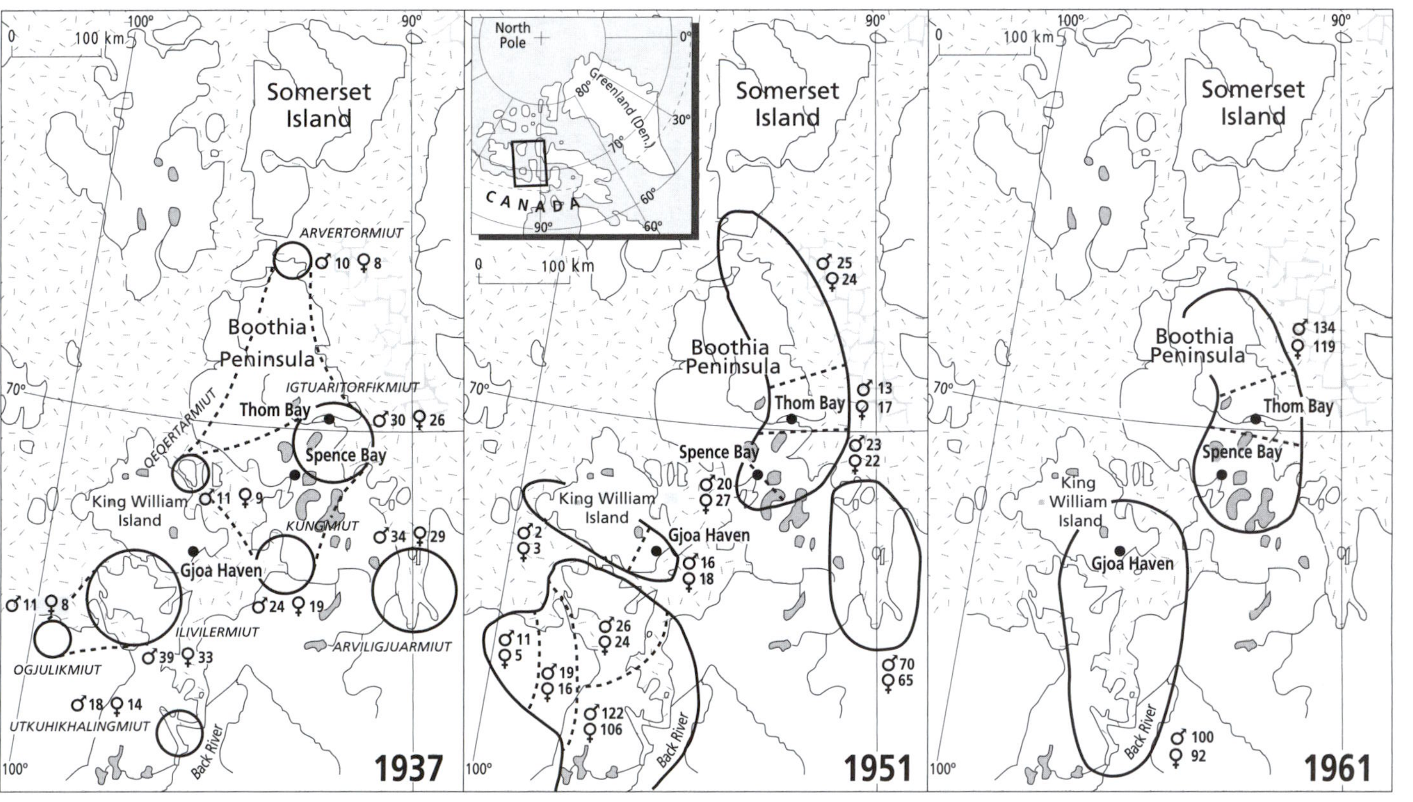

Demographic growth in the hunting areas of six Inuit groups on Boothia Peninsula, King William Island, Adelaide Peninsula, Back River, and Pelly Bay, the entire area covered by the RCMP post in Spence Bay, 1937–61. (Ice conditions on 30 March.)

policy that, while simplifying the work of the relevant departments, threatened to kill their reason for being.*

A few figures illustrate the pattern of population concentration. In 1923 the Boothia Peninsula was inhabited by 259 Netsilingmiut (Rasmussen). In 1930 there were 8 camps. In August 1953 there were 11 camps comprising 43 tents and a total of 200 inhabitants, including 141 Netsilingmiut and 59 Kingarmiut. At Spence Bay there were 7 tents and 40 inhabitants, at Thom Bay 3 tents and 12 inhabitants. In 1955 there were 10 camps outside of Spence Bay.[26] In 1963 only the Spence Bay and Thom Bay camps remained. By 2000 Spence Bay would be the only locality left, a "Canadian" town of 900.

In 1961 trapping represented no more than 5% of the territory's income, versus 44% in 1920, while mining – a white-owned enterprise – provided 80% of the income. The "urbanized" hunter was in the process of becoming a social cadaver, the ghost of an ancient civilization. What did Canada want? A vast North populated by aboriginal people (3,700 in 1910, 6,000 in 1920, 11,000 in 1970)[27] or a neocolony dotted with mining towns, relief posts, hunting and fishing camps for tourists, military bases, and weather stations?

"The sedentarization of the Inuit will be their ruin, as a hunting and fishing people at any rate," said one of the men, quite accurately. "I don't think we really know what we're trying to accomplish. They are nomadic by tradition and we should be going where they are, not forcing them to come to us. For me, the current policy is contradictory, negative on balance. In our cities, the youth will learn the laziness that their ancestors never knew. They won't be hunters anymore. They will emigrate, and who will replace them in this god-forsaken land? But I only carry out what other people decide. I'm speaking as a citizen here, not on behalf of the body to which I have the honour to belong."

In essence, this man was paraphrasing what Amundsen wrote in 1904 at Gjoa Haven, after wintering two years on King William Island: "And I must state it as my firm conviction that ... the Eskimo living absolutely isolated from civilization of any kind, are undoubtedly the happiest, healthiest, most honourable, and most contented among them ... My sincerest wish for our friends the Nechilli Eskimo is, that civilization may *never* reach them."[28]

Mathias Warmow, a Moravian missionary who accompanied William Penny's whaling expedition to Cumberland Sound (Baffin Island) in 1857, was another acute observer of the Inuit's deteriorating condition: "I am always sorry to see the Esquimaux ... imitating the European in all respects. They

* In 1950 the Ahiarmiut (Kazan River Caribou Inuit) were "deported" to Ennadai Lake and then to the coastal cities, where the prospect of their assimilation loomed after the slow degradation of a lifestyle maladapted to the coast. Slum housing, homelessness ... a journey to the end of the night.

were undoubtedly better off in their original state, and more likely to be gained for the kingdom of God. But when they begin to copy our mode of life they are neither properly Europeans nor Esquimaux and will speedily die out, in consequence of the change."[29]

HISTORICAL ENCOUNTERS WITH THE NETSILINGMIUT

On 9 January 1830 John Ross met the Netsilingmiut thirty kilometres north-east of Spence Bay at Lord Mayor Bay (no longer inhabited in 1961):

I proceeded accordingly in the direction pointed out, and soon saw four Esquimaux near a small iceberg, not far from the land, and about a mile from the ship. They retreated behind it as soon as they perceived me; but as I approached, the whole party came suddenly out of their shelter, forming in a body of ten in front and three deep, with one man detached, on the land side, who was apparently sitting in a sledge ... The rest of my party now coming up, we advanced to within sixty yards, and then threw our guns away, with the cry of *Aja, Tima*; being the usual method, as we had learned it, of opening a friendly communication. On this, they threw their knives and spears into the air in every direction, returning the shout *Aja*, and extending their arms to show that they also were without weapons. But as they did not quit their places, we advanced, and embraced in succession all those in the front line, stroking down their dress also, and receiving from them in turn this established ceremony of friendship. This seemed to produce great delight, expressed, on all hands, by laughing, and clamour, and strange gestures: while we immediately found ourselves established in their unhesitating confidence ... They were all well dressed, in excellent deerskins chiefly; the upper garments double, and encircling the body, reaching, in front, from the chin to the middle of the thigh, and having a cape behind to draw over the head, while the skirt hung down to the calf of the leg, in a peak not unlike that of the soldier's coat of former days. The sleeves covered the fingers; and, of the two skins which composed all this, the inner one had the hair next to the body, and the outer one in the reverse direction. They had two pairs of boots on, with the hairy side of both turned inwards, and above them, trousers of deerskin, reaching very low on the leg ... With this immense superstructure of clothes, they seemed a much larger people than they really were ... Their sledges were singularly rude; the sides consisting of pieces of bone tied round and enclosed by a skin, and the cross bars on top being made of the fore legs of a deer. One of them was but two feet long, and fourteen inches wide, the others were between three and four feet in length. On the under part of the runner, there was a coating of ice attached to the skin, rendering their motion very easy ... The knives that we first saw, consisted of bone or reindeer's horn, without point or edge, forming a very inoffensive weapon; but we soon discovered that each of them had, hanging at his back, a much more effective knife pointed with iron ...

The wind without, howled round our walls of snow, and the drift which it brought sounded against them with a hissing noise ... During the whole day they were employed in removing the meat from the upper half of the ox; cutting it off in long narrow slips, which, in the usual manner, they crammed into their mouths as far as they could push it in, then cutting the morsel from the end of their noses by the means of their sharp knives, they bolted the mouthfuls as a hungry dog would have done. Thus passing the slice from one to the other, alternately, they contrived at length to swallow all the meat from the neck, backbone, and ribs, of one side of the ox: suspending their motions, however, every now and then, to complain that they could eat no more, and lying back on their beds, but still retaining their knives in one hand, with the unfinished morsel in the other, and again beginning with as much energy as before, as soon as they felt it possible to get down another lump.[30]

In March 1859 McClintock found the Netsilingmiut to be proud, well dressed, and friendly when he encountered them along the Boothia Peninsula coast and on King William Island:

These Esquimaux had nothing to eat, and no other clothing than their ordinary double dresses of fur; they would not eat our biscuit or salt pork, but took a small quantity of bear's blubber and some water. They slept in a sitting posture, with their hands leaning forward on their breasts ... These Esquimaux were all well clothed in reindeer dresses, and looked clean; they appeared to have abundance of provisions, but scarcely a scrap of wood was seen amongst them which had not come from [Franklin's] lost expedition ... The men were stout, hearty fellows, and the women arrant thieves, but all were good-humoured and friendly ... They had fine eyes and teeth, as well as very small hands.[31]

Forty-five years later, Amundsen wrote:

Otherwise we did not see anything on our first meeting with the Nechilli Eskimo [at Gjoa Haven] which would suggest any intercourse with the outer world, with the exception of some few iron bars and knives they had obtained by barter from Eskimo tribes dwelling further south [Repulse]. We were suddenly brought face to face here with a people from the Stone Age: ... who as yet knew no other method of procuring fire than by rubbing two pieces of wood together, and who with great difficulty managed to get their food just lukewarm, over the seal-oil flame, on a stone slab.[32]

Amundsen had found the Inuit of Greenland to be ugly, but

here we encountered a tribe of which some could be called really handsome. A couple of them looked like Indians ... They were also tall and muscular ...

Like most other Eskimo women she had lovely shining white teeth and beautiful eyes, brown on a light blue ground. She was tattooed like the rest on the chin, cheeks, brow, and hands. We learnt afterwards that these women also tattooed themselves on other parts of the body ...

Their teeth are of peculiar shape. Ours are pointed and thin; theirs have a large broad masticating surface. They wear their teeth quite down to the fangs, which, of course, is quite unknown with us. I never heard toothache mentioned among the Eskimo.[33]

Elsewhere, he wrote: "These people, previously so reserved, now exhibited the most deplorably loose morals. Among these Hyperboreans, the connivance of husbands and mothers was beyond all imagining."[34]

Knud Rasmussen, whose complex Danish personality was strongly inflected by his Greenlandic ancestry, produced what is undoubtedly the most authoritative and lively account of the region that I find myself visiting forty years after his famous expedition. His was also the first account in the history of these far northern peoples (particularly the Caribou Inuit) to denounce the endemic poverty and famine they suffered. Rasmussen wrote in Danish but also, in his expedition diaries, in Inuktitut. One must hew to the original text in order to catch all the nuances of his thought.

In his descriptions of the Netsilingmiut, he emphasized their joyfulness in the face of adversity:

The main result of my visit there was, however, the strong and intimate impression I received of the summer joys of the Netsilingmiut. Life round my tent was so vigorous ...

Never in my life have I seen such frolicsome and happy people, so gaily starving, so cheerfully freezing in miserable, ragged clothing. I will always remember Sâmik's brisk boys ... The Netsilingmiut imagine the "Land of the blessed" as a place where joy never dies and where every day it must manifest itself in play. It would seem that this ideal existence had already been realized in life at that fishing place, where every single day they played and carelessly noised and laughed for at least five or six hours – people of all ages and of both sexes ...

"Oh! You strangers only see us happy and free of care. But if you knew the horrors we often have to live through, you would understand too why we are so fond of laughing, why we love so food and song and dancing. There is not one among us but has experienced a winter of bad hunting, when many people starved to death around us and when we ourselves only pulled through by accident."[35]

Finally we have the account of the irascible Gontran de Poncins from 1939: "I had not expected them to be actually sordid, physically repugnant, and possessed by a nature in which I could see none of the generous hospitality of

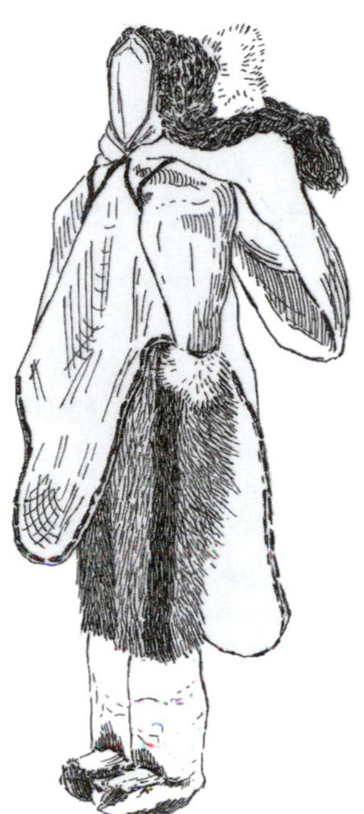

Back River doll made in several days during my expedition in April 1963.

primitive people elsewhere, none of the frankness I had known in other parts of the world, but only suspicion, cunning, slyness."[36]

MY FIRST IMPRESSIONS, 1961

Apart from guns, domestic utensils (including matches), canvas tents, canvas clothes used in summer, coffee, tea, sugar, flour, tobacco, wood for making sleds and canoes, iron, and tools, the population's lifestyle has hardly changed since Amundsen visited. The same probably goes for patterns of thought, with shamanism remaining a potent force. The people endure.

The police interpreter Tootalik* has been placed at my disposal, and with him I go to visit each family. Initial notes: half the people wear animal skins in summer, nine-tenths in winter. Only the older women (aged 40–50) are tattooed, on the forehead, chin, cheeks, forearms, and hands, as in the time of Ross, Amundsen, and de Poncins. No tattoos on the younger women: the Church has exercised its powers. As at all the settlements that I will visit in

* Born 1924 (his wife b. 1932), four children (three boys and one girl). Anglican.

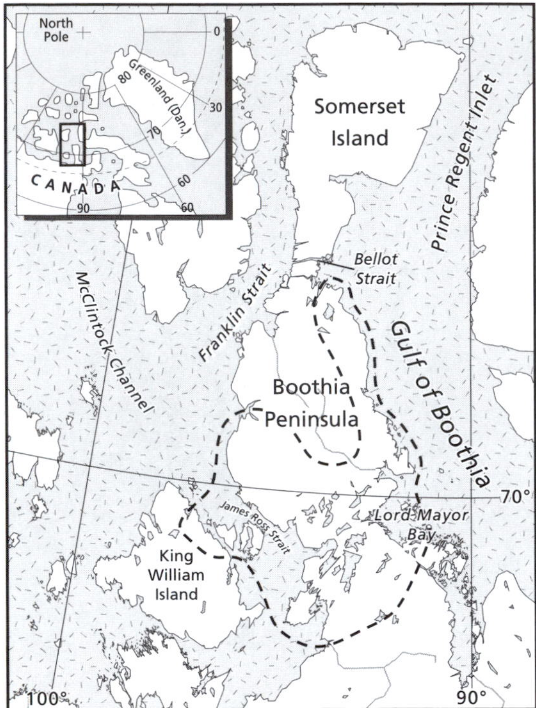

Boothia Peninsula. Netsilingmiut territory (trapping).

Canada, the men and women are warm but reserved, unpresumptuous. I begin a systematic microeconomic survey. The portrait is very different from that of Igloolik, where a greater proportion of hunting is for the HBC. Five to ten seals and ten caribou are taken per family per year, enough to live on but without inordinate expenditure of energy. They earn some income from sealing and trapping, but all families are on relief, which covers the basic necessities at the store. As for the HBC, it is a private corporation making a profit for its shareholders (including the Queen) by buying pelts at the going rate (no multiyear guarantees) and selling staple goods at monopolistic prices determined by adding a generous profit margin to the cost price. There is no shopping alternative, no other Crown-owned or privately owned competition. In the late nineteenth century, HBC earned enormous profits from trapping; today, with the collapse of the fur trade, it has transferred its profit margin to its retail operation. Its suppliers (the hunters) have become customers, their family allowance and relief cheques being milked for new revenues. In essence, an indirect tax is being paid by the Inuit, in addition to the direct value-added tax.[37] Much more important as a revenue source, however, are the purchases of the cooperants "working for" the Inuit (teachers, nurses, in-and-out government experts), who are in no way embarrassed by the yawning gap – as much as ten to one – between their income and that of the people whom they serve. Characterizing colonial outposts generally, and this one in particular – apart from pitifully small-minded gossip – is a sort of mental laziness among the whites that is reminiscent of slumber. These upstanding citizens, who have never learned how to conceptualize the genius of Inuit civilization, would be stupefied if one were to confront them with concepts such as historic justice, social duty, ethics, or Christian life. The Inuit as master artists? An alien idea. These imported employees know which solutions "work" and which should be dismissed out of hand. Gustave Flaubert's comment to George Sand in a letter of mid-June 1867 from Croisset captures the attitude nicely:

> A week ago I was enraptured by an encampment of gypsies who had stopped in Rouen. This is the third time I've seen them, each time with new pleasure. The wonderful thing is that they were arousing the *Hatred* of the Bourgeois, even though they were harmless as lambs. The crowd looked its great disapproval when I gave them a few sous. I heard some delightful remarks a la Prud'homme. That hatred stems from something very deep and complex. It's to be found in all "champions of order." It's the hatred felt for the Bedouin, the Heretic, the philosopher, the hermit, the Poet. And there is fear in this hatred. I'm infuriated by it, being always on the side of minorities.[38]

In summer, as I have mentioned, the resort to Western clothing is limited – mainly shirts, dresses, and pants collected by charities in the South and distributed by the churches. Sealskin boots remain in standard use; no modern sneakers or rubber boots. And no linens; everyone sleeps on and under caribou skins.

Carving and sharing out a beluga whale. Drawing by Inutersuak, North Greenland, 1967.

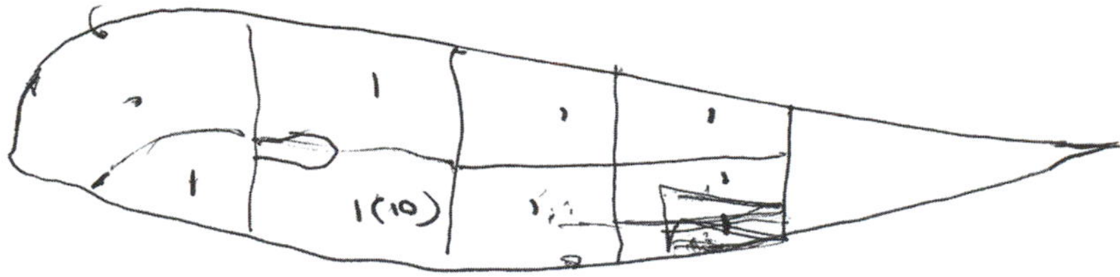

Poverty is visible and in some cases extreme. Indebted to a three-centuries-old monopoly but living in a social service vacuum, the families experience harrowing famines, whose outcome is high infant mortality and euthanasia of the elderly. However, adult suicide has been nonexistent in recent years, to my knowledge, and alcohol is still unknown.

My initial impressions are confirmed: the living conditions of these nineteen families are truly precarious, if not destitute.[39] Before entering each tent and becoming more a guest than a researcher, I ponder the distance between us and the Netsilingmiut. We see ourselves as Good Samaritans, as democrats advocating social justice and human rights, as businesspeople, teachers, police officers, or priests dispatched to "serve" them. What monstrous hypocrisy! But more to the point – and this idea becomes my leitmotiv – what can the low-level custodial administrators do if there is no political will above them in Ottawa? Very little, apart from buying time. Meanwhile, they set up headquarters in huge oil-heated houses with aggressive stores of food while their subjects shiver for all to see in snow houses or tents. Truly, the class structure is never more blatant than in primitive societies under colonial rule. Straining against this conclusion, trying to speak with more reflection than passion, I reason that the only justification for conquering, "civilizing," the Canadian North must be an awareness of a dilemma in which neither of two evils is the lesser: modernize them and destroy their society in the process, or do nothing and condemn them to self-destruction since they are already infected with our pathogenic virus.

As for the Inuit themselves, they are resigned but clear-sighted, exhibiting a characteristically hard, penetrating stare.[40] I observe two women at the Bay store, head propped in hands on the counter, staring philosophically at the products that they cannot afford (fabrics, oil stove, canned food, rice, pasta, fruit, marmalade) while their husbands make a few meagre purchases. Meanwhile, the white administrators' wives buy great quantities of whatever they please, with cold, detached eyes and not the slightest embarrassment.

I come and go, and people gradually get used to my presence in the neighbourhood. The survey progresses with increasing spontaneity. I appear to be regarded by the Inuit not as an "inspector" from Ottawa but as a different sort of Kablunak, standing apart from the priests, policemen, administrators, geologists, and anthropologists, the white hunters on their expeditions, and the whole system encompassing them. People call out to me, inviting me into their tents for a chat. Inquisitive as magpies, they "explore" me, feel me out with questions, to which I provide brief answers. I sense that our interviews are appreciated for their coherence, their focus on pragmatic matters such as time and money budgets. I explain that I am interested in the eternal, universal calculus of what they have, what they buy, and what they sell, their equipment, hunting income, work schedule (routes and calendar), allowances, expenses, and the rest, all the rest – life and its train of doubts and aspirations. And the rest of the rest: those tiny, hidden secrets that each of us clutch to ourselves. Increasingly emboldened, the obstinate scribe that I have become asks cautious questions about marital arrangements and taboos.[41] I learn that the dowry (*akki*) is payable by the groom and usually consists of a dog, a gun, and one or two years of work with/for the wife's family. Sexual relations with adopted girls and daughters-in-law, between first cousins, between persons whose parents have swapped wives, and recently, between Catholics and Anglicans are forbidden. The perception of consanguinity fades beyond the second degree, whereas in North Greenland it remains taboo-laden out to the fifth degree (1950). In ancestry discussions, the father's lineage takes precedence.

I dwell on a contradiction: adoption is very much extant, but the adopting family always prefers the biological son over the *tiguak*, who may nonetheless have been taken from his mother only a few days after birth. Children adopted after weaning (age two) are likely to be treated even more coolly. Why? I am told that it is only natural.

Finally we get to the question of wife swapping, or *kipuktut*, the real reason for my trip. But as tongues begin to loosen, the interpreter is called away to accompany the RCMP on a nocturnal criminal investigation, and I am left to my own devices. I am told that *kipuktut* is a vanished custom here. All agree that I must cross the isthmus to Tuat or Igpik (Thom Bay), where the tradition persists. I inquire about the locality, note family names and relationships, peruse police, social assistance, and HBC documents. It is becoming evident that the routine of a police station, although instructive, does not facilitate close communication with the Inuit. For all the credibility with which the policemen's implicit endorsement invests me, I am not sure that it opens people's hearts. These and other considerations converge on a decision: I will trek the eighty-five kilometres to Igpik.

The competent, experienced Ernie Lyall is my preferred travelling companion, but unfortunately, several days after agreeing to accompany me, he is laid up with a broken rib. The kindly constables assure me of their continued hospitality and promise to introduce me to the next Thom Bay hunter who shows up at the post. Hunters do come, albeit rarely, for a handful of tea or tobacco. A remark is casually dropped about an Oblate missionary, a Frenchman as it happens, living at Thom Bay. When I inquire further, there is silence. A "tough customer," apparently; their rueful smiles betray sympathy for anyone who is unable to avoid crossing his path. A photograph depicts an interesting but hard face, that of a saint or a fundamentalist. A face out of Bernanos.

Yesterday I took out a Beaulieu 16 mm camera, and I instantly felt like a voyeur. It is the first time in my life that I have taken one along. I promptly put the camera back in its bag, where it stayed. The observation of a people calls

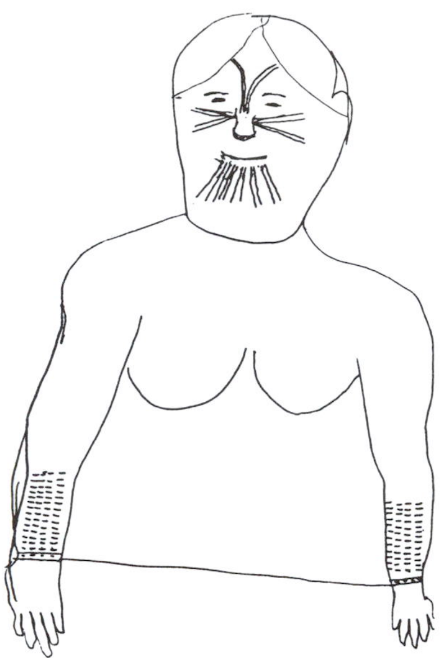

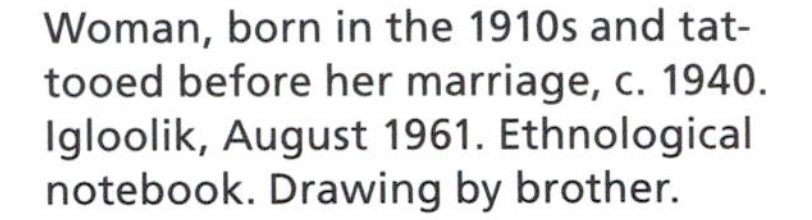

Woman, born in the 1910s and tattooed before her marriage, c. 1940. Igloolik, August 1961. Ethnological notebook. Drawing by brother.

for slow immersion, a second state that excludes all other activity. These two functions get in each other's way. The filmmaker, his eye glued to the lens, is attentive to technical problems, particularly in a cold climate where lenses are sensitive to temperature change. His focus is on the *mise en scène*, itself envisioned in terms of a particular audience, a predefined agenda. He lacks the freedom of ethnologists or travellers to look where they wish. But my reticence has a deeper source. I am the guest of a people whom I am hoping will gradually open up to me. When I do make films as a director, it will be within a formal, structured context and assisted by a crew. During this solitary humanistic research – perhaps I am a bit behind the times? – photography is a violation, an act that distorts all relationships by freezing and making theatre of them. The caméra-vérité has no place in these hours of reciprocal giving. As it is, my presence disturbs the peace of the day and complicates relationships. I am like a migratory bird in this ancient society, curious about the nature over which I fly; landing on a lake, the bird comes to realize that the ripples and eddies must subside before he can attune all his senses and dialogue with the people of nature. Only among them, living as they do, will I achieve this to some small extent. With a camera, it would be impossible. Since then I have never used a camera in individual encounters.

14 August, a blessed, sunny, windless day. I am apprised that a "Tuat" named Krokiarq* has just arrived, and I hasten to meet him. He is a young man with closely cropped blue-black hair, a long face, and yellow-brown skin speckled as if bitten by deerflies. Head down, nervous at being face to face with a white, he initially responds only with rumblings and gesticulations. He indicates agreement with a blink of the eyes, negation by screwing up his nose. Not an intelligible word comes out of his mouth. The interpreter summarizes this fog of impressions by telling me that Krokiarq will be most honoured to travel with a Kablunak. In haste to return to his young son, he will depart Taloyoak after a modest barter transaction at the store. We agree to meet at his tent tomorrow morning at six.

THE TREK TO THOM BAY[42]

15 August. Krokiarq harnesses his three silvery-haired dogs. Six o'clock, it turns out, was presumptuous. The Inuit have no fondness for dawn departures, and it is eight before we are underway. The three dogs each carry two white, mould-dotted canvas bags balanced awkwardly on their spines. The bags contain ten kilos of purchases for three families, including gas, ammunition, tools, and tobacco. The tent, stove, provisions, and tape recorder are in our backpacks; Krokiarq secures his with a sealskin strap around the forehead and another around the chest. He also has a rifle in a shoulder strap fashioned from a length of rope. We depart at a brisk pace.

It brings a rare joy to pace the Archean plateaus of the tundra, to soak in its washed-out hues and feel the springy, half-frozen soil underfoot. Our path toward the Krusenstern Lakes starts out along the oblong Middle, Jekyll, and Angmaluktoq Lakes, cutting diagonally across the Boothia Isthmus. These lakes and streams are nested one inside the other (see maps, pp. 70, 101).

The marshy tundra has no real relief, topping out at ninety metres east of Spence Bay (near Middle Lake). A graceless landscape that beguiles the visitor only gradually. The sandy clay soil (*maraq*) is spongy, soft, at times viscous. Sporadic tufts of downy aquatic plants peek out of the sunburnt clay (*irjuk*). The wind ruffles clumps of white daisies, buttercups, the odd fern, snow gentians. In the hollow of a rock, I study a common flower, the purple saxifrage (*Saxifraga oppositifolia*). I walk ahead with long strides while Krokiarq follows two metres behind, torso bent forward, his short, supple, elastic pace covering less than a foot with each step. The sky is clear, the light damp. Eleven o'clock: our first rest stop near a cheerful whispering stream. I lie down next to the

* Born 1 July 1926, married to a woman ten years his elder named Anasalak (b. 1916). They have a two-year-old son, Kakeanook.

current and lap at the clear water. For a snack, we tear off small squares of dry salmon with our teeth. The stream is easily forded on large, smooth slabs of rock at the foot of a waterfall.

The soil changes. The stones (*ujarak*) of the rocky tundra, stood upright by freezing and thawing, become sharp-edged under the soles of my sealskin *kamiks*. The summital substrates are fragmented. As I examine the flaky, desquamated skin of the rocks, Inuktitut words resurface in me like bursts of air. Hare (*ukaleq*) scat is recent and abundant, while caribou (*tuktu*) scat is older and less common. The earth is punctuated by numerous small holes, home to the millions of lemmings (*avingaq*) whose subterranean paths are an unknown universe. I imagine their mazes and labyrinths.[43] Walking stimulates my physical geographer's mind, oxygenates it. My eye becomes a microscope, and my path zigzags along a route determined by my curiosity. I observe the gelifracts, the mat of harsh green moss around the stones, the interlacing of rust-coloured lichens.

Along our effortful way over the muskeg, I identify certain plant associations underfoot, recalling the charming botanical classification of plants according to their "fidelity" as exclusive, elective, accessory, indifferent, or alien. Like humans, plants cannot live here alone. They display affect, huddle together, interweave. Who can say that they are not engaged in some amorous dialogue? In the Arctic, whenever I am feeling restless and ill-humoured indoors, I put on my parka and head out. Now, my five senses are honed and watchful as nature instils its vigour in me. In the silence, indifferent to the cold, I get in tune with the latent energy, the unfathomable harmony, the

left: *Oxyria digyna*, edible plant, a puree of which is prepared with caribou milk. Author's herbarium.

right: *Plantago maritima borealis*, seaside plant. Height, 10–15 cm. Author's herbarium.

assembly of the dead who reveal themselves only to those who respect them.* The icebergs, the streams, and the wind all have their secret lives. The spirits (*tonrar*) speak to passing travellers in the Inuit language. Krokiarq observes me, discovers me, lending an ear to the brush of the breeze and finding a certain kinship with me.

Toward two o'clock we arrive at a stream (*kuk*), or rather a wide torrent (*kuksuak*), seven metres across, still in full spate and requiring fording. Krokiarq strips to his boots and parka. We divide up the dogs' packs. Unburdened and fearful, they watch their master, then follow him into the water, swimming at the end of a bridle. I leave on only my wool shirt and lace my sealskin boots up to the knee, trusting the stitches that the Labradorian's wife assured me were well done. Unfortunately, the Inuit are losing their know-how through contact with the whites: the seams are loose, and my *kamiks* take on water. I will have them redone in Igpik. Luckily the sole (folded back at the tip as in a gather) is in *ugjuk* (large seal), a stronger material than the caribou used by Krokiarq in the absence of sealskin (*kresik*). The water is very cold, no warmer than 2°C. I lend an ear to its murmuring, perceiving the shivering, crystalline transparency, feeling the wonder of the earliest days of humanity. Fascinated by the polished stones of the thalweg, I bend down to touch them with my hand, bracing myself so as not to be swept off balance by the glacial current.

Naked on the bank, Krokiarq hesitates to touch this Kablunak, this bearer of evil portents and powers; then he bravely rubs me down, and I reciprocate. His body is stocky, long in the torso, with the strong thighs of a walker and the calves of a cyclist. We get dressed. A fraternity is being established between us, and I hear him speak for the first time: "Tîgukpok!" (I need a cup of tea). We decide to make camp soon. After drinking a silent tea, I fall into a deep sleep, exhausted from these first thirty kilometres.

KINA IGVIT?

The next morning at seven o'clock, while we eat our dried salmon with tea, Krokiarq finally speaks. Slowly, cautiously. The word stems of this language resemble those of North Greenland and especially Igloolik (Foxe Basin), which I visited in 1960. I am not entirely at a loss. If he has remained silent until now, it is because he feared this eating and sleeping, this prolonged contact with a Kablunak, and a heretic for good measure. As for him, he is a "professed" Anglican. But he believes in spirits, and all the more so when in danger. If I

* In Kotzebue, Alaska, in March 1976 an elderly shaman explained to me that by staring fixedly at an anthropomorphic stone, one is permeated with its energy and that of the man or woman petrified within.

had evil powers (*iliasuktuq*), he would be afraid (*sajuktuq*); he would become nervous and run away. And so, the first question: "Kina igvit?" He wants to know who I am and what I am doing. I answer that I am studying the stone (*ujarak*), what goes on inside of it, its contradictory existence, the malevolent forces of frost that seek to destroy it and the others that seek to preserve it. The stone is alive, and I am on the trail of its hidden spirits. I observe the cryergic tears in the earth (*nuna*), the animal holes (*sitik*), the solid rock (*kaertok*), and the sand overlying it as a product of geochemical disintegration. I examine the stones detached from the bedrock, the pebbles (*tuapait*) rounded differently depending on whether they are of morainic, marine, or torrential origin. Concerning these last, I determine their distance of travel by calculating the ratio of length to width, the facies of the stone (blunted, rounded).[44] Then I turn my attention to the great heaps of stone, the rockslides (*ujarasugssuit*; literally, many stones). Krokiarq points out that the Inuit distinguish the east side of a lake (*kitliniq*). The south slope of a hill is *uquqkiniq*, while the north side is *aggurkiniq* and the east side *isuaruq*. I find the asymmetries of *sarqaq* and *alangoq*, caused by differential exposure to cold, wind, and sun, which I mapped at the same latitude on Disko Island (Disko Fjord) on the west coast of Greenland. Shades of the French concepts of *adret* and *ubac*.[45]

I tell Krokiarq, "I am studying human beings and – well, you. The harmonious balance of the Inuit with the air, the water, and the rock as they go about their daily lives on the tundra and the ice floes. Is Inuit thought irrigated by the energy of the stones, the wind, the ice?" That occluded energy, what are its trajectories? Frost (*kruarq*) is the destroying genie of the stone, but there is also a conserving spirit incarnated in aggregating, crystallizing forces. Using the few simple words that I know in his language, I dare to put forward complex ideas, positing that the physical ecosystem, by osmosis, informs the social ecosystem. From stones to people: anthropogeography. Krokiarq watches me intensely, mouth half-open, nostrils questioning, torso stiff as if prepared to dodge. I make two drawings in an attempt to explain how his ancestors tactfully handled these alliances, using the example of kinship taboos.

He follows the pencil with his eyes. After a long silence, he answers: "I live on seal meat, every day, every year, from birth until death. You see," he says, slapping his legs, nape, abdomen, "all that is seal, it is all I eat. The seals live in me. With some caribou. They go well together in my fat, my flesh, my blood. *Inuk*, the man, *issuma*, the idea: these two govern the whole. It is as you say: from the animal to the man, the animal in the man. I am dual."

As I write these lines, I find myself growing nostalgic for the quasi-sacred gravity of these attempted meetings of the minds of two men whom everything divides. Step by step, day after day, observing good sense and a scout's caution, we grow closer – understanding what the other doesn't know he has said. No big speeches: brief remarks, casual touches and retouches. Tuning in to the systole and diastole of tundra, tide, and confidences is the *sine qua non* of our attempts to understand each other. Outside the humanized enclosure of the houses and the tents, I advance in an ancient temple; hand to ear, I perceive the echo of the subconscious mind that underlies intelligence and gives free rein to the irrational and the sacred. I can still hear the murmuring of wild nature, the crunch of the schistoid scree under our feet, still sniff the stench of old pollock emanating from our bodies huddled together in the tent. (And an overriding olfactory memory imprint, that of hareskin socks drying on a rope twenty centimetres above our faces.) Outside, my fingers rub willow bark and ericaceous plants.

Yesterday, before fording the stream, I relived the fragrances of Kuukkat near Siorapaluk (North Greenland) and smiled inwardly. Oh, how I loved Siorapaluk! Or, at least, how I enjoy remembering those blissful days when the Inughuit and I lived in quest of harmony, in a pagan intimacy steeped in epic legends. They were charmed by my romantic elation upon discovering the universal harmony reigning between animals and man, such that (despite the superficial Anglican Puritanism inculcated into them for three or four decades) they could let their ancient mythology rise to the surface of their wounded consciousness. I felt this vitality, this vitalism, with exceptional force in winter, in the formidable mineral silence of the polar night, or in June, in the juvenile awakening of a multiple spring that is ever renewed. I shall remember until my last breath the strident cries of the guillemots roosting in rookeries on pink sandstone cliffs, where festive life explodes in barbarous symphony.

My senses are solicited from all sides, and I decide to devote the morning to soaking up colour: the iron-gray rocks, the reddish-brown tufts of grass, the straw yellow corolla of Arctic poppies, the rusty undersides of rhododendron leaves with their immaculate pink or white petals, the rich, luxuriant green of rough bog plants, the last white snow patches at the bottom of slopes, soiled with flecks of dirt. Genesis tells us that the colour of plants appeared only on the third day. What is order? A construction of the eye, a memory, an inner peace. I have hardly begun to sketch out some thoughts when I am dive-bombed by a white-tailed, ochre-legged bird: an Arctic tern (*Sterna paradisaea*). It dodges away just above my head. *Imiqqutailaq*! An omen of bad weather. As the sun rises higher, the tundra comes alive. A female ptarmigan (*aqiggiq*) waddles after me beating its wings, chasing me away from its nest. Earlier, we were greeted by the joyous chatter of a flock of snow geese (*mitiq*, *Anser caerulescens*) as they flew over, bound for lakes further north. My eye is caught by the smallest details: a black rock outcrop with lichens forming pale arabesques, a bright streak of feldspar, a quartz-veined escarpment, a tear in the mossy carpet. Welcome! The word is written everywhere in the esoteric language of creation.

Dreaming and walking do not make a very good pair, and I have lagged behind. I pick up the pace, yanking hard on my calves as I follow in the tracks of the three dogs. But just across a stable rockslide, my old devils catch up with me again. Here, I am at the school of my discipline, the study of weathering processes. Kneeling, armed with my micrometer and a ruler, I measure the glacio-isostatic phenomena on the speckled rock, identifying the glacial striae, awestruck by the size of the polygons making up the patterned ground. I resume walking, my mind waxing dialectical on the geological structures of the landscape, large blocks stood upright like columns of a Romanic church. When? How? By nature, over the long term, over cycles lasting thousands of years (e.g., 8,000 years for the postglacial period); however, there were interglacial periods throughout the four million years of the Ice Age, and 100,000-year intervals must be distinguished. I lose myself in the calculations ... thousands, millions of years. This evening I will say, as the Inuit do: "many, many years" (*amissuit ukuit*). The crustaceous lichens grow on the rocks by only a millimetre a year. With duration comes complexity. The same is true for the isolated human groups that, in our myopia, we deem primitive and uneventful.

Nevertheless, for almost fifteen years, trade and Kablunak "ideas" have been infusing the Inuit with new thoughts in this desolate space; thoughts of buying and selling, a strong God who can be severe or compassionate depending on the circumstances, sexual equality, prohibitions on murder, polygamy, euthanasia, and infanticide. "We don't understand. Why let unhappy people live if they are too old or too sick? It makes no sense," Krokiarq tells me in a whisper. I stop and draw: north (*kanaknaq*), south (*kivataa*), west (*kangia*), east (*kitaa*), noting the landform elements and their orientations.

My attention gravitates toward what has always held it: basic structures and their logic, ordered series. "And thus as we descend the scale of being, Nature speaks to other senses – to known, misunderstood, and unknown senses: so speaks she with herself and to us in a thousand modes."[46]

We set up a small tent under a corbelled rock. Lying next to each other, he on his back, I on my side, we talk before sleep, my face straining toward him. It is harder for me while walking, when his syllables are frayed and dispersed by the wind. He tells me about a recent tragedy in which a man's son was frozen to death in a blizzard while hunting. Head in hands, indifferent to everything, the father no longer speaks to anyone.

17 August, cold weather. We wake up huddled against each other after a night full of rain. While repairing the tent flaps, scrambling about in the mud of the thawed, fibrous tundra, my mind wanders to France, to images from

a child's history book ... the Valmy volunteers, Gavroche's cheeky humour, Foch's soldiers in the Saint-Gond marsh, feet soaking in water before the offensive. Why has France, with its bloodthirsty national anthem, so liberally shed its blood all over the world? Such a dismaying, depressing mixture of Cornelian republican grandeur and petit-bourgeois effeteness. Could this people, even though laid low in defeat after resounding victories, be rehabilitated by the meaning that it gives to its anarchic pursuit of the noble ideal of 1789? Will Anglo-Saxon pragmatism, with its racist and imperialist overtones, get its ethical comeuppance when all is said and done?

We eat our twice-daily salmon, dried *pipsi* this time, cut lengthwise and shared fraternally. At dawn, the snorting of the three dogs impels us onward, and we resume our journey. Most of our breaks are taken standing up since it is impossible to sit down: everything is wet. Due to a deplorable habit of mine – for my summer field seasons I tend to prepare my equipment on the eve of departure – we are wretchedly equipped, without proper oilskins. Our clothing is soaked. I am the victim of my own heedlessness. Toothbrush, sweater, wool shirts ... what matters to me are my notebooks, scientific instruments, camera, and tape recorder. For the rest, I have always entrusted myself to the Inuit. But while their winter clothing, including caribou parka (*qulittarjuaq*), pants (*qarliik*), mitts (*pualu*), and boots (*kamik*), is top-notch and can be made by hand in two or three days, their summer clothing is makeshift and mediocre. At this rate they'll be wearing sneakers in the 1980s.

Our route takes us along glacial hilltops, rosaries of lakes sitting on the austere Archean shield. For our brief rest stops, we look for a boulder so that it will be easier to reshoulder the load. Now, a thirty minute stop for tea; we undo the dog packs, root out the Primus and pot, search for water, and shelter the stove from the wind with our bodies. Stiffly encased in my old sheepskin jacket, hands amorously clasped around the white enamel cup, I take small sips, Inuit-style, like Krokiarq. Actually, suckling is more like it. How curious that under physically demanding circumstances, moments of comfort and relief take the form of childhood gestures. The sibilant sound warms us. Krokiarq drinks more than I do, nearly three litres a day.

18 August, 8:00 A.M. Still raining, a dense mist turned penetrating by a sour northwest wind. We dawdle over tea, breaking camp only at 10:30. We walk with heads down, bodies buffeted by the wind like the misshapen, hunchbacked cypresses along the Breton coast. Our rest stops are limited to five minutes every hour at first, five minutes every half-hour after five hours of walking. We cross the lower foothills of the Thom Bay Peninsula, a mighty thrust fault, via a low pass. Exhausted, we must nonetheless keep up the pace, for we are out of fish, and the game on which I had counted is scarce: a few hares, ptarmigans, and snow buntings are all we see. We also note fox holes

(*siggat*). It is out of season for caribou. If a multiday storm were to blow, our situation would degenerate alarmingly.

I try to remember a few rules learned at the Lycée Hoche de Saint-Cloud when we ran track and field at the Stade Français (I took great pride in being a front runner in the interschool tournament at La Courneuve): pace yourself and breathe deeply through the nose from time to time. I am gaining muscle tone but am still very much out of shape. At each stop I am truly weary. We are not eating enough – it may be only that.

Krokiarq shows me the shelter where he stopped on the reverse trip. He tells me of his son, his reason for living, and explains one of the festivals to which his people are particularly attached: the one celebrating the son's first steps (*ablureortoq*), when relatives and old friends are invited to share fish and meat stored up during the year. Although the Netsilingmiut are individualistic, they seek out every opportunity for company in this physically oppressive environment.

He goes on to offer an account of the Tunit, those legendary bearskin-clad giants from the west whose civilization preceded that of the Inuit. They were stronger and could throw their spears a considerable distance with their feet. They raided Inuit camps, he says, to copulate with the women. They were also capable of swimming straits or catching caribou on the run and spearing or stabbing them to death. Here and there at Rankin Inlet, Igloolik, and Spence Bay, I was shown huge walls, the vestiges of buildings built by these giants. Their graves were surrounded by big stones stood on edge as supports for a large slab covering the body (see figure, p. 138).[47]

Tundra funeral. The body is laid out in a caribou skin sewn up to the chin. The exposed face is covered with a thin skin in which small holes have been cut out for the eyes, mouth, and nose. The body is surrounded with stones but never covered with a slab. Sketch by Arnaja, a Thom Bay resident (b. 1913), who drew it during our southwesterly trek across the peninsula to Spence Bay (28 August 1961).

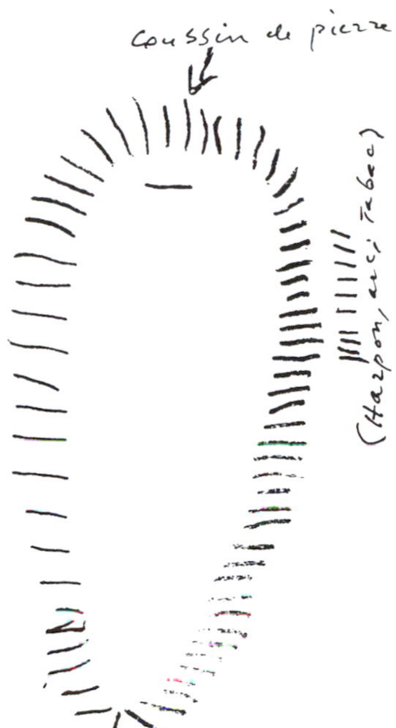

Caribou hunter's tomb on the tundra, stones surrounding the body. At the top of the tomb is a stone serving as a headrest; at right, within reach of the dead hunter but outside the circle of stones, are his weapons (harpoon, bow) and tobacco for the trip into the afterlife. If the deceased is a woman, her thimble and round knife (*ulu*) are at hand instead. Drawing by Homaok, Gjoa Haven, May 1963. Ethnological notebook.

The weather turns foul, the wind gusting and whipping piles of icy snow into our faces. My teeth are chattering and my lips, like his, are blue. To boost my spirits, I try but fail to light a cigarette (I am not a smoker). With a humble look, I ask Krokiarq for help. He lights it and we share it.

The dogs eye us with distress, as they have eaten practically nothing all day. The yellow dog whom I have nicknamed Iliarjupaluk ("unhappy orphan" in the language of North Greenland) walks alongside me. He seems to be showing me some fellow feeling since I started giving him my fish scraps. Last night he got lost in a rockslide. I awoke to his heartrending cries and rousted myself in the white night to go look for him. His fur bristled when I approached, but a hushed, fraternal whimper was his only response when I forcefully seized him by the harness.

We are truly weary as the Maneetkalig mountains and their 700-metre peaks come into view. We skirt them to the west. My legs are so stiff that I walk mechanically; it feels as though these pole-legs would snap in two if I made a false step into a heap of rocks. Nine o'clock. We follow the shore of a lake and finally reach the sea at the edge of the fjord: 70°05'N, Eek-to-ak-shorvik (Thom Bay) at last!

A group of dirty white tents is dimly visible along the north shore of the small bay, illuminated by their lamps. We call out, but our voices are lost in the wind and mist. So much the better. We shall camp here in the damp dusk and take the opportunity to refashion an appearance worthy of our hosts. On the horizon is Victoria Harbour, where Captain John Ross wintered in 1831–32. "Keel-anak-toon," says Krokiarq, pointing out Cape Margaret to the northeast, which marks its inlet (see maps, pp. 70, 101).

TRIALS AND TRIUMPHS OF JOHN ROSS

My thoughts are drawn with empathy to my illustrious predecessor Sir John Ross, the Arctic giant with whom my path has curiously coincided. Ten years ago I was at Melville Bay in North Greenland, where in August 1818, on his first Arctic expedition, Ross became the first European to make contact with the northernmost people on the planet, the Polar Inuit, whom he termed "Arctic Highlanders." Now I am at Thom Bay, which he named for his faithful meteorological officer William Thom. Only a few kilometres east of here, Ross, his nephew and second-in-command James Clark Ross, and their crew* spent four icebound winters (1829–32) on board the proudly christened *Victory*, the first steamer to visit the Canadian Arctic.

It was 1828 and Ross's public reputation had been at stake ever since his return from his first expedition. "Captain Croker," they snickeringly called him in every officers' club, for thus, on 31 August 1818, had the unfortunate man named a "mountain chain" that he claimed to have glimpsed in the middle of Lancaster Sound, the entrance to the Northwest Passage. In the grip of a hallucination caused by the reflection of the bordering cliffs off the water, he had mapped the mountains and named them after the first secretary of the Admiralty. Particularly scathing on this and other points was the soon-to-be-knighted John Barrow, who had become his staunch enemy. Barrow was seconded (mostly in private) by two of Ross's former shipmates, the pious and ambitious William Parry, who detested him, and the vindictive Captain Edward Sabine, who despised him. One slander had led to another, and the three increasingly found themselves invested in their dreadfully arrogant role of judge and jury.

Any man of honour will seek redemption after such a disastrous gaffe by redoubling his efforts to succeed, and it was in this spirit that Ross, ten years later, sought to lead a second expedition in search of the Northwest Passage.

* Three volunteer officers (they generously took no pay), a surgeon, three noncommissioned officers, a steward, two engineers and three mechanics (for the steam and wheel machinery), a carpenter and his apprentice, a cook, and nine sailors.

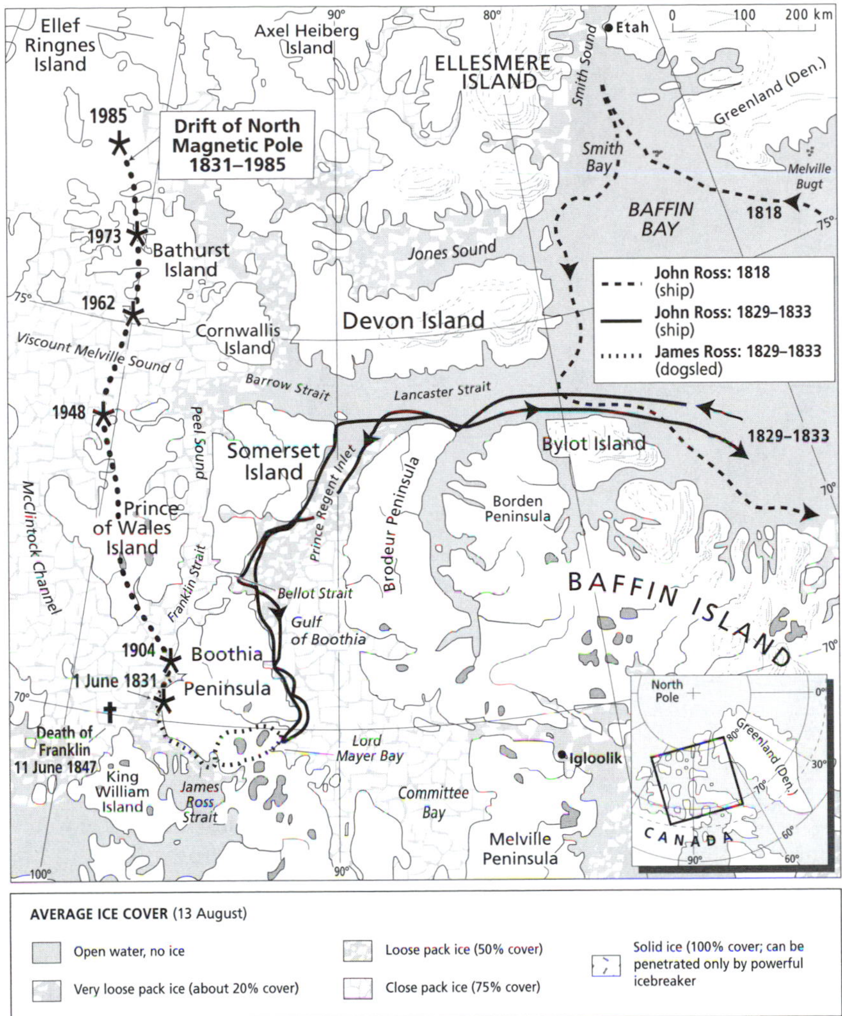

Routes of Ross's 1818 expeditions on the *Isabella* and *Alexander* and the 1829–33 expedition on the *Victory*. Also indicated is the route of James Ross's dogsled excursions in 1831.

He had another motivation: he wanted to even the score with Barrow and company – jealousy being one of the great drivers of polar history – by showing that the body of water south of Prince Regent Inlet was a readily navigable strait (it was where Parry had turned back on his own expedition) connect-

Captain John Ross and his resentment.

ing southwest to the Great Fish River estuary along the northern edge of the continent. If this was true, it would represent a crucial link in the Passage. But Ross was wrong again, as he would sensibly conclude. The Gulf of Boothia has no such outlet (leaving aside the narrow, shallow Bellot Strait further to the north).[48] It is a dead end.[49]

Rebuffed by the Admiralty (a foregone conclusion with Barrow still its second secretary), Ross turned to private sources of financing. He found a patron in Felix Booth, the public-spirited London brewing magnate, whose backing enabled him to fit out the *Victory* with the latest steam machinery, and the ship got underway on 23 May 1829. But Ross was no longer the man of a decade earlier. He knew that he was both physically and mentally out of shape. Older and heavier (too old and heavy to run behind a dogsled), dreading the thought of making another navigational blunder (and he would, for there is no commanding fate in the Arctic), he spent long hours in his cabin. Here is Ross, later in the journey, in one of his depressive moods: "The sameness of everything weighed on the spirits, and the mind itself flagged under the want of excitement ... had there even existed a beauty of scenery, everything was suffocated and deformed by the endless, wearisome, heart-sinking, uniform, cold load of ice and snow."[50]

Ross's writing is captivating for the candour with which he describes his various states of mind, but one must read between the lines to discern a major cause of his general ill humour: the contrast between his self-image and the handsome, active figure cut by his nephew and protégé. While the uncle moped, the younger Ross was busy exploring the Boothia Peninsula by dogsled. On 2 June 1831 during one of these forays, he reached a point on the southwest coast where the compass needle did not settle on any point of the horizon – the Magnetic Pole, a major discovery for any navigator and one of the expedition's main objects.[51] It was one of many important scientific and ethnological observations made by both Rosses.

However, in naval terms the expedition proved another disaster. With its innovative technological features and low draft (150 tons, half the weight of the Admiralty's ships), the *Victory* was – in theory – an advanced vessel well suited to the task of threading through ice floes. But the steam machinery, the object of much comment in the British press, had begun to fall apart even before they put in to a Scottish port for a final pre-Arctic stop. The next three years would become an extraordinary trial for captain and crew.

After making their way down Prince Regent Inlet to Felix Harbour (69°59'N, 92°W),[52] they readied the *Victory* for winter on 8 October 1829, expecting to be able to continue the journey the following summer. To their dismay, they found the ice slow to break up and realized that they were its prisoners. Strenuous efforts to free the ship were to no avail. From one year to the next they moved the ship within a small area of Lord Mayor Bay known since by the Inuit as "Kablunaq-Shorvik" – from Sheriff Harbour in 1830–31 to Victoria Harbour in 1831–32, this last only a few kilometres from our current location. The future was dark, but the crew had absolute confidence in the legendary humanity of its captain. A night school was set up to teach the largely illiterate sailors to read, write, and count, while Ross's pioneering approach to health kept scurvy at bay. Only one man died in four years due to the conditions of the expedition, compared with the abysmal death rate of nine officers and fifteen men over the first thirty-two months of Franklin's subsequent 129-man expedition, his authoritative reputation at the Admiralty notwithstanding. In fact, the members of that expedition, instead of eating fresh seal and other game, poisoned themselves one after another with the tinned meat that they all preferred.

Even under Ross, however, the fare remained British. Pristine fish taken from lakes and streams was polluted by boiling in copper pots, and the officers and men had to hold their noses to avoid the stench. Why not eat the fish raw, like the Inuit? On Sunday, work and hunting were forbidden. Every-

East coast of Boothia Peninsula, John Ross's 1832 headquarters at Felix Harbour, a few kilometres east of Thom Bay. Wall of snow for protection from the weather. The *Victory* was abandoned here in 1832.

one put on their finest clothes, and mass was held. The three-master was surrounded in winter by a high wall of snow to shelter it from the wind and cold. From October to May the nights were lit by the aurora borealis.

As the months and years went by, Ross felt luck slipping away from him. Lord Mayor Bay is the oddest of cul-de-sacs,[53] a place where the peninsula narrows to a nine-kilometre-wide isthmus and a string of frozen lakes. Its allure is akin to that of the elves of Celtic legend or the sirens of the *Odyssey*; travellers giving in to it are called on to despair. The time came when it was clear that the *Victory* could not be saved, and in May 1832, for the first time in his life, Ross made the decision to abandon ship.[54] The flag was nailed to the mast, tears streamed down the weathered cheeks of the rugged seamen, a parting glass was drunk, and they were northward bound with two boats and several sleds, retracing their effortful steps.

Their goal was to reach ice-free Baffin Bay before winter, where they might find salvation in the form of a Scottish whaling ship. They made it as far as Creswell Bay (Fury Beach), 400 kilometres up the Boothia coast, where they were forced to winter a fourth time. Finally, in the summer of 1833, they arrived at Lancaster Sound, where, in an amazing coincidence, they were saved by Ross's 1818 flagship, the whaler *Isabella*.

All things considered, John Ross had proved himself a great expedition captain. His geophysical and cartographic results were important, a hitherto unknown people had been observed, nearly his entire crew had been saved, and arguably the crowning achievement, the Magnetic Pole had been found. Sadly, however, this discovery became a bone of contention between Ross and his nephew, contributing to the continuing deterioration of their relationship (a process that had begun even before their safe return).[55] James wanted sole credit for this and other scientific successes of the expedition, neglecting the fact that his work had been made possible by the best ship and instruments (compass, sextant, chronometer, thermometer, barometer) that science and his uncle could provide. John was unwilling to give way. He had invested his honour and part of his fortune in the expedition; on it he had pinned his hopes of earning his due renown as an Arctic explorer, and for the Pole he would take the credit. Upon his return to London in 1833, John Ross, whose strength of character had stirred the imagination of all England, wrote:

> [I]f I myself consent to award that palm [credit for discovery of the Magnetic Pole] to him [James Ross] ... [and so] surrender [my] personal claims ... I should not be justified in thus surrendering the rights of the brave, and patient, and enduring crew of the *Victory*, nor perhaps those of him, the noble-minded and generous [Booth], who sent the *Victory* ... to the Polar regions. It must be hereafter remembered in history, and will be so recorded, that it was the ship *Victory*, under the command of Captain John Ross, which assigned the north-west Magnetic Pole, in the year 1831.[56]

A soothing night. Krokiarq sleeps, first in a sitting position, then with arms outstretched and palms open like a crucified heron. I observe his features: tousled hair; sparse, slim childlike eyebrows; worn, uneven, yellowed teeth; short strong hands and black nails ... a "primordial" Inuk, is he, or a man of mixed ancestry? Including English ancestry, perhaps? Miscegenation began with the *Victory* sailors, as Ross reported, and continued at the whaling port of Repulse on Hudson Bay, a good month by dogsled southeast of our current location. There, since 1800, the Central Arctic has traded its ivory, furs, and women for British iron, wood, and guns. News swiftly made its way to all points of the territory; Captain McClintock, after speaking with the Inuit at Pond Inlet in August 1858, wrote, "We were of course greatly surprised to find that Dr. Rae's visit to Repulse Bay was known to this distant tribe."[57] In 1903, upon arriving on King William Island, Roald Amundsen observed that four Netsilingmiut (whom he termed Nechilli Eskimos) had gone to "Eivilli" (Repulse Bay or Naujat)[58] to trade furs for utensils (see maps, pp. 5, 15).

The scope of trade was, of course, rather broad. In 1903 at Gjoa Haven, Amundsen observed: "All shame was cast aside, and men offered their wives, old cronies, their daughters or step-daughters for sale like any other merchandise."[59] Genes propagated rapidly in this tiny isolated group, and by 1920 people whom outsiders – explorers, ethnologists – had begun to study as "pure" were no longer true aboriginals but physical and intellectual half-breeds of Inuit, English, Scottish, and Norwegian descent. And if these societies must be "reread" with this knowledge, so must the many anthropological works purporting to describe traditional Inuit patterns of thought. Upon reexamination, many of them suffer from this failure to take the long historical perspective.

At daybreak, the rain has stopped. We hang our clothing out to dry between two stakes. The nomad's code: arrive as a victor, not as a tramp. At eight o'clock, while looking through my binoculars, I spot a boat and a kayak coming toward us. The normal practice is to lie down on the kayak behind the paddler. I opt for the boat. I am a Kablunak and a certain stiffness of character has always prevented me from pretending to be Inuit. The Inuit welcome me with gravity, their keen black or brown eyes a question mark. "Kina? Kina?" (Who is this?). (They have had no notice of my arrival in this radioless land.)

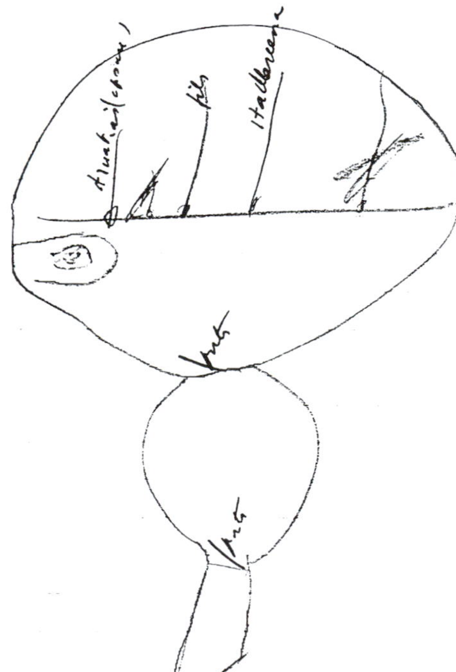

Snow house inhabited in winter of 1959–60 by Hadlareena (b. 1909, Catholic); his wife, Angnatiak (b. 1914); their son, Nalugiark (b. 16/7/1951); and to Hadlareena's left, a visiting relative, lying in the same orientation as the others, head pointing inward. Facing the wife is a small stone seal-oil lamp for light and heat. Thom Bay, September 1961. Ethnological notebook.

Pentagonal faces, strong brown hands, worn clothes – and close-cropped haircuts, a telltale disfigurement indicating that the priests, the "men in black," have gotten to them already. Proudly overlooking the bay stands the mission, a fifteen-square-metre cabin wrapped in tar paper.[60] A young man with a pale, angular face and thin lips, the only Kablunak in Thom Bay, is at the door, feigning ease. In the belt of his cassock is a prominent copper-tipped crucifix that I fancifully imagine being pointed at the base like a stylet. We shake hands in silence. He knows nothing of me but is already on his guard, obeying the prudent reflex of the seminarist.

Krokiarq stands two steps back, waiting for ... what, exactly? For the resolution of the eternal problem faced by the visitor in foreign territory: who will be the host? Uncertain, I whisper to him, "Leave the bag where it is. I will come get you later."

THE VICARIATE AND THE RIGHT OF INTERFERENCE

"Good day, Father! I am here from France, and I am staying a week. Pardon my directness, but Krokiarq's relatives are expecting me. Would you prefer that I stay in their tent or here with you?"

He hesitates a moment.

"The bishop would not condone such close cohabitation."

I fail to stifle a laugh. "Forgive me, but it would amaze the Inuit and perhaps also my Canadian friends in Spence Bay if two whites isolated in these solitudes, compatriots no less, were unable to live under the same roof."

He agrees but adds in a muted voice, "There is only one bed, that is the rule. You shall sleep on the floor."

I cross the holy threshold. The Oblate invites me to sit and share his meal of caribou, wine, and homemade brioche. He is a gourmet. I devour it hungrily, without a fork. Indifferent to my savage ways, he takes pleasure in speaking his language once again. His speech is rapid, jerky. As for me, my fatigue lends a breathless quality to my account. Choosing my words carefully, I explain my research project, telling him that I am interested in processes of change, but also in ethnography, particularly among the Netsilingmiut. I have come to study shamanism, family and matrimonial structures, and wife swapping (*kipuktut*), a little-known phenomenon.

He recoils in horror. "That is paganism, satanism. Don't expect me to help you."

I specify that it is an official mission, that infant mortality is very worrisome, and that it is a matter of observing customs as they are. Since my official interpreter was detained in Spence Bay, I greatly need his help.

"No," he says, "that is not the job of a priest. My life is given up to the parishioners, the Catholics. Shamanism is the Devil's work. Wife swapping, a vile pagan practice. On other subjects, if you really need an interpreter, I may perhaps be able to help. We will see."

I do not insist, as I must stay in his good graces. Tomorrow will tell. But an idea is already going through my mind: I will include this singular priest and his methods of evangelization in my study. "A door opens and it is the one we had not seen" (Marcel Proust).

Evening comes to the small room, with the priest in his bed and me on the modest floor. *Sancta humilitas* ... The ground is very cold. I lay out a caribou skin under my sleeping bag and hunker down in it wearing my sheepskin jacket. The dear man alerts me that I will have to get up by seven o'clock to free up the floor for mass. Worn out from the ninety-kilometre trek, my legs a solid, uncoordinated mass, I drop like a sledgehammer into a deep sleep.

Morning ... the humble altar sits on a small shelf facing me, two metres away. May God forgive me! I am still too weary. Despite my best intentions and to my great embarrassment, I remain lying down during the holy sacrifice, listening to the orison from my worm's-eye view of the Oblate's big black shoes, a foot from my face. He stands and kneels in sequence, while my gaze follows the movements of his soles: vertical, horizontal, vertical ...

Shortly before nine o'clock I abruptly vacate the space, shoving my pack and animal skins against the wall panelling, and we sit down to an amicable breakfast. I explain my research in greater detail, attempting to put it in perspective. If this man cannot be convinced, I think, perhaps he can at least be drawn in by discussing matters that might interest a priest. I remind him of the maxim that in research, everything is connected. Since Inuit thought is consubstantially animist, evangelical work among them must, in my modest layman's opinion, be primarily ecumenical in nature. I describe my comparative work in Greenland and the Canadian Eastern Arctic on microsocieties whose conservatism is a response to perceived threats. His interest is barely piqued. His brow furrows with renewed distrust: too many intellectual words. Spying the potential dangers, he reacts instinctively with a stiffening of the body, a tightening of the buttocks, and a pursing of the lips. The seminary has taught him to guard against this kind of seduction. What is a French anthropologist doing here? What is his hidden agenda? Strange, very strange.

I try to mollify him by mentioning a student of mine at the Hautes Études who was an Oblate seminarist. I had encouraged him to do a thesis on the history of evangelization in the Canadian North. He had gone to Rome, to the Vatican archives ... The priest remains stony-faced.

"I do not know him."

-23-

PENANCE

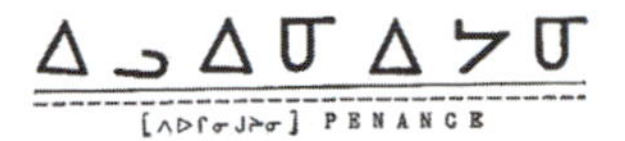

Guide to confession informed by the moral prescriptions of the catechism. Oblate Father Eugène Fafard's Inuktitut prayer book.

I take a new tack: "I would like for us to be fellow researchers during these few days. There can be no productive research if the interpreter is uninterested and doesn't encourage the Inuit to search their memory." A distanced silence is his response.

Cooperation will be difficult. We are a badly matched pair, this priest and I. No, not all men are brothers, and baptism has not necessarily made us allies. "How they mistreat you, they who know not how one must whimper and sigh to understand something of God" (Saint Augustine). "Does charity dictate that the weak shall be tormented and the strong spared?" asks Diderot in his *Lettre à mon frère.* Perhaps I am nothing more than what he takes me for, a wicked, ungodly man ... Time to go out and get some air.

Thom Bay is eight families consisting of thirty individuals (13 male, 17 female). I am told that several families are camped a few kilometres up river where they have built two *saputit*, or stone weirs, a time-honored system for catching wintering char[61] and salmon as they swim up river. The weir creates a bottleneck for the fish, which are speared with leisters (*kakivak*) as they emerge. This time of year is biologically and sociologically vital, for fish

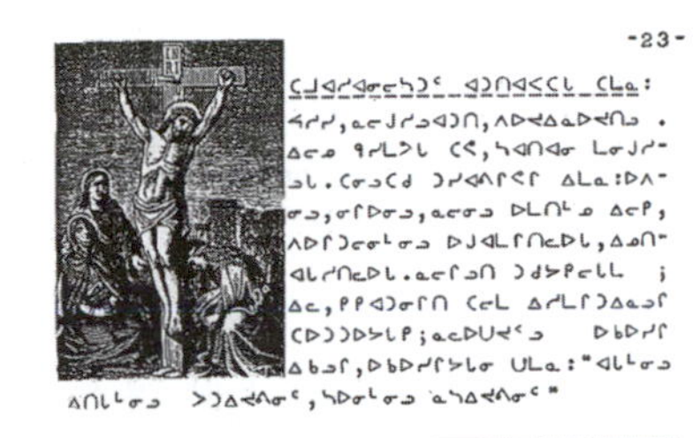

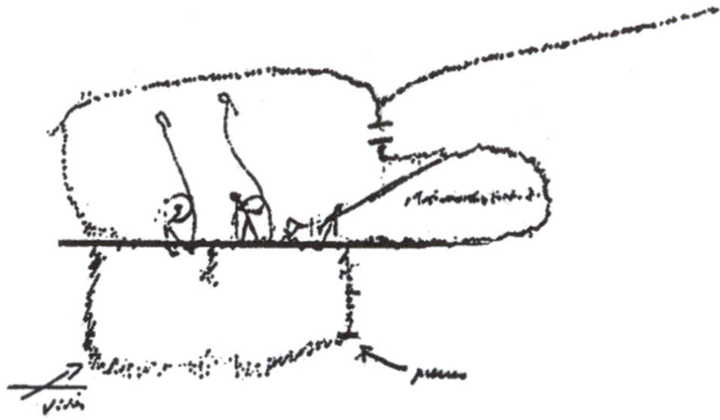

Stone dam (*saputit*), two metres high, at Back River. The Inuit caught salmon by casting lines from the bank or, as at right, in a narrow pond created by the dam, spearing them with leisters. Nets were forbidden by Inuit tradition. Drawing by Kikiak (b. 1922), April 1963.

are, with seal, the dominant food source. Their life cycle dictates the Inuit's calendar: from the river to the ocean in July, from the ocean back upstream in mid-August. In these isolated populations, communal fishing is a time of great conviviality that attenuates power struggles or jealousies between men who might be trying to steal each other's wives. In these groups composed of strong personalities, "weird" individuals, and lazy folks, collective hunting and fishing act as a unifying force, keeping an undercurrent of hostility from becoming overt.

The weirs stand nearly 1.5 metres high and a half-metre wide and represent a week's work for the entire group.* Behind each weir is a pond where the catch is collected. Each family needs 4,000–5,000 fish, calculated at one fish per adult per day in summer and one and a half in winter, with extra for the dogs; any shortage is supplemented by ice-fishing for lake trout in winter. A carved ivory fish used as a lure is shaken with the left hand and the fish is speared with a *kakivak* held in the right. In order not to exhaust the resources, the Inuit use a different watercourse each year according to a cycle determined by the elders (generally triennial). The use of nets, as the missionary does,

* Some of these weirs are very old and are attributed to the Tunit (Back River, camp 2); see sketch, p. 289.

is contrary to *saputit* tradition; the Inuk must spear the char (*iqalukpik*) one by one. Fish is generally abundant here. In the summer of 1831, James Ross netted 3,378 in a single day not far from the *Victory*.

As we walk up the stream toward the camp, the Oblate's step reveals something more of his inner character. He walks ahead briskly, his cassock slightly aloft, at home on "his" turf. *Nunaga*, my country. The slight influence that I thought I had gained over him during our tête-à-tête in the little mission disappears in the immensity of the tundra. Here in the great outdoors, he is back in touch with his inner self, feeling pugnacious like a boxer bouncing back from a blow. The disparaging discourse of the young seminarist at large is painful to the ears: the Sorbonne, atheism, anthropology, progress ... all old-fashioned nonsense. Too many professors harbouring false ideas, making the Inuit in our own image, interfering with the work of the poor missionaries. "His" Inuit no longer know what to believe. I hear overtones of the directives mocking the vanity of knowledge that were published in 1665 by the vicars apostolic of the Société des Missions Étrangères: "Astronomy and the other mathematical sciences, painting, the mechanical arts and others – all of this, for the missionary, is a burden and a hindrance rather than a real help. All the time that he devotes to it is taken from prayer and other apostolic functions. Furthermore, the consideration and renown that these activities earn the missionary fill him with the smoke of vainglory, excite the curiosity of the listeners, and distract them from matters of salvation."[62]

I am also reminded of the Congregation of Propaganda's instructions of 1659 to Eastern missionaries, which facilitated the penetration of Christianity into China: "Be not in any way zealous, make no argument to convince these peoples to change their rites, customs, and manners, unless they are obviously contrary to religion and morals ... never compare the customs of these peoples with those of Europe; quite the contrary, be assiduous in learning to accept them."[63]

While the priest discourses on the dangers of nondenominational schooling and false science – "Oh yes, there are many leftists among you!" – I drink in the wonderfully pure air. What a sublime landscape! What magnificence in the strength of the clear, swift current![64] I watch as fat trout, five to eight pounders, leap amid a confused murmuring punctuated by cries and cackles.

Reaching the *saputit*, we find the eight families gathered. Everyone is present, including the men, women, children, and dogs. The *saputit* is a sacred place ruled by numerous taboos, especially in relation to women. For example, any who are pregnant or premenstrual or have recently miscarried are forbidden from entering the water. Most of the women are on the bank (in an area called *saunaviik*) cutting up and cleaning the fish, arranging them on stones to dry, and separating the fat.

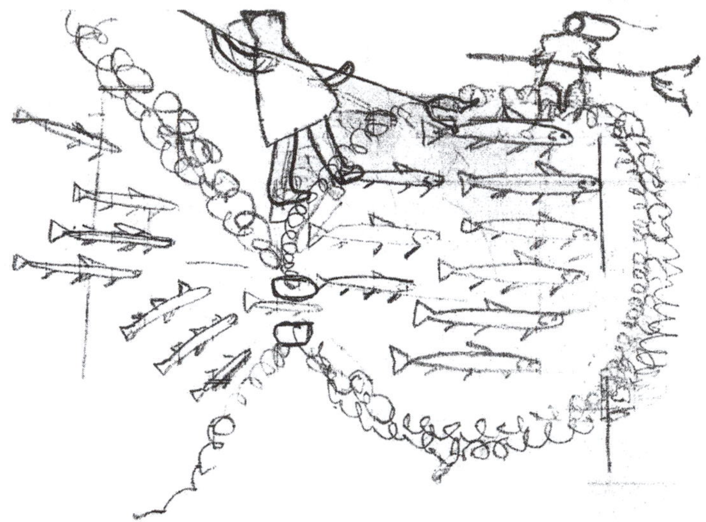

Saputit at Back River. Woman in background, participating. Drawing by Koenakunak (b. 1935), Gjoa Haven resident, April 1963.

The river is seething with glistening salmon, their skins a studied disorder of black spots. The men, bare-legged, *kamiks* tightly laced below the knee, attend to the unending job of repairing the weir, piling up the stones until they jut above the current. Others are spearing fish with impressive two-metre *kakivaks*. The catch is skewered on the central tip, made of iron or sharpened bone, then transferred to lateral tips made of caribou bone. Using a caribou-antler marlinspike (*krupkavut*), the fishermen thread a strand of seal leather (*nuvikerut*) through the fish heads in groups of fifty and toss them on to the bank. Ten or twelve year olds are standing in the water up to their waists, lending a hand. Salmon try to jump over the wall of the *saputit* in a splash of crystalline water. The Inuit exchange smiling glances, their faces bright with good cheer. May their joy endure for all time!

Two men emerge from the river, approach us slowly, and energetically shake my hand. Krokiarq has no doubt informed them of my arrival, and they know that I am cooperating with the universally respected RCMP. An old hunter and a young nursing mother sitting on a boulder join in the conversation. The children move off, uninterested in this adult affair. Traditions remain strong here, and it is the rule (as at Thule in 1950–51) for young people never to look an adult in the face.

Caught up in the ambiance, the Oblate becomes human again, giving generously of his time and revealing himself to be devoted and precise. From the way he handily administers the economic questionnaire that I have distributed to each family, it could indeed be said that he is directing the survey. The various options for them to check off are labelled in the remarkable syllabic script invented in the nineteenth century by Wesleyan and Anglican missionaries, of which they are proficient readers. They answer the brass-tacks questions about hunting and fishing honestly but uninterestedly, their eyes hazily focused on some other horizon. How many fish did you catch? Where did you spend the winter? How many dogs, guns, harpoons, nets, and seal-oil lamps are you using? It appears that they expect me to probe deeper matters, that their imagination is fired – like yours and mine – by the beyond, the mysteries of life and death, all of what concerns the shamans. But with the Oblate as my interpreter, they remain silent on these fundamental aspects of their tradition. As soon as the interviews move on to "social" aspects – whether shamanistic customs (they are on their guard) or kinship, and hence women and sexuality (they let their guard down somewhat) – the Oblate becomes increasingly nervous, his voice cold and halting. I think of the verse from the Apocrypha: "Of the woman came the beginning of sin, and through her we all die" (Sir. 25:24). But familiarity bears us onward, and each Inuk in turn comes to me with clear, vivid eyes. The weather is superb. Just upstream, the fish are drying on large slabs, lined up in the same direction as the watercourse, as ancient tradition requires. They are stacked in groups of five hundred under

Traditional bow of caribou antler, 60 cm.
Netsilik, 1961.

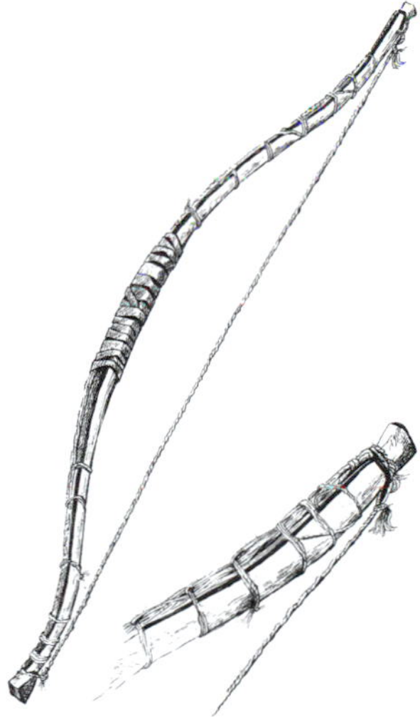

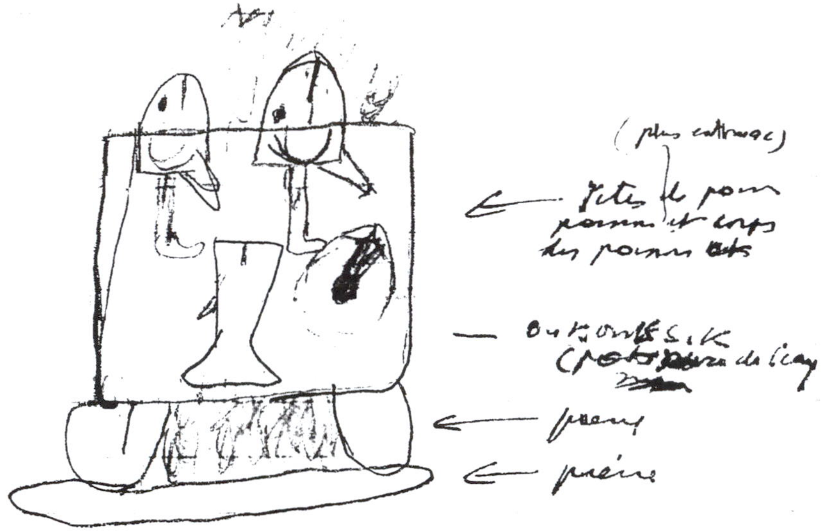

Fish heads, bodies, and innards. The pot was formerly made of soapstone, nowadays metal. Base, two small stones resting on a longer one. Fuel, roots, and twigs collected on the thawed tundra. Typical meal: boiled fish or fish soup. Drawing by Krokiarq, Back River, April 1963.

two-metre-high mausoleums of stones with the openings blocked by larger stones to prevent predation by the wily fox and bear. Five or six of these caches per family constitute essential winter provisions.

On the bank, women are boiling fish in large aluminum pots over ground-willow fires; some are eating it raw. Ah, the pungent smoke! It reminds me of the west coast of Scotland, in the Highlands or the Hebrides. I am taken with the arrhythmia of the Inuit, their nonchalant gestures, the lingering casualness of their rest stops and camps. They know how to recharge their batteries. Cooking is a two- or three-hour process that starts with the melting of snow and ice in an old dented, blackened pot. Sharp-eyed alertness while hunting becomes nonchalance in the igloo, with nostalgia for an age when people were on familiar terms with *netserk* and *nanuk*, the masters of the animals.

I am casting a wide net with my questions, but so far, apart from the systematic socio-economic data, the catch is slim and time is moving fast. Then I notice that their remarks are taking a more personal turn. Intimacy appears to be setting in. I can hardly complain that it has taken this long since such forthrightness is not often in evidence even after much longer periods. Kroki-

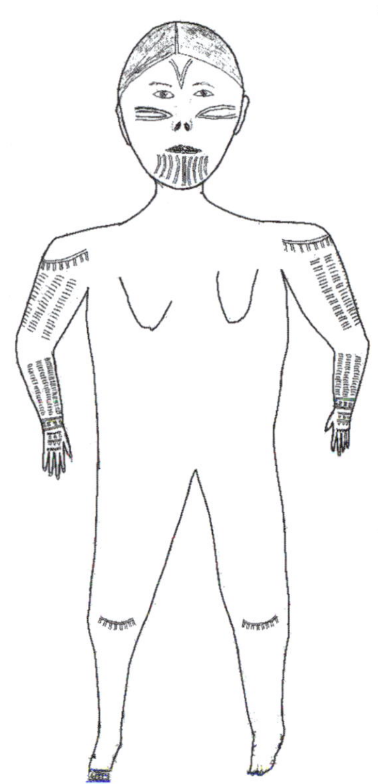

above: Mother-in-law of one of my respondents, tattooed by her mother before being married in the 1920s. My respondent's wife (this woman's daughter) was born in 1935 at Igloolik; this drawing was done by her brother, born about 1930. Igloolik, 1960. Ethnological notebook.

right: Netsilik woman (1900–61) tattooed four years after marriage. Drawing by 35-year-old son. Ethnological notebook, 1961.

arq surely has something to do with my success. On the matter of marriage and reproduction, they are candid: "We don't have enough women.* It is difficult to find a spouse [the two widows living here apparently will not do] and we are all related. This is not good. Too many couples are sterile." One of them, a widower, went to Arctic Bay to look for a wife, whom he did not find. A four-month, eight-hundred-kilometre journey for nothing.

* The deficit is on the order of 10–12 per cent. Is this due, as I have suggested above, to infanticide committed against infant girls? The semi-nomadic population of Thom Bay fluctuates widely (as indicated by censuses of 1950, 1953, 1955, and 1962), and interestingly, a sex ratio reversal appeared to be taking place: in 1937 the Inuit population was 56 (30 M, 26 F), while in 1951 it was 30 (13 M, 17 F). This phenomenon was probably due to the decline of infanticide with the onset of social assistance.

Their intense, troubling stares are almost unbearable when they come to rest on you. The statuary quality of these busts, these high-cheeked faces of a reddish-brown, almost fruity, complexion are burned into my memory.[65] But the Oblate edits their responses. For him this is all paganism and obfuscation. It is not his affair. He is a priest, not a government employee. Marriages must take place between Christians, which means Catholics; the rest is sin and satanism, as he repeats three times an hour. I let it go with a "quite so" and compliment him. But now he is irritated. These people are worse than pagans – they are heretics, by virtue of being Anglicans. "In any case, not Catholic." Excommunication: the terror of terrors evoked by these missionaries after tormenting the people's souls. Intermarriages between their catechumens and the "heretics" would, he says, destroy the small parish that he has worked so hard to build. I, however, know of a real-life tragedy elsewhere in which one partner in a mixed Catholic-Anglican Inuit couple was threatened with exclusion if he continued to associate with "apostates" (as the putative threat was tersely summarized) – in other words, with people outside the parish. The girl committed suicide. Here, the three terrorized Catholics are among my respondents.

A young boy takes us to his family's tent, where we strike up a conversation with a clear-eyed elder. A woman of forty, teeth worn to the gums from chewing on skins, follows the interview at a conspicuous remove, masking her discomposure by sewing a child's sealskin pants with broad hand movements.

It's six o'clock and the sun is already low on the horizon. "Nerreyok ilibsi!" (Come eat!) "Alût!" – the woman with the worn teeth offers me the family's only antler spoon. Curtly, the Oblate announces that he must say the rosary at the "church" (translation: the hut where we are living) at seven.

"I'm late," he says.

I turn my head and stare aghast: "But father, we are in a fishing camp, and they have invited us for supper. Say the rosary here. God is everywhere."

"No. I have to go to the mission. The true faithful are waiting for me."

"But there are only three of your Catholics! A sociological survey is a rare opportunity. No scientist has ever been here. I beg of you, stay with me! Help me to help these Netsilingmiut improve their lives. Put off your rosary!"

"No, I must go." And he is off, his long strides lifting the tails of his black cassock. An elder standing meditatively to one side has observed the exchange. "Kablunaks! Always rushing somewhere," he must be muttering.

The Anglican missionaries, it should be said, are neither better, nor more tolerant, nor more open-minded. At Igloolik in August 1960, I saw some Inuks sitting in quiet desperation in front of their one-room stone, peat, and wood house (*q'angmat*) because they had been forbidden to hunt on Sunday, the Lord's Day, despite their extremely precarious situation. The Puritan spirit

Manellia and Adelik, Netsilik women who frequented the *Victory* while it was iced in off Boothia Peninsula. Taken from Sir John Ross, *Appendix to the Narrative of a Second Voyage in Search of a North-West Passage and a Residence in the Arctic Regions during the Years 1829, 1830, 1831, 1832, 1833* (London: A.W. Webster, 1835).

of John Knox was very much in evidence. Some officiants are more tolerant, of course. Nevertheless, a war of religion, a rekindled Franco-English war, rages in these once tightly knit communities of the Boothia Peninsula. On one side are the long-robed Catholics ("Papists"), rough-hewn Oblate sons of stubborn francophone peasants, builders united by an intangible credo; on the other and in fierce opposition are the Anglicans ("Orangists"), amiable liberals more attached to ritual than doctrine, supported by Ottawa, the capital of the "maudits anglais."

Most of the Inuit wear hungry smiles and observe me with sympathy. I believe they have understood many things. Poor Kablunaks, always quarrelling. So it was long ago on the *Victory*, they know, for they have inherited a dim memory of the events from their clear-eyed, discriminating ancestors. We eat standing up, women and children in one group, men in another two or three metres away. The meal consists of raw fish and some boiled fish eaten with the fingers. The many small bones are chewed up and swallowed.

SOCIALIZING WITH THE INUIT, 1830–31

We could now easily see that their appearance was very superior to our own; being at least as well clothed, and far better fed; with plump cheeks, of as rosy a colour as they could be under so dark a skin ...

... twelve snow huts ... had the appearance of inverted basins ... each of them having a long crooked appendage, in which was the passage, at the entrance of which were the women, with the female children and infants ... The passage, always long, and generally crooked, led to the principal apartment, which was a circular dome, being ten feet in diameter when intended for one family, and an oval of fifteen by ten where it lodged two. Opposite the doorway there was a bank of snow, occupying nearly a third of the breadth of the area, about two feet and a half high, level at the top, and covered by various skins; forming the general bed or sleeping place for the whole. At the end of this sat the mistress of the house, opposite to the lamp, which, being of moss and oil, as is the universal custom in these regions, gave a sufficient flame to supply both light and heat; so that the apartment was perfectly comfortable. Over the lamp was the cooking dish of stone, containing the flesh of deer and of seals, with oil ... Everything else, dresses, implements, as well as provisions, lay about in unspeakable confusion ...

The females were certainly not beautiful; but they were, at least, not inferior to their husbands, and were not less well behaved. All above thirteen years of age seemed to be married ... All were tattooed to a greater or less extent, chiefly on the brow, and on each side of the mouth and chin ... Their features were mild, and their cheeks, like those of the men, ruddy ...

They seemed now to relish the preserved meat; as they did some salmon, more naturally: but they did not like the salt meat, and equally rejected pudding, rice, and cheese ...

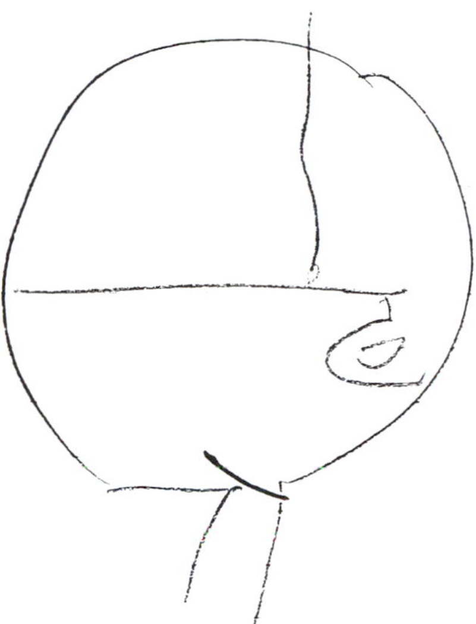

Igloo of a widowed hunter who did not remarry, a rare case. Neeveea-cheak (b. 1923, Anglican) had recently lost his wife and son. Near his bed, a stone seal oil lamp for light and heat. Spence Bay region, winter 1960. Ethnological notebook, 1961.

[On a later occasion] [t]hey had proposed to dine with us ... they preferred their fish raw ... one salmon, and half of another, was more than enough for all of us English, [while] these voracious animals had devoured two each. At this rate of feeding, it is not wonderful that their whole time is occupied in procuring food: each man had eaten fourteen pounds of this raw salmon ... Nor is it wonderful that they so often suffer from famine: under a more economical division of their food, with a little consideration for to-morrow, the same district might maintain double the number, and with scarcely the hazard of want ...

We were weary for want of occupation ... To-day was as yesterday, and as was to-day, she would be to-morrow ... while if there was no variety, as no hope of better, is it wonderful that even the visits of barbarians were welcome, or can anything more strongly show the nature of our pleasures, than the confession that these were delightful ...[66]

[They recognized the places marked on our map] and Ikmallik, then taking the pencil, proceeded to prolong the sketch from Akullee, following very nearly, for a very considerable space, the line already traced by Tulluahiu. After this, he prolonged it still further westward, instead of turning to the north, as the latter had done; then continuing it to the north-west, in a direction more favourable to our views.[67]

As they were in 1830, as they remained in 1923 when Rasmussen studied them (they then numbered 259), so they are in 1961,[68] minus tattoos on the youngest women, plus guns, steel traps, tools, canvas tents, canoes, sugar, and tea. Most are still wearing furs. They still eat copiously and immediately when fish or seal are abundant, clutching large knives with shiny, thirty-centimetre blades. Any of them will talk or call out to another with a quarter of a raw char in his mouth or laugh while simultaneously spitting bones onto the ground, as if to swallow more quickly and catch his breath. The man next to me is picking his teeth with a nail.

They try to persuade me to stay, but what can be done without the interpreter's assistance? At two o'clock in the white, wakeful night, I walk back downstream alone.

RIGHT OF INTERFERENCE, REDUX

A moment's hesitation at the door of the hut. I go in and undress in silence, lay my two caribou skins out on the modest floor, and add a dog skin for extra warmth. This makeshift bed is always cold, colder than in a tent.* I lie down in the heavy silence. His bed creaks as he tosses and turns, breathing noisily. He is not sleeping.

An unhappy man, this. Too isolated, perhaps friendless. It sounds as though there is a weight that he must get off his chest. A hushed word in the darkness, the dam is burst, and out flows a torrent of sarcasm:

"Scientist, hah! What does that mean? ... How should I know what's going on in your head and if it's all on the level? ... Like to get to know me, eh? Get to know a poor little priest? Do your worst!" A pause. "No. Confound it. It's all wrong." Does he want me to confess? Or to confess to me? The latter, it seems; he is getting there without my help. Little by little, he opens up and reveals the secret resentments that every man nurses, rehearsing his loathing of Parisians, atheists, nondenominational schools, and so forth. "You really humiliated us with Bécassine!"[69] He opines that the Breton people should speak Breton and go to Catholic schools only: "Away with the secular schoolteachers and all your wise men, Renan, Combes[70] ... You've all done tremendous harm." The verbal delirium continues. Without saying so outright, he conveys that his life is difficult. "You come and go like the wind, independent ... always 'thinking' ... Who are you? I have no idea. What do you think of me? No idea ... You fall into my life like a Martian ... Me, all alone, an Oblate priest posted here straight out of the seminary, living among the pagans and the heretics ... Enough! You're the Devil, that's what you are, here to throw my life into chaos!"

* The tundra is "hot" on the surface where the vegetation or a rock formation absorbs the rays of the sun.

Air: Minuit chrétien, c'est l'heure solennelle . . .

Refrain: utertartok

Okperpogut, Jesuse tikingmat,
Jesu. Jesu, kuwiagilawut; Jesu, Jesu, kuwiagilawut.

1	2
Ibjornaitok unnuarli tamanna	Okpernipta k'aumaksârmattigut
Nunaliyok atk'arealermat.	Jesuseli illitâriyawut
Sivudlipta piunginevininglt	Ajorniwut kappianalermatta
Akilereartorlugit tagva;	Uwagudli, kappiasukpogut
Inûluktât kuwiasulerput	Inôsaiyib tikilermattigut
Piuliyetârtitaugamik.	Kappiasugungnailerpogut.

Lyrics to "Minuit chrétien" (French version of "Oh Holy Night") in Inuktitut.

Perhaps I represent what he thought he could find by becoming a missionary in the Far North: adventure, exoticism, freedom, all the ideals that haunt the imagination of so many daydreaming young Bretons. Perhaps they are drawn to this place by visions of ocean and fairies and korrigans, those magicians of the wide Breton coast who dance by the light of the moon in the forests of Brocéliande with Merlin the Enchanter, blowing into little horns behind thick hedges. From my bed on the floor, I listen to the voice issuing from this singular pulpit, this psychoanalyst's couch perched higher than the analyst. Abruptly, he switches focus to his pet peeve – gossip – a cancer he sees as ravaging the parishes. Acting the lofty judge of manners and conduct, he visits anathema on various individuals, blaming X and criticizing Y as the Holy Scripture taught him to do. As for my colleagues and I, we are fairly worthless. Ottawa is spending far too much money on our foolishness, while the priests are humiliated and looked down upon as miserable beggars. His voice swells: "We've never forgotten the Freemasons!"

I interrupt, telling him he is wrong, that his words are mad and that they darken my vision of the church. And truly, this witness of Jesus leaves me pensive. What is a priest if not an example according to the Sermon on the Mount, a person who takes its message ("I am meek and lowly in heart"; Matt. 11:29) to heart?

"I think you have relied too much on the use of coercion, Father, or you have been its victim. After all, I might have liked to have your spiritual guidance."

His response is cutting.

"I do not minister to scientists with tortured souls. I am here for the Inuit."

"I like you nonetheless, Father, and if I were a believer, I would pray for your salvation. Good night."

I hear him breathing in the darkness. Clearly, this hapless Oblate is unhappy. Solitude gives poor counsel. How is he to experience the Christian faith and transmit that experience to others when he feels so alone in such a hostile land? Like so many graduates of the seminaries, those forcing houses where the sons of impoverished peasants were in many cases literally seduced, he has been trained in the ways of submission. From every Sunday pulpit and in every confessional, their mothers were exhorted to give one of their sons to the church for redemption. The young men became God's functionaries, corseted by vows of poverty, chastity, and obedience. This one in particular has been forced to endure a long ordeal among a haughty people whose mentality is far removed from the spirit of the Beatitudes. True, he speaks Inuktitut, but he observes through a filter and finds celibacy a challenge. Gratitude? Why should the Inuit show any to these tormentors turned judges and moralists?

The Oblates, it occurs to me, ought to be posted in pairs for mutual support! In fact, there were two at Thom Bay in the time of Fathers Henry and Papion. But the Order observes no such prudence; its goal being to spread the gospel from east to west and from pole to pole, it disperses its missionaries over a wide area.[71] It could do better if it tried to do less.

"The Lord knoweth them that are his," perhaps, but – to take one example – not all priests possess the virtue of chastity. How many have voluntarily been defrocked so that they could marry? Were it not for one's natural reverence for these men of God, these great inquisitors and preachers of morality whose activities are, after all, a matter of public consequence, we laymen too could gossip. We might assess their virtue and those sacred customs – such as cohabitation and paternity – that the future will reveal to have been common in the Canadian North. A little less drama, please. Granted, I am troubling this priest's serenity. Why wouldn't he envy my life and education, he who is so ill-prepared to face his pagan flock, he who was taught no anthropological or psychological methods for analyzing ancient religions, complex thought processes, untainted philosophies with their extraordinary wealth of myths (whose millenarian message he dares to combat with rote sermons when his faith falters)? There is no worse experience for a man solemnly committed to a cause than to discover that his certitudes need rethinking. One suspects that this man is already on the defensive against anything that might weaken his faith. He is young, inculcated with the "canonical truths," and backed by his Order. "A few days with this annoying foreign layman will be over soon enough," he thinks unconsciously. Such is the ecclesiastical prudence that has taught him to judge the Other rather that to listen to or dialogue with him. Must I infer that he abhors the free discussion of ideas? Most important, what are his views on the value of critical self-examination? After the seminary, he would have been better off clearing his thoughts for a time before deciding what to do with his life, and in doing so he would have learned that others share his doubts. Perhaps he would have sought inspiration from Kierkegaard, for whom the church, by becoming institutionalized, turned away from Christianity.[72] He might have realized that faith is not behind us, a settled issue, but ahead, still to be imagined. He might have looked to John Newman, for whom "there is something true and divinely revealed, in every religion all over the earth."[73] But the ecumenism advocated by Vatican II is barely in evidence here.

Let me ask bluntly: by what right have the apparatchiks of ritual and dogma destroyed age-old Inuit beliefs? What has possessed them to terrorize the faithful by invoking the spectres of mortal sin, damnation, and hell, thus stepping into the role of the "sorcerers" with their redoubtable taboos? Surely, there is no disrespect in asking the question. The Christian parish is a locus of fraternity, as one could only hope, but also an instrument of control. Confession, in particular, whose power in this desolate land has yet to be fully measured, allows the priest to exercise omnipresent ideological, moral, and social surveillance. Strict rules laid down in the Inuktitut prayer manuals[74] prescribed (among other things) the examination of conscience (*erk'asarvik*)

Excerpt from Oblate Father Eugène Fafard's Inuktitut prayer manual.

with respect to each of the ten commandments. The sixth (Thou shalt commit no impure act) and the ninth (Thou shalt have no impure desire) were grouped: *Nulliarma asia ... uima asia ... kanôq.*

The concept of "sins of the flesh" was foreign to these innocent societies, yet the "directors of conscience" busily went about demonizing the act of love, depicting it as something akin to a stain. Sexual repression of this sort lays waste to primitive joyfulness. It is reminiscent of Saint Paul's well-remembered admonition: "But this I say, brethren, the time is short: it remaineth, that both they that have wives be as though they had none" (1 Cor. 7:29). Or of the *Decretum* of Burchard of Worms, the eleventh-century German canonist who proscribed the pleasure of orgasm and ordained that certain practices constituted "abuses of marriage": "Hast thou copulated with your wife or with another woman from behind, in the manner of dogs? Or with she on top of thee? If so, thou shalt do ten days' penance on bread and water."[75]

In Christian fundamentalist tradition, sex is constrained by numerous taboos (e.g., it is forbidden on the Sabbath and during Lent). Moreover, once a child has stirred in the uterus, it must be irrigated by the father's sperm, whereupon copulation ceases. In the privacy of confession, exactly what words passed between the confessor – a man condemned to perpetual abstinence – and the Inuit penitent? Can we assume that the one routinely threatened the other – the maverick, the ladies' man, the "heretic," the "reprobate," the "apostate," the man or woman "living in sin" – with the terrors of hell? It was a closely guarded secret, but one needed only listen to the anxieties and repressed desires of young Christians and defrocked priests to infer the punitive tone that must surely have characterized some of these encounters.

What instructions did Quebec confessors' manuals contain in those years? One thing is sure: religious control extended beyond sexual matters to include social ones. For example, marriage was decreed to be monogamous and indissoluble; divorce, formerly common among the "pagan" Inuit (for reasons of temperamental incompatibility, sterility, etc.) was a grave heresy punishable by permanent expulsion from the parish and the community. It was the worst form of punishment imaginable for a communitarian people. The resulting distress was so agonizing, so anxiety-provoking, that suicides resulted.

The Catholic and Anglican missionaries also used their sweeping powers to engage in continual disparagement of the shamans (*angekkut*). This might have been tolerable in a system of educational free choice, but such a system did not exist here. The Inuit were forced to deliver their children to the priests and reverends for schooling, a domain over which the churches, by some special dispensation, had secured considerable control. Many of these schoolmasters lacked the ability to give the children, by word or example, a solid mooring in a new religion, yet this did not stop them from lambasting the parents' mythical worldview in the schoolroom.[76] Oh, there were exceptions, admirable ones, and I shall mention those saintly priests. But the right to meddle with people's souls: who granted it? Ottawa and its colonial administration. Such a subversive right should, at least, have been tied to a duty of transparency. As a researcher concerned with processes of change, I considered myself duty bound to include the missionary, that pivotal actor of change among my objects of study. Need it be said, the church did not appreciate such academic scrutiny.

My thoughts meander. After taking a few notes by flashlight, I fall asleep. Tomorrow is Sunday, the Lord's Day. I will be up early. Perhaps a propitious surprise awaits me.

Sunday, seven o'clock. A short night. The mass, early again, begins with a very long meditation on the Virgin in the form of repeated Ave Marias, as in a rosary: *Kuwianamik Mari, illumertauwutit Saimanermik, Nunaliub illagiwâtit ... Ernîdlu Jesuse*. At first I am the only congregant, then two women enter. The Lord's Prayer is recited in Inuktitut: *Atâtab, Ernerublu, Anernerublu, Pioyub atingani. Taimâk ilerli* ... In the name of the Father, the Son, and the Holy Ghost. *Atâtawut krilarmitutit* ... Our Father who art in Heaven ...

After mass, the Oblate approaches me carrying the coffee pot, bread, and powdered milk and apologizing profusely.

"You'll have to get used to it, it's in my nature. I am a stubborn man, a true Breton!"

I agree that our initial dispute was ill-advised. We vow to treat each other fraternally, and I propose a way to limit our discussions: "In each mission, Father, there is a codex in which everything – nearly everything – is recorded. Your codex must be fascinating, since this place was 'pagan' all the way up to the founding of this mission by the admirable Father Henry not long ago.[77] You and your predecessors surely must have taken extensive notes on the Inuits' initial reactions to the many unfamiliar aspects of Christianity: a suffering, crucified God-Man; a single God divided into three parts; the Comforter, transubstantiation, the Second Coming, the Communion of Saints; the Virgin Mary, free of original sin, the Immaculate Conception; the concept of sins of the flesh attaching to what the Inuit see as a natural act; hell and eternal damnation. What are the effects of evangelical teaching? Where has it run into difficulty? How do the Inuit relate to the fifth commandment (Thou shalt not kill), the sixth (Thou shalt not commit adultery), and especially the ninth (Thou shalt not covet thy neighbour's wife)? For the pantheist, conversion is a break with a millenarian reading of Nature in which primal fears coexist with a keen awareness of a preexisting order. Myths are his alphabet primer, whereas for the Christian, 'God is elsewhere, the distance infinite.'[78]

The codex may contain notes about that mental revolution that would be absolutely fascinating to a historian.[79] I would like to have a look at it in the light of your comments and experience."

His eyes are ablaze as he takes a book from under his pillow.

"Here it is, your codex! I had an idea you'd like to get your hands on it. You're the Devil himself, you are! Drat it, I won't give it to you! I have to have the Bishop's authorization."

"I requested it by telegram on behalf of the Department of Northern Affairs (Ottawa) and the Centre National de la Recherche Scientifique [CNRS] in (Paris) but didn't get a reply. Look, we are thousands of kilometres from the authorities. In all likelihood I'll never return to Thom Bay, so let me propose this: I will commit in writing to never disclose what I have read without the consent of the religious authorities."

"Never, do you hear?" he cries, brandishing his little book. "Never will you have it without written permission! No one warned me that you would drop in out of nowhere, and this document belongs to the parish. When I sleep, it goes under my pillow. When I go out, it comes with me." The little priest is overjoyed at his noisy victory.

Several Inuits arrive around eleven o'clock dressed in yellowed sealskin pants and tattered fabric anoraks. The meek whom Jesus Christ loved; the "little people of Our Lord," as Joinville might have put it. Intuitively sensing that the house is trembling on its foundations, they want to know what is going on. This modest missionary's hut, equipped with coal stove, wooden furniture, and copious provisions, is, for the Inuit, a mansion inhabited – remarkably – by a man who preaches poverty, self-abnegation, and penitence. Ah, the church and its mysteries! They know that my stay will be brief, and they want to speak with me, tell their own story, be recorded. But there is a language barrier, and the blasted Oblate will be stingily meting out his assistance from now on. The incident of the codex has transformed him into a holy dispenser of justice, a vigilante. His hackles are raised; "right" is on his side. That document is private property. I invite my respondents over toward the river bank, away from the tense environment of the "church." Nine-tenths of them are Anglicans anyway, and these quarrels annoy them.

Visibly glad to speak without an intermediary, my respondents entertain questions for an hour or so, but sadly, my two-hundred-word vocabulary is far from sufficient to carry on a real dialogue, to catch the subtleties. Among the Inughuit of Greenland and at Igloolik, I could speak freely with everyone. Here, I tape-record the conversations and will have them translated in Ottawa, but as a research technique it is woefully inadequate. I take a break and wander away from the camp, stopping to rest against a large boulder. This tormented priest has tired me out. The air is warm with the rays of the autumn sun, but the sky is already a wintry hue. Icicles lie shattered on the beach. Yawping dogs, laughing children, whistling wind. Tatters of ice floes on the horizon.

Night returns to Thom Bay. Merciful peace! The unquiet missionary has been silenced – by my departure from the mission, weary of his histrionic intensity. Today at dawn I decided to set up my tent on the shore, feeling free of an encumbrance. The Inuit are delighted.

Around ten o'clock, the Oblate comes for a visit. "This is not good, you know. The Inuit will wonder why we've had a falling out. Let's keep things civil. Come have lunch with me this noon."

I thank him. I do not like conflict. The man is not spiteful; it is my innocence that has exacerbated our dispute. His anger has subsided and, as for the codex, it is safely stowed. He graciously renews his offer of interpretation assistance, and we proceed to conduct a series of health-oriented interviews. The illnesses most frequently mentioned are flu, diarrhoea, impetigo, pulmonary ailments, epilepsy (seven cases in Spence Bay), deafness and dumbness (three cases), rheumatism of the hands, knees, and back, and eye inflammations worsened by the albedo of the snow in spring. No cancer. They sensibly assess the causes of their epilepsy cases and other abnormalities as follows: "We are all interrelated (*arnaqat*) and that is not good; too many babies are abnormal at birth. So we look for women elsewhere to 'renew the blood.' That's the problem: not enough new women here." In fact, many of the men are married to women from Back River. When the topic of shamanism arises* to what appears to be general approval, the Oblate announces that he must make an urgent visit to a Catholic family.

At noon, a distressing surprise awaits me at the mission: a huge padlock on the door. The priest is afraid that the Inuit might steal from him. What an insult for a people whose houses and tents are open to all! The RCMP never commits this kind of gaffe. Spying me at a distance, he hastens toward me and unlocks the door, uttering unctuous apologies.

I decide to return to Spence Bay on foot, the way I came. I will not take the plane scheduled to pick me up on 27 August. The Inuit would like me to stay the winter, but they respect my freedom. "Our thoughts will accompany you." Arnaja, the person most competent on the matters of interest to me, is designated as my companion. "He will talk with you. He will stay as long as necessary to help you with our cousins in Spence Bay. We are with you."

* George MacDiarmid, the *Victory* surgeon, suffered from painful toothaches. An Inuit shaman examined him, patted his cheek three times, blew into his face repeatedly – and he was cured, wrote Captain Ross. The last generation of Inuit had excellent teeth.

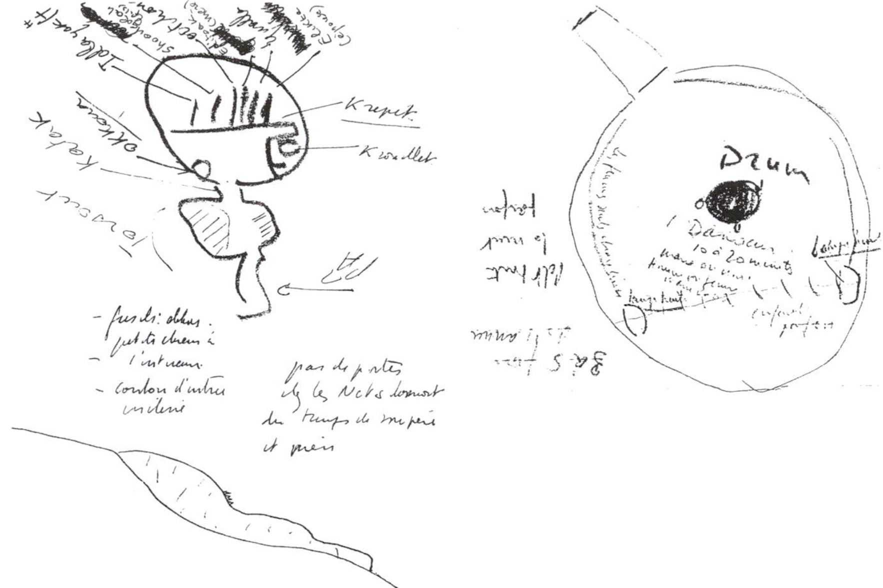

left: Snow house at Thom Bay, winter 1959–60, occupied by the hunter Ikadlyuk (b. 1932, Anglican) and his family. Far right, his wife, Elikta (b. 1929); centre, his elderly mother, Editoak (b. 1905); left, his son Shoongolah (b. 20/10/1957); two related children. In front of platform, right, oil lamp; left, frozen meat on a slab. In the *torsut* (hallway), rifles and clothing. As the figure indicates, the entrance hallway and house are laid out on a slope. No doors in Netsilik homes. Ethnological notebook, 1961.

right: *Q'assigi* or common house. Dances take place 3 or 4 times a year to the rhythm of a large sacred drum. A male or female dancer in the middle of the floor dances and sings for 10 to 20 minutes. At far left, choir of women; the children stand at the back of the house. Two seal oil lamps, right and left, provide light and heat. Author's sketch, Spence Bay, September 1961. Ethnological notebook.

In my tent, I prepare my departure, sorting out and recopying my notes. Arnaja arrives in a good mood, and we talk while sharing a meal. He explains his hunting and fishing calendar; then, in my notebook, sketches the hierarchy of men, women, and children in each house (winter) and tent (summer): husband (*ui*), wife (*nuliak*), father (*atata*), mother (*anana*), grandfather (*atatatsiarq*), grandmother (*anânatsiark*), son (*irnik*), daughter (*panik*), paternal uncle (*akka*), father's sister (*atsak*), mother-in-law (*arnaksak*), father-in-law (*angutiksaq*), brother-in-law (*ningau*), namesakes (*avvarriik*), eldest brother (*angaju*), youngest brother (*nukaq*), child named after a relative (*atsiara*). The conversation ebbs and flows like the tide, creating an ambiance conducive to the Inuk's self-expression. On birthing: "It's not like where you live. I've been told that white women give birth on their backs. Here, the woman kneels. A female relative squeezes her belly between her legs to speed the delivery. For strength, a sip of seal's blood. She is up and about in only a day or two. Very few women die in childbirth, but many infants die before their first birthday."

Asen Balikci noted that at Pelly Bay, a pregnant woman was considered extremely unclean and was confined to a small igloo for four to five days; nobody was allowed to touch her. Kneeling on the snow platform, she delivered her baby in a hollow dug beneath her, and the baby was not wrapped in skins. An elderly woman was occasionally allowed to assist with the naming but not the actual delivery. For the next month, the young mother was isolated in a larger igloo, forbidden from sexual intercourse. In the year that followed, she had to observe a whole series of dietary and behavioural taboos; for example, eating only in the early morning and late evening, keeping her drinking bowl bottom upward, and avoiding eating raw meat.[80] I also observed, at Thule (1950), Igloolik (1960), and with the Netsilik (1961) that newly married women would not look a man in the eye while her husband was absent and that young people would lower their gaze in the presence of elders. Observance of this custom depended, to a degree, on personalities, relationships, and circumstances.

I go and settle my accounts with the Oblate, with whom I have boarded for five days, although I was often hosted by the Inuit. I triple the quantities consumed, figure in the cost of shipping the food to the Arctic, and pay for it all, even rental of the floor space.

The next morning, Arnaja arrives at eight o'clock and we leave an hour later. The cassocked missionary – I have never seen him dressed any other way – stands at his door with a grave face, a likeness to the calcified witnesses of the faith that one sees on cathedral porches. Adieu, Father! An honest man such as you does not deserve to be just one more victim of the narrow-minded seminaries. No doubt you started out with a thirst for knowledge, but all you got were preconceived notions. I suggest to him that he meditate on our failure, and request his consent to publish an account of our meeting.

"No objection; I have nothing to hide. This is the house of God." No further comment is forthcoming.

Arnaja waits, indifferent, staring offshore at the bay congested with drifting ice. The Inuit are used to these spats between whites. We must be off.

"Father, you can take my place in the plane that is coming for me. Like an insect, I prefer to stick to the ground. I will go my way with Arnaja as an explorer of the infinitely small. Adieu."

Dear reader, please do not mistake me. I know of the heroism – indeed, martyrdom – of certain missionaries. In several cases, in fact, I have had the honour of their friendship: Father Pierre Henry, the first missionary at Pelly Bay (1935); Father Louis Fournier, admirable and always helpful, whom I met at Igloolik in 1960 and 1961 while he was building his masterpiece – a stone church – with his own hands; Father Didier at Rankin Inlet, whose keen intelligence and sophisticated theological ideas were on display throughout our long correspondence; Father Joseph Buliard, who froze to death on a dogsled in Keewatin in 1956; Father Lucien Schneider of Ungava, an accomplished, meticulous philologist and author of an Inuktitut dictionary, some of whose works I published at CNRS in Paris; Father Arthur Thibert, who so obligingly helped me translate many of my recordings and notes back in Ottawa; and others besides. I trust that I may be forgiven if I do not make an exhaustive list of my friends! Any whose names I have omitted will recognize themselves.

Bearing witness to Christ is an elevated ambition. However, divine providence has its mysteries, and this trip had the formative merit of causing me to reflect on the crisis of the churches and their evangelism in Inuit societies. In later years I contributed to this reflection, in collaboration with the Dominicans, by publishing a groundbreaking work on the terminal crisis of the worker-priests.[81] In the West, where our churches are empty, the crisis is profound, visible, much remarked upon, but the Arctic, too, is beginning to reread the faith that it has been (badly) taught. By 1980 Inuit of all denominations (Lutheran, Anglican, Catholic) were deserting the churches. In truth, during a century of exploration and colonial occupation, they had always put incommensurably greater effort into adapting to our ways of being than vice versa. One can understand why their intelligentsia are now at best condescendingly tolerant of the priests and ministers, why they put up with the church and its rites but keep our dogmas at bay. And the disenchantment goes much further, of course. Lawsuits have been filed against priests and ministers by Natives infuriated at their thirty-year-old abuses of power, including sexual abuse and paternity cases.[82] The hatred of lying is ingrained in Inuit culture; those who had respected the clergy are profoundly wounded by the way their holy vows have been held up to ridicule.

"We are starting to believe what we want to believe," one young writer from South Greenland told me in 1991. Their evangelization by the West? "A racket," wrote another, a Canadian, in 1990. (A racket that deserves to be investigated and brought to light, I might add.) "What the reverends and priests actually taught us was to submit to the colonial powers. What is Christ, anyway? A bank manager?" The precepts of the Sermon on the Mount have become a boomerang, hurtling back toward the men who first flung it. Yet the Inuit are still willing to accommodate missionaries who want to live among them in a spirit of charity and tolerance for others' beliefs; they simply have no use for religious colonialists. As the Tlingit Indians told the reverend accompanying John Muir on his travels in Alaska in 1879, "We are children ... groping in the dark. Give us this light and we will do as you bid us."[83]

Did these holy men, these dyed-in-the-wool moralists, hold the mystic flame of the Beatitudes high enough in the Arctic? Didn't they, for want of charisma, of "mysticism in the wild state" (Paul Claudel), abuse the trust of these "children of the dark"? Let each of them judge in all conscience.

DIALOGUE WITH A SAGE ABOUT WIFE SWAPPING

We stop briefly at the Inuit camp, where I have begun to make friends. I sense Arnaja's sadness when he kisses his young daughter in the tent and murmurs, "Sleep well! Siniktaralu!" I give her my last biscuits, and we cross the fjord by boat.

The track is straightforward at first as we work out the kinks in our muscles. The sky is bright, the horizon clear. It will be less demanding than the reverse trip, when the boggy ground yanked at our feet with every step. Now winter is near, and the icy muskeg crunches pleasingly underfoot.

The Oblate's welcome, Arnaja tells me, was not appreciated by the largely Anglican Inuit. I feel consoled for the preceding days' trial by the fellow feeling that he shows me. His speech is more elaborate and fluid than Krokiarq's, and my proficiency is improving day by day. I mention the first words of peace exchanged by Ross and Amundsen with the Netsilingmiut: *Taima! Manik-Tumi!* Arnaja smiles. These words are archaic, no longer in use between whites and Inuit. Pronouncing phonetically, I cite the names of people whom Ross met on his second expedition: Tulluahiu, who had a wooden leg made for him by the *Victory* carpenter to replace the one that he had lost while bear hunting; the hunters Otoogiu, Awack, Pootwwutyook, Ooblooria, Ikmallik, Awack, and Illictu; Kunana, the best hunter; Hibluna, a woman who leapt for joy at the gift of an iron knife; Adelik, the mischievous one, who mimicked the English; an old woman named Nimna Himna. Arnaja recognizes the names and corrects the pronunciation. He explains his own hunting calendar: sealing on the bay in the fall; at the breathing holes on the ice floes in winter, a day away from camp; collective seal hunting on the pack ice (*uutuq*) in spring, and collective hunting of spawning salmon (discussed above) in summer. He also hunts caribou with a small group during the June and September migrations, two to five days away on foot. He is not much interested in birds. He plots his seasonal movements on a map and teaches me various Inuit toponyms.[84]

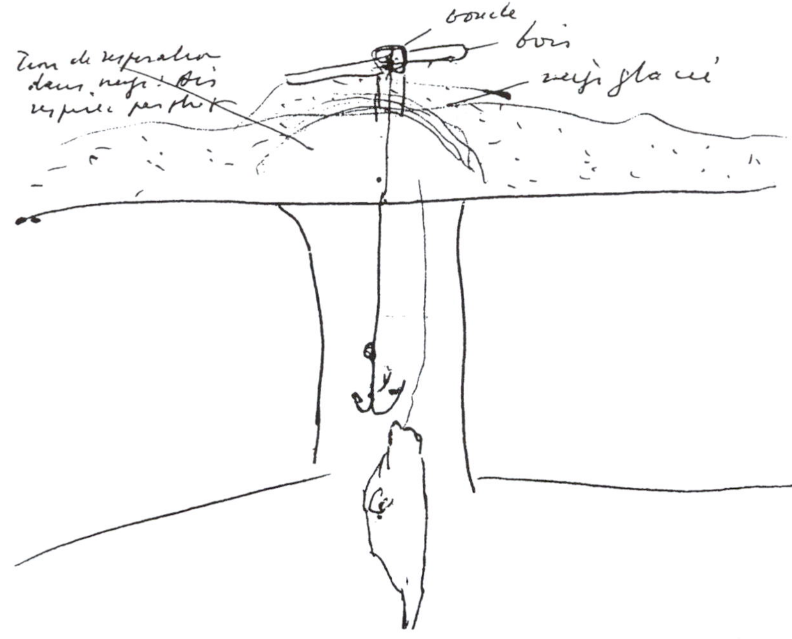

Fishing with a hook hung from a Primus tripod. This is a recent modification of the traditional technique of spearing seals at their breathing holes (*aglu*) on the pack ice. Seals create a living space of several square metres under the 2–3 metre thickness of pack ice. They have 20 to 25 breathing holes through which they periodically come up for air. The presence of the seal near one of these holes is sniffed out by the dog, and the hunter blocks all the others. Sketch by Arnaja, Spence Bay, August 1961.

27 August dawns still sunny but with a little snow coming down. Around the tent, on the rich, peaty soil, I observe decayed organic matter, dew forming on the moss. I repeat to myself the insight of Simone Weil, whom Albert Camus considered the only great mind of our times: "We must certainly have committed crimes which have made us accursed, since we have lost all the poetry of the universe."[85] I kneel for a closer look at an alpine bistort (*Polygonum viviperium*), at spider webs woven between willow leaves. A mite slips through my fingers along with some unidentified insects. "Kopilrok!" (a worm), says Arnaja disdainfully. A few kilometres farther, golden bearded spikes of beachgrass line the shore of a lake. I spend some time identifying and counting all plant and animal species within a five-square-metre quad-

rat. The soil is granular, inert, poor, but scattered peaty areas support mosses, lichens, grasses, flowering plants, and a wealth of small animals, including spiders (*nigjuarjuk*), moths (*tarralikitaaq*), snails, collembolans, flies, and the last few mosquitoes (*kikturiat*). The bright midnight sun shining week after week has accelerated plant growth, and the flowers have bloomed in a few days. But fall is already here. The willow leaves are yellowing, with purple spots appearing on their edges; the dwarf birches are turning orange, the *Vaccinium* red. A butterfly flutters around our feet, avoiding the snow patches, hugging the warm, humid ground. I believe that it lays one hundred eggs, but I do not know where, and Arnaja is unable to say. Its territory is poorly known. The hairy larvae take a season or more to form. In northwestern Greenland, certain moths remain deep-frozen at the larval stage for three winters. The Inughuit showed me one under some stones. The transformation into the adult form takes place once enough heat has built up. (Some insects

Portrait of Tulluahiu, who lost a leg while bear hunting. The wooden leg was made by the *Victory* carpenters. Lord Mayor Bay region, 1829–33.

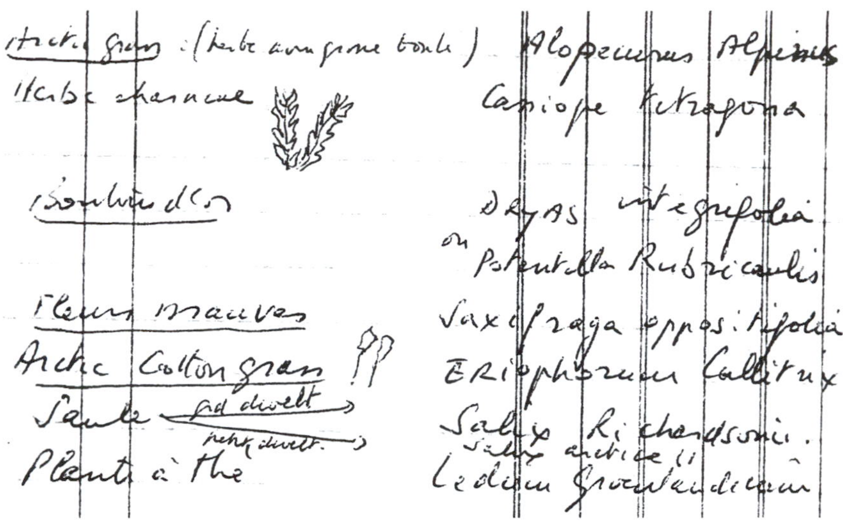

Plants observed on the tundra during my east-west crossing of the Boothia Peninsula, Thom Bay to Spence Bay, August–September 1962.

embed themselves in the tundra, producing antifreeze-like substances that enable them to withstand freezing down to -50°C. Since the life cycle from egg to adult can progress only during the three to four weeks of summer, it takes twenty years to complete.)[86] In early afternoon a plane flies over at moderate altitude. I know whom it has come for and who will be taking it. I am the insect, the *uumajuarusiq*, sticking to the ground, with a discreet feeling of pride and humility. We eat a half-cooked hare whose pink flesh becomes cloying after awhile. The great torrent has begun to freeze and is shallower than on the reverse trip. As we ford, I drop the Primus. Arnaja picks it up and patiently separates the water from the gas.

An opal-streaked purple sunset blocks the horizon in the direction of Pelly Bay. I notice that I am being observed by something that looks like a man with a tuft of plants for a wig: a cairn (*inukshuk*) whose purpose is to channel bands of wild caribou. The marshy lagoons hampering our progress glimmer in the evening light.

At the bivouac, Arnaja expounds on *kipuktut*, which some men practice from time to time, although he does not. "It's natural between men," he says. "Where is the harm in it? It deepens friendship." When a man leaves for several days, he may lend his wife to a friend. The reverse may also happen, where a husband asks a friend to lend him his wife since his own is sick, menstruating, or pregnant and cannot accompany him on the hunt. These exchanges are rarely permanent, but serious conflicts can arise if the woman falls in love with the temporary companion. As for the wife and the swapped woman living together in the husband's igloo or tent, this almost never occurs. Contrary to Captain Ross's impression that the woman's opinion was ignored, the wife may refuse the swap (*naruguifamiu*). "Often, it is the woman who requests it," says Arnaja. "It reinforces their power over us. They direct the group from below." Husbands who swap wives are called *aïparerq* and owe each other assistance. Polyandry is rare.*

Gontran de Poncins, in 1939, gave the following account of wife swapping among the Netsilingmiut at Gjoa Haven:

> Kakokto and Kukshun have been exchanging wives, and as usual the wives were not consulted. Lady Kakokto does not find Kukshun to her tastes; a little briny, shall we say? It's put her out of sorts. She's one of the few women around here who is in love with her husband. Kakokto doesn't care specially about her, and he'll lend her to anybody who asks for her. For one thing, it's a tradition that has to be observed; for another, friendship has its obligations ... Between husbands there was never any question of compensation. On the other hand, a "well-bred" bachelor whose friend accorded him this courtesy would expect to make his friend a little gift as a token of appreciation. The lady, the object of the courtesy, was as little compensated as consulted ... the privilege of disposing of the lady belonged exclusively to the husband.[87]

John Ross wrote on 30 April 1830:

> I was at first surprised to hear my guide Poo-yet-tah call Pow-weet-yah his father; since, to my eye, there were not many years of difference in age. On asking the reason, I was informed that he was only the step-father, and that he was even the second in this relation which Pow-weet-yah had possessed; while both of them were such during the lifetime of his own father, who had taken another wife and left his own to the first of these two. It was, however, an amicable separation. The man had desired to migrate to the westward, and the wife, on the contrary, preferred staying among her own relations; they therefore separated, a short time after his birth, and the woman then married a man called Arg-loo-gah, by whom she had four more sons. This husband was drowned; leaving his widow a large fortune in the shape of these five sons, who are here

* At Rankin Inlet in 1962 I went to the tent of an old man and his wife of thirty years who had willingly taken in a young hunter to survive. All three sat with me, and no one was embarrassed. "At least we're eating, thanks to him. It's only natural. Age comes," said the old man.

considered a valuable estate, since the maintenance of the parents in old age devolves on them. Thus she easily procured another husband, Pow-weet-yah, the brother of her first one; but by this marriage there were no children ... they had adopted two grandsons as such; and the boy who had been killed was the eldest of those. The original husband, Ka-na-yoke's true father, had also procured a son by adoption, among the tribe at Oo-geoo-lik, to which he had gone, and he was now living in a small island called O-wut-ta, three days' journey to the westward of Nei-tyel-le.[88]

The custom of marriage arranged at birth is still practised, but some young people, encouraged by the priests, no longer accept these arrangements. I learned of such a case at Igloolik in 1960. A young couple were about to take the vows with their parents present: "Do you, X, take this man ..." In one breath came the response: "No." The plans were cancelled, and the parents noisily left the church, understandably furious. Arnaja thinks that priests and ministers should not interfere with Inuit customs. He confirms the frequency of adoption – one child in four – a custom intended to help the most destitute families. Arnaja himself, who has two biological daughters, Angnuya (b. 1944)

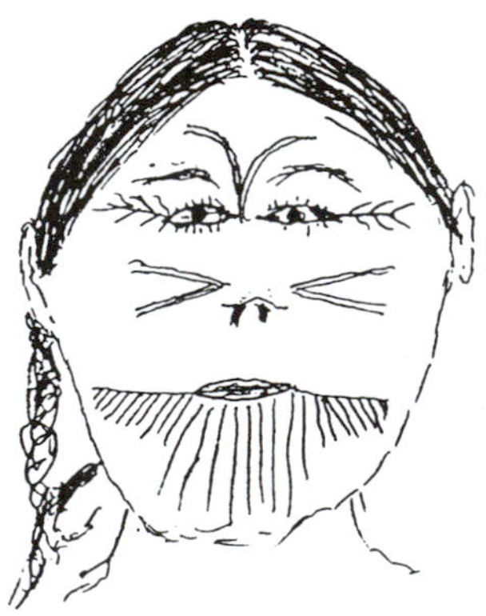

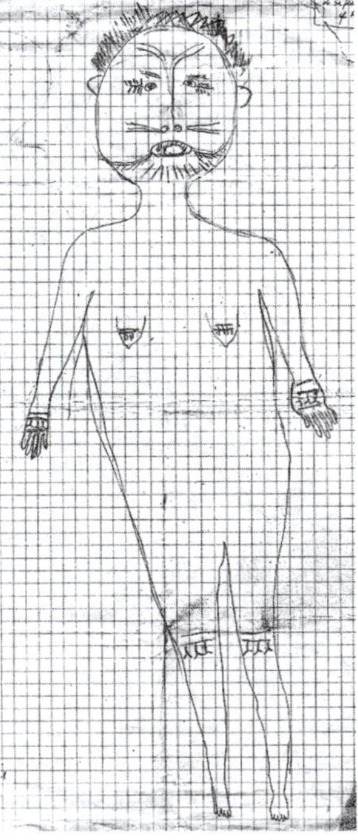

above: Mother of one of my respondents (drawn by him), tattooed before marriage in the 1920s. Thom Bay, before 1960.

right: Tattooed woman at Spence Bay, died before 1960. Apart from the facial tattoos, note lines symbolizing breaching whales on the wrists, knees, and breasts. Sketch by a 40-year-old hunter.

and Elihaping (Elisapee, b. 1952), adopted the son of a handicapped hunter in 1954, as well as two girls, Starr (b. 1939) and Nimirakjuak (b. 1948).*

On our last evening, Arnaja becomes more confiding, and I venture to ask him about infanticide. To avoid misinterpreting his response, I record him. During periods of severe famine, he says, families needed hunters and hoped that their women would have boys as soon as possible. They did not conceive of the killing of unnamed girls as a crime (see note 20).

And that was only yesterday. It's true: there are still some incidents in very remote camps, in late winter, in the poorest families. Here is what would happen. The child was asphyxiated immediately at birth under caribou skins, sometimes in front of the whole family. The body was placed outside, far enough away that it would not be eaten by the dogs. No tombs were ever made for those babies, as they were not considered living Inuit. Naming the baby, thus infusing it with the spirit of a dead person, brings it to life. The name is tried out by the grandmother on the mother's belly. Several names may be under consideration but the final decision is made at birth. We carefully gather together animal skeletons [seal, caribou] side by side, vertebra by vertebra. The spirit of the dead person [the real dead person who had a name], aided by his most familiar *tonrars*, may slip into the body of this animal.

I listen with emotion and respect. A rough people. Formerly, when food was scarce, old people went out to die with ancient dignity so as not to be a burden on the group. It still happens. One morning last year an old man walked out of a snow house, put his gloves and pipe on the edge of the pack ice nearby, sat down with his legs immersed in the ice water, and slowly froze from foot to head.

Paying rapt attention, I follow Arnaja's account of the founding myths. At first there was night, with no human beings. Then came the halcyon days in which androgynous beings (masculine sex, small, sparse beard, woman's breasts, body generally hirsute) lived with their animal cousins, everyone speaking the same language. They had a mouth in place of a navel, one eye, hare's ears, and the canine teeth of the castrator. Then came the flood, after which two shamans copulated, giving birth to two girls. There is an upper world, where souls live happily; an underworld, down deep, where life is much harsher and people must pay for their violation of taboos or other lapses; and finally, a world right under our feet, below the tundra but above the underworld – a middle space – for those guilty of only minor infractions.

* Arnaja (b. 1913), his wife Shaunua (b. 1918), and all the children, biological or adopted, are professed Anglicans.

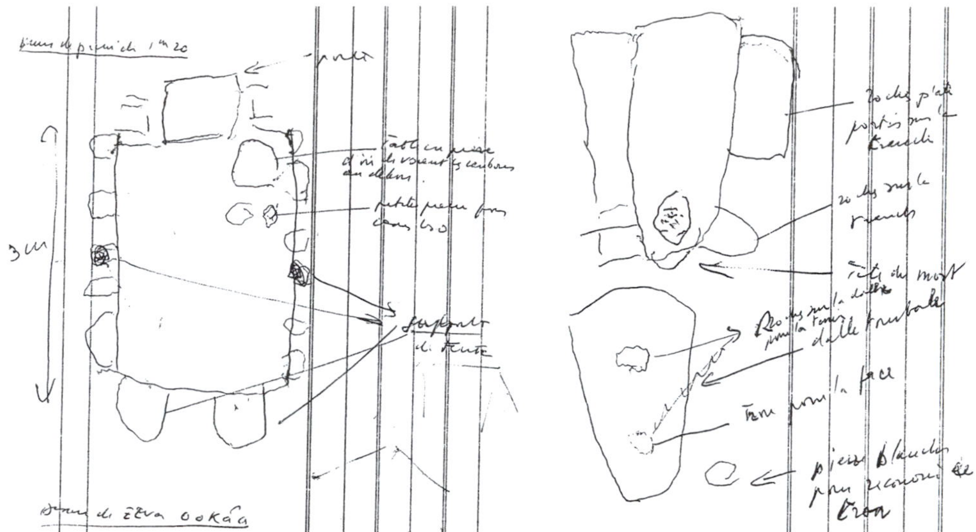

Tombs of the legendary Tunit people. A race of giants, they were said to surround their houses with large stones. Left, large Tunit house, 1.2-metre-thick stone walls. Inside right, stone table where they sat watching the caribou outside; nearby, small stones used by the Tunit to break the bones. Right, Tunit tomb. The corpse was laid out face up with a stone for a headrest. Around the body, stone slabs set on end. Unlike Netsilik tombs, which are always left exposed, Tunit tombs were covered with a slab in which a hole with a removable cover was cut for the face. Drawing by Arnaja, Thom Bay, September 1961.

I am cautious in my interpretations of these descriptions, reminiscent as they are of heaven, hell, and purgatory, punishment and reward. They are evidently the result of a syncretism (see above) with white Christian religious ideas distilled homeopathically over a century and a half since the arrival of the missionaries. A complex process of sedimentation thus took place, with the heavy sediments falling into the depths and the flock, the floating matter, remaining visible to the eye. In the long run, different mentalities overlap and interact. Future research will have to trace the strands of this tangled skein of thought. I must reiterate that the Inuit have not had authentically aboriginal thought patterns since the mid-nineteenth century. One need only refer to the maps and stories of exploratory expeditions since the eighteenth century to gauge the density of cultural interaction in the Central Arctic during that time.[89]

Evening routine: write down the words that I have learned and repeat them aloud. Arnaja enjoys the process. When I mention the seal-oil lamp (*quullirvik*), he tells me that it was traditionally a very valuable object; his own wife cost him a large soapstone (*ukkusiksat*) lamp in dowry (*akki*).[90] The lamp had come from his mother, who had obtained it through barter with a widower at Back River, where the raw material was available in great quantity. In the last decade, a few lamps have been made out of sheet metal from the American radar bases, but this remains a rare material.

Arnaja leisurely cleans the bowl of his antler pipe, gathers the ashes, and cuts the flower heads off some plants that he has gathered on the barren ground. After a quarter of an hour of silent preparation, he lights his pipe and puffs aromatic smoke.

House of Arnaja (b. 1913, Anglican) indicating position of parents and children. From far right near oil lamp, visiting woman, Arnaja, children, Arnaja's wife, Shaoonooa (b. 1918), all sleeping with heads pointed inward. The children, between the adults for warmth, are Starr, adoptive daughter (b. 1/7/1939); Angnaooya, daughter (b. 15/1/1944); Nimirakjuak, adoptive daughter (b. March 1948); Elihaping, daughter (b. 30/5/1952); and Okraluk, adoptive son (b. 12/3/1954). In the antechamber preceding the house, seal meat at left, caribou meat at right, rifles at left on entering. Inside the house, two seal-oil lamps in front of the sleeping platform, one on either side. Thom Bay, winter 1960.

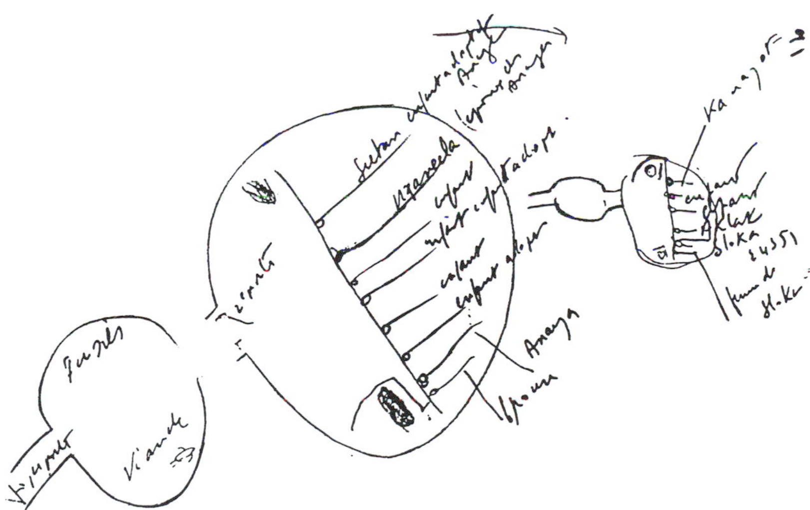

"Tell your wife that you saw a poor Inuk make tobacco that way. Why are you so interested in us?"

"I hope I can be of some help to you."

"How?"

"By letting people know about your situation. And what interests you about the whites?"

"We want to learn from you. You are stronger than us." He wants his children to go to our school, to learn what we know, so that they can free themselves from our domination and power.[91]

The tundra has taken on the colours of autumn: faded yellow and pink with rusty tinges here and there. Withered swamp flax. The cold has already left its mark, killing the sap.

When I arrive at Spence Bay, the two constables welcome me amicably as if I were returning home. They surmise that things did not go smoothly at Thom Bay but withhold their inquiries. I have eight days left here, and I spend them going from family to family in an unusually friendly atmosphere. They all want me to tape-record their remarks on taboos, life stories, death, and hunting. The women glance over frequently, nervously, to make sure that I am writing down everything that they say, all the while sewing skins with caribou-tendon thread. Winter is approaching, and the skins must be ready before the men go out seal hunting. If they do not finish the sewing now, they will have to do so in a snow house or tent on the tundra, in isolation. They report this fact without comment. Should one be surprised, appalled? No: they are still to a large extent bound by the Inuit taboo against allowing spirits of land and sea to mingle. Roald Amundsen observed in 1903–05:

Spence Bay children playing ball on the coast on a spring day. August 1961.

Igloolik, 1821–23.

As far as I could see, the moon had to have a certain position before they dared go seal catching. They look upon the moon as an important sacred body, according to which they divide their time ... A great number of women folk had constant sewing work from us ... but one fine day they all declared that they could not work. We questioned them and learnt that the first seal had been caught and that the women had eaten its flesh; it was consequently impossible for them to do any work other than their own before the sun was at a certain height in the sky ... We promised them higher wages, indeed almost begged ... them to continue their work for us, but all in vain; they were proof against all ordinary human arguments.[92]

My respondents specify the values of barter goods: a snowhook for a six-year-old male dog, a leister for a pair of sunglasses. Krokiarq, my first guide, gave Poodlat a two-year-old bitch and a new net in exchange for a three-year-old canoe. In Ross's time, the terms were less advantageous, to say the least ... a seal for a file or an iron fish hook or six nails. Information on their sex life is finally more forthcoming. Sex education is simple and visual. Puberty for girls may be quite early, at age twelve to thirteen or even ten to eleven. Precocious sexuality with girls aged eight to ten is frowned upon but does exist in isolated camps. "It is not good," says Arnaja. "Nature has its laws." Incest, Arnaja says with his Anglican conscience, is a sin.

The prostitution mentioned by Amundsen appears to be unknown today. Likewise homosexuality, once frequent in Chukotka, Siberia, the historical starting point of the great Inuit migration, is nonexistent here as far as I can determine.[93] A few cases of zoophilia (with dogs or dead caribou) are mentioned. I am given a list of six sterile men and adult men who have been without wives for more than one year. There are two widows. Unfortunately, I am not at leisure to clarify these matters. The oldest man in the district of Spence Bay, Kavavaoo, is seventy-five; only two women, Poocheyoo and Oonalikjuak, have reached the age of sixty-five.

Why must I stick to my prearranged schedule? Why leave this place? The obligation-bound academic is a vassal, a prisoner of himself. How shall I become the nomad that I imagine myself to be? By rebelling? It is already late in life. Besides, the mindset necessary for this kind of research is one that adapts readily to constant changes of pace, from field study of the peoples in question to distanced reflection at the university in Paris, where reports and books are written. And then back to the site for more, ever more observation.

At the small farewell dinner, the senior constable says, "I am not big on religion, but I get the impression that somewhere up there your prayers have been heard. The Anglican minister still hasn't returned from London and your Catholic missionary has gone south; to 'consult,' is what he said."

4

On Hudson Bay, 1962

Ottawa, July 1962: fourth expedition to the Canadian Eastern Arctic. Awaiting departure. Five empty days to while away.

In the evenings, the bars are filled with disjointed chatter about inflation, the dollar, unemployment. Snide remarks about the "Papists" (Catholics), the "French," and the "reds" or "Orangists" (Anglicans) fly this way and that as the natterers of all stripes carry on. Dubious weekend clients come and go from anonymous hotels. Doors slam at six o'clock behind sales reps – the ambassadors of our West – swarming out like termites to conquer their markets, monogrammed, combination-locked attaché cases in hand.

At the Department of Northern Affairs, I am attempting to negotiate an extension of my current expedition (Rankin Inlet, Chesterfield Inlet, Baker Lake) to the Central Arctic (Back River, Chantrey Inlet), where I surmise the existence of a unique, practically unknown society living under extremely harsh conditions. After reviewing the internal report of my 1961 Spence Bay expedition, the department has given me advance written approval for the endeavour. But now that we are face to face and the agenda for the expedition has to be definitively established, that approval has morphed into de facto rejection. The bureaucrats consider this expedition risky and uncharted. As my insistence grows, so does their mysterious reticence. What should I read into this dithering? Time is tight; the division's budgets are about to be finalized. I ask the director of the department, Eugène Bussières, to intervene, and the two of us meet with the person in charge. Bussières, after scanning his notes, expresses his shock at the obstacles being underhandedly put in my path and crisply orders the official to grant my request without further hesitation. He proceeds to thank me on behalf of the department for my willingness to carry out this difficult exploratory expedition to Back River, about which the government considers itself ill-informed after the famine of 1958. Unfortunately, the delay has been such that, despite my best efforts, I will not be able to go to Back River this summer. The expedition is postponed to the following year, when I plan to winter over. Was the delay intentional? The civil service has its logic and its secrets. As we shall see, the consequences for me will be considerable (see ch. 5, note 94).

Nevertheless, Rankin Inlet and the other destinations are still on the agenda. One important goal of the journey is to investigate the situation of inadequately trained Inuit nickel miners working in Rankin. I also have a personal motivation for the trip in that I want to see a good friend, a hunter from Igloolik who has decided to resurface with a new personality by taking a job in the mines. The catalyst for this life-altering decision was the emotional trauma – alcoholism, depression, suicidality, alienation from his community – that resulted from a serious accident. When last we met, I encouraged him to chronicle his distress by keeping a diary. "Write about your life," I advised him. "It will be your life buoy. You are your own best friend." The resulting diary is unique in that it gives us a close look at a man's real-life vanishing act, his descent to the status of a "nobody," to use his word. The work is revealing of the cynicism of Western capitalist society, which considers the Inuit nothing more than a labour force and renounces its social, pedagogical, and human responsibility toward them (as witness the authorities' staunch anti-union position; see below). It has been my experience in life that the maverick, the outcast, the excluded, the walking wounded teach me much more about the mysteries of the human condition, our extraordinary ability to rebound, than the contented and the well-off, whether they be champion Inuit hunters revelling in their power, millionaire businessmen, or self-important university academics.

Montreal airport, six o'clock. A departmental two-seater bound for one of the confidential radar stations on the DEW Line is waiting on an isolated portion of the runway reserved for official use, the baggage already in the hold. While the pilot does the routine checks, he encounters serious mechanical problems, and the flight is delayed at least twenty-four hours but perhaps as much as three days. I opt for a more dependable conveyance, the train to Churchill via Winnipeg, a sinuous 2,500-km ride out to the edge of the Prairies followed by a twenty-four-hour northbound leg. I remain in good spirits; after all, even the most propitious expeditions must begin by surmounting hummocks.

Crossing the snowy fields of Manitoba, I think of Louis Riel, the charismatic rebel leader of the Métis and the province's founding father, who was hanged at Regina in 1885. "Those who are right too soon are always wrong" (Pierre Teilhard de Chardin). Riel's statue in Winnipeg faces the Parliament buildings.

At Winnipeg I switch to the trapper's train bound for Churchill. A train out of Disneyland, with braziers at the entrance to the cars. People wear checked shirts and gold-digger's hats and speak a French Canadian-sounding vernacular in which the "sh" sound is prominent. The place names are such as to fire the imagination: Portage Embarras, Fort Qu'Appelle, Lac Brochet, Lac Ile à la Crosse, Le Pas, La Rouge, Flin Flon, Cormorant. This is all Chippewa, Cree, and Athapaska territory, once explored by light-hearted *coureurs de bois*, the famed French Canadian *voyageurs* whose epic history as "white Indians" remains to be written. One thinks of Franklin's companions Gabriel Beauparlant (who also travelled with Back), Pierre Saint-Germain, Régiste Vaillant, Joseph Peltier, Jean-Baptiste Adam, and seventeen other intrepid men and women to whom history has not fully given their due. French gaiety and boldness are apparent at every stop. At the door are crowds of long-haired people with laughing brown eyes and lilting, melodious voices. We emerge from the spruce forest onto stunted taiga, and then onto the desert of rocks and lakes known as the tundra.

CHURCHILL[1]

20 July. Enormous silos of wheat from the Manitoba plains stand on the shore of Hudson Bay awaiting Soviet ships. Churchill is a western town with a muddy main street flanked by saloons, bars, and stores for Natives. Intrigued by a sign reading "Eskimo Museum," I enter and am greeted by the jovial lay brother Jacques Volant, who was born near Quimper, France, and immigrated to the Canadian North in 1925. His age shows; his jet-black cassock is worn. This museum represents fifteen years of his work collecting documents and artifacts of northern exploration history, some of them very rare. It is a pity that this well-intentioned man never got the requisite museological training, as he would no doubt have wished. His museum is fascinating, unpretentious, and a bit anarchic; space is at a premium. "I did my best, Professor,

with my limited knowledge. Frankly, I haven't got much time for books of ethnology or sociology. I fought to save these precious objects, these amulets and sacred drums. Never got any help or budget. I was always being told that this is all just foolishness, but the peasant in me refused to give up, and I collected *everything*. If the Eskimos believed in it so fervently, it must be because there was some value to it." While he talks, the lyrics to a Bach aria come to my mind: "Be thou with me and I shall fear no evil." The church has long held that the ignorance of pagan religions is a providential springboard to faith.

On the doorstep of the apostolic vicariate of Hudson Bay, where I have an appointment with the bishop in charge of all the Oblates in this immense region, the secretary curtly conveys Monsignor's regrets: he has had to leave at a moment's notice. Yet I have prudently called in advance from Ottawa and, for good measure, arranged for a formal referral from the Vatican through my father's old friend Gabriel Le Bras, the renowned canon law jurist, sociologist, and advisor on religious matters to the Quai d'Orsay. Worried, I inquire as to the date of Monsignor's return. Unknown. "Monsignor is often away!" I leave a written message reiterating my request for access to the mission archives and amble off, pensive, down the muddy road. Laymen who take too keen an interest in church activities – especially laymen from the Freemasonish Sorbonne – aren't appreciated around here. The Vatican is far away, the Oblates are an autonomous order, and prudence is an episcopal virtue when confronted with such highly recommended – hence eminently suspect – visitors. The church does not like to open its archives to free thinkers. A big black car emerges from the vicariate's garage: Monsignor's car, with him at the wheel, splattering me with its omnipotence as it passes. Sometimes the causes of reflexive anticlericalism are not far to seek ... Bishops, what have you done for the people of God who walked with you and so humbly devoted themselves to your holy cause?

Science, it is claimed, lives within the mind of God. If so, who shall be admitted to its labyrinths? His faithful wait silently for those in the know to deign to explain the mysteries of the faith from on high. Ultimately, the church would pay dear for this churchly distance, this fear of transparency. Consider the case of Quebec. In the late 1960s two centuries of authoritarian domination exercised by a distant, silky-voiced hierarchy, as well as a series of scandals, provoked a revolt of the clerics that led to the province's emancipation. Full-fledged schisms would endanger the church's continued existence and ever more priests would become deserters, asking to be reduced to lay status so that they could marry. So much for your solemn undertakings, you blessed priests, you whose faith proved so fragile when you found yourselves alone behind closed doors. One can hardly blame the many Christians who came to consider themselves agnostics or even atheists. And the reverberations were bound to be felt in the North, where the church's prestige among the Natives, so great until then, began to weaken. During the ensuing period of tumult leading to Native autonomy, the fissures would become gaping faults. "Occasions for stumbling are bound to come, but woe to anyone by whom they come!" (Luke 17:1).

I decide to go see a movie in a theatre half-full of drunk Indians wearing gloomy stares, their faces a closed book. The projection is punctuated by the dull thud of empty bottles hitting the sloping floor and rolling toward the screen. The rough Chipewyans* and the Inuit ignore each other. The brutal wars fought ages ago still weight heavily on today's generations. No mixed marriages span the invisible divide between these groups.

INUIT MINERS IN RANKIN INLET: A RUDDERLESS POLICY

24 July, Rankin Inlet (Kangiqliniq),[2] a one-hour flight from Churchill on the west shore of Hudson Bay, 450 kilometres to the north at the head of a wide fjord. Its lattice of huts gives this Inuit settlement the appearance of an anonymous mining town, and that is what it is. A mournful siren greets my arrival, announcing the first of two seven-hour shifts per day (six o'clock). Helmeted men pass on their way to the nickel mine, operational since 1957 and steadily being worked out. The ore is shipped to the port of Churchill and travels from there by rail to southern Canada. The Rankin mine is unique among Arctic mines in employing Inuit labour. By contrast, at Ivigtut on the southwest coast of Greenland, nineteenth-century Danish governments took wise measures to keep the Inuit from becoming cryolite miners and to preserve, insofar as possible, their traditional way of life. Similar measures were taken in northeastern Siberia. Here, the liberal economy is sovereign, and any profitable transformation is considered acceptable. The displaced ("relocated") seal and caribou hunter is "re-skilled." No uncertainties or hard thinking.

Just inland is the territory of the Caribou Inuit (380 families in 1950), a group that remains little known despite the distinguished work of Kaj Birket-Smith in 1924. Since 1930 their precarious, semi-nomadic way of life has been marked by tragedy, forcing some of them to move closer to the posts, schools, and mines.† The government has encouraged this process along with its attendant sedentarization; indeed, it is has been quite authoritarian in its decision to group together various bands. "It is recommended that ... Serious study be

* Athapasca Indians living between the Churchill River and Great Slave Lake, population 5,100 in 1970.

† See pp. 240–1 for more about the famines at Garry Lake in 1950, Keewatin in the winter of 1957–58, and Back River in 1958.

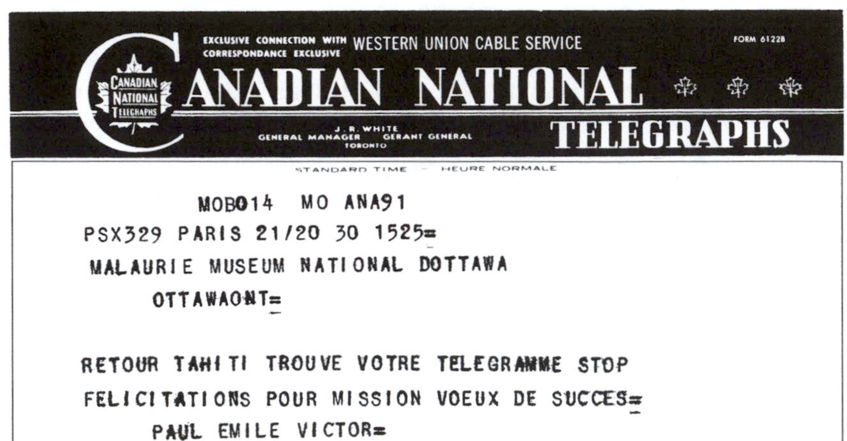
EXCLUSIVE CONNECTION WITH WESTERN UNION CABLE SERVICE
CORRESPONDANCE EXCLUSIVE
FORM 6122B
CANADIAN NATIONAL TELEGRAPHS
J. R. WHITE
GENERAL MANAGER GÉRANT GÉNÉRAL
TORONTO
STANDARD TIME — HEURE NORMALE

MOB014 MO ANA91
PSX329 PARIS 21/20 30 1525=
MALAURIE MUSEUM NATIONAL DOTTAWA
OTTAWAONT=

RETOUR TAHITI TROUVE VOTRE TELEGRAMME STOP
FELICITATIONS POUR MISSION VOEUX DE SUCCES=
PAUL EMILE VICTOR=

made of the rationale of relocating a small group of Eskimo families to southern Canada," said one report; "the Eskimos of Keewatin require to be educated to understand the economy of modern life, the need for organization, the need for supervisors – and bosses."[3] But now it appears that Rankin Inlet will be only a stopping place. The mine will soon close, and they will have to go. Where? Back to hunting? The clock cannot be turned back. This legendary people is at an impasse, and I am at the heart of the crisis.

In the Northwest Territories of 1962, nothing less than the modern equivalent of a Controversy of Valladolid was needed.[4] But mentalities in the Canadian government and public opinion (as in historical Spain) were not ready for such a reversal of forces. It would have been not only naive but subversive to abruptly ask the director of the mine, "Who does the ore really belong to? Who is the owner of the soil and subsoil in the Canadian North?"

"To the people of Canada," he would have replied with surprise and annoyance. "To the Canadian government, that is.* And our company has an agreement with the government."

Yet the same question posed to an Inuk in Rankin Inlet or Igloolik in those pivotal years would have produced a different and unequivocal answer: "It is ours. Nunavut is our land." The disarray and confusion was plain in their faces.[5]

* To the Crown, in fact, by virtue of the *Rupert's Land Act* of 1867, which transferred "Rupert's Land and the North-Western Territory" from the HBC to the Dominion of Canada.

SPEAKING THE PRESENT WITH EYES ON THE FUTURE

At the sound of the siren calling the Inuit to the next shift, a daydream would come over me: wasn't this prophetic siren sounding to remind the whites that it was time for them to pay tribute to their new masters, the Inuit? But it was still August 1962, and the Inuit were off to the mine in the rain, heads down. Autonomy was a long way off. For the time being, Ottawa and the whites were still the masters of the entire Northwest Territories. Naturally, the transfer of the capital to Yellowknife on 18 September 1967 was celebrated as a historic event. Said Commissioner Stuart Hodgson, "Finally we are at home" – implying "the home of the white citizens who control the government." I have here on my desk the report of the opening ceremonies of the Council of the Territories' thirty-seventh session, dated 27 June 1968. In a photograph of the thirteen members (including several friends of mine), I recognize the first two Natives to sit on the council: Abraham Okpik, appointed in 1965, and Simonie Michael, elected a year later. During the thirty-four-week session, the council passed 180 motions and 37 bills, studied 24 individual presentations and 16 recommendations, and referred 1 bill to committee, but not a single debate dealt with the prospect of autonomy. However, a door was left ajar: an amendment to the *Municipalities Act* allowed for the creation of elected village councils.

When, at the first pan-Inuit conference at Rouen (followed by the first conference on Arctic oil and gas at Le Havre, 2–5 May 1973), James Wah-Shee, president of the Indian Brotherhood of the Northwest Territories, in the presence of Tagak Curley, president of Inuit Tapirisat, expressed with extreme moderation the Inuits' desire for emancipation and their inalienable right to sovereignty over their despoiled territory, the Canadian delegation responded with glacial silence. Such was Canada's legislative backwardness with respect to its Arctic minorities. I still recall Commissioner Hodgson's brief response to Wah-Shee: "The last time I came to Le Havre was twenty-seven years ago. I came here to fight. Today, such is not my intention. And it is on this note that I will conclude my statement."[6]

It was not until early 1983 that the first formal steps toward Native self-government were taken, when the Province of Quebec proposed a gradual transfer of administrative powers to Nouveau-Québec. Premier René Lévesque, a visionary statesman, said, "if the Inuit can become unified, in the sense of autonomy within Quebec, in a way that allows them to better manage their affairs, to make laws in areas directly concerning them, to organize their lives, we would be willing to talk with them without delay and to take this into account. We can negotiate on this basis whenever they wish ... it is up to them to decide."[7] And so a process began that would lead successively to the creation of Nunavut (1 April 1999) and Nunavik (5 November 1999). How far the Inuit had come![8]

THE GERM OF AUTONOMY

There are no certainties but what is hidden.
– Gaston Bachelard

August 1962. Some of the governing ideas that would make history in thirty years were beginning to germinate, although their emergence was masked by an inchoate crisis. "The bond one does not see is stronger than the one that is visible" (Heraclitus). The crisis had worsened in the preceding thirty years, leading to the disintegration of age-old Inuit groups under the authorities' indifferent eye. To the west, in the Mackenzie region, Canadianization was well under way, and the indigenous language was threatened with extinction. In the east, only the groups of the Central Arctic, the subject of my previous three years' research (the Igluligmiut, Netsilingmiut, and Utkuhikhalingmiut), were more sheltered from these developments.

Judging by appearances, by their genial smiles, the people were resignedly bearing up under the terrible ongoing clash of civilizations in these high latitudes, their spines bent as they had been for a century. But their muteness and passivity masked things going on under the surface. Murmurs were already audible among the men and women whom I met on the street, at the store, at the mine, in the movie theatre, and especially, in the Inuit miners' village, which was off limits to the whites without special permission.

In the "laboratory of the future" that was the mining town of Rankin Inlet, the eight dozen Inuit mine workers (the majority of them men but also including a few women) had got a glimpse, through a kind of mental alchemy, of what fate had in store. Since the spring of 1956 they had been thrown willy-nilly into their new duties as labourers above ground or, in some cases, two to three hundred feet under it. Some fate, indeed, working underground or in a mechanized factory, when only yesterday they had been independent hunters on the vast tundra and could fully inhabit their pantheistic worldview. And as if this radical change of surroundings were not bad enough, a shockingly strict apartheid system governed their lives from the pithead and the mine cafeteria all the way to the town movie theatre. A transformation by forceps had catalyzed the mental processes of these hunters and their wives. They were coming to understand, as the Far North was invaded and colonized, that to the whites they were just a labour force and that the government was uninterested in protecting their rights.[9]

Surely, another fate was imaginable. One might have hoped that a more elevated philosophy would guide the government's approach to these legendary aboriginal peoples, but a more short-sighted policy could not be imagined. Truly, it defied all common sense. American liberalism had laid waste to the Inuits' hunting culture, reducing them to cheap labour for a capitalist corporation whose every feature was foreign to them. The first consequence would be the disintegration of their social structures and their dispersion into an ethnic no-man's-land.[10]

When, during my interviews, I launched a few trial balloons in the way of political psychology, they were met with silence, stares, or even aggressive gestures toward the anonymous enemy, the occupying white civilization, which, under the guise of cooperation, had relegated the Inuit to second-class status. These wordless exchanges were a clear indication to me – one would have had to be deaf and blind to miss it – that the Rankin Inlet Inuit were already undergoing a cultural alchemy of the kind described by Jean Duvignaud,[11] in which subversive ideologies, fragments of slogans borrowed from our democratic vocabulary – "our" land, "our" government, injustice – are grafted onto preexisting concepts. When I talked to the few more specialized Inuit mine workers, their wounded consciousness was evident in stares and gestures of anger, in a kind of contained violence. Naturally, not a word was spoken that could cause them problems with the management. The diary of my miner friend from Igloolik (see Appendix 2) typifies the trajectory of so many Inuit thus displaced. Either they would give in to alienation and, ultimately, inner silence or suicide, or they would make radical demands. The middle way, that of political diplomacy, was unthinkable at the time. The anarcho-communalist Inuit had not yet integrated such skills and concepts into their political arsenal. But I can attest that invisible barriers had already been erected between the Inuit miners and the whites. "A bunch of liars!" was an insult that I heard the former mutter about the latter more than once.

At pan-Inuit conferences such as those held in Rouen (November 1969), Le Havre (May 1973), and Point Barrow, Alaska (June 1977), a young intelligentsia (teachers, unionists, priests and ministers, journalists), until then confused and complex-ridden, asserted itself before our eyes. And it was at events such as these that a will to self-determination gradually built strength, that they dared to stand up and look us in the face. When the impassioned debates of these conferences are reread, they must in fact be "infra-read." What is most important – the implicit assumptions, the underlying tension – is between the lines.[12] The Rankin Inlet mine ordeal, the Inuit cooperatives at Povungnituq shepherded by my dear friend Father André Steinmann, and especially the Inuit Circumpolar Conference of 1977 were the laboratories of what would become Nunavik, Nunavut, and Kalaallit Nunaat (Greenland). As an involved spectator, I tried to descry the birth of this collective awareness – let us be more direct, this political awareness – but I must confess that it was faint, embryonic, in 1962. The only sign of it was the slow emergence of reciprocal fear and distrust.

What was transpiring in these Canadian Inuit groups, for which the administrative regime was far behind that of Greenland? Was it a labour dispute involving a group of Inuit workers discontent with their lack of access to professional development opportunities? Or could it be construed as a gradation into ethnic revolt? Were these the seeds of nationalism and independence, slowly growing under the influence of the first intellectuals produced by the primary schools? Only the long term would provide the answer, but I could not help observing then that Canada had done little to prepare for this ineluctable confrontation, whose consequences might be unpleasant if the authorities did not take the urgent measures that I constantly recommended in my scientific writings and administrative reports. At Igloolik, Rankin Inlet, and Spence Bay, I met no Inuit physicians, engineers, journalists, or writers whose existence might attest to a growing consciousness. If anyone was working to reinforce the Inuit's awareness of their civil rights, it was the much-disparaged Christian missionaries, even though the pacification that they effected might be considered colonial in spirit. As Christians, the Inuit began to consider themselves equal to their masters, whom they judged severely in the name of the Gospel.

Dear Professor

Voulez vous venir partager notre maigre pitance. Votre parole réchauffera nos cœurs pendant une bonne tasse de thé – – – – –

Cheerio –

Fr. Fournier

Letter of August 1960 from Father Louis Fournier, OMI, an Igloolik resident. The only other whites there were HBC manager Bill Calder and myself. Inuit population: 494.

INUIT REPRESENTATION

As I mentioned, the first Inuk was appointed to the Council of the Northwest Territories on 19 October 1965 at Yellowknife, resulting in a tiny minority of one vote versus twelve white ones. Nearly a century had had to pass before an Inuk could have a word to say about the future of his people and their territory. Abraham Okpik represented Rankin Inlet, where he had been dispatched (urgently, something like an envoy from a social Red Cross) to help the Inuit miners "adapt to urban life," as it was euphemistically put. "I don't want any special treatment because of my background," he boldly declared after his appointment. "I just want to express my beliefs, and I will not hesitate to criticize what I think deserves to be." Writing in 1962 in the syllabic-language journal *Inuktituk*, he issued a warning and a challenge to his compatriots: "There are only very few Inuit, but millions of *qallunaaq* [white people] just like mosquitoes. It is something very special and wonderful to be an Inuk – we are like the snow geese. If we abandon our Inuit ways, or no longer find it important to use our language, we will be nothing but just another mosquito." It is up to the Inuit of today, he wrote – and especially the youth – to capitalize on the power of their words and ideas. I read the article with pleasure, but it did not apparently cause much of a stir. The Inuit at that time, although perfectly literate in syllabic script, were not used to reading and commenting on pamphlets. For them it was the same old political song. Soporifics. Bathwater.

But events were quickening. In October 1965, spurred on by the good-hearted Gordon Robertson (deputy minister of northern affairs and commissioner of the Territories) and his successor, Arthur Laing, Ottawa worked out a large-scale development program for the Inuit. Twelve million dollars were allocated for the construction of 1,600 homes, adding to the 1,000 already built. Permanent structures would replace the snow houses and tents that I had visited, measured, and sketched at Spence Bay, Thom Bay, and Igloolik in 1960–61. In the decades to follow, the Inuits' political awareness would lead to constitutional negotiations, carried off masterfully by negotiators such as Senator Charlie Watt, John Amagoalik, and Tagak Curley (see pp. 51–5).

Now, what of today, and what of the future? I would first acknowledge that justice has been done, if tardily. Two or three generations of remarkable Inuit individuals were sacrificed, and it gives me sorrow to think of the exceptional men who were my guides and comrades as I travelled from camp to camp and how their talent was wasted. Awa, Piugatu, and Arnaja would have made first-class diplomats, statesmanlike ministers.

Second, with the acknowledgment that the Inuit have power over the soil and subsoil on their territory, a federated policy for the North is finally a reality. But now the more perilous phase begins. As John Amagoalik told me in 1969 and as he publicly repeated in 1999, "That will be the most difficult and demanding part. We will have to show that we are capable, in a modern culture, of being worthy of our ancestors." The pact signed with the whites may be a pact with the Devil, a remark that unfortunately applies to all such agreements involving first peoples. The wealth that they acquire often, by successive shifts of perspective, leads them to relinquish their greatest asset, which is their pantheistic philosophy of nature, the product of their harsh life in the environment. They are drawn into white civilization, to varying degrees, by the laws of money, markets, and power. Is it at all plausible to believe, without believing in fairy tales, that the Western economy and democracies will not attempt to manipulate the Inuit authorities? It is already happening, and one may count on Western cynicism to ensure that it continues. The relentless race for money has its inevitable price: the loss of identity.

Until the Inuit have their Hampaté Bâ (the great Malian writer discovered by Théodore Monod); their Léopold Sédar Senghor, writer and prime minister of Senegal; their Félix Houphouet-Boigny, physician, minister under General de Gaulle, and prime minister of the Ivory Coast; or their Nelson Mandela, the autonomous Inuit territories will remain fragile spaces. The danger – I cannot overemphasize it – is that they will lapse into welfare or succumb to the neocolonialist designs of our insatiable industrial societies.

It is often supposed that cultural fusion leads to renaissance, but where the two cultures are of unequal power and influence, nothing could be less certain. Destruction of the less powerful culture is the more likely outcome. The history of civilization records, for example, that the likes of Montaigne, Pascal, Rousseau, Goethe, or Tolstoy did not emerge with the birth of their respective civilizations but centuries later, and the Canadian Inuit do not have the leisure of waiting that long. Their small numbers and cultural fragility are such that they must assert themselves immediately through the formation of elites and the training of officials, as we are attempting to do at the State Polar Academy of Saint Petersburg and as has been done for two centuries in Greenland. The disastrous fate of indigenous groups in the Americas following their clash with white culture provides any number of cautionary tales, notwithstanding the United States' reserve policy or the activities of the National Indian Foundation of Brazil (FUNAI), to take two examples of attempts to limit the negative impacts in some small measure.

FIRST PEOPLES AND GLOBALIZATION

What to do? While the world marches lockstep toward globalization, it behooves us to meditate on the dramatic future of these first peoples. They are the life blood of human history, which only advances by borrowings and, consequently, cannot make progress unless societies different from ours remain vibrant on our small planet. I have recently been rereading the expedition diaries of my colleague and friend Darcy Ribeiro, the great Brazilian anthropologist – indeed, one of the greatest the profession has ever known. He writes:

> The remains of a moribund tribe living out its last days of despair have brought forth the prophets and saints of a hitherto vigorous community that will itself be extinguished, since it is following the same inevitable path of peaceful contact with our society. On the facades of the Indian posts we could write the same thoughts as Dante did on the Door of Hell. And yet these posts are, up to now, the best thing our society has been able to give the Indians in a legitimate effort to save them ... But the disease is progressing; no tribe can elude it and all will go extinct through contact with us, sooner or later. Is there any hope to be found? ... What can we do to protect them? Could another society, a less individualistic, profit-oriented one, save them? Are they not, as the victims of their passion for our trinkets and the lights of our cities, the cause of their own downfall? ... One of the things I find most enchanting about my beloved Kaapor is precisely their ever-vivid curiosity, an eminent quality that goes hand in hand with their remarkable sense of communal life, and with the fervent need for beauty that is expressed in all that they do. It is sad to see how all of this has been lost to us. The monopoly of scholastic knowledge, operating like an oppressive sledgehammer, keeps the people ignorant and forces them to accept their ignorance. They know that they know nothing, just as they know that they are poor and can do nothing to obtain whatever it is they lack.[13]

These profound thoughts concern an Amazonian aboriginal group, but what is remarkable with the Inuit is their political adaptability and pragmatism, combined with an extraordinary pride and a traditional thirst for knowledge. Not only have they never thought of themselves as poor: they consider themselves our intellectual superiors. They have succeeded in building a state that can dialogue on their behalf as the equal of other states. And, after the long, sad experience of the Indian reserves, the years of poor policy that I feel obliged to analyze in this book, the intelligence of the Canadian government is finally manifesting itself in the third millennium. Canada is finally acting as a multinational state and adopting a highly innovative legal structure.

To be sure, the battle is not over. Deculturation and assimilation caused by schooling, the market economy, tourism, and the omnipresent power of television are daily realities for the Nunavik and Nunavut authorities, as are substance abuse and government corruption, just as much a scourge here as in our democracies. It is hardly surprising to discover among the Inuit one of the world's highest suicide rates, a phenomenon that could presage ethnic and cultural annihilation. Or, alternatively – who knows? – the Inuit may undergo an intellectual, moral, and political renaissance. Let us hope that the youth of the new generations, particularly the women, blossom into full-fledged political leaders and that a new church, purveying a Christianity with shamanistic overtones, makes its appearance. With such assets, Nunavik and Nunavut will be well on their way to the success that history has long denied them.

Realistically, all births, including the birth of the Inuit nation, involve an element of pain. *Alea jacta est*; history is a continuing, long-term process. In a geographical setting of extraordinary cruelty and inter-ethnic violence lasting for millennia, the Inuit have managed not only to survive but to transmit a civilization and a philosophy of life. And, to be fair, Western civilization has not always been single-mindedly bent on subjugating them to cynical capitalism in the guise of progress. History, which is Darwinian, witnesses surprising turns of events that call for a careful analysis of geographical facts, civilizations, and mentalities. My scientific spirit of observation and analysis has always explored with cautious optimism, particularly so in those rainy days of August 1962 on the street leading to the Rankin mine. Let us pick up the story there, with our knowledge of what came after.

A FIRST LOOK

I was greeted by representatives of the Department of Northern Affairs, who assured me of their utmost assistance. Knowing that this research would be difficult and at times unrewarding, they displayed the professionalism characteristic of the British civil service: no judgment, no useless chatter, just faithful cooperation. An obliging word, a sympathetic look, a clap on the shoulder evoked inner echoes of gratitude. They pushed you to outdo yourself, reminded you that your results were eagerly awaited and that every day counted.

Rankin's mining potential had been discovered in 1928, when the area was populated by only ten hunting families tied to the Chesterfield Inlet trading post. Construction of the mine facility began in 1953. The enterprise experienced initial financial difficulties and decided to offer employment opportunities to Inuit labourers. By 1965 eighty Inuit men and a dozen women – my interview population – were on the payroll. The total Inuit population was 352, most of them from Chesterfield Inlet but some from Eskimo Point (Arviat) and Repulse Bay and a few from Baker Lake. The inland Inuit, with their refusal to eat seal meat, were looked down upon by the Chesterfield Inlet people.

Sample average monthly wages calculated over a three-month period in 1958 were \$108–\$134 for unskilled Inuit mine labourers, \$227–\$246 for skilled labourers, and \$294–\$417 for the highest-paid skilled trades classification.

Wage workers earned $0.75–$1.50 per hour. The houses were built and rented out by the mine for $30 per month, a relatively high amount on such salaries.[14] The Inuit paid for their own food. In spring and summer, hunting and fishing supplied their traditional food needs, including seal and salmon (abundant), birds (duck, goose, ptarmigan, eider, and goose eggs), blueberries, and roots. Other items were available at the HBC store, which got away with charging excessively high prices due to its retail monopoly. The Inuit, with no experience of money or budgeting or saving, spent their entire salaries there. Daily food purchases, in decreasing order of importance, consisted of frozen beef (pork was disliked), lard, butter, margarine, sugar, flour, biscuits and cookies, dry cereal, canned chicken and fish, prepared soups, canned spinach, fruit (raisins and dried apples), and orange juice. Nonfood items included clothing, radios, phonographs, perfume, and tobacco. Alcohol was unknown, and its sale and importation were prohibited.

The town had a medical clinic serving the Inuit population. Diseases of note were bronchitis, pleurisy, tuberculosis (declining), gastrointestinal conditions (e.g., diarrhoea), influenza, nosebleeds, epilepsy (one case), dental caries, bleeding gums, ear infection, cystitis, impetigo, and other skin diseases.[15]

The overall impression was that of resistance by the Inuit culture in terms of its language, family structures, marriage networks, and physiological and circadian rhythms. But also palpable, as the diary of my miner friend attests (see Appendix 2), were the psychological and cultural solitudes experienced with respect to the dominant society. This observer noted an appalling absence of interaction between the white managers and the Inuit families transplanted into such a foreign setting. Also surprising, as I mentioned, was the federal government's failure to protect Inuit union rights. Although salaried, many of these workers found themselves perpetually poor, unable to save due to their new underground working conditions, their unfamiliarity with the use of money, and the amazingly strict apartheid system in which they lived. At the mine, the white and Inuit workers ate in separate cafeterias, and the food was served out of separate kitchens. In the movie theatre, the lone cultural facility, Tuesday, Wednesday, and Friday evenings were reserved for the whites and Mondays, Thursdays, and Saturdays for the Inuit. The mine manager's authorization was required in order to visit the Inuit in their village. (Being on an official mission, I had a standing authorization to do so, and also to interview all mine employees, white and Inuit, on the premises.) "At Rankin Inlet, the Eskimo is being trained to be a labourer – not a citizen," wrote Robert and Lois Dailey.[16]

To be sure, the Inuit could pride themselves on holding paid employment in a new setting that might well be their future metropolis. But the transition was effected American-style – that is, there was no transition at all. In cultural terms, it was a forced march into the future. No educational, psychological, or vocational support was available from the mine management or the government. No, nothing so forward-looking. And it was not a matter of indifference or slapdash policy. Rankin Inlet was truly worrisome as an embodiment of 1960s federal Inuit policy precisely because it evidenced a policy vacuum for the aboriginal North. So long left to their traditional ways and then thrown pell-mell into industrial society, the Inuit would succumb to alcoholism, drug abuse, despair, and one of the world's highest rates of youth suicide in the 1980s. Was the sacrifice of two generations really necessary to make way for the future?

Yet it seems to me that something positive may be salvaged from this dreadful experience; to wit, the Inuit may have benefited from the absence of an assimilationist approach such as France applied to its overseas territories and departments. As a result, they avoided the "anesthetization" of the next generation of Inuit, the one coming of age in the year 2000, which might well have hindered the emergence of Nunavik and Nunavut. That is, perhaps the initial series of hummocks that they encountered was actually a catalyst to autonomy.

THE INTERPRETER AND THE ANTHROPOLOGIST

After moving into my room, I go out to look for an interpreter, as I do not speak a word of the coastal Inuit dialect. I am introduced to Sally Tootoo, a young Jewish Canadian married to a Caribou Inuk and employed at the mine office. She is enthusiastic about the project and generously offers her time, even though it means doing a "double day," attending to domestic chores for a chauvinistic husband when she gets home.

At eleven o'clock we go out in high spirits to explore the town. Our first respondent is a parched, wrinkled, tattooed Netsilingmiut woman with an impassive, absent gaze. We talk while she busily makes biscuits (*biknik*) on a homemade stove consisting of an old barrel. Also present is a young woman staring at the ground; with her husband absent, her behaviour must allow no room for misinterpretation. A snot-nosed child stands at a safe distance, staring at me distraughtly.

To fall in out of the blue is the worst calamity in this kind of research. The old woman's attitude is reserved. She has no idea what I am driving at, and in truth, as the dialogue drifts, I too lose track. The role of mentor to Sally begins to seem more rewarding, her particular mental *métissage* more interesting, than the respondent's recalcitrance. The conversation meanders through a haze of smoke, while the oil crackles in the pan. I cast a multihooked line and pull as adeptly as I can, trying to sort out anything that may be useful, but my questionnaire clearly still needs work. This first interview proves a comical failure.

After two hours of disjointed remarks, we beat a retreat, and my assistant steps into the breach: "Why don't you start with me? I know more about that stuff than she does. I've read some anthropology, you know – the great Franz Boas, for example. I understand what you're trying to do. Come to my house."

Amid a spare decor consisting of a table, a sink, and a gas stove, Sally Tootoo is back at her usual job, ironing her husband's blue jeans, while I ask her about taboos related to food, hunting, death, and naming. *Illigerik*: I bring up the case of two people who are not allowed to speak each other's names. It is common, for example, for children to have a godfather whose name remains unspoken. All their lives they owe each other assistance, especially in moments of crisis. To survive in their solitude, the Inuit need allies, so they multiply kinship structures.

She puts down her iron for a moment and with bright eyes reveals the *idlertuara*, a taboo related to naming and godfathering, that her husband observes.[17] I have begun to question Sally (still surprised at her revelation) on burial rites when the telephone rings. "Hi, honey ..." Iron in hand, visibly contented with her submissive role, she reassures her husband that lunch – steak and fries – will be ready when he gets home.

In the vigorous week of activity that follows, I am able to clarify various points of ethnology, some of which are already familiar to me from my two previous expeditions to Igloolik. Here, however, everything is more complicated because the coastal Inuit society is in contact with a very different, traditionalist people, the Caribou Inuit, who abstain from eating seal meat. I try to elucidate the main features of the mentalities of these two antagonistic groups, so mutually opaque that they do not speak to one another. What is a mentality? As Jean Duvignaud explains, it is a river of ideas and beliefs that is either contaminated by foreign influences or develops complexity in order to better resist them.[18] Inflecting the metaphor, I would say that a delta builds up and washes away from season to season, leaving certain accretions behind. The differences between these groups are partially a function of hunting and fishing taboos that vary according to geographical area – from inland hunting to hunting of marine mammals to collective fishing. But running deeper than these obvious differences are opposing understandings of the universe, existential passions, which solidify as techniques are abandoned and people travel to new places. I must discover the key to these juxtaposed cultural ghettos, this "will to exist" within difference, so evidently a response to a fear of annihilation. Various accounts allow me to trace the vital threads. There is no implicit institution or organization among the Caribou Inuit, who constitute more a collection of bands than a group. Rather, what unites them is a space of imagination and a collective representation of the fate of the world.

A good week, all told; I am beginning to assemble the scores of disparate pieces of information and get a broader view. Logical relationships are falling into place. But a change of plans is imposed on me. Sally receives a telephone

Excerpt from my expedition diary, Rankin Inlet, August 1962.
August 30. Windy and rainy. Morning: Economic Survey still there. Stuck [no seaplane]. Discussion on coordination among them [the various departments]. Father Didier kindly invited me to lunch. A born monk. Very interesting afternoon with Margaret [my Inuit respondent]: accounts of sorcery, which she clearly believes in. I hire the police assistant for late afternoons.
The priests' radio vice: breaks isolation [but] favours gossip. Certainly does not enhance these communities' spirituality. My term for it: "having a chat."
August 31. Rainy and windy. Last day of the month. Putting my morning's notes in order. Worked this morning with a Caribou Eskimo from Garry Lake [south of Back River] who wore what seemed like a perpetual, distant smile. Two hands simultaneously: speaks fast and without embarrassment even when recounting most intimate details. Availability and generosity of spirit, clarity of the strong races. Never doubting what they do, their way of life, for [they are totally committed to it]. Evening: my second interpreter, Luki, absent. When I call back, tells me reserved by HBC. Tomorrow, 6:30 P.M.

Excerpt from my expedition diary, Rankin Inlet, August 1962.
Afternoon of the 13th: successive visits to the school, where I set up my field office of sorts. Interview with three women. Failure. "Nauk! Nauk! We don't know anything about the past and we don't want to. It's bad." Even if Reverend James – 32 years here – had wanted to support my research, he could not have. Minds have been changed [made more resentful]. They are afraid. Evening met American biologist studying lemming population dynamics. Interesting as any biologist but genially (or contemptuously – their lack of awareness is so huge that one can never tell) ignorant of France and even Europe. To bed at 1:00; the woman annoyed me with her continual questions. Her feminine presence aroused in me a foolish instinct of male domination.

call from Montreal: her possessive mother is arriving for two weeks and will not tolerate having to share her daughter. I will have to find someone else.

A man named John who interprets professionally for the doctor and the police is put at my disposal. I resume the survey, beginning with John, but the easy complicity is lacking; first, because Sally is a woman and, second, because she knew or, with rare finesse, could sense what I was looking for. To my chagrin, John and I make a cool, distant pair. He never meets my gaze as he delivers the straightforward translations of a proud, assiduous fact-finder, rarely straying off topic. He permits himself none of those asides that often yield new discoveries, nor does he encourage them in my respondents. I vaguely sense that he derives some enjoyment from the knowledge that the researcher is lost without him. My successive respondents listen but are hardly encouraged to express their personal thoughts. We come off as investigators.

Obviously, the police interpreter is not the best intermediary for obtaining information on wife swapping and taboos. But more generally, the make-or-break role of the anthropological interpreter in all such interactions cannot be overstressed. As the person who sets the tone of the interview, he can make the researcher's reception chilly or warm depending on his mood and good will. Moreover, he may often filter questions and answers. To echo Clifford Geertz's famous phrase, one must read over the interpreter's shoulder.

As the interviews proceed, John becomes more assertive with me and puts new distance into our relations. Ever the law enforcement professional, he asks for a written questionnaire that he can study in advance so as to avoid making any mistakes – a typical fear that I have found among the Inuit. I write up a questionnaire as a guide, but the weave of the questions is so loose that at first it nets only trivialities and clichés.

A family's survival here depends on a subtle network of alliances, marriage obviously being the most important. *Ui* (husband); *nuliak* (wife). The society is endogamous. Marriage only takes place between *ilatgit*, first or second cousins, on one's "territory," which is inhabited by related *tonrars*, or spirits of the dead. Their benevolence must be earned. But there are many other kinds of kinship that entail mutual assistance: that of namesakes (*awariik*), or "halves of a whole"; wife swapping (*kipuktut* – here the obligation of assistance extends to the children); the so-called "joking partnership," consisting of two men in the habit of making others laugh; and commensalism, the hunting and eating of seals together. Sharing the flesh of an animal is a copulative act. If I give seal meat (*kuyak*) to an unrelated neighbour, by eating it he becomes my *kuyara*, and we two commensals are collectively *kuyaré*. Thus kin are as numerous as game animals, although only seal, walrus, whale, and bear count for this purpose.

I attempt to delve further into the unique aspects of Inuit naming practices. Until the age of ten to twelve, children are said to be inhabited by the *tonrar* of the dead person whose name they bear. They are never criticized or abused, for this would be an insult to the *tonrar*. At Neqe, North Greenland, in November 1950 I saw the five-or-six-year-old son of my neighbour Q'aungna break an expensive alarm clock. The parents laughed. Children may even behave violently without reproof. Rochfort Maguire, during his stay at Point Barrow in 1852–54, described the case of a four-year-old child who demanded a lump of tobacco. When he did not receive it immediately, he violently struck his father on the face with a piece of wood. Apparently nobody felt justified in criticizing or punishing him.[19] Collective and quiet, childrearing is a perpetual process. Anyone in the group, whether kin or not, will intervene if the child hurts someone, calmly showing him how to "do right": how to shoot better, or how to set a trap in the right place, arrange it on the snow, and cover it with a layer just thick enough to trick the fox. Children learn quickly by watching, by example. "But we measure our efforts." It is a step-by-step process in which there is little or no need to repeat. The jury – that is, the talk among the members of the group – is benevolent until the threshold of adulthood. Then, when the child has killed his first seal or bear, he is considered to have joined the race of men, and his behaviour and mistakes are appraised pitilessly. The ideal is to further one's accomplishments continually and to absorb new knowledge like sand absorbs water. I personally attended this school without walls in 1950–51 in North Greenland while learning to guide my sled and navigate in the dark.

I receive a visit from a Caribou Inuk, a man with noticeable body odour who even here, in his new surroundings, declines to eat seal meat. He stares briefly – a bony, elongated face, a study in angles, the forehead prominent as in one of El Greco's hidalgos – before stating that he wants to participate in my study. It is a disinterested act, no remuneration expected. At first he sits half-on and half-off a chair with some embarrassment. Then he gets a caribou skin from under the awning and moves to the floor, where he sits at ease. Chest erect, legs spread at an angle, he speaks not only with the voice but with small, vivid eyes, fine-boned hands (knife-trimmed nails), and torso movements that obey his verbal expression. His precise, descriptive, leisurely narrative (*uqaluktuaq* in Thule) is free-ranging and impulsive, something I am finding to be characteristic of the more traditional Inuit.* I discover a significantly different mental structure from those of the people who live at Thule and Igloolik, although I am as yet unable to fully describe it.

The air suddenly fills with shouts: whales have been sighted. In seconds all the hunters, my interpreter John included, jump into their canoes. The Caribou stays behind, indifferent to anything that touches the sea. We stare at each other, powerless. Without my intermediary, I am an invalid. As soon as John returns, someone announces that a cargo ship is approaching, and the Caribou goes down to the shore to lug crates without a look backward. Another day lost.

Lately, I have been eating with the Inuit only every third day so as not to impose on them. To live in their homes would be very artificial. Mostly, I eat alone, making meals from the rice and salt water biscuits that I've purchased at the store. On my table is the seal meat that I eat standing up from the point of a knife (although I'd prefer a caribou steak). Also my daily half-gallon of tea – my luxury, and I sit down to drink it. My porridge breakfasts, which I prepare in various ways, are a moment of enjoyment.

* Inuktitut is a highly descriptive language. For example, the word lawyer is literally translated as "one who lies"; judge, as "one who convicts."

I harbour no illusions; I know that I am seen by the Inuit as having fallen in out of the blue. Everyone knows that I work for a government department, for the "Queen," and my reception, although kind, is rather stiff. On my sporadic visits to the whites, they welcome me with open arms, while I try to maintain my distance. I want to avoid being sucked into the mire of the provincial family circle in which the teacher entertains the nurse, who entertains the policeman, who entertains the HBC manager, who entertains the pilot, who entertains the missionary, who entertains the pious couple – in which cookies are baked, time is killed with trifles, and the eternal simplistic gossip of colonial towns makes the rounds.

In an unusual situation, not one but two priests live at the Catholic mission founded in 1957. There is Father Eugène Fafard, a French Canadian with a rabbinical beard and blue eyes who radiates goodness, as he has throughout a thirty-year career in the North; and Father Didier, from France. They invite me in and provide sincere offers of assistance. Sunday is their big day, the day when "bells" chime – actually a recording of bells on an LP record. The town's several Catholic and Anglican churches hold mass at different times, allowing the Inuit to attend different services in succession. For many of them it is a diversion, a form of entertainment, a chance to sing well-loved hymns. At the Oblate services in Igloolik, I had recorded the Mass of the Angels, which was said and sung in Latin. The Inuit knew it by heart. Everyone's attention was rapt, their eyes closed, the rites and words deeply experienced. "I believe in one God, the all-powerful Father, creator of Heaven and Earth. Okperpunga Naliortemut. Atâtarmut ajugak' angitokmut pingortitsiyeomut. Christ, have pity on us! Kriste nikatigut!" Several hymns were sung in Inuktitut. At the end of the ceremony, the congregants deposited their modest offerings in a gilded metal plate in front of the altar.

On Sunday nights the two priests at Rankin Inlet have their moment of great human joy when they tune in to the Oblate short-wave radio channel. Apart from distress calls, no outside messages are allowed – that's how rumours get started. It is a confined world, as at the seminary; the family circle has taken them back within its circumference.

Second week. My new interpreter says he is glad to work with me and is interested in shamanism. "The priests try to keep us from talking about those practices, but they are still very important to me. Kappiasutuq!" But the next morning, when he fails to show up, I learn that he has suffered a puncture wound by stepping on a nail while wearing rubber boots. Decidedly, an evil spirit has it in for me.

Interpreter number four! We meet at the HBC windmill, where he is greasing the gears, and he agrees to work with me. At lunch, consisting of seal soup with half-frozen potatoes, he opens his mouth wide as if to breathe and

Bear hunting at Qaanaaq, North Greenland, 1991. The Inughuit consider the Igloolik Inuit to be their distant ancestors. Drawing by Kiutikaq Dunek.

swallow at the same time, revealing rotten teeth. Some of his relatives arrive, one of whom resembles Kutsikitsoq, my friend and companion on my 1951 expedition to the North Geomagnetic Pole.[20] The interpreter tells me that the man is moody, irascible, quick-tempered and that he is one of several people who fought off a polar bear with a knife. The man shows me the scars on his chest.

The afternoon finds us in a tent by the sea visiting an irascible, freckle-faced Inuit woman. Soft light filters in through the pale fabric, but I quickly sense that the atmosphere is hostile. She and her family would like me to be elsewhere. I am too big for the space, my legs are a foot too long; I am too much of everything, and a Kablunak to boot. I annoy because I observe. Some young girls delicately raise a corner of the fabric to see what is happening outside: a cold rain is sweeping over the shore. Occasional passersby are described to the people sitting at the back of the tent in an increasingly loud voice. A little girl at the entrance sings quietly to herself. The interview quickly goes sour. To terminate it, the interpreter asks an abrupt question that I had taken elaborate care to phrase circumspectly. For my comparative research on birth intervals among the Inuit (e.g., twenty-eight months for the Inughuit), I must obtain accurate information on all births, including miscarriages, which may represent disguised cases of infanticide. The woman is incensed. "You don't ask questions like that to a woman! That's sacred. Get out of here." I blush inwardly with shame, and prepare my departure like a sage lost in thought, while the son pokes about noisily in his stove. The atmosphere is heavy, the retreat turning into a debacle.

I have no choice but to pursue a rather technical research agenda, using a set of related, systematic questionnaires in an attempt to derive more general conclusions. For example, one questionnaire seeks to determine food consumption patterns by gathering data on types and quantities of food consumed by age, sex, and size of locality (hamlet of two or three dwellings versus town of forty or more); another compiles typical activities by age, sex, and psychological traits. The reader should bear in mind that this field work was done before computers existed, yet it had to be systematic, covering the largest possible number of families. This was the reason for my perseverance and for these dogged visits from tent to house, family unit to family unit. Columbo on the job – even Saturday nights, when admission to the many parties was a bottle of gin, whisky, or beer, which I refused to proffer. Acrimonious remarks: "Who are you? [the ubiquitous *kina igvit*]. Describe your job. Ah! Writing reports? I can't stand bureaucracy. Who pays you? White people? This is not their place. Inuit land!" The masks drop, aggressivity reappears. *In vino veritas*.

The interpretation problem is becoming comical. The latest has disappeared, probably hung over. I go looking for him. His one-night stand tells me that he has gone to work for the HBC and will be back tomorrow. And so the days pass. Obviously, it would be more reasonable to have a single interpreter with a thorough understanding of my agenda, but the government classifies Inuktitut interpretation as casual employment due to the variety of dialects. We anthropologists and sociologists have no easier a time of it than the doctors. Ah, humility ... an essential asset for scientists, rebuffed and insulted as we are! The work is a matter of finding crumbs, looking for wheat grains scattered through a pile of chaff. I have always searched for the hard kernel; although infinitely small, it may be the catalyst for a system's transformation. I am driven by a trapper's obstinacy, on the prowl for bits of gossip, arriving too soon or too late in a conversation whose hidden meaning I fail to grasp. To create an impression of composure, I give a piece of candy to the kid with the yellowish snot.

My ideas on the importance of names and naming (*attierq* here, *atiq* in the North Greenland dialect) are gaining clarity.[21] The single given name (there are no surnames) is that of a recently deceased person, and as such it connects the person to an ancient lineage. It is the medium of what may be called

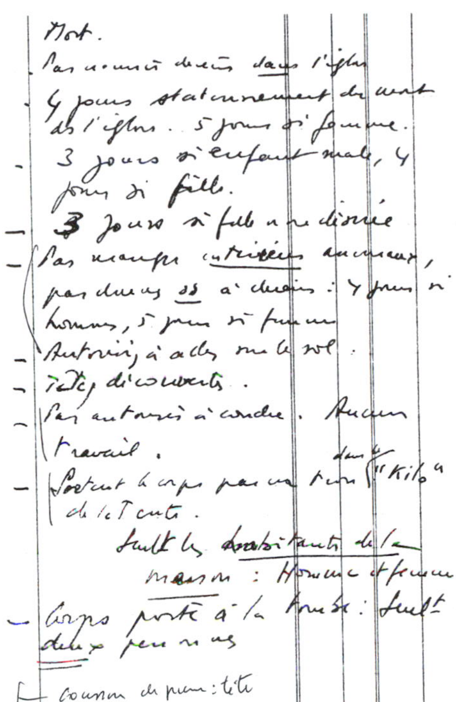

Notes of interview with Homaok, observations concerning Utku death rituals prior to their conversion to Anglicanism. Back River expedition, May 1963.
Death
No feeding dogs in house.
Corpse laid out four days in igloo, five days if woman.
Three days if boy, four days if girl [mourning].
Three days if unwanted girl.
No eating innards of animals, no giving bones to dogs: four days if man, five days if woman.
Allowed to walk around.
Heads bare [after four or five days].
Sewing not allowed. No work.
Body removed through hole in side of tent.
Only the inhabitants of the house: man and woman.
Body brought to tomb: only two people.
Stone headrest.

the breath. "Everything moves on and nothing is at rest ... Immortal mortals, mortal immortals, one living the other's death and dying the other's life" (Heraclitus as quoted by Plato). *Attierq* is the vehicle of reincarnation for recently dead namesakes, although this is not totally clear-cut, for the "spirit name" (*inua*) must be distinguished from the "soul name." Parents like to give their children several names of dead persons, thus conferring heightened powers on them. There is a stock of names (about one hundred) that are transmitted from generation to generation, many of them unisex. In a spirit of androgyny dating back to a time when the sexes were not differentiated, a newborn may bear the name of a dead person of the opposite sex. Interesting work could be done to elucidate the androgynous identity of boys bearing a grandmother's name or girls bearing a father's. However, such interpretations would have to be derived with extreme caution given the vast differences between Inuit and Western worldviews.

A southeast seawind (*niggingajuk*) has picked up again this morning. Damp snow turns to rain, the wind to a windstorm. For twenty-three hours I am cooped up in my house – a prefabricated one-room miners' hut guyed on all four sides by cables attached to iron stakes, these latter driven deep into the bedrock. The tar paper on the roof has come loose and beats erratically; to calm my nerves, I try to make it fit a measured, musical pattern. My morale is not very high ... Is it in any way reasonable to dedicate hours, days, months – let's face it, many years – of one's life to the microproblems of microsocieties of which only rags and tatters remain? A memory from June 1978 haunts me: I am at the Palais de l'Élysée as a luncheon guest and am introduced to the president of the republic, Valéry Giscard d'Estaing. I am about to speak the few words I have prepared for the occasion when he pronounces this historic sentence: "So, professor, tell me why you've devoted so many years of your life to such a little people."

To clear my head, I resort to the age-old chore of washing my clothes. There is a knock at the door. It is the friend from Igloolik to whom I lent a sympathetic ear during his period of depression. The face, all hollows and bumps, tells of his battle-scarred life. A mandragora's face, bloated, the skin drab, lifeless, and rumpled, the eyes swallowed by the pockets under them, leaving only a small opening for the yellow pupils. A conjugation of the verb "to drink" in the past, present, and future.

Darkness liberates: with our features obscured by the night, our conversation is confiding. He tells me that he has followed my advice about continu-

Autobiography of an Inuk living in Rankin in August 1962, which I am preparing for publication. It is not the autobiography discussed in Appendix 2, whose author's name is withheld for reasons of confidentiality.

MOI ,JEAN AYARUA E 3-54,actuellement résident à RAKIN INLET, N.W.T.
ᑕᐸᓂ,ᐅᐸᓚ,ᔮ-ᐊᔭᔪᐊ E3-54, ᒪᓇ ᑲᒥᓂᓂᒥᐅᑕᐅᓗᒐ

donne à Monsieur le PROFESSEUR J.N. MALAURIE de LA SORBONNE , la permission
ᐃᓂᓂᐊᑎᓯᔮᐊᓗ J.M. MALAURIE. (ᒪᓗᕆ) , ᐊᒥᐱᒥᒐᑯ ᐃᒪᓇ:

de publier à son gré une COPIE AUTHENTIQUE traduite des SOUVENIRS que j'ai rédágés
ᑕᐃᑯᐊ ᑎᑎᒐᑕᐱᓂᑲ ᐃᑲᐅᒪᔾᒪᓂᒃ ᑕᐃᒪᒪ ᓄᑕᒐᐅᓂᒪᓂᑦ,ᐃᓄᑐ ᑎᑎᒐᑕᑲ

en 112 pages de texte syllabique en passant par le Père THIBERT,O.M.I.
ᐊᓂᓚᔦᐃ ᓇᓴᐅᑎᓂ 112, ᐊᑕᑕᑎᕙᑯᑎᓚᐅᑕᑲ 12-10-1960,

ing to write his autobiography and entrusts several volumes to me. The text, written in both syllabic and roman script, is exceptional, demanding, at times touching. I encourage him to stick with the daily writing routine. Twelve months from now he will be sober, and I will have played a small role in midwifing his rebirth – one of the most positive results of my expedition.[22]

No sooner has he left than there is another knock at the door ... the wind, perhaps? From out of the darkness there emerges a shadow, a very old man with rough-cut features, once a "sorcerer," his brown-black eyes set deeply in a smooth face that is the maroon colour of old roman tile. In 1923 he was one of Rasmussen's respondents while the illustrious Dane of Eskimo ancestry spent eight months researching the Netsilingmiut. All he wants is to touch me, to touch a white man who shares Rasmussen's interest in the history of his people. No words are spoken. The suspicious eyes brighten. He grips my shoulder with three fraternal fingers, stares with satisfaction, then dissolves into the night.

A new problem has arisen in the past two days: I have fallen sick. I am lucky to have a sturdy constitution, and what little I have in the way of medication in my first-aid kit – the universal aspirin – is enough to speed my recovery. Forty-eight hours on spring water and tea is still the best medicine. I spend the time organizing my notes, writing them legibly in my journal, rereading my ethnographic notebook, touching up various figures and lines, making an attempt at synthesis theme by theme. In the evening, weary of scribe's work, I go to a screening of *Ivanhoe* at the mine cinema. Whole Inuit families are there in their blue or white khaki parkas and rubber boots, some dressed like the Kablunaks. A few people, mainly women, wear traditional dress. A group motions for me to join them after the show: "Come on! Forget about your boring paperwork!" On leaving the theatre, I am handed a message from the RCMP. One of their seaplanes is leaving for Chesterfield Inlet tomorrow. Welcome aboard!

CHESTERFIELD INLET: MEETING WITH A HOLY MAN

Chesterfield Inlet (Igluligaarjuk),[23] a very old HBC post eighty kilometres north-northeast of Rankin Inlet at the head of a 280-kilometre fjord flanked by a red and gray granite shoreline. The area was visited in the mid-nineteenth century by whalers and in the early twentieth century by Anglican and, especially, Catholic missionaries. The Oblate mission was founded by the legendary Father Arsène Turquetil of Normandy in 1912.[24] The first conversions, of four families, took place in 1917, and Father Turquetil became the first apostolic vicar of Hudson Bay in 1931. I wanted to come here to meet a holy man: Father Pierre Henry, one of the first Christian missionaries to live among the

Netsilingmiut.* He is a pivotal figure in the transition from a pagan, traditionalist society to a Christianized one. I had heard much about him from my friend Gontran de Poncins, who had met him in 1938 and who had described him in his book *Kabloona*. On my visit to the Netsilingmiut of Spence Bay and Thom Bay, I found that he was remembered with emotion and respect.

The early morning of 6 August 1962 dawns clear and sunny as the seaplane lands on the water, a pneumatic canoe drops down, and I deplane. On the beach I am warmly welcomed by the post manager, the Department of Northern Affairs representative, and Father Roland Courtemanche, the director of the Catholic mission. Word of my arrival has reached them over Oblate radio. The department has reserved a small house for me, but, my desire being to live with Father Henry, I am guided by Father Courtemanche to a severe wooden dwelling, whose uniform, faded gray facade is decidedly ecclesiastic in tone.

"My dear professor, please make yourself at home," he says.

On the ground floor is my austere five-metre-square bedroom: I could not have asked for more. What is an evangelical mission? An odour, half-voiced or unspoken words, doors softly closed. Small rugs here and there in front of the cells. Aboriginal lay nuns in brown robes shuffling or gliding from place to place, their carriage humble.

"Father Henry is resting," they whisper.

He is an old man now. Born in the Côtes-d'Armor region of Brittany at Corman-en-Plouguenast, he lived ascetically for nearly twenty years (1935–50) in snow houses, hunting and fishing like his flock. Now retired, he wants to end his days in the Arctic. As soon as I enter the room he gets up, and his first words open hearts: "Your visit from France does me a great deal of good. I know of your work and have great esteem for what you are doing. I want you to know that." With his smiling blue eyes and noble, russet-streaked white beard, he reminds me of a Russian hermit. There is also something of the Abbé Pierre in him.

"I will do whatever I can for you during these few days," he says. "But do you think I can be of any help? I doubt it ... I don't know much about the subjects that interest you. These days, I doubt everything, in fact. I'm not good for much anymore. You see how old I am. What was my purpose here? The Church is in crisis, at the top and at the grassroots. Help us poor priests, simple men, men of little means. We can't all be like the Curé d'Ars.[25] Pray for us. I am at times wracked by doubt. Believe me, we despair of everything, just

* I also wanted to visit the starting point for one of the greatest but littlest-known journeys in Arctic history, that of US Lieutenant Frederick Schwatka; see pp. 196–7.

as you laymen do; unfortunately, we are vulnerable to despair. Oh, pray for me, a poor priest among the Eskimos! My nights have become a trial."

We agree that I will interview him in his room every morning after mass, taking care not to abuse his valuable time. Depending on his level of fatigue, he either remains lying down or sits on the bed, under an image of Saint Thérèse de Lisieux. In regard to the Netsilingmiut, his cooperation proves inestimable. I cautiously phrase my questions referring to the emotional transmutation from animistic to Christian thought, to shamans (*angaqut*) and shamanism – "sorcery." These phenomena were at play during his time in Pelly Bay combating a world of evil spells and amulets. As is to be expected, he considers all of this inconsequential, pagan.

"Oh, you know, sorcery, all those things, I pretty well ignored them. I teach the Gospel: Jesusib Ajok' ertûta."

I dwell on his vows as a priest. What methods did he use to teach these people, Christianize them? How did he effect their shift of faith, if he actually succeeded? Decades earlier, Father Turquetil wrote:

> When I begin to preach, they pay strict attention at first, then look about at the faces as if mystified by their expression of rapt absorption ... we are in no hurry to take them aside and suggest that they prepare for baptism. God alone opens hearts. Our work is to prepare the way, waiting till their perseverance proves that the time has come to put the question plainly to their conscience.[26]

Father Henry carries the sentiment further: "Christianity liberated them from the oppressive taboos of animism. They wanted to live more freely but they were afraid to break the rules and the *angaqut* took advantage of that fear. I tried to help them. Still, the Inuit are stubborn and cautious. Tradition is their compass. What I did was to notice that there were many exceptions to the rules. To be perfectly frank, if you want to know the key to thirty years of close relations, they were willing to cooperate because they understood that we are stronger. They are, of course, very, very intelligent and practical. Together we contemplated death, sin, and the sanctifying goodness of Jesus: tokonerk isumagilago. He is like they are, they are as poor as He was. Now that they need us, they suffer us with difficulty because they are proud.

"Their social organization is like that of a dog team: they all follow the leader. Mind you, they are always watching one another, and the best competitor takes the leader's place at the first opportunity. So there is emulation and there is competition. Ah, the fiery characters I've met during thirty-three years of priesthood! Staunch opponents, apostates, informers, real bullheads! Sometimes with perverse ideas. But the group doesn't tolerate them for long. They are absolved by public confession or expelled with the consent of all.

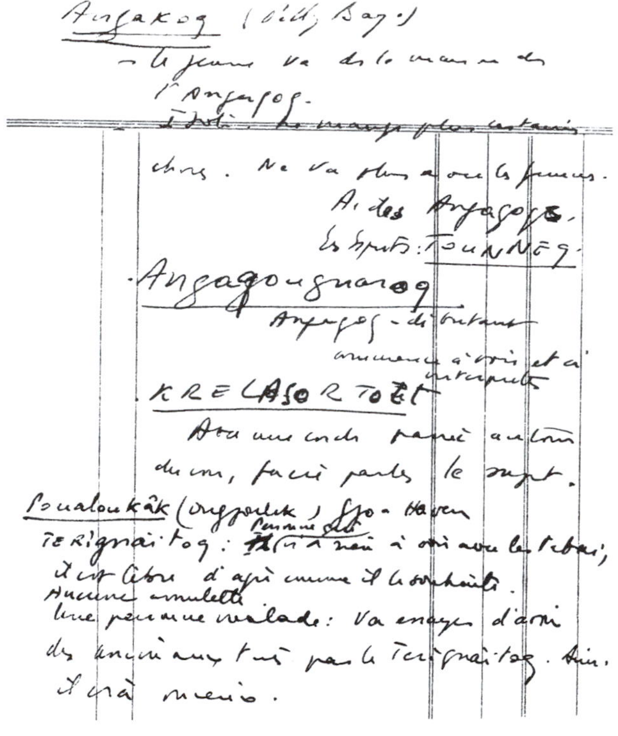

Angakoq (Pelly Bay)
– Le jeune va dans la maison de l'Angakoq.
– Isolé. Ne mange plus certaines choses. Ne va plus avec les femmes.
Aides des Angakoqs.
Les Esprits: TOUNNEQ.
Angagougnaroq
Angakoq – débutant
commence à voir et à interpréter
KRELASORTOTIT
Avec une corde passée autour du cou, faire parler le sujet.
Poualoukâk (Ugjulik) Gjoa-Haven
TERIGNAITOQ: personne non soumise aux tabous; il est libre d'agir comme il le souhaite. Aucune amulette.
Une personne malade: va essayer d'avoir des animaux tués par le Terignaitoq. Ainsi il ira mieux.

Education by the *angakoq* at Pelly Bay. Interview with Father Henry at Chesterfield Inlet, September 1962. Ethnological notebook. Youth goes into Angakoq's house. Isolated. Refrains from eating certain things and from female company. Angakoq's assistants Spirits (*tunneq*) ANGAGUGNAROQ beginning Angakoq beginning to see and interpret KRELASORTOTIT With a rope around neck [can] get individual to talk [man or woman] PUALUKAK (Ugjulik) Gjoa Haven. *Terignaitoq*: person not bound by taboos, free to act as he pleases. No amulet. Sick person will try to have animals killed by the *terignaitoq* so as to get better.

They have no choice but to think through the group. Meanwhile, over the many years in which I have solemnly practised my faith by administering the Holy Communion (*Tamuasugiarsiutit*), I have met people who were most fraternal in their adversity because I intimately shared their existence."

Leaving, I pass a sister of the Quebec-based order of the Grey Nuns, who wears a bright smile.

"I understand that you went to Thom Bay," says Father Henry straight away the next morning. "I was informed of your visit by Father X, a young Oblate whom you met there. I gather that you didn't get along. How odd: two Frenchmen, a missionary and a professor, alone in that place of great transcendence. You are the first lay Frenchman to go there. Father X was angry with himself. He regretted his obtuseness and ill temper. No help for it, he's a Breton like me! And he is young. He has been having a difficult time, that is for certain; after your departure, he travelled five hundred miles south to consult with his fellows, to get a weight off his chest.

"I know that little mission well; it was I who built it in 1948–49. I spent long months there, a solitary white man meditating before the ice desert of the Magnetic Pole, experiencing moments of loneliness as any priest might. We are so very alone! Nor should one assume that we all think alike. After all, an Oblate is only a man. People tend to forget that. I wish I had been there to welcome you and to offer you my brotherly assistance in interpreting the codex that I wrote myself."

He allows me to see the Chesterfield Inlet codex, and we discuss the future of the Inuit. "Right," he says, "let's talk about what the government has in store for them. It will not be good at all. These people are like family to me. I worry about them sometimes; often, in fact."

I explain the purpose of my carefully thought-out recommendations to the government: "The guiding principle is autonomous government *immediately*, while their culture is intact, with simultaneous selection and on-the-job education of elites. Autonomy means self-management, full empowerment, promotion of self-sufficiency rather than creeping dependence on relief. An Inuit university, with its own pedagogy, remains to be conceived and created in the North. These people are steeped in oral culture and have different neuronal patterns from ours. It is not a matter of churning out bureaucrats, teachers, or technicians but of helping people to choose what is good for themselves, rejecting the elements of our culture that are perverse or contrary to theirs. They are people of character who should invent their own schools and systems of government. Give them responsibility for an increasingly broad range of services and departments. They are adults, not children. Let time do its work as these societies transform themselves from within, with the whites on the sidelines if possible."

Father Henry reacts with a start, his eyes shining. Seizing my hands, he exclaims: "That's exactly right, and that is the mission of the Church! We have been too silent. Like the Jesuits in Paraguay with the Guarani, we should have organized model villages with appropriate pedagogical methods. I proposed my own mission for Chesterfield Inlet and Pelly Bay, but the hierarchy was cautious and always refused; "ambitious," "premature," the comments were always carefully worded. I found this painful since I was as keen to help them as you are. With the Inuit, one must set the example, then leave them to themselves. Quite true, what you've said. Learn by doing, in action. That's the nature of Inuit education. I beg of you, never give up. And if you are attacked, consider it a good sign. But what can we do to carry out this magnificent project? How I regret being too old!"

Theology is of little interest to him, and we spend little time on it. However, he tells me that he has reflected a great deal on the meaning of suffering while sharing the hard life of the Inuit. The Greek word *pathos*, he reminds me, means suffering but also passion, deep emotion.

"It was difficult, but I tried to convey that I accepted the harshness of their lives – which they did not measure, they were so accustomed to it – as a school of transformation. At any rate I did my best, living like Job in my snow house with a few frozen fish and a tainted seal rib. No, it was not easy living among the Eskimo, who are so pagan, egotistical – no, really – so brutal and ill-prepared to comprehend the idea of purification through suffering. There were murderers, perverts among them, whom the group dealt with in its own way. As for the poverty, it was evangelical in its simplicity, a thing to be endured. Hardship is second nature to them, a condition of survival. To transform their second nature into a supernature would have taken more charisma than I had. Evangelism is hard and at times thankless; when we compare ourselves to others, we are humbled ...

"I prayed a great deal during my solitary life among the Eskimo. The Pelly Bay mission was founded way back in 1935. No one visited me in those days,

Excerpt from my expedition diary, Chesterfield, September 1962.
September 10. Fine weather. Morning with Father Henry who gave me list of shamans [at Pelly Bay]. High-minded spirituality always in evidence. Some interesting observations. Afternoon with Norman Ford, always a fount of history. Padlei trapper. Seaplane picked up the mail for Churchill. Decided to leave for Baker Lake by HBC boat *Fort Ross* [actually *Fort Severn*] which was ready to depart, waiting for pilot. He arrived by boat from Baker Lake and prepared to leave immediately. Went to see the captain. Just as one would expect of a cargo captain who has spent a long time in harbour: unshaven, disgruntled, book in hand. Agreed to take me. Spoke again with Father Henry, [asked him] to pray for me from time to time.

10/ Beau temps. Matin avec Père Henry. Me donne une liste sorciers. Toujours hauteur spirituelle chez vous. Quelques observations intéressantes. Après-midi avec Norman Ford, toujours riche d'histoire : trappeur chez les Padlei. L'hydravion prend le courrier pour Churchill. Décide de partir à Baker Lake par le bateau HBC. « Fort Ross » qui peut partir ayant reçu le Pilote qui est arrivé d'un bateau venu de Baker Lake et parti aussitôt. Vais voir le Capitaine : identique à ce que l'on peut attendre d'un Capitaine de cargo stationnant depuis longtemps en rade : hirsute, mécontent, un livre à la main. Accepte de me prendre.
Parlé de nouveau avec P. Henry, lui demande de prier, à l'occasion pour moi.

and at times I was on the point of caving in, but somehow I was protected. You will come around to it, my dear professor. To prayer. I understand you better than you think."

He focuses his pale blue, innocent eyes on me. "There is active prayer, in which one dwells on the words, on their apparent or implicit meaning. There is the virtue of silence. And then there is the grace of spontaneous prayer, which comes from the heart. Bless you."[27]

TO CONVERT OR BE CONVERTED

12 August 1962. I have boarded an old cargo ship bound for Baker Lake (Qamanittuaq),[28] the westernmost post on Chesterfield Inlet. It is at the eastern edge of the great Keewatin desert, adjacent to the territory of the semi-nomadic Caribou Inuit, who are now undergoing a process of sedentarization. More than half of them have gathered here following the measles epidemics of 1956 and 1957 and the recurrent famines caused by the steady decline of the caribou herds since 1930.[29] The post dates back to 1913, and the population of the whole administrative district is 520. The Anglican and Catholic missions were founded here in 1928 and 1929, respectively.

A federal report from the summer of 1962 declared that "Keewatin ... has been aptly described as the Land of the Desperate People ... [it] cannot support its present population ... the demoralized state of many of the local people [at Baker Lake] plus the distress caused by caribou decline and fox cycles has made a high assistance bill to some extent unavoidable." The report stated that 35 per cent of the population lived in extreme poverty, while annual direct government relief amounted to $145, or the cost of keeping a local bureaucrat on staff for ten days. Its disabused conclusion was that "[unless] there is prompt action ... the increasing population will lead to an extremely depressed situation in which the Eskimos of Keewatin will exist in social and economic stagnation."[30]

The *Fort Severn* weighs anchor at three o'clock in the morning. I accompany the captain to the command post, which is equipped with radar, instantaneous readings, depth sounder, and gyroscope. Just behind us is the map room. The Inuit pilot sits impassive, his right elbow nonchalantly draped over the window sill, indicating the route to the sailor at the helm with weary gestures. His very presence, his aged face serve as a reminder that this has been Inuit land since time immemorial. The day dawns in a diaphanous mist. Purple sun rays shine on the stern, on the smooth surface of the water, and on the micas and jagged quartz seams of the red and gray granite cliffs. We sail up the inlet to the steady heaving of the engines, feeling their reverberation through the ribs of the ship. Having given the instructions, the captain returns to his cabin. No need for him to stay above decks, since he can detect every impulse in his sleep. Like a horseman travelling a familiar path, he is wedded to the regularity of his mount, her shudders, nervous respiration, momentum. When the ship approaches a narrows or a rocky sill, he gets up semiconscious, his eyes half-closed. Certain channels, he points out, are only passable at high tide, hence the early departure.

Another passenger awaits me on deck, amid the magnificent landscape of mountains and icy cliffs: Father Robert Haramburu, the Oblate provincial and Basque country native.

"I am familiar with your qualms about some of our missionaries," he says. "But don't forget that these men have given up their lives for the cause of evangelization. I must help them, and you should try to understand them."

I reply that the admittedly few conversations that I have had with certain Oblates have left an appalling impression of acrimony and narrow-mindedness. These men do not live up to the congregation's venerable reputation, its exceptional charitable efforts in Hudson Bay and the Mackenzie Delta over the past half-century. Showy religiosity and venomous backbiting do not do justice to the revolutionary message of the Sermon on the Mount. These people are starving for the sacred, and they expect a nobler discourse. Among Christ's last words were his vow to remain in mortal agony until the end of the world, and now that I have discovered the personality of some of "God's functionaries," I have new insight into the dramatic meaning of his words. To be sure, there have been giants among the Oblates, such as Fathers Petitot, Falaize, and Turquetil, and I am well aware that forty of them have died by freezing, drowning, violence, or other causes over the years.[31] But encounters with the new generation have given me cause to doubt a certain manifestation of the church. The narrow-minded fundamentalism of priests set up in a life as dogmatic, judgmental functionaries of God is truly hard to take.

"They may be few, but they most definitely exist," I continue. "And I have given long consideration to their proselytizing methods, this utterly inappropriate alternation between seduction and pressure. As well, the churches need to reexamine their complicity with conquering states. And finally, the animosity between Catholic and Anglican missionaries must be curtailed immediately.[32] The native people convert to the religion of the masters. Which sect is the right one? It's a matter of chronology; they line up behind the first to arrive. Yet the Inuits' strength is in their unity, and here they are divided into Catholics, Anglicans, Presbyterians, Episcopalians, Pentecostals, and Mormons,* a rosary of words that's just mumbo-jumbo to them. Now, after thirty

* See p. 116 for discussion of the consequences of the Catholic strictures concerning mixed marriages.

years of teaching, they have begun to assert themselves. How will matters stand twenty years from now once they've gone to university or our technical schools and can make their own judgments? Don't you fear a boomerang effect?"

To convert, one must first attempt to be converted, to comprehend the other. Knowing the language is not enough; it is necessary to respect the vertical religious vision of these Inuit groups at all costs. All the first peoples have a sense of the sacred and have reflected on death and the afterlife. There is no single truth, as the church teaches, but multiple truths. The Recollets of the seventeenth century, in their work with the Huron and the Micmac, understood this principle. They testified to Jesus but did not baptize. The history of humanity is a slow coming to awareness of the varieties of truth corresponding to the specific cultural histories of different peoples.

"The Church is not behind but ahead of us, still to be forged, and it will have to grow increasingly ecumenical if it values its continued existence. That is the message that the Inuit are looking for in the Oblates' discourse."

Father Haramburu is a friendly man with a keen, open, constructive mind. His smile of complicity encourages me to continue with my indictment.

"The missionaries should always keep in mind that the Inuit, too, have a long history. Before daring to convert these people in the literal sense, it would be wise for them to do the reverse: to be 'converted,' 'incultured' to the Inuit worldview, in order to gain a better understanding of their religion. There's nothing reprehensible about pagan philosophy. It is different but of equally sacred inspiration. And what matters is not the number of priests deployed but their example. To the average person – a Frenchman like me, a Canadian bureaucrat, an Inuk – the priest is the avatar of Jesus.* Yet for too long the seminaries have been schools of repression. Some of their pupils undoubtedly lack the necessary moral fibre, and the results are worrying. The clergy's example is perhaps the primary agent of de-Christianization."†

Having listened in silence, Father Haramburu responds: "You're right, there are no specialized anthropology courses in the seminary curricula, and undoubtedly some of the missionaries lack the necessary social science training. And it's not enough to be fluent in the native language. That all has to be profoundly changed," he says with a mischievous smile. "If I accepted this position as provincial, it is because I think that our order must reform

* The Franciscans, in their spirit of humility and original poverty, or the Quakers, with their rigour and generosity, might have been more open to the Inuit worldview.

† The crisis has only deepened. In 1991 in the Ungava Peninsula, I met an Oblate representing the Japanese company Yamaha. The Inuit expressed surprise at such obfuscation, and who could blame them?

and take up the challenges that the modern world poses to the church. I'll grant you that our seminaries have not always prepared our priests for today's world. The ones you met are country folk, and they've been straitjacketed by their compulsory reading of outdated books of piety."

At Baker Lake, I spend a week pursuing my comparative family-by-family survey. Oh, they are miserable, indeed; the federal report is accurate in its description of them as impoverished and humiliated at having to depend on relief. Yet I find, for example, a matchless artistic sense that is expressed in bone and soapstone carvings, drawings on fabric and paper. These are historically recent techniques. The Dorset artifacts typical of the period between 200 B.C. and A.D. 1200 were small objects made with rudimentary tools, in which the shamanistic dimension had an incomparable force. Since the spirit inhered in the matter, the form followed the hard core of the bone or stone, dialoguing with the dead – a dialogue that endures.

I speak with several former "full-time hunters" who are now artists. "All sculpture and painting has a meaning. We aren't motivated by aesthetic ideas; we don't know what the word 'art' means. We're only trying to put images to a story. We are narrators, people who converse with the Spirits." While listening to them, my mind remains occupied with recurring thoughts on the role of missionaries. In the Gambier Islands of Polynesia in 1903, Victor Segalen wrote in his diary: "Every serum is a globulicide for the red corpuscles of other species. Thus every civilization (and religion, a quintessential feature of civilization) is murderous to other races. The Semitic Iesu, as transformed by the Latins ... was fatal to the Maori Atua [spirits] and their adherents."[33]

The Oblate in charge at Baker Lake is visibly straight-laced. Instead of engaging him in dialogue, I spend an evening with Reverend James, the Anglican minister from London, discussing Biblical themes with a thoroughly British serenity; he reads me passages from Ezekiel. Borne on the words of the great prophet, I return home on a night illuminated by the moon and the aurora borealis, pursuing my conversation with myself. Have the Inuit truly accomplished a mental cleansing of their former religious beliefs? Is Mary Nirrivik? Satan, Krevitok? What does it mean to believe in a dual truth? The Inuit, as I have said, are hungry for the sacred. They do not especially care for uncertainty but detest dogma. Since their conversion, they have developed a deep attachment to the Jesus who made common cause with the poor and the humiliated, but not to the dogmatic quarrels of Christianity – transubstantiation, the Trinity, Mary's virginity. These are the concerns of white people, the people of the book and the word. For the Inuit, a people of extreme sensitivity, Christianity is an intense emotion and an encounter with the beyond, with the invisible dead. In their hearts they have not renounced the practices that long gave succour to their ancestors, the shamanism that is the ultimate expression of their cosmic-dramatic pantheism. My Inuit respondents, seemingly so traditionalist in their techniques, are inhabited by ontological angst in the face of death, which leads them to reflect on the meaning of life. I have a vivid memory of one Wednesday evening in a snow house when, after the weekly reading of scripture, a group of these new Christians engaged in a commentary on the Sermon on the Mount (*beati pauperes*). In short, the Inuit are building a neo-Christianity informed by shamanism: they are "Inuitizing" Jesus. It is a process similar to the one taking place among the Pueblo Indians of the United States and various Mexican indigenous groups. The new *mestizo* church is not behind but ahead of them. Future research should attempt to elucidate such interlacings of worldviews past and present as well as their effects on a person's entire existence, including their most intimate sexuality. Roger Bastide's work on Candomblé in Brazil is exemplary in this respect.[34]

In 1949 at Ilullissat I had sought further enlightenment on these matters in conversation with Assistant Bishop Mathias Storch. A full-fledged Greenlander and a man of elevated ideas, Storch gave me a glimpse of Luther's essential message: that Christians are justified by faith alone. *Sola gratia, sola fide*. The Calvinist can spend a whole life hopelessly looking for – in fact, calling forth – signs of divine election. The Calvinist, more than the Catholic, seeks signs that some member of the narrower community is among the elect. The Catholic, by virtue of sanctifying grace, is attached to the sacraments and hence the priests. Baptism is vital; by means of this lustral water, he becomes a son of God. But so are confession, whereby he reveals his sins and obtains forgiveness from God's representative; Communion, an act of intimate alliance for Christians, particularly for the Inuit, in which God's flesh is eaten and his blood drunk; and Extreme Unction, a viaticum for eternity. But does the concept of original sin have any meaning for pantheists nostalgic for a lost paradise? How have the Greenlanders reacted? The Canadian Inuit are too scarred by the violence of the preaching, the priests and ministers too vehement, the Lutherans, Calvinists, Anglicans, and Catholics too recently converted within the same parish for this issue to allow for dispassionate examination. Another researcher will have to take up where I leave off.

Before returning to Churchill, I bid goodbye to the provincial. "I have thought a great deal about our conversation," he says. "You are too harsh. The missionaries' lives are difficult, and it may happen that in their solitude their spirit becomes parched. Do not judge them. Let alone those who disagree with you and gravitate toward the others."

I respond that it is not my place to judge but that I do not want to be judged either. "Too often, the missionary journals such as *Eskimo* contain jaundiced comments about scientists and the government. A missionary journal is not a tribunal, much less a prosecutor's indictment of those who do not share his views. It should not take after the European church's reckless condemnation of any and all dissidents as heretical and pagan. Before the wars, in a Catholic or Calvinist parish of Quebec, the priest's authority was absolute, and parishioners made it their business to submit. Not anymore. I have seen letters of complaint written to the embassies of foreign researchers or the relevant Canadian government departments. Some of them concerned me. It is not very appropriate. What business is it of theirs? In church the priest is sovereign, granted. But outside of it, he is a citizen like any other and is expected to act with dignity and generosity. If they wish to help the Inuit in their crisis of confidence and identity, the missionaries should partake of the worker-priests' mystique of extreme tolerance and humility, not set themselves up *hic et nunc* as moralists on a mission to whip up the natural anguish of the 'heretical,' 'pagan' Inuit by threatening them with eternal damnation for their mortal sin. Please do not misunderstand: there is no unconditional anticlericalism in me. I greatly enjoyed the several days I spent in the company of Fathers Henry, Fournier, Fafard, and Didier, all of them saintly men."

I wish him good luck in his attempts to revitalize the Order. It is long past time; not much longer and the emperor will be naked. He has kindly allowed me to speak without interruption.

"What if I took you at your word and sent one of these priests to you for an education after your fashion?" he asks with another mischievous glint in his eye. I unhesitatingly agree to his proposal.[35]

I board a southbound RCMP seaplane, disappointed and weary of my short-term surveys. I cannot say that the trip has been a success; still, it has given me an opportunity to clarify my ideas about missionaries and their critical role in the disruption and overturning of traditional societies. Missionaries should be transparent about their plainly revolutionary goal of Christianizing societies with millenarian pantheistic cultures, for, in so doing, they risk laying waste to a heritage lying within each of us, one that we have denied or disowned.

SUMMING UP

Despite a few courageous reports, the federal government's policy for the Inuit of Rankin Inlet, that emblematic town of the future, lacked foresight. The putative (and utterly demagogic) justification for the de facto apartheid policy that I witnessed was "We shouldn't interfere with the Eskimos' customs if we have nothing better to offer." Meanwhile, the North was in the process of being conquered by Canadian and American industry. In fact, for many years the government department responsible for the North was prosaically called the Department of Mines, while in a subsequent incarnation,

"Northern Affairs" was augmented to include "National Resources." This department's purview was essentially the industrial development of the vast northern territories with which the nation's fate was bound up. As specific and complex as they are, Indian and Inuit affairs were of secondary importance, particularly in budgetary terms. There was no encouragement for the formation of political leaders, for the young elite that would eventually administer the Inuit municipalities and territories still to be conceived. The Canada of the 1960s lagged fifty years behind Greenland on Inuit policy.

The church, anxious to preserve its privileges in education and health care, remained prudent, silent. For the other government agencies concerned – and God knows they were numerous – "wait and see" was the order of the day. Let the two civilizations coexist, even though one was numerically weak, complex-ridden, bitter at being duped, and technologically backward, while the other was swaggering and all-powerful. The outcome was obvious: Canadianization, creeping assimilation by English-speaking Canada.

The leitmotiv of my interventions was that the Inuit should be empowered without delay, while their society was still intact. That was the time to identify leaders among them, to create an autonomous territory within the federal framework. Discussion between the federal government and the Inuit elites on the creation of an autonomous Inuit territory had to begin without delay. These common-sense ideas appeared utterly utopian and farfetched to the government officials with whom I interacted in 1963, although they ultimately proved prophetic when Nunavut and Nunavik were created. Autonomy as a political concept was seen as unrealistic – not revolutionary, merely irrelevant in view of the Inuit's level of intellectual and political development. A.B. Yates, director of the Northern Economic Development Branch under the Department of Indian Affairs and Northern Development (a man of high calibre in other respects) could not hide his irritation with such proposals, calling them unrealistic on camera in my film series *Inuit*.[36]

In short, the future would not be bright for the generation of Inuit that I watched coming up. The confrontation would be brutal, the outcome alcohol and drug abuse, violence, incest, battered women, and very high rates of youth suicide – a knockout punch thrown at a generation of exceptional men and women. The political roots of such social problems should have been addressed promptly back then, in the socio-political laboratory that was Rankin Inlet in the 1960s, where Inuits and whites lived and worked at close quarters.[37]

Back in Churchill with its white houses standing amid patches of grass, its solitary empty warehouses along the port, I meet Norman Ford, a mixed-blood who tells me of his life among the Padlermiut ("people of the willow"). I listen to him through the evening and into the night.

Arctic poppy, *Papaver radicatum.* Height: 10–35 cm. Yellow flower. Author's herbarium.

"Come with me, why don't you?" he says. "We can go trapping all winter long!"

The sky there is tinted with the colours of water. There is great poetry in their summer camps, their villages of snow houses set within vast expanses of white.

"I know you don't like the priests, at least some of them. I don't either. The Great Judges have divided us. But you know, my uncle taught me all about shamanism. I will initiate you. I've read a bit and I think I understand what you're looking for. We could take our snowshoes and sled and head right off to visit the Padlermiut at Arviat [Eskimo Point]. Come with me. Who knows? The beauty of the women (*attigi*) may captivate you. They will love you, the whole community will. You will become one of us."

My son is ten. I love my own family, and see them so rarely. For four years now I have been off on these expeditions every summer, all spring long, practically never at home. I hesitate, decline – and will never forgive myself for such a mistake! One should follow one's impulses,[38] or as the complex André Gide wrote in his mature years and was fond of repeating, one should "follow one's inclination, provided that it leads up hill."[39] I was wrong not to go with Norman; the trip beckoned invitingly, and there would not be another chance.

A stepladder stands before the door of the Churchill-Winnipeg train. A black steward helps me up, putting his hand under my forearm ... shades of the India Office. With a hesitant gesture, I wave goodbye to Norman, who watches with a sad, dignified expression as I erase him from my life.

5

The Spartans of Back River

April 1963 finds me making ready for departure on a dogsled expedition to Back River (Kûnajuk), the home of the Utkuhikhalingmiut (or Utku).[1] Starting point: Gjoa Haven (Uqsuqtuuq)[2] on King William Island, a town 150 kilometres to the north consisting of a few snow houses and three buildings: the trading post, the church, and the school. This is Qikiqtarmiut territory.[3]

I arrived yesterday from Cambridge Bay as the only passenger in a two-seater propeller plane. It took two attempts; on the first, the bush pilot was unable to make out Gjoa Haven in the blizzard, and we had to return to Cambridge Bay, while on the second, the weather had cleared sufficiently to reveal the HBC buildings, and we managed a landing on the pack ice. My three companions for this voyage were waiting for me: Koorsoot, a Netsilik hunter and guide; Tootalik (Christian-named Peter Adams), my Inuktitut interpreter;* and an RCMP constable assigned by Ottawa to assist me. We have spent only

* Netsilingmiok (b. 1924), married, three children, sons Ohoodlik David and Munga Raph (b. 1951 and 1953), daughter Ananok Mary (b. 1958). His wife, Angnasha, and his children

one night in the town, just long enough for me to assemble my gear before departure.

Now en route, our sled dogs pant as they plough their way over the bumpy pack ice. A snowstorm has blown up hours before our departure from the small post, situated at the place where Roald Amundsen wintered on board the *Gjøa* during the first complete ship traverse of the Northwest Passage (1903–05). His astute innovation was to use a small ship to navigate the narrow, shallow Simpson Strait and Storis Passage (as little as twelve metres deep and less than a kilometre wide), the final link in the legendary route to the Pacific Ocean.[4]

For the Inuit of Gjoa Haven, the Norwegians are now but a dim memory; tall, bearded, but otherwise formless men.[5] A few foreigners live on in the naturalized versions of their names: "Amuya" (Amundsen), "Maiki" (de Poncins), "Gobsi" (Gibson, the manager of the Gjoa Haven trading post during de Poncins's visit in 1938), "Kayonaluk" (Father Pierre Henry). Hygiene appears to have made some timid progress here since Amundsen's time, although they still blow their noses into their fingers, and flu sufferers, both children and adults, casually swallow their snot. Amundsen recounted that in 1904 "an Eskimo named Akla had come to see us with a child [on board the *Gjøa*]. The boy had a bad cold and was coughing and spitting without respite. At first I said nothing, but finally, nauseated by this filthy display, I sharply commanded Akla to obey the rules. Frightened by my severe countenance, the Eskimo precipitately knelt, scooped the sputum off the floor with his hand, and swallowed it!!!"[6]

The first encounter with the Norwegians in 1904 was friendly:

> When within about 200 yards distance the Eskimo halted ... But suddenly they deployed in skirmishing order and advanced ... Suddenly, there flashed through my mind ... the word "Teima!" and "Teima" I shout with all the power of my lusty lungs. The Eskimo stop short ... Then I hear the call: "Manik-tu-mi!" ... In a moment we fling away our rifles and hasten towards our friends, and with the universal shout of "Manik-tu-mi!" ... we embrace and pat each other, and it would be hard to say on which side the joy is greater ... At noon [near King William Island] we hit upon a little Eskimo camp of six huts [Ichyuachtorvik] ... These Eskimo were on an average taller than the Nechilli, and stood about six feet high.[7]

In 1939, twenty years before my trip, the French traveller Gontran de Poncins described the Netsilingmiut of Gjoa Haven as living in a state of abject

are Catholic; he is Anglican. I mention this detail for its rarity and the fact that it concerns a representative of the authorities. The union was only allowed when the wife swore that she would raise the children in the Catholic religion, as its rules require.

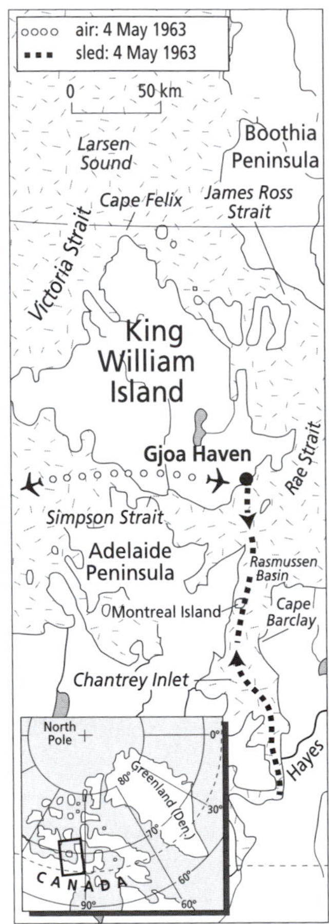

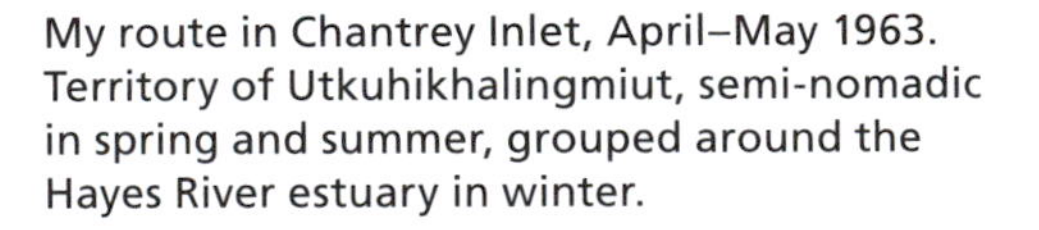

My route in Chantrey Inlet, April–May 1963. Territory of Utkuhikhalingmiut, semi-nomadic in spring and summer, grouped around the Hayes River estuary in winter.

poverty: "These Netsilik are now the most abjectly poor people in the world. Yet they stay, they do not think of migrating to better hunting grounds. King William is their land ... You have seen nothing at all until you have seen this Shongili, in the igloo, scrape with a knife between his toes, lick the blade, and look up at you with a great coarse laugh."[8]

April 17. The frigid north wind blows at our backs as the blizzard builds in intensity throughout the day. To the west, I spot the long, low, sandy peninsula of Ogle Point (Siorartôq, 68°16'N, 96°15'W), the furthermost point reached by George Back (1796–1878) on his remarkable overland voyage to the mouth of the Great Fish River (renamed Back River by the Europeans) in 1834. Dease

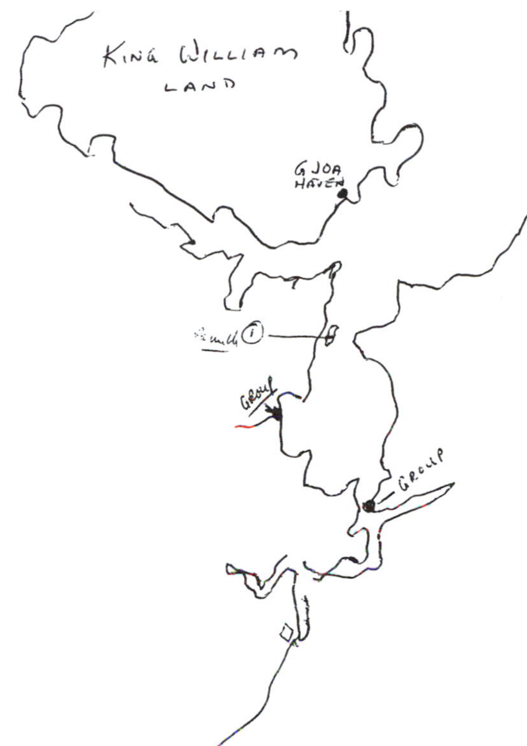

Map of Utku territory, Chantrey Inlet, December 1962. Seven families divided into two groups, plus one isolated family on Montreal Island. Sketch by the RCMP constable.

and Simpson passed this point on their westward journey along the Arctic coast.* In the evening, reaching the mouth of Chantrey Inlet ("Utkuhikjalik Fjord," 150 kilometres long and 25 kilometres wide at this point), we etch a circle in the compact snow with a large knife and hastily build an igloo. The job is done in half an hour. It is –35°C and all four of us pitch in, chopping blocks and carrying them to the "architect" at the centre of the circle. Later, we sit on the six-square-metre platform inside and eat our meal of frozen caribou and speckled char, chewing in silence. The Inuit and I spit out the bones and push them into a corner with our feet; the constable has better manners. The abrupt transition to the cold air has hit me like a sledgehammer since my arrival: I am exhausted. Half-dozing, I check my gear. The key to surviving

* They turned back at the estuary of the Castor and Pollux River south of Shepherd Bay, the starting point of my canoe trip to Spence Bay in August 1961; see pp. 61–8.

the cold, the unforeseen, and the snow (indeed, the Inuit have made these forces their allies) is to stay warm in sturdy, loose-fitting clothing, eat high-energy foods (5,000 calories daily), and keep to a slow, measured pace. What may look to us like impulsive decisions in this climate are actually the fruit of considered reflection. Willpower – even heroism – are insufficient to withstand nature's sovereign rule for any length of time. Amateurism and misdirected effort can be suicidal, and agitation inexorably leads to tragedy.

During the night, the blizzard drives snow through the interstices in the wall blocks, covering our hair and faces. With more time the blocks would be welded together by freezing. Tootalik goes out to fill the spaces one by one. With the frost on our eyebrows and lashes, we look twenty years older.

The indispensable *tiluktût*, a caribou-antler snow brush, is passed from hand to hand, and everyone removes the snow from their clothing. If allowed to stay damp from snow melting in the relative heat of the igloo, our clothes would instantly freeze upon exposure to the outside air and become our shrouds. The north wind howls incessantly, plaintively. The air is very cold, even though "heated" by the humidity that it takes on over the fissured pack ice of the James Ross and Rae Straits (see maps, pp. 5, 186). We observe the Inuit watchword – wait – hunkering down in our bags and sleeping until noon. Thursday, 18 April: still waiting, sunrise to sunset.

Trek to the Utkuhikhalingmiut winter camp. Plan of snow house that I occupied on 17 April 1963 south of Ogle Point, a prolonged bivouac made necessary by a blizzard. L. to R., my baggage, Tootalik, the RCMP constable, myself, and Koorssut. Other bags are outside under a tarp consisting of a piece of fabric draped over the dome. To the left of the entrance are the frozen fish, seal, and bear meat; two urinal buckets at right. The dogs are tied up in a line a dozen metres from the house.

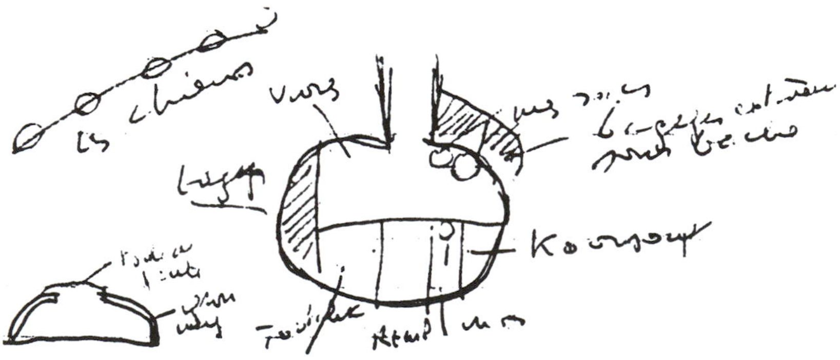

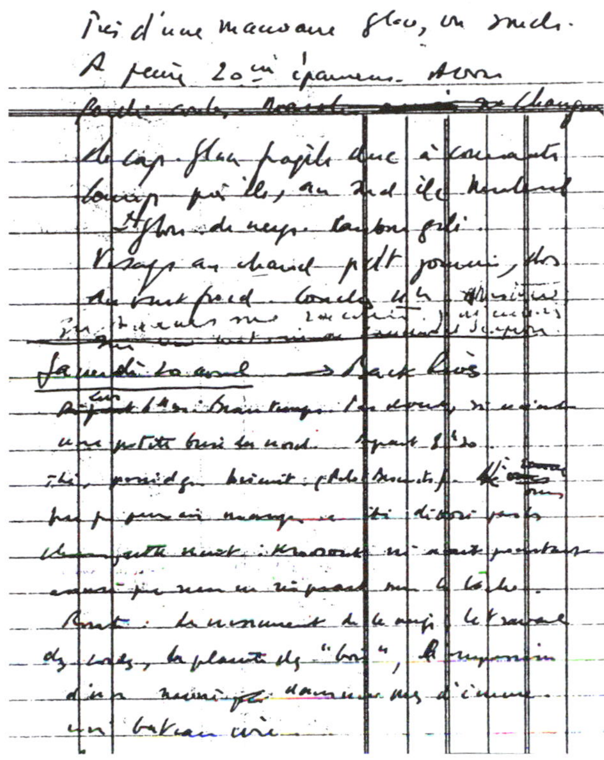

Toward the Utku winter camp; page from my expedition diary for 19–20 April 1963: We probed an area of thin ice. At most 20 cm thick. Nearly fell through, changed course. Ice fragile due to currents. Camp near islands south of Montreal Island. Snow house. Frozen caribou. Face warm today, back to cold wind. To bed at 11. Story told me by Adams [Tootalik]. Fell asleep to a story of [illegible]. Saturday, April 20. Toward Back River. Up at 6 [A.M.]. Good weather. No wind except for a slight breeze from the north. Departure at 8:30. Tea, porridge, pilot biscuits [hardtack]. Bear meat I had planned to eat devoured by dogs last night, yet Koorsoot had assured me it would be perfectly safe under the tarp. On the way: crunch of snow underfoot. Ropes straining, "wood" complaining, sensation of ship on choppy sea. A drunken boat.

I am an early riser, and I quickly tire of this lethargic state. Noticing me sitting up in my bag, Koorsoot turns to me with a mischievous, self-assured expression. His is a stern face, with the mouth bracketed by furrows of bitterness, the soft lower lip never participating in a smile, the nose abnormally stout, the pupils yellowed, the corneas bloodshot.[9] His stare is more attentive than intrusive but can become implacable at times. After examining me for several seconds in a silent, atypical pose, hands clasped under chin, he tells me without preface that he has four names: Koorsoot, Krolitalik, Nivanguak, and Kretluk, given respectively by his father, maternal grandfather, maternal aunt, and a sick neighbour hoping to be cured through association with a healthy namesake.

The Inuit detest boredom. Tentatively, he sounds me out: "Kina ivdlit?" (Who are you?) I play along and, opening my notebook, respond with a question of my own: "Know any games?" The whites are so strange; who would think of games at a time like this? But Koorsoot is a willing confederate, and he takes up my suggestion, mentioning several that he has played or heard of.

Among the Qikiqtarmiut, the most popular indoor games are *ayagaaq*, a cup-and-ball game with sexual connotations, where the object is to toss a humerus bone in the air and catch it by inserting the point of a stick into the larger of two holes (symbolism of vagina and anus);[10] *inughat*, seal bones of various shapes used in geomancy; *ajarautit*, a string game played and enjoyed by people of all ages; *nuglutkaq*, a game of great skill that involves throwing darts into holes drilled in a bone; and *taptaujarnik*, blind man's buff. Also of note are games of skill or balance, games that get the blood flowing, such as *nalukatuq*, in which a walrus skin is used as a trampoline; *idehortaqtut*, a dance in which the dancer undresses and dresses while crouching; *ablaqetertut*, separating the legs and bringing them together in a single jump; and *akracheak*, kicking a suspended ball with both feet. And then there are games of strength:* *paajarnik*, wrestling; *adgamitut*, two-person tug-of-war with one finger; *taliriunnik*, pushing or pulling with arms folded; *aksaraq*, seated, two-person tug-of-war; *tunumiu/dunnumik*, back-to-back pushing; *niaquriunniq*, adversaries try to pull each other forward while kneeling face to face, heads butted together. Summer games include *aqsarniq*, sealskin ball;[11] *qimuksiraujarnik*, in which a sled is pulled by another person or a dog; *arrangminin*, walking on hands; *pangakkartaq*, four-legged race; *kaliviktaq*, rope; *amaruujarniq*, a game of tag in which, if you are "it," you are a wolf in the night; *ujauktarniq*, rotating one's body around a sealskin cable without letting the cable touch the chest; *qaniriunniq*, a standing two-person tug-of-war in which the adversaries pull with a finger inserted into each others' mouths.

"Purposeless acts," to quote Jean Duvignaud, are not a game; they "wrap us in a narrative without which history would be nothing more than a puppet show."[12] Later, no doubt, in the course of an interview, I will grasp the explanatory importance of each of these games. They have obvious elements of attack and strategy, as may be expected in a hunting people embedded in a culture of violence. But they also serve two additional functions: building skills through play and emulation, and keeping the players warm.

My two other companions continue to sleep, their heads poking out from under the covers (a sleeping bag covered with a caribou skin), Tootalik snor-

* In physical combat, the adversaries stand face to face and punch each other alternately, always hitting the same part of the body (e.g., temple or shoulder) until one of them falls. In some cases the fighting is limited to verbal assaults before a referee group; the winner is the person who provokes laughter at the other's expense. In these small, fragile groups of the Canadian Central Arctic, every effort is made to avoid combat or to play down one's victory if it occurs; each man is vital to the group.

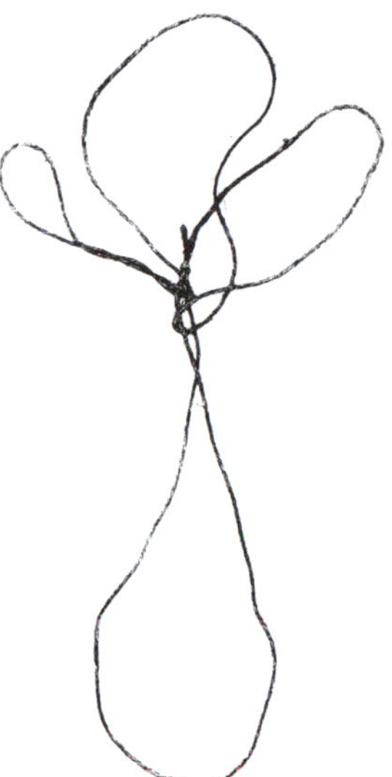

Ajarautit, string game. This configuration, with its three loops, represents a traditional tent. Siorapaluk, January 1951.

ing lightly. Koorsoot explains some of the taboos current in Gjoa Haven. If an adult is sick, a healer (*angekkok*) may give him the name of a healthy child, and sometimes he will recover. Concerning burial, the corpse must be removed from the house through a hole cut specially for the purpose. The pallbearers, usually kin, must wear gloves. The body is laid out east to west and symbolically surrounded with stones. It is dressed in new clothes and wrapped in a caribou skin, the seams facing outward, the fur inward. The face is covered with a thin skin in which a hole is cut for the mouth (the corpse must breathe) and sometimes for the eyes. The deceased is given the tools of his or her activity: harpoon and knife (*savik*), if male; crescent-shaped iron knife (*ulu*), needle and thread, if female. He or she must be visited and spoken to placatingly for one to three years so as to dissuade the deceased from casting an evil spell.

A snort or two from my companions. Cramped quarters. We get up one at a time so as not to stumble over each other. Tootalik melts snow for water, and we take our tea and frozen char in silence, waiting ... In the Arctic one must master the art of tactical delay. Nature gives the orders. When the wind dies down in late afternoon, I go out and make a quick topographic sketch. To the west is the Adelaide Peninsula, the territory of the Ilivilermiut, a group whose numbers are declining after having suffered massacres at the hands of the more bellicose Netsilingmiut. Ogle Point is still visible, and I sketch Pech-

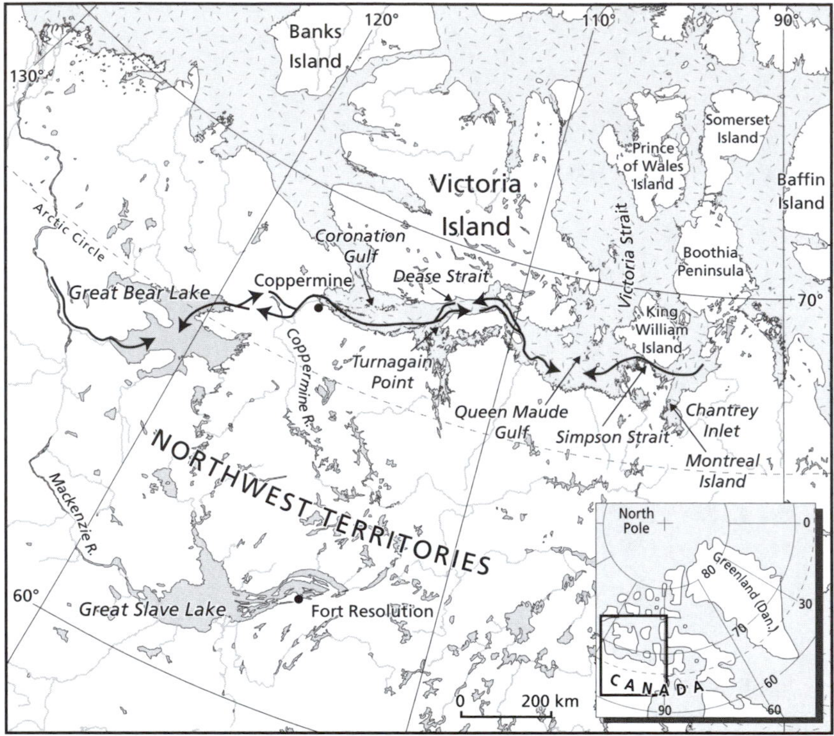

Dease and Simpson's spectacular voyage of 1837–39, when they mapped the coast from Point Barrow to Chantrey Inlet. (Ice conditions on 20 August.)

ell Point with its four islets. We are twenty kilometres southeast of the well-named "Starvation Cove" at the northeastern tip of the peninsula, the end of the line (along with nearby Montreal Island) for the last half-dozen survivors of Sir John Franklin's mid-nineteenth-century expedition (see maps, pp. 193, 199).

FRANKLIN: POLAR EXPLORATION'S GREATEST TRAGEDY

While advancing across the smooth ice, my thoughts are drawn over and over to this, the greatest tragedy in the history of polar exploration.[13] All that is known for certain was gleaned from the contents of a message written in haste by one of the officers and left under a cairn on 25 April 1848. The crew had just abandoned the majestic three-masters *Erebus* and *Terror* (respectively 370 and 340 tons) in the Victoria Strait, where they had sat icebound

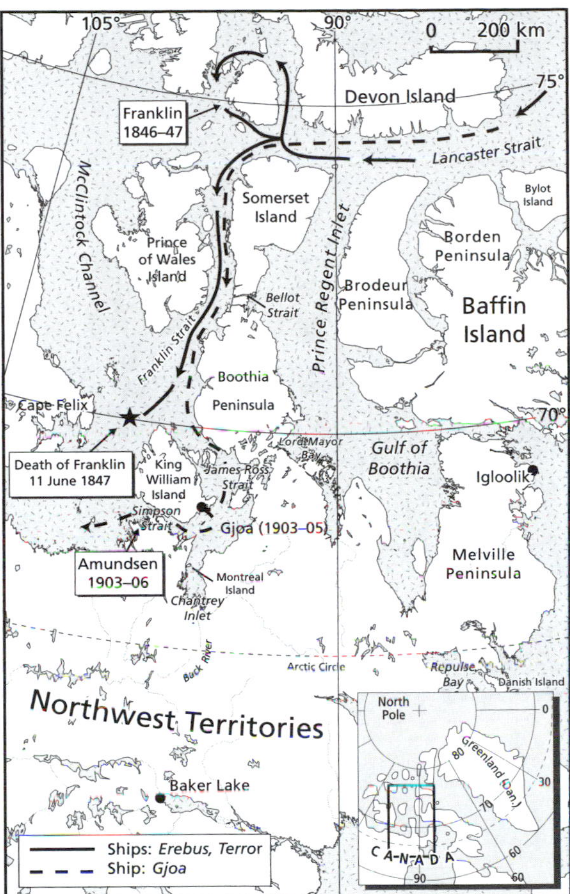

Routes of Franklin (1845–47) and Amundsen (1903–06). (Ice conditions on 15 August.)

for nineteen months. This is much wider than the James Ross and Rae Straits and lacks the violent currents and countercurrents that keep the latter open.[14] The note stated that Franklin had died 11 June 1847 at the age of sixty-one and that nine officers and fifteen sailors had also died, representing an abnormally high mortality rate for a polar expedition. The 105 survivors, led by Captains James Fitzjames and Francis Crozier (the latter a charismatic veteran of Arctic exploration who had previously wintered at Igloolik with Lieutenant William Parry) struck out for the Back River estuary, where George Back had found fish to be abundant in 1834. They left in a hurry, apparently suffering the effects of lead poisoning from tinned food. It must be remembered,

Lyon's sled expedition (1822) during a blizzard. The sleds were dragged by sailors teamed together as dogs, as was the British method.

however, that these volunteer officers and sailors were exceptional, the elite of the Navy. The ship carpenters built an oak sled and a whaleboat twenty-eight feet long and seven feet, three inches wide. On his May 1859 search expedition to the west coast of King William Island, at the site later known as Cape Crozier, Francis Leopold McClintock found the sled with the boat lashed to it as well as some four to six human skeletons. He estimated the total weight of the sled and boat at 700 kilograms. The extra weight (six small books,[15] silverware for the officers, crockery for the crew, etc.) gave him the impression of a group in distress, overwhelmed by the situation: "a mere accumulation of dead weight, but slightly useful, and very likely to break down the strength of the sled-crews."[16] Yet all they had to travel were 350 kilometres over smooth ice floes harbouring a large seal population, and they were armed with plenty of ammunition. It became a voyage of bitter suffering, and no one made it to Back River.

What can explain such a disaster other than the proposition that these naval men must have been out of their element once they left the ship? They were admirable men, but the sled was too heavy, burdened with useless items and tins of poisoned food.* Although excellent, brave, athletic sailors, their sedentary winter had rendered them ill-prepared for such an ordeal, their clothing was singularly unsuited to the conditions, and they proved to be poor walkers. (Captain Ross, by contrast, had required his crew to walk several miles a day back and forth over the silted deck of the *Victory*.) McClintock, judging from the orientation of the boat that he had found, surmised that a group of Franklin's crew members, in a fit of pure, desperate common sense, may have doubled back toward the two abandoned ships. According to Inuit witnesses who looked on powerless, some of the men turned to cannibalism. It seems significant that Franklin's officers never, although famished and decimated by scurvy, considered turning to the hunters of Boothia and King William Island for help. Such fraternal cooperation had been readily accepted by John and James Ross seventeen years earlier.

Crozier, the expedition's second in command, had apparently had considerable reservations about the organization of the voyage from the outset. Various hearsay accounts – they are fragmentary, contradictory, open to interpretation – suggest that he and a small band survived for months or years, perhaps accompanied by some Inuits. It is surprising that none of the many contemporaneous search expeditions conducted any methodical surveys among the Inuit; any information collected from them was noted casually and with much incredulity.

One document that has not been given all the scrutiny that it deserves is Charles Francis Hall's fascinating report of his second expedition of 1864–69, which I examined at the Smithsonian Archives in Washington.[17] On his first and second solo expeditions, this remarkable explorer lived and travelled with the Inuit, and on the second, he reached Shepherd Bay, the starting point for my July 1961 canoe trip to Spence Bay with two Netsilingmiut (see ch. 3). From here, he proceeded to the southern end of King William Island in May 1869, convinced that some of Franklin's men were still living there. Four Inuit families, he grumbled, had apparently seen Crozier and could have saved his life if they had been so inclined. Hall is one of the great neglected figures of Arctic history, and he is frequently in my thoughts.† Here is Hall, the warm, voluble outdoorsman:

* It is a tradition in the British Navy to consider Inuit food unworthy of an Englishman. William Parry reported that some of the men on his 1821–23 expedition to Igloolik had been revolted by the odour of raw blubber, although he was not.

† There are others; the intense public focus on a few names has obscured remarkable explorers such as USArmy 1st Lt. Frederick Schwatka, Richard King (see below), and the exceptional Scotsman Dr John Rae (see p. 64).

When Too-shoo-ar-thar-i-u first saw Crozier and the men with him, he was moving, having a loaded sled drawn by dogs; he was going from place to place, making Igloos on the ice – sealing – he had with him his wife, whose name is E-laing-nur, and children. Crozier and his men had guns and plenty of powder, shot and ball. The cousin took Crozier and his men along with him, and fed them and took good care of them all winter ... Crozier was called Ag-loo-ka by the Innuits. Crozier's name was given to old Ook-bar-loo's sister's son, whose name was Ag-loo-ka ...

Crozier was the only man that would not eat any of the meat of the Koblunas as the others all did ... Crozier, though nearly starved and very thin, would not eat a bit of the Koblunas, – he waited till an Innuit who was with him and the three men caught a seal, and then Crozier only ate one mouthful ...

Crozier with his two men ... started ... traveling to the southward ...

[H]e (Ag-loo-ka) knew all about how to hunt and kill took-too (rein deer) and nearly everything else that the Innuits could kill; knew how to keep himself warm, how to live, just as the Innuits do ... Ag-loo-ka knew all about everything that the Innuits knew.[18]

It would appear that these reports have not been mined for all their potential conclusions. Hall was an American outsider, not a member of what may be called the establishment, and at that time London's relations with Washington were not as fraternal as one might suppose. Similarly, a keen-eyed visionary such as English naturalist and surgeon Richard King, Back's second-in-command on the 1834 expedition (see map, p. 198), was scarcely paid any attention by the Admiralty in subsequent years. King's acerbic criticism of its cumbersome, costly expeditions grew out of his disbelief in the value of maritime Arctic expeditions generally. He had become convinced – and history has borne him out – that the only sensible approach to completing the Northwest Passage was to explore the coast by canoe from Back River through the Chantrey Inlet area and eastward to the Melville Peninsula, working up the Boothia Peninsula as necessary to locate the first open channel. King's close relations with the Indians and Inuit, whom he admired, led him to engage in a continual tirade against their exploitative treatment at the hands of the Hudson's Bay Company. His books, letters, and pamphlets were ignored.*

Then there is the Polish American Frederick Schwatka (1849–92), another neglected Franklin searcher. Accompanied by William Gilder as second-in-command, Heinrich Klutschak (a civil engineer), Frank Melms (an experienced whaleman), Joseph Ebierbing ("Esquimau Joe," a member of Hall's

* A nod in passing to King Island as it comes into view southeast of Montreal Island and north-northwest of Cape Barclay. Its naming in honour of Richard King by the Canadian authorities proves that history sometimes gives the deserving their due; see map, p. 203.

earlier expeditions), and twelve Inuit men, women, and children, plus three sleds and forty-two dogs, he showed in 1879–80 that it was possible, in the same "desert" where Franklin's 129 men died of starvation and exhaustion, to survive on what they could shoot and by engaging in fraternal cooperation with the Inuit.

The expedition began in 1878 when they sailed to Chesterfield Inlet and wintered over. The following spring on 1 April, they departed Camp Daly, adjacent to Depot Island on the north side of the inlet, carrying 5,000 pounds of weapons, ammunition, provisions (one month's worth), and gifts on three sleds. Reaching the Back River area on 15 May, Schwatka met a group of Utkuhikhalingmiut (his transliteration was "Ooquee-sik-sillik"), who were then in the process of being squeezed off their land by the more warlike Netsilingmiut. An elder in the group had met George Back and, years later, gone on board Franklin's deserted ship.

Then, on 1 June on the Adelaide Peninsula, Schwatka encountered a group of Netsilik who had more precise information about Franklin's expedition. A fifty-five-year-old woman named Ahlangyah remembered that a group of ten Kablunaks had been seen many years ago dragging a boat lashed to a sled. She even remembered a name, "Doktook" (Doctor). It became apparent that four members of the expedition might have survived until 1849 and that one of the last survivors died inland on the peninsula, ten kilometres from Richardson Point (i.e., only one or two days from Back River).

At Schwatka's return on 4 March 1880, 334 days later, he and his companions had travelled 5,230 kilometres before reaching their farthest point, Cape Felix at the northern tip of King William Island. They had killed 522 caribou as well as bear, seal, and musk oxen. Of all the Franklin search expeditions, none collected as many accounts and relics. Schwatka brought back the bones of four to six crew members, one of the sleds, and the stem of the boat found previously at Erebus Bay by McClintock. His findings made it possible to follow the survivors' ordeal to the vicinity of Montreal Island – presently we skirt it to the east – where as many as twenty-nine of them died. They also force us to return to the nagging question, even today unanswered: did four crew members survive until 1849?[19]

What McClintock, Schwatka, and Ross accomplished should have been possible for Franklin and his men. Why did they fail? Despair has unpredictable effects. Its causes, as I mentioned, were poisoned tinned goods,[20] failure to seek cooperation with the local people, insufficient use of seal, walrus, musk ox, and fish as food sources, and appalling dietary and food preservation habits. Any birds that the sailors caught, for example, were immediately salted down, giving this fresh food a familiar taste but destroying its vitamins. The despair ensuing from their grave lack of organization was comparable to

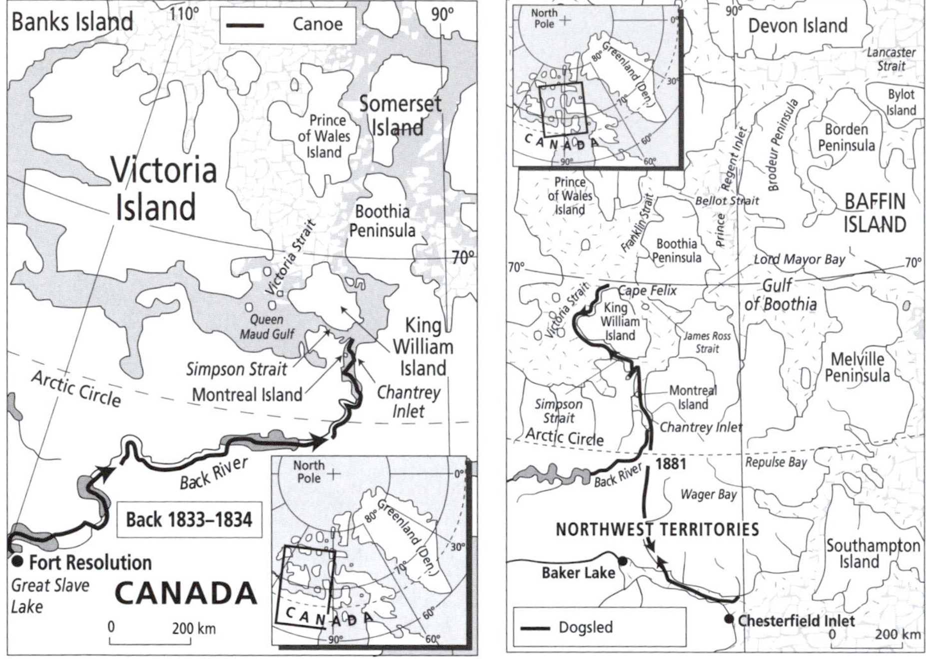

left: Back's expedition of 1833–34. (Ice conditions on 20 August.)

right: Schwatka's expedition of 1878–80, which covered 4,539 kilometres. (Ice conditions on 15 March.)

that which gripped the expedition led by US lieutenant Adolphus Washington Greely, nineteen of whose men died of starvation in the winter of 1884 at Cape Sabine on Ellesmere Island, only fifty kilometres from the busy North Greenland Inuit village of Etah. Yet in June 1951, carrying no European provisions other than tea and coffee and living exclusively by hunting, I was able to verify the exceptional abundance of seals in that area.[21] If further proof is needed that extreme weakness and despair were the cause of this great, moving tragedy, the modest group of Inuit whom I have now joined easily covers the 300-plus kilometres down the pack ice of Chantrey Inlet to the Back River estuary. The ice is broad and smooth all the way from Gjoa Haven; we encounter no hummocks or crevasses. We are using a primitive conveyance (peat-runner sleds)[22] and eating mainly frozen meat and fish. McClintock accomplished the same feat in 1858–59.[23]

A "HOT" DAY AHEAD

The lull has been brief. The violence of the coming storm is augured by snowflakes flying past as if terror-stricken, streaking the pack ice as they land. We decide to stay at the bivouac on 18 and 19 April. Perseverance and prudence: two Arctic virtues.[24] In the evening I go looking for the bear haunch that I bought in Gjoa Haven, but unfortunately, it has been inadequately stowed on Koorsoot's sled, and the dogs have eaten it. If I were not possessed of a cheerful disposition, I might very well hold it against him.

At dawn on 19 April the sun finally shines. Koorsoot ventures a glance out of the exit hole at the base of the snow house: "Looks like a hot day!" We emerge. The sky is a pale, mist-enshrouded blue. In the aqueous light, the air seems suffused with a palpable humidity. The day breaks slowly in superimposed bands, a series of dissolves. A thin streak of yellow and red arches over Cape Barclay far away to the east. Ensconced in the snow, the twenty-eight dogs arch their scrawny backs spasmodically, sensing our readiness. Clumps of icy snow stick to their fur and down. Like their owners, whose moods they mimic, the dogs will be glad to get moving again. The Inuit pay them no atten-

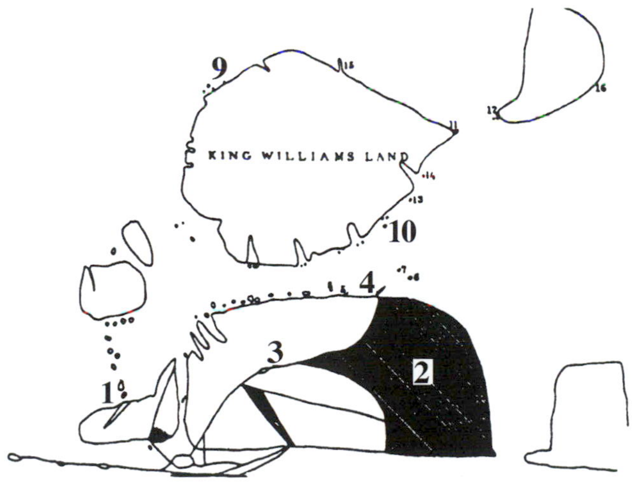

Map of King William Island and Adelaide Peninsula as seen from Chantrey Inlet, made by In-nook-poo-zhe-jook in 1869. (1) Kee Wee Woo, alleged site of the sinking of one of Franklin's ships. (2) Oogloolik. (3) Great Fish River (Back River). (4) See-er-ark-tu. (9) Too-Noo-Nee, coastal area where the sketch's author found one of the two lifeboats dragged by the survivors. (10) Kee-û-na (Todd Island), where he found five skeletons.

tion. We clear out the house, load the sleds, and harness the dogs, each man doing his part in silence. The nomad's routine. Koorsoot punches in the peak of the house with his fist: evil spirits must not be allowed to occupy it.

Our progress is unimpeded except for a small barrier of hummocks that force us to look for a negotiable route. To vary the conversation, I move from one sled to the other, from Tootalik to Koorsoot, when they draw up alongside each other.

Late in the day we set up our second bivouac south of Montreal Island, thus named by Back on 2 August 1834 while en route to Ogle Point. That year, Back (a member of Franklin's first expedition) descended the river that now bears his name accompanied by twenty men, travelling 700 kilometres from Great Slave Lake on a boat weighing 1,500 kilograms empty. By the time they reached this point, they had negotiated eighty-three rapids, in one instance portaging the boat a hundred kilometres over boulder-strewn tundra. These were men of incredible daring and indomitable courage.[25]

> I had for some time cherished the notion of dividing the party, leaving four to protect the boat and property, whilst the remainder, with Mr. King, would have accompanied me on a land journey towards Point Turnagain; but this scheme was completely frustrated by the impracticability of carrying any weight on a soil in which at every step we sunk half-leg deep; destitute of shrubs or moss for fuel, and almost without water; over which we must have travelled for days to have made even a few miles of longitude; and where, finally, if sickness had overtaken any one, his fate would have been inevitable. Thus circumstanced, therefore, and reflecting on the long and dangerous stream ... that we had to retrace, the hazards of the falls and rapids ... I felt that I had no choice, and, assembling the men, I informed them that the period fixed by his Majesty's Government for my return had arrived; and that it now only remained to unfurl the British flag, and salute it with three cheers in honour of His Most Gracious Majesty, whilst his royal name should be given to this portion of America.[26]

Montreal Island is snow-covered when we pass, and I regret not being able to stop there, for its history is one of poignant tension. An Ugjulik met by Schwatka on his 1879 journey claimed to have found a cairn from Franklin's expedition there. Schwatka's attempts to follow up on this valuable information bore no fruit. Earlier, on 17 May 1859, McClintock had killed a hare and a pair of ptarmigan on the island. No animals are visible today as we pass. My itinerary is tight and I have no time to stop.

To meet the Utkuhikhalingmiut – that is my objective. I try to imagine this isolated population, its taboos, its rules. The harshness of their lives, as described in the RCMP reports, evokes an image of a people at the end of a world that has not been explored since Back's 1834 expedition. But are they

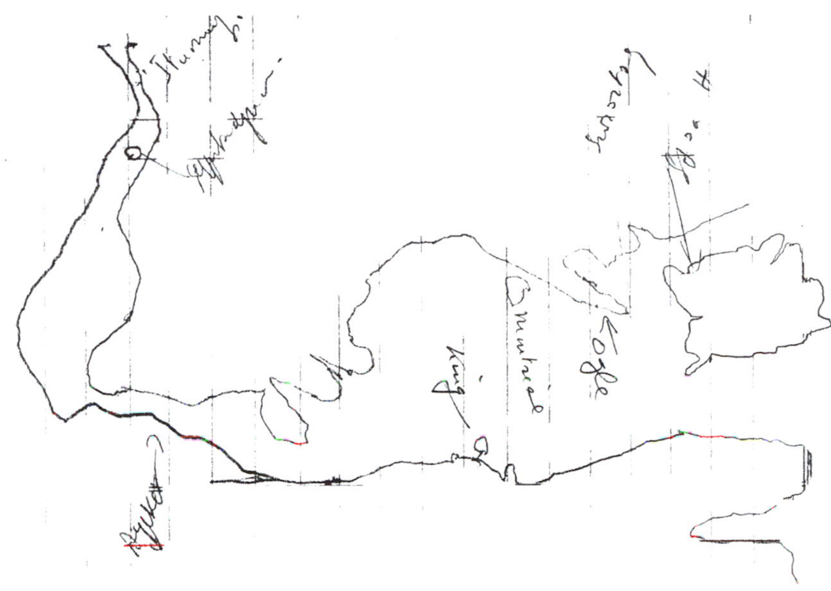

Map of Chantrey Inlet sketched for me in April 1963 by Nanordloo, a hunter (b. 1923). Clearly visible on this sketch (oriented east to west) are the Back River estuary and the rapids at the outlet of Lake Franklin, the site of the Utku's usual summer and winter camp. At the mouth of the Mistake River in the estuary, oriented north-south, an island representing another of their winter camps can vaguely be discerned. Finally, Montreal Island (drawn rather small) and little King Island are drawn east to west. Also visible is Ogle Point to the north of Montreal Island. At the far north is Victoria Island (not drawn to scale but properly oriented), with the Gjoa Haven post.

really so isolated? As I shall soon discover, this tribe is exogamous, exchanging women with groups on the Boothia Peninsula; they are not as separate from the other Inuit as might have been supposed. Moreover, the people living on Franklin Lake were observed in possession of objects from Franklin's expedition as early as July 1855, when James Anderson and James Stewart paddled down the Back River in search of the lost mariners. Dease and Simpson (1839) had came close to encountering them, and Schwatka (1879) actually did, but none of the elderly people interviewed by Rasmussen in June 1923 claimed to have ever met any whites. Oral accounts and their shadows.

20 April, 6:30 A.M. Good weather, a fine mist to the north. Breakfast is a big cup of tea, a hearty bowl of porridge (which the two Inuit refuse), and frozen

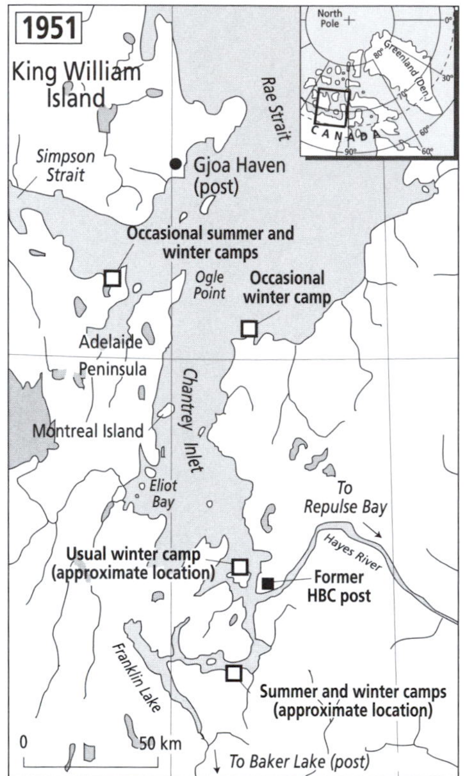

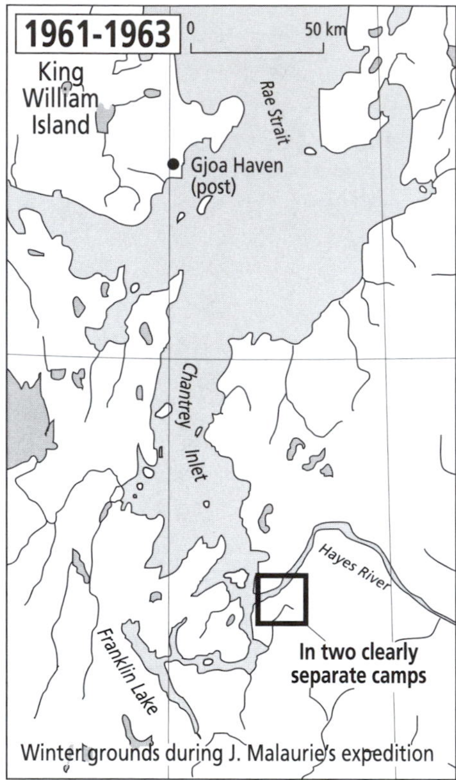

Utku territory, 1951 and 1961–63.

seal ribs eaten convivially from the tip of a knife. We tear off the last reddish-black shreds of meat with our teeth.

What with the crunch of snow under the peat runners and the creaking of the sled during rough passages, it feels as if we are on a ship sailing a choppy sea. Against a backdrop of off-white drizzle lit by the albedo of the snow, the ice is spangled with translucent green patches of water. The sides of the peat runners are protected from the sun by cakes of snow that the Inuk repairs frequently, every hour now, every half-hour as the day goes on. Yet the sun itself remains invisible, masked by the gauzy, frozen air. Not a bird in sight. We advance at four kilometres per hour, keeping our distance from the snow-bound west shore of Chantrey Inlet. The low plateau of the Adelaide Peninsula peering above it is distinguishable by its different hues. After crossing

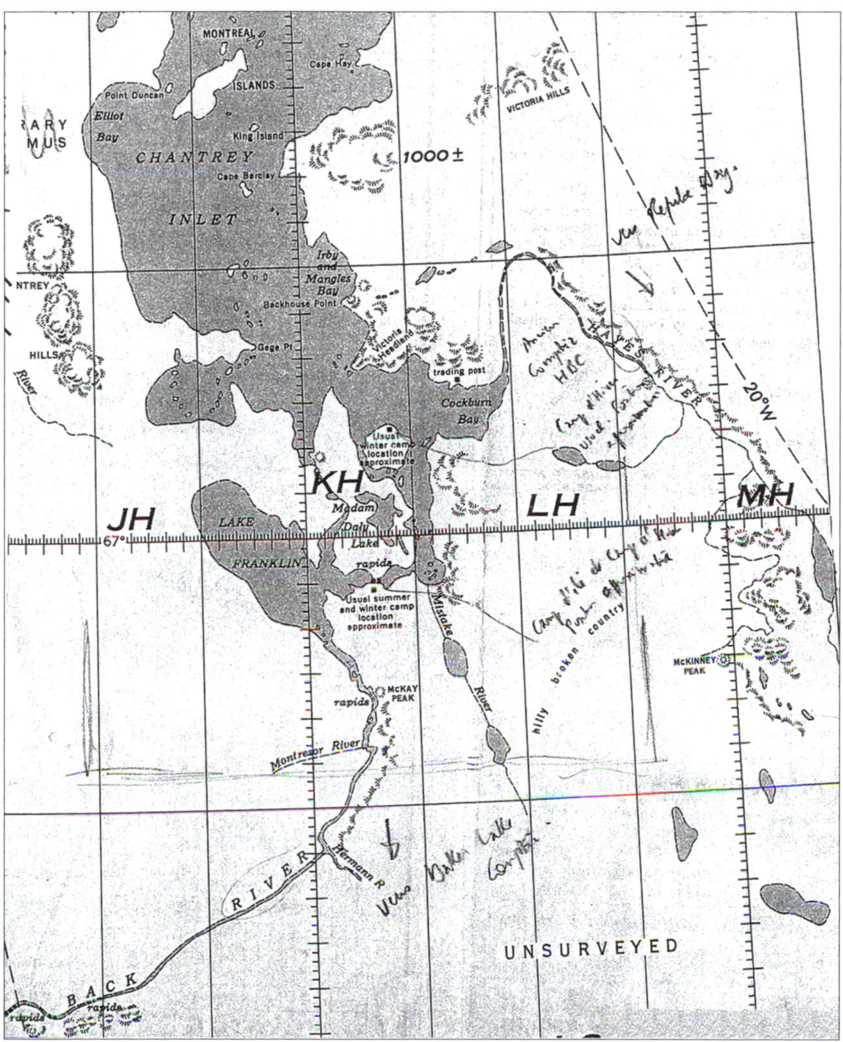

ICAO 1:1,000,000 map of Chantrey Inlet and environs with author's annotations.

Elliot Bay (Tarajunuaq, "little salt bay"), Koorsoot abruptly halts the dogs in the middle of an anecdote about bear hunting. Are we approaching the great delta? The ice will be treacherous at the far end of the bay, where the violent currents of the Hayes River outlet interfere with freezing. Koorsoot goes forward courageously, probing the ice with his spear. It is only fifteen centimetres thick. Terrorized, we streak toward the centre of the estuary.

FIRST CONTACT WITH THE UTKUHIKHALINGMIUT: JULY 1834, APRIL 1963[27]

Suddenly, underfoot, the first yellow plants. With all the strength of our dog teams, we make for three snow houses that we have glimpsed to the south-southwest. They are abandoned, their domes stove in, but their sooty gray walls attest to routine habitation here during the winter months. The solitude leaves us perplexed: where are the people? A dot appears on the horizon, steadily growing in size. It is a man approaching on foot across the frozen Kûnajuk delta. We are off at a gallop. Reaching him, men and dogs surround the Utkuhikhalingmioq in a cloud of snow and a halo of steam. He had spotted us while on his way to his fish cache. We shake hands, staring gravely at one another as protocol dictates. He leads us to his camp.

George Back wrote on 28 July 1834 about his first meeting with this group:

These were the Esquimaux, of whom we had so long and ardently wished to get a sight ... As the boat grounded they formed into a semicircle, about twenty-five paces distant; and with the same yelling of some unintelligible word, and the alternate elevation and depression of both extended arms, apparently continued in the highest state of excitement: until, landing alone, and without visible weapon, I walked deliberately up to them, and, imitating their own action of throwing up my hands, called out Tima – peace. In an instant their spears were flung upon the ground; and, putting their hands on their breasts, they also called out Tima, with much more doubtless greatly to the purpose, but to me of course utterly unintelligible ... [I am] strongly opposed to the customary donation of knives, hatchets, and other sharp instruments, which may be so easily turned to use against the party presenting them ... I went with them to their tents, which were three in number, one single and two joined together, constructed in the usual manner with poles and skins. On our arrival, I was struck with the sight of a sort of circumvallation of piled stones ... arranged, as I conjectured, to serve for shields against the missiles of their enemies ... Many dogs, of an inferior size, were basking in the sunshine, and thousands of fish lay all around split, and exposed to dry on the rocks, the roes appearing to be particularly prized ... The women and children, about a dozen in number, came out of the chance to see me ... The men were of the average stature, well knit, and athletic. They were not tattooed, neither did their vanity incommode them with the lip and nose ornaments of those farther west ... they could not have nurtured a more luxuriant growth of beard, or cultivated more flowing mustachoes ... The women were much tattooed about the face and the middle and fourth fingers ... [One woman had] six tattooed lines drawn obliquely from the nostrils across each cheek; eighteen from her mouth across her chin and the lower part of the face; ten small ones, branching like a larch tree from the corner of each eye; and eight from the forehead to the centre of the nose between the eyebrows ... They had only five keiyaks or canoes; and the few implements they possessed were merely such as were indispensable for the procuring of food; viz. knives, spears, and arrows. The blades of the first and the heads of the last were sometimes horn, but oftener rough iron, and had probably been obtained by barter from their eastern neighbors ... There might have been about thirty-five altogether; and, as far as I could make out, they had never seen "Kabloonds" before. They had a cast of countenance superior to that of such of their nation as I had hitherto seen, indicating less of low cunning than is generally stamped on their features.[28]

Back saw these people in July 1834; 129 years later, two families of their lineage are standing before me at a distance of two metres. The men are assembled in front, wearing wide caribou-skin parkas (*qulittarjuaq*) and pants (*qarliik*). Behind them are the women and children, including one infant carried in his mother's hood (*amaut*). Three snow houses. A hermetic ambit of civilization. A savage beauty; an antique innocence. The dogs' belligerent yelps as they make one another's acquaintance.[29]

Utku man and woman whom Back encountered in August 1834. Note that the man is bearded, something rare today.

After a silence whose duration I am unable to estimate with precision – perhaps three to five minutes – the men advance ceremoniously. Still silent, their postures erect, arms held high, they extend their hands in greeting. The women and children approach but do not participate.

I make a few remarks: "I will stay with you for about ten days. I am on an official mission from the Department of Northern Affairs, and I am here to speak with you about the famine you have experienced. Do you wish to be settled around a *niuvirvik* (post), in Uqsuqtuuq (Gjoa Haven) or Iqaluktuuttiaq (Cambridge Bay) for example? I will listen to each of you and faithfully report what you have to say." Silence, another long one. The ice is broken by a practical-minded man named Toolegaak,[30] who stands to one side. He wants to know where I wish to sleep. While riding on the sled with the young hunter, Tootalik has learned of the existence of an *iglurjuaq* ("big house"). I hesitate, then point at a nearby structure. A lucky choice: it is the house in question and is inhabited by a man named Inukshuk[31] and his wife and children. It will be warmer than that of Toolegaak, a widower since his wife died of hunger.

THE ICE AGE

We examine the house. Built on 4 March, it is six weeks old and will be particularly "warm" because the porous snow inside is not yet covered with a film of ice. I enter the wide vestibule (*tuqsuq*) and make my way under the snow, mole-like, down the three-metre-long hallway (*kataq*) into a double-celled structure. The cell that I am to occupy, to the right of the entrance, is still occupied by a bitch, her pups, and their strong odour. What meets all my senses is the shock of living prehistory. I learn my first words of their language: "yes" and "no" are *aià* and *ija-kak* (*é* and *nâkâ* in Thule, *hap* and *namik* in South Greenland).

Due to the humidity in the air, I decide to set up my tent in the cell and ask Tootalik to get it from his sled. In the presence of the Utkuhikhalingmiut, whom he regards condescendingly, his Netsilingmiok graciousness has undergone an abrupt change. He complains that the house is too small and goes out, grumbling. Back inside, he fumbles unproductively with the aluminum poles. No tent will arise out of this activity, that much is obvious, but neither his knowledge nor the tent itself are at fault. I risk losing face. The Inuit are natural surveyors, capable of estimating volumes at a glance. It is a matter of minutes before the laughter begins. The RCMP constable hesitates, immobile, silent, not wishing to be their buffoon. But I am in luck: Inukshuk's son Akretoq jumps in, and with his spontaneous, energetic assistance, we find the proper arrangement for the poles. We were just a few centimetres off.

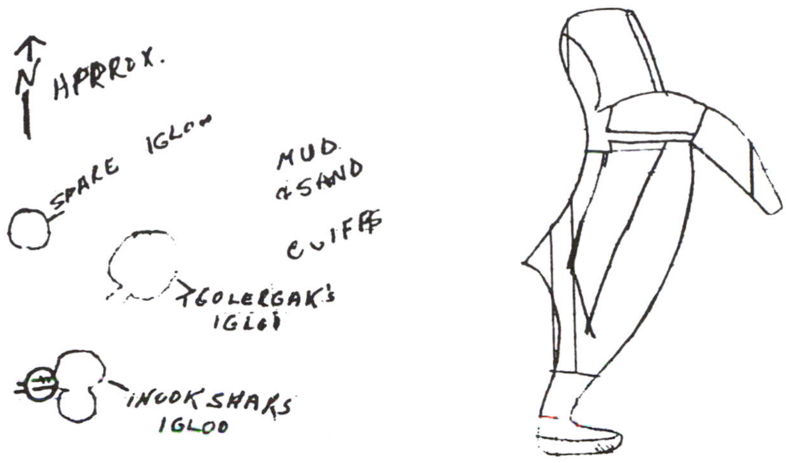

left: Houses of Toolegaak and Inukshuk, April 1963. Entrances to the west and southwest, sheltered from east wind by a low rise. RCMP sketch.

right: With the Utku. Humoristic view of a man walking. Sketch by Kiggiark (b. 1923) in my notebook. Back River, April 1963.

My three companions and I, like wise men from afar, unpack our things in the room next to the fabric shelter. I then join the two Inuit families in the other room, where they obligingly gather around me on the *iglerk* (bench-like platform, pronounced *igle'q* here, *igliq* in North Greenland). The only source of light is an ice window (*igalaak*). Assisted by the interpreter, who translates sentence by sentence, and followed with rapt attention, I give them more details about the purpose of my research. I tell them that I would like to make a complete survey of everything they own as well as a precise accounting of what and how much they hunt and fish month by month, including itineraries and approximate times spent. I tell them that I have conducted the same type of family inventory with the Igluligmiut in Igloolik, the Netsilingmiut, and also with the Inughuit, far away to the east in North Greenland. Naturally, they have never heard of these last, but they make their own mental map: "East of here ... other Inuit." I specify that I will complete the survey by consulting the RCMP archives and the HBC figures and accounts at the store in Uqsuqtuuq, where I will stay a week or more. While speaking, I observe Inukshuk

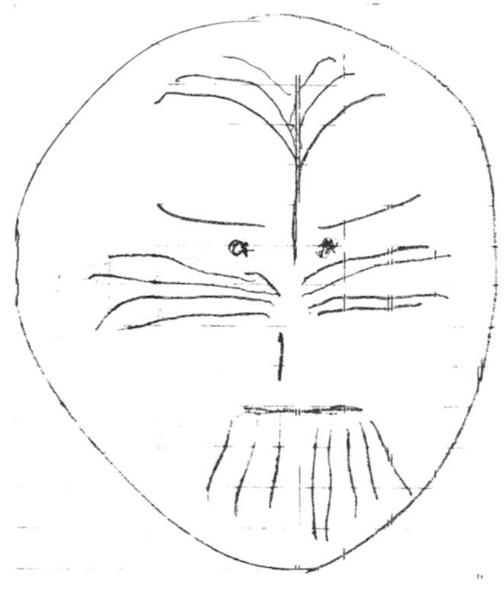

Inukshuk's drawing of his mother. Tattoo done with soot, point by point, before her wedding. The last tattooed woman in the group, Arnartak, died in the 1960s. Back River, April 1963.

obliquely. He listens attentively, immobile, mouth ajar, eyes keen and bright, his only motion the soft rubbing of a caribou skin with his left thumb. The others' heads are lowered, yet their eyes are fixed on the speaker, following his every movement: a silent meeting of insular minds. Blackish brown faces, heads partially covered by caribou-skin hoods. Will they eat separately, as at Thom Bay? When I am done speaking, two of the men retrieve a sixty-centimetre-long frozen raw char from a sort of internal excrescence serving as a pantry or ice chest to the right of the entrance hallway. It contains about twenty fish. The wet sound of tongues is punctuated by that of bones cracking under incisors.[32] Here, too, they spit the bones onto the ground, but nobody bothers to kick them away; they are simply walked on. We eat in reflective silence. The foul-smelling bitch whom I have supplanted with my tent comes and goes at the foot of the *iglerk*, her teats hanging low.

Remarkably, there is no continuous heating source[33] nor any *kutdleq* (oil lamp made of soapstone or another rock material). A cloud of condensation accompanies every word. The floor (*natiq*) is made of packed snow. The indoor temperature of −5 to −10°C, depending on the time of day, is maintained with the occasional ground-willow-root fire, which they kindle in an annex (*ishavik*) off the entrance hallway (*turhuuq*), a fireplace of sorts with a chimney consisting of a stove-in, funnel-shaped red can.[34] When they have tea or a substitute, they heat water on the Primus. But gas is rare. They are as poor as Job, and the austerity appears to be deliberate. No stone plates (*uvkusik*) or meat rack (*igliviaq*). One surprising luxury is a red aluminum pot and some white cups bought at the store; another is a set of shelf brackets planted in the wall. Apart from these and the indispensable snow beater (*anautaq*) stored to the right of the entrance, they appear to be devoid of imported possessions.

My every movement is watched. I suddenly pat my right front pocket, checking for my switchblade, but it is not in its usual place. A child gestures toward my back pocket, where I have stowed it ... the nervous tension of our encounter, no doubt. Inukshuk, the head of the household, presents me with a small bag of tobacco. He asks whether the large can of tobacco that I gave them upon arrival is for him or for all the Inuit. "For all the Inuit, but for you, my host, there is an extra share," I reply, and hand it to him. He receives it without comment or show of gratitude.

We all retire around 11:00 after conversing for a time. All of us are on our guard. The gloves and boots hang outside on stakes, to either side of the entrance. I discover that my tent platform is too short, and I use my kit bag as a footrest. During the night, the muted sounds of the two couples' intimate conversations – especially the one taking place a foot from my head – carry me far back into my childhood.

The next morning at 8:00 I hear Inukshuk moving about in the other room, and he leaves shortly afterward. Tootalik and the constable are still snoring. Koorsoot has already gone out. The morning light offers a better view of our dwelling, a snow house with a film of blackish, crystallized snow clinging to the vaulted ceiling. An intense feeling of elation wells up in me at being on this side of the great divide between the poor and the rich; I am surprised to find myself discreetly hugging the snow wall. How I love this people in all their innocence and original intensity – how wonderful that such Inuit actually exist! The floor, packed down under their boots, is dotted with fish heads and bones and streaked with blood. This detail escaped my notice yesterday, gripped as I was by the ambience of this venerable people. Their snow sleeping platform is covered by a delicate latticework of roots held firmly in place by a board and four caribou skins. On a shelf are an alarm clock, small sacks of herbs (*igwit*) and moss, a hurricane lamp, and two women's crescent-shaped knives (*ulu*). On the ground are a small wooden box serving as a table for a tin cup and a red-and-white-striped can used indiscriminately as a spittoon and a urinal (*q'orwik*). This is placed to the right of the entrance tunnel at night. The hallway door is made of wood (*ookoak*) but would formerly have been of caribou skin (*taluaq*). One enters the open, unsheltered vestibule by descending some uneven steps. Austerity is not necessarily synonymous with misery; still, I find myself ill at ease as I move in among these unspeakably poor men and women. As far as they are concerned, my gear and provisions – sleeping bag, gas lamp, well-fuelled Primus and copious supplies of tea, tobacco, and sugar – make me a millionaire.

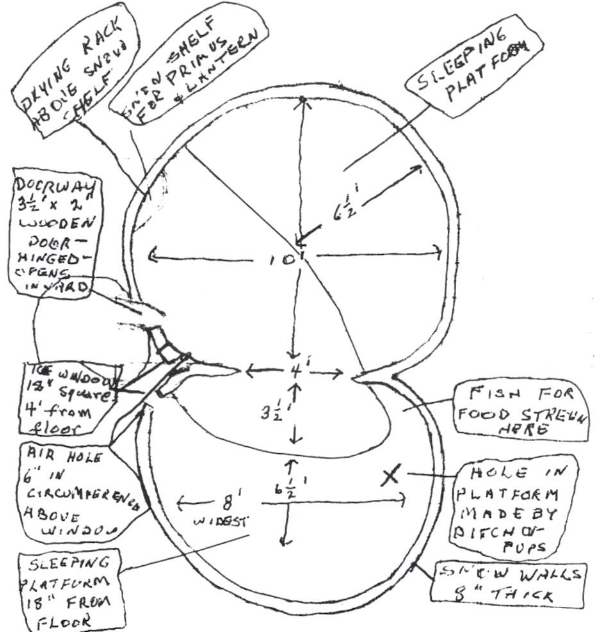

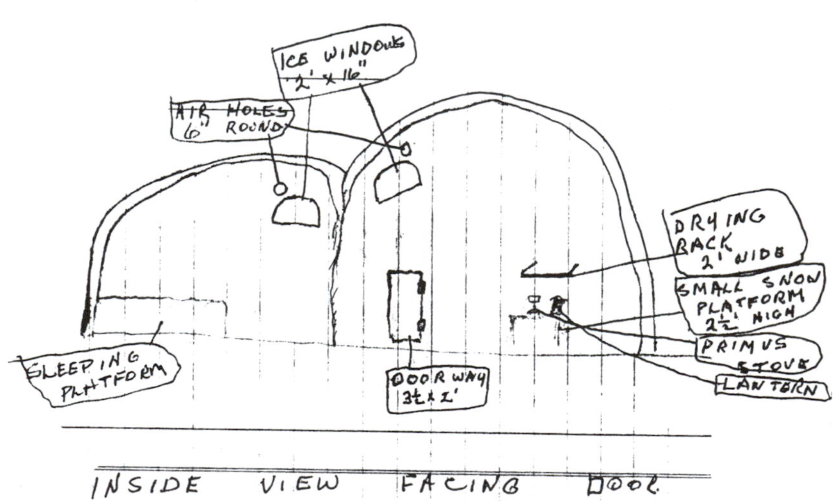

With the Utku. Plan and cross-section of Inukshuk's house. Sketches in my notebook by the RCMP officer, who as a duty constable preferred to remain anonymous. See also photos in my *Call of the North*.

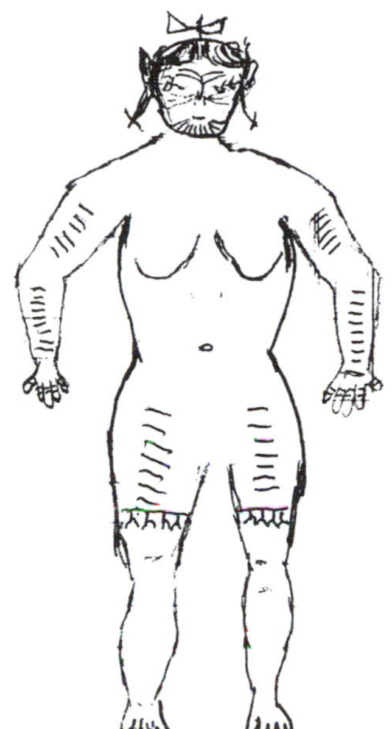

With the Utku. The mother of one of my respondents (the latter b. 1923), drawn by him. Tattooed in 1910, before her marriage. Back River, April 1963.

Only a low ridge of translucent ice[35] separates me from the room where Akretoq* sleeps lying face down on a caribou skin. His newlywed wife Kresuk ("wood") sleeps to his left; they were married 16 March. With her petite stature, soft, sad eyes, and pale gray face, I have given her the secret moniker of "Little Fish." My gift for her is a kilogram bag of tea, which I delicately place under her head. Also present is an old woman who was widowed last year when her husband drowned. Her plump, chubby cheeks turn crimson pink when she makes any physical effort. She is an actress who can put on the face of a stupefied Inuit woman at will, like the ones depicted in historical engravings. My secret nickname for her: "Great Whale."

Akretoq is awake now, giving me sidelong looks instead of stares as he did yesterday. Both of us feel vulnerable. With his yellow skin, small, darting brown eyes, and keen intelligence, he gives the impression of a Parisian kid. It is a standoff; both of us beat a retreat. I find myself casting around for

* Adoptive son of Inukshuk, born 1 January 1940 at Garry Lake in central Keewatin, which underwent a great famine in the 1950s. Like everyone here, he is a professed Anglican. His easy rapport with me may have something to do with the indebtedness that he must feel toward his adoptive father.

the stereotypical Eskimo of my imagination, here in my risibly small headquarters, in this cloud of thoughts and ideas separating the outsider from his hosts, in the no-man's-land growing between us. Sensing himself surveyed, spied on, he withdraws behind a mask. Slowly, the roles are reversing. In the torpid icy cold of this early morning, I am the game for a wily hunter who very much looks the part, his tousled hair worn short with a hint of a part, his skin dirty and abraded. Worse: I am his prisoner, and I am being put on trial. I simply must escape from the silent, tightening grip of his courtroom. The roof weighs in on me, the walls press together: the space becomes a confinement. I attempt to use my limited vocabulary to provoke Akretoq. But the hunter has no intention of becoming the game or giving up the prerogative of setting the traps. His face colours. Laughter is in his eyes, tension in his jaws, muscle spasms under the skin. His lips and eyes take part in the smile. Doggedly, I endeavour to shift the weight of my presence, to shake off the stigma of the Kablunak, the person who takes up space now only to take control later. In a flash, I spot an opportunity for us to collaborate in the hunt for a different sort of prey, namely the other Inuit, his relatives and rivals. We will conduct the survey together.

The house awakens to Kresuk's elation upon discovering the bag of tea; she will be my ally. In the course of the morning, she goes from house to house (first to her close relatives) showing off her treasure. The sight of her pretty, gleaming teeth gives me pleasure. The others go about their chores with a characteristic morning air of affliction. Inevitably, the visitors' presence sets the tone of the proceedings. I rather wish that I could slip into the rhythm

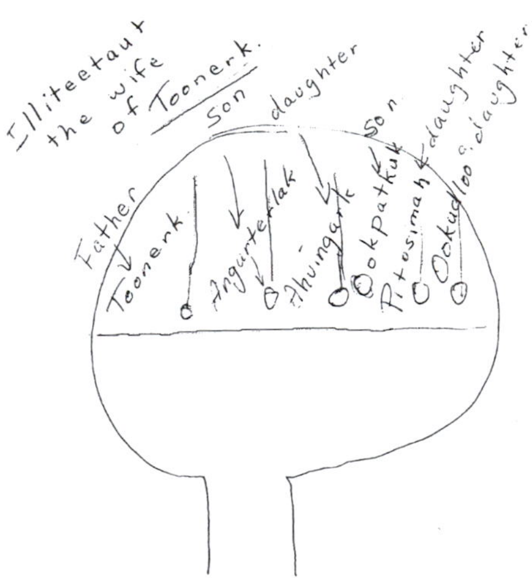

Left and facing page: Five houses composing the Utku group in the winter of 1960, 1961, or 1962. Sketches by Awagashee, a Back River emigrant whom I met at Baker Lake in September 1962.

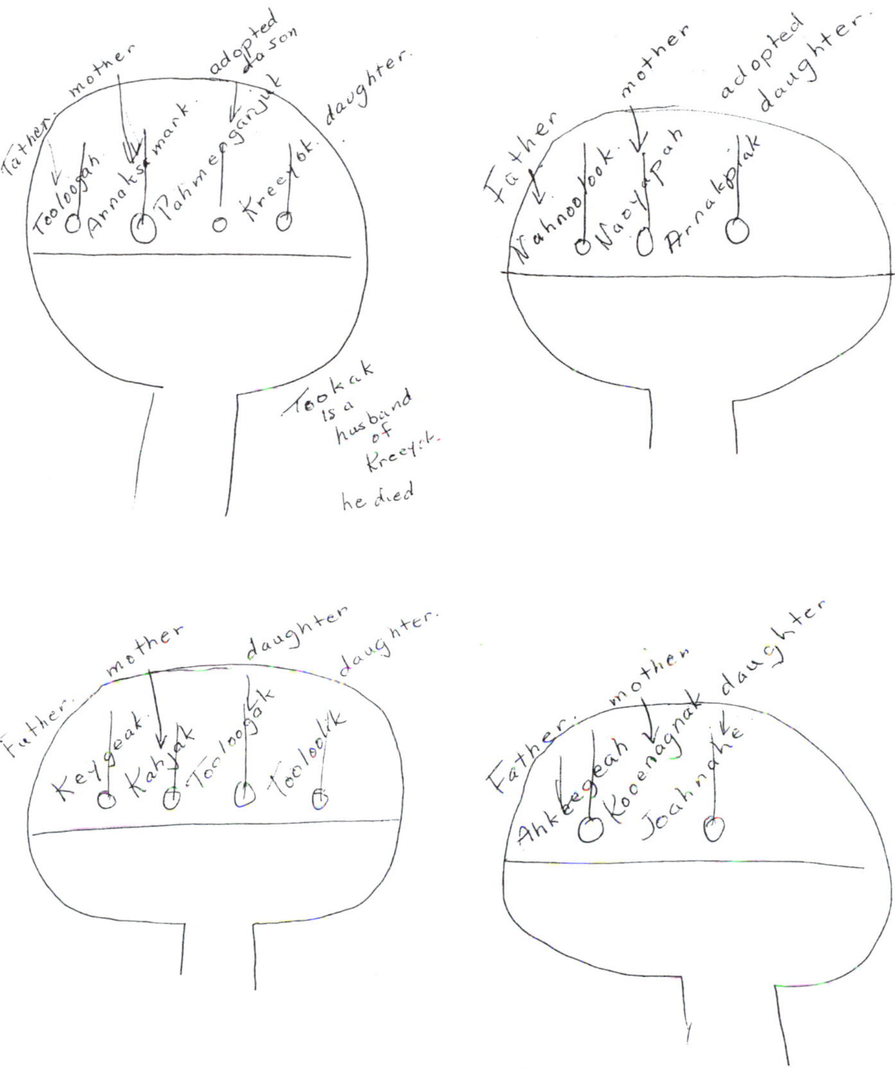

of this society inconspicuously, without a ripple, make myself invisible. The best I can do is to remain silent and try to position myself in a blind spot. But my speech of yesterday, like a stone thrown into a lake, has made waves that are now breaking on the shore. They are all awaiting "instructions" from the Kablunak and the policeman who have travelled so far to visit them. They are wondering about our hidden agenda.

Trade among the Netsilingmiut, according to Tootalik, my respondent and interpreter from Spence Bay, 13 August 1961.

– A dog (leader) for a two-year-old gun (300). Joe (no. 62) traded his gun to Igjookjuak (no. 17) for a dog, c. 1959 (fall), Natsegsirvik.
– A dog (female, big) for a telescope. Jonnie (no. 20) sold his telescope to Kilnik (no. 27), c. 1957 (spring), Thom Bay.
– Adams [my interpreter Tootalik] traded a leader dog (1 1/2 years old) for a one-year-old gun (22) to Inugssuk, a Back River Inuk, at Gjoa Haven, 1958 (winter).
– A sewn tent for a dog.
– Kilnik traded a one-year-old dog to Itunga (Spence Bay) for a gramophone (value $20).

I make no move. In the weighty silence, the constable speaks up, asking me in the solemn voice of the professional if he can be of assistance. So he can. I entrust him with the task of taking the dimensions of the houses, identifying their occupants, and plotting each one's position on the *iglerk*. He accomplishes this expertly, doing work that would be the envy of any novice ethnologist.[36] Later, I ask the women to sketch male and female costumes in my notebook.

PRELIMINARY INVENTORY

The seven families are divided into two neighbouring camps. My survey begins with questions covering household items and hunting and fishing gear, their year of manufacture and barter value, calendars of activities and routes travelled, buying and selling history at the trading post, and government assistance. Aided by Rasmussen's report, and with Akretoq correcting my pronunciation, I learn to count: *atauheq*/one, *atlra*/two (rather than *matlruk* for the Netsilingmiut at Igloolik and the North Greenlanders), *pinajuat*/

three, *sitamat*/four, *taglimat*/five, *arwinat*/six, *atlra*/seven, *pinajuat*/eight, *sitamat*/nine, *taglimaujoertut*/ten, *atqaane*/eleven, *amissut*/many. Thus identical words are used for two and seven, three and eight, and four and nine. Where clarity is necessary, the word *arwinat* is added: *atlra arwinat*/seven, *pinajuat arwinat*/eight, *sitamat arwinat*/nine. That is, the word for "six" has the meaning of "five" in these expressions. The Netsilik say *atauheq arwinat* (as if six equaled seven!). Seven is *matlruk arwinat*, eight is *pinajunik arwinat*, and nine is *sitavamik arwinat*.

They smile at my French-inflected North Greenlandic (I do not speak their language). It seems they are touched by the effort. This fraternization, so natural to me, takes the other members of my party aback – in truth, it puts them ill at ease. Their Anglo-Saxon manners dictate that one's distance should be kept when on official missions. We are guidance counsellors, as it were, and it is up to the student to come to us. None of this is stated overtly, but I sense that they would have preferred for us to sleep apart from the Inuit. Rasmussen had his own tent, did he not? Then again, that was in the month of June!

The most painstaking process is that of ascertaining the hunting and fishing calendars. I manage to get only three complete calendars for the seven families. The exercise confuses Akretoq. On his first try, his year has thirteen months; when Tootalik asks him to start over, it has ten. He will get the idea eventually ... we let the question rest. The hunting territory, Franklin Lake and its environs, is delimited on the map. It comprises *amujat*, a winter camp, where they gather in one or two related groups; *kajat*, a spring camp; and *itimnaaqjuk*, a spring-summer camp that was probably the location of their encounter with Back on 28 July 1834 (see map, p. 198). Two other camps, *kuuttiq* and *uyuqpa*, are at the northern tip of the Adelaide Peninsula, a few kilometres from Montreal Island. North of there runs a string of outpost camps along both shores of Chantrey Inlet. This all adds up to two large, broadly rectangular areas in which to hunt for caribou and musk oxen, measuring 300 kilometres north to south along the river and inlet and 200 kilometres east to west, for a total of 60,000 square kilometres. In fact, the hunters range over only one-tenth of this area. They correctly interpret the details of inlets, capes, and rivers on my 1:1,000,000 World Aeronautical Charts (ICAO standard; see map, p. 203) and draw me four maps of their own (see maps, pp. 201, 237, 272, 287). Qeqertaq is King William Island; Uqsuqtuuk, Gjoa Haven; Ilivileq, the Adelaide Peninsula; Ko'najuk, the river estuary; Utkuhikjalik, the eponymous upstream camp where soapstone is found; and Taherjuaq, Franklin Lake (as named by George Back).

I record the names of objects: *eqalujaq*/fishing lure, *kakivak*/leister (*kakivvak* in North Greenland), *qarhorsaq*/hook, *pilaut* or *saviut*/knife; *nigshik*/caribou-tipped spear used only at the *saputit*/stone weirs erected for river fishing, according to Rasmussen and confirmed by my respondents. Noticing my interest, Akretoq goes to get the one planted at the entrance to the hallway (*torsut* or *torhuq*). The word *ipo* here designates the handle of a dog whip, while in North Greenland, it designates a net used to catch birds in spring or char in summer; *ulu*, as in North Greenland, is a woman's knife. The two languages are similar, but how different are the accents! This one is much more guttural, with numerous aspirations that are palatalized in some words or syllables, velarized in others. Their speech is rapid among themselves; at first I find it difficult to recognize even the words that they share with the language I already know. But I stick at it and fluency returns in spurts. Other objects are pointed out: *ilaut*, an antler-handled shovel used to clear away the ice debris from fishing holes in order to gain a clear view of the water; *kumut*, a lice scratcher – an invaluable item.

On average, each Back River Inuk catches 2,500 Arctic char (*hîlor* or *iqaluk*) and/or speckled char (*iqalutqik*) and 1,000 whitefish (*kakkiviaqtuuq*) and

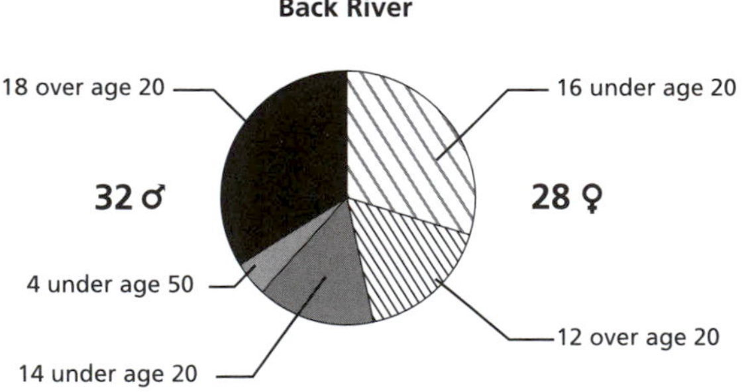

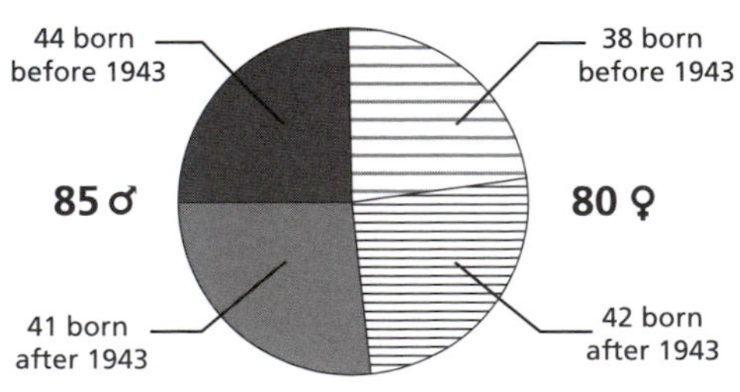

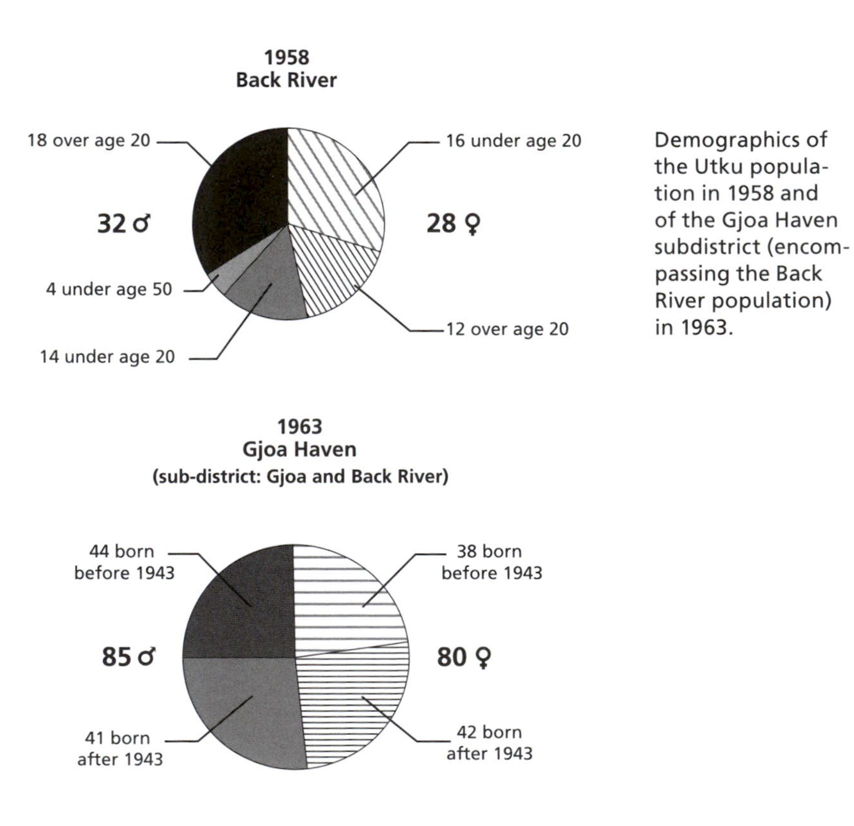

Demographics of the Utku population in 1958 and of the Gjoa Haven subdistrict (encompassing the Back River population) in 1963.

shoots one or two caribou annually.* Summer foods include birds, eggs (raw or boiled), and blueberries. What with the taboo on seal hunting (see below) and the increasing scarcity of caribou, the Back River Inuit are ever more dependent on fish. But fish cannot clothe them (although Rasmussen notes that fish skin was being used in his day to make bags and soles for indoor boots). A family of four needs about fifty caribou skins every five years for clothing, bedding, and tent fabric. Since game resources are clearly insufficient to meet this demand,[37] they would need an annual income supplement of $500 per family of four to five – the same level as the Netsilingmiut of Spence Bay and Thom Bay. As far as clothing goes, the benefits of church charity seem dubious. The fabric dresses and sweaters that they are wearing hold too much moisture to be of value in this climate; donations of caribou skins would clearly be much preferable. Kayaks have not been in use since 1925–30; they were extant after Rasmussen but had disappeared when de Poncins visited in 1939, as all here concur.

THE SEAL TABOO

My survey has turned up an enigma. Seals are abundant only a day away from their camp and could provide them with oil for heating as well as meat in times of scarcity, yet the taboo against hunting them is powerful. A few "modernists" who turn up during the course of my research are merely the exception.

Is the objection cultural, technical? Whatever the case, many of them even refuse to give seal meat to their dogs, and they are not much inclined to discuss the matter; "Inuit tradition," goes the refrain. When Nanudluk accompanies me on my return trip to Gjoa Haven, he will bring along enough fish to feed his nine dogs. Every people may be defined by its dietary taboos – we are what we eat. Inukshuk delivers a meandering, idiosyncratic explanation of the taboo. At first, I listen distractedly, with a historian's arrogance, yet who can say that his reasons are not perfectly sensible?

> Yes, there is a seal taboo, dating from the introduction of rifles when I was nine [1920?]. At that time, food was so abundant, there were so many caribou, people left them on the ground during the spring hunt. That was when the Inuit stopped hunting seals. Then the caribou became rare, so the Inuit began to fish. There are many, many fish ... The elders died and the young people no longer have the skills to hunt seals. Waiting at

* Other species sometimes taken are Atlantic tomcod (*ogaq*) and redfish or scorpionfish (*kanajoq*).

the *aklo* [seal breathing hole; *aglu* in North Greenland] is a long, tedious process. You spend too much time waiting for the seal to come up for air. Fishing is less work.

At the second camp, where Kiggiark ("beaver") is the only person who occasionally hunts seals, old Toonee will tell me more or less the same thing. Rasmussen recorded fifteen seal hunting terms in 1922, when the taboo was coming into force. I observe that these terms (*aklo*, for example, and *iglak*, bubbles at the surface of the *aklo* indicating the seal's presence) are still in their vocabulary; even the young people (born 1935–40) know them. Toonee* recalls seal hunting on the Adelaide Peninsula:

Years ago X lived at Ugjulik [Queen Maud Gulf]. I was a child. We used to hunt seals at Ugjulik forty or fifty years ago, that would be around 1910–20 [before Rasmussen's first visit to the Utku on 21 May 1923.] We hunted them with harpoons at the *aklo* before everyone got guns. People gradually migrated away from Ugjulik due to illness and especially famine. They moved to Back River on the shores of the big lake. There was always abundant fresh water there, and in the spring they hunted the many caribou that were found inland to the south [at Garry Lake], pursuing them onto the lakes in the fall. Caribou were abundant then. Sometimes they returned to Ugjulik in winter for seal hunting. Usually only the men, sometimes the whole family, but only for short periods [i.e., several months]. Then the custom was lost.

Tootalik proves a worthy interpreter. He lets the respondents express themselves at length with no prompting, and these people need none anyway, for they are excellent narrators. Give them space and time and they produce a vivid account. In their typical pose, hands clasped, forearms propped on thighs, they appear to be gathering themselves for a confession. In contrast, when expressing a political idea, they sit erect, carry their heads assertively, and produce solemn, even-toned, Indian-style pronouncements, with some introductory ethical considerations and a firmly stated conclusion. The final syllables may be summarized thus: "I have spoken." Whereupon they lounge back on their seats like satisfied senators.

Together we read several pages, line by line, from the black binder in which I have placed Knud Rasmussen's seventy-four-page report.[38] At first they are keen to continue, but boredom overtakes them. "Yes," they say, "he's the one. He was here." One of them turns around and points northeast. Tootalik

* Born 1906, widower, father of four children, two sons whom he proudly introduces as "hunters," Oopootkak and Naruk (b. 15 May 1950 and 3 December 1938), and two daughters, Avingnak and Aniknik (b. 1944 and February 1953). His granddaughter, Ookooshook Tunulik (b. 3 February 1952), lives with him as well. All are professed Anglicans.

informs me that his father, Uvdleq, was Rasmussen's respondent and that he had used his persuasive powers to placate certain members of the group who detested foreigners. "He was with an Eskimo woman from Greenland."[39] Our communal reading exercise turns out to be a poor research method, for they agree with every statement, not wishing to contradict the whites or the elders. Besides, they grow tired of hearing what are, for them, mere truisms. It should be recalled that in Rasmussen's day paper was a novelty among the Inuit, and they mistook the sheets on which he wrote for fox pelts. For the women drawing me objects and costumes, the Rasmussen binder mainly serves as a hard surface to write on.[40]

I produce a comparative lexicon of Utku and Inughuit terms using the method that the Danish explorer modelled on that of Kaj Birket-Smith for the Caribou Inuit. The respondents pronounce words from Rasmussen's lexicon, and I enter these and their North Greenland equivalents, which I learned during my 1950–51 expedition, in two columns of a table; the Netsilik equivalents are given by Rasmussen. Akretoq takes visible pleasure in this process. The 135-word lexicon that I have collected by the end of my stay at Back River and Gjoa Haven (see selections in Table 5.1 on the following page) clearly illustrates the linguistic continuity between the two languages.

To encourage old Toolegaak to recount a legend, I turn on my tape recorder and ask him to listen to songs and stories of the Spence Bay and Thom Bay Netsilingmiut that I recorded in August 1961. Everyone pays rapt attention. The use of this machine (a Swiss Perfectone) in these bare environs endows me with the power of another age – until it abruptly stops.

I have long had absolute confidence in these people's powers of observation, the natural pride that they take in solving their own problems. Yesterday, Akretoq watched me operating the magic machine, noticing how I took the batteries out to check them and warm them in my hands. Without hesitation I hand it to him, and without much surprise, he takes it. The constable, Koorsoot, and Tootalik are reserved, keenly intrigued, mentally gathering around Akretoq to observe what he will do. Everyone sits in a broad semicircle on the *iglerk*, taciturn, thinking as with one mind; one has his legs stretched out horizontally, his back braced against the ice wall.[41] Akretoq places the tape recorder on his lap, turns the central screw with the tip of his knife, and begins to raise the cover of the battery compartment. As if unnerved by his own audacity, he hurriedly screws it back down. Glancing at me momentarily for approval, he opens the receptacle, removes the twelve batteries, reinserts them – then removes them again and lodges them between the generous breasts of the three women present.* The porous silence endures for several

* In those older times, Inuit women did not wear brassieres.

TABLE 5.1 A COMPARATIVE LEXICON OF UTKU AND INUGHUIT TERMS

UTKUHIKHALINGMIUT (BACK RIVER)	INUGHUIT (NORTH GREENLAND)	TRANSLATION
tautsamani	taimanngali	long ago
unuaq	taaq	night
anoré	anuré	wind
qiläk	qilak	sky
ubloriaq	ulluriaq	star
nuviya	nuigaq	cloud
arksaq	arharniq	aurora borealis
qe'meq	qimmiq	dog
panneq	–	male caribou
ivik	iviq	herb, grass
tinaussat	maniq	moss (dry, combustible)
iteq	itiq	anus
amamak	amaama	teat
iksuk	ighuit	testicle
usuk	uhuq	penis
utjuk	utsuit	vulva
uksuk	ughuk	large bearded seal
ukiaqsaq	–	autumn
ano	anuq	harness
erneq	irniq	son
iglok	illuq	cousin
nerrivoq	nirihuq	eat
oqalupoq	uqaluktuaqtuk	speak, tell
iklarpoq	iglaqtuq	laugh
pisukpoq	pihuktuq	son he walks
anana	anaana	mother
atata	ataata	father
ninio	aanaq	grandmother
it'o	aataq or aanaghaaq	grandfather
akak	akkak	paternal uncle
pilaut	havik	ordinary knife
ulo	ulu	woman's round knife
kakivak	kakivvaq	leister
kunut	kunngut	back scratcher
saputit	haputit	stone weir
é	é	yes
ijakäk	naka	no
qanukiak	ammaqa	maybe
qaqugo?	qanga?	when (in the future)?
illibse	ilissi	you (plural)
uwana	uvanga	me
uwagut	uagut	you (formal singular)
isfit	illit	you (informal singular)

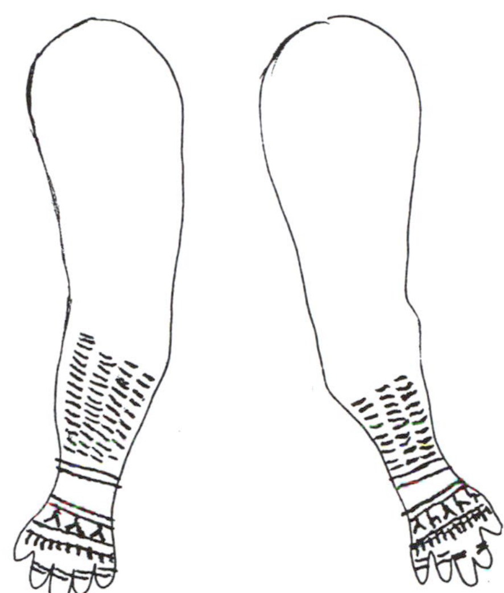

With the Utku. Sketch by a respondent showing the tattoos on his mother's arms and hands (b. 1890–1900 at Back River). April 1963.

long minutes. Akretoq puts the batteries back in the machine with the positive and negative poles in the correct orientation and closes the compartment. He nods for me to press play: the tape rolls. In an icy cave out of prehistory, this young hunter has just shown us that batteries run down in the cold.

The recording resumes. Old Toolegaak's gaze is one of profound disenchantment, then absence, as if he is elsewhere, an actor waiting to face his audience. "Just one and that's it," he stipulates. After two or three abortive attempts, he casually, easefully, raises his voice in song. I am crouching at the entrance to the *kataq* wearing headphones to control the input volume when Inukshuk enters without warning, his face half-paralyzed by the cold, and knocks over the recorder. I am in the wrong place; the *kataq* is a thoroughfare. Someone goes down the hallway to the entrance to stand lookout, and the recording of Toolegaak proceeds.[42]

The Bear and the Caribou: A bear and a caribou meet. The bear says to the caribou, "You are skinny." The caribou replies, "I may be skinny but I can walk, I go where I please." The caribou adds, "Look at your fat haunches." The bear replies, "Those are fighting words." They run at each other. The caribou skewers the bear's paw with its horn. The caribou drives the bear back. They go at it again. The bear is in retreat, hurting, its leg tendons and muscles injured. The bear is furious and tries to sink his teeth into the caribou, but it runs away.

The Snowy Owl and the Hares: Two snowy owls, male and female, see some hares. The male tries to catch one but gets two. The female tells him to let one of them go. The male replies, "If I keep the two hares for the entire lunar cycle, the Inuit will have plenty of food." He releases the two hares, and they try to run away. He catches them again, and again lets them go. This time they reach safety in a boulder pile. The owl cannot catch them again without breaking one of his legs.

I am offering to make tea for some refreshment when a boy of about ten goes into what is evidently an epileptic seizure. He trembles, emits a few brief cries, rights himself momentarily, then lurches forward with outstretched arms and chattering teeth, smashing his fists and feet together. His eyes are haggard, his face pallid ... he briefly loses consciousness. Inukshuk intervenes, grabbing the boy by the neck and wrists and clamping him between his powerful legs as if applying a straitjacket. Shivering, prostrate, trying to catch his breath, the boy slouches back against the wall to general indifference, if not contempt. Was the episode triggered by my irruption into the life of the group? I venture to suggest that the boy be placed in my sleeping bag for warmth. Toolegaak opposes this categorically, with distance: "Just watch how I take care of him. Inuit business. Keep out of it!"

With that he sends the boy to the other side of the estuary to get fish from the stove-in houses, kilometres of walking in the cold, with the return into a headwind. Life resumes without ado; the scene has taken place to the apparent indifference of all present.

"If he returns – and he will, you'll see – then he is not sick." He does return, the poor boy, a vacant, pained look in his eyes. His gray-hued skin has taken on some colour. "You'll see how we treat this sort of 'disease.' This 'sick' boy, as you put it, is shamming. When the weather is cold, the trouble enters his body. Inside in the warmth, it is released. So it is not a big problem. The Inuit have learned to cure these false, deceitful diseases. Years ago, orphans slept and ate in the *kataq*. That is where you would have found him then since you would have had to step over him to get in the door. All they got was leftovers,* and as for hunting, they had to manage on their own. That's how we made men out of them, the hard way, each one according to his status. This boy is very lucky; he sleeps with us on the *iglerk*. He lives just as we do. We are Christians." The next day, the seizures intensify; the day after, he has eight in the space of two hours.

* Orphans ate standing up at one house or another; sometimes they had to wait a half-hour or more before someone disdainfully gave them a morsel. During my time in the Central Arctic in 1960–63, I witnessed a few of these humiliating scenes. Decidedly, anarcho-communalism is not all primitive charm.

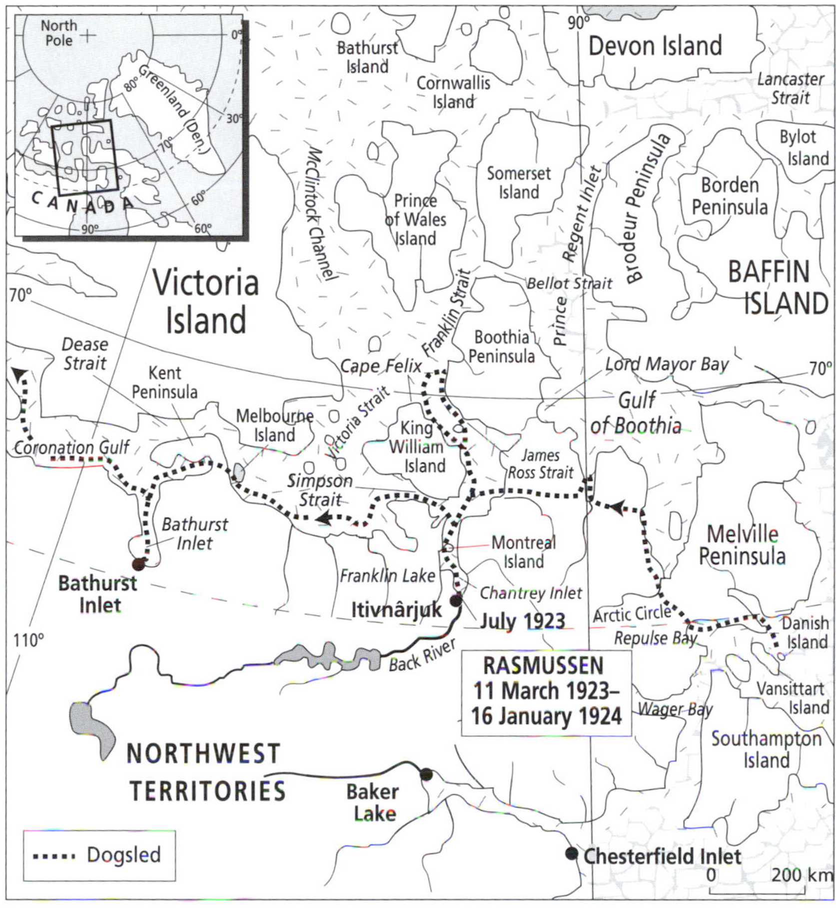

Route of Rasmussen's 1923 dogsled expedition from his base near Repulse Bay to Coronation Gulf.

That night, I reread Rasmussen's reports of the Fifth Thule Expedition by flashlight. I keep turning over the seal taboo in my mind, as it is evidently a key factor in the difficulties that this society is experiencing.

The present-day Utkuhikjalingmiut round about Franklin Lake say that their forefathers originally lived at Ugjulik, the eastern part of Queen Maud's Sea. Not so very long ago they were there visited by a famine which claimed so many victims that nearly all the families moved up to the great river [Back River], where food could

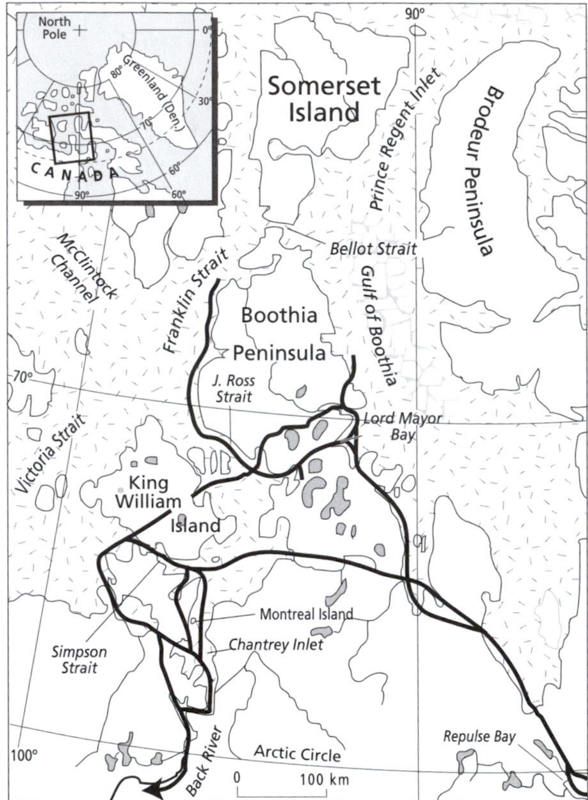

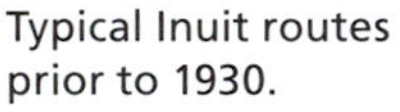

Typical Inuit routes prior to 1930.

always and at all seasons be secured in the form of caribou, musk oxen or trout. After their removal to the interior, however, they maintained their connection with the sea right down to the last generation ...

... [S]ince an Eskimo trader from the Qaernermiut, Ilangnaq by name ... introduced the first guns [about 1908] ... they turned their backs on the sea and adapted themselves entirely to trading ...

Fifteen or twenty years ago [before 1922, the Utkuhikhalingmiut] always made their way out to Elliot Bay as soon as caribou hunting was at an end and the winter clothing finished. The sealing area stretched from the so-called Tarajunuaq, just outside the delta of the river, to Cape Britannia, where they used to meet the Netsilingmiut, who there had the eastern boundary of their hunting grounds ... They hunted the seal not so much for the sake of food but to procure blubber for the autumn and the first part of winter.[43]

The gun has made life easier by removing some of the uncertainty from hunting; formerly, with the bow and the spear, it was a more tenuous enterprise, as these implements necessitated a closer approach over cracking snow. Trout fishing was a suitable complement to hunting, and this new abundance appears to be what encouraged the Utkuhikhalingmiut to give up the "long, tedious" practice of seal hunting, what with the Caribou Inuits' longstanding and undeniable repugnance for everything that comes from the sea. Rasmussen kept his interpretation cautious, concluding that "it was only the establishment of the trading post at Baker Lake that induced them to turn to fox trapping and trading and entirely abandon sealing."[44]

Fine – but why invent a taboo? Perhaps the revolution of the gun confirmed what was already their natural inclination: to remain caribou hunters and turn their backs on the traditionally hostile world of the sea. But everything has its price, and in times of scarcity corresponding to the caribou migration cycle, the Utku have lived in spartan austerity. As Ikinilik told Rasmussen in June 1923, "We admit that our houses are sometimes cold, but as they always are like that we do not become soft ... When the Netsilingmiut have no more blubber, their huts seem to be even colder than ours, for they have accustomed themselves to a heat that we never have."[45]

The statement is clear: for both cultural and technical reasons, it is the will of this people to live under harsh conditions. It is their ethic. *Aurea austeritas!* They know that if they acquiesced to the luxuries available during "times of plenty," they would be unable to bear up under austerity again. "Here we have a group that has been accustomed to have warmth in the huts in winter, but has now turned to the cold, unheated snow huts of the inland Eskimos, strangely enough without feeling the slightest privation."[46]

In the decade after Rasmussen's expedition, around 1930–35, caribou were becoming scarce for complex biological reasons. Their population was no longer experiencing normal cyclical fluctuations but a sharp decline, a crisis

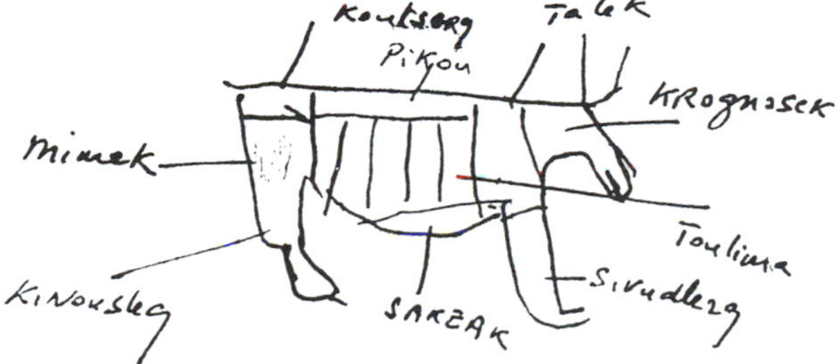

With the Utku. Caribou with traditional cuts of meat indicated. Drawing by Homaok, Gjoa Haven, May 1963.

whose spectre has always haunted the Inuit in their symbiosis with the animal world. Or to look at it another way, the period of the cycle lengthened to such an extent that the decline took on the proportions of a natural disaster. According to a centuries-old tradition that I subjected to ethnohistorical analysis for the period in North Greenland history known as the "Little Ice Age" (1840–90),[47] the onset of hardship would cause the Inuit to assemble like musk oxen in known favourable hunting areas. They would follow their rules with narrow conservatism and live according to strict dietary and sexual taboos. The fate of the elderly was euthanasia, that of infant girls infanticide if their fathers died before weaning. It was at such times that the seal taboo probably came into being. Things have changed since their encounter with Back. Most significant, their interactions with various Franklin search expeditions (Dease and Simpson, Anderson and Stewart, Hall, Schwatka, Rae, etc.) and their short stays at the white-dominated Repulse Bay[48] trading post, two months overland to the east (400 kilometres as the crow flies), have heightened their attraction to a strong God, the God of the conquerers, whalers, and gun merchants. These interactions were intensified by the interbellum establishment of a Hudson's Bay trading post at Cockburn Bay, only ten kilometres from the Back River estuary. The post was connected via the Hayes River system to a now-abandoned trading post at Wager Bay, a deep inlet of Hudson Bay 250 kilometres away. Back River was actually less isolated than it is now, its situation less primitive and precarious than the reports suggest (see maps, p. 5, 198, 202–3, 223–4).

EXISTENTIAL CRISIS

> Here at Utkuhikjalik there are no shamans now ... The shamans of our day do not even serve an apprenticeship ... Now that we have firearms it is almost as if we no longer need shamans, or taboos, for now it is not so difficult to procure food as in the old days ... the result is that we have lived ourselves out of the old customs.[49]

So said Ikinilik to Rasmussen in June 1923. Ikinilik, like all the Inuit, was silent on the crisis of conscience that had led them to switch allegiances from the "pantheistic God of the shamans" to the "strong God of the whites." It was their living secret, a mental revolution. The Inuit, as we know, have traditionally had nothing but scorn for the defeated and abhorrence for the weak, yet they were now being asked to adore a flagellated, humiliated, crucified Christ. Their consciousness would be overturned at the very moment of their spiritual starvation, their vigil for eternity. It was a crisis as much cultural as it was technical. At Clyde River in 1987, I verified the existence of this mental conflict among my Inuit students. Their most intense worries concerned, on the one hand, shamanism, death, and the afterlife and, on the other, the prospect of being jobless in the land peopled with their dead now that hunting was a thing of the past. "What shall we do? What will become of us? We couldn't bear it if we had to leave our dead far behind, and we would soon die."

By 1950–60 the caribou population was at a historic low, and they were living in the depths of anxiety, wondering whether they had made the right choice in giving up their ancient gods and shamans.[50] And it was to this existential worry that the reverends and catechists addressed their affirming message about the virtues of poverty, even as they attacked the churches' old, inflexible enemy, the *angekkok*, hoping to finish him off for good. The Inuit gave themselves over spiritually to the church, while the *angekkok* was likened to Satan. For chronological context, in 1912 a Catholic post was founded at Chesterfield by Father Arsène Turquetil, who set the pattern for Oblate policy in the Canadian Eastern Arctic; another was founded at Pelly Bay in 1935 and two more at Spence Bay and Gjoa Haven in 1950 and 1952, respectively, all three by the indefatigable, radiant Breton Father Pierre Henry. The Anglican ministers and their catechists have been equally active since 1930. In only a few years, the Utku all became fervent Protestants, even though the reverend does not reside in the community.

What is the dread fear of a people in crisis? That they have fallen out of favour with the supernatural forces surrounding them. If so, why has this group apparently failed to express any spiritual retrenchment or revolt? Because, for one thing, few observers have thought to look for it. The anthropologists' approach is quite secular; in their analysis of ritual, they are disinclined to allow for the metaphysical and the sacred. Further, the Inuit would be hard pressed to discuss this crisis under the conditions of our interviews, assuming it ever came up. The Christian church in the broad sense, irrespective of denomination, has become all-powerful in these communities, and it stifles all dialogue on this subject. Instead, it inculcates Jesus' essential message of humility and poverty, instilling in the poor a spirit of submission to an established order. Now, there is a fundamental difference between the priest and the minister: while the former lays down the law and interprets the sacred texts, the latter's approach is to continually consult the parish assembly. He is not God's representative but the "shepherd of the flock." Still, both the priest and the minister preach that poverty must be accepted because it is the passport to eternal life in the Heavenly Jerusalem that has usurped the Inuit Elysium. Even the most envious of these proud, destitute Christians may, in his fervour, regard the rich – you or I – as the ultimate losers. Reading Ikinilik's remarks to Rasmussen (May–June 1923) by flashlight, I am surprised to find myself pronouncing each word aloud: "The shamans have also told us that they have seen groups of people playing about, happy people who did nothing but laugh and amuse themselves. That is why we believe that the Land of the Sky is a land devoid of sorrow and anxiety, a good place to be."[51]

Of course, the doors to this syncretic heaven – the Christian heaven conflated with its predecessor – are narrow. The missionaries constantly repeat that eternity is reserved for the poor, off limits to the colonizers: "Sell that ye have, and give alms," Jesus enjoined his disciples (Luke 12:33), "for it is easier for a camel to go through a needle's eye, than for a rich man to enter into the kingdom of God" (18:25). Most famously, Jesus' Sermon on the Mount begins by emphasizing that the oppressed have special entitlement to his intercession: "Blessed are the poor." Reiterating these principles in more contemporary language, the *Catechism of the Catholic Church* of 1992 reads, "The precept of detachment from riches is obligatory for entrance into the Kingdom of heaven."

After a few days I proceed with extreme caution to ask some highly indelicate questions. They are bemused and, I sense, on their guard. What has their reverend told them? Has he forbid them to listen to foreign voices expounding on issues that are held to be the exclusive province of the church? I also sense that I am being watched by the constable and the Netsilingmiok interpreter (an Anglican whose wife, as I mentioned, is Catholic). In view of these constraints, I step circumspectly beyond the bounds of my official mandate, if at all, knowing that I may face bitter reproof. I know – I have been forewarned – that these people are fervent Anglicans and fanatical anti-Catholics into the bargain. Tensions between these two parishes are rife: Gjoa Haven for the Catholics, the "Papists"; Back River for the Anglicans, the "Orangists." Hence

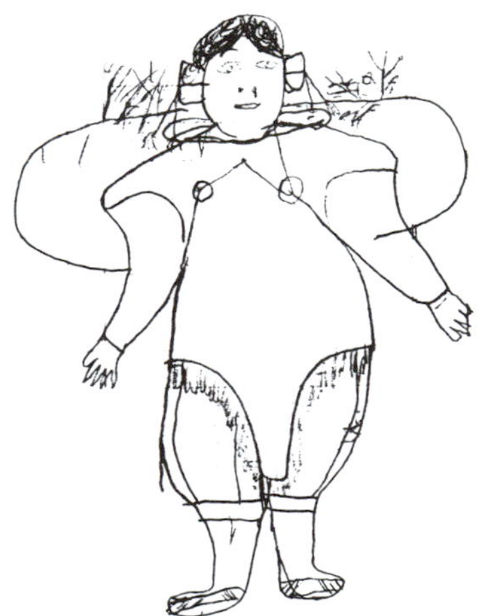

With the Utku. Winter costume. Drawing of woman carrying caribou-skin bundle horizontally, using chest strap (more commonly a forehead strap) to stabilize the load. The bundle is filled with brushwood and roots constituting the winter's provisions, and mother and daughter also gather blueberries in a container. Sketch by Kiggiark, Back River, April 1963.

they linger only as long as necessary on their infrequent trips to Gjoa Haven, the home of a zealous Oblate who has been coming to Back River from time to time since 1955. He is a French speaker; do they know that I am, too? I have not told them. They would swiftly make the equation to my detriment. I have also been told in the course of a conversation that they are angered by the Oblate's intention to put up another building in Back River. One suspects that if the Protestant Church encourages the Utku to preserve their traditions, it is because this keeps them on the land, far from the "long black robes," the corruptions of luxury (i.e., the post), and the heretical Catholic commentary on the Word of Christ.

As plausible as they are, these are just suppositions; I have not "searched the heart and tried the reins." But such are the facts. I have spoken with the missionaries in this area enough to know that the philosophy of segregation central to their thinking is instilled in the Utku by a guided weekly reading of the Gospel. And there is more. The Inuit regard me with the distance of the newly converted. My rich man's equipment (tape recorder, hurricane lamp, Primus, sleeping bag) is, to them – and this is palpable – inspired by sacrilegious thoughts. The sight of it buttresses their belief in their moral superiority. Like their ministers of religion, they now feel justified in passing judgment: you are rich; therefore, you are an infidel. They are surely coming to wonder about the hypocritical divide between word and deed among "Christian" Kablunaks. Unflattering rumours about us – they are more than rumours, in fact – have been circulating since the Franklin search expeditions and the short incursions of prospectors, geologists, surveyors, anthropologists, and others. We are sowers of discord, unprepared for the rigours of the climate, rapacious, domineering. We are worshipers of Mammon and the dollar, purveyors of violence and brutality against women. White men have wives in the South, yet they cohabit with, impregnate, and abandon Inuit women in the North. We may claim to be Christians, but clearly we are infidels of the kind whom Christ held in contempt. How is it, for example, that after initially supporting and encouraging our missionaries, we Kablunaks have now turned away from them? Why do we so rarely attend mass? What is this obscure cynicism? Such reasoning, I think, underlies the Inuits' loftiness, provides the germ of their mystique of poverty. The strong God is the God of the weak, the oppressed, the humble: theirs is the kingdom of heaven.

I do not know how Christianity was first taught to them, but I have heard the sermons of today, with their continual revisitation of a few narrow themes: Christ crucified for our sins, then resurrected; Christ the good, but also Christ the smiter of nations; contempt for worldly goods and exaltation of poverty; the Last Judgment, with heaven for the elect and hell for the damned. It has been drummed into the Inuit that the poor man is the personification

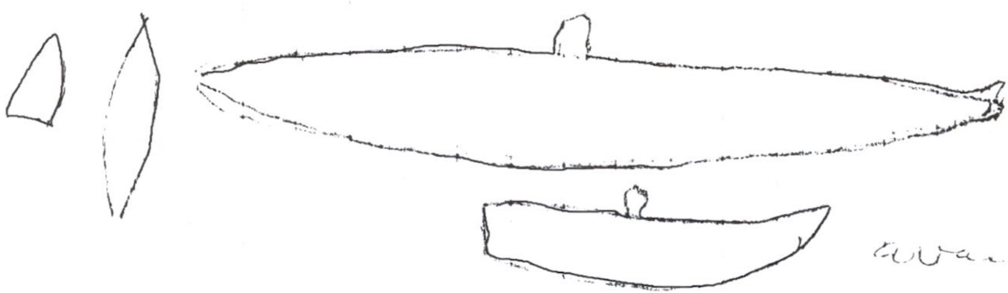

Rough cross-sectional sketch of kayaks used for sealing in Elliot Bay off Adelaide Peninsula, 1900–10. Sketch produced by Inukshuk after four attempts; dubious accuracy. Back River, April 1963.

of Christ, the man who will save the world. This is what the church has glorified since its beginnings, particularly since the Middle Ages. I am reminded of the images of St Martin portrayed in the stained-glass windows of medieval country churches. The poor man is the master of rich men's souls, the defender of the true faith. Granted, I never had the chance to meet any of the Anglican reverends who came to proselytize at Back River and cannot vouch for the content of their sermons. But this message is clearly at the heart of the evangelical discourse that was transmitted to every Inuit group, with nuances according to denomination. I would have liked to hear more on this subject from one of these new converts. In private, unrecorded conversations, I tried to elicit comment by mentioning, for example, the names of great mystics: St Francis and his visions and stigmata; St Thérèse of the Child Jesus and St Teresa of Avila and their transverberations and levitations, and so forth. The subject was visibly taboo, out of bounds. I was skating on very thin ice.

Monday, 22 April, 7:00 A.M. I have been giving thought this past evening to an admirable text by Charles Péguy about money, and I find myself continuing to reflect this morning on the mystique of poverty. My evangelical musings continue as Inukshuk joins me and we take our fraternal tea. The beverage is indispensable to them now. On average, an adult drinks ten ten-ounce glasses per day, some much more. Formerly – only yesterday – they drank lake water and fish stock.

The constable and an Inuk attempt to fish behind a snow berm through a hole in the river ice, even though the first fish do not normally return to this area until early June.* Each is armed with a lure (*eqalujaq*) – a bit of red cloth

* The gaunt char descend the river in June and July; having built up their reserves for the winter, they swim back toward the lake in August and September. It was during this season (September 1961) that I visited the Inuit of Thom Bay; see ch. 3, note 61.

for the one, a fish carved in bone for the other. They shake the lure with the left hand and hold the leister (*kakivak*) at the ready with the right, waiting to spear the char. Nothing biting. The other Inuit are all outside going about their business. A moment of great calm descends over the snow house, and I take advantage of it to silently review the historical facts, which I provide here in chronological order (see maps, pp. 186, 198, 202–3, 224–4):

(1) July 1834: Back's encounter with the Inuit at Garry Lake (upstream of the estuary) and Chantrey Inlet (my present location).

(2) 1900: famine. The Utkuhikhalingmiut, hunters of both seal and caribou, have occupied the area all the way to the northeastern part of the Adelaide Peninsula (Ilivileq). They go sealing in Elliot Bay and as far as Cape Britannia.

(3) 1900–10: migration from Queen Maud Gulf to the Back River estuary for a pragmatic purpose – to eat. Their primary food sources are fish and caribou, both abundant at close range.

(4) 1910–20, shortly before Rasmussen's arrival: guns come into widespread use, facilitating caribou hunting; start of fox trapping to meet demand at the Wager and Repulse posts. Renunciation of seal hunting as "a long, tedious process."

(5) Before 1923: the gun and what it made possible encouraged these pantheists to cast off their ceremonial life, to renounce their shamans.

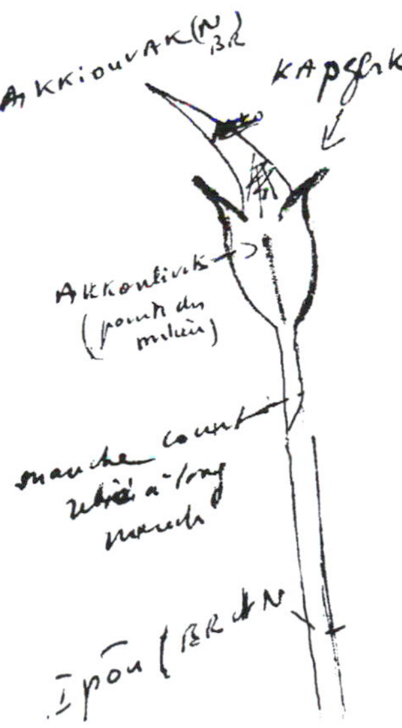

Leister. Drawing by Krokiarq, Back River, April 1963.

(6) 1930 and after: swift decline of caribou population, perceived as a punishment. The use of the gun has broken an ancestral pact, and the Inuit are living in a state of existential angst.
(7) 1920s and after: arrival of Anglican missionaries, who encourage the Inuit to accept adversity while labelling their neighbours the Netsilingmiut – not all of whom are Catholic – heretics. Establishment of the Oblates at Pelly Bay in 1935, Spence Bay in 1950, and Gjoa Haven in 1952. Arrival of charismatic missionaries such as Fathers Henry and Van de Velde. The Back River Inuit, Anglicans who have renounced seal hunting, might, I hypothesize, have come to consider this practice the greatest of sins, its practitioners heretics. Poverty became a virtue. One may posit this as the process whereby Christ took the place of the shamans.

But the image of Jesus differs in many ways from that of a master hunter. Hence the Inuit, in their pragmatism, drew two conclusions from all these developments (again, my conjecture). The first is that by being "poor," by living in a state of passivity – to the point of wearing totally unsuitable, often damp charity clothing, as my photographs attest – they might meet the missionaries' expectations and please Jesus, the new great shaman. With me, their speech is abnormally "humble," sententious when discussing topics related to their Christian duty. Second, they must take care to observe the ancestral taboos, to respect the Master of the Animals to whom their animistic mental makeup unconsciously or subconsciously looks. They may be seeking help from both the Christian God and the Master of the Animals in restoring the caribou to their former numbers. Consequently, they strictly limit themselves to fishing and hunting the vital but increasingly rare caribou, while the seal, as an animal of the sea, remains taboo.

These are merely suppositions regarding a people whose behaviour is manifestly the expression of self-imposed discipline. What makes the evolving Inuit consciousness especially resistant to straightforward anthropological analysis is their amalgam of traditional hardness with high-minded solidarity, the latter a feature of both their traditional and Christian worldviews. On the one hand, their brutal response to a traumatized child testifies to an absence of pity, an implacability toward the infirm and the weak; on the other, the current crisis demands that they obey the precepts of the strong God's missionaries, exalting humility as a virtue and repressing their violent tendencies. And so they have. "Never in anger" – or, to quote Knud Rasmussen, "a great capacity for resignation" – is indeed an Inuit characteristic.[52] But we have had too much of a brand of anthropology that is willfully blind and deaf, hence mute, to the cruelty routinely practised in Inuit society. Quite apart from infanticide and euthanasia during hard times, the Inuit are no strangers to murder as

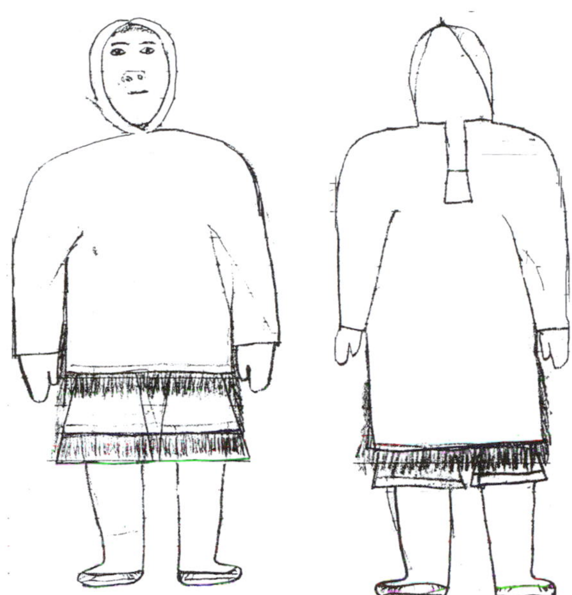

Male winter costume, front and back. Sketch by Kiggiark, Back River, April 1963.

the dénouement to particularly intense conflicts. This underlying tension in contemporary Inuit culture appears to be kept subjugated by the force of the absent minister's authority; it is as if they wore a corset. In particular, they are instructed to abjure relations with their Netsilingmiut brethren of Gjoa Haven, where Roman Catholic teaching and preaching hold sway.[53]

Another observation and a constant throughout this book: when any particular matter remained unclear, perhaps because the information provided by the Inuit was insufficient to elucidate it, I did not hesitate to engage in informed, exploratory speculation. The missionaries, with their Western cognitive systems and their abhorrence of shamanism, had no direct point of entry into the mind of the Inuit. They did what they could to establish their authority and impose a moral code, but it is unclear to what extent the Christian message that they were transmitting came through intact or altered. No research has been done in this region to elucidate the vital issue of whether this group identifies more with the eschatology of evangelical thought or with its ethic.

For example, it would be interesting to know whether they continue to believe in ancestor worship and the realm of the dead, where nearly everyone expects to wind up (except perhaps reprobates, those whose souls wander resentfully) or whether they accept the Christian barrier between heaven and purgatory. In Inuit tradition, souls move off into limbo after a probationary period of three to five days. By means of certain practices and under certain circumstances, notably the naming of newborns, they can be called back among the living, reincarnated. The Catholic Church, in an effort to impose its law, opposed this belief in the power of the ancestors, inculturating itself by taking control of naming. Baptized children were given saints' names (Suzanne, Louis, Alice, Jacob, Bernadette, Thérèse, Sébastien), and the Inuit name was relegated to the status of a patronymic – a foreign concept to the Inuit. Then, in the 1970s, a second factor conspired to deprive the Inuit of the power of naming: in so-called "Project Surname," the Canadian government (without discussion with the Inuit authorities, whom it did not recognize) required each person to choose a surname and pass it on to his children. Now they had two names instead of one, neither given in accordance with their ancient traditions, both responses to white demands. In this way, the Christian God, in collaboration with the government, appropriated the power of the ancestors, annihilating the Inuit logic of reincarnation and abrogating a whole world of shamanistic thought.

As I watch them tonight, pensive, brows furrowed, I think of the biblical prophet Jeremiah who rose in the night to lament that if Jerusalem had been destroyed it was because the Jews, the chosen people, had sinned against the Lord and broken the holy covenant. The time of repentance had begun. This is my provisional conclusion, yet I sense how arbitrary it is. Who knows if,

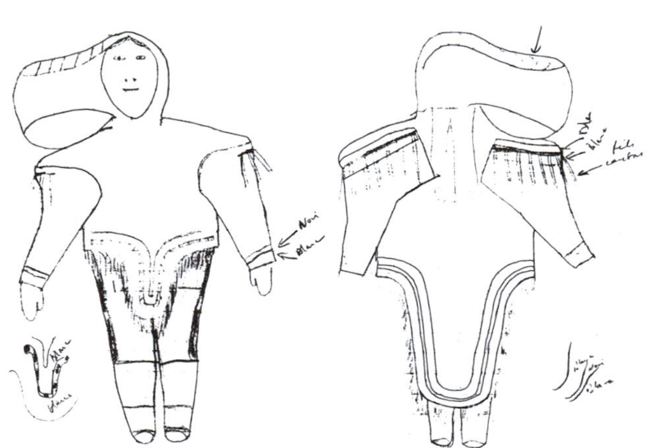

Woman's winter costume, front and back; caribou skin coat with hood for carrying a child. Drawing by Kiggiark, Back River, April 1963.

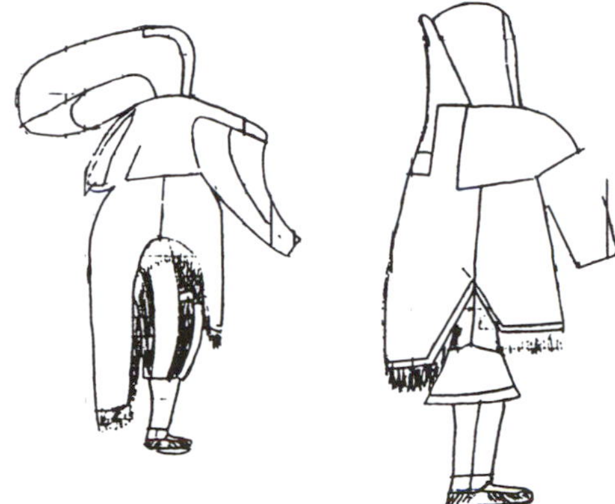

L. to r., female and male winter costumes. Drawing by Kiggiark, Back River, April 1963.

for the Back River Inuit, these times of austerity are experienced as punishment for having sinned? Who knows if they are not, in their apparent passivity, living with a new feeling of guilt? The caribou have shunned them, the Master of the Animals has abandoned them; perhaps the time of a new diaspora (similar to their withdrawal from the Adelaide Peninsula in 1900) is not far off. If so, then it will be because they have sinned against Nature. It is extremely difficult for the Inuit to leave their land, to cut the umbilical cord; it means leaving behind their dead along with the familiar environments where the *tonrars* (spirits of the dead) inspire them.* But they see that the caribou are growing scarcer with each migration. The young people no longer observe the ancestral hunting rites, and the white people's guns kill efficiently. Game is no longer called on; the pact between humans and animals is broken. The inner disillusion of the Inuit, as indicated by numerous psychological tests in other regions – such as my Rorschach tests in North Greenland (1951) and Chukotka (1990) – is visible in their faces. It will not be long before despairing acts on the part of young people displaced to the cities (alcoholism, suicide) become the manifestation of this break with the past.

I shall leave these reflections here since I sense how they are tainted with a Western connotation that makes them tenuous.[54] The human spirit is a product of age-old cognitive structures. Christian ideals simply could not have totally supplanted the animistic mindset of these proud hunters and fishers

* The 1953 Resolute Bay and Grise Fiord relocation affair is significant in this regard; see pp. 42–3.

in the space of a generation or two. Let us consider the prohibition on sealing again. The kernel of the problem is twofold: first, the dietary taboo per se; second, the frequent exogamous marriages with seal-hunting Netsilingmiut men and women in Spence Bay and especially Thom Bay. The dietary taboo may hark back to an ancestral cultural taboo observed by the Caribou Inuit, one that in turn descended from a kinship taboo. (This dietary taboo, it occurs to me, was extant at Rankin Inlet during my visit there in 1962. The Caribou Inuit émigrés abstained from seal meat, and marriages between them and the coastal Inuit were rare.) Now, there is a new prohibition: Catholic Netsilingmiut women are not eligible to participate in these intermarriages. True, they are a small minority in the two towns, where Anglican families outnumber Catholic families 53 to 11. Likewise, there was fierce opposition between the 15 Catholic families and the 30 Anglican families at Gjoa Haven. It is rare, of course, for anyone to renounce their faith. I sense that I am repeating myself, and if so, it is because I am discovering my reasoning to be tenuous. Two interpretations are possible: the synchronic, structuralist one that I have just set forth; and one of a more historical nature. I tend to believe that both pertain.*

THE CULT OF FISHING

The fishermen return carrying whitefish and tomcod in their bare hands. The house is noisy. I take a few flash photos, and the children pick up the scorching blue lamps, observing them with the attentiveness of experimenters. Around eleven o'clock, a child and a woman enter exclaiming, "Inuit! Qaamutit!" Three sleds arrive. A hunter enters, crouching, then stands up before us, powerful, wearing his *kulitak* and caribou-skin boots. It is Nanudluk ("great bear," b. 1923), a resident of the upstream camp, who is on his way to Gjoa Haven. No sooner has he removed his heavy fur jacket than he is pushed to the back of the house and into the cold entryway of the *torhuk*. I don't want to miss anyone, and he will probably not be staying long; with his mouth full of frozen salmon, he graciously responds to my systematic questionnaire.† I take inventory of what he owns and has caught in the last three months. He locates his trap lines on the map. The accounting is brief: trapping is, for him as for all the Utku, something to be stooped to.‡ Nanudluk spends most of his

* See Appendix 1 for the interpretation of my colleague, the Africanist anthropologist András Zempléni (of the CNRS), whom I asked to read the manuscript.

† I paid the respondent only if the interview was in-depth, a half-hour or more. Attempting to pay them would have been an affront, for they considered me their guest.

‡ I verified all these figures by examining the books of account at the Gjoa Haven HBC post, which were graciously opened for me. These books are destroyed every five years.

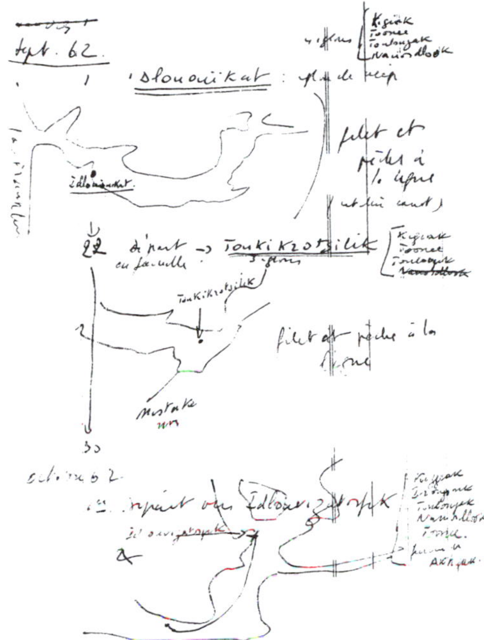

Kiggiark's hunting routes and calendar, beginning in September 1962 and continuing to my arrival in April 1963. I recorded versions of this calendar provided by five hunters. They show that, as in all Inuit societies, the men did not expend all their energy on hunting and fishing, which only accounted for about one-half of their waking time and was limited to specific periods. The other half was reserved for socializing, dialogue, and interaction, including singing, dancing, and religious rites.

time fishing, with one month for hunting caribou and only six days for trapping, as if in perfunctory compliance with the long-held expectations of the white-owned trading posts. With the exception of four annual five-day trips to Uqsuqtuuq, his travels are limited to the vicinity of Franklin Lake.

Around three o'clock we eat another fish, a lovely black-speckled char with a satiny sheen. The head and bones are scattered on the snowy ground. Each of us has been consuming about half a char every four hours.* Each fish weighs about five and a half pounds after removing the head, tail, and bones. The colder the weather, the more they eat. The Inuit heat themselves discerningly, from within.

The well-named Little Fish, who has charmed me with her nonchalant gait and the graceful sway of her hips when she stands up, teaches me various fish preparation words: raw (*mikegiiak*), frozen (*kroar*), dried (*pipsi*), high (*kringnerk*), boiled (*pataorq*). She speaks slowly while I write these words in my green notebook. The Utku are not culinary boors; they prepare their fish in

* A healthy diet, incidentally. Apart from a bit of porridge, all I ate was frozen raw fish, and upon my return to Gjoa Haven I had gained a kilogram.

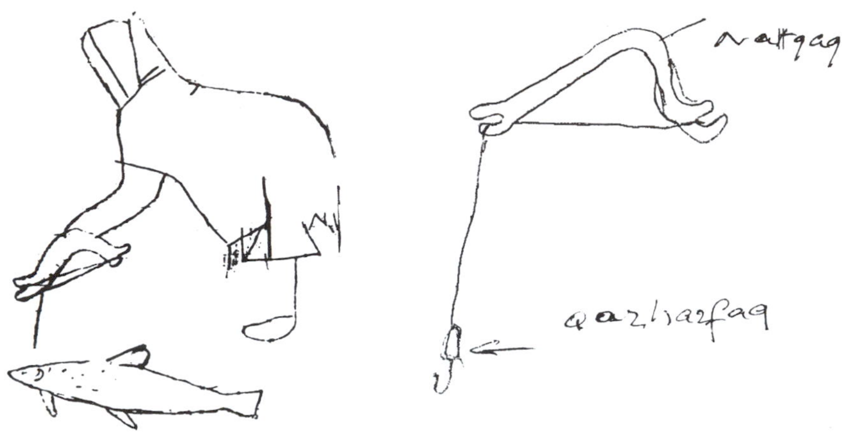

left: Ice fishing on the river in February–March. Drawing by Kiggiark, Back River, April 1963.

right: Winter ice fishing for trout with homemade iron hook (*qarharfaq*) on the lake and the estuary. Caribou antler (*natqaq*) handle. Sketch by Akretoq, Back River, April 1963.

various savoury ways – in soups, for example, or on a grill at the entrance to the *torhuk*, adding various aromatic plants (*ixiutetaq*, *tingauya*, *orpigit*). In the summer, they boil the heads. When it comes to caribou, that too-rare delicacy, "We eat everything we can, even the stomach lining." But never, ever do they mix caribou with ocean fish or seal, and this taboo holds for all the Inuit. Land and sea must remain separate, or else hunting and fishing could be jeopardized for good.

Toolegaak quantifies the dogs' fish ration: one fish per dog per day during the eight-month winter, one every four days in summer, one every three days in spring. He then explains his calendar as I follow along in the Rasmussen report,[55] making changes as necessary (see calendar according to Amundsen and Koorsoot, note 24). The phonetic spellings are as follows, to the best of my ability: June/*nore'rwik* (caribou giving birth), July/*it'avik* (birds moulting), August/*itavik aipa* (other birds losing their down), early August/*ameraerwik* (old caribou shedding velvet from their antlers), late August/*teritorqät ameraerwiät* (young caribou shedding velvet from their antlers), September/*amerasukapa* (female caribou losing their antlers), October/*ukighäp-aipa* (beginning of winter), November/*seqin'aut* (sun is gone), December/*ubluilaut*

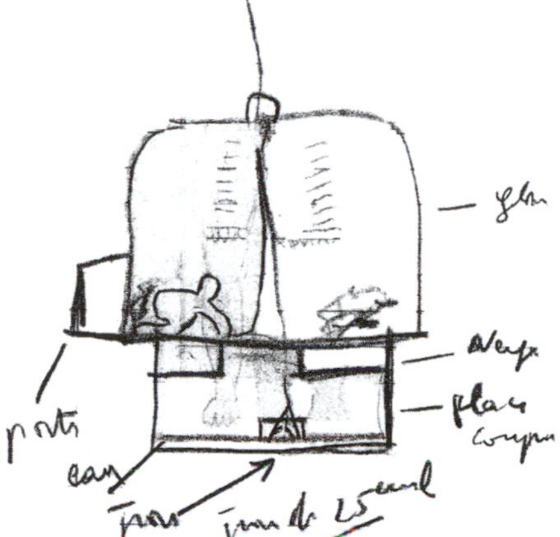

Winter fishing in the bitter cold under a snow house. Drawing by Kiggiark, Back River, April 1963.

(no daylight or dawn), April/*nätsialeriwik* (seals giving birth), May/*qava'sfik* (young seals molting, shedding their white down).

Akretoq takes me to the ice fishing hole. In the shelter of a snow berm, a consummately skilled fisherman shows me his method; he has watched the constable jiggling his line in vain. As an aside, he mentions that ten or twenty years ago, snow shelters were built on top of fishing holes. (Later Kiggiark draws me one, adding some details; see figure above). Within five minutes he catches and hands me a small char, then graciously gives me the antler rod, line, and lure. "Here! This is for you." I still have it sitting by my bedside in Paris.

At four o'clock, the hum of a motor is heard in the damp late-afternoon light – an airplane, landing. It is ... the x-ray program? Decidedly, this place holds nothing but surprises. I had believed myself to be in the Paleolithic, at the end of the world, and here is the government taxi taking the Back River Inuit (in several groups) for a medical examination in Gjoa Haven, a fifty-five-minute flight. In an instant, everyone is bustling toward the cabin with an air of aristocratic indifference to the flying men and their modern gadgetry. Inukshuk comes running and hands his whip to a relative; he had been about to leave by sled when the plane arrived. I give the pilot a note describing the convulsive boy's symptoms and recommend that he be given special care. The pilot is not thrilled at the prospect. Toonee,* the pilot's appointed interpreter,

* Born 1906, professed Anglican. Four children (b. December 1938, 1944, May 1950, February 1953), respectively named Naruk (M), Avingnak (F), Oopootkak (M), and Aniknik (F); also a young girl, Ookooshook Tumulik (b. February 1952), living with them.

speaks no English, while the pilot knows no Inuktitut. But an "official interpreter" is mandatory, and the letter of the law is observed.

A SUBSISTING SOCIETY

Despite these medical programs and the five-minute exams that they mete out to each patient, infant mortality continues to take its unacceptable toll. In the recent past, demographic regulation was achieved by infanticide against girls;* today, dire austerity plays this role – no sex discrimination. Famine remains a reality in this land of great hunting and fishing potential, naturally striking the weakest (children and the elderly) first. During the tragic winter of January–March 1958 – only yesterday, really – Back River was left to its fate. Upstream at Garry Lake, seventeen people (5 per cent of this ethnic group) died of starvation. All the dogs were eaten (they are back to their former numbers and size). A forgotten tragedy. I note the names of those who died at Chantrey Inlet. Nuliarpok died 20 May 1958 after leaving this camp on foot for Gjoa Haven; his last act was to point his daughter in the same direction. The exhausted, emaciated girl alerted the post, which immediately dispatched two sleds. This was followed by an army-supervised aerial search on 13 June at a cost of $8,273, including $3,800 for food, clothing, nets, traps, and other equipment. Again, the money should have been spent, the problem solved, much earlier. It was not. A policy framework for the future of these ancient peoples remained to be found.

The Inuit gave me a confusing explanation of the famine: the summer's fishing had been poorly organized and had not yielded sufficient provisions for winter. Rereading my notes on the RCMP reports, I find them pervaded by the assumption that poverty here is intrinsic and endemic. Famine? These people are used to it; it goes with the territory and the tradition. But this is Canada, a rich nation with all the resources necessary to protect a few thousand people occupying one-third of the country's area. No mention is made of the various entities at the disposition of the state. The police, the Catholic and Anglican missions, and the HBC were perfectly aware of the crisis. And although the reports acknowledge adult deaths from starvation, silence reigns over the high rate of miscarriage as well as the high neonatal mortality rate (one-half to two-thirds of all babies). Subsequent reports and ethnological studies have tended to gloss over the tragedy; some do not mention it at all. It is as if this were the normal course of events in such a cruel land, so no comment is necessary; or perhaps the prevailing social climate made it inapposite to acknowledge the events in writing, to get exercised about them.

* See Arnaja's description of this custom, p. 137.

Caribou hunting. A sled approaches. The hunter cleverly arrives from downwind so as to catch the two caribou unawares. It is very cold and the caribou-skin hood is pulled down over his face. He is in shooting position with his rifle at 3–5 metres, as in hunting with bow and arrow. Drawing by Kaomayok (b. 19/08/1952), son of my companion and guide Q'ipsiga (b. September 1936), Q'apuivik, Igloolik, September 1960.

It was certainly not an isolated case. As winter gives way to spring in the Central Arctic, shortages are commonplace; caribou are lacking and fish not always abundant. At Ennadai Lake, west of Arviat, the Inuit suffered a terrible famine in 1950, one that had been looming since the closing of the trading post a decade earlier. The photographer Richard Harrington published a gruelling account of this unspeakable tragedy, pointing out that it took place within a short distance of a post and a Christian mission. The RCMP reports from this area are equally dramatic. In March and May 1961, shortly before my trip to Spence Bay, serious shortages occurred at Levesque Harbour on the Boothia Peninsula. "They don't want to go south," wrote the constable. "They are too proud to beg." Harrington's photographs are heartrending.[56]

At ten o'clock in the evening, all the Inuit are back with a "clean bill of health," perfunctory though it is. Only the convulsive boy was kept for observation; he has had another seizure on the plane, corroborating my account. He will be sent south to a hospital for a complete examination. I plumb the cold, revealing stare of the pilot, which seems to be saying, "We whites are too good for these basket cases; why do we bother?" In 1962 government anti-poverty assistance is a reality here. Each family gets a fishing net as well as $9 for groceries, $3–4 for gasoline, and $9–12 for ammunition, depending on the month. Seven families were eligible from February to April 1963.[57] The authorities face a dilemma: either let the people alone to face an arduous transition in the absence of sufficient caribou, or take them under the government's wing and turn them into museum pieces. The choice is eminently philosophical – and political.

In the houses, the children stamp restlessly around the floor at the base of the platform, while the adults strut about like dukes. The journey has electrified them. I regret having discovered the Utku only now. They are a rough people but more keenly spontaneous than the Netsilingmiut, whose sentiments are held in check. Here, news plays a vital role in the culture; reports of the littlest event travel from one house to another. Their sense of family is refined. It is a small community in which one is never alone. As soon as a visitor arrives, he gives a precise account (and a livelier one than the Netsilingmiut, I think) of what he has seen and done.

As for me, I am slowly being adopted. At one point Little Fish and Great Whale kneel in front of me to remove my boots (*kamik*). This greatly embarrasses me, and I decide that it will not happen again. The boots with their chewed-up soles are immediately put outside to dry on a hanger, as I have only one pair. Little Fish decides that the seams on my *kulitak* need mending and does so without a word.

COMPARATIVE ACCOUNTS

In my view, it is a crucial obligation in anthropological research to compare, contrast, and interpret all the different voices speaking about a given region or problem during a given period of time. Only such a contrapuntal approach can yield an approximation to the truth. Before leaving Ottawa, I have reviewed all my predecessors' publications, beginning with the classic work of Back, published following his August 1834 meeting with the Utkuhikhalingmiut, and continuing with Schwatka's account of 1878–80. Most of the explorers, however, mention the Inuit only tangentially since they could not speak the language and were indifferent to their civilization. The real groundbreaking work was Rasmussen's, irrespective of the short duration of his stay. It is the keen eye and competence of this extraordinary man that make his work the standard of reference. I am continually referring back to it, not to mention his two great works on the Caribou Inuit and that of his companion Kaj Birket-Smith, my Danish colleague and friend, whose work on this Inuit group (the forebears of the Utkuhikhalingmiut) is first-rate. To all these accounts, I add the annual reports of the RCMP, a gold mine of information consistently neglected by anthropologists. I cite these below as relevant. Unfortunately missing are the confidential Catholic and Anglican codices. Not that I did not make every effort to obtain them; I even contacted the Vatican, although its intervention in Anglican-dominated Chantrey Inlet, off limits to the Oblates by tacit agreement, would have been of no use anyway.

I variously cite the texts, read them in tandem with my own observations and remarks, quibble about or take outright issue with them. In the historical sciences as taught by the masters, Lucien Febvre and Fernand Braudel, this is what is called an internal critique of an account, and it is the historian's responsibility to adhere to it. History, after all, is not activism – that would be to distort reality. By meticulous internal critique, historians verify the veracity of the facts.

The Canadian Central Arctic (the Boothia, Melville, and Adelaide Peninsulas and King William Island) has, for many years (in fact, centuries if cyclical "little ice ages" are considered) been the theatre of famines aggravated by intertribal tensions and violence. Rasmussen writes: "All hunters (Caribou Eskimo) have to base the whole of their livelihood upon caribou hunting, disaster very quickly arrives when this fails. The most dangerous time is always the two months that precede the great caribou migration at the end of May, when the animals come from the woodlands to work their way down towards the coast. If the Eskimo have no cached supplies to fall back upon, March and April are always fateful."[58]

Cruelty increases when survival is of necessity at someone else's expense, a zero-sum game. The little-known Indian-Inuit wars were the scene of vendettas, abduction of women, and massacres (without slave taking), and the same can be said for intertribal struggles between Inuit ethnic groups. Since 1900–20 these peoples have come under Canadian law and RCMP policing, but tensions remained acute. On 19 May 1923 at Kazan River, Rasmussen wrote: "the fear of the Indians was especially great, as century-old feuds had been waged with equally great cruelty on both sides and were still fresh in mind ... It was a custom that had come right down from the coast dwellers by the Northwest Passage, whence people used to come up to the timber line to fetch wood sleds, kayaks and tent-poles. This greeting was: 'il ranik tikit'una,' and means: 'I come from the right side, from the proper side.'"[59]

But worse – in the domain of the irrational, there is always worse – tensions have not ceased between different Inuit groups;[60] reflexes are all the more unthinking and violent for the obscurity of their origins. Judging by the Netsilik and Caribou accounts that I have read and compared, every hunter fears the stranger. According to the RCMP report of 22 May 1956 for the year 1955, the arrogance of the Dorset* immigrants in the northern Boothia Peninsula toward the local Netsilik was visible, even though they were both – particularly the Dorset – destitute at the best of times, starved at the worst. The ethnic cleavages were stronger than any solidarity that might have been displayed. There was an exaggerated sense of honour here that was best left unprovoked. In July 1962, at Rankin Inlet and particularly at Baker Lake, I witnessed such inter-ethnic tension between the local Inuit and the Caribou, who had been transplanted there by Ottawa to avert a new famine.

The collapse of the formerly three-million-strong Canadian caribou herd – reduced to 300,000 since 1930 – was the official explanation for these endemic tragedies. The truth, as the Back River Inuit told me (echoing the Thom Bay Netsilik), was that the explanation also involved a technical component. As Arnaja said during our September 1961 foot traverse of the Boothia Peninsula (see pp. 131–42), "It was easier with bow and arrow because the caribou (*tukto*) were less fearful; they followed well-known paths that we knew well. Today, they fear our guns and are constantly changing paths. We arrive to see a heaving mass of caribou, thousands of them, headed for the coast; most of the herd is gone by the time we get there."

Toonee of Back River gave a similar account during our early-morning talks in the snow house in April 1963, and both accounts are nearly identical to what Rasmussen wrote in May 1923 when he visited the Kazan River:

> In these parts of the Barren Grounds there are enormous numbers of caribou, which follow their old migration paths and cross rivers and lakes at quite certain places. As long as the Eskimos only used bow and arrow, their kayaks and their special kayak lance, the animals were not scared to such an extent as they are now, when the hunters shoot away at the animals opposite the crossing places with long-range magazine rifles. When the caribou have experienced this disturbance for a few years they take other paths, whereas the Eskimos remain at the same villages, and this causes the catastrophe. They think there are no caribou, whereas the truth is that the caribou have merely chosen another road.[61]

According to Father Turquetil, a missionary with a great talent for regional history who lived at Chesterfield from 1910–20, there were then 600 Inuit living at Hikoligjuaq at the headwaters of the Kazan River; in 1923 Rasmussen counted only 100. The population had been decimated by famine.[62] Evidently,

* Hudson Bay seal hunting group transplanted to the Boothia Peninsula by the authorities due to famine in the 1950s. The outcome of such forced migrations is usually negative, as with the Resolute Bay and Grise Fiord relocations of 1953; see pp. 42–3.

technical progress can be devastating for a people so closely tied to their culture and beliefs that they are unable, as here, to emigrate to the coast to hunt seals as a substitute for the missing caribou. Lack of technical ability, know-how, was surely operative, but in the hour of great perils, human history is not driven by such factors alone; it responds to individual and collective fears, unconscious impulses, attempts to divine the abiding purpose of the group's predicament by reading the forces of nature and adhering to its dictates. Otherwise, chaos ensues; it is anything goes, and every man for himself.

I should stress that my daily caloric intake on their raw fish diet was almost 5,000 calories during my brief stay, and to my benefit, I gained weight. (I did not follow their example and eat the heads or eyes.) They also drank a great deal, two to three litres per day. No nutritional deficiencies were to be found among these eaters of fish, caribou in season, berries in summer, eggs, birds, and the occasional Arctic hare. The problem was not diet but the uncertainty of being able to obtain the elements of that diet due to fluctuating caribou numbers and other seasonal irregularities. Relative abundance gives way to scarcity. In truth, several generations of Central Arctic people had suffered great adversity. On 19 May 1923, at Tugliuvartalik near the Kazan River, Rasmussen wrote: "These people told us at once that they had just managed to survive the winter, and in many places both man and dog had starved to death."[63] Among the Padlermiut, he wrote, "I was told that only a month before they had all been on the verge of starvation. In spite of endless hunting, there had been no game to find, and all the caches from previous hunts had been emptied."[64]

As I read the RCMP reports for the Spence Bay and Gjoa Haven districts, covering the whole of the Back River and Netsilik territory, I am dumbfounded at Ottawa's phlegmatic response to ten years of repeated sounding of alarms. Boothia Peninsula, 22 May 1956: "Three of the Dorset families are practically destitute and the hunter in these cases appears to become more indigent every year. It could be said that in the winter of 1955, if not for the assistance of certain friendly 'Netchilik' Eskimo in providing fresh meat, the three Dorset families would surely have starved."

A conservative society, the Dorset, rooted to its place and governed by apparently suicidal dietary (indeed, cultural) taboos, the prevailing one being the contrary of the Utku's: the Dorset refused (or did not deign) to fish in the rivers or hunt caribou, to eat land animals, even during times of famine. Born on Hudson Bay, they considered themselves sealers, even if married to Netsilik women, who, by perspicacious tradition, espouse a "hybrid" dietary culture – both land and sea animals allowed. RCMP, 22 May 1956: "Regardless of the fact that 'Dorset' women have made successful marriages with 'Netchilik men,' the attitude of the Dorset is still that they are superior in all respects ...

to a Netchilik Eskimo ... Thom Bay: six Eskimo families. Laziness. There were some days that the camp had no food at all. Most of the Eskimo of the camp are 'Dorset' and depend greatly on there being a floe-edge to hunt from. This is never a good idea as there is not always open water."

Another RCMP constable wrote that on 2 March 1961, in a camp of seven families at Levesque Harbour on the northern Boothia Peninsula, he observed an extreme shortage liable to lead to famine; he reported no change on a second visit in May. Although the report preserves silence on the matter out of discretion and propriety, these famines were accompanied by voluntary euthanasia – suicide – on the part of older persons who considered themselves, in Cornelian fashion, to be burdensome to a group in jeopardy. The sick and weak were eliminated, the mortality rate due to lowered resistance was shocking, and the appalling practice of killing girls at birth was pervasive. Telling in this regard are the abnormally imbalanced sex ratios that I determined in 1960–61 for this region, particularly in the Fort Ross area near Bellot Strait and at Thom Bay (August 1961), where there were six marriageable bachelors and one marriageable widow among a population of seven families. These observations are confirmed by RCMP and other data: "A definite shortage of marriageable females ... Only five marriageable girls and women are in this area compared to 17 eligible young men or older widowers." "There is a preponderance of males and difficulties in finding prospective brides are encountered."[65] "The percentage of males and females is a bit better than in Spence Bay subdistrict with nine eligible single females and sixteen males."[66] Here, then, was the proof of hidden crimes committed among these groups living at the edge of the ecumene, a fate to which geography had pushed them. I must reiterate that it was not considered murder. For the Inuit, a child was born alive only when the community had named it. The name is the bearer of life. And once life was recognized, the group members would share their wealth as equitably as possible in order to preserve it.

To these hecatombs, as I mentioned, may be added a very high child and adult mortality rate. RCMP, 1960 annual report for the Spence Bay district: "Under one year: 14 deaths, the majority within the first two months after birth, four of these were sickly children who died very shortly after being born, and the remaining deaths were apparently from respiratory diseases. Between 1 and 13 years, five deaths, all apparently from respiratory diseases. Between 13 and 21 years, one death caused by pneumonia. Over 21 years, 13 deaths, one from tuberculosis, and the remainder apparently from respiratory diseases ... There were a total of 36 births and 33 deaths for the area during the year."

The previous report for the Spence Bay district, covering 1 January 1958 to 31 December 1959, noted 60 births for a population of about 500. There were

26 deaths in infants under one year of age, including 3 stillborn, 5 aged under one day, 4 from one day to one week, 6 from one week to one month, 7 from one to six months, and 1 from six months to one year. The causes (hearsay evidence) were flu, pneumonia, malnutrition, or other pregnancy complications. There were 8 deaths in children under thirteen, 3 from an unknown illness, 3 from pneumonia, 1 from starvation, and 1 from smallpox; 4 deaths in the thirteen to twenty-one age group, 2 from measles and 2 from starvation; and 16 deaths in people over twenty-one, 1 from a miscarriage, 2 from measles, 5 from old age, 4 from starvation, and 4 from drowning.

Respiratory problems, including tuberculosis, were among the main medical concerns for this population of snow house dwellers. In the spring when the air begins to warm up, the men and women were afflicted by the damp cold. The tradition, as I observed it in April 1963 at Back River, and as can be seen in the photographs published in my *Call of the North*,[67] was to let clothing dry on one's body, while mittens and boots were hung on stakes outside. Rasmussen made a similar observation in 1923: "If they have enough skins, the wet garments must be thrown away and replaced by new ones; if not, they must be dried during the night by means of placing the wet parts against the naked breast."[68]

This people of subsistence did not appear to have any spare animal-skin clothing when I visited in April 1963. Instead, they wore donated fabric clothing, with disastrous consequences for their health.[69] They were distressingly cash-poor. The RCMP report of 20 February 1952 for Spence Bay noted a particularly bad year for trapping, with a scandalously low price of $5.50 per pelt.* At this rate, the average annualized family income would be about $120–150 (this figure corroborated by the above-mentioned report), as much as a Hudson's Bay Company employee earned in a single month,[70] not including benefits. I found the same income disparities in all the societies that I studied in the Canadian Eastern Arctic in the early 1960s: the maximum annual income was $300–600. At its widest (i.e., in bad years for the Inuit) the gap between their incomes and those of the Northern Affairs bureaucrats was on the order of 1 to 12, as it was at Kuujjuaq (Ungava, Nunavik) during my research there in 1968–69.[71] It is deplorable that geological, anthropological, cinematographic, and museological expeditions (admittedly few in this remote area) have kept so quiet about the day-to-day drama of these impoverished men and women

* Trapping required exceptional skill and long treks. The fox, once caught, had to be skinned and its pelt carefully prepared, this latter work being done by the women. A day's work – anywhere from five to twenty-four hours – might yield one to five pelts, making for a meager hourly wage.

over the past thirty years, their literal struggle to survive. Apart from the diligent, harrowing accounts of Rasmussen, Birket-Smith, Jenness, Harrington, and Mowat, most travel or ethnological texts mention the harshness of their lives casually, without dwelling on the cruel, tragic outcomes that I have been discussing. And this, I must reiterate, was all taking place in the great, rich, Christian, democratic nation of Canada. In the Canadian Central Arctic, child mortality was a whopping two out of three, people over fifty were committing suicide to save the young, and infant girls were being put to death. Only the exacting, courageous truthfulness of the annual RCMP reports gets to the heart of the problem, and it is amazing that I should be the first anthropologist to make systematic use of this essential source of information as part of a "contrapuntal" study, giving it the public forum that it deserves. The reports make for painful reading, particularly when one realizes that this elite body sounded the alarm in vain for at least thirty years. And it was not a matter of putting thousands of needy people on welfare. Only 200–300 families among Canada's founding peoples were at stake, suffering with dignity through a biogeographical and cultural crisis that had overwhelmed them.

The RCMP reports are eloquent on the harsh primitivism of their daily lives. For example, even when the outside temperature fell to –30 to –50°C, they did not heat their homes. Back River, 1955: "When there were large herds of caribou to shoot, there would be plenty of fat for their lamps. Nowadays all they have, is the belly fat from the white fish which does not add up to much. For cooking and making of tea, they use the ground willows, which are abundant, and the fire is made in a separate porch to the living quarters. It appears that no attempts were made to make a little stove for the living quarters that could burn the willows and to supply much needed heat."[72] Likewise, Rasmussen commented: "The people here, by the way, have never had large blubber lamps like the Netsilingmiut or the Kitlinermiut. They were small and intended for economy. Nowadays, the soapstone lamp is no longer used. They are content with a hollow stone in which burns a moss wick in melted caribou fat, the so called pun'ernaq. They also render down oil from the fat bellies of the autumn trout and preserve it in throat skins."[73]

Exhausted by recurrent famine, these populations were ravaged by disease – deadly influenza, measles, and odd cases of diarrhoea such as those observed in the winter of 1957 at Spence Bay. The 1956 RCMP report noted secondary problems occurring throughout the Spence Bay district, including ear, eye, throat, and urinary infections. It may come as a shock to learn that as late as 1960, the emblematic Back River people were not even entitled to a regular, comprehensive, government-funded check-up. This fact, like all the rest, is mentioned and deplored in the RCMP reports for 1955–62 in their typically reserved administrative style.

In short, these men and women were fatalistically engaged in a relentless struggle to exist. An even worse situation had occurred in the northern Ungava Peninsula twenty years earlier, when a terrible famine wiped out one-third of the population, a tragedy met by total silence on the part of the media in Québec City and Ottawa and by inaction on the part of the all-powerful church parishes, dioceses, and universities. Relief came only with the arrival of US military bases during the Second World War.

At Back River, where the men and women stared at the floor when answering any sensitive question (they never looked me in the face during the initial days of my socio-economic survey), I sometimes wondered – so great was their economic misery – as to the veracity of their statements. Some individuals told me, for example, that they had not shot a single caribou in 1962–63, while another said that he had shot twenty-six. Yet a family needs at least forty to sixty every three years. Perhaps there was some mistake on my part – or might they have been deliberately misstating their catch? Both possibilities seem unlikely. The police interpreter Tootalik (who also accompanied me on the Boothia Peninsula from August to September 1961) did a magnificent job, and the respondents' willingness to communicate openly was plain. Further, the English-speaking RCMP constable later congratulated me on the uncommonly warm fellow feeling between us.

One needed only look at the state of their clothing, particularly the children's, to see that they were experiencing a grave crisis.[74] The charity clothing worn by the women and children was worrisome in the extreme. The ambient humidity and the presence of tuberculosis made them likely candidates for pulmonary disease. Consider the Ona, Yaghan, and Alakaluf peoples of Tierra del Fuego, who were exterminated by a similar process. The Franciscans, shocked by the way that their animal-skin ponchos left certain parts of the body exposed, had encouraged similarly inadequate forms of dress: the one that they replaced had possessed the notable merit of letting water trickle off the wearer's body. The RCMP report of 26 August 1960 for 1959–60 remarks: "Back River, ten families ... usual shortage of sleeping-bags and clothing-skins early in the winter."

The litany of woes goes on. Back River, 1959: "Nine families. Their main diet and for the majority, the only diet, was fish. And the fish run throughout was very good all year ... The trapping of fox was practically negligible and hardly any caribou were killed in this area." 30 June 1957: "14 families, one large camp during winter months. In the spring and summer months, they divide up for caribou hunting. Poor year, each family averaging approximately five caribou a piece." 30 June 1959: only ten caribou were shot in the Back River region during the 1958–59 season. No musk oxen. One to three fish caches (char and whitefish) per family.

My family-by-family inventories revealed that they had surprisingly large numbers of traps – not purchased, it turns out, but loaned by the Company. An utterly futile gesture. These people, proud of their autonomy, clearly wanted to avoid what they saw as a dissolute occupation, one whose outcome would be to bind the hunter to the trading post, to engender a dependency on a cyclical socio-economic phenomenon. Consequently, they refused to trap fox even when bearing up with stoicism under extreme economic hardship. It is alleged that the HBC subtly encouraged them and other Native groups in the Arctic to become indebted, forcing them to assimilate into white civilization to varying degrees.

RCMP report for 1955: "Trapping at Back River is a standing joke; as it is said that an Eskimo can leave after tea-time, cover his whole trap-line and be back in time for supper. The Eskimo here are of a very primitive type and are content to live according to old standards ... The Eskimo of this area are not dependent on seals but are solely caribou hunters and fishermen. Each family averaged a dozen caribou for 1955 which is not very many."

Annual report for year ending 30 June 1957: "The true Back River Eskimo do not show any desire in moving into different hunting grounds. They seem to take hardships and starvation as a matter of course and something that cannot be helped."

They were proud of their traditionalist stance to the point of pampering their dogs at the risk of self-sacrifice. RCMP report of 22 May 1955, corroborated by my observations of April 1963: "The Back River Eskimo seems to take pride in their [*sic*] dog teams, as all the dogs are big, healthy and fat looking."

When I brought up the tragedy of 1958, the Inuit (particularly the elders) gazed at me with faraway looks.* Their words, gestures, and facial expressions all seemed to state that these famines were just an episode, a detail in their long history. I am reminded of Fernand Braudel's concept of geohistory (*histoire non-événementielle*), a phrase originally due to the economist François Simiand, which signifies an awareness that in history the short term and the long term are two different things. As tautological as this sounds, the distinction is often neglected. Braudel's geohistory puts events into multigenerational perspective. The whole of Inuit history is like the play of systole and diastole, with rather long intervals of comfort and prosperity broken up by short, terrible periods of famine and war.

* During my interviews with the men, the women stood slightly behind them in near total silence. They were always very obliging with material assistance and would spontaneously give me gifts, such as dolls with finely sculpted caribou-antler heads. I had only to ask and they would produce drawings of their costumes and other items in my small green notebooks; almost as an afterthought, they would press modest gifts into my hand.

20 juin 63

Commissioner C.W. HARVISON
R.C.M.Police
H.Q.
Tremblay Road
OTTAWA, Ont.
Canada

Monsieur,

Je tiens à vous remercier personnellement des éminents services que la Gendarmerie Royale du Canada a bien voulu assurer à mon Collègue, le Prof. J.-N. MALAURIE au cours de la mission scientifique qu'il a assurée en avril-mai 1963, conjointement pour mon Institution et le Northern Research Coordination Center, Department of Northern Affairs, dans la région esquimaude isolée de l'Arctique Central Canadien, à Chantrey Inlet (Territoires du Nord-Ouest).

Le Prof. MALAURIE m'a fait part de l'aide efficace qu'il a reçue du Surintendant J.T. PARSONS, "G" Division, à Ottawa, ainsi que des facilités que ses services lui ont fait accorder localement.

Au nom du Prof. MALAURIE et de notre Institution, je vous en suis très reconnaissant.

Veuillez agréer, Monsieur, l'assurance de mes sentiments très distingués.

F. BRAUDEL
Professeur au Collège de France
Président de la VIe Section de l'Ecole Pratique des Htes Etudes

The Caribou Inuit do not move voluntarily into an unknown hunting area, however favourable, unless literally forced. Because of their knowledge of geography and game, but also their shamanistic relationship with the dead, the Inuit are attached to the tundra, their traditional home. Fernand Braudel writes, quoting Claude Lévi-Strauss: "Cultures ... are societies 'which produce little disorder – what doctors call "entropy" – and tend to remain indefinitely as they originally were: which is why they look to us like societies that lack both history and progress.'" Braudel goes on:

Almost all civilizations are pervaded or submerged by religion, by the supernatural, and by magic: they have always been steeped in it, and they draw from it the most powerful motives in their particular psychology ... A civilization generally refuses to accept a cultural innovation that calls in question one of its own structural elements. Such refusals or unspoken enmities are relatively rare: but they always point to the heart of a civilization ... Marcel Mauss has remarked that every civilization worthy of the name has refused or rejected something. Every time, the refusal is the culmination of a long period of hesitation and experiment. Long meditated and slowly reached, the decision is always crucially important ... A civilization, then, is neither a given economy nor a given society, but something which can persist through a series of economies or societies, barely susceptible to gradual change.[75]

It seems to me that these observations apply quite germanely to the Utku. When I asked Toonee, Toolegaak, Nanudluk, and Kiggiark why they had stayed at Back River after the 1958–59 famine, I was focusing on the short term; in answering, the men were showing me that their actions are best interpreted from a long-range perspective. Each was silent for some time, then looked at me and repeated approximately the same words:

But this place is good to us. There is running water all year long, and since we have no animal fat, or very little, it is essential not to have to melt ice or snow. Running water is our most precious capital. And there is also fish, three per person per day, not counting fish for the dogs; here, we can always drink and eat when we want. It's different for the Netsilik. They go through cycles and lengthy famines, and when there are no seals they have a drinking water problem, too, because they need oil to melt ice.

In answering thus, they were essentially invoking this piece of age-old wisdom: when in crisis, keep what you have unless you are absolutely certain that change is better. It was, after all, such pragmatic wisdom that had originally led the Inuit to abandon the Adelaide Peninsula during famine times and move to these hallowed ancestral grounds, where they have stayed through thick and thin. All things considered, Back River was a secure place of refuge, one of the safest in the Central Arctic. Recall RCMP sergeant Fryer's remark that "an abundance of fish is what keeps the Eskimo living in this country and even, in the deep winter, an active Eskimo can haul thirty fish a day."

Prudence counselled them to keep clear of the trading posts: "A bad place, full of diseases; one gets lazy there," said Toolegaak. This is corroborated by the following remark from an RCMP report on the Boothia Peninsula Inuit: "Brentford bay (including Nydlukta inlet): eight families: four Netshilik, one Dorset and three Arctic Bay [Tununermiut] ... it is customary for Eskimo from this area to make only one or two trips a year to Spence Bay to trade, usually in fall and spring. With this infrequent contact, they are more or less isolated from the frequent diseases that occur amongst the Eskimo living near Spence Bay."

They knew, moreover, that game is scarce at Gjoa Haven, myopically chosen by the authorities as the place to assemble the entire local population of hunters, this despite the RCMP's oft-repeated and judicious counsel. Gjoa Haven, 22 May 1956: "This location has never been known to have abundant game."

One understands why life at Back River, as austere as it was, was perceived as safer than disease-infested, game-poor Gjoa Haven. No famine there, perhaps, but harsh austerity all the same during that difficult period of history.

SEMI-NOMADISM

There is a prevailing misconception that the Caribou Inuit were nomadic. While at Back River, I perused the 4 July 1962 report of the RCMP detachment to the G Division office in Ottawa.[76] An agent from the Baker Lake detachment wrote of four camps comprising fourteen hunters upstream of the Back River estuary,* each of whom shot forty-three caribou in 1961–62. He noted: "There is an increase of twelve caribou per hunter over the previous year," and added, "Twenty-three trappers averaged 18 fox each, total for the area being 416 white and 6 blue."[77] Oh, bountiful tundra! A radically different situation from what was happening in the Back River estuary that same year, only 300 kilometres away as the crow flies, a moderate distance for semi-nomads to travel. That is to say, a bird's eye view of the geography obscures significant local differences that may not be exploitable by the people living on the ground. The Inuit groups lived within defined, or "marked," territories. They had perfect knowledge of their game characteristics and an intense awareness of how they are inhabited by the spirit of the dead. But they knew that game numbers fluctuated with each migration. "This is a good year; next year might be terrible!" *Imaha* (perhaps) – the cornerstone of their philosophy. Randomness is the rule. Time and changing faunal distributions govern their destiny. And so, come what may, they stayed on their "good," thousand-square-kilometre fishing grounds, even though the catch was not always sufficient to support seven to nine families.

A revision of the concept of "nomadism" in this connection is thus long overdue. When one thinks of nomads, the Huns, Mongols, and Visigoths come to mind, epochal upheavals that caused the hordes to spread out over thousands of kilometres into *terra incognita*. The Inuit exhibited true nomadism of this kind only when one takes the long view of their movement from the Bering Strait to Greenland as a response to century-spanning climatic and faunal crises. Over shorter time spans, they were only semi-nomadic, ranging over a well-known area for decades at a stretch. And why go elsewhere? Away from the spirits of their dead, they would be orphans: "We wouldn't be welcome where the other Inuit are. It's their territory." Or as Toonee put it: "We've got to stay here at all costs. Back River is the land of our ances-

* I was planning, as part of my winter activities in 1964, to travel up the Back River, particularly to Garry Lake, whence the forebears of the Back River ethnic group had migrated, to inquire into the endemic famine in the region over the previous decade.

tors." A sentiment recognized by the RCMP report of 30 June 1957: "the true Back River Eskimo do not show any desire in moving into different hunting grounds."

Steeped in fatalism and tradition, the people preferred to wait, to stay put. On the individual level, their extraordinary patience could be measured in hours, days, or weeks; as a people, in years, centuries. I reread my careful transcriptions of the profound RCMP observations that I had found in their annual reports while staying at the Spence Bay post in August 1961, observations that were the genesis of my decision to carry out this exploratory expedition at once: "fatalism in the face of adversity ... vigour derived from isolation ... pride in their traditional customs."[78]

ISOLATIONISM

The point should be stressed that traditionalist Inuit groups do not intermingle during famines. Their natural aggressiveness keeps them conscious that the neighbour is always a potential enemy, especially when resources are scarce.[79] Toonee's and Toolegaak's accounts of tribal warfare in the Adelaide Peninsula took place in the not-too-distant past, perhaps twenty years ago, perhaps fifty; it is impossible to be certain. Not yesterday, but the day before. If they did not make their way up the river in 1959, it is because they knew – sensed – that they would not be welcomed. An RCMP corporal expressed similar surprise that the Boothia Peninsula Inuit did not migrate during a famine. Migration had never crossed their mind, he was told, and he concluded in essence that it was a matter of natural pride (1960–61).

They did not want to beg from Inuit groups who had already helped them, so they opted to live with endemic famine instead. RCMP report of 22 May 1956 for the year 1955: "15 Eskimo families resided at Back River during 1955 but only 10 of them are considered the true 'Okoseeksalingmiout' or Back River Eskimo. These particular 10 families always remain at Back River, whereas the others periodically go into this area." Visitors were accepted on a seasonal basis only. No Catholics allowed.

CHEERFULNESS

They loved their land and were in good health. RCMP report of 30 June 1959 for Back River: "Nine Eskimo families, the natives in general were in excellent health and spirits." In my presence the group members were vigourous and jovial. Moreover, those who had worked with whites on a small American DEW Line site had done so only for the money, before getting married. They wanted to return to their snow houses even if it meant suffering from hunger and cold. "It quickens the blood, makes you stronger," said both a youth and an elder whom I interviewed. They would have to be forced to return to the

American base. "You become a *kiffak*, a lackey. You do women's work, sweeping. No initiative, no promotion. Those comfortable barracks wear you down, make you want to sleep all the time." The RCMP report of 22 May 1956 made the same observation: "At the present time, none of them would like to return on work there ... [there was] no difficulty getting them to adapt themselves to the native way of life and most of them it could be said that they are better men for hunting and trapping than before they went to work on the American air base (DEW Line)."

INTEGRATION?

Yet how bereft they seemed, how fragile their will to remain themselves! A people living on the edge, apparently destined for dispersal and extinction. In 1923 Rasmussen counted 147 Utkuhikhalingmiut (30 families) at Back River. This figure, he clarified, comprised both the settlement at the mouth of the river and the upstream settlements of Itivnârssuk, Ilôrtôq, Orssugiut, and Kibvaluk Lake. Therefore, his figures cannot be compared with later counts unless adjusted for this factor. I did so and found that the number of families at the estuary in Rasmussen's time was 13. In 1937, according to Gibson, the total population was 32 (18 male, 14 female). In 1963 it was 25 (7 families), outnumbered by about 40 expatriates (10 in Gjoa Haven, 5 in Rankin Inlet, 8 in Whale Cove, others at Baker Lake). Famine had led to emigration. I later met and conducted individual interviews with the ten who had gone to Gjoa Haven as well as with several others at Rankin Inlet and Baker Lake.

Our Cartesian rationalism impels us to give paramount importance to economic factors in societies as bereft as theirs, but we fail to perceive essential

Detail of hand tattoo. Back River, April–May 1963.

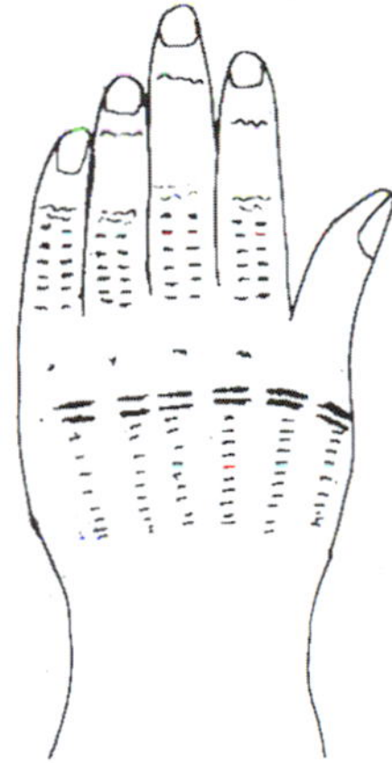

things of which the first peoples, with their more developed neurons, their finely attuned dendrites, are conscious.[80] There are powers ungraspable by rational thought, realms of consciousness to which the first peoples, by virtue of their sensory acuity, have privileged access. The Utku in particular, having only just converted to Christianity, possessed an especially intense version of this vertical vision; in fact, like the Pueblo and the Sioux before them, they were in the process of "Indianizing" Christ, devising a neo-Christianity with shamanistic overtones.[81] With hindsight, the observer, historian, ethnologist, and geographer gains a deeper understanding of the data that he collected long ago. Thus, for example, the issues discussed in my *The Last Kings of Thule*, in the course of its five editions, have taken on deeper meaning for the man of reason that I am. The relationship between humans and their environment is akin to what are nowadays called networks. There is a holistic interpretation of the forces of the earth, the air, and our planet's place in the cosmos alongside the sun, the moon, and a certain number of stars, which first peoples such as the Inuit perceive but which we, with our reason, can discern only with great difficulty. This interpretation of such anthropogeographic networks, the cognitive systems of the far northern hunters, can be better apprehended by computers. Barbara Glowczewski, in a superb recent book on the Aborigines of the Australian deserts, emphasizes this relationship between transcendence and such terrestrial and cosmic networks: "I am convinced of the existence of a kind of wisdom prevailing since the dawn of time that is expressed in certain religious mystiques, although that is not its only *raison d'être*. The Aborigines taught me that matters held by Occident and Orient to be within the realm of religion partake, for them, of a phenomenology of being, an immanence of the spirit with respect to the body and its universe."[82] Among the Inuit, this network-oriented relationship is perceptible in rites, taboos, socio-economic refusals, shamanistic scenes, and the characteristic geometrically patterned representations found in women's arm, thigh, and facial tattoos as well as on the ivories placed in tombs (Bering Strait). In all this, there is something like an alliance between humans and the forces of nature. "If there is no one left to 'read' changes, to interpret them and actualize the traces of the past through song, painting, and dance, life will have neither foundation nor future, and people will be more akin to stray dogs than to human beings."[83]

THE ENCYCLOPEDISTS AND THE SOCIETIES OF NATURE

Diderot or Rousseau would have been fascinated by people such as these, by their lives of stark subsistence on the margins of history. What might they have written if they had been in my place? What are the factors that may help a "natural" society to emerge from its "rootedness"? And what better way to fire the imagination in this chilly snow house than to attempt to analyze the initial forms of organization of a primitive society, with its overlapping, interpenetrating strata borrowed from other cultures?

The Encyclopedists wrote about these problems with emotion and eloquence; I am reminded of Rousseau's famous comment in his first draft of the *Social Contract* (the "Geneva Manuscript"): "I describe [the machine's] mechanisms and its parts, and set them in place. I put the machine in running order. Wiser men will regulate its movements."[84] What keeps a "natural society" in running order? The will to exist is first and foremost economic; human beings must eat and protect themselves from the elements, an imperative at which they will fail in isolation. So they come together in an aggregate of hunting groups. Gradually, these take the shape of a polity that is also a moral community since, after millennia, its thought becomes anchored within a purposive, pantheistic, shamanistic worldview. Rousseau's "whole greater than the sum of its parts" aptly describes the subtle anarcho-communalism that I experienced in 1950–51 and described in detail in *The Last Kings of Thule* and in *Ultima Thule*. It is this system that maintains the human ecology – those few points of equilibrium between natural, savage man and "social" man – within a shamanistic worldview. But beyond the social contract, are the Inuit impelled into the future willy-nilly by larger historical forces? To answer this question is to resolve the conundrum of their disintegration following a rapid conversion to a foreign religion and economy, not to mention their flight or migration to towns offering only commerce and government assistance, a move that has condemned them to a life of welfare.

Their society had apparently adapted with the flexibility visible throughout much of Inuit history. But the organism was wounded somehow, pierced to the heart; I could see it, feel it. The introduction of guns forty years earlier represented the initial break with the past. Then came Christianity, just decades ago – only the day before, as it were. The profound effects of the resulting spiritual upheaval were perceptible. What force must be causing them to dig their heels in before me with such obstinate conservatism if not the conviction that any additional change – most pertinently, to leave their historical home – would hasten their annihilation? Their tiny population of seven families could subsist only in determined isolation, and determined they were: it was there that they must remain, as if with the instinctive strength of an endangered species. To assimilate with the Netsilingmiut would be fatal to their ethnic group and to their spartan philosophy of life. Marry their women and let them emigrate from Thom Bay? Yes, said Toonee, provided that they adopt "our ways and our vision."

To remain at Back River was therefore a deliberate choice, and we are brought face to face with Rousseau's observation in the *Discourse on Inequal-*

ity: "Nature lays her commands on every animal ... Man [alone] ... knows himself at liberty to acquiesce or resist: and it is particularly in his consciousness of this liberty that the spirituality of his soul is displayed."[85] "In the state of nature, history is dammed up, as it were; but the least breach in nature's perfection allows the pent-up waters to pour forth."[86]

And so I returned to the leitmotiv of my thinking here in the Central Arctic: the future, what might it hold? Who would shape it? Certainly not the RCMP; the force could only assist, lend a helping hand in times of duress. It was the central government's responsibility to make a dignified, statesmanlike decision. Back in Ottawa, in conversations with government officials, I put great emphasis on this imperative. But life went on as if these first peoples had not already acquired the historical and political legitimacy to which they have been entitled since the birth of the Dominion in 1867.

With the end of tribal warfare around 1900–10, this ancient society had not only the conditions for survival, but also, in two generations, the time to deepen and develop its civilization with the formation of elites concerned with affirming the creative aspects of both cultures. The crisis was not inevitable. It was brought to a head by the sedentarization of the Inuit around the trading posts, where civil servants operating within a banefully dogmatic ideology of relief meted it out in homeopathic doses. To what ostensible end? Continuity without loss of colonial control, an English Canadian education, and over the long run, assimilation. A comprehensive political vision was entirely absent. Instead of dealing with the underlying problem, the authorities opted to address its direst manifestation, their unspeakable poverty. The

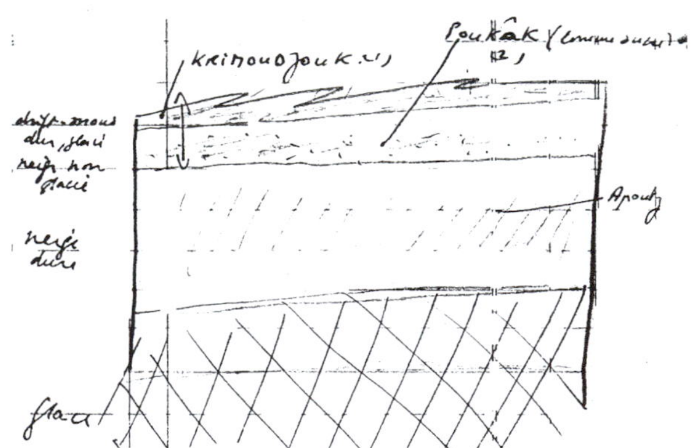

Author's sketch at bivouac on return trip from Back River to Gjoa Haven, from information provided by my guide Nanordloo. Top, layer of drift snow (hard-packed, icy snow ranging up to 10 cm thick). Below that, 10–20 cm layer of looser, granular snow (*pukak*); below that, thick layer (up to 20 cm) of hard snow (*aputj*), from which blocks are cut for the snow house. This is sitting on a layer of ice, as for example on the ice floe. April 1963.

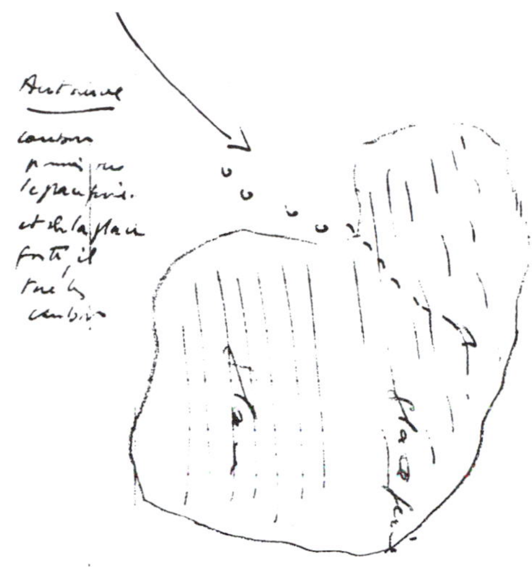

Autumn caribou hunting technique. The hunters make a commotion along a corridor marked out by cairns (*inugshuko*; four small circles in the drawing), attempting to drive the caribou herd onto the thin ice of a half-frozen lake. The drowning caribou are shot by hunters from the far shore. Drawing by Walter Porter, a mixed-blood Inuk who managed the Gjoa Haven post, May 1963.

resulting "relief" was the work of the tinkerer and does not stand up to serious examination. What good, for example, was an income supplement without price controls on hunting and fishing supplies? But no such toying with the sacrosanct liberal economy would be brooked, and the consequences were grievous. Out of a growing need for security, the hunters settled ever closer to the posts or missions and, consequently, ever farther from their hunting grounds, which were now as much as four to ten hours distant.

The Back River holdouts had rejected the system, refused to assimilate. But how long could they hold out? A few years at best. The new needs of the young dictated that ampler resources be allocated, while the fabled physical strength of this ancient people was being biologically undermined. Endemic disease – respiratory ailments, tuberculosis, measles, ear infections, impetigo, eczema, and so forth – was an early consequence of their sedentarization. An RCMP report for 1956 found that the only Inuit apparently in good health were those living far from the posts, while the annual report for Spence Bay of 30 June 1961 stated: "19 families ... Typically, many of the people in the area lack the foresight to put up substantial winter caches and rely heavily on day to day hunting ... The trend towards the settlement is slow and mainly includes the less self-reliant individuals. It seems reasonable to expect that this pace may be quickened and the scope widened as a result of the pending government expansion here. Should this prove to be the case, we will have a predominantly welfare society at Spence Bay, unless steps are taken to counteract such a transition."

These semi-nomadic Inuit were beginning to feel the bodily effects of a devitalizing relief program. Nunaluk, a hunter living at Spence Bay, told me that he had received the following utterly inappropriate ration: 4 pounds of flour, 1 pound of yeast, 6 pounds of oatmeal, 2 pounds of margarine, 10 pounds of sugar, 2 pounds of tea, 4 pounds of fat, 8 pounds of jam, and 4 pounds of rice. If food dependency was the goal, what better way to achieve it? Relief, store, and church charity were at best anesthetics, poultices on a wooden leg, balms for a bad conscience, while at worst they deepened the recipients' dependency.

But what could be done? At the risk of repeating myself, the most pressing need was for a determined, radically different policy conducive to the endogenous development of societies representing one of the most singular civilizations in history. The inevitable consequence of the Inuits' centuries-long submission and indebtedness to the HBC had been to vitiate their autonomy, such that they expected everything to be provided by social assistance. This process had been abetted by a species of Christian ideology that inculcated an ethic of submission in the "children of God," teaching them that their highest goal was to be among those favoured by Divine Providence at the time of the final judgment. But a different future was imaginable. Price supports and the creation of cooperatives could empower the Inuit to return to hunting and fishing, to disperse over the territory instead of staying close to the posts. A bilingual school system could give pride of place to the creative energy emanating from traditional values, offering a dynamic education designed to help them shape the future as a continuation of their heritage. The key task would be the formation of political elites and the achievement of administrative autonomy – "national defence" of a kind. Thus empowered, they would draw their own lessons from the famine and might perhaps turn toward the only supplementary activity available to them: sealing. Kiggiark, a fisherman living at the second camp, had already done so, others had done likewise, and no one seemed to hold it against them. They had begun to adapt – but time was running out, and they did not see it.

"Modernism consists in not believing what one believes. Freedom consists in believing what one believes and accepting – in fact, demanding – that one's fellow human being believe what he believes."[87] The Back River Inuit were in the process of losing their freedom of choice, which they were then exercising by clinging fiercely to their traditional ways in the face of the government's assimilationist designs. I sensed, in the courteous distance they kept from me, how earnestly they wished to remain master of their own decisions. Stay here or move? Preserve the taboos or abandon them? "These things are our busi-

ness, not you government people's," they repeated over and over. Yes, I would respond, but the time available for them to marshal their forces was limited. All the agents of "development" were standing by to "trap" the group once and for all: the police, the market economy (via the post), the schools, and of course, the ministers and catechists, whose omnipresent power extended into their daydreams and inner thoughts.* Counterfeiters' techniques, drawing the Inuit ever further into a process of assimilation, depriving them of their bearings and the hunter's sixth sense. The environment would no longer have any meaning for them.

They listened with condescending courtesy, and still they resisted. By their rejection of trapping and being trapped – the two were synonymous – the elders gave voice to their unwillingness to be uprooted, along with their ancient civilization, by a risky foreign system. But they could not delude themselves forever. The donated gray fabric shirts were harbingers of increasing dependency; one more generation, and the listlessness of the defeated would hang upon them. They would be herded into "open reserves," and slow death would ensue for one of the most prestigious and mysterious of the first peoples. In these crucial years, it would have been naïveté to imagine that this tragedy would be loudly and persistently denounced for what it was – so much easier for most of its observers to keep quiet and avoid the fate often reserved by the powerful for the bearers of bad news.

* Tomorrow, prospectors, industrialists, and tourists; soon, scientists and collectors for the "museums of civilization," the cemeteries of peoples eliminated by colonialism.

THE NUMBERS DID NOT LIE

It is easy to criticize. Still, one could not avoid noticing, for example, that nothing was being done to help these fishermen export a portion of their high-value catch of salmon and char, which they were forced to sell cheap on the local market. The situation should have been reversed: the Gjoa Haven bureaucracy – store, school, police, missions, fifteen well-paid civil servants – should have been at their service. This was its putative *raison d'être*. Trapping incomes were declining due to a depressed market? There should have been no great shame in raising them artificially by means of a supply-management system similar to the ones that dairy farmers in southern Canada are familiar with. Assistance levels could then be reduced to one-fifth of income, and thus empowered, the Inuit would understand that it was up to them to build their future.

The figures in Table 5.2 were gathered on my visit to the Hudson Bay and Gjoa Haven trading posts (founded in 1927).* The poverty of the Utkuhikhalingmiut can be measured by comparing the prices of staple goods with the average 1959 family income of $170 reported by the RCMP, an insignificant proportion of this from trapping.

Budgets were strained. The purchase of basic supplies of sugar, tea, and a few utensils for one family required the kind of careful control over spending that is foreign to the typically prodigal Inuit. The Gjoa Haven trading post bought fox pelts for the absurdly low price of $4.25 apiece – the price of two knives – and seal pelts for $0.25–1.18 – the price of one to five pounds of sugar. For the aggregate Inuit population of Gjoa Haven and Back River, hunting and fishing income amounted to $3,660, while relief (family allowances and other forms) provided $12,660. The average half-yearly family income (1 November to 1 May) was on the order of $200–400, half of it from family allowances.

The method used to produce the inventory in Table 5.3 consisted of personal interviews with various heads of households. As regards household items, I believe that it is incomplete to a very insignificant degree in view of the pervasive poverty. With regard to the essential – hunting equipment – it is undoubtedly highly accurate and indicative of truly meager stores of "capital." It appears that any and all revenue (from trapping, family allowances, and

* Until 1860 purchases were made at the faraway Baker Lake (Qamanittuaq) trading post, a six-month round-trip voyage; prior to its founding, the Inuit had to travel to Akilineq fair (Rasmussen) or to Wager, 450 kilometres round trip. Travel time was variable, depending on weather conditions, hunting success, and any incidents that might befall the voyagers. Baker, Wager, and Repulse were major expeditions.

TABLE 5.2 PRICES OF ITEMS AT THE HUDSON BAY AND GJOA HAVEN TRADING POSTS, 1959

ITEM	PRICE ($)
Ten pounds of tea	17.50
Ten pounds of sugar	3.42
Wool blanket	8.50–13.50
Snow glasses	3.42
Sleeping bag	13–45
Tent (depending on size)	28–65
Canoe	380–450
Knife	2
Teapot	8
Fishing net	7
Single-shot 22-caliber rifle	16
Repeating rifle	28
Telescope	45–60
Primus	10.50
Shirt	4.30
Pants	5
Dress	10
Sewing machine (manual)	80

TABLE 5.3 UTKU HOUSEHOLD INVENTORY, APRIL 1963, SIX FAMILIES

FAMILY #1			
Equipment	Dogs	13	oldest age 4
	Sled	1	average size; obtained by trade at Back River
	Traps	50	
	Rifles	1	(22), 4 years old; purchased at HBC
		1	(25/35), 5 years old; purchased at HBC
	Tent	0	
	Canoe	1	from government
	Nets	3	from RCMP antipoverty assistance
Domestic items	Primus	1	
	Hurricane lamp	1	
Living conditions	No heating in winter 1962–63		
Animals taken	Seal	0	
	Caribou	0	
	Fox	0	

FAMILY #2

Equipment	Dogs	5	1 female, age 3; 1 dog age 2; 3 dogs age 1
	Sled	1	self-made with wood from Gjoa Haven, inherited from son-in-law (drowned)
	Traps	11	1 fox (1963)
	Rifles	1	(22), 16 years old; obtained in local barter
		1	(30/30), purchased at Gjoa Haven HBC
	Tent	1	purchased
	Net	1	RCMP donation (1962)
Domestic items	Plane	1	2 years old
	Saw	1	
	Primus	1	
	Sewing machine	1	purchased 1960
	Accordion	1	
	Hurricane lamp	1	2 years old
Living conditions	No heating in winter 1962–63		
Animals taken	Seal	5	spring
	Caribou	0	
	Fox	1	

FAMILY #3

Equipment	Dogs	8	oldest age 4
	Sled	1	average size; obtained from deceased brother
	Traps	40	
	Rifles	1	(22), 5 years old
		1	(35), 11 years old
	Tent	1	purchased with family allowance money
	Canoe	1	
	Net	1	1 year old
Domestic Items	Caribou-skin sleeping bags	4	
Living conditions	No heating in winter 1962–63		
Animals taken	Seal	1	
	Caribou	7	taken one day away from camp (summer 1962)
	Fox	1	

FAMILY #4

Equipment	Dogs	8	4 age 5, 4 age 1
	Sled	1	average size; obtained as dowry from father-in-law
	Traps	30	
	Rifles	1	(22), 5 years old; purchased with family allowance money
		1	(300), 12 years old; purchased with family allowance money via HBC
	Tent	1	1 year old
	Canoe	1	from government
	Net	1	from RCMP antipoverty assistance
Domestic items	None		
Living conditions	No heating in winter 1962–63		
Animals taken	Seal	0	
	Caribou	22	summer 1962, 11; fall 1962, 6; winter 1963, 4
	Fox	3	

FAMILY #5

Equipment	Dogs	4	oldest age 6; 2 age 1
	Sled	1	obtained in barter with brother-in-law
	Traps	15	
	Rifles	0	uses brother-in-law's rifle
	Tent	0	
	Canoe	1	obtained with family allowance money
	Net	0	
Domestic items	None		
Living conditions	No heating in winter 1962–63		
Animals taken	Seal	0	
	Caribou	1	fall 1962
	Fox	2	1962–63

FAMILY #6

Equipment	Dogs	5	oldest age 5
	Sled	1	average size, 6 years old, built with wood from Gjoa Haven store purchased with family allowance money

	Traps	28	
	Rifles	1	(22), 2 years old; purchased at store with family allowance money
		1	(30/30), 2 years old; purchased at store with family allowance money
		1	(25/35), obtained in local barter
	Tent	1	1 year old; poor condition
	Canoe	1	1 year old; from government
	Net	1	1 year old; from RCMP antipoverty assistance
Domestic items	Soapstone seal-oil lamp	1	
	Soapstone fish-oil lamp	1	
Animals taken	Seal	3	
	Caribou	0	
	Fox	10	

other sources) was invested in this equipment. I indicate the ages of the dogs because the teams were broken up and eaten during the famine of 1950–51 and had to be restored in subsequent years.

As for the numbers of animals taken, the figures for seals are surely accurate, being in all cases nil to negligible. Fox trapping figures were very low but could be crosschecked with transactions at the post. I am more cautious about the caribou figures; they seem inordinately low – indeed, dubious. It would normally take 50–70 of the increasingly scarce caribou or 50 seals (taboo, as we have seen; see Appendix 1 by Andras Zempléni for further commentary) to supply a family's needs for two to three years. Yet four families (#s 1, 2, 5, and 6 in Table 5.3) reported almost no animals taken, while the highest annual take (family #4) was only 22 animals.

The pattern emerging from the figures is clearly one of harrowing poverty. The sole earned income evidently derived from trapping, which they considered an unworthy occupation. In truth, they subsisted on fishing alone, for which I provided the figures earlier. My respondents also corroborated the RCMP reports to the effect that they hardly heated their homes in winter. When fish were abundant, they said, they might indulge in the luxury of heating their one-room homes to dry their clothes. Mostly they used their own bodies as clotheslines by wearing their damp clothes outdoors in the cold, dry air. I did the same.

One of the hunting equipment inventories I conducted at Back River in April 1963 with Utku hunters, in this case for Toolegaak (b. 1891 or 1906). He had a wife, Hitveak (b. 1911) and an adopted son, Pameogarak (b. 11/02/1950). Transcription:

Toolegaak W1 110 [number appearing on the aluminum disc he was required to wear]
Dogs: 5 (1 female age 3, 1 age 2, 3 age 1, 4 age not indicated, undoubtedly puppies)
Traps: 11
Sled: average size, 1 year old
Inherited wood from son-in-law in Gjoa Haven who drowned last year.
Old sled lost.
Rifles: 22: 16 years old. Bought from Eskimo. Traded 22 for 30/30 (HBC)
3 years old [with] pelts and F.A. [family allowance]
Tent: 1 year old [bought with family allowance]
Boat: 0
Net: 1, donated last summer
Small items: plane (2 years old)
Primus, 1 hurricane lamp
1 sewing machine. Purchased.
3 years old.
1 accordion.
Seal: spring full year: 5
Caribou: 0
No heating in winter.
Drying *idem* [clothing dried on body and outdoors on stakes, as seen in photographs in *Call of the North* or the Inuit sketches in this book]

Table 5.4 presents the detailed accounts of nine members of Back River Utku households at the Gjoa Haven HBC post for various periods during 1961–63. Names are withheld to preserve confidentiality.

These credit and debit entries give an indication of the frequency and regularity of the hunters' visits to the post: not monthly, and for some (#s 6, 7, 8) quite irregular. With a few exceptions (#s 1 and 6, as well as #s 7 and 8 for a single trip on 19 September, undoubtedly facilitated by the authorities), they did not travel to Gjoa Haven in the summer since July, August, September, and October were taken up with fishing and caribou hunting. The Utku travelled by dogsled in winter and spring; I did not see any motor canoes. Some of

TABLE 5.4 DETAILED ACCOUNTS OF NINE MEMBERS OF BACK RIVER UTKU HOUSEHOLDS AT THE GJOA HAVEN HBC POST, 1961–63

DATE	CREDIT (CAN$)	DEBIT (CAN$)
Household member #1		
December 1962	48	61.75
March	24	20.35
May	12	20
July	6	4
August	12	12
September	10	6
October	6	6
February 1963	6	5.99
April	12	12
Household member #2		
10 November 1962	0	38
16 December	47.50	18.35
12 January 1963	57.50	32.45, 6.35
6 February	0	8
19 February	11.50	11
11 March	11.50	8.8
2 April	15	13
29 April	5	5
Household member #3		
18 November 1962	32	32, 25, 20
16 December	57.5	52
5 January 1963	16	8
22 February	23	17.40
16 March	11.50	11
12 April	69	65.80
5 May	69	65.80
6 May	10	19.98
11 May	0	10
24 May	3	0
Household member #4		
11 September 1962	0	29.63, 26.80, 23.57
6 November	16	15.99
27 December	16	8
29 December	0	8
19 January 1963	0	25.21, 2.73
19 February	11.50	11.50
9 March	16	19.39
10 April	16, 15	1.61, 16.62, 15
15 April	16	16.58

DATE	CREDIT (CAN$)	DEBIT (CAN$)
Household member #5		
10 November 1961	0	55.15
16 December	107.35, 19	36.25, 25.90, 19
5 January 1962	16	2, 15, 7.50
28 January	8	0
7 March	11.50	11
14 March	66.25	6
12 April	23	22.65, 50.25
25 May	11.50	11.50, 16
22 November	40, 16, 8	18.22
19 February 1963	0	24
11 March	16	10, 19.8
2 April	8	8
29 April	3, 131	5
11 May	5	68.5, 29.11, 34.8
Household member #6		
7 March 1962	0	11
20 April	54, 11.50, 2.50	115.55, 20.95
3 July	14, 14	14, 34.75
22 November	70	27.7, 26.8, 151
19 January 1963	28, 11.5	25.9, 11
3 March	141	25.7
29 April	28, 43.50, 31, 101	25.7, 2.93, 38.55, 3.45, 101
Household member #7		
10 November 1961	0	62.90
6 January 1962	67.30	0
7 March	32	32
19 September	32	32, 4.40
22 November	8	8
19 January 1963	24	23.90
19 February	8	8
23 April	16	16
29 April	15	14
Household member #8		
10 November 1961	24, 18.50	19, 4, 18.5
16 December	9.50	0.50
22 February 1962	11.50	9, 11.50
7 March	24, 11.50, 8.50	11.50, 24
24 April	52	24
24 May	54	75.70, 13.40
19 September	48	39.80, 24.5
22 November	24	19.8, 4

DATE	CREDIT (CAN$)	DEBIT (CAN$)
28 January 1963	24	0
19 February	12	12.20
29 April	24, 3	22.5, 11.48, 3
Household member #9		
10 November 1961	24	20.8, 3.20
5 January 1962	117, 50	38
6 January	0	43.9, 62.55, 12.70
22 February	6	10.5
7 March	11.50	0.5, 11.50
12 April	12	11.90
24 May	11.50	11.50, 6
6 November	28	25.90, 3.10, 32.50
25 December	10	8.50
19 February 1963	6	16.48
29 April	14, 15, 5	14, 15, 5

them stayed at the Gjoa Haven post for a day or two, but others left that "place of heretics" the same day for Back River. It is the men who made these trips, sometimes for very small purchases (e.g., $3, #3; $5, #2; $6, #s 1 and 9). Relief or family allowance payments were spent the same day that they were received; no hoarding or banking. This is all perfectly understandable since the ethnic tradition of this society – its ethical tradition, in fact – was to show contempt for anything connected with the whites, particularly trapping. Moreover, as recent converts to Anglicanism, they had turned away from the Catholic seal hunters – the manager of the post, a mixed-blood Inuit, being one of them.

The data also show that the main source of income was family allowances and relief payments. Family allowances were $6 per month for children aged 0–10 and $8 for children aged 11–16. In very recent years seniors had been receiving a pension of $65 after age 55, an age that very few of them reached. At the time of my visit, only two – Toolegak (b. 1891, aged 72) and Toonee (b. 1906, aged 57) were eligible. The oldest woman, Hitveak (Toolegaak's wife), was only 52.

"RELIEF"

Family allowances and antipoverty donations were administered, in May 1963, by the very competent Gjoa Haven schoolteacher Miss Armstrong, a

TABLE 5.5 FAMILY ALLOWANCES AND ANTIPOVERTY DONATIONS GIVEN TO UTKU AT GJOA HAVEN, SEPTEMBER 1962 TO MARCH 1963

NETS	DATE	RECIPIENT			
	Sept. 1962	1			
	Sept. 1962	2			
	Nov. 1962	3			
	Nov. 1962	4			
	Nov. 1962	5			
RELIEF OR SOCIAL ASSISTANCE (1962-63)	**RECIPIENT**	**GROCERIES**	**GASOLINE**	**CLOTHING**	**AMMUNITION (TWO BOXES OF 30/30)**
	1	9.66	4.00	0	12.80
	2	9.66	4.00	0	11.90
	3	9.66	4.00	0	12.00
	4	9.01	4.00	0	0
	5	9.01	4.00	0	0
	6	9.01	2.90	0	0
	7	8.89	3.50	10.00	9.00
FAMILY ALLOWANCES	**RECIPIENT**	**SEPT.–FEB.**	**FEB.–MARCH**		**TOTAL**
	1	10.00, 28.00	14.00, 28.00		80
	2	24.00, 12.00	24.00		60
	3	40.00, 5.00	16.00, 8.00		69
	4	18.00, 24.00	8.00, 16.00		66
	5	42.00, 28.00	6.00, 14.00		90
	6	16.00, 16.00	32.00, 16.00, 32.00		112
TOTAL					477

native of Saskatchewan. My thanks to her for kindly providing the figures on these payments shown in Table 5.5.

Over the period in question, September 1962 to March 1963, the total amount of assistance allotted to this group – the poorest, most traditionalist group in the North American Arctic – was $477 for seven months, or $11 per family per month on average.

In my reports to the authorities, I tirelessly repeated my recommendation, as if hammering away at a nail, that production prices should be subsidized and commercial fishing encouraged, this if they wished to avoid plunging

Map of Utku hunting and fishing grounds by Kamimalik (b. 1936), Back River, April 1963. At left, Franklin Lake, oriented toward the west, and Back River (shortened). Top right, north of Ogle Point, a dot indicates Gjoa Haven. Far right, Hayes River and its wide bend leading to the lake east of McKinney Peak. Bottom, Mistake River and its first lake upstream.

the people further into dependence. The destitute Inuit (*Beati pauperes!*) and the civil servants – the Inuits' servants, theoretically – constituted a pool of compulsory consumers who yielded a sales volume of $26,260 for the post by spending their family allowances or salaries there.

To sum up, the impoverished heirs to one of history's most fascinating civilizations, in facing their gravest crisis, had to depend for support on a system inspired by one of history's smallest-minded ideologies: the liberal economy. It was, of course (and still is today) dissimulated behind a hodgepodge of humanistic-sounding slogans: "development for the less-developed countries (LDCs)," "globalization," "competitiveness," "human rights," "spreading democracy," "freedom of initiative." But such words can hurt – "competitiveness," for example. How could they be expected to compete, and with whom?

Commonsensically, the Canadian government should have been modelling its interventions on those of Knud Rasmussen and Peter Freuchen in Northwest Greenland (1910–33), which enabled the northernmost people on the planet – the Polar Inuit – to manage their own natural resources and to triple their numbers in forty years.[88] In the face of such blindness, such hypocritical inertia, the Canadian churches should have alerted their hierarchies and taken initiative, setting up alternative trading posts (following Father Henry's example at Pelly Bay) and fish-marketing arrangements and, in general, encouraging local Inuit autonomy; they contented themselves with apologetics, catechism, and sweater handouts. How they loved proselytizing poor people's souls and whimpering in their parochial newsletters about adversity! Meanwhile, the crosses of those dead of starvation and poverty lined up in the cemeteries.

RELOCATION?

One of the objectives of my too-brief exploratory mission* was to assess the option of relocating the Back River families. Relocation? They listened, heads held high, then responded slowly, as if emphasizing the seriousness of their thinking: "Out of the question. This is our land!" Seek nowhere else for the verities of the humble. To be sure, starvation had claimed some of their members, but this is the law of the tundra. As I understood the genesis of the crisis, their normal practice was to observe a three-year rotation between different rivers. That year they chose the wrong one. They realized their mistake too late and, upon reaching the "right" river two or three weeks later, found that most of the fish were already gone.

"Preserving our language, our people; dispersing in summer looking for caribou, gathering in winter around the lake, where there is always fresh water, and the river estuary with its abundant fish stocks: those are our traditions. Having drinking water available all year long from the lake, under the ice, is vital to us. No need for oil or blubber for the lamp to melt ice and snow. At Uqsuqtuuq or Iqaluktuuttiaq [Cambridge Bay], people live on seal meat. Here we always have fish." They would add with a sad smile: "One or two canoes. That's all we need. Try to get them for us ... and three paddles." They repeated that to group the people around a school and a post would be to misunderstand them – indeed, to ignore their wishes. "Here are our dead, here is our land; here, and nowhere else."

* Back River: 15 April–26 April 1963; Gjoa Haven: 26 April–6 May 1963, the date of my departure for Cambridge Bay. In 1962 at Baker Lake, I had begun to survey the members of the Back River Inuit community displaced to this locality.

I promised that I would be their faithful interpreter. "It all begins with *the* mystique," Charles Péguy wrote, "a mystique, its (own) mystique, and it all ends in politics."[89] The mystique: the shamanism of the place where the ancestors are reincarnated. The politics: resistance to being uprooted.

UPSTREAM

23 April 1963. I set off for the second camp, near the rapids, with the ever-present RCMP man and with Akretoq as my assistant. Along the way we stop at three recently built sheds. Two were built to house emergency provisions after the famine of 1959, as if in atonement for the government's scandalously inadequate response. The third is for the use of the Catholic missionary, who is absent during my visit. The RCMP constable tries various keys, attempting to unlock the two government sheds for inspection; as for the Inuit, no key has been issued to them. While this goes on, Akretoq stands to one side, his back turned with a degree of condescension, idly kicking a stone. I wonder silently about the utility of this safeguard in the event of a crisis and about the glaring distrust shown this ethnic group.* When will they be allowed to administer their own affairs?

Drifting snow follows clear weather, and we move along the bank unhampered. On our arrival, the three families living at the camp have massed in a small crowd in front of the house of an elder named Toonee. Word of our arrival has preceded us. The women and children shake our hands, staring straight at us with the gravity of those who live in the constant presence of death. Laughter accompanies an invitation for me to take tea and eat a piece of frozen caribou, chopped with an ax on the ground. The snow houses are monastic in their austerity. When evening comes, I hang my spare gloves and *kamiks* on stakes and take a short walk to warm up. Long periods of sitting on the *iglerk* are tiring. Reaching a height of land, I collect moss (*tinaussat* here, *maniq* in North Greenland), grass (*ivik*), and the roots of dwarf ericaceous plants (*iksutit*); ground willow roots with their long rootlets pull out easily, too. Back at the house, they burn at the snap of a match. Akretoq is asleep in one of my sleeping bags. He is adapting to modern life very quickly.

Wednesday and Thursday, 24–25 April: a "warm" wind from the south. Time flows by without measure as in happy days. Each minute is held intensely. Drop by drop. Late in the evening, the children play ball on the icy river. Is it a modern ball or a traditional one made of caribou skin? I am not at leisure to

* During a previous famine at Ennadai Lake, a group of famished people had plundered a depot.

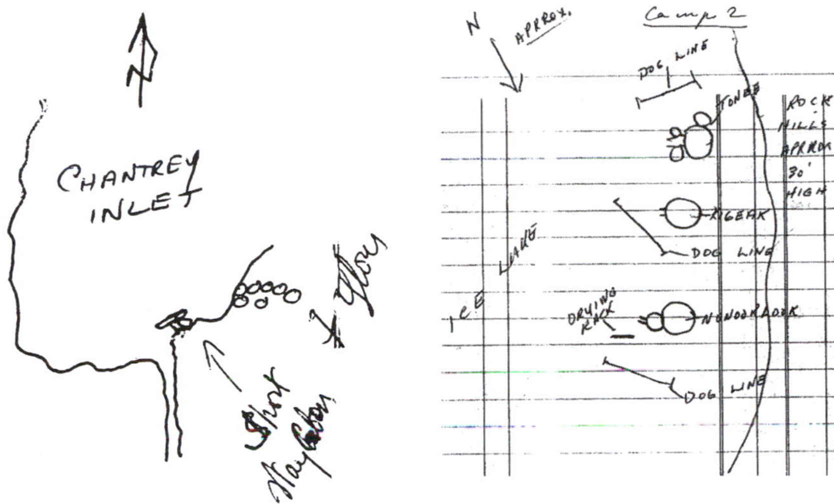

left: Sketch of the locations of the two camps in my notebook. April 1963.

right: Sketch of upstream camp at Back River and its three houses by RCMP constable. April 1963.

find out. In the house of Kiggiark,* his wife Anahlook attends to her chores. With her red-topped cheeks, she reminds me of one of Gauguin's women at Pont-Aven.[90] Such a round head. My survey continues with an inventory of possessions, routes, and toponyms as well as the demographic data necessary to calculate fertility rates for the seven families. I am trying to get a true picture of neonatal mortality since unnamed dead children and miscarriages are not accounted for in the official statistics. When I probe the matter of ancient and extant taboos, they confirm the prohibition on mixing meat and fish. As for the recent famine, they have little to say about it: it is forgotten, or at least this is the image that they wish to convey. Indeed, they may wish to believe it themselves. I have so little time ... but I will, I must come back. I am already

* Born 1923, married to Anahlook (b. 1930). Two daughters, Tolohlik (b. February 1949) and Toolegaak (b. 28 January 1957) living with him. All Anglicans. He was a maverick, a seal hunter who took liberties with the tradition and, as such, a person whom I absolutely had to interview first thing next winter – but it was not to be.

Burial: Notes from my dialogue with Homaok. "An unnamed child is given no tomb to make sure that it will be eaten by animals. Infanticide is even practised in the presence of the family. In general the child is nameless [in fact, always: infanticide is always practised on a nameless victim. For the Inuit, the child is unborn since the spirit of the name does not yet inhabit him]. Infanticide is always [practised on] girls. Abandonment of old people: before Knud [Rasmussen]." Gjoa Haven, May 1963.

girding myself mentally to arrive around 15 August and stay the winter. I have chosen my assistants and confided my plans to them.

Meanwhile, the essential problem of my upcoming research is taking shape in my mind like a leitmotiv: how do these men and women, once so profoundly holistic (the great, female governing spirit of the Inughuit, called Nuliajuk or Nirrivik, "married" her father's dog) understand and interpret the Christian message? "We fear it," said Ikinilik to Rasmussen in June 1923. I ask the same questions as I did in the first camp; they find them troubling. After the death of the body, what is the fate of the spirit, the vital energy? It wanders, patiently waiting in the realm of the dead (eyes open or closed, a skeleton?) for its temporary reincarnation in another body. How do they reconcile this migration of souls with the dogma of the resurrection of the flesh? As people who feared evil spirits, how do they imagine Satan – as pure spirit? A fallen angel who thrice attempted to seduce Jesus and will show his fearsome power in the time of the apocalypse? Can he be likened to a super-Tupilak or a giant *tonrar*? And the angels, the archangels as "spiritual, incorporeal beings" – a truth of the faith? And the prophets: how could they have had foreknowledge of God? I sense the tension. To overcome the barriers put up by new converts, to earn enough trust to obtain frank responses on such emotion-charged matters, I would have to spend much more time building close relationships. When asked about ancient customs and taboos, they parry with a laugh before speaking. Akretoq skillfully phrases the questions and returns the answers. There is no bad faith on anyone's part. "You surprise us with your questions," he says openheartedly, staring at me with a clear, confident eye. "You disconcert us by questioning our beliefs and encouraging us not to forget. This is very, very new, this encouragement not to lose sight of what the elders taught us. We've been trying to do as the Christian minister asks and not look like pagans, so we never discuss the past ... The past? That's sorcery![91] Surely we are wrong to be so ungrateful to our elders. They were sages. Christianity, shamanism: in our solitude, doesn't the one lead to the other, to the God of Truth? I confide these thoughts to you. They trouble me."

Toonee tells a story of the Tunit (Dorset) people. Before beginning, his aged, failing, cataract-ridden eyes rest on me slowly, scrutinizingly: "Tautsamani (long ago) ..." Guardian of memory, he hesitates, wanting to assure

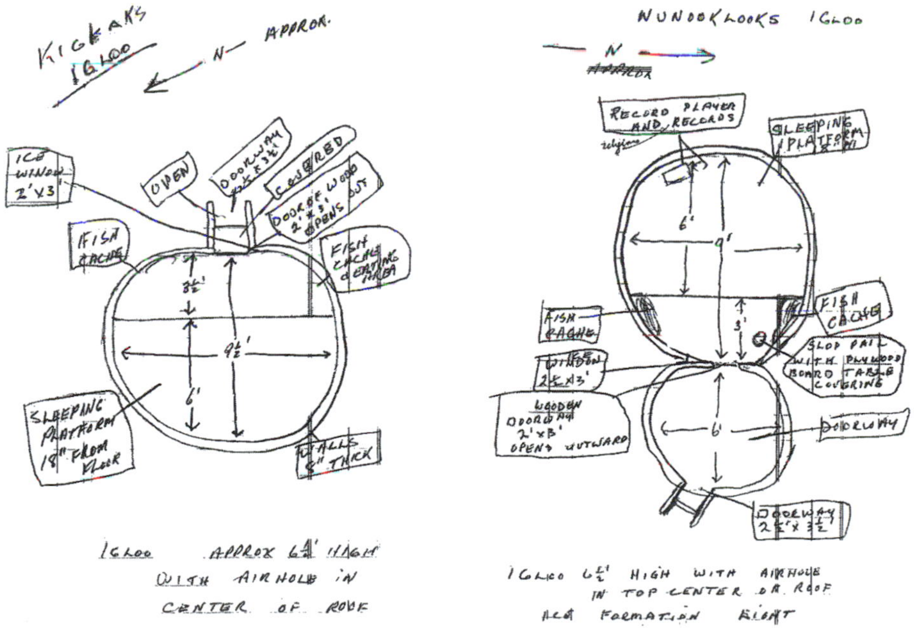

Sketch of two houses (Kiggiark's and Nanordloo's) by the RCMP constable (his orthography). Back River, upstream camp, April 1963.

himself that I am worthy. Premature old age veils the strength and pride of the young hunter of musk ox and caribou. He is fifty-seven, and, as at Thule in North Greenland, a person becomes "old" here after fifty. Old people here rarely have the imposing presence of the Indian sachem.

Some children were playing on the ice. The giant Amayorolu picked some up, put them in his bag, and took them home to his rocky cave. The opening of the cave was barred by leather mesh. After making sure they were securely locked inside, Amayorolu went to look for some ground willow roots to make a fire. The oldest girl called to a bird to open the door. The bird freed the children, and they all returned to their families. When Amayorolu returned, the snowbird was still standing at the entrance to the cave. Amayorolu suspected the bird and became furious. "Don't make such a fuss," said the bird. "They are long gone." Amayorolu cried, "Umiktik! I will kill someone!" The bird replied, "One of my toes is hungry." Amayorolu said, "If one of your toes is hungry, it will eat me." And he left.

The clever Kiggiark proposes to tell a fable and proves particularly eloquent. He takes great pleasure in being recorded and hearing the recording played back, as I do for each of them. Here is his recounting of "The Ptarmigan and the Smelt":

A ptarmigan was flying when he saw a big-headed fish, a smelt, lying on the bank not far from a crack in the ice. "Hey, smelt! Go lie down at the bottom of the lake! Your belly is fat, your mouth is wide, and your eyes are tiny." The smelt looked at the

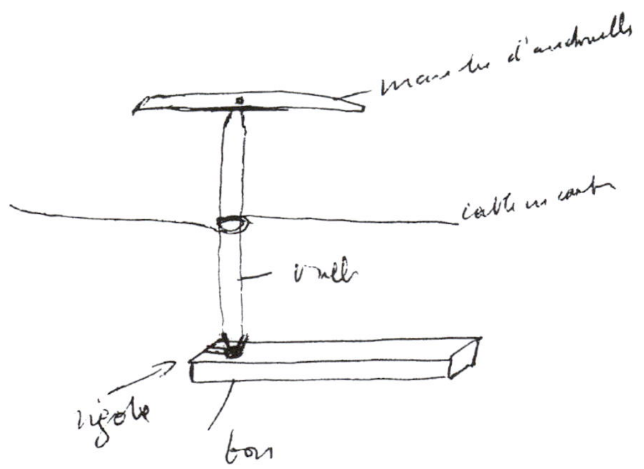

Traditional fire-making technique. Tip of stake rubbed rapidly in pit carved in block of dry wood. Back River, April 1963.

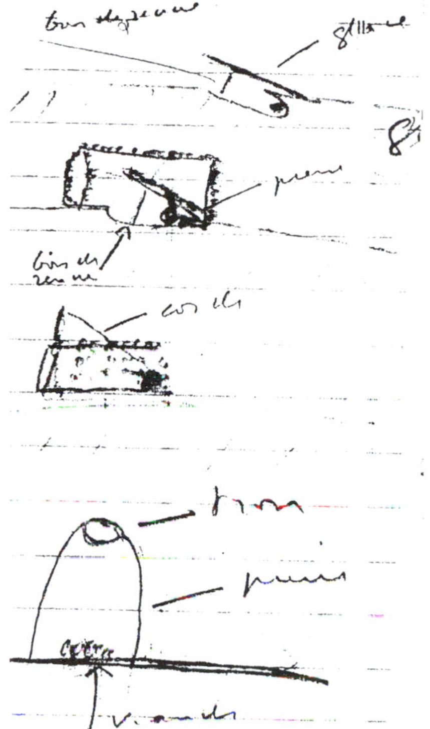

Two Utku and two Netsilik traps, sketched by Akretoq or Toonee at Back River, and Homaok at Gjoa Haven, May 1961, respectively. T. to b.: (1) trap consisting of recess under snow and ice roof, bait at bottom, caribou-antler door; (2) stone slab held up by caribou antler; (3) stone tunnel baited at back, door (slab) tripped by animal near bait; (4) stone shaft, bait at bottom.

ptarmigan and said, "How's that? You, ptarmigan, have a fat beak and you can talk. You have big intestines and you must have a lot of blubber and you tell me about all that." The ptarmigan took to the air, flying about and crying, "This flesh of my belly is blubber."

The ptarmigan went away, then came back. Landing on a stone by the sea, he saw a fox coming toward him. He said, "Females who walk must walk endlessly." When the smelt saw and heard the ptarmigan talking to the fox, he told him, "Look closer and raise your head."

DEADLY VENDETTAS

I was given several accounts of aggression and war in this region. The stranger – even if a member of your ethnic group – may be your enemy. On the Adelaide Peninsula, vendettas were frequent: "A caribou hunter had a wife who slept around. Returning from the hunt one day, he killed her. The father-in-law was furious and decided to kill the husband. He stood in front of the man's house with a long knife and ordered him to come out. The husband did. The father-in-law advanced, but the husband jerked away to avoid being stabbed. He killed the father-in-law by stabbing him with his own knife. The brothers-in-law witnessed this scene from a distance and retaliated, stabbing the jealous husband in the ribs."

Toonee told of a duel between a Netsilik and a man from Repulse: "The two families hated each other. The two men agreed to a mutual challenge: they would walk toward each other in grave silence, then simultaneously and very slowly insert the blades of their long knives into each other's bodies. The hunter from Repulse collapsed first. The other, the Netsilik, fell to his knees. He survived, and an igloo was built for his convalescence."

Conflicts would sometimes be settled through community-regulated combat. The entire group would gather around in the common house (*q'agsigi*) while the two adversaries took turns punching each other in the side of the head, each gathering his strength to deliver the next blow. The loser was the one who fell and struggled to get up.

In group conflicts before 1930, a messenger – usually an old man or woman – would be sent to announce a coming attack. The combat was hand-to-hand with spears and knives; defenceless individuals were left unharmed. After a few casualties, the assailants withdrew. Male prisoners were not taken as slaves, but girls were sometimes kidnapped.

The fear of being murdered by a stranger was persistent, as the following legend from the first three decades of the century illustrates:

A hunter went looking for his *aklo* [seal breathing hole in the pack ice] but could not see it. He realized he had become snow-blind from staring at the ground. He could not see or hear. A man walked up behind his back, approaching slowly from a distance. Suddenly the stranger spoke: "Your eyes hurt? You can't see?" The blind man was only half-blind. He saw the sooty face of the stranger and became furious when the man leapt on him, pinning him against the ice. He told the stranger to turn his head to one side. When the latter did so, the blind man stabbed him in the neck with his spear. The wounded man moved off, his body bent double in pain. At a good distance – beyond striking distance, that is – he turned around to the half-blind man and stood erect: "You almost broke my neck!"

RETURN TO UQSUQTUUQ

Friday, 26 April, 6:00 A.M., my day of departure, by prior arrangement with the RCMP. At 8:00, the red-cheeked women stop by for tea and fish, radiating

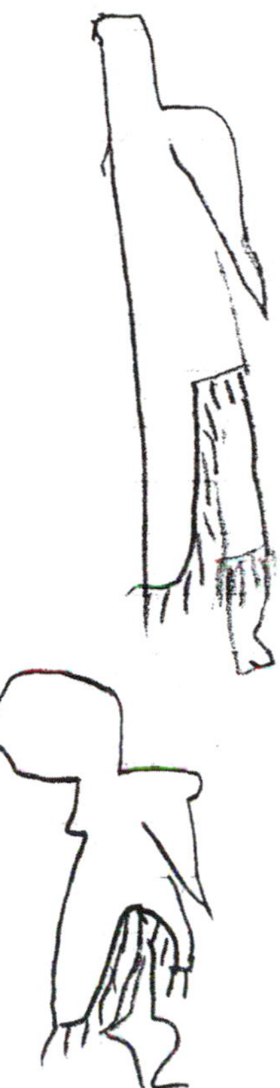

Top, man; bottom, woman moving away. Note how the man is depicted larger than the woman. Drawing by Homaok, Gjoa Haven, May 1963.

good health. Goodbyes are said with a look, and our group departs on three sleds. Tootalik and the RCMP constable are in the rear on a sled weighing 365 kilograms (including 135 kilograms of fish), hauled by fourteen vigorous dogs. I am a passenger on Nanudluk's sled. Although taciturn indoors, his speech is impassioned now as he comments on the places where he has hunted and fished. I memorize the essential facts, writing them down at each rest stop in my personal shorthand. As we reach the first camp, Inukshuk leaves his fishing spot and comes running to greet us. In the hallway of the double-celled house where I lived for a few days, my indelible friends Little Fish and Great Whale hasten to put up water on the Primus. Their cheeks too are abnormally red. Inukshuk takes me aside to tell me the nickname that I have been given:

Igloq, cousin. I present Akretoq with my switchblade as a symbol of friendship, and I give an avuncular tug on Little Fish's pigtail. Inukshuk accompanies me to the sled, whispering that he would very much like me to stay. Otherwise, it is a wordless, Inuit-style departure. Northbound.

After two days of travelling, we are caught in a storm off a barely visible island called Umanak by the Inuit. We bivouac, one group in a snow hut, another in a tent. Inukshuk points out the two spring camps on the island, Qavvik and Ipuituk, whose locations were shown to me earlier on the map. Suddenly I am aware that the cold is taking hold of me, penetrating to the bone: I am wrapped in a shell of ice. Something is wrong with my gear, and I react at once. The first order of business is to remove one of my two sweaters; they are too tight-fitting and do not provide the necessary cushion of insulating air. I ask Nanudluk to stop and block the wind for me. In haste I remove the stylish RCMP parka loaned to me obligingly by District Chief Parsons at Cambridge Bay, then the sweaters and wool shirt. I put the sweater back on, followed by the shirt, the other sweater, and instead of the parka, the loose-fitting but deliciously warm caribou-skin *quulitaq*, and we are off on our solitary way again. North of Montreal Island (see maps pp. 186, 202–3), we make another stop when Nanudluk loses one of his gloves. He goes looking for it while I mind the dogs, standing in front of them with a seven-metre-long whip. The blizzard intensifies, the minutes pass. I start to worry. Where is he? Nanudluk can't find the sled ... Finally, after what seems like a very long time, he returns with his glove but, shortly afterward, drops his whip. We stop again.

We become separated from the group. It feels like we are going in circles. I surmise that we have passed Ogle Point to our left, and we strain for a glimpse of Hovgaard Island ahead. If we miss it, we risk straying northeast of Gjoa Haven into the Rae Strait. We have no compass nor any need for one: I am with the Inuit. Direction finding is by detective work. We take bearings on the hazy sun and examine furrows in the icy snow, which indicate the direction of the prevailing winds. Visibility is no more than ten metres. The dogs walk very, very slowly. After miles of gliding over the rough ice, one of the frozen peat runners comes apart and is hindering our progress. Nanudluk proposes to stop and make repairs. We remove the load and turn the sled over – but the Primus is on one of the other two sleds! At that moment, they emerge from the blizzard, pushing through the billowing cottony wall of snow. Confirmation: with our slow progress we have only reached Pechell Point; Ogle Point is still ahead of us. In the lee of a crate, we melt snow on the stove. Nanudluk bends over the peat runner, exposing the small of his back – this at a temperature of –30°C with the wind-chill factor, perhaps lower. As I watch, he slowly,

Ethnological notebook, Spence Bay, September 1961. Two respondents.
Transcription:
Respondents:
Taraizook E4 507 [b. 1896]
Tukiagnu E4 508 [his wife, b. 1906. Two adopted children, Ibuceak Colu, daughter (b. 8 September 1949) and Ottoktook Munga, son (b. November 1942); all Anglican].
After famine:
Second famine of which the RCMP learned by chance in mid-May after having ordered that such situations be reported. "Yes, good idea," they had responded.
Mid-May: famine. Game scarce.
Still not moving.
Causes: no kinship with camps to south and north. Check this.
Even if kin, can't request that much support from neighbouring camps.
Fatalism.
Integration difficulties [of] Dorset.
Asked Adams why the group did not send someone to report the situation. Answer: "I can't say. I'm not one of them."
Yet these Eskimos have been living among – and intermarrying with – the Netsilingmiut for ten years!

patiently dribbles a thin stream of saliva onto the peat layer and smoothes the resulting film of ice with his gloved fingers.

A few more long hours of travelling, and Uqsuqtuuq is close at hand, as heralded by bits of rope, dog turds, pieces of sheet metal, and other debris on the track. On the evening of 28 April, with the blizzard still raging, we are welcomed back to the small community of Gjoa Haven. The charming, fifty-ish schoolteacher Miss Armstrong is busily preparing for our arrival in front of her house. How pleasant are her humour, her keen sense of observation, her generosity after my plunge into a literally extraordinary world! Also present are the sombre but cooperative Oblate Father Lorson, from the Lorraine, and the young mixed-blood Walter Porter, who manages the post. True friends all. I am given a lord's welcome.

My short stay in Gjoa Haven (until 6 May) affords me an opportunity to survey the Utku émigrés.[92] How do they live? What are their thoughts – about themselves, others, the people still in Back River, the Netsilingmiut? One of them, a woman born before 1900 (whose name I withhold here to protect her privacy) provides a fascinating account of Inuit marriage and childbearing customs. Her excellent memory enables her to answer my questions in great detail, and she willingly does so.

According to custom, she was betrothed at birth to her first cousin. While still an infant, her father died. She was married in the winter at age fourteen or fifteen. For a dowry (*akki*), her maternal uncle gave the groom's father a dog. Commonly among the Inuit, the interval between commencement of sexual relations and first conception is three or four years, and so it was with this couple. The newborn girl, however, was eliminated immediately after delivery due to the endemic famine in the region, as tradition dictated. They had been hoping for a boy who could join the hunt as soon as possible. (The woman made this admission to me without comment.) In late summer of the following year, she had a boy, who was kept, and the following summer she had another. Because of the extreme hardship of their lives, the second boy was given up for adoption to her maternal aunt. The following spring, she had a miscarriage while two or three months pregnant – sex of the child unknown. Several years later in winter, she had a baby girl, the first to be kept alive. The girl was given a name and is today married to one of the hunters in the group that I interviewed at Back River. Two years later, with winter coming on, another girl; this one was killed. Misfortune struck again when her husband died shortly after this birth.

Soon, however, she had another husband, a cousin once removed, with another dog as dowry. One or two summers later, perhaps more, she had another boy, whom she kept. The year was then about 1933, and she was in her early forties. Although still menstruating, she became sterile. She then became involved in a polyandrous marriage by taking and living with a second husband, who lived for about ten years more. No dowry was given, for this was uncustomary in such cases. Thirty years later, this heroic woman, quietly chuckling at the cruel life that she had experienced – "ayorama! no help for it, our life is hard" – introduced me to her husband, two years her elder. With the double old-age benefit that they had been receiving since 1940, their standard of living had improved.

Before interviewing the émigrés, each in turn, I study the statistics and household accounts at the post. My "office" is an empty classroom in late afternoon. After my time in the houses of snow and ice, I find the white peo-

Note in syllabic script from manager of small Hudson's Bay post concerning 1961–63 data that he has supplied. Gjoa Haven, April 1963.

ple's houses insufferably hot. During the first night, I am beset by a violent and inhabitual migraine. Before departing on the return trip to Back River, my three travelling companions from the second camp – Nanudluk, Kiggiark, and Toonee's oldest son – help me clarify certain points concerning toponymy, spelling, taboos, the thirteen spring and summer camps, and two life histories. I tape-record the session. They delay their departure until everything is checked. Even indoors they remain men of the cold, proudly keeping on their heavy caribou-skin *quulitaq*. To take them off would signal comfort in a white person's home – unthinkable. Sweat trickles down their faces. They phrase their thoughts prudently, deliberately. After answering some specific questions, they talk freely – hold forth, in fact – on various topics. Soon they are joined by Akkimalik, who spent thirty years at Back River, and old, tattooed Homaok Shomoak, an accurate and inexhaustible source of information.* At Back River, in a snow house, supported by the group, she might have answered certain questions with a burst of laughter. Here, in a white person's home, she is rather ill at ease but, intuiting that a service is required of her, strains against her own inclinations. If only I could stay longer, six months, a year ... surely I could convey to her that the survey is being done in the interests of her people. For this to happen, however, our relations would have to be built on a foundation of true, equal cooperation. We could write a book together, model it on Talayesva's inspired *Sun Chief.* I would truly need an extra life, and, in my mind, I am already making preparations for one: in the

* Born at Ugjulik (Queen Maud Gulf) in 1895. Anglican. Married to Ongoyomenak (b. 1894, Anglican).

winter of 1963–64, Back River will be another pole for me, like Thule. I visit the Hudson's Bay post, where I have the pleasure of meeting its manager, George Porter, a mixed-blood Inuit, and his son Walter, who has been helping him for the past few months. Trading post ambiance, "Inuit" disorder. All the books of account are graciously opened for me. Walter's wife Theresikulu is a pretty mixed-blood from Herschell Island at the mouth of the Mackenzie River on the Alaskan border (an island with a particularly tumultuous past, visited by rapacious Californian whalers at the end of the nineteenth century). At home in her slender, supple body, she goes seal hunting alone on her sled. Now she sits on a box at the counter, head resting casually on fine-boned hands, setting a calm, deliberate, scrutinizing gaze on each visitor. Walter, a Catholic with an Anglican mother-in-law, was raised by priests and goes to mass each morning.

Never have I felt such nostalgia as when rereading these travel diaries, turning their yellowed pages greasy with seal and fish oil, reviewing the sketches of routes, maps, costumes, objects, tattoos, evil spirits, familiar spirits, and *tonrars* made by the Utku men and women. Back River was – I sensed it as soon as I began to read the RCMP reports in July 1961 at Spence Bay – a hallowed place, one that was destined to mark me forever. This group was unique. Across the years, to this very evening, my thoughts have stayed with those seven families, those men, women, and children of the cold, in their cheerful austerity, their obstinate defiance. The memory of their stares still evokes doubts and misgivings. Might the oral societies, the poor, have a singular call-

Tattoos on four fingers of woman's hand but not thumb. Drawing by Koorsoot, Back River, April 1963.

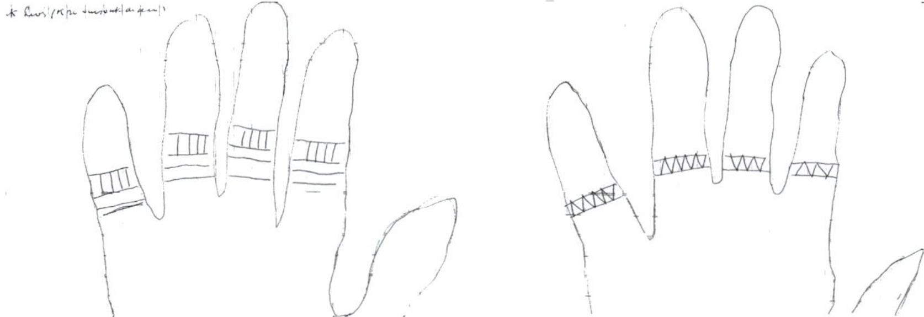

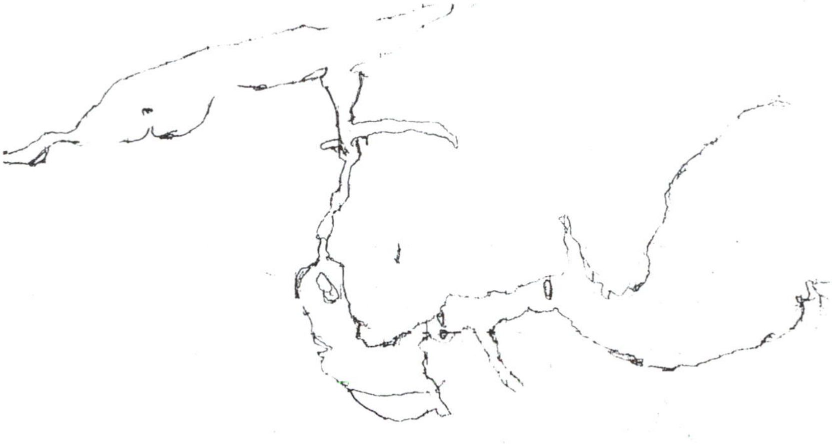

Map of Franklin Lake, first lake upstream of Back River, drawn by Naruk (b. 3/12/1938), Toonee's son. Oriented east-west. Bottom right, Hayes River estuary. Downstream of Franklin Lake, rapids. Island of Nilak site (spring and summer camps) and Itimnaaqjuk site. Back River, April 1963.

ing to eternal life? Bernanos wrote: "The merciful priesthood of poverty was established in this world to redeem it from misery ... The poor man ... is a man who lives poorly, in the age-old tradition of poverty, who lives from day to day by the labour of his own hands; who ... eats from the hand of God, as the popular saying goes."[93]

Yes, meeting them was, for me, a flash of inner lightning, a dawning awareness of their vast history as well as of the sad state in which they then found themselves. Only the Inughuit of Thule and the Yuit of Savoonga (St Lawrence Island, Bering Sea) and Yttygran (Chukotka, Siberia) have inhabited me as forcefully. My stay among this isolated group of the Central Arctic was brief, for, as a young, recently appointed professor at the École des Hautes Études (1958), I had been unable to obtain more than a six-week leave of absence while university was in session. It was my intention, on returning to Paris in May 1963, to request a sabbatical year (1964), an administrative formality that my chairman at the École, Fernand Braudel, would surely have granted. In the tradition of the Annales School, I would have expanded my research agenda to include an ethnohistory of mentalities and a more comprehensive anthropogeography. It was essential to study the conjunctions, or the syncretism, as the case might be, between Christianity and shamanistic animism. But several days later at Cambridge Bay, I learned of the imminent arrival of a young American anthropologist in Back River for her field season. I blame myself for not rushing back to my friends at Back River immediately after she had completed her work. Back River, the river of return ...[94]

Instead, in July 1965 I was drawn westward, captivated by the prospect of studying ceremonial life in the Bering Strait region. The proverb has it that we lead two lives, the one we catch sight of in the mist every now and then, from early childhood onward, and the one that our daily existence imposes on us. With the years, the poetry of this people of dreams has continued to inhabit me. I find myself seized with regret – and a bad conscience. Ah, Back River, the river of return ... I hear Piuvkaq singing:

A wonderful occupation
Making songs!
But all too often they
Are failures.

A wonderful fate
Getting wishes fulfilled!
But all too often they
slip past.

A wonderful occupation
Hunting caribou!
But all too rarely we
Excel at it
So that we stand
Like a bright flame
Over the plain.[95]

1987. I am teaching for several days at Iqaluit (Frobisher Bay) as part of my circumpolar survey of pedagogical practices. At the college cafeteria, a military barrack housing the elite of the Canadian Eastern Arctic, a loudspeaker plays blues in the background. On the menu are hot dogs, hamburgers, fries, cold milk, ice cream and cake ... the bulldozer of "progress." In a corridor I meet a bright-faced young Inuk who speaks English. "Where are you from?" I ask.

"Utkuhikhalingmioq. Born on the tundra. I am twenty. My family left Back River. We were waiting for you to come back."

"What are you doing here?"

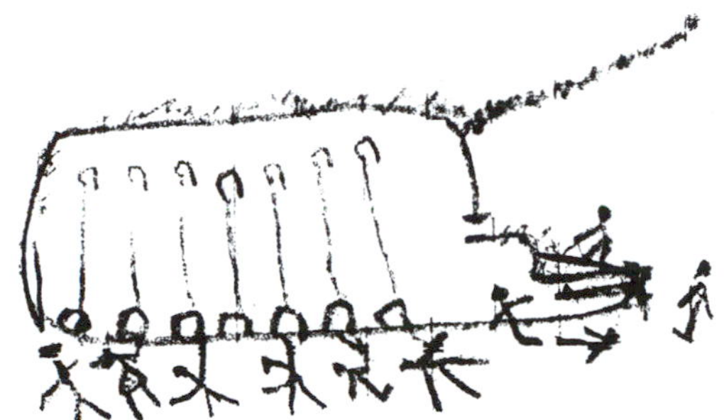

Fishing at *saputit*. Back River, Drawing by Kiggiark. April 1963.

"Hotel management school."

Rumour has it that the site of the *saputit* is now occupied by an outfitter's lodge, a tourist attraction for North American millionaires.

BACK RIVER: THE RIVER OF RETURN

I wrote the following notes for the second French edition of *Hummocks* after rereading and giving further thought to my little green field notebooks from April to May 1963. Back River was one of those inner places that one spends a whole lifetime trying to revisit; a hallowed place imbued with an intensity, an attraction all the more haunting in that the community living there, by being dispersed, was annihilated. I shall always be thinking back to that time, and with remorse. It was a missed opportunity that is still sorely missed. For me, Back River has taken on the mythic dimensions of a place that will live for the ages.

Unless one aspires to mere drudgedom in the realm of ideas, a life is constructed as a quest after the meaning of what one desires to become. Thule/Siorapaluk, Back River, and Whale Alley are not run-of-the-mill places; they are the inward awareness that we have found that hazily glimpsed space of the imagination where we breathe easier, become better. They epitomize what I believe I came looking for in the Arctic: an answer to the riddle of my existence, a return to the source. Echoes of Stepan Trofimovitch's dying words: "The one essential condition of human existence is that man should always be able to bow down before something infinitely great. If men are deprived of the infinitely great they will not go on living and will die of despair ... Even the stupidest man needs something great."[96]

To put it differently, these seven Back River families were, in their Trappist austerity, the sum of free individualities held accountable by the group. But for me their life trajectory has an eschatological meaning as well. Against all odds, staring at death, they continued to believe themselves fated to live out their lives at the double estuary of the Back and Hayes Rivers. Would they cling to it without good reason? Any society, even the most elementary, lives with an awareness of its destiny; when the people cease to believe in it, the society is bound to disappear.

Lamarck: "The influence of the environment as a matter of fact is in all times and places operative on living bodies; but what makes this influence difficult to perceive is that its effects only become perceptible or recognisable (especially in animals) after a long period of time."[97] Were his words applicable to Back River and its twenty-five Utkuhikhalingmiut? On 20 April 1963 I arrived in force (accompanied by an RCMP constable, an interpreter, and a guide), resolved, on this initial fact-finding mission, to comprehend and analyze their exceedingly strong will to persevere despite overwhelming adversity. This arrival in force was perhaps not the optimal introduction, although (as the RCMP experience attests) the aura of an official mission does tend to facilitate initial encounters with traditionalists such as these. They were united in their destiny, these men and women, self-isolated within an anarcho-communalist structure and doggedly following a path that they dimly sensed was now a dead end. The attitudes of the group's elders and youth bore witness to a durable emotional bond that endues these people with legendary qualities, a bond forged since the earliest days of the Inuit utopia. The youth in particular, after spending time on the American bases, felt almost duty-bound to return to their snow houses to live out their lives and share their ancestral rites. Over the long arc of history to which the myths that they recount with such pleasure attest, Utku society has structured its forces as an inner struggle to fulfil a destiny. Their desire to impress upon me their fidelity to these beliefs was evidenced by the fact that, by the end of my stay, they were the ones insisting that I tape-record their stories. "Don't forget," said Inukshuk, "I still have a few stories for you; many, in fact. We are coming to understand why you are here." A group is the sum of elementary factors that are ordered as they gain in complexity through specialization. Advances in knowledge of Inuit society show us that a regular gradation in traditional Inuit social organization exists across the brow of the Arctic, from Greenland to Siberia. At Back River, I was on the lowest level of this sociological grammar.

After the 1958 famine (six out of twenty-five dead), how could the strange forces undergirding the life of a people be brought to their awareness? Naturally, there were oppositions, winners and losers, perhaps even a Judas in the group. I sensed competition, subterranean struggle between factions, although the men and women standing before me were silent on the existence of intergenerational and interpersonal conflict. It seemed that their line of conduct when faced with the outsider, the Gil Blas* that I so wished to be, was to keep the wraps on such internal matters. And I was not so deluded as to suppose that I was getting any other than stereotypical answers from the members of this relict of communitarianism, whose seven families were surely experiencing the humiliation of the defeated in the presence of the conquering people, whom I represented. My mission was difficult.

There were no specialized hunters that I could see, nor was anyone specialized in a craft or trade such as teacher, nurse, interpreter, or guide. Each person represented the whole. Back River was a sum of free individualities held accountable by the authority of an omnipresent virtual entity, the group. In the case of a transgression, this entity immediately intervened to enforce the traditions constituting their unwritten body of law.

There was a catechist who played an important role similar to that of Piugatu, the Anglican catechist whom I had met among the isolated walrus hunters at Kapuivik. I had learned in Gjoa Haven that the Utku had, since their conversion around 1930, become devout, ritualistic Protestants. They were under the authority of an Inuit deacon in Gjoa Haven, Nakliguhuktuq, who reported to a British-born Anglican missionary in Spence Bay, and he in turn to a superior in Cambridge Bay. I did not meet the Spence Bay missionary since he was on holiday in Europe while I was there. Wanting to keep my distance from the authorities so as to appear more independent and credible in the eyes of the Inuit – an enterprise handicapped from the outset by the official nature of my mission – I did not seek out Nakliguhuktuq, said to be a person of great authority and prickly temperament. His wife spoke English fluently and was probably the real power, as Inuit women generally are. I was told that the catechist whom he delegated to Back River normally held two Sunday services – work was forbidden that day – as well as a Wednesday prayer meeting; such was his duty of state. But they were not held during my stay at Back River. Were they cancelled, perhaps, due to the presence of my official mission? How accurate was the epithet "devout" as applied to the Utkuhikhalingmiut? A study of the Anglican hymnology inspired by the Book of Common Prayer – prescribed by the *Act of Uniformity* of 1662 for the English but not, my luck, for me – might have helped me to refine my thinking into an "experimental and practical theology."[98] By noting and comparing the frequency of references to Old Testament, New Testament, Epistles, and Acts and by identifying

* Translator's note: *The Adventures of Gil Blas of Santillane* is an eighteenth-century French picaresque novel by Alain-René Lesage and one of the earliest realistic novels.

the recurring theological themes appearing in the hymns, I might have been able to reach some conclusions about their spiritual orientation.

When in peril, this communitarian group* withdrew into a prudent, wait-and-see attitude. I must note the sexual division of labour observed by Rasmussen in May 1923 and still in effect in April 1963. The men's duty was hunting, travelling by dogsled, caring for the dogs, building and maintaining the snow houses, and buying at the post, while the women attended to domestic chores, sewing, childrearing, and food preparation. The women ate separately from the men and in silence. More food for thought: do such people, living in such marginal conditions, have a concept of their lives' purpose? If so, it must certainly have been modified by their conversion to Christianity, but in what way? Was there a transnatural state leading them to ponder what Michael Francis Gibson calls "the unknown laws" of human history according to which society is prior – I would add internal – to the individual?[99] I return to this matter in my discussion of their recent conversion, which changes the picture substantially.

THE PERILS OF CONSANGUINITY

Were these seven families necessarily condemned by their voluntary isolation to atrophy and disappear? An initial observation, corroborated by the RCMP reports, is that the Utku (apart from the seven- or eight-year-old epileptic boy whose case I discussed earlier) appeared to be in good health as compared with the populations of Gjoa Haven and Spence Bay, the district capital; appeared, I say, for I did observe the deplorable state of the older people's dentition and eyesight (one of the women had evidently had some dentistry done)[100] and noticed that they all coughed constantly at night. I am not a medical doctor and can say no more; still, a 1951 RCMP report readily concluded that the people at Back River "are the healthiest looking natives in the whole district," while a 1959 report said that they "in general were in excellent health and spirits."

For the wider Spence Bay and Gjoa Haven district, serious genetic disorders were appearing despite the churches' thirty-year-old bans on consanguineous marriage. The RCMP noted in a report for the year 1961, covering the whole district and hence Back River, "The occurrence of deaf and dumb Eskimos and presumed epileptics is startlingly high for so comparatively small a population."[101] My 1961 census of the Boothia Peninsula district found the same

* I could not discern any rules of exchange; nevertheless, judging by the results of my inventory, the existence of income and wealth disparities in this group (i.e., the beginnings of social stratification) seemed probable.

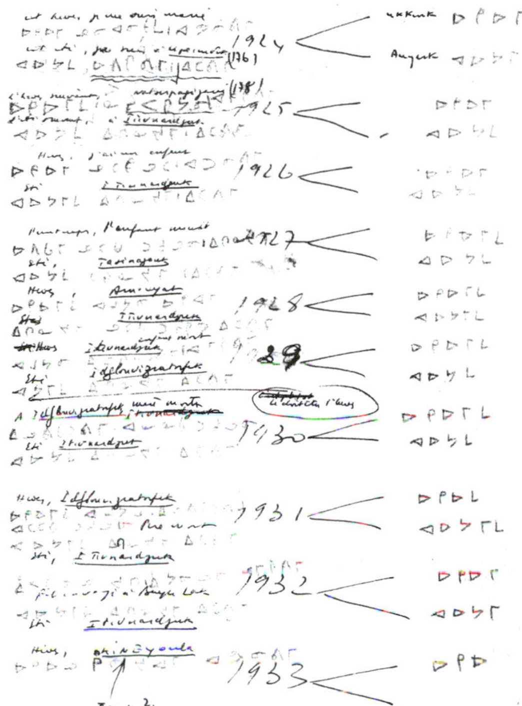

Calendar completed by five different hunters in syllabic script as part of my survey. The questionnaire was administered on a snow platform with the whole group present. Excerpt: "1942: The minister told me we must be united. I heard that God is with us. God always helps. Adieu. We must follow the path of religion…" "1943: I received instructions from Kritjulik [Gjoa Haven catechist], the minister [Spence Bay], and Tajurnark." "1944: The white man comes to our country. We pay no attention." More extensive interviews were planned for the second expedition.

pattern. Out of a population of 450, there were 3 deaf mutes and 6 or 7 epilepsy cases, including a sixteen-year-old girl at the small Josephine Bay camp.* Such consequences of inbreeding bolstered the converts' resolve not to proceed with a marriage unless the priest or minister approved. Consanguinity was undoubtedly also a factor motivating the exogamous unions between Utku men and Thom Bay Netsilik women (who would adopt their husbands' seal taboo even though they themselves had not observed it since childhood).

The introduction of Christianity had, of course, put a stop to the free exercise of the law of nature according to which the weak, the sick, and the elderly

* 1961 census for Spence Bay district, not including Gjoa subdistrict: in a population of 245, there were only 115 males. Gjoa Haven, however, had a population of 190 and a perfectly balanced sex ratio. See maps, pp. 5, 186.

were eliminated.* Canadian law had done likewise, and the RCMP was there to enforce it, more strictly than before 1960. Historically, the force had used discretion in bending the law to accommodate harsh Inuit customs. It was a matter of living within the constraints imposed by the environment; limited fish and game and generalized poverty traditionally made it impossible for the group to support individuals (e.g., the handicapped) who could not fend for themselves. For them to have abided by the law would have required massive assistance that was not forthcoming from Ottawa, as attested by various internal government memos made available to me. The unfortunate experience of the Indian reserves deterred the federal government from developing a policy of active intervention, which would have evinced a radical change of attitude. But the question would arise in the future, especially since, in this isolated and probably highly inbred group (despite the exogamous marriages), their genetic predisposition to deafness and epilepsy would be likely to increase – a hypothesis that remained to be confirmed. In centuries past, the incidence of deafness and epilepsy among the Netsilik and Utku – indeed, among the Caribou Inuit in general – should have risen markedly, yet the reports of nineteenth- and twentieth-century explorers give no reason for believing that this actually occurred. Traditional eugenics was probably the reason.

FATALISM AND EXTREME AUSTERITY

The population decline at Back River was precipitous: from 15 families in 1955 down to 9 in 1959 and 7 in 1963. Obviously, this society had reached a critical demographic and sociological threshold. What to do? "Wait," repeated Toonee, Toolegaak, and Nanudluk, fatalistically entrusting themselves to the future. Echoing this sentiment, the RCMP report for 30 June 1957 stated, "They seem to take hardships and starvation as a matter of course and something that can't be helped."

A burning question: did they have a vision of the future? Again, it appears not: they were leaving it to fate. For several thousand years the estuary had provided fresh water and abundant fish. Caribou were eagerly awaited on their spring migration, while stragglers could be shot throughout the summer and fall only a few days journey away. As discussed, caribou numbers had been declining from year to year since 1930, a biological event of uncertain causation, and their migratory routes were increasingly unpredictable. Still,

* There were old people among the Netsilik; the oldest man and woman were Kavavaoo (Anglican) and Angmardlok (Catholic), aged 77 and 70, respectively. When we met and shook hands, they sported heads of black hair with a few white strands. Although somewhat arthritic in the hands, they were still agile and sharp-witted.

the Utku anticipated that adversity would give way to better times as it always had. In the meantime, they worked on improving their shooting skills so as to maximize their collective catch. Their traditional fatalism, like that of the Bedouins, say, took the form of an extraordinary confidence in Providence – their pantheistic version of it especially. They expected to be shown favour because of their conversion to Christ and his message of the Beatitudes, believing that they were, if not the elect, at least dear to his heart.

What is a generation, thirty years, in the five-thousand-year history of a people who have known guns only since 1908 (introduced, according to Rasmussen, via the Baker Lake post and an Inuit trader)? Was their resistance any surprise when one considers that they carried within them the memory of terrible untold tragedies? When I questioned them about the prohibition on sealing and the resistance to trapping, they responded with demure silence, apparently a form of mental resistance to the temptation of doubting tradition. They were physically staying put but, more than that, warding off uncomfortable thoughts. Perhaps they were unsure of the soundness of their group's decisions; perhaps they felt that discussion of any aspect of these decisions with an outsider would expose the group to collective doubt and that individualism and anarchy would ensue. Whatever be the case, the Utku's withdrawal into self-enforced isolation and conservative adherence to tradition was uninflected by any food shortage that they might experience. RCMP report of 31 December 1953: "The Back River natives do not hunt seals although some can be obtained within a days travel from the river mouth. They depend almost entirely on fish oil, caribou fat and willows for their heat. In many instances, the snow house [*sic*] of that area had no light or heat even during the coldest weather."

This description indicates a situation worse than the one that Rasmussen described in June 1923. The great ethnologist noted that although they did not heat their houses, they did at least light them:

> The snow house is the only dwelling of the Inland Eskimos, and as they have neither blubber nor train oil, they are quite unable to have any warmth inside, although in the cold period the temperature often falls lower than 50 °C below zero. But they are so accustomed to living in these cold houses, where of course they keep their frocks on, that it is usually said that a snow house is only comfortable when the temperature is so low that one's frock does not become damp by coming into the living room ... As a rule a small tallow dip burns in a hollow stone, not warming the room but merely illuminating it.[102]

In April and May 1963, indoor heating was still absent or minimal. There were a few Primus and Coleman stoves, but the limited supply of gasoline was hoarded to make tea, which was also in rather short supply (see Table 5.3 above). I was unable to ascertain whether they used lamplight in winter since daylight is continuous in late April. I assume that they did since, for example, the hurricane lamp appearing in the photograph on pages 234–5 and 246–7 of my *Call of the North* belonged to the family depicted. While visibly intent on preserving their traditions, they displayed cautious openness to technical innovation.

An inland people, they refused to hunt marine mammals (see the excellent analysis by the ethnopsychiatrist András Zempléni in Appendix 1 and the photographs in *Call of the North*),[103] a resistance rooted in interrelated psychohistorical factors that I was unable to discern fully in the three weeks that I had available. But the fact remained that even during periods of famine, they did not hunt the seals available nearby. To enforce this taboo must have required a harsh exercise of authority; perhaps violence had been used to repress the famished. Was there, perchance, any of the pathetic aggressiveness displayed by the Ik of Uganda, who made a game of taking food out of elderly people's mouths?[104] I could not get them to speak about this period; the requisite climate of trust had not been established. It certainly must have been a difficult and painful experience, especially for the elders – was their authority challenged by the young? Everyone kept their feelings on the matter under wraps, in a manner reminiscent of the French deportees in 1945.[105] They simply refused to speak about the unspeakable, deflecting the interview into talk of ancient legends every time I attempted to bring up the topic. One does not share one's pain with a stranger.

What other options were available to them? They clearly had little interest in the income-generating potential of trapping: "It's a joke," they would tell the RCMP, and they used the same language with me, evincing some annoyance when I returned to the subject. As to my idea of a school for nomads, they categorically rejected it: "It would not be Inuit," said their elders. In so concluding, they would settle back on the *iglerk* like great sages while the younger ones bowed their heads as if to signal their approval of the conventional wisdom and their irritation with my insistence. I observed that imported items among their possessions were limited to a few basics – pots, knives, cups, lamps, fishing nets, rifles, boards, watches, and tools such as saws, hammers, and screwdrivers. I do not know the source of these last, but the rest had been purchased at the store. They also had some fabric clothing, much of it donated but some obtained through barter with other families. One constant, according to the RCMP, is that they bought no women's or children's clothing, although they clearly lacked enough caribou skins for bedding. Everyone slept on one snow platform from which they were insulated by a layer of fine, interlaced ground willow roots and twigs[106] covered by an unidentified animal skin and another dog or caribou skin. For blankets, they used a caribou skin that left parts of the body exposed, covering the rest with a filthy, threadbare quilt. A bitch and her pups were also present.[107]

I remained mindful of the confidential mission with which Ottawa had entrusted me, that of encouraging them to move closer to the Gjoa Haven post or to the village itself so as to avoid a repeat of the 1958 tragedy and its potentially disastrous political exploitation by the press and the parliamentary opposition. But when I brought it up, however subtly, Toolegaak leaned back like an old sage, repeating "we will wait" and intoning "Inuit, Inuit," as if Inuit tradition could compensate for the events of history. RCMP annual report of 30 June 1961 for the Spence Bay district: "Typically, many of the people in the area lack the foresight to put up substantial winter caches and rely heavily on day to day hunting." This observation was valid for the Boothia Netsilik but not for the Utku, who would put up as many fish caches as they could, pro-

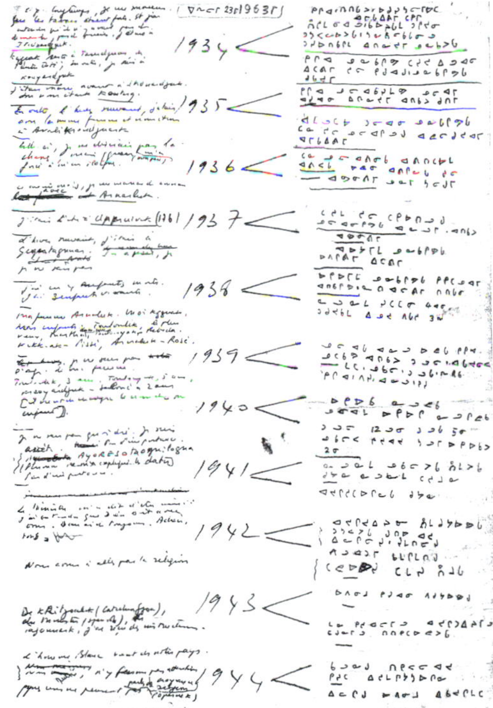

Calendar of life events and hunting trips for a Back River hunter, April 1963.

vided they could reach the spawning sites in time (see pp. 110, 112, 289). Using the *saputit* technique described above, they could catch 500 to 1,000 fish per day. But if they were delayed by caribou hunting and arrived too late, as in 1958, the consequences were catastrophic. The short spawning period allowed them a narrow margin for error.

However, the RCMP's observation remains valid for all the Inuit, including the Utku, in the general sense that they were closing their eyes to the future. Having no experience of what they sensed was coming, instinctively believing it to be too complex, they did what imperiled peoples everywhere do: bow their heads and stick to tradition, their Ariadne's thread.

THE INUITIZATION OF JESUS

I had initially become convinced that I was dealing with a primitive group as conceived of by Durkheim, Mauss, and other writers of foundational anthropology texts, but considering their recent conversion to Protestantism, was this a sound conclusion?

Clearly, my respondents were worried and, as such, open to prudent, gradual change. In this they displayed the pragmatic flexibility of their philosophy. The proof: they gave me cautious hints of the religious dualism that they simply had to be experiencing. Even as they put all the energy derived from their conversion into living "the Christian way," the past remained too present not to influence their consciousness. What was the catechist's discourse? It would be useful to analyze each of his sermons and religious statements, the influence of his speech over the faithful. A third way was stealthily being enunciated, an Inuitization of Christ and Christian thought, a new Christology. The official census listed them as Protestant Christians (Anglicans), and they identified themselves as such when asked.[108] But in my brief one-on-one conversations with Akretoq, for example (who had offered to assist me throughout the mission and during the winter to come), his Protestant faith, so totalizing and supercilious in the presence of the others, did not prevent him from musing about shamanism and spirits and daring to sound me out on the subject. His dreams were visited by the same Satan with whom Luther was so preoccupied, and he asked me how I conceived of the Evil One's power. There was, in his manner, a kind of obsession with salvation. "If we are bad Christians," he would say, "we will burn in hell." To be sure, the dominant tendency of modern-day Anglicanism is liberal-minded and attaches no great importance to Lucifer, but an evangelical variety predominates in the Canadian Arctic, and I found it being preached by the ministers and catechists whom I visited. Thus it is no surprise that the Anglican Inuit, like the Catholics, came to believe in the physical existence of Satan, hell (but not Purgatory), and the archangels, while scorning the various "Papist inventions":

devotion to the Virgin, Immaculate Conception, Communion of the Saints, the Seven Sacraments. Akretoq's memory was gradually being destructured by new dogmas.

Nevertheless, I sensed that it would not take much for the group – or at any rate some of its members – to listen to my general comments on religion, my account of the history of Christianity from Jesus' death onward. We could discuss my explanation of the crises that the church had undergone and how they had given rise to the Reformation of which these people were disciples. I sensed that they were grateful to me for such explanations, provided that I did not proselytize. Agnostic that I am, yet interested in the religious dimension of life, I described my own inner path with sincerity and infinite respect for their faith, speaking as if listening to them, as if saying, "Help me to understand." This was the essential precondition for their allowing me to talk of religion. If I had wintered with them, the issue would have been central to my research. Provided that we treated each other as equals, each drawing on his own Christian background, I have no doubt that they would have generously discussed their doubts and convictions.* There is no strategy to gaining a person's confidence. Nothing touched the Inuit more deeply than being treated as fellow human beings, and this sensibility was integral to every one of my expeditions, as it was to Rasmussen's.[109] "Every serious philosophy has a biographical dimension."[110]

As my early-morning conversations with Akretoq (outdoors, apart from the others), Inukshuk, Toonee, and Toolegaak bore witness, the Utku appeared to have preserved their questing openness and creativity. They seemed more open-minded than the more prosperous folk in Igloolik, who were sharply divided between Catholics and Anglicans, each group heaping anathema upon the other. The Utku told me that they were eagerly awaiting my arrival in the coming winter so that we could reexamine their relations with the government, which they considered to be on a poor footing. For example, why were they given no paddles or nets? "We're not welfare bums. We just want to fish better," they said. They wanted to avoid the welfare rolls at all costs and cringed at the word "relief." (They did ask me to pass on a very modest request to the authorities for some canoes, and I complied.) Nor did they want to be in any way dependent on the HBC, a fate that they vaguely sensed to be as bad as any imaginable. I did not see a single dollar among them. An autonomous people living outside the white economic system, they wanted to plot their future at their own pace, one which, although normally slow, could become

* This statement does not contradict my profession of agnosticism; or rather, this contradiction is an integral part of my Christian identity.

lightning-fast when the urgency of a decision loomed. They did not much care for the obscure purposes of ethnologists, government researchers, and their kin. The Inuit found extremely unpleasant this hypocritically courteous spying, this false warmth; "like offering cookies to a child," was how one put it. This reaction was a constant across all my expeditions, including Rankin Inlet in 1962 and Kuujjuaq in 1968. They hated being asked questions about their personality, psychology, and private life. In fact, I am not aware that there is a more private people in existence. Moreover, outsiders never saw fit to send them copies of the photographs and reports published following their visits. In later years – at Kuujjuaq in 1968, Clyde River in 1987 – I would be told bitterly and angrily by more politicized individuals how offensive they found the whole practice: "We're like animals in a zoo, on display." To put it bluntly, our careers were built at their expense.

If they willingly accepted the RCMP's visits, it was because, since 1940 (in fact, earlier in the Northwest Territories and this remote region), it had always detached upright, respectful men with a genuine desire to help them. The police were responsible for distributing the modest family allowances and old-age benefits, as well as conducting the excellent censuses and writing the annual reports that I have cited at length. Continuing to receive food aid was ruled out; as one RCMP report stated, "It would be their ruin." Cooperating with the Gjoa Haven HBC post would compel them to gradually become its employees, and this, too, was out of the question. "We are Inuit, hunters of tukto and fishers of eqaluk," they insisted, as if weary of such foolish ideas. They were, in fact, the last free people that I saw in the Arctic, and it was moving to observe how gamely they fought to preserve their freedom.

RCMP annual report, 1951: "When one of the Back River natives obtained his first issue in Gjoa Haven, the writer was present and on inquiries being made, the natives only wished some ammunition and a fish net; no food stuff at all." They knew that by becoming dependent on utterly inappropriate white food aid (butter, marmalade, flour, etc.), they stood a good chance of becoming integrated, in dietary terms, with the life of the post. For illustration, the following was the contents of a six-month food ration, as told to me by Munaluk (an Inuit man whom I met at Thom Bay; after sustaining a spinal injury in a fall from a sled at Fort Ross, he had spent three years in hospital): 24 pounds of flour, 1 pound of yeast, 6 pounds of oatmeal, 2 pounds of butter, 10 pounds of sugar, 2 pounds of tea, 4 pounds of fat, 8 pounds of jam, four dozen boxes of matches, 3 pounds of rice, and 4 gallons of gasoline. A white's ration. What they really needed, apart from the tea, sugar, and gas, was animal fat, meat, and skins. To a government more attuned to their culture and circumstances, this would have been obvious.

SHUNNING GJOA

Why did they dislike Gjoa Haven? Because "[t]his location has never been known to have abundant game and only in good years and by hard work, are Eskimo families able to live comfortably on their caches. The desire to be around [the trading post] is the only reason that would keep Eskimo living there." This statement appears in the stinging RCMP annual report of 1955. Is it any wonder that life in Gjoa Haven, with its poor seal hunting and absence of other game, held little interest for the roving caribou hunters and fishermen of Back River?

To repeat: their leitmotiv was to hold fast to Amujat, where all the Utku would gather to spend the winter. As of April 1963, there was no question of their leaving the Hayes and Back Rivers estuary. No one would bother them there, not even a related ethnic group. I was given to understand that the arrival of Netsilingmiut from the north would be accepted only if they did not stay too long and kept a scrupulous distance from the camp. In truth, the Utku were open to all sorts of transitions on the condition of being allowed to stay where they were. They wanted to live in harmony with their history, at their tempo, without criticism. They alone would decide which aspects of their traditions and beliefs to retain and which to discard. They would not tolerate any attempt to push them onto a path different from the one that they had collectively marked out.

Christianity, as I quickly perceived, was the major factor in the cultural and technical impasse affecting this society. Nakliguhuktuq, an Inuit theologian with very particular ideas, was the pivotal figure in the Back River parish, as the astute Father Lorson told me during my short stay in Gjoa Haven. He intimated that caution would be necessary in my interviews there if I wished to avoid this man's wrath. If hell was real for the people of the early sixteenth century, it had become equally real for these new Protestants, a menace invoked to keep their minds in thrall. But coexisting with such fire and brimstone was the Lutheran idea according to which all Christians, by virtue of baptism, are "truly of the spiritual estate,"[111] members of a universal priesthood. On the dogsled trip south, I spent time contemplating the liberating idea – in essence, the foundation of Christian thought – that faith alone saves a person by bringing him closer to Christ. It is the kind of thinking that could lead a Protestant to reason, "If God did us this honour, what do we need priests for?"

But was I likely to find a priestly community of the kind that Luther might have approved of? This was not so certain. Anglicanism, while closely related to Lutheranism, is an established episcopalian church with its hierarchy of bishops and ministers. One certainty was that the seven families saw themselves as active members of the universal, invisible church, a community of the faith experienced by various Protestant movements – Lutherans, Calvinists (Wesleyans), Anglicans certainly – as the "body of Christ." As a guest of this Christian community, I wanted to understand how, for example, the Inuit converts interpreted the Eucharist, an immense theological issue central to profound upheavals since Luther's day – indeed, since the origins of Christianity. Whereas for Lutherans, the body and blood of Christ are substantially present in the bread and the wine, the Anglican ministers at Rankin Inlet and Baker Lake informed me that the Anglican Church considers this issue to defy the understanding. "We are pragmatic," they said: "substantiation, consubstantiation – we leave the interpretation to the local minister."

More visibly here than elsewhere, religion represented what economics represented for Marx: the substrate of social and individual thought. But the Gospel and Luther's commentary imposed an especially severe constraint. No longer were the Inuit masters of their own thinking since the "good news" of the Gospel provided the signposts that they had to follow. At the time of their conversion, the Inuit probably did not imagine that they would be asked to rethink their shamanism from a radically new angle. One of their cultural characteristics is to attempt to master new skills and knowledge piece by piece, as if learning a mechanism. They want to understand what they undertake. No doubt they would have liked to observe this fundamental shift in the same way, stand outside of it, but of course this was impossible. Only recently still a "free" people (in fact, bound within a corpus of taboos), they were subjected to a new law imposed by outsiders, whites, whose rigour and complexity would be revealed only in the course of their practice of Christianity. By means of a conversion that they were assured would free them spiritually, they gave themselves up as prisoners. The word "conversion," from the Latin *conversio*, designates the action of turning to God; to submit to His will is not merely to switch from a "false" belief to a theological truth, but also to undergo an inner revolution.[112] Total adherence to the new dogmas is required. "I am the way, the truth, and the life," said Christ. Your eternal salvation depends on it. Christianity demands a wholesale conversion and does not allow for negotiation. The resulting submission to a set of moral and ethical dictates undoubtedly represented an upheaval for each of them individually and, *a fortiori*, for the group as a whole.

Whereas their traditional memory space was almost consubstantially bound up with pantheism and the spirits of the dead, the Anglican teachings were characterized by a broad church spirit that sought to reconcile all Protestant tendencies within a "humility of reason." Inner psychological conflict was unavoidable. It would be extremely interesting to interview these people about all aspects of the change: their conception of the fall from grace and original sin, faith in consubstantiation, the duty of compassion, the Communion of the Saints, heaven to be gained and eternal hell to be feared, the sacraments of baptism and Holy Writ. I would have inquired into the nature of their faith in the Holy Communion; did they actually see themselves as eating Christ's flesh and drinking his blood, as opposed to symbols thereof? A huge distinction, famously divisive among Christians. Here, it took on a connotation of cannibalism, of which they had a longstanding horror because they had been fated to practise it under extreme circumstances. But although the inner conflict was predictable, there was no overt evidence of its occurrence, none of the retrenchment or revolt that one would expect to find. Perhaps emigration to Baker Lake, Repulse Bay, and Gjoa Haven after the 1958 famine had been, for some, a way of expressing tacit revolt against what non-Christians might flatly regard as religious tyranny. In my 1962 interviews at Baker Lake, these émigrés did not say that this was so, but in truth, I did not nudge the conversation in this direction since I was then unaware of Nakliguhuktuq's existence. It may be that some of these proud men and women resented him. As for the twenty-five neophytes at Back River, they were too close-knit to tolerate dissent. My cautious interviews showed them to be skillful diplomats who responded with precision or evasion depending on the topic at hand. Their adherence to Christian ideas had not caused them to become vocal detractors of tradition; rather, they appeared to be in the process of weighing the resulting political issues. The central pillar of their faith was the figure of Jesus, defender of the humiliated and the wronged, not the dogma surrounding him. What I was witnessing was the ongoing Inuitization of Christianity.*

This was, it must be stressed, a tiny Inuit community with a twenty-to-thirty-year history of fervent Christian belief, a community visibly chary of any waywardness. As well, I sensed that my small, modest survey was circumscribed in its possibilities by the surveillance of the constable, who was anxious to keep the peace between Catholics, Protestants, and traditionalists, although he was so silent, so discreet that I would forget he was there. As I mentioned earlier, he took an active role only once when, finding himself at loose ends, unable to relate to the intensity of the interviews, he offered to perform the ethnographic survey of the community, the results of which he later entered in my little green notebook. The shadow of Nakliguhuktuq preceded me wherever I went, at times becoming an intervening presence; I ventured into the opaque domain of religious experience most cautiously. Particular care was needed since my interpreter, Tootalik, an Anglican, was married to a Catholic woman in Spence Bay who had vowed before the Oblate to raise her

* I observed a similar process taking place with the Pentecostals in Alaska (at Shishmaref and Savoonga in 1965 and 1967).

children in her own faith. The research that I planned to conduct in the winter of 1963–64 might have helped to firm up these inchoate hypotheses about an Inuitized Jesus.

Another question: how did they feel about having been abandoned by the civil and religious authorities during the famine of 1958? Anyone observing the living conditions of this small, remote group, the inadequacy of their provisions, might have seen it coming, but help arrived only after the tragedy struck. The authorities in Ottawa were mum on the subject, evidently taken by surprise. Apparently, they had no choice but, with great reluctance, to make the epochal decision to relocate the tiny Inuit groups in mortal danger. My respondents made no comment, offered no criticism of the church, in regard to this issue.

Another remark: the Sermon on the Mount is the kernel of Jesus' message. *Beati pauperes!* Poverty is the passport to heaven. But this was not the only new idea injected by the Gospel into the Utku's vitalist worldview: they were asked to show love for every fellow human being, an abiding spirit of charity and compassion, respect for all human life. For hunters who killed not only game but, at least in former times, the weak and the superannuated of their own number, it was a radical mental revolution. The Protestant missionary (the English-speaking minister in Spence Bay or the Inuit deacon in Gjoa Haven) had evidently got the message across – there were now a few older people, the sex ratio was returning to normal – but had he convinced them to do away with the practice of infanticide? This is not certain. Judging by what they told me, they evidently believed that life emanates from God. If so, then I would add, in the spirit of the Gospel, that to interfere with it is an offence to God, and to be Christian is to submit to His will.

Christianity, whether of the Protestant or Catholic variety, henceforth obliged them to keep deaf mutes and epileptics alive, to cease the kind of harsh treatment that I saw meted out to an epileptic boy – ultimately, to treat everyone as equals. To act otherwise in such cases, to violate the Ten Commandments, is a mortal sin according to the Gospel, not to mention a crime under Canadian law. Judging by the parents' uncharitable attitude toward the boy, conversion was still a work in process – a process that would continue with the destruction of their antique social system and mentality.

Looked at another way, however, Christianity worked to reinforce the unity of the group. Their adherence to Protestantism welded them together in an ethnocultural unit defined, among other things, in opposition to the Catholic Netsilingmiut, the heretical Papists who hunted and ate the seals that the shamans had proscribed. Moreover, by Protestantizing the Inuit, the evangelical church granted them the same immediate relationship to Christ that every other Christian enjoyed. They became the equals of the whites, who had supposedly come to this land to guide them, help them administer their affairs, enlighten them. As Christian as their Canadian administrators, they could now, in the name of the Gospel, the invisible church, turn around and judge the latter's customs and actions. They could consider themselves superior. Baptism had given them an extraordinarily powerful civic voice. From one Sunday sermon to the next, through various comments on the Scriptures, the parish presided over by the Inuit catechist became the crucible of autonomous power. Not enough consideration has been given, perhaps, to the influence of Christianization on Inuit thinking about self-government, which would gain ground in the following twenty years, increasingly being wielded in opposition to the colonial authority. In fact, a good number of catechists were among the first Inuit political leaders.

The influence of Christianity was, to say the least, complex. Apart from its authentic, revolutionary Christian message that salvation is reserved to true followers of the evangelical word, Lutheran- and especially Anglican-inspired Protestantism has a more conservative face. In a well-known text, Luther emphasized the duty of loyalty to the established secular authority[113] – here, the colonial authority. Bernard Cottret, in his remarkable history of the Protestant Reformation,[114] reflects on the following remarks of Friedrich Engels: "Luther had given the plebeian movement a powerful weapon – a translation of the Bible ... Now Luther turned the same weapon against the peasants, extracting from the Bible a veritable hymn to the authorities ordained by God – a feat hardly exceeded by any lackey of absolute monarchy."[115] The Canadian Inuit, at the mercy of a monopolistic corporation in the service of the colonial authority, converts to an Anglican Church whose highest authority (*defensor fidei*)* is the Queen of England, could appreciate that the history of the conquest had left them with a singularly narrow margin of autonomy. It took political genius for these men of the tundra and the igloos to stand up and affirm their identity as free citizens of a free people, to demand and achieve debate on their status within Confederation.

THE CRISIS

But there and then I did not get the sense that these resolutely autonomous people fully grasped the width of the chasm yawning before them. Like all neophytes, they trusted in the new religion, in Providence, in this "foreign" God the omnipotent father, creator of heaven and earth, to solve their insoluble problem. Christianity? Yes, but within Inuit tradition and autonomy. They were proud of their conversion and unabashedly optimistic. God does not

* "Defender of the Faith." Title given – rather incredibly, in light of the simmering crisis and the rift that would soon appear – to Henry VIII by Pope Leo X in October 1521.

abandon his chosen people, they said, and we are the chosen people by virtue of our poverty. With the faith and vanity of new converts (echoing the sentiment of long-established believers) they maintained that tradition makes it possible to endure the great trials of history. Still, the coexistence of these two bodies of thought inevitably engendered contradictions; how, for example, was one to reconcile the practice of infanticide with the Christian doctrine of respect for all life? When I elliptically referred to these matters in one-on-one interviews with Akretoq, Toolegaak, and others, they sidestepped the questions with talk about hunting and place names and heroic Knud Rasmussen from faraway Greenland.

ETHNOPHOTOGRAPHY AND THE GAZE

My photographs appear to depict a people assured in their ancient traditions – "the igloo people." Looking at them differently, one can see that anxiety about the future inhabits these misty, inward-looking eyes, these distant gazes.[116] How much joy did their newfound Christianity really afford them? There was no telling. Given the mindset of their sect, which partook more of Calvinism than of Lutheranism, doubts had to be hidden from one another and perhaps even from oneself. My questions concerned complex, vital matters bearing directly on their future and faith, and they may have regarded being interviewed without the guidance of their "shepherd," their minister, as a dangerous prospect.

LAUGHTER AND SORROW

I hope the reader will not mistake me: there was plenty of laughter in these camps, and it was not mechanical laughter. Whether or not you believe it, these men, women, and children loved a good joke as much as anyone else. I sensed their comfort with themselves as well as their openness to my survey. But I also had no illusions. Serious or smiling, all except the children – perhaps even the children – had their masks on. The alacrity with which they submitted to the daily interview routine was something of a pretense. It would be a stretch to say that they were trying to win me as an ally; rather, it seemed as though they were testing me in order to determine whether to treat me as their guest. When I told them that I had decided to winter over that year, the elders emphasized that they were looking forward to my arrival and had arranged for my accommodations with Akretoq and Inukshuk. Nor did it take great intuition to see that my gifts – the bag of tea that I put under the pillow of Akretoq's wife every morning, the knives, and so on – were appreciated, although their acknowledgment was characteristically uneffusive; my gift, my business. The expatriates whom I interviewed at Gjoa Haven in early May 1963 on my return from Back River, and at Rankin Inlet and Baker Lake in 1962, all expressed sorrow at having had to leave this "good and beautiful place, where we were happy." They described the summer, the fish, life's joyfulness. In contrast, there was absolute silence on those who had starved to death during the famines and on the cruel elimination of infants considered deformed, sickly, or unviable. Not a word about the old people who committed suicide when they had begun to feel burdensome; not a word about the wholesale conversion to Protestantism and the attendant repudiation of shamanism and its myths, everything that had constituted the backbone of their culture. Not a word, naturally, about their internal quarrels and apostates. Discretion toward a come-and-go investigator was a matter of course. It seems that the Utku, at this watershed moment in their history, had not left behind any of their baggage, even if they did not say so openly. They had held on to the customs from which their past was forged, customs that would allow their intact ethnic group to ply a course into the future. Moreover, as I watched the six hunters identify toponyms and trace hunting routes on the map with amazing precision and recall (including a recounting of various humorous incidents), I realized the fullness with which they inhabited their land in both space and time. The purposiveness of their daily life had allowed them to preserve their ancestral dynamism. This was especially relevant in view of the object of my mission, which was to assess the advisability of relocation.

All these factors – home territory as a sacred place, dietary sufficiency, isolation, coherent religious identity, simultaneous emotional attachment to the elders and the Anglican Church, Inuitization of Jesus – typified the Utku identity for me as a researcher and a consultant to Ottawa.

The missionaries like to claim that the Inuit conversions took place in a manner similar to Saint Paul's revelation on the road to Damascus. If this is to be believed, then the Inuit (with the odd exception) became convinced in an inspired moment that their shamans were nothing but liars. Biblical truth and the crucified Son of God took hold in their minds, and they were liberated from the suffocating strictures and taboos of yesteryear. This version of events cropped up frequently in missionary journals such as *Eskimo*. For my part, I became increasingly certain, based on what I observed in April and May 1963, that the group had effected a gradual syncretism between traditional shamanism and Anglicanism. The missionaries, of course, never mentioned shamanism except to vilify it, to warn the Inuit against slipping back into their pagan ways. By all accounts not a single murder or suicide had been committed in the wake of this radical conversion. Could it have been that profound? If so, at what psychological cost? What becomes of a Back River convert when he finds himself alone on the tundra doubting the white gospel, a gospel that he has heard but not read, while his subconscious mind appeals to the elders, the beliefs that were their greatness and that still dwell in his sorrowful, divided heart? I cannot say. That they still lived austerely in their snow houses is no reason to lapse into the telling of fairy tales, to regard these traditionalist believers as pure-hearted innocents, comforted by a conversion to a religion that would allow them to go straight to heaven if they were baptized and followed the rules.

I relate what I saw. Their religious unity and resolve resembled that of the little Protestant societies of eighteenth-century England or Scotland. Within their community, apparently, they never doubted or challenged any aspect of their faith – no theologians there, it seemed. But the last word had not been said. At Kangiqsujuaq (Wakeham), Nunavik, in July 1987, I was present when one Inuk launched into a discourse on the text of Numbers and Deuteronomy. He clearly felt entitled to offer his own interpretation of various Bible passages, and I engaged him in conversation about it. It was his contention that the Inuktitut translation provided during Sunday Mass was in many respects a corruption of the English version with which he was familiar, and that it did not correspond to the idea of the Beatitudes that he had formed as a fervent Anglican. This man (not the catechist but a congregant close to the minister) expressed his desire to retranslate the sacred texts that he so loved. Such theological activism in the Arctic was entirely new to me. I had not observed it at Back River, Gjoa Haven, Spence Bay, Igloolik, Rankin Inlet, or Thule/Siorapaluk. I was unfamiliar with the Sunday sermons of the catechist and Deacon Nakliguhuktuq – which leads me to a new avenue of exploration. In 1963–64 a local catechist told the anthropologist Jean Briggs: “If people don’t want to believe Nakliguhuktuq either, then Nakliguhuktuq will write to Cambridge Bay, and a bigger leader, the Kapluna king in Cambridge Bay, will come in an airplane with a big and well-made whip and will whip people. It will hurt a great deal.”[117] Based on my experience of Inuit Christians, whom I have always found to be possessed of deep, reflective thought, I find myself reading irony into this remark (Never in anger? Think again!), interpreting it as that of a person tired of being questioned about his Christian beliefs. To him it must have been obvious that his new worldview represented an upheaval, a radically different approach to death and eternity, so he dispensed with the anthropologist’s question by evoking the pat image of a colonial whip-wielding bogeyman, and Briggs let the remark pass without comment. One RCMP report that I read expressed annoyance about the Flemish Oblate’s possessiveness toward his Catholic Netsilingmiut “flock” in Pelly Bay.

AN EMOTIONAL ATTACHMENT TO PLACE

Let us recapitulate the essential facts about Back River in order: emotional attachment to the beauty of the place; isolation; fecund families; good health; austere but stable economy; high-calorie diet; apparent survival of preexisting Inuit spirituality in the form of a syncretism with Christianity; pride of the new convert to an established church; youth exposed to modern technology on the American bases before returning to their families. Their adaptive mechanisms had integrated all these parts into a cohesive whole, making them increasingly open to the outside world. The seeds of development had been planted. On the surface they remained a primitive society of raw-fish-eating, igloo-dwelling spartans smilingly waiting ... for Godot, for the caribou, for fate to take its course. They inhabited the long perspective with extraordinary confidence in their destiny.

To the east of them, the 302 Inughuit of Thule lived in harmony with technical innovation in a structured anarcho-communalist society. Their healthy financial situation resulted from a vigorous fur market (seventy hunters, one thousand pelts per year). To the west, in the Bering Strait, the proud whalers of Saint Lawrence Island, Ipiutaq, Point Hope, and Chukotka had formed redoubtably complex societies that ritualized the sacred with great, inspired metaphors.[118] Here in the Central Arctic, I found this same Inuit people, but in its rudimentary expression. Space and time, geography and history, had constituted "a general series ... in conformity with nature";[119] the globalization of the gaze inevitably leads us to reflect on the magisterial idea of evolution. Here again is Lamarck, writing more than two hundred fifty years ago: "Man should not consider it beneath him to study the laws of nature, the observed facts which must show him in all obviousness that these phenomena, seemingly so singular, so marvelous, are in fact perfectly organic, subjected to the powers and laws of nature and that, consequently, the knowledge of these laws has become for Man an absolute necessity in his present state of civilization."[120]

At Back River I witnessed the embryo of social life and collective thought that had already burgeoned into a complex *naturphilosophie* among the Inughuit in 1950 and the Alaskan whalers in 1965. Everything was in place for its full flowering here, if time were allowed to do its work. As Lamarck wrote concerning evolution in his penetrating *Zoological Philosophy*: "I was then convinced that it was only in the simplest of all organisations that the solution of this apparently difficult problem was to be found. For it is only the simplest organisation that presents all the conditions necessary to the existence of life and nothing else beyond, which might mislead the enquirer."[121]

HISTORY ACCELERATES

But – and this "but" is heavy with implications – the Back River Inuit, in their proud isolation, were unaware of the laws dictating the acceleration of history. In the next twenty years, the far-reaching political events taking place in this region would shuttle them from the time of discovery to the time of the

DEMOGRAPHIC STATISTICS

Social facts are not things. I do not judge, I relate. Due to lack of historical perspective and appropriate social policy on Canada's part, the Nunavut and Nunavik authorities have inherited a tremendous burden. Demographic statistics are one revealing way of depicting this situation:

- In the early 1990s, the Canadian Inuit birth rate was 35 per 1,000, while for Canadian women generally it was 13.1 per 1,000. The Canadian Inuit infant mortality rate was 16.9 per 1,000 live births, while for Canada women it was 5.2.
- Mean life expectancy (2001): 60 in Labrador, 62 in Northern Quebec, 66 in the Northwest Territories; in Canada, 75 for men, 82 for women.

Source: Indian and Northern Affairs Canada, *Canada and Aboriginal Peoples: A New Partnership: Report of Hon. A.C. Hamilton, Fact Finder for Minister of Indian Affairs and Northern Development* (Ottawa, 1995).

TABLE 5.6 SUICIDE RATES, 1995 (PER 100,000)

	BOTH GENDERS	MALE	FEMALE
Canadian Indian and Inuit population	33.3	51.5	15.1
Canada	14	19.2	4.9
France	19.5	29.2	9.8

Sources: *Report of the Royal Commission on Aboriginal Peoples*, vol. 3, (Ottawa, 1996); Direction de la Recherche des études de l'évaluation et des statistiques, Ministère de l'Emploi et de la Solidarité, Paris, 2002.

invasion. The RCMP would become stricter in enforcing laws that interfered with nature's commands, and likewise Christian morals would compel the parishioners to accept and protect every living being. It would no longer suffice to call themselves Christians; they would have to prove it by withstanding the wave of alcoholism, drug abuse, and violence washing over them in the 1980s. Deaf mutes, epileptics, orphans, antisocial individuals – formerly snuffed out – would become increasingly numerous. This factor among others would induce the Inuit to assimilate further with Canadian society in order to enjoy the benefits of its social-democratic assistance regime. Not coincidentally, the 1970s saw the region's most rapid population concentration. Yesterday, they were semi-nomadic peoples dispersed among eighteen camps north

and south of Spence Bay and Gjoa Haven;[122] today, they lived in these two villages, by now rather large towns, each with a population of 800 and, be it repeated, the worst places to hunt and fish. If Ottawa chose them as administrative capitals, it was because of their logistical convenience. A people thus "globalized" was condemned to watch its traditional history fade away, while relief as a principle of development would become a metastatic cancer. School and Canadianization would become burning necessities for the young elites. People would have to be trained rapidly to occupy new positions in computer science, biogenics, and law, thereby integrating into the market economy. A new people was in gestation. The elders – Toonee, Toolegaak, Nanudluk – had been prophetic: salvation meant clinging to the ancestral land. By relocating, the Utkuhikhalingmiut signed their death warrant as an ethnic group. Gjoa Haven would mean schooling, food dependency, and all the illusions of capitalist commerce; a journey to the end of the night, with alcohol, drugs, broken families, battered women, and incest marking the way. Christ would be in agony once again. One may well ask whether Christianity, by undermining their traditional ways, facilitated this major crisis of deculturation by acculturing the only God that business will recognize: the dollar. But at the same time, we must acknowledge that Christianity was probably one of the best bulwarks against demoralization. The time has perhaps come for these Anglicans and Catholics to assert that they are, for the time being, neither Christian nor Inuit, and that they will have to relearn to be both rather than being forced to make a choice between them. A time of terrible trials – for a generation or two or ten – may be necessary for them to be reborn as a new people with a different culture.

DISPOSSESSION

I would add one final remark: if the liberal evolution of our Protestant churches and other white institutions had somehow been accelerated by just a few years, it might have helped to assure a smoother transition of these traditional societies, with their draconian customs, to the more humane and permissive aspects of our civilization. One thinks, for example, of the liberalization of attitudes in the area of birth control (elective abortion, ultrasound, the pill) in the 1950s and 1960s. Such serendipity did not happen, and it was necessary for me to be there as a witness to the difficult transition that the Utku were undergoing. The Inuit customs of the past were cruel, they might have said, but no worse than the inhumane life extension and eugenic abortion that goes on in the old-age homes and birthing clinics of your allegedly civilized societies. And there is much truth in this. In view of how our pro forma Christianity and failing democratic spirit have resulted in policies that privilege form over content, policies that do no more than give lip service to human rights, we would do well to look to the Utku for insight into the deeper meanings of community.

appendix 1

From Tactic to Expiation: Thoughts on the Utku's Abstention from Sealing

Paris, 6 February 1996

Dear Jean Malaurie,
The epistolary form seems the one best suited for me to respond to your superb, moving text. What moves me is the keenness of your concise observations, the way you laser-etch them into the Inuit landscape, and also your tenacious nagging away (like a toothache) at a deep ethical and theoretical question, spurred on in this by your love for a people who are dying. Some will say that the captain of the *Terre Humaine*, that twilled fabric in which so many different human odours are instilled, has succumbed to an attack of mysticism at the icy doors of his Eskimo Sparta, if not his ethnologist's earthly Jerusalem. But no matter. Really, what do such complaints matter when stood next to the image of an afflicted little boy – wracked with convulsions, shivering in a chilly igloo – being "educationally" put out to freeze for lack of the warming blubber of the seals that his relatives obstinately refuse to hunt for some enigmatic reason? In sum, what do the reactions of the timid matter in

the face of this block of ice of a real anthropological question: why have the Back River Inuit forbidden themselves from hunting the fat and meat of the only animal that can assure their autonomous, if not comfortable, survival? It goes without saying that, given my incompetence in this area, I have no solution to offer you, only a few thoughts and naive questions to ask on the subject of the social "double knot" of the Utku. The first is academic but implies others that are not, to wit: Is this a taboo in the strict sense, identifiable by the characteristic that its transgression automatically produces an anticipated and feared mystical punishment? Judging by your account, I would say definitely not, since you yourself provide a counter-example of a "real" dietary taboo against mixing caribou meat with fish, food from the earth with food from the sea, a taboo that, if violated, could "jeopardize future hunting and fishing" (the mystical punishment).* This is a far cry from the prohibition on sealing that manifests itself in two guises in the lives of your hosts: as a mere dislike and as ascetic abstinence in the religious sense. Let us dwell on the first of these, returning to the second as we must. You write that the Utku have an "ancient and undeniable repugnance for everything that comes from the sea"† and, furthermore, that their longstanding attitude (noted by Rasmussen) is that sealing is "a long, tedious process" in comparison with fishing. Whether indicative of dislike or abstinence, these remarks are foreign to the language of taboos, it seems to me.

In saying so, I may be giving the impression of going against the grain of your Judeo-Christian interpretation of the Utku's abstention from sealing. Quite the contrary, for the concept of a taboo is diametrically opposed to the Judeo-Christian concept of sin. Its transgression automatically provokes a punishment, whereas the breaking of rules regarded as sins calls for human repentance, atonement, in order to avert or lift a divine sanction. As Lévi-Strauss would put it, seals are "good to think," suitable vehicles of violation or sin among the Inuit, precisely because they are not, or are no longer, taboo as such.

But you know better than I that this is not the end of the matter and that the Utku "double knot" is much more intricate. Again, I do not claim to untie it; but three other questions come to mind that I would put to you following the chronological order that you lay out, enriched by that of Rasmussen. My understanding is that the introduction of guns around 1908 – which allegedly sounded the death knell for the "tedious" practice of sealing – dates roughly from the time when the starving Utku migrated from the Queen Maud Gulf to the Back River estuary – that is, from the time of their transformation from

* See pp. 217–36.

† See p. 225.

coastal Inuit (accustomed to eating seal, walrus, and whales) into land-based Inuit (hunting caribou and musk ox and, especially, catching fish). Which leads to a first question: Wasn't the seal already at that time – leaving aside guns and the abundance of caribou – an animal tediously emblematic of this radical departure from their elders' way of life? In other words, perhaps the white people's guns gave a boost to their preexisting inclination to rub out such an awkward witness to their break with the traditions of the sea – whose products might now repel them for the same reason.

Second question: Wasn't this amphibious animal and its ambiguous method of capture (does one "hunt" seals at a breathing hole or "fish" them?) the very incarnation of the aforementioned taboo on mixing foods from the sea and the land? In sum, didn't abstinence from sealing during this period help to simultaneously resolve two enduring contradictions imposed by the Utku's history: on the one hand, their infidelity to their ancestors' maritime way of life and, on the other, their ancient habit of consuming this hunted-or-fished, half-terrestrial, half-aquatic animal in violation of a "strict" taboo on mixing caribou meat with fish flesh? Finally, my third question brings us down to the icy earth of Back River, which your historical geographer's eye has scrutinized: Were there really all that many seals at a not-too-"tedious" distance during that remote epoch of migration and newly introduced guns?

Once again, I may be giving the impression of going against the grain of your interpretation, this time using the vehicle of an Africanist's unverifiable speculations. But I am getting to the heart of our matter, which these tentative conjectures may just help to untangle. For the reader's benefit, here is a brief recapitulation of the facts you summarize (my emphasis):*

(1) Famine of 1900 followed by migration of these "multiprey" hunters of seal and caribou to Qamanittuaq ("widening river"), where they commence catching fish and hunting caribou, these toothsome prey being abundant there.

(2) 1908–30: *introduction of guns* and resulting golden age of hunting, *period of relative prosperity, abandonment of "tedious" seal hunting.*

(3) (Apparently) simultaneous decline of traditional ceremonial life and *progressive abandonment of shamans.* Ikinilik to Rasmussen in 1923: "Now that we have firearms it is almost as if we no longer need shamans, or taboos."†

(4) Starting in 1930 – after simultaneous abandonment of sealing and shamans – *rapid decline of caribou population*, interpreted a posteriori as a *punishment* for their having broken an ancestral pact through their use of guns, this situation engendering a *state of existential angst.*

* See pp. 231–2.

† See p. 226.

(5) 1920–30 (before this ecological and social catastrophe): arrival of Anglican missionaries preaching the acceptance of misfortune and the virtues of poverty while labelling as heretics the Utku's *neighbours*, the Netsilik, who *continued to hunt and eat seals.*

(6) The exogamous Back River Utku nonetheless *continued to marry the women of these "heretical" seal hunters and eaters*, who in the eyes of the Utku would have been indulging in the worst of sins.

I hope that I have done a modicum of justice to your passably complex history of the prohibition in question. But this picture remains unintelligible without your interpretation, which structures it, and which I will summarize with insertion of my own remarks and questions. As of 1923 (before the golden age of caribou was over), the remarks of one of Rasmussen's respondents on the subject of the thermal comfort of the Netsilik igloos (heated with seal blubber) attest, you say,* to an ethic of austerity characteristic of the Utku, a cultural and technical insistence on doing without this precious fuel. The decisive question: How can this ethic of austerity, this thermal asceticism, shall I put it, be reconciled, in those times of prosperity brought on by the gun, with the equally evident dietary hedonism of eating caribou, then an abundant treat? Wasn't the former in some sense the price to be paid for the latter? Couldn't we make profitable use here of the distinction between the energetic and dietary aspects of the seal prohibition?

In any event, it was against this backdrop of *aurea austeritas* that the massive social reaction of the Utku to the catastrophe of the disappearing caribou (the "dread fear of the Inuit") took place, and it was then, in those times of profound existential angst, that "the seal taboo came into being." The aforementioned dislike, abstinence, or indolence would then have given way to a taboo per se. Your argument is plausible and rings true to an Africanist who has more than once witnessed the divinatory imposition of similar group prohibitions following comparable catastrophes and states of collective angst. However – and apart from the aforementioned problems related to the automatic nature of the mystical punishment characteristic of taboos – this argument leads to several questions, some of which you yourself have posed with great clarity.

In my estimation, the first relates to the logic of taboos itself. In this logic, akin to that of sociobiology (but coincidence is no evidence!), shouldn't the Utku have imposed a taboo *not on seals but on caribou*, whose overhunting with the white people's guns was perceived as an offence against the Master of the Animals; whose catastrophic disappearance was seen as a punishment – and here is the kernel of the matter – not only for the allogenic overhunting

* See p. 225.

of caribou, but also, and especially, as you clearly state, for the simultaneous abandonment of shamanism, "the gods and the shamans," with the advent of the golden age of guns? At the risk of going astray, I would say that if they had displayed the standard, oft-observed reaction to situations of existential crisis, your Inuit hosts should and could have rehabilitated their shamans and, through them, should and could have imposed a taboo on caribou while taking up the "tedious" sealing of their maritime ancestors.

The contrary happened, and that is what intrigues me in your saga of the Utku. They did not turn back to their shamans, and they gave up sealing. Why? One could no doubt hypothesize the pragmatic (and not unprecedented) stratagem of a taboo shift – they may have abstained from "tedious" sealing as a way of bringing back the succulent caribou! But in that case, one would still have to explain the sacrifice of sealing in a crisis situation not very conducive to substitutions of other than archaic origin. Let us look further. We might conjecture instead that abstinence from sealing was both a reminder of and a ritual atonement for a much older transgression than the allogenic overhunting of caribou, namely the abandonment of the land and traditions of their maritime ancestors who hunted (or fished) the amphibious seal. But even in that case, where the role of the seal taboo would be to legitimate a break between the two ways of life, one would still – indeed, a fortiori – have to explain why your hosts did not rehabilitate their shamans, something that constantly happens in Siberian societies, for example.

One is ineluctably led to acknowledge the legitimacy, not to say the necessity, of your Judeo-Christian interpretation. What does it say? That the Anglican ministers, who arrived before a natural catastrophe aroused an overwhelming sensation of punishment in the Utku, attempted to build an ethic or mystique of poverty and submission on the assuredly fragile foundation of a preexisting ethic of austerity, in which thermal asceticism and abstinence from sealing still vied with the dietary hedonism of the happy caribou hunters, an ethic in which the "strong God of the whites" would replace the "pantheistic god of the shamans,"* Christ would stand in for the Great Shaman,† and the Utku would become the true defenders of the faith – provided that they renounced their "sins" and worldly lust while awaiting collective salvation in an afterworld modelled on the paradise that their shamans had promised.

I realize that I am confounding (but can anyone tease apart?) the missionaries' normative discourse with the presumed but not readily explorable psychic realities of the Inuit.‡ Whatever be the case, the rapid disappearance

* See p. 226.

† See pp. 231–4.

‡ I must say that the otherwise estimable book by Jean Briggs (*Never in Anger*) that you lent me is not of much help on the matters of interest to us here.

of the caribou and the ensuing crisis of collective angst were a magnificent godsend and adjuvant to the enterprise of proselytizing among the Utku. The latter did not rehabilitate their shamans, nor did they impose a taboo on caribou; instead, they "Christianized," hence internalized, the oppressive punishment applied to them for having abandoned "their gods and their shamans." They may then have transformed it into a punishment for their sins and sought redemption through a (demonstrably existing) mystique of poverty and asceticism, the most costly and convincing manifestation of which was their abstinence from the precious fuel provided by seal blubber. By living in poverty in their icy igloos, these "new converts" would be proving to the rich, cozy whites (including the ethnologist) that they were the true faithful, the true Christs of the Arctic. "The strong god is the god of the weak," the Inuit, and "eternity is reserved for the poor," the Utku.

If I am repeating or paraphrasing you, it is to underscore along with you the evident shift toward an appropriation of the proselytizers' faith by the proselytized, the latter turning it against the former as has been commonly observed elsewhere. I, for one, have noted the same phenomenon in Africa. But the Senufo catechists with whom I am familiar commonly exhibit two motives that appear to be missing here. The first is that of charity, a quality usually inseparable from fervent conversions of this kind. What shall we make, for example, of your hosts' hard-hearted act of kicking the trembling boy out of the igloo, a spectacle that shocked you? Could the doors of the Utku's new heaven be wide open to the poor and the weak but slammed shut in the face of the sick, even those who commit the venial sin of shamming? The second enigma, it seems to me, is the strange tolerance or indifference toward individual transgressors of the seal "taboo," especially as represented by the privileged ties of intermarriage with those collective transgressors, the Netsilik. Keeping within the framework of your Judeo-Christian approach, I see only one rather convoluted interpretation: the abstinence from sealing does not represent the expiation of a sin or (relative) enjoyment of luxury, nor of the transgression represented by allogenic hunting back in the beatific days of caribou abundance, nor even of the "paganism" represented by the traditional religious life and the practice of shamanism. Rather, if expiation is at play, then it involves the (older if not original) sin represented by the abandonment of their maritime ancestors' customs and way of life, a sin that concerns only your hosts the Utku, not the Netsilik. I willingly admit in advance that this "explanation" verges on pure speculation and is easily refutable by Inuit specialists such as yourself.

Forgive me for cavilling at such length about a matter you undoubtedly view as much simpler and more pragmatic; is there any need to adduce yet again the comical excuse of my incompetence? Better to invoke my keen interest in a fundamental ethical and theoretical issue – the human history of a lethal taboo – that your lovely, impassioned book raises with a prudence and empathy that I find most moving.

Yours sincerely,
András Zempléni

appendix 2

Diary of a Hunter Turned Miner

During my Thule expedition of 1950–51, no Inuk that I knew of kept a diary or other such personal record of events,[1] apart from the official statements of the Inuit representatives at the annual "Fangeraad." Subsequently, in the Canadian Central Arctic (1960–63), certain autobiographical texts were made available to me, allowing me to further the socio-demographic research and the analysis of mentalities that I had carried out at Thule.

It is interesting to note the similarities between the ways that "modernization" (i.e., Americanization) had affected the lives of the Inughuit of Thule and the walrus hunters at Igloolik (northern Foxe Basin), with whom I stayed for a lengthy period in 1960–61. (This was, in fact, the original population from which the Inughuit, guided by Qritdlarssuak, migrated to Thule around 1860.) The establishment of radar bases on the DEW Line was one element in this process; another was exposure to mining. In Canada the government provided inducements to hunters to hire on as nickel miners in Rankin Inlet.

One Igloolik hunter reacted to these and other developments by keeping a diary, as I gleaned from someone's offhand remark on my first trip to his camp. We became friends, and I encouraged him to pursue the exercise, which he diligently did in the ensuing years. When I met him at Rankin Inlet for the third and last time in August 1962, he entrusted his writing to me for purposes of study. The analysis presented below was originally contained in an unpublished report to the Northern Co-ordination and Research Centre (NCRC) in Ottawa.

The diary captures three major phases in the life of X (as I shall call him to protect his privacy), a Catholic man in his late thirties to early forties. In the first phase, as a husband, father, and hunter – a good one when he applied himself – he is relatively prolix, expressing vivid curiosity about everything and readily taking the reader into his confidence. In the second, while living in a sanatorium near Toronto due to ill health, he puts on a mask, becomes cautious, saying no more than necessary. His return to Igloolik as an alienated (although not physically isolated) man was painful, for his wife had died in the interim and he found it difficult to resume his traditional activities. Thus began a third phase consisting of a move to Rankin Inlet, where, along with dozens of Inuit men and women from varying backgrounds, he was employed as a labourer at the nickel mine. In his new surroundings, he experienced the same material and psychological conditions (company housing, shift work, movies, radio, dancing, night life, occasional hunting opportunities in the back country, proximity of two hunting communities) as any Canadian miner. However, these conditions were totally unfamiliar to him, and he was in some sense a psychological exile.

His newly chatty writing at Rankin betrays a mood that could easily be misconstrued as upbeat, but this would be to overlook the increasingly monothematic nature of his remarks and the secrecy, if not outright silence, about his thoughts, feelings, and hopes as well as other core issues. Such reserve is, of course, an Inuit characteristic, but the remarkable thing is that, outside of his home setting, the diaphragm of expression closes down even further. At the very time that his material security, daily food, and comfortable "white" housing were guaranteed, X the miner, in marked contrast to X the hunter, contents himself with trivial, purely chronological remarks, displaying no desire for self-improvement, no technical curiosity. Concerns that we know to be vital for him are never voiced now, whereas he made clear references to them in Igloolik.

Why a diary? Why this painstaking effort to annotate the days when the author knew that his efforts would be appreciated neither by his own people – he took care not to let the content be circulated – nor by the whites, apart from one or two to whom he gave it in confidence? The mere fact of his assiduous, years-long pursuit of an activity unusual for an Inuk, under frequently difficult material conditions (snow house, hunting, fatigue, discouragement, poverty), suggests a signal, a call for help, a psychological self-defence mechanism, or an attempt to connect with a community in which the author was psychologically ill-adapted for reasons that will shortly become evident. One may assume that there is an element of banter intended to hide the essential – all of us blush when faced with ourselves – and it is tempting to speculate about the inner man hidden behind his often matter-of-fact comments. Tempting – but inappropriate. X's written opinions, his displays of affection, his rare (hence revealing) euphoric outbursts followed by flat statements, his shutdown of expression once he leaves his community of origin, and the sea of technical and hunting-related details surrounding these are all the documentary evidence that we have. Therefore, and given the particular events that have marked the author's life, it seems entirely justified to limit my analysis to the text of the diary itself.

I performed a qualitative content analysis of all 2,288 sentences composed between 10 May 1957 and 28 August 1962, a period of 1,534 days (1.49 sentences/day), working from the word-for-word English translation by R.P. Thibert, OMI. To do this, I carefully perused the entire text, enumerated the main sentence topics or themes (18), and grouped them into a small number of categories (functional, social, sleep, etc.) to reveal certain general patterns. I categorized each sentence of the Igloolik and Rankin Inlet sequences according to its most prominent topic and computed the absolute and relative numbers of sentences for each topic, taking pains to do this objectively and without arbitrary psychological speculation. The aggregate analysis of the diary is presented in Table A2.1. (Note that aggregating the data without reference to time hides the considerable seasonal fluctuations in the frequency of certain topics; e.g., trapping and hunting.)

The functional category, composed of topics 5 (marine mammals), 12 (trapping), 15 (fishing), 17 (caribou; note the implications of this decreasing frequency), 1 (ecology), 2 (technical aspects), and 18 (food), includes 42.1 per cent of the sentences. The social category (topics 4, 7, 9, 13, 14, 16) accounts for 27 per cent, followed by references to the need for sleep, at 10 per cent, leaving an insignificant proportion of the text for residual, specifically allogenic topics. In the terminology of Linton and Kardiner,[2] the total personality coincides in practice with the basic personality to a very striking degree. X is literally only himself as an Inuk in his typical setting. This observation is especially remarkable in that the very existence of a diary presupposes an element of marginality and psychological trauma, which the author did in fact undergo. Evidently, this trauma was not so severe as to impair his deep functional coherence within his ethnic context. A priori, an average Iglooliker such as the author is inherently fit for the traditional way of life that fashioned the very stuff of his psychology, as the following comparative analysis of the Iglo-

TABLE A2.1 AGGREGATE ANALYSIS OF DIARY SENTENCES

	TOPIC	RELATIVE FREQUENCY
1	Ecology (weather, snow, geography)	14.7
2	Technical aspects (dogs, routine work)	12.0
3	Need for sleep	10.5
4	Catholic friends	10.3
5	Marine mammals	9.5
6	Personal judgments	7.5
7	Inuit in general (other than family)	6.0
8	Work	4.3
9	Anglican Inuit	4.1
10	Catholic priests	4.0
11	Whites	4.0
12	Trapping	3.5
13	Family	3.0
14	Dancing	2.6
15	Fishing	1.4
16	Acknowledgments of various people	1.0
17	Caribou	0.7
18	Need for food	0.3

olik (hunting) and Rankin Inlet (mining) sections of X's diary makes even more plain.

Here the patterns glimpsed in Table A2.1 come into clear focus. When the analysis is restricted to the Igloolik data set (Table A2.2), the functional category (topics 1, 2, 5, 12, 15, and 17) jumps from 42% to 60.8% of the sentences. The social category remains stable at 26.7%, but the total of these two rises to 87.5%. The Rankin Inlet data set (Table A2.3) is strikingly different in two respects: references to the need for sleep undergo a tenfold increase (from 2% to 19% overall, and as high as 30.5% during the initial period of adaptation from 26 August 1961 to 26 January 1962), and general references to the Inuit also increase markedly (from 18% to 28%), both displacing topics in the functional category. In particular, the halving of references to weather, snow, and geography (topic 1) evidences the erosion of contact with the aboveground ecology, predictable for a miner who spends part of his time underground. Likewise, there is a precipitous drop in personal judgments, suggesting an inhibition of his reactive capacity.

In the functionally alien role of the miner, X reacts with self-induced lethargy and a shutdown of expression; he puts on a mask, seals himself off hermetically. References to family (topic 13) almost vanish, as do acknowledg-

TABLE A2.2 ANALYSIS OF IGLOOLIK DIARY SENTENCES, 18 NOVEMBER 1957 TO 16 MAY 1958

TOPIC		RELATIVE FREQUENCY
5	Marine mammals	23.0
1	Ecology (weather, snow, geography)	17.5
12	Trapping	12.0
9	Anglican Inuit	11.7
2	Technical aspects	8.3
6	Personal judgments	9.0 (4 positive, 4.5 negative, 0.5 neutral)
4	Catholic friends	0
13	Family	6.0
3	Need for sleep	2.0
18	Need for food	2.0
11	Whites	1.0
16	Acknowledgments of various people	1.0

ments of other people (topic 16). A new Inuk emerges, one reduced to reflexes, to a "baseline chatter" intended to reassure himself that he exists. The person, or rather the expressed personality, goes into voluntary eclipse, minimizing his vulnerability to the growing external solicitations and threats – represented by the fivefold increase in references to whites.

It might be protested that all this is merely typical of the emigrant experience. True enough, the emigrant often experiences worries provoked by a new and alien environment and defends himself by keeping his sensitivities under wraps, by withdrawing protectively into himself, by entering a state of lethargy. Any concerns or susceptibilities not instrumental in facilitating his desired integration remain marginal, unexpressed. The essential support structures persist and are even, through the psychological phenomenon of compensation, reinforced. But with X, references to these drop sharply; in contrast to his writing as a hunter, there is now little talk of family, little politeness or gratitude expressed toward the new environment, no special attention paid to mastering the craft associated with his new job. (Not surprising in that he has been reduced to the role of a labourer.) And a diffuse impression emerges (from both the diary and our interviews) of a gradual attenuation of reactions, the rise of an inner silence, a subtle drift toward self-abnegation. In truth, he is not an emigrant but a wanderer, an exile still profoundly connected to his community of origin, which, as it happens, considers his departure unfortunate and unnecessary. After all, it is still a living, functioning,

TABLE A2.3 ANALYSIS OF RANKIN INLET DIARY SENTENCES, 26 JANUARY TO 28 AUGUST 1962

TOPIC		RELATIVE FREQUENCY
2	Technical aspects (mine work)	28.4
7	Inuit in general (other than family)	27.8
3	Need for sleep	19.5
1	Ecology (weather, snow, geography)	8.6
11	Whites	5.3
6	Personal judgments	5.0 (2 positive, 2 negative, 1 neutral)
14	Dancing	1.8
13	Family	0.6
18	Need for food	0.6
12	Trapping	0.3
16	Acknowledgments of various people	0.3

economically viable unit, and his departure has left a hole in it. Had he been simply departing for a seasonal job, had he still felt the strength of his bond to the group, the psychological situation would have been radically different. But he has fled to an alien environment for reasons all his own, without social articulation or economic justification. Thus it is not surprising that the man of before is replaced not by a new man but by a void pure and simple.

The man whose profile emerges uneasily from Table A2.2 is still there in Table A2.3, for he still feels ties to his Igloolik camp, to material and psychological possibilities, to an environment, a tradition, a long proud history in which his expressive and functional capabilities remain intact. Nothing has convinced him of the decadence of his traditional society. X is only "passing through" Rankin Inlet; he is lending but not giving of himself. If this is not sufficient to remind him of his connection to home, the ecological setting of Rankin Inlet resembles that of Igloolik (tundra, seaside, availability of seals, fox, and caribou), and everything, even the tiresome proletarian work, reminds him of that living society. Had he found himself working a white person's job for an extended period in the forest or in southern Canada, the break with his ecological background would have been sharper, and X might have truly felt like an emigrant, with all the hazards, the risks of total assimilation, and also the capacities for reaction that such a situation would entail.

Tables A2.2 and A2.3, it seems to me, encapsulate the conundrum of X. They explain how apparent psychological disintegration can coexist with the survival or rebirth characteristic of the emigrant. X carries no nostalgia, no regret, no strength; quite simply, his very survival was contingent upon his departure. He has temporarily lost his status as a full-fledged Inuit hunter (he knows that he will return to hunting in his native land), and the self-abnegation, the silences highlighted by Table A2.3 represent the negative image of the aptitudes, the adaptedness, the powers evidenced by Table A2.2. X is still too thoroughly what he is, what he was, too aware of the living reality represented by his community of origin, to pretend to be someone else.

When individuals from traditionalist communities undergo such processes, the forces of deculturation tend to do their work faster than the forces of acculturation can compensate. Cultural dislocation is the inevitable outcome. While the individual is functionally persistent – he is employed at a different job – he may well be psychologically and culturally annihilated. In the case of X, his mood declined from distraught to despairing, and he told me that were it not for his diary, which I encouraged him to continue writing, suicide would surely have been his fate.

I would have liked, of course, to publish the whole, singularly monothematic text, but space permits only a selection of illustrative excerpts. One may note the prominence of the expressed need for sleep (after the initial satisfaction of discovering a new environment) that characterizes the latter part of the diary:

26 August 1961: I am in Rankin Inlet. There are many people here. We know some of them; the child of some relatives is here, and I have other relatives. Alianai! I am happy!

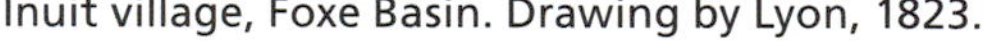

Inuit village, Foxe Basin. Drawing by Lyon, 1823.

20 September (on detached sheet): At eight o'clock we return home and go to sleep; at midnight we start again.

26 October: I slept a lot since I needed a lot of sleep. As soon as I wake up I go to work at midnight with W. and U. We do not stop until nine o'clock in the morning.

25 December: At six o'clock N., U., and myself return home to sleep; at ten o'clock I am awakened to go to church and at midnight we return to work. There.

3 May 1962: This morning at eight o'clock, we stopped working. We came back and I went to sleep. At eight o'clock in the evening, back to work to replace the previous team; at K., some have five dogs, others three, others none at all; all we do is work continuously, especially evenings.

25 June: When I woke this morning I ate; I received my paycheque and went back home. I stayed in bed and did nothing. In the evening I felt better and went to sleep like everyone else.

21 July: At eight o'clock I went to work; the night shift people were returning. T. and I prepared the ore. E. didn't come. People arrived from Tikerardjuark [Whale Cove]. At eight o'clock we returned home and went to sleep. Others went to work in our place.

27 July: At eight o'clock we returned home, others were starting work. A white arrived [Malaurie]. I had met him in Igloolik. It is a pleasure to see him again here. When we stopped working, others started and we went home to sleep. At eight o'clock we went to work. E., T., and I were together, always working to prepare the ore; and I am nearly sick.

28 July: At eight o'clock in the morning, we stopped working. Right.

appendix 3

Glenn Gould's Fascination with the Arctic

One of my deepest regrets – I still muse about it often – is never having met the Canadian pianist Glenn Gould. I might have had that opportunity while filming in the Canadian North in the summer of 1973 with Jacqueline Vischkoff, who had also worked on Bruno Monsaingeon's film about Gould. But the extreme admiration that I bear him as a man and a musician is not the only reason for my wistfulness.

I learned (after his death, alas) that he had written, "Ever since I can remember, I have been fascinated with geographic studies ... of the Arctic."

In the mind of this visionary, the Far North, plunged for months into the long polar night, was the ideal place for solitude and isolation, conditions that engender an infinitely creative process of adaptation in an individual.

While producing a radio series, "The Idea of North," about which he was particularly passionate, he contacted a friend of mine, the anthropologist James Lotz, an administrator in the Department of Northern Affairs,[1] who four years earlier had supervised my four missions to the Canadian Eastern Arctic (Igloolik, Spence, Rankin, and Back River). Shortly afterward I was to learn that Gould had formulated the wild project – to which he claimed to be absolutely committed – of giving a concert in the polar night. I may be deluding myself, but I am sure that I would have been able to persuade him, by recounting my experience of these "desolate lands" (which, of course, have always deeply fascinated me, too), to take the plane once again – despite his dread of that conveyance – so that he could fulfil his desire to play alone in the polar night, in Tuktoyaktuk at dusk, where the navy blue would dominate, as he imagined it, or – why not? – in Thule, or at Back River, the Inuit Sparta. There, the Last Puritan might finally have found the place of rebirth and regrowth that he sought in vain his whole life long in the profound religious music of Johann Sebastian Bach. "The only environments to which he had ever wished to belong were the limitless expanses of the Far North or the storyless walls of motel rooms."[2]

"The God who touched Glenn Gould is the one who visited Hölderlin: not Dionysus, the saturnine, hot-tempered one but Apollo, the upright, the transparent."[3] Apollo the androgynous, god of the Hyperboreans; the handsomest, most mysterious god of Greek mythology; the wolf god, the archer god, the musical god who played the lyre at Zeus's table.[4]

"It's an ambition of mine," he said in an interview, "to spend at least one winter north of the Arctic Circle ... and so help me I'm going to do it one of these times."[5]

Final memory flashes: Need I mention that Chanel No. 5, the immortal feminine perfume, was first conceived – perceived – by Ernest Beaux in the Far North, in the cold clarity of the icy, misty night?* Or that Franz Schubert wrote a letter on his deathbed requesting a copy of a new book by James Fenimore Cooper?

* "Creating a perfume is like composing music," wrote Beaux. Born in Moscow to a French father, he travelled to the vast regions above the Arctic Circle where "the lakes and rivers give off a very special fresh fragrance."

appendix 4

The Spirituality of the Polar Night

To my friend Charles Watt, Inuit senator, Ottawa; in homage to the first peoples, to all aboriginal people of the Americas, and in particular to the Inuit:

As life would have it, I had a brief but enjoyable meeting with a distinguished Canadian statesman, former Prime Minister John Diefenbaker. We spoke of his patriotic vision of a Canada worthy of its founding fathers, his "dream of the North," in which the Confederation's centre of gravity would shift toward the Pole. But alas this dream, among other factors, ultimately proved his undoing.

The immense, magnificent country that is Canada had not yet, back when I was still but a modest consultant to the Department of Northern Affairs, gained any deep awareness of the riches represented by its ethnic and cultural diversity. We Europeans, however, are keenly aware of how difficult it is for Canada to bring to fruition its founding dialogue between francophones and anglophones from ocean to ocean. At our remove we see all too clearly that an obscure hundred-year war has stifled and provincialized the country's creative energies.

But there is another great challenge facing Canada: that of the first peoples, those hundreds of aboriginal nations, and particularly the Inuit, who are asserting their rights with increasing vigour and independence.

When government representatives speak to them, it is always with words such as "education" and "development," as if – in these deserts suffused with transcendent light – it were not incumbent upon us Westerners to do the listening rather than the speaking, to learn the foundations of their pantheistic philosophy from the source.

The longstanding bitterness of the Huron, the Ojibway, the Dene, the Piegan, the Montagnais, the Cree, the Chippewa, and especially the Inuit bespeaks a mutual existential incomprehension.

And the policy of Indian "reserves" obstinately deployed for over a century certainly does no honour to the multicultural and multiethnic conception of a modern nation that is supposedly inclusive of all Canadians.

On another matter, there is truly no need for me to reemphasize the extraordinary creative genius and international fame of the Canadian pianist Glenn Gould, who took musical Europe by storm at age twenty-five. His magical, fervent interpretations of history's greatest composers, such as Beethoven and J.S. Bach, have enthralled listeners the world over.

Bruno Monsaingeon was one of the first Frenchmen to apprehend the spiritual dimension to which Gould aspired. In his introduction to a volume of Gould's writings, he wrote:

> On 3 March 1972, the date when I first received a letter from the planet Glenn Gould, a small space probe was launched in the direction of Jupiter. Pioneer 10 left the solar system a few months ago and is now forging forward into the unknown at nearly 50,000 km/h, headed for Ross 248, a star it will reach in some 30,000 [*sic*] years after travelling several billion [*sic*] kilometers. On board, whirling through space, are the following decipherable symbols: a plaque displaying drawings depicting a man and a woman, several mathematical formulas, and the earth's location in the galaxy, as well as a recording of Glenn Gould playing a fugue by Johann Sebastian Bach. Who shall I thank for the immense privilege that this vessel crossed my path, in the coordinates of time and space, if only for a moment?[1]

After reading these lines and later discovering that Gould had, his whole life, been possessed with a yearning to spend a winter in the Arctic, I reflected on the reasons Canadian political and cultural leaders never (and more pointedly not in 1967, during the Centennial of Confederation ceremonies) saw fit to offer this gifted native son the means to bring about what he called his "fascination": to play in a far northern village in the heart of the polar night.

In 1965 he wrote, "Ever since I can remember, I have been fascinated with geographic studies ... of the Arctic and I finally determined to see a small part of it for myself this year. In sum, next to visiting the Soviet Union,[2] it was perhaps the most fascinating two weeks I have ever spent."[3] He later said in an interview, "It's an ambition of mine, which I never seem to get around to realizing, to spend at least one winter north of the Arctic Circle. Anyone can go there in the summer when the sun is up, but I want to go there when the sun is down, I really do, and so help me I'm going to do it one of these times."[4]

That the great Arctic nation of Canada could not, or would not, allow one of its most prestigious prodigies to realize one of his most fervent wishes calls for a political explanation. Was the Canadian government ever informed of his wish, as often and as ardently as he expressed it? I am willing to believe that it was never brought to the prime minister's attention, but why did the Centennial Commission regard it as just a whim, a matter of no particular importance?

While the Canadian government could not have been unaware of the virtuoso's extraordinary reputation, it probably failed to understand what truly motivated him: the possibility that one of his recordings could embody not just technical but spiritual perfection. Judging from his published correspondence, it seems as though the commission did not discuss this problem with Gould or explore his project in any detail. This is the reality: his ardent wish was never granted during his lifetime.

If Gould, visionary that he was, had become so deeply convinced of his duty to venture into the Arctic solitudes, then his wish should have been the government's command. Yet as the great pianist acknowledged with a touch of modesty, he was certainly not the only one to experience this attachment to the North. As stated by one of the four contrapuntal voices that he sampled in his "The Idea of North" (part one of a radio trilogy broadcast in CBC's "Ideas" series for the first time in 1967 as part of the Centennial celebrations): "Sure the North's changed my life. I can't conceive of anyone in close touch with the North being ... untouched by [it] for the rest of his life."[5]

It seems that Canada, a crossroads for such a wide variety of cultures, remains insufficiently aware that the Inuit people – who, with the various First Nations occupy nearly half the country's land area – embody values infinitely more elevated than the economic and political ones currently holding sway in the Arctic.

The history of white-Inuit relations should not be reduced to a conquest, nor to a desire to convert or educate these peoples, nor (as at present) to a multiculturalist policy of so-called tolerance. This last, indifferent to their deepest aspirations, purports to assist and even defend their values but in actuality has sent them marching down the dead-end street of pharisaic capitalism.

Lyon's portrait of Nee-A-Kood-Loo, an Inuk from Southampton Island met during the 1824 expedition of the *Griper*.

Here we have proof (alas, as if more were needed!) of a real communication barrier imposed by our perception of ourselves as possessing technical, religious, and philosophical superiority. The West would deny the possibility that the Inuit, who have lived for millennia in symbiosis with the upper reaches of this world, could, before coming under attack from "civilization," have been the keepers of a body of wisdom that the world has never needed more than it does now.

It can be gleaned from his correspondence that Gould was discouraged by the commission's rejection and by the implication that his country's governing authorities considered his project whimsical. And what, pray tell, was so eccentric about the idea that the Inuit could be touched by the music of Johann Sebastian Bach? The whole episode leads me to conclude that Glenn Gould should have been given a chance to show the world that two apparently distant cultures could meet on musical ground in the polar night in a sort of intuitive, shamanistic recognition. This was not just symbolic but *vital* for us and the so-called "primitive" peoples of the North.[6]

Canada will have no notable place in history except insofar as it gives expression to the idea of its founding fathers, thereby distinguishing itself from the great assimilationist giant to the south. Its economic potential and geographic magnitude aside, where can Canada's wealth lie if not in the diversity of its cultures? Beyond the coexistence of the French and English civilizations, it is imperative to acknowledge the inspiration of the first peoples, who will probably be the wellspring of humanity's rebirth in the third millennium. The beat of their drums catalyzes an intimate interpenetration with the shadows and spirits of the afterworld, which find their maximal expression in the polar night.

When I was a volunteer elementary school teacher in Clyde River, on Baffin Island, the Inuit told me, "What we need are not ordinary teachers, not managers, but visionaries; not just industrialists, bankers, priests and psychologists, but Nobel Prize winners, artists, poets and mystics; people who can perceive that behind deceptive appearances, we are the heirs to the cosmic worldview of our elders, the Great Shamans."

Through the ages of human history, the Pole has remained one of the great, mystical realms. This being the case, it is no surprise to find the following thought inscribed on the façade of the Scott Polar Research Institute of Cambridge University: *Quaesivit arcana poli, videt Dei* (He plumbed the mysteries of the pole and found the hidden face of God).

Knowing what we do about Glenn Gould's spiritual calling, the phrase seems remarkably apt and prophetic.

Perhaps the Canadian Parliament should set aside its constitutional debates, however briefly, to reflect on this phrase, as well as on the words of Ernest Renan: "A nation is a soul, a spiritual principle." For I happen to be deeply convinced that the North may well be the place where Canada finds its soul, its hidden God.

Jean Malaurie, April 1998

appendix 5

Excerpt from notebooks of Monique Malaurie, May 1996: Glenn Gould

I have not yet described what I felt upon learning, while reading his published letters, that Glenn Gould had a genuine obsession with the Far North, particularly with the polar night.

I suddenly became conscious of a surprising connection between Glenn Gould and Jean-Noël Malaurie, a connection entirely independent from my own relationship to the two of them. And it touched me in a special way, much more surely than if Jean-Noël had merely experienced the same spiritual certitudes as I did on first encountering the Gouldian sound, namely that I was hearing music for the first time, whereas until that moment I had merely been listening to it.

What a remarkable fact that two people so dear to me would turn out to be so intimately connected by their strange fascination with the Arctic! On the one hand, Jean-Noël the nomad has never been happier than on a spring morning at Disko Bay, or while mapping Inglefield Land, or on an autumn evening at Siorapaluk when the day is slowly disappearing, not to return for four months to a glacial land where the quality of the light, he feels, reflects the beauty of the most fully consummated world. On the other hand, the sedentary Glenn was inhabited his entire life by "the idea of North" and by his desire to melt into the polar night for a whole winter.

All of what Jean-Noël has repeated to me a thousand times about these places to which he is irresistibly drawn at regular intervals, places where he now feels entirely at home and has even decided to spend his "eternal life," takes on full meaning for me (and I get physically and spiritually cold just about anywhere, except perhaps in the winding streets of Siena!) when his irresistible attraction is paired with Glenn's tenacious desire – one that, unfortunately, was not to be fulfilled during his lifetime.

It is unthinkable, I tell myself, that no one in the huge crowd of Gould's unconditional admirers around the world, myself included, ever responded to the many feelers that he put out, particularly in 1965–67, by finding a way to convey him (not by air, for he dreaded flying) into the very heart of the night, where he could play on the ice floes, surrounded only by the howling of the lone wolves that he so greatly resembled.

What was he hoping to find in the crystalline peace of the North? Was it that state of wonder and serenity he sought as a young man on the shore of Lake Simcoe and worked ceaselessly to cultivate throughout his life?

If so, then one could hardly imagine a greater joy than if Jean-Noël were to succeed in his ardent intention to create a shrine to Glenn Gould on the Diomede Islands in the Bering Strait (under the sign of Apollo, that upright god who went into the mountains of Hyperborea for renewal each winter before returning to the oracle at Delphi). Visitors to this sacred place of spirituality in the long Arctic night would hear Glenn's music (his beloved Partita No. 5 by Bach, or the Larghetto from Mozart's B Minor Concerto, or the Adagio from Haydn's late Sonata in E-flat major that he recorded in 1981, a late year for him as well) emanating from a small, low, apparently empty chair behind a white piano.

In truth, my life will not have been lived in vain if Glenn could finally – at the age of seventy, in 2002, had he lived – reach the far-flung places of his imagination at the summit of the world. The millions of those living and still to come for whom his genius is eternal could then go there to look for him and, finding him, discover that "desire to cry or to die for the beauty emanating from his fingers in the darkness."[1]

appendix 6

How a Liberal Economy Suffocates and Kills a First People

The following is a list of standard items and their prices in Canadian dollars at Iqaluit in 1997 (at auction, pelt prices were 20 per cent lower):

White fox: $40
Blue fox: $40
Ringed seal: $30
Bear: $150–175 per foot
Skidoo: $8,000
Gasoline: $0.731 per litre
22-calibre rifle: $800
20 cartridges: $20

"It is extremely difficult if not impossible for a Native person to have a decent life in the trapping economy. This is due to the high cost of the required capital investment – skidoo, guns, cartridges, motor boat, gasoline – and the low market value of furs. Fur prices should be supported by the government to a certain extent. The Cree hunters were able to obtain such terms in the context of the James Bay Agreement with the Québec and federal governments."

Thanks to the Iqaluit-based historian Kenn Harper for this quotation from Jack Hicks, which he kindly communicated to me on 17 December 1997.

notes

PREFACE

1 André Malraux, during a 1959 speech in Brasilia.
2 Jules Michelet, *The People*, 150–2.
3 Charles Péguy, *Basic Verities*, 92.
4 Jean-Antoine-Nicolas de Caritat, marquis de Condorcet, *Cinq mémoires*, 349.
5 Jean Michel Huctin, "Eskimooq Imminorneq"; "Jean Malaurie: enn eskimo begar ikke selvmord."
6 Fernand Braudel, *A History of Civilizations*, 35.

CHAPTER ONE

1 The North Magnetic Pole is the point where the earth's magnetic field points vertically downward. It was discovered near Cape Farrand on the Boothia Peninsula in the Canadian Central Arctic at coordinates of 70°5'17"N and 96°46'45"W by James Clark Ross on 2 June 1831 during a dogsled expedition. Since Amundsen's expedition in 1904, which found roughly the same coordinates, it has moved

1,300 kilometers north-northwest. In 1985 it was located northwest of Bathurst Island on the southern tip of Longhead Island (77°0'N, 102°3'W). This rapid northward movement presages a polar reversal of a kind that has recurred at intervals in geological history. As a result, the biosphere may be more exposed to cosmic rays, with ensuing increases in human genetic mutation rates. However, this is only conjecture. The diametrically opposite North and South Magnetic Poles define the magnetic axis of the globe.

2 Three centuries before Jesus Christ, Taoist thought had defined this internal order: "The harmonious cooperation of all living beings was not decreed by a higher authority but, rather, results from the fact that they all partake of an overarching hierarchy constituting a cosmic order and obeying the internal dictates of their nature"; Chuang-Tzu, quoted in Pierre Douzou, *Les Bricoleurs*, 10.

3 Pierre Clastres, *Chronicle*.

4 Jean Malaurie, *Les derniers rois de Thulé*, 528–30, 532, 568, 570, 627, 634; Jean Malaurie, *Ultima Thule*.

5 Michael Servetus, *Christianismi restitutio*, quoted in Georges Haldas, *Passion et mort*, 239.

6 Jean Piaget, *The Science of Education*, 153.

7 Charles Péguy, *Basic Verities*, 92–5.

8 Jean Malaurie, *Call of the North*, 330–1.

9 Elsewhere, I have described the attempts at subversion made by "mavericks" during people's assemblies. I have attempted to discern the subtle play of talk and action in egalitarian groups subtly dominated by elites. Three profiles emerged: those of the "good hunter," the "shaman," and the "maverick"; see my *The Last Kings*.

10 Johann Wolfgang von Goethe, *Conversations*, 480.

11 Maurice Maeterlinck, *The Life*, 222.

12 *Erkrelardjuk* (F): pretty curl of the lips. *Tuluardjuk* (F): young raven. *Tonrrar* (F): spirit. *Alianakoluk* (M): minor hitch or misfortune. *Pikuyar* (F): hunchbacked woman. *Oreortok* (F): one who spits. *Mamatiar* (M): edible. *Erqroaluk* (F): fat buttocks. *Iktuardjuark* (F): aging woman. *Tapatsiar* (F): monopolist. *Makki* (M): Get up! *Umik* (F): beard. *Piugatu* (M): good, kind, generous man. *Uteardjuk* (F): smaller of the large vulvas. *Utokrutiuk* (M): nice little vulva. *Paomik* (F): itch. *Anguvasak* (F): grave man. *Issigaitsoq* (M): no feet. *Krangut* (M): snow goose. *Anguiliainun* (M): person who is scared shitless. *Kattalik* (F): that which has a bucket. *Kadluk* (F): thunder. *Ikkuma* (F): lamplight. *Aerut* (M): root. *Kramukka* (F): small sled. *Kigutikardjuk* (M): small teeth. *Arnatiar* (F): beautiful woman. *Akkiterk* (M): pillow. *Alakat* (F): large soles. *Krimmerdjuark* (M): large dog. *Krillak* (F): sky. *Tatigat* (M): gull. *Arnadjuark* (F): tall woman. *Kugatoloriktok* (F): smiling kindly. *Kopak* (M): half. *Angutautok* (M): it's a male. *Ivaluardjuk* (M): small thread. *Arvaaluk* (M): large whale. *Saumik* (F): left-handed. *Uyaralak* (F): large stone. *Nanorak* (F): bearskin. *Pialak* (M): fast. *Anangorar* (M): shithead. *Angutimarik* (M): true male. *Ittikusuk* (M): small anus. *Iktoriligak* (M): handsome old man. *Nasuk* (F): turned-up nose. (With thanks to Father Louis Fournier of Igloolik for his assistance.)

Inuit interpreters Junius and Augustus. Drawing by George Back (1820).

13 At Kapuivik I had the pleasure of meeting up again with an American colleague, the estimable, genial David Damas. Younger than I, this Detroit native was then just starting a thesis on kinship structures using the methods of the Chicago School. We had first met upon his arrival in Igloolik in August 1960. We spent an evening together that time, and on my second trip to the island in March 1961, specifically to meet and dialogue with him, I slept in his rudimentary *q'angmat*. Our methods and approaches were different (at his request I brought my genealogical map of the Polar Eskimos of North Greenland), but our mutual honesty as witnesses to such a "primitive" and intense society made conversation easy. No sourness; he was jovial and at ease with me, as I was with him. What more could one ask? The winter had been long, and the Inuit not always approachable. I sensed that he enjoyed my visit. His Inuktitut proficiency had initially been poor, the Igloolik hunters knew no English, and local interpreters were not to be found. An excellent researcher, he scrupulously stated this fact in his thesis.

Ah, the predicament of interpreters, and the perils of translation: the great unknown (but rarely mentioned) factor in academic anthropological work on the Inuit. One thinks of the great Malian writer Hampaté Bâ's novel in which the narrator wittily recounts how, for years, his uncle's friend Wangrin misled the colonial officer to whom he served as official interpreter; see Amadou Hampaté Bâ, *The Fortunes*. Serious scientific research involves (1) knowledge of the language, however imperfect; (2) return to the site with an official interpreter to verify the results obtained; (3) cross-referencing and citation of all works in all languages on the subject concerned. Only with such a research protocol can one begin to isolate the variables and build structured models in a spirit of scientific inquiry; see my "Pas à pas vers les Inuit."

CHAPTER TWO

1 François-René de Chateaubriand, *Memoirs*, 139.

2 Specifically, to Igloolik (1960–61), Spence Bay (1962), Rankin Inlet (1962), and Back River (1963). I also travelled to Fort Chimo (now Kuujjuaq) in northern Quebec in 1968–69, as part of a Franco-Quebec cooperation program, and to Clyde River on Baffin Island in 1987–88; see fig. page xvi. See maps, pp. xvi–xvii, 5.

3 Diamond Jenness, *Eskimo Administration*. For a tribute to this great scientist and courageous man as well as a complete bibliography of his works, see my "A French Homage."

4 Stefansson (b. 1879 in Iceland, d. Aug. 1962). Taught anthropology at Harvard University and led three expeditions: Mackenzie (1906–07), Central Arctic (1908–12), Canadian Arctic Expedition (1913–18). For an alphabetical listing of Arctic specialists and explorers from 1700 to 1960, see my *Hummocks*, vol. 2, *Alaska*, 591–9.

5 When the expedition ship *Karluk* became icebound and sank off Wrangel Island, Siberia, the crew – twenty-five explorers, including scientists, sailors, and Inuits – endured the horrific saga of an expedition abandoned without its leader, for Stefansson had by that time left the ship, ostensibly to hunt caribou for provisions. Eleven crew members, including Henri Beuchat, the admirable archeologist and colleague of Marcel Mauss who might have been the great French Arctic anthropologist, died tragically from starvation or other causes, the victims of indiscipline and inexperience. A survivor, William Laird McKinlay, recounted the forgotten tragedy in a book that stands as an indictment of its leader, *Karluk: The Great Untold Story of Arctic Exploration*. We met in Edinburgh in 1970, and I tape-recorded his detailed version of the events. Jenness, too, had become Stefansson's circumspect but implacable critic following the *Karluk* disaster.

6 Canada had not been very assiduous in its exploration of the region, and in fact the majority of the expeditions to the Inuit of the Northwest Territories during this period were non-Canadian. A report on the Keewatin (Caribou) Inuit produced for the Department of the Interior in 1914 stated: "The permanent inhabitants of the Barren Lands are about two thousand Eskimos, who live either along the coast or on the banks of Kazan and Dubawnt rivers" (Canada, Railway Lands Branch, *The Unexploited West*, 312). More precise population estimates and locations would emerge only with the 1922–25 expeditions of Knud Rasmussen.

7 The initials HBC were often jokingly expanded to Here Before Christ. I should note that I always maintained cordial relations with the HBC employees, who were generally of Scottish background, honest, and dedicated to the company and its customers.

8 This chapter was written prior to publication in 1996 of the long-delayed five-volume report by the Royal Commission on Aboriginal Peoples.

9 Quoted in R.A.J. Phillips, *Canada's North*, 161.

10 According to Diamond Jenness, in 1939 the Canadian government spent $17 per person on RCMP policing of the Inuit, compared to $0.41 in Alaska, while Denmark had no budget for policing the Greenlanders and did not build a prison there until 1955. Canada budgeted only $12 per person for education, health care, and social security, $5 of which was taken from a tax on pelts (Alaska, $13; Greenland, $44).

11 The results of these expeditions dealing with hunting ecology and microeconomic structures will be the subject of a subsequent publication. An English language journal, *Anthropologica* (Ottawa), offered to publish my report in English immediately. I preferred to postpone it *sine die*, wishing to take some distance from my conclusions. These precautions were unfortunate, for at the very least a preliminary report should have been published without delay. My internal report, "Igloolik Report," is available from the National Archives in Ottawa.
12 Frank James Tester and Peter Kulchyski, *Tammarniit (Mistakes)*, 16–17.
13 My genealogical work on the Polar Inuit of North Greenland for the period 1860–1951 puts the average life expectancy at twenty-two years for women and twenty-seven for men. The population in 1951 was 302; see Jean Malaurie, Léon Tabah, and Jean Sutter, "L'isolat des Esquimaux." In the Canadian North, this calculation is difficult since no comparable genealogy exists for the regions that I studied.
14 At Igloolik in 1960–62 the Anglican presence took the form of a single catechist – Piugatu, an Inuk – while the Catholic mission was staffed by the venerable Father Louis Fournier.
15 Expedition members included the great Danish writer and explorer Peter Freuchen, the archeologist Therkel Mathiassen, and the geographer and ethnologist Kaj Birket-Smith, who produced the founding study of the Caribou Inuit; see Kaj Birket-Smith, *The Caribou Eskimos*.
16 Jean Malaurie, "Les Esquimaux du Keewatin."
17 The Oblates of Marie Immaculate (OMI) was founded in 1816 by Eugène de Mazenod of Aix-en-Provence to spread the gospel in the French countryside, where Christian fervour had waned after the Revolution. The overseas missionary work of the order commenced in 1841 in the Far East, Latin America, and Canada; until recently it held authority over numerous educational institutions around the world. The Oblate missionaries in the Canadian Arctic are francophones, and many are natives of France (Brittany, Franche-Comté, Lozère, Bourgogne). Priests such as Fathers Dion, Bazin, Étienne, Courtemanche, Fournier, and Didier were highly respected. The headquarters of the Order is in Rome.
18 A third settlement was initially planned for the Bache Peninsula, where I had gone with my expedition. However, this had to be postponed and eventually abandoned when the progress of the *D'Iberville*, a large ship bound for the police post, was blocked by the ice and it could not make landfall on the peninsula or at nearby Cape Herschell; see photos in my *Call of the North*, 126–31.
19 Letter from Commander Ripley, 23 June 1953.
20 Later, during his term as premier of Quebec from 1961 to 1963, Lesage would distinguish himself as the father of the "Quiet Revolution."
21 See Regitze Margrethe Søby, "Rink, un visionnaire," which includes a complete bibliography of works by and about Rink.
22 A complete bibliography of Rasmussen's works is given in my "Knud Rasmussen, 1879–1933."
23 The putative role of the northern service officer (NSO) positions, the first six of which were created by Northern Affairs in February 1955, was to coordinate

government interaction with the Native people in northern communities. For a discussion of the numerous ways that they fell short of the mark, see Tester and Kulchyski, *Tammarniit (Mistakes)*, 326–30. Lesage offered one of these positions to me at our Ottawa meeting. October 1958 saw the creation of the Northern Welfare Service.

24 Jean Malaurie, director, *Les Esquimaux canadiens et le Canada: L'incommunicabilité*, documentary film, 55 min.

25 Canada, *Report*.

26 Mackenzie Valley Pipeline Inquiry, *Northern Frontier, Northern Homeland*. Also influential on the process of decentralization was a 1980 report by a special committee of Parliament known as the Unity Committee, headed by C.M. Drury, Prime Minister Pierre Elliot Trudeau's special representative on constitutional development for the Northwest Territories, which recommended division subject to a plebiscite involving the inhabitants; see Special Representative for Constitutional Development in the Northwest Territories, *Report*. Trudeau (b. 1919), an ardent defender of Canadian bilingualism and federalism, was prime minister of Canada from 1969 to 1979, when his party was defeated in an election. He returned to power within nine months. When he retired from politics in 1984, John Turner, the new Liberal Party leader, succeeded him as prime minister.

27 Diamond Jenness autographed a set of these volumes to me with a phrase that became an obligation: "To Jean Malaurie: may he go ever further."

28 John George Diefenbaker (1895–1979), prime minister of Canada from 1957 to 1963, strove for a policy of Canadian independence vis-à-vis the United States by strengthening economic ties with Britain and opting for the accelerated development of the Canadian North. He was a true Canadian patriot whom I had the chance to interview at length in 1962 on my return from Churchill. He eloquently explained to me his position that Canada could regain its unity in the South, from coast to coast, vis-à-vis the United States, only by affirming its sovereign power in the North.

29 In my film *Les Esquimaux canadiens*, A.B. Yates, a Department of Northern Affairs representative with certain responsibilities for economic development in the Northwest Territories, stated his view (in October 1974) that to give ten thousand Inuit the administration of a territory as large as one-third of Canada was unrealistic. This eminent administrator was proved wrong in 1999 with the creation of Nunavut and Nunavik, which cover one-fifth of Canada's land area.

30 James Cook, *The Journals*, vol. 2, *The Voyage*, 175.

31 I also had some acquaintance with and appreciation for Walter Rudnicki and the likeable, open-minded Alex Stevenson.

32 Fondation française d'études nordiques, *Le pétrole et le gaz arctiques: problèmes et perspectives*; Fondation française d'études nordiques, *Le pétrole et le gaz arctiques: problemes et perspectives: débats*.

33 See my *The Last Kings*, 422–31, for an account of these extremely busy and productive days.

34 Quoted in my *The Last Kings*, 68.

35 Fondation française d'études nordiques, *Le Peuple esquimau aujourd'hui et demain*; see also discussion from the conference in Fondation française d'études nordiques, *Le Peuple esquimau aujourd'hui et demain: débats*.

36 This process formally began in January 1973 with the Special Committee on Home Rule and continued in 1975 with the Greenland Home Rule Commission, chaired by Professor Isi Foighel, a constitutional law specialist.

37 The media in the English-speaking world, including Canada, are certainly no strangers to anti-French sentiment. To pick a random example, in 1995 a major Australian daily published a front-page story criticizing President Jacques Chirac and French nuclear policy. The title, left in French for extra provocation: "Pourquoi les Français sont des connards." One descries, in similarly aggressive verbiage put about by the popular British press (*Sun*, *Daily Mirror*, etc.), an intolerable underlying racism that spares the admirable British people from having to sharpen their critique of their own oligarchy.

38 Laporte was minister of immigration, manpower, and labour in the Liberal government of the time. I still recall the state of emergency imposed on Québec City while I was staying at the Château Frontenac in October 1970, with all its military consequences. In the early morning, I heard the noise of tanks outside my window, indicating that Ottawa's forces had moved into the nerve centre of the province. That morning I breakfasted with colourful Huron chief Max Gros-Louis. His comment: "Oh, it won't change anything for us. It's just another episode in a long, drawn-out quarrel between Ottawa and Quebec. For Ottawa, the 'Frenchies,' the 'oui-oui,' – the Inuit call them 'Ui-Uit' – are just noisemakers. They'll come to terms eventually, at our expense. Quebec may be up in arms, but it can't go very far: Ottawa is stronger." He added, "Our problems as Natives are much older and more serious than Quebec's problems; 80 per cent of the province belongs to the Indians and the Inuit." For further comments by the Huron participants in my film, see my *Les Esquimaux canadiens*.

39 In 1968–69 I was the rapporteur and program director for a Franco-Quebec cooperation program to study rational development in the Ungava Peninsula, then known as Nouveau-Québec, now Nunavik. The resulting 300-page report, complete with critical notes and constructive observations, was a collective endeavour resulting from work conducted in the towns of Kuujjuaq, Kangiqsualujjuaq, and Tasiujuaq by myself, by Paul Adam, the head of the OECD Fisheries Division, and by Jacques-Robert Bel, a director of the SODETEG engineering corporation (Paris), respectively. Also participating in the project was Pierre Laurent, assistant director of the Institut National de la Recherche Agronomique (Paris), responsible for livestock policy. The final report was filed in 1970 with the Fonds Polaire Jean Malaurie (Muséum National d'Histoire Naturelle) in Paris and with the Ministry of Intergovernmental Affairs in Québec City.

Our intention was that the report, which is of more than mere historical interest, be translated into Inuktitut and distributed widely among the Inuit in order to obtain their reactions; these would have been published in a conclusion. I urged the Quebec minister of education to fund this initiative when he visited

Paris, but it did not come to pass. Years later, starting in 1994, the report was distributed at the impetus of Senator Charlie Watt. Our results have now been published in abridged form as a special supplement to *Inter-Nord* consisting of four articles, an introduction by Mark Malone (former staffer to Prime Minister Trudeau and current advisor to Senator Charlie Watt), some prefatory remarks by Senator Watt, and my brief history of the cooperation program; see *Inter-Nord* 20 (2003): 291–367.

40 David Pelly, "Footprints in New Snow," 7–10.

41 The Centre d'Études Arctiques of the École des Hautes Études en Sciences Sociales (EHESS) (founded by me in 1957 and incorporated into the Centre National de la Recherche Scientifique in 1979) has some experience in this region. In 1961 I was visited in Paris by the eminent Canadian ethnobotanist Jacques Rousseau after he was forced into exile by the perpetual scheming of a certain segment of the Quebec university intelligentsia who could not abide forceful personalities. He had faced the music and was considering accepting a position as a librarian in Addis Ababa. I immediately appointed him assistant director of the Centre d'Études Arctiques, and in 1964 we edited the first collective study of the human occupation of Nouveau-Québec; see Jean Malaurie and Jacques Rousseau, eds, *Le Nouveau-Québec*, reprinted as *Du Nouveau-Québec au Nunavik* in the Polaires collection with new prefaces and afterwords. This appointment was not destined to win me the unanimous friendship of the Quebec university milieu. Pierre Trudeau, too, as a young jurist in 1960s Montreal, was subjected to small-minded incomprehension and malice on the part of Quebec university intellectuals envious of the illustrious figure that he had already become.

42 The relevant letter from de Gaulle reads: "It appears that the great national enterprise of the advent of Quebec, as you are pursuing it, is now well under way ... Therefore, the time is right – don't you think? – for our French community to intensify what has already been undertaken. In the financial, economic, scientific, and technical domains, my government will shortly be in a position to offer yours specific proposals on the subject of our common effort. As to culture and education, Mr. Peyrefitte, to whom I am dictating this letter, will indicate to you what Paris is willing to do right away, which is quite considerable." De Gaulle to Johnson, 8 September 1967, *Lettres, notes et carnets,* vol. 11, *July 1966–April 1969* ([Paris]: Plon, 1980–88), 132–3.

43 Credit is due Révillon for sponsoring Robert Flaherty's classic, widely viewed documentary *Nanook of the North*, the first film to introduce Inuit culture to a wide audience.

44 I was introduced to Quebec juridical circles by my brother-in-law Pierre Azard, dean of the Faculty of Law at the University of Ottawa in the 1960s and author of an authoritative treatise on Quebec civil law.

45 Victor, after an initial expedition during which we explored the socio-economic development problems of northern Quebec, village by village, told me that he did not wish to continue. "I'll stick to the ethnography of Eskimo societies as I knew them when they were still following Eskimo traditions, at Angmassalik on the east coast of Greenland, in 1936. You can have this job. Good luck!" A great

explorer to whom contemporary progress in French polar history owes a profound debt, Victor eventually retired to Tahiti; see photo 72 in my *Hummocks*, vol. 1, *Nord Groenland*.

46 Quebec had begun developing its hydro-electric resources in the 1960s without consulting the Native people. On 15 November 1973 a group of the latter won an injunction in Quebec Superior Court (the Malouf decision) blocking development in the absence of an agreement with the Native people. The outcome was the JBNQA, signed by the Quebec and federal governments, Hydro-Québec (the publicly owned hydro-electric company), and three associations representing the principal Native groups concerned.

47 Jean Malaurie, *Les Derniers Rois de Thulé*, 631.

48 See also Charlie Watt, "Message du sénateur Charlie Watt."

CHAPTER THREE

1 The results of these two expeditions, among the most fruitful of my career, remain to be published. So it goes. It is my intention to publish the trip diary as well as the many results obtained in the areas of microeconomics, ethnogenesis, and comparative history of mentalities. At that time the population of Igloolik was 99 Inuit families comprising 494 individuals; 61 of the families were Anglican, 38 were Catholic. In addition, there were three whites: the obliging Scotsman Bill Calder, the manager of the HBC store; Father Louis Fournier, an Oblate missionary from the French department of Lozère; and myself. My Inuit guide was Pacome Kolaut, who was to become a legend in this part of the Arctic. The wise Piugatu offered his whaling boat to help complete, by sail and paddle, my detailed survey of the villages and camps in northern Foxe Basin in the fall of 1960.

In 1959–60 the post bought $37,376 worth of pelts (54 seal, 1,681 white fox, 8 blue fox) and sold $83,092 worth of merchandise. My family-by-family survey of buying and spending habits and of hunting routes and calendars is especially interesting in that the society was then still isolated.

2 Military command in the Central Arctic was essentially American at the time; despite Ottawa's annoyed requests, authority would not be shared until 1965.

3 See also my *Ultima Thule*, 110–27.

4 Maxime Du Camp, *Souvenirs littéraires*.

5 Most of the civilian employees never left the confines of the base. They had no geographic or ethnological curiosity whatsoever.

6 Roald Amundsen and his seven-man crew followed this segment of the Northwest Passage in July 1903 aboard the *Gjøa*, a 47-ton sloop equipped with a 13-HP motor and five years of provisions. They circumnavigated King William Island via the James Clark Ross and Rae Straits after wintering in what would become known as Gjoa Haven close to the southern tip of the island. A light ship (like William Baffin's 60-ton *Discovery* of July 1616) can navigate the ice here, whereas to the west of King William Island, it is impenetrable. Such was Amundsen's breakthrough: avoid the fatal ice along the route followed by Franklin at all costs.

Even so, he admitted that he nearly shipwrecked in the James Ross Strait off Matty Island (my present location) because the reefs could not be spotted accurately from the crow's nest. In 1845 the glorious John Franklin had opted for very heavy ships, the 340-ton *Erebus* and the 370-ton *Terror.* Older in spirit and body, he had forgotten the lessons of his magnificent 1821 canoe expedition to Kent Peninsula in the company of bold, jovial *voyageurs*. The James Ross and Simpson Straits were then unmapped, and King William Island was believed to be a peninsula of the mainland. Having no knowledge of these, Franklin could not hug the Arctic coast and instead tried to make his way through the dangerously icebound Victoria Strait west of the island – the fatal mistake; see maps, pp. 192–3. I have opted for the canoe, the more appropriate vessel as the Inuit know. It is a matter of slipping through tight spaces everywhere, as if on a commando raid. For the route we followed from Shepherd Bay to Spence Bay (with a brief bivouac at Balfour Bay), see maps, pp. 67, 70.

7 Rae was spartan in his frugality, and he lived entirely from what he could catch. A crack hunter, he shot as much game in the Melville Peninsula (west of Igloolik) as all twelve Indian and Métis *coureurs de bois* on his 1847 expedition. Too perspicaciously critical of the Admiralty, the remarkable Rae was one of the few British explorers of the era not to be knighted. The spitefulness of the military establishment proved enduring. See Kenneth McGoogan, *Fatal Passage*.

8 The younger Ross (1800–62), a hero of British polar history, made his first voyage, with his uncle to the northwest coast of Greenland, in 1818. He joined Parry on his first two expeditions (1819–20, 1821–23). In later years he commanded a major expedition to the Antarctic with the *Erebus* and the *Terror* (1839–43), where he discovered the Ross Sea and Victoria Land and mapped part of Graham Land. See map, p. 101.

9 See also my *Ultima Thule*, 20–45.

10 See also my *Ultima Thule*, 48–57.

11 Certain ice floes form by breaking off the continental landmass, carrying rocks formed of alluvial deposits and pebbles dozens of kilometres out to sea. The blackish ooze with which these deposits are often coated creates a resemblance to a shredded piece of animal flesh, attracting the attention of the dogs.

12 Armchair critics of Rae, sitting in their academic ivory towers, have tendentiously argued that he and his Inuit crew were only a few days from Franklin's men and their desperate southward trek. Had he continued, his detractors claim, Rae might have found the survivors – but how could he have known where they were? See maps, pp. 193, 199.

13 In April to May 1859, when McClintock travelled down the Rae Strait by dogsled (the reverse of our direction), he and his companions Allen Young and William Hobson unearthed important clues to the tragic fate of Franklin, most remarkably a note dated 25 April 1848 from second-in-command Francis Crozier indicating that Franklin had died the previous spring.

14 Ross explored the Boothia Peninsula in tremendously cold weather in April 1830 with two Inuit guides and an English sailor, who suffered severely frostbitten feet. They reached this promontory by dogsled from Thom Bay, where the *Vic-*

tory was icebound, and he named it for his sister Isabella. Spence Bay is another toponym due to Ross. It is an irony that Franklin's two ships sank within sight of two capes further north on King William Island, discovered and named Franklin Point and Cape Jane Franklin by Ross seventeen years before the tragedy; see map, p. 101.

15 Pop. 19 families (1961), 247 individuals (1966), 250, including 230 Inuit (1970), 430 (1984), 560 (1991), 900 (2001).

16 Prior to his time at Spence Bay, the warm, friendly Lyall (b. 17 April 1910) worked at the now-abandoned Fort Ross post at the northeast outlet of the Bellot Strait (near Hazard Island). He and his wife Nipisha (b. 1917) had nine children.

17 The Canadian laws criminalizing murder, euthanasia, and incest are strictly enforced; such cases lead to dogsled pursuits and arrests. In other cases the officer, aware that the legal backwash is likely to be disproportionate, well-advisedly suppresses the matter – just as in the French countryside.

18 Roald Amundsen, *Roald Amundsen's "The North West Passage,"* vol. 1, 250.

19 The mean life expectancy for women, factoring in neonatal mortality, was 22, while for men it was 27. Puberty in girls occurred at age 12 to 14; in boys, at age 16 to 18, or as much as two years later, and the age of puberty varied according to the severity of the cold weather. The birth interval in the absence of contraception was thirty-two months (see my genealogy of four generations of Polar Eskimos in *Les derniers rois de Thulé*, 95–101).

20 This custom was common until 1960 and is doubtless still practised here in secret. Babies considered infirm or weak were eliminated, as (I suspect) were twins, considered a freak of nature, and babies lacking the typical "Mongolian spot" at the base of the spine. Indeed, infanticide, along with euthanasia, sexual and dietary taboos, and other regulators, has long been part and parcel of Inuit family-planning practices. I stress that a baby was not considered human until it was named, usually one or two days after birth. Therefore, in the minds of the Inuit, infanticide was not a crime tantamount to murder.

21 John Ross, recounting his expedition to the Boothia Peninsula, commented: "The terms husband and wife are words of usage ... and the term marriage is one which equally excites neither reflection nor commentary ... it was not uncommon for a man to have two wives ... my friend here informed me that he and his half brother had but one wife between them ... [In a different case, a man's] present wife and children belonged to another man who was his particular friend, and an angekok, to whom he had ... lent his own two wives; a loan which is here considered a peculiar mark of friendship, and, it must be admitted, not very unreasonably ... we had subsequent occasion to believe that [this practice] was universal among this tribe; the inhabitants of Boothia ... the women had no voice in the matter ... It is the custom to interchange wives ... In this country, the views of the citizens may be physiologically philosophical ... though it remained to discover whether they proved sound in practice. The people thus considered that they should have more children"; John Ross, *Narrative of a Second Voyage*, 230–1, 278, 334.

22 One example: we wondered at length about the high rate of suicide (*ingmilik toqroioq*) among the Inuit, particularly the Netsilingmiut. In fact, it appeared to be a tradition. Asen Balikci, who meticulously studied the Arviligjuarmiut of Pelly Bay (a subgroup of the Netsilingmiut, according to Knud Rasmussen) between 1959 and 1965, noted that in a neighbouring population of 300 Netsilik, there had been some fifty suicides or attempts in an equal number of years. Men of all ages were more suicidal on average than women. The usual methods were hanging, shooting, or drowning. Those who wished to hang themselves would put the rope around their necks, tie it to a horizontal board running between the walls of the igloo and, with the energy born of desperation – the board's height was insufficient – leap into the air, straining to keep their legs bent underneath them. Balikci and I met and discussed these problems in the autumn of 1962 in his office at the National Museum of Canada in Ottawa. As we turned the pages of our respective trip diaries, we were surprised to discover that unbeknownst to one another we had been doing research only 170 kilometres apart.

23 Joseph Chamberlain, *Foreign and Colonial Speeches*, 6, 89.

24 Permanent relief was set at $60–100 per month but only applied to extreme cases during periods of famine. In the whole of the Spence Bay district only thirteen individuals were entitled to it. The underlying worry was that the people would be made into welfare bums of one sort or another. The strength of the Inuit resides in their courage, their defiance in the face of hardship. All three of us were deeply convinced that "social security" would be their ruin.

25 I took extensive notes, line by line, on a rare book consisting of a scathing critique of John Ross's second expedition: Robert Huish, *The Last Voyage*. Huish's book was essentially a ghostwritten version of the account of ship's steward William Light, one of Ross's personal enemies. A great man as seen by an underling: may God preserve us from such rats, whether on an expedition or in the laboratory! One of Light's characteristic techniques is to invidiously compare the aging, portly, miserly Captain Ross – especially miserly when bartering with the Inuit – to young, alert, ambitious Commander Ross, a friend to sailors and Inuit alike. Uncle against nephew. John Ross did not deign to respond to this slander, but the tarnishing that his image underwent was a bitter trial for him. Truly, thugs like Light would besmirch the whitest snow. He reports the facts without the psychological intelligence necessary to understand the inevitably complex relationships between two exceptional men of different generations and complementary concerns. The uncle knew his nephew to be ambitious; after all, glory, in the Cornelian sense, has been the great motivator of many an explorer – not to mention vanity. After the Greenland expedition of 1818, the young James had conducted himself quite shabbily toward his uncle in the matter of Barrow's smear campaign (see p. 105). This behaviour notwithstanding, Ross chose him as second-in-command for this decisive expedition to the Magnetic Pole. That is what William Light might have striven to understand if he had not been so blinkered and ill-intentioned.

A piece of advice for you, dear reader: do as Captain Ross and avoid dialoguing with such venomous dwarfs, which only gives them credibility that they do not deserve. Remember Ross's prideful motto, *Aquila non capit mergulas*.

26 Distribution of Netsilingmiut families in 1955 outside Spence Bay: Lord Mayor Bay, 5 families; Cape North Hendon, 15; Thom Bay, 4; Avatootsiak, 1; Brentford, 8; Cresswell Bay, 4; Tasmania Island, 6; Josephine Bay, 1; Netsilik Lake, 4. In 1989 the whole Boothia Peninsula outside of Spence Bay was deserted.

27 Pop. 36,215 in 1991, divided among the Northwest Territories (58%), Quebec (19.4%), and Newfoundland (13%). In 1996 the population was 41,080, divided 59.88%, 20.20%, and 10.38% among the three regions, respectively.

28 Amundsen, *Roald Amundsen's "The North West Passage,"* vol. 2, 48, 51, original emphasis.

29 *Periodical Accounts Relating to the Missions of the Church of the United Brethren, Established Among the Heathen* 23 (1858): 89, quoted in W. Gillies Ross, *This Distant and Unsurveyed Country*, 108.

30 Ross, *Narrative of a Second Voyage*, 242–4, 246, 357–8.

31 Francis Leopold M'Clintock, *The Voyages of the 'Fox,'* 232–3, 236.

32 Amundsen, *Roald Amundsen's "The North West Passage,"* vol. 1, 294.

33 Ibid., vol. 1, 116–17, 168, 315.

34 Roald Amundsen, *Le passage du Nord-ouest*. Translator's note: The French and English editions of this work are substantially different in content.

35 Knud Rasmussen, *The Netsilik Eskimos*, 62–3, 138.

36 Gontran de Poncins, *Kabloona*, 37. A singular testimonial from 1938–39 without the slightest scientific pretension that is nonetheless one of the best pieces of writing on the Inuit of the Central Arctic. De Poncins – very much an odd-man-out among the Inuit – also produced an invaluable photographic album of mainly aesthetic intent: *Eskimos: Photographs and Text by Gontran de Poncins*.

37 Trapping revenue was much more substantial in the Hudson Bay region. In 1960–61, 6,300 arctic fox pelts brought $94,500, in 1961–62, 7,592 pelts earned $76,300, while in 1964–65, 11,133 pelts earned only $97,525. However, sealskin, previously without market value, was becoming profitable: while in 1960–61, 262 pelts sold for $1,268, the figures rose to 8,357 and $88,723 in 1964–65.

38 Gustave Flaubert, *The Letters*, vol. 2, 106.

39 The corollary of this appalling situation is a population growth rate much below the birth rate, which is nearly double the Canadian average. Why? Because infant mortality is shockingly high. The solution would be to offer price supports for pelts to raise their value above, for example, the paltry $5 that they were worth in 1950. Living standards would gradually be raised at the Inuit's initiative, a development criterion that I consider essential.

40 Jean Malaurie, *Call of the North*, 174, 177, 179.

41 In this gossipy colonial village, I am under constant observation by the various colonial representatives, including the police, the HBC, the priests, the administrators, and their wives. For the time being, the murmuring appears to be sympathetic, but that could change in a day. Francophones – Frenchmen especially – are suspect due to an ancient quarrel exacerbated here by Anglo-Saxon and Anglican provincialism. The epithets "Papist" and "Orangist" persist.

42 See my *Call of the North*, 196–207, for a photographic account of this trek.

43 It was long the conventional wisdom that lemming population dynamics were regulated, among other factors, by collective suicide, with whole troops of lem-

mings leaping into the sea before the onset of extremely cold winters. This fanciful idea has been definitively refuted; see, for example, Dennis Chitty, *Do Lemmings Commit Suicide?*

44 In this I followed the ingenious method of André Cailleux, a good friend and colleague during my first field season on Disko Island in August 1948.

45 Jean Malaurie, "Sur l'asymétrie des versants," 1461–2.

46 Johann Wolfgang von Goethe, *Goethe's Theory of Colours*, xxxviii.

47 See also my *Last Kings of Thule*, 213.

48 Discovered by William Kennedy and Joseph-René Bellot on 5 April 1852 and well known to the Inuit as Ee-Karashak, the Bellot Strait is a passage leading out of Brentford Bay between the Boothia Peninsula and Somerset Island. It is more than 30 kilometres long, less than 1.5 kilometres wide at its narrowest, and 122 metres deep. Travelling by dogsled south from Batty Bay, where their ship, *Prince Albert*, lay icebound, Kennedy and Bellot were alerted to the possible existence of a strait when they noticed a dense fog over an "inlet" (John Ross's term, for he had twice overlooked the strait while carefully mapping the Boothia Peninsula in 1829 and 1832), indicating open water. Inland exploration enabled them to confirm the discovery. The following year Bellot died in a tragic accident in the Wellington Channel while participating in a Franklin search expedition on the *Prince Albert*.

If Ross had been able to elicit this information from the Inuit during repeated discussions with them over three winters – he hadn't – the Northwest Passage would have been his to claim. McClintock, in 1858, was unable to navigate the strait with the *Fox* and had to negotiate it by dogsled. The first ship traverse, by the HBC's *Nascopie*, took place in 1937.

49 This became clear when his nephew reached the western ocean during a reconnaissance of Boothia by dogsled. His Inuit guides indicated that Boothia was continental and that their present location could be reached only by sea via a long detour north, west, and south through the Lancaster and Peel sounds; see maps, p. 101.

50 Ross, *Narrative of a Second Voyage*, 384–5.

51 The wandering North Magnetic Pole had long been a source of fascination for the British, exerting an attraction almost as strong as the Northwest Passage: "it almost seemed ... as if our voyage and all its labours were at an end and that nothing now remained for us but to return home and be happy for the rest of our days. There were after-thoughts which told us that we had much yet to endure [but they] did not intrude; could they have done so, we should have cast them aside, under our present excitement," wrote James Ross in his diary; see Ross, *Narrative of a Second Voyage*, 357–8. See also map p. 101.

52 Another tribute to Felix Booth, Ross's friend through good times and bad. Booth was scandalized by the insidious smear campaigns being waged against Ross at the Admiralty.

53 Discussions with the Inuit confirmed that the Gulf of Boothia has no outlet to the west: "there was no way into this sea from the south ... if our ship desired to

reach Ney-tyel-le from our present position, she must go round a long way to the northward"; Ross, *Narrative of a Second Voyage*, 206.

54 The wheel, rods, and levers – the remains of the steam machine – were subsequently found scattered on the shores of Lord Mayor Bay. "In future, our ship was to be a sailing vessel, and nothing more. I therefore determined to lighten her ... With this view, arrangements were made on the last day of September [1829], for taking to pieces the boilers"; Ross, *Narrative of a Second Voyage*, 123. Amundsen confirmed in 1903 that the Netsilingmiut of Gjoa Haven had no iron despite the veritable mine of it that is, or was, ready to hand. Their cultural conservatism had led the Inuit to spurn a good part of these gifts of fate.

55 The expedition had obviously been gone much longer than planned, and in order for the crew and patrons (Ross and Felix Booth) to receive government reimbursement, a twenty-six-member parliamentary committee of inquiry had to consider the scientific merits of what they had achieved. Of this episode, Sir John Ross wrote bitterly in the 1840s: "Since that day [of the parliamentary hearing] my enemies received their warmest ally: in private and in public, in every club and in every society ... did I hear of efforts to depreciate my talents, my acquirements and my services; but I have borne all in silence because I knew the quarter from which these efforts emanated, and grief subdued my indignation. Now, however, silence becomes impossible. To all the calumnies in Sir John Barrow's works, Sir James Clark Ross has affixed his signature"; John Ross, *Observations on a Work*, quoted in M.J. Ross, *Polar Pioneers*, 291.

56 Ross, *Narrative of a Second Voyage*, 368.

57 M'Clintock, *Voyages of the 'Fox,'* 148.

58 Inuit population in 1991: 480.

59 Amundsen, *Roald Amundsen's "The North West Passage,"* vol. 1, 202.

60 The mission was built in 1948 by Father Henry as a summer hermitage for the missionary from Spence Bay (mission founded in 1950) or Pelly Bay (founded 1937). All the Inuit here are Anglicans, but subtly couched remarks by various parties suggest to me that their Christian faith is quite superficial. They are still pantheistic animists in the most ancient of traditions. At Pelly Bay, half the Inuit population (135 in 1951) is Catholic, a testament to Father Henry's magnetic personality. See maps, pp. 70, 80.

61 Arctic char is a handsome salmonid fish that divides its life between fresh water and the sea. Hatched in lakes and large ponds, they descend to the sea in their fourth or fifth year to feed on coastal plankton. After a summer spent there, they ascend the rivers again and are ready to mate and spawn on reaching their lake breeding grounds; see Bernard Stonehouse, *Animals of the Arctic*, 57.

62 Francis Pallu and Pierre Lambert de la Motte, *Monita ad Missionarios*.

63 Bernard Jacqueline, "Les instructions de la S.C.," 624.

64 See photograph in my *Call of the North*, 210–11.

65 See photos in my *Call of the North*, 208–9, 215.

66 Ross, *Narrative of a Second Voyage*, 162–7, 287, 379–80.

67 Ibid., 171.

68 1951 Census: Fort Ross, 49 (25 M, 24 F), Thom Bay 30 (13 M, 17 F), Lord Mayor Bay, 45 (23 M, 22 F), Spence Bay, 47 (20 M, 27 F); total for Boothia Peninsula, 171; King William Island, 39; Pelly Bay, 135.

69 Bécassine was a character in a comic book that made its appearance around the same time (1905). Its plot involved the adventures of a naïve yet commonsensical Breton housemaid who worked in the homes of the Parisian upper class. Bécassine was severely criticized for its condescending image of the Breton people – an image that would no longer be tolerated today.

70 French philosopher and eminent philologist Ernest Renan (1823–92) caused a scandal in nineteenth-century Europe with his historical work on the life of Jesus, which earned him the wrath of Pope Pius IX. Renan presented Jesus as a holy man and a prophet but not a god. Émile Combes, as prime minister of France from 1903 to 1905, presided over the secularization of the country's school system, an act that led to a breaking-off of relations between France and the Vatican. Church resistance to these developments was at its most strenuous in Brittany, whose population is largely Catholic.

71 I must stress that the behaviour of the missionaries was such that not one Native priest was to be found in these territories of the Canadian Northwest at the time of my research – none until 1970, in fact. Only catechists and, at Chesterfield, two nuns. History records that the message of the Church of Jerusalem, which spread throughout the Mediterranean and the entire world with dazzling speed, has become singularly insipid over the past hundred years if not longer. Sex will be its eventual downfall.

72 "It is a matter of shedding light on the Christian crime whereby an attempt was made to remove Christianity from God, piece by piece, such that Christianity today is poles apart from that of the New Testament."

73 John Henry Newman, *The Arians*, 80. Newman (1801–90) was an English churchman and author whose spirituality gave inspiration to the British Catholic and Anglican Churches.

74 See, for example, Eugène Fafard, *Prayers and Hymns*, 220–5. This manual was distributed to all the missions.

75 Burchard of Worms, *Decretum* 19.5 (Migne *Patrologia Latina* 140: 959–60).

76 It is of great interest to reflect on this avatar of practising Christianity. Consider, for example, the fierce backlash against Christianity in 1970s and 1980s Quebec; the religion was so totally routed that one may well wonder at the spirit of religious teaching dispensed in the nineteenth and twentieth centuries in a once-fervent province. Bishops, what have you done for this people of God to retain your sweeping privileges?

77 My friend Gontran de Poncins described to me in 1955 his edifying encounter with Father Henry in an igloo at Pelly Bay sixteen years earlier; see de Poncins, *Kabloona*, 225–31.

78 Paul-Louis Combet.

79 With a few rare exceptions – and what treasures they are! – the codices that I read were of middling interest, full of interviews with parish leaders or statistics attesting to the intense rivalry between Roman Catholics and Anglicans. I

remember one missionary on Hudson Bay whose great joy was to display a curve that he had painstakingly plotted on graph paper showing that thanks to his parishioners' fecundity, the Catholics would soon outnumber the Anglicans in the vicinity. The spirit of Vatican II had not moved upon these waters. The virtue of repentance had barely grazed certain congregations led by headstrong individuals whose authoritarianism was at times all the more disastrous for being thought virtuous.

80 Asen Balikci, *The Netsilik Eskimo*, 220–1.

81 François Leprieur, *Quand Rome condamne*.

82 Since 1990 Canadian churches of all denominations have been calling on the government to bail them out financially, claiming that they have been ruined by lawsuits (paternity, sexual abuse, etc.) stemming from the residential school experience.

83 John Muir, *Travels in Alaska*, 127.

84 Subsequently, through the RCMP, he sent me the completed questionnaires of every Inuk in Thom Bay. Arnaja was a man of honour. Our travels together are detailed in my *Call of the North*, 213.

85 Simone Weil, *Gravity and Grace*, 138.

86 See Richard E. Lee, Jr, and David Denlinger, *Insects*. Cryobiology is equally complex in rocks, where, due to the density of the compressed water, the microchannels freeze at 10°C; see my *Hummocks*, pocket ed., vol. 1, *De la pierre à l'homme*, 76–8.

87 De Poncins, *Kabloona*, 118.

88 Ross, *Narrative of a Second Voyage*, 230.

89 I discuss this issue in relation to the west coast of Greenland in my *Hummocks*, pocket ed., vol. 1, *De la pierre à l'homme*, 164–6. See also my *Ultima Thule* as well as my preface, "Jésus-Christ indianisé," to Joëlle Rostkowski, *La Conversion inachevée*, 11–19, and maps, pp. 34–6 above.

90 The typical dowry today is a dog or a boat. Historically, if the bride was a *tiguaq* (adoptee) or an *illiyardjuk* (orphan), the price was lower or sometimes nil. I plotted the fluctuations in the amount of these dowries over two generations (1900–60) and found the bride price to be relatively stable throughout the period.

91 See photograph of Arnaja, his steady gaze, during our conversations on the tundra, in my *Call of the North*, 213.

92 Amundsen, *Roald Amundsen's "The North West Passage,"* vol. 1, 277–8. The scene happened on board the *Gjøa*. The Inuit village of Gjoa Haven (Uqsuqtuuq) on King William Island grew from a mere stopping place in 1903–05 to its 1962 population of 121 (64 M, 57 F) after the founding of the Hudson's Bay post in 1930.

93 "There was never such a master of pantomime as this infinitely strange, perpetually agitated, and yet extraordinarily self-possessed rogue who dropped in one afternoon from Back's River ... he would sit stiffly down, motionless in a sort of comical dignity while he watched you out of the corner of his eye. But his hands never ceased from fluttering, and even in the air they did not draw forms, they caressed them. His eyelids fell into folds when he shut his eyes, and there was something about them both pink and obscene ... To heighten the impres-

sion of inversion this man dragged along with him, behind him, a child whose features were no less astonishing than his own – a little Aiglon with romantic locks brushed across his forehead and immense, incredibly ringed eyes that were a little melancholy and rather protuberant. What was this? Was it a girl, a boy? A boy, yes, said our Louis XIII, turning round to stroke the passive forehead; and a very good trapper. He got two foxes the other day. The word 'trapper' went very ill with the look of the boy, and I was sure that the man was lying about his minion. As the evening wore on, and the child began to droop with sleep, he refused to allow the boy to go off to the igloo alone, explaining with inconceivable gestures that they always slept together (gesture of rocking the child to sleep in his arms) and saying that the boy was never able to go to sleep without him"; de Poncins, *Kabloona*, 135–8.

CHAPTER FOUR

1 Churchill, (pop. 2,450 in 1961, 1,089 in 1996, 963 in 2001), was a very active military base during the Second World War and a centre of scientific and technical research. In the eighteenth century with its bloody French-English battles, Fort Churchill witnessed the exploits of two great explorers, Louis Antoine de Bougainville and Jean-François La Pérouse. It was the determined La Pérouse who captured the fort from Samuel Hearne (1745–92) in 1782 without a shot being fired. Hearne, the legendary HBC agent, traded with the Inuit northwest of Churchill on his famous exploration of the Mackenzie River in 1770–71. He was the first explorer to cross the Canadian tundra to the Arctic Ocean and map the route, one of the great epics of Arctic history. Ranging up to the Coppermine River, this tenacious expedition represented a whole series of accomplishments. During his expeditions, Hearne lived like the Chipewyans, eating caribou meat (and hides) and buffalo fetuses (which he considered a delicacy).

Starting in the nineteenth century, small HBC steamers ranged up the west coast of Hudson Bay with barges in tow, stopping at coastal Inuit summer camps. The Inuit societies of this whole area clearly have been subject to acculturation for a much longer period than is normally posited in historical and anthropological work. An in-depth revision, a semiological rereading of the original texts on supposedly "pure" native thought, based on observations from 1840 to 1925, should be undertaken in view of this internal acculturation.

2 Pop. in 1970, 495 Inuits, 30 whites; in 1984, 1,110 total; in 1995, 1,450 Inuits; and in 2001, 2,177 Inuits. Rankin Inlet is now the site of a large university college.

3 D.M. Brack and D. McIntosh, *Keewatin Mainland Area*, 124, 145. My severe criticism of this report is provided in my "Les Esquimaux du Keewatin."

4 A debate held in 1550–51 at the behest of King Charles V of Spain that pitted the Dominican priest Bartolomé de las Casas (1474–1566) against Juan Ginés de Sepúlveda, the advocate of the Spanish colonists (*encomenderos*). The epochal question: should the peoples of the New World be converted to the Christian faith by waging war on them or by setting "an example of good and holy living"? The Dominican took the latter position on the basis of Pope Paul III's bull *Subli-*

mis Deus of 1537, which held that the Indians were human beings equal in law to the Spanish colonists. Although the tangible results of Valladolid were limited, it was probably the only time in history when a conquering sovereign halted his conquests to hear learned testimony on whether they were just; see Lewis Hanke, *All Mankind Is One*.

5 See my *Call of the North*, 175–9.

6 Jean Malaurie, ed., *Arctic Oil and Gas*, 252.

7 René Lévesque, remarks to the Nunavik Commission of the National Assembly of Québec, 23 November 1983, quoted in Commission du Nunavik, *Partageons*, 1.

8 I had a long conversation with Premier Lévèsque in Paris, where he encouraged me to keep up the fight for minority rights, particularly in Quebec: "Never give up! Here in the province, there is still much 'Great Darkness' in people's minds in regard to the Indians and the Inuit. I greatly appreciate what you have done with the federal and Quebec governments for the Inuit. Of course we still need you. Come see me in Quebec City."

9 In particular, according to a courageous contemporary report by Robert and Lois Dailey, the impersonal mining company was "unalterably opposed to any form of unionization of the Eskimos," as it informally admitted, although the Daileys were unable to obtain written confirmation of this; see Robert C. Dailey and Lois A. Dailey, *The Eskimo of Rankin Inlet*, 96.

10 Unfortunately, this initiative was as emblematic of Canadian Arctic policy as the 1951 agreement to allow an American offensive military base at Thule without the Inughuit's consent. One-fifth of their land was expropriated in 1953, and their waters were polluted with the crash of a bomber carrying four H-bombs on 21 January 1968.

11 Jean Duvignaud, *Le Pandémonium du présent*.

12 I reiterate here these references, all edited by myself, in order to drive home their importance: Fondation française d'études nordiques, *Développement économique de l'Arctique*; *Le peuple esquimau aujourd'hui et demain*; *Le pétrole et le gaz arctique: problèmes et perspectives: débats*; and *Le pétrole et le gaz arctique: problèmes et perspectives*. Numerous North American sources simply ignore this chronology of Inuit autonomy, as if the French language were some sort of vice.

13 Darcy Ribeiro, *Carnets indiens*, 538, 595–6. In addition to his anthropological work, Ribeiro is one of the charismatic political figures of the last half-century in Brazil, as well as the founder of the University of Brasilia. In his view, the problem does not affect the Amazonian Indians in the same way as the Inuit. In the Mato Grosso, the contact is often brutal, deadly, whereas in Canada, contact with the whites dates back much further than the Inuits' stage of technical advancement might indicate. Contact with explorers and whalers on the coast has been occurring since 1840. The Inuit have also had time to adapt physiologically by developing flu antibodies in the wake of the epidemics, and there has been mental adaptation as well. Indeed, throughout their 5,000-year history, the Inuit have shown adaptive ingenuity and the ability to distinguish what is favourable to their culture. This is a good foundation, but it is still necessary to see to the education of elites, and this is what the two of us sought to achieve, Ribeiro

with FUNAI, I with Canada's Department of Northern Affairs. Our immediate priority was a radical reform of the primary school system for these first peoples.

14 Here, I refer again to Dailey and Dailey, *The Eskimo of Rankin Inlet*, which is highly critical of the mine administration and the federal government. The figures in their report are corroborated by my own surveys.

15 Ibid., 28–32.

16 Ibid.

17 Jean Malaurie, *The Last Kings*, 162–3.

18 Duvignaud, *Le Pandémonium du présent*.

19 Rochfort Maguire, *The Journal*, 521.

20 My Inuit companion Kutsikitsoq and I reached the Geomagnetic Pole on 29 May 1951 with two dogsleds. I was the second explorer (after the American R.E. Peary, August 1895) and the first European to do so.

21 See my *The Last Kings*, 161–3.

22 A few years later the mine closed, and the diarist was reduced to unemployment. We corresponded, never losing sight of each other. His valuable diaries are still in my possession, and their author is still alive. He has never asked to have them back. I have in my possession two other autobiographies from this region of the Canadian Eastern Arctic that I intend to publish in a multivolume compilation of my publications and research findings.

23 Pop. 225 Inuit (185 Catholics) in 1935; 200 Inuit, 30 whites in 1970; 295 Inuit in 1991; 300 Inuit in 2001. At the time of my visit in 1961, the total population of the Chesterfield Inlet administrative district was 863.

24 Father Turquetil was born 1876 at Reviers, died 1955 at Washington, DC.

25 Reference to Saint Jean Vianney, a French parish priest who was canonized for his piety and simple life.

26 Adrian G. Morice, *Thawing Out the Eskimo*, 100–1.

27 On 4 February 1979 at 7:30 P.M. near Québec City, Father Pierre Henry (Kayonaluk by his Inuit name) died at the age of seventy-four.

28 Pop. 640 Inuit, 70 whites in 1970; 955 total in 1984; 1,120 Inuit in 1991; 1,507 total in 2001. First maritime exploration by Captain William Christopher in 1762; see maps pp. 5, 34–6.

29 In 1953, 217,500 caribou were counted in an area half the size of France in which 380 nomadic families lived. In that year 3,650 caribou were shot at Baker Lake. Brack and McIntosh, *Keewatin Mainland Area*, refer to Keewatin as "the most desolate region in the Arctic."

30 Ibid., ii, 101, 143.

31 Founding dates of Catholic missions in the Hudson Bay vicariate: Chesterfield Inlet, 1912; Eskimo Point, 1924; Southampton, 1926; Baker Lake, 1927; Pond Inlet, 1929; Churchill, 1930; Repulse Bay, 1932; Igloolik, 1933; Pelly Bay, 1937; Arctic Bay, 1939; Cape Dorset, 1948; Thom Bay, 1948; Garry Lake, 1951; Gjoa Haven, 1952. Milestones of evangelization: Father Turquetil's first trip among the Inuit, 1901; first Inuit conversion, 1916; first hymnal and Catholic prayerbook in Inuktitut, 1934; Sister Pélagie's profession of faith at Chesterfield Inlet, 1954; Sister Blan-

dine's profession, 1953; founding of Catholic residential school at Chesterfield Inlet, 1954, where I stayed on my visit to Father Henry.

32 Étienne Bazin, *Les lettres*: "A conversion! That's one more snatched away from the protestants and the devil!" (70). Father Clabaut, Repulse Bay, 1933: "Protestant prayer books, calendars, and bibles are very common here ... it is a scourge, and many of our Eskimos give us ill-favoured looks just because of those books." In 1910–11, Father Turquetil, the founder of the Catholic missions in the Canadian Northeast, noted the resistance put up against them by the Anglican ministers operating out of Churchill during the previous century, who protested bitterly against the Catholics' encroachment on their turf. Likewise, on each of my visits, the Anglican and Presbyterian ministers expressed their irritation at the attempts of Roman Catholicism to subject all Christian faiths to a single orthodoxy. "Luther considered himself a Catholic reformer," I was told. "Never will we accept the dogmas of papal infallibility, Immaculate Conception, the preeminence of the Virgin Mary. The Gospel is silent on these dogmas." One of them added, "We find the spirit of self-deprivation – celibacy, poverty, solitude – exhibited by some Oblates amazing; indeed, frightening. Is it any wonder that it produces such scandalous lapses of judgment?"

33 The function of the church is to proselytize, to win souls by threatening them with eternal damnation. Mgr Turquetil was perfectly open about how far from Christian ideals he considered the Inuits' customs to be. In 1926 he wrote in the journal of the Archdiocese of Saint-Boniface, Manitoba, "Each conversion of a pagan adult is a true marvel of grace, considering the frightful mistakes or practices from which we must dissuade them in order to bring them to God"; Mgr Arsène Turquetil, "Au Pays des Esquimaux," 128. In eschatological terms, the religion of the book still has a long way to go before it will acquiesce to a constructive dialogue between priest and shaman in a spirit of tolerance. It is imperative for us to rethink the pluralistic complexity of beliefs in the sacred and to respect the primitive polytheism dwelling in each of us – our lost heritage.

34 Roger Bastide, *The African Religions of Brazil.*

35 Unfortunately, the project proved abortive. The following year a priest from the Mackenzie came to study in Paris at the Centre d'Études Arctiques, but he was reticent to engage fully in an exploratory dialogue due to the Sorbonne's reputation as a Masonic institution. Moreover, he was ill and had to return to Canada on short notice. He died there, and the experience was unfortunately never repeated. The Oblate equivalent of, for example, Don C. Talayesva's *Sun Chief: The Autobiography of a Hopi Indian* remains to be written. The French translation, *Soleil Hopi*, was published in Terre Humaine, the anthropology series at Plon that I founded in 1954 and have been editing ever since. Terre Humaine also published a successful collaboration emerging from my many years of discussions with Jesuit Father Éric de Rosny, the lovely volume translated into English as *Healers in the Night* – not to overlook François Leprieur, *Quand Rome condamne*, which chronicles the demise of the worker-priests movement.

36 Jean Malaurie, director, *Les Esquimaux canadiens et le Canada: L'incommunicabilité*, documentary film, 55 min.

37 I have written extensively on the political roots of the Inuits' social problems in *The Last Kings of Thule* as well as in the following articles: "Le développement industriel"; "Promotion indigène"; "Du droit des minorités esquimaudes"; "Les Esquimaux du Keewatin"; and "Les peuples arctiques." See also Tagak Curley, "Policy Issues in Nunavut." Curiously, during my time as a consultant in the four territories of Inuit habitation (Alaska, Canada, Greenland, Siberia), the only national government that grasped the essence of my recommendations was the Russian government. The year 1991 saw the founding, at the initiative of President Gorbachev, of the State Polar Academy of Saint Petersburg, a leadership training institute housed in a 27,000-square-metre building and attended by 1,600 students from forty-five ethnic groups. I am one of its founders and its honorary president for life. The institution is unique in the Arctic. French is the first mandatory foreign language, while Russian is the working language.

38 The Padlermiut were an especially interesting, little-studied tribe living under harsh conditions. They are gone today, dispersed and assimilated. There is grace in the sensitive paintings of their traditional customs by Winifred Petchey Marsh (wife of the respected Reverend Donald Marsh), which have always exerted a great pull on me; see Winifred Petchey Marsh, *People of the Willow.*

39 André Gide, *The Counterfeiters*, 327.

CHAPTER FIVE

1 The encounter was long overdue. The Utkuhikhalingmiut were among the last representatives of the "Caribou" people, the hard core of Inuit civilization. The Danish ethnogeographer Hans Peder Steensby has argued that the Mackenzie was probably the cradle of proto-Esquimaux civilization. The Caribou Esquimaux, descendants of these proto-Esquimaux, migrated to the coast and evolved into the eschato-Esquimaux. This central group, bearers of a dual (i.e., inland and coastal) culture, then expanded outward from east to west. This interpretation, one among several propounded, locates the origins of Inuit history in the Canadian Central Arctic as a branch of an older Arctic aboriginal group. Linguists today tend to situate the cradle of Inuit culture in the Bering Strait and beyond, in northeastern Asia, since it is there that the oldest word roots are found. Physical anthropology concurs, taking its cues from the work of the Soviet physical anthropologist Maksim Levin; see my *Hummocks*, vol. 2, *Alaska*, 320.

2 Pop. 34 Inuit (16 M, 18 F) in 1951, 121 Inuit (64 M, 57 F) and 12 non-Inuit in 1962, 235 Inuit and 15 non-Inuit in 1970, 760 Inuit in 1991, and 960 Inuit in 2001; see map, p. 186.

3 In 1951 the following groups inhabited Boothia Peninsula and its environs: the Arvertormiut of the Bellot Strait area (25 M, 24 F); the Igtuaritorfikmiut of Thom Bay (13 M, 17 F), Lord Mayor Bay (23 M, 22 F), and Spence Bay (20 M, 27 F); the Arviligjuarmiut of Pelly Bay (70 M, 65 F); the Qikiqtarmiut of Gjoa Haven and the western portion of King William Island (18 M, 21 F); the Utkuhikhalingmiut of Back River (12 families in 1952); the Ilivilermiut of the Adelaide Peninsula

(26 M, 24 F); and the Ugjulimmiut of the Queen Maud Gulf area (30 M, 21 F). The Kuungmiut of Shepherd Bay were absent from the area during the census and at the time of my July 1961 trip; they are partially grouped with the Spence Bay Inuit.

4 This final link was discovered by the uncommonly courageous Scotsmen Peter Warren Dease and Thomas Simpson (cousin of George Simpson, the governor of the Hudson's Bay Company) on 11–13 August 1839 while exploring from the west on an HBC-backed canoe expedition. The paranoiac Simpson was killed in mysterious circumstances while returning to London. They were exceptional explorers to whom history has not paid sufficient tribute; see map, p. 192.

5 Whereas the memories of the shipwrecked sailors from Franklin's expedition, the "Tuluit" as the Inuit called them, were fresher in 1903–05. "Of all these tribes the Ogluli Eskimo was the one that had been most in contact with white men. In their districts many members of the Franklin Expedition breathed their last. It was also this tribe, that M'Clintock, Hall, and Schwatka met, while on their search for Franklin documents, and they were also the first we encountered. Several of them could remember the members of the Schwatka Expedition, and they still retained among them some remnants of English words"; Roald Amundsen, *Roald Amundsen's "The North West Passage,"* vol. 1, 293.

6 Roald Amundsen, *Le passage du Nord-ouest*, 102.

7 Amundsen, *Roald Amundsen's "The North West Passage,"* vol. 1, 115–16, 173.

8 Gontran de Poncins, *Kabloona*, 30, 219.

9 See photo of Koorsoot in my *Call of the North*, 219. In Emmanuel Levinas's subtle formulation, the face is a bareness, an absence of cultural adornment.

10 For the symbolic aspects of the game, see my *The Last Kings*, 274.

11 This game was very popular on the southwest coast of Greenland in the eighteenth century. I found it being played in Chukotka in 1990, where the balls were adorned with geometric motifs. It is described, along with several other of these games, in F.H. Eger, comp., *Eskimo Inuit Games*.

12 Jean Duvignaud, *Le Pandémonium du présent*.

13 See also my account of the Franklin expedition in *Ultima Thule*, 48–57.

14 Francis Leopold M'Clintock, *Fate of Sir John Franklin*, 267.

15 Devotional books, except for Oliver Goldsmith's *The Vicar of Wakefield*, as well as the covers of a New Testament and a prayerbook.

16 M'Clintock, *Fate of Sir John Franklin*, 267.

17 The self-taught Hall (1821–71) was, for his time, a model of intercultural tolerance and respect whose love for the Inuit was genuine. He conducted three Arctic expeditions, the first (1860–62) to Baffin Island (Frobisher Bay), the second (1864–69) to Hudson Bay and King William Island, and the third (1870–71) to North Greenland in search of the Pole, sailing on the *Polaris*; see map, p. 199. Recent scholarship indicates that he died of arsenic poisoning, possibly at the hand of Emil Bessels, chief scientist on the *Polaris*; see my *Ultima Thule*, 110–27.

18 Charles Francis Hall, *Narrative*, 589–94.

19 Frederick Schwatka, *The Long Arctic Search*. See maps, pp. 193 (Franklin) and 198 (Schwatka).

20 A remarkable recent Canadian expedition analyzed the bones of a sailor from the expedition (found at Booth Point on the southeast coast of King William Island near Gjoa Haven) and found lead levels of 228 ppm, as compared to an analysis of contemporaneous Inuit bones yielding a figure of 22–36 ppm. Hair analyses were equally significant. As the report indicates, the well-established effects of lead poisoning include anorexia, weakness and fatigue, irritability, stupor, paranoia, abdominal pain, and anaemia; see Owen Beattie and John Geiger, *Frozen in Time*, 83–4; Owen Beattie and Roger Amy, "A Report."

21 Malaurie, *Ultima Thule*, 357; and *The Last Kings*, 356–60.

22 Malaurie, *Call of the North*, 224.

23 "Since our first landing upon King William's Island we have not met with any heavy ice; all along its eastern and southern shore, together with the estuary of this great river, is one vast unbroken sheet"; M'Clintock, *Fate of Sir John Franklin*, 244.

24 During our bivouac, my Netsilik guide, Koorsoot, reviewed their calendar with me. I transcribe it here phonetically and with all the usual caveats: *Norervik* (June); *Itavik* (July, birds molting); *It'avik aipa* (August); *Amerasuvik* (September, male caribou losing their antlers); *Amerasuvik aipa* (October); *Sikuvik* (November, first sea ice); *Ukiak aipa* (December, winter approaching); *Ubluilaut* (December, days short); *Qa'mataut blaksaut* (January); *Ikiakparvik* (February); *Avungnivik* (March); *Natsianerik* (April, baby seals); *Kravasivik* (May, baby seals getting new coats). This resembles the calendar transcribed by Amundsen (1905), which I provide below in his orthography: *Hikkernillun* (December), "The sun disappears"; *Kapidra* (January), "It is cold, the Eskimo is freezing"; *Hikkernaun* (February), "The sun is returning"; *Ikiakparui* (March), "The sun is ascending"; *Avonivi* (April), "The seal brings forth her young"; *Nechyialervi* (May), "The young seals are taking to the sea"; *Kavaruvi* (June), "The seals are shedding their coats"; *Noerui* (July I), "The reindeer bring forth their young"; *Ichyavi* I (July II), "The birds are brooding"; *Ichyavi* II (August), "The young birds are hatched"; *Amerairui* I (September), "The reindeer is migrating south"; *Amerairui* II (October); *Akaaiarvi* (November), "The Eskimo lay down food depots"; *Hikkernillun* (December), "The sun disappears"; Amundsen, *Roald Amundsen's "The North West Passage,"* vol. 2, 46–7.

25 Back's five expeditions took place in 1818, 1819–22, 1825–27, 1833–34, and 1836–37. In England there was great concern at the absence of news from John Ross's second expedition to the Canadian Central Arctic (1829–33). Back's publicly funded overland expedition of 1833 aimed to reach the estuary of the "Great Fish River" and, with the help of the Natives, to rescue the shipwrecked *Victory* crew. Apprised along the way of Ross's return and his exploration of Lancaster Sound and Baffin Bay, Back set about exploring new territory. However, he did not get far beyond Ogle Point, falling shy of discovering the missing piece of the Northwest Passage that follows the Simpson and Rae Straits to the south of King William Island. If Simpson or Back had been able to establish that the island is separate from Boothia Peninsula, Franklin would have followed the route that

proved to be the only viable passage, as Amundsen demonstrated in 1903. See map of Back's 1833–34 expedition, p. 198.

26 George Back, *Narrative*, 426–7.

27 See maps pp. 198 (1834) and 186, 202 (1963).

28 Back, *Narrative*, 379–85.

29 In June 1923 Rasmussen became the first anthropologist to visit this remote region during his famous Fifth Thule Expedition. I am the first scientist to follow him. He stayed six days, leaving 6 June 1923 for King William Island. He wrote, "the inhabitants of the delta region round about Back River, and in fact all their kinsmen further inland, were among the least known of all Eskimos"; Knud Rasmussen, *The Netsilik Eskimos*, 467. See maps, pp. 223–4, and also my *Call of the North*, 218–61, for an ethnophotographic account of my Back River journey.

30 Born 1891 according to our interview and other evidence, 1906 according to the RCMP census.

31 Born 1911.

32 See my *Call of the North*, 248. The necessary provision is three fish per adult per day. I am told that not long ago, when people met, fish was eaten communally, passed from hand to hand. I estimate the average weight of each fish after removal of head, tail, and scales at 2.5 kg (char), 1.5 kg (lake trout at second camp), and 0.5-0.75 kg (whitefish).

33 RCMP Sergeant A.C. Fryer's report of 22 May 1956 (covering 1955) concurs: "An abundance of fish is what keeps the Eskimo living in this country, and even in the deep winter an active Eskimo can haul in thirty fishes a day. A lack of seal blubber is a real handicap ... In the olden days, when there were large herds of caribou to shoot, there would be plenty of fat for their lamps. Nowadays all they have is belly fat from the white fish, which does not add up to much. For cooking and making of tea, they use the ground willows, which are abundant, and the fire is made in a separate porch to the living quarters. It appears that no attempts were made to make a little stove for the living quarters, that could burn the willows, and to supply much needed heat."

34 Malaurie, *Call of the North*, 228–9.

35 Ibid., 146.

36 Gibson's census of the Utkuhikhalingmiut (further to Rasmussen's account of 1923 and updated using Hudson's Bay Company data) found a population of 32 (18 M, 14 F); a 1953 census found 12 families. See the constable's sketches, pp. 187, 207, 210, 275, 277. My 1963 census found 7 families, 25 persons (10 M, 15 F), including 7 girls and 3 boys (1 adopted) under the age of 15. The mean age was low. There was 1 man aged 72 (Toolegaak), 1 aged 57, 2 over 50 (1 M, 1 F), 2 men over 40, and 2 women aged 30–40. The largest household, headed by a widower, had 3 children at birth intervals of six and three years. The census included only the people living on the Back River estuary, not those living on the large inland lakes (MacDougall, Garry, and Pelly).

37 Four years earlier, RCMP constable E.J. Giesbrecht made similar observations: "Back River. Nine families. Their main diet and for the majority, the only diet,

was fish. And fish run throughout was very good all year. And the natives, in general, were in excellent health and spirits. The trapping of fox was practically negligible, and hardly any caribou were killed in this area ... With constantly decreasing caribou, there is very little hope foreseen of this people ever being completely independent in the future. Clothes will always have to be supplied as well as nets and ammunition, and their existence in this area will depend largely, if not entirely, upon the fish run"; "RCMP report of conditions amongst Eskimo generally," 30 June 1959.

38 See chapter on Rasmussen in my *Ultima Thule*, 254–83.

39 He is referring to Arnarulunguak, a young Eskimo widow who accompanied Rasmussen on the Fifth Thule Expedition of 1922–23, as did Kravijarssuaq, a young hunter. I got to know the latter well and interviewed him many times about Rasmussen and the Thule expedition. He was particularly struck by Inuit who did not heat their homes and added, "They were clean compared to the Netsilingmiut, who were nearly black with filth, but darker-skinned than us Inughuit." Likewise, Rasmussen remarked, "it is always refreshing to be among clean people, clean right down to feet and hands. The Netsiliks, whom I had just left, had a thick layer of indescribable filth and fat on thigh, shin, feet and face, not to speak of ears, throat and neck"; Rasmussen, *The Netsilik Eskimos*, 471. Arnarulunguak had died at Upernavik before I arrived in Thule on my first expedition to North Greenland in 1950–51. Her fame was widespread, and she was said to be beautiful and charming.

40 See photograph in my *Call of the North*, 234–5, in which a hunter sketches a map of his routes.

41 Malaurie, *Call of the North*, 234–5. The photograph evokes the atmosphere of subdued tension in the group.

42 Brief excerpts from these recordings were issued on two LPs: *Chez les Esquimaux Netsilingmiut*; and Jean Malaurie, *Chants et tambours inuit*. Many, unfortunately, remain unissued.

43 Rasmussen, *The Netsilik Eskimos*, 473–4, 485. Cape Brittania lies to the northeast of Montreal Island at the entrance to Chantrey Inlet. It is an occasional winter camp for the Utku but was unoccupied during my visit.

44 Ibid., 473. Baker Lake is at the head of Chesterfield Inlet, 300 kilometres from the Back River estuary; see maps, pp. 5, 198.

45 Ibid., 487.

46 Ibid., 486.

47 Malaurie, *Ultima Thule*, 214–19, 394–5.

48 Discovered in 1742 by the English navigator Christopher Middleton, who concluded that the Northwest Passage was not to be found in this area. In 1821 William Parry confirmed Middleton's report. Industrial whaling began there in the 1860s, with American whalers employing Inuit crews. It is unlikely that the Caribou Inuit engaged in barter on the coast, but rumours travelled fast from group to group.

49 Rasmussen, *The Netsilik Eskimos*, 500.

50 Charles Francis Hall's fascinating interviews with the Inuit on his exploratory voyage to the south end of King William Island (Douglas Bay, Todd Islands) – of which only short excerpts were published – give us an idea of the terror aroused by the presence of two "white" ships in these waters. The entry for 7 December 1864 reads: "Relative to Sir John Franklin's Expedition, mother Ook-bar-loo says (very reservedly – in a way of letting me know of a matter that is a great secret among the Innuits) 'that two annatkos (conjurors [*angekkok*]) of Neitchille [Boothia Peninsula] ankooted so much, that no animal, no game whatsoever would go near the locality of the two ships ... The Innuits wished to live near that place (where the ships were) but could not kill anything for their food. They (the Innuits) really believed that the presence of Koblunas (whites) in that part of the country was the cause of all their (the Innuits') troubles'"; Hall, *Narrative*, 590.

51 Rasmussen, *The Netsilik Eskimos*, 500.

52 Knud Rasmussen, *Report of the Fifth Thule Expedition*, vol. 7, *Observations on the Intellectual Culture*, 23.

53 In August 1960 at Igloolik, I witnessed this tension between Anglicans and Catholics. The two young Catholic hunters paddling the canoe that took me from Igloolik to Jens Munk Island (Kapuivik) refused to set foot on the island. It was a land of heretics, three tents occupied by Anglican walrus hunters. They slept uncomfortably in the canoe before returning to Igloolik the next day.

The American anthropologist and psychologist Jean Briggs reports how in the summer of 1963, a few months after my visit, she visited Back River with a view to studying "the social relationships of shamans"; she had been "assured" that the Utku were pagan and hoped, in a place so far from missionary influence, that she could find practising shamans. After an incident in which she rebuked some white fishermen from the South for breaking a canoe, she was subtly ostracized by the Back River community for her "un-Eskimo volatility" for about three months; Jean L. Briggs, *Never in Anger*, 2–3.

54 But who will attempt such an analysis if not a Western anticolonialist motivated by the utmost respect for the Inuit and attempting to grasp the contemporary existential difficulties that they encounter as they confront the conqueror? Who will help them to become aware of their ethnic and religious uniqueness so that they may rebound and look to the future with optimism? They must be helped with a kind of psychoanalysis to express themselves freely on these religious problems. Nietzsche's polemical tract *On the Genealogy of Morals* is relevant here, as is Rousseau's "Discourse upon the Origin and the Foundation of the Inequality among Mankind," in *The Social Contract; and, the First and Second Discourses*, 122: "man, heretofore free and independent, was now in consequence of a multitude of new wants brought under subjection."

55 Rasmussen, *The Netsilik Eskimos*, 463–4.

56 Richard Harrington, *The Face of the Arctic*.

57 The family allowances were essential to balance the budget. I was given a breakdown at Gjoa Haven. Six of seven families were registered. Monthly allowances ranged from $16 to $70 per month depending on family size. The old-age pension

(starting at age 55) was $65, but because of low life expectancy, few people were entitled to it.

58 Rasmussen, *Report of the Fifth Thule Expedition*, vol. 7, *Observations on the Intellectual Culture*, 9.

59 Ibid., 13.

60 Intertribal warfare in Alaska, particularly between groups on Saint Lawrence Island and in Chukotka, is described in my *Hummocks*, vol. 2, *Alaska*, 29–33.

61 Rasmussen, *Report of the Fifth Thule Expedition*, vol. 7, *Observations on the Intellectual Culture*, 36–7.

62 Ibid., 36.

63 Ibid., 14.

64 Ibid., 33.

65 Report of 22 May 1956 from Spence Bay.

66 Report of 30 June 1961, Gjoa Haven district.

67 Malaurie, *Call of the North*, 232, 236–9.

68 Rasmussen, *Report of the Fifth Thule Expedition*, vol. 7, *Observations on the Intellectual Culture*, 45.

69 Malaurie, *Call of the North*, 234–47.

70 "As I have said, I was only making $185 with the Bay"; Ernie Lyall, *An Arctic Man*, 217.

71 See more details of this analysis in my "Kuujjuak (Fort-Chimo) 1970."

72 Annual report of 22 May 1956 (for 1955).

73 Rasmussen, *The Netsilik Eskimos*, 486.

74 See photographs and captions in my *Call of the North*, 218–61. These nineteen photographs, taken in April and May 1963, are a unique and unimpeachably objective depiction of the most traditionalist Inuit group in the Arctic. See also the legends collected in that volume. I intend to publish my remaining Back River photographs in a subsequent book.

75 Fernand Braudel, *A History of Civilizations*, 17, 23, 29, 35.

76 TP-20-181-22 (vol. 3). Baker Lake, NWT, 4 July 1962. The Officer Commanding, "G" Division, RCM Police. Re: Game Conditions – Baker Lake District.

77 Ibid.

78 I have already narrated my misadventures with certain bureaucrats in Ottawa and how they prevented me from reaching Back River in 1962 as I had planned, even though I was supported to the last by the department's senior officials. A year was lost – disastrously, for my purposes, as another researcher's field season in the same locale had been planned without my knowledge. I have too often heard remarks to the effect that Europe and especially France are provincial and old hat, while the United States, with its prestigious universities, is the future. At any rate, as this case shows, history is often made by self-important pencil pushers. See my *Hummocks*, pocket ed., vol. 1, *De la pierre à l'homme*, 177–8.

79 Malaurie, *Hummocks*, vol. 2, *Alaska*, 29.

80 Marc Tadié, "Perceptions extra-sensorielles," 31–54.

81 Joëlle Rostkowski, *La Conversion inachevée*.

82 Barbara Glowczewski, *Rêves en colère*, 51.

83 Ibid.
84 Jean-Jacques Rousseau, *On the Social Contract*, 157.
85 Jean-Jacques Rousseau, *Social Contract and Discourses*, 208.
86 Jean Starobinski, *Jean-Jacques Rousseau*, 293.
87 Charles Péguy, *Pensées*, 50.
88 Malaurie, *Ultima Thule*, 395.
89 Charles Péguy, *Notre jeunesse*, 30, original emphasis.
90 Malaurie, *Call of the North*, 241.
91 Toolegaak's description of mourning taboos: three days for a deceased woman, four or five days for a man. Hunting is prohibited. Raw meat is eaten before any other food. The widow must refrain from sewing until the warm summer months return. An Inuk who has behaved badly toward the group has his eyes left open in the tomb. Are these rites still observed? The answer is unclear. Although the belief remains, the practice may have died out.
92 There were ten: Ilisuitoq (b. 1919, Catholic), his wife, Sheriak (b. 1939, Anglican), and their daughter (the first case I found of a complex intrafamilial religious configuration, the husband's emigration to Gjoa Haven having been motivated by his conversion to Catholicism); Ilisuitoq's mother Uyarosudja; Sheriak's sisters Ipuitoq and Kuniangna; Kamimalik, Pokangna, and Palla; and Sauga, Antiguar's brother-in-law, whom I met on Perry Island. At Rankin Inlet I met five more émigrés. However, since I did not go to Whale Cove, I was unable to interview the eight émigrés living there.
93 Georges Bernanos, *La Vocation spirituelle*, 240–1.
94 The anthropologist was Jean Briggs. Naturally, I did not want my presence to interfere with her research, so I was unable to winter over at Back River with a view to delving further, in the spirit of the "Annales" school of history to which I belong, into the many ethnohistorical issues raised by my highly promising preliminary expedition. (In passing, my thanks to the staff of the Department of Northern Affairs for their organizational and logistical support.) I trust that I may be forgiven for admitting my annoyance at how this unexpected event interrupted my research in a microcommunity to which I had become profoundly attached.

As one would expect, I read Ms Briggs resulting book, *Never in Anger*, a personal and at times moving work on the behavioural psychology of one family. Regretfully, it does nothing to resolve the complex problems of ethnohistory that I had discerned in 1963, which I hoped to address by spending the winter at close quarters with the people in question.

I have provided some preliminary remarks about these issues in my seminars at the École des Hautes Études en Sciences Sociales (EHESS) and in this chapter, but unfortunately, I was unable to organize a new solo expedition to the Canadian Central Arctic in 1965 and during the years that followed, as I so desired. I was prevented from doing so by my pressing engagements in Alaska, particularly in connection with Inuit autonomy in the Bering Strait. The promise of my 1963–64 winter research project thus turned into a missed opportunity due to an entirely fortuitous event. This ethnic group per se has now vanished, annihilated through relocation and dispersal. Toonee had been right: "Leaving Amujat will be our ruin." Numerous questions raised by this extraordinary – for me, nearly mythic – people will remain unanswered forever. The photos published in my *Call of the North* are a modest tribute to these men and women who welcomed me with such generosity.

Back River is one of the most painful regrets of my scientific career.

95 Piuvkaq, quoted in Rasmussen, *The Netsilik Eskimos*, 511 (in a remarkable chapter devoted to Back River).

96 Fyodor Dostoyevsky, *The Possessed*, 674–5.

97 Jean Baptiste Lamarck, *Zoological Philosophy*, 106.

98 Bernard Cottret, *Histoire de la réforme protestante*, 262.

99 Michael Francis Gibson, *Ces lois inconnues*.

100 Malaurie, *Call of the North*, 241.

101 Annual Report, 30 June 1961.

102 Rasmussen, *Report of the Fifth Thule Expedition*, vol. 7, *Observations on the Intellectual Culture*, 45. The word "frocks," as an English rendering of a Danish word (Rasmussen's notebooks are in Danish), is ambiguous: does it refer to a hooded jacket specifically or to clothing in general? The reality behind this word, as well as any other apparent ambiguities found in Rasmussen's writings, should be analyzed insofar as possible with reference to the original text. This is particularly important when drawing on his work for analysis of sensitive issues such as shamanism. *Traduttore, traditore* ...

103 Malaurie, *Call of the North*, 218–61.

104 Colin Turnbull, *The Mountain People*, 261.

105 Amicale d'Oranienbourg-Sachsenhausen, *Sachso*.

106 Malaurie, *Call of the North*, 238, 250.

107 Ibid., 238–9.

108 The spirit of the Anglican church is that of open-minded Christian humanism; thirty-nine articles represent its foundational declaration. It may be considered a middle way between the various currents of the Reform (Presbyterian, Calvinist, Anglo-Catholic) as set out by Martin Luther and later Philipp Melanchthon (Schwarzerd) (1497–1560). The Anglican Church sees itself as unified not so much by doctrine as by rites. Anglicans practise the sign of the cross, which I saw several times during mass, genuflection (less frequent), and benediction (de rigueur). There are two sacraments: Holy Communion and baptism. The latter is a very important ceremony for the Inuit. In the Roman Catholic version of this rite, they add a Christian name to their name, which is that of their father, the founder of their lineage. I did not attend any communions in these communities since I mainly visited Anglican communities administered by catechists.

109 See, for example, my *The Last Kings*; see also my "Pas à pas vers les Inuit" and, with Jan Borm, "My Hummocks: An Interview with Jean Malaurie."

110 Henri Gouhier, *Bergson et le Christ*, 83.

111 Martin Luther, *Luther's Works*, vol. 44, *The Christian in Society*, 127.

112 "True religion consists in annihilating self before that Universal Being, whom we have so often provoked, and who can justly destroy us at any time"; Blaise Pascal, *Pensées*, 155.

113 During the German Peasants' War of 1524–25, Luther wrote a pamphlet, *Against the Robbing and Murdering Hordes of Peasants*, lending his support to the ensuing brutal repression by the nobility and the church.
114 Cottret, *Histoire de la réforme protestante*, 67.
115 Friedrich Engels, *The Peasant War in Germany*, 62.
116 Malaurie, *Call of the North*, particularly the photos on pages 234–8.
117 Briggs, *Never in Anger*, 59. Another translation is possible, given the anthropologist's admitted difficulty learning Inuktitut. One may suppose that the catechist spoke in a sort of pidgin that I would venture to reconstitute as: "If Inuit not want believe Nakliguhuktuq, Nakliguhuktuq write Cambridge, very big chief, airplane Cambridge whip, make big Inuit boo-boo."
118 Malaurie, *Hummocks*, vol. 2, *Alaska*, 58–82.
119 Lamarck, *Zoological Philosophy*, 134.
120 Jean-Baptiste Lamarck, *Arcticles d'histoire naturelle*.
121 Lamarck, *Zoological Philosophy*, 2.
122 In the years 1950–63 Fort Ross, Josephine Bay, Lord Mayor Bay, Thom Bay, Levesque Harbor, Cresswell Bay, Back River, Avatoocheak, and Brentford Bay were temporarily inhabited in the winter or the summer, as were, less continuously, the Franklin area, Elizabeth Harbour, Nudlukta, Tasmania Islands, Kayashukjuak, Murchison River, Felix Harbour, Netsilik Lake, and Shepherd Bay. In 2001 the entire Inuit populations of Boothia (828) and King William Island (835) were concentrated in Spence Bay and Gjoa Haven, respectively.

APPENDIX TWO

1 Subsequently, my friend Inuterssuaq Ulloriaq (b. 1906), one of my best respondents in Thule, published *Beretningen om Qillarsuaq*, an autobiographical work.
2 Abram Kardiner, *The Individual and His Society*.

APPENDIX THREE

1 Gould to Lotz, 1 September 1967, in Glenn Gould, *Glenn Gould: Selected Letters*, 104–5.
2 Michel Schneider, *Glenn Gould, piano solo*, 18.
3 Ibid., 169–70.
4 Malaurie, *Ultima Thule*, 8.
5 Glenn Gould and Jonathan Cott, *Conversations with Glenn Gould*, 104.

APPENDIX FOUR

1 Bruno Monsaingeon, "Introduction," in Glenn Gould, *Écrits*, vol. 1, *Le dernier puritain*, 20. Mr Monsaingeon, a violinist and filmmaker of great talent, produced seven black and white films – each 52 minutes in length – with and about Glenn Gould for French television (ORTF). These films are divided into two series. The first series, composed of four films directed by François Ribadeau-

Dumas with Jacqueline Vischkoff assistant directing, is titled "Musical Paths"; the second, directed by Mr Monsaingeon, is titled "Glenn Gould plays Bach." The first series as well as the first two films of the second series were shot in Toronto, while the last film was shot in New York.

In a strange coincidence, I was assisted shortly thereafter by Ms Vischkoff on my own series of seven films, titled "Inuit," which were made for ORTF and Antenne 2. These were shot in the Canadian Arctic and Alaska (November–December 1974), Greenland (September 1976), and Siberia (November 1976).

Ms Vischkoff's vivid recounting of her collaboration with Gould, of whom she is a most fervent admirer, enlivened the long evenings that we spent together in the Inuit houses – an experience that I still recall with emotion. I am most grateful to her for her consummate skill and genuine good will.

2 Glenn Gould embarked on his first European tour in 1957, playing eight concerts in Moscow (7, 8, 11, 12 May) and four in Leningrad (14, 16, 18, 19 May). The Canadian Press presented this Soviet tour as an affair of state, for Gould was the first North American personality to be invited by the Soviet Union.

Not only were all 1,300 seats of the Leningrad Philharmonic filled, but an additional 1,100 concertgoers were admitted on a standing-room-only basis; every last recess of the room was occupied. His manager, Walter Homburger, telegraphed home to the *Toronto Star* that it was a show he would not soon forget. The orchestra members stood in the wings listening during his solos and applauded when he came out for a bow.

My friend Valeriy Selivanov, assistant director of the Hermitage Museum, recently told me that he attended this extraordinary concert and saw many people of all ages in tears.

3 Gould to Kitty Gvozdeva, 6 September 1965, in Glenn Gould, *Glenn Gould: Selected Letters*, 80.

4 Glenn Gould and Jonathan Cott, *Conversations with Glenn Gould*, 104.

5 Glenn Gould, *Glenn Gould's Solitude Trilogy*, sound recording.

6 I must mention – and this will come as a surprise to many – that the USSR, the standard-bearer of atheistic dialectical materialism, once attempted such an encounter at the summit of the world. No doubt Glenn Gould would have been intrigued.

I could not resist including in one of the films of my "Inuit" series, *The Siberian Eskimos*, a strange scene taken from a Soviet film, which some viewers found comical (stupidly, I thought): on the shore of the Bering Strait, a large, besuited Russian orchestra plays Vivaldi for a group of quiet Eskimos dressed in animal skins, while sled dogs meander about to the sounds of violins, cellos, harp, and rolling waves; see photo 94 in my *Hummocks*, vol. 2, *Alaska*.

Logistically, Glenn Gould's trip to the Great North would have been complex, yet it was within the means of a great polar nation such as Canada to facilitate it.

APPENDIX FIVE

1 Michel Schneider, *Glenn Gould, piano solo*, 135.

bibliography

Amicale d'Oranienbourg-Sachsenhausen. *Sachso: Au cœur du système concentrationnaire nazi.* Paris: Plon/Terre Humaine, 1990.

Amundsen, Roald. *Le passage du Nord-ouest.* Trans. Charles Rabot. Paris: Hachette, 1909.

– *Roald Amundsen's "The North West Passage"; Being the Record of a Voyage of Exploration of the Ship "Gjöa" 1903–1907, by Roald Amundsen, with a Supplement by First Lieutenant Hansen, Vice-Commander of the Expedition; with About One Hundred and Thirty-Nine Illustrations and Three Maps.* 2 vols. c.1908. Reprint, London: A. Constable, 1966.

Back, George. *Narrative of the Arctic Land Expedition to the Mouth of the Great Fish River, and Along the Shores of the Arctic Ocean, in the Years 1833, 1834, and 1835.* London: J. Murray, 1836.

Balikci, Asen. *The Netsilik Eskimo.* Garden City, NY: Natural History Press, 1970.

Bastide, Roger. *The African Religions of Brazil: Toward a Sociology of the Interpenetration of Civilizations.* Trans. Helen Sebba. Baltimore: Johns Hopkins University Press, 1978.

Bazin, Étienne. *Les lettres d'oncle Étienne.* Dijon: N.p., 1974.

Beattie, Owen, and John Geiger. *Frozen in Time: Unlocking the Secrets of the Franklin Expedition.* Saskatoon: Western Producer Prairie Books, 1988.

– and Roger Amy. "A Report on Present Investigations into the Loss of the Third Franklin Expedition (1845–1848), Emphasizing the 1984 Research on Beechey Island." *Inter-Nord* 19 (1990): 77–86.

Bernanos, Georges. *La Vocation spirituelle de la France.* Paris: Plon, 1975.

Birket-Smith, Kaj. *Report of the Fifth Thule Expedition, 1921-1924: The Danish Expedition to Arctic North America in Charge of Knud Rasmussen.* Vol. 5, no. 1, *The Caribou Eskimos: Material and Social Life and their Cultural Position.* New York: AMS Press, 1976.

Brack, D.M., and D. McIntosh. *Keewatin Mainland Area Economic Survey and Regional Appraisal.* Ottawa: Projects Section, Industrial Division, Department of Northern Affairs and National Resources, 1963.

Braudel, Fernand. *A History of Civilizations.* Trans. Richard Mayne. New York: Allen Lane, 1994.

Briggs, Jean L. *Never in Anger: Portrait of an Eskimo Family.* Cambridge, MA: Harvard University Press, 1970.

Burchard of Worms. "Decretum" 19.5. Migne *Patrologia Latina* 140: 959–60.

Canada, Advisory Commission on the Development of Government in the Northwest Territories. *Report.* Ottawa: 1966.

Canada, Railway Lands Branch. *The Unexploited West: A Compilation of All of the Authentic Information Available at the Present Time as to the Natural Resources of the Unexploited Regions of Northern Canada*, by Ernest J. Chambers. Ottawa: printed by J. de L. Tache, 1914.

Chamberlain, Joseph. *Foreign and Colonial Speeches.* London and Manchester: G. Routledge, 1897.

Chateaubriand, François-René, vicomte de. *Memoirs.* Trans. Robert Baldick. New York: Knopf, 1961.

Chez les Esquimaux Netsilingmiut: Arctique central canadien. Sound recording. Paris: Le Chant du Monde, 1969.

Chitty, Dennis. *Do Lemmings Commit Suicide? Beautiful Hypotheses and Ugly Facts.* Oxford: Oxford University Press, 1996.

Clastres, Pierre. *Chronicle of the Guayaki Indians.* Trans. Paul Auster. New York: Zone Books; Cambridge, MA: distributed by MIT Press, 1998.

Commission du Nunavik. *Partageons: Tracer la voie vers un gouvernement pour le Nunavik: Rapport de la Commission du Nunavik.* Québec City: 2001.

Condorcet, Jean-Antoine-Nicolas de Caritat, marquis de. *Cinq mémoires sur l'instruction publique.* Ed. and comp. Charles Coutel and Catherine Kintzler. Paris: GF-Flammarion, 1994.

Cook, James. *The Journals of Captain James Cook on His Voyages of Discovery.* Vol. 2, *The Voyage of the Resolution and Adventure.* Ed. J.C. Beaglehole. Cambridge, UK: Cambridge University Press for the Hakluyt Society, 1955.

Cottret, Bernard. *Histoire de la réforme protestante: Luther, Calvin, Wesley, XVIe-XVIIIe siècle.* Paris: Perrin, 2001.

Curley, Tagak. "Policy Issues in Nunavut." *Inter-Nord* 16 (1982): 407–11.

Dailey, Robert C., and Lois A. Dailey. *The Eskimo of Rankin Inlet: A Preliminary Report*. Ottawa: Northern Co-ordination and Research Centre, Department of Northern Affairs and National Resources, 1961.

De Gaulle, Charles. "Letter to Daniel Johnson, 8 September 1967." In *Lettres, notes et carnets*, vol. 11, *July 1966–April 1969*, 132–3. Paris: Plon, 1980–88.

de Poncins, Gontran. *Eskimos: Photographs and Text by Gontran de Poncins*. New York: Hastings House, [1949].

– *Kabloona*. New York: Reynal and Hitchcock, 1941.

de Rosny, Éric. *Healers in the Night*. Trans. Robert R. Barr. Maryknoll, NY: Orbis Books, 1985.

Dostoyevsky, Fyodor. *The Possessed*. Trans. Constance Garnett. New York: Modern Library, 1936.

Douzou, Pierre. *Les Bricoleurs du septième jour: Nouveaux regards entomologiques*. Paris: Fayard, 1985.

Du Camp, Maxime. *Souvenirs littéraires de Maxime Du Camp, 1822–1894*. Paris: Hachette, 1962.

Duvignaud, Jean. *Le Pandémonium du présent: Idées sages idées folles*. Paris: Plon, 1998.

Eger, F.H., comp. *Eskimo Inuit Games: Book One*. Vancouver: X-Press, [1980?].

Engels, Friedrich. *The Peasant War in Germany*. Trans. Moissaye J. Olgin. New York: International Publishers, 1966.

Fafard, Eugène. *Prayers and Hymns*. Ottawa: Institut de missiologie de l'Université d'Ottawa, 1957.

Flaubert, Gustave. *The Letters of Gustave Flaubert*. 2 vols. Ed. and trans. Francis Steegmuller. Cambridge, MA: Harvard University Press, 1980–82.

Fondation française d'études nordiques. *Développement économique de l'Arctique et avenir des sociétés esquimaudes; débats du 4e colloque international de la Fondation française d'études nordiques, Le Havre-Rouen, 24, 25, 26, et 27 novembre 1969*. Le Havre: Fondation Française d'Études Nordiques, 1972.

– *Le pétrole et le gaz arctiques: Problèmes et perspectives = Arctic Oil and Gas: Problems and Possibilities, Fondation française d'études nordiques. Ve congrès international. Le Havre, 2–5 mai 1973. Rapports scientifiques*. Ed. Jean Malaurie. Paris: Mouton, 1975.

– *Le pétrole et le gaz arctiques: Problemes et perspectives: débats = Arctic Oil and Gas: Problems and Possibilities: Discussion*. Ed. Jean Malaurie. Le Havre: Fondation française d'études nordiques, 1975.

– *Le Peuple esquimau aujourd'hui et demain: Débats*. Ed. Jean Malaurie. Le Havre: Fondation française d'études nordiques, 1972.

– *Le Peuple esquimau aujourd'hui et demain = The Eskimo People To-Day and To-Morrow, Quatrième congrès international de la Fondation française d'études nordiques, Rapports scientifiques*. Ed. Jean Malaurie. Paris: Mouton, 1973.

Gibson, Michael Francis. *Ces lois inconnues: Pour une anthropologie du sens de la vie*. Paris: Métaillié, 2002.

Gide, André. *The Counterfeiters*. Trans. Dorothy Bussy. New York: Modern Library, 1955.

Glowczewski, Barbara. *Rêves en colère: Alliances aborigènes dans le nord-ouest australien*. Paris: Plon/Terre Humaine, 2004.
Gouhier, Henri. *Bergson et le Christ des Évangiles*. Paris: Vrin, 1999.
Gould, Glenn. *Glenn Gould: Selected Letters*. Ed. and comp. John P.L. Roberts and Ghyslaine Guertin. Toronto: Oxford University Press, 1992.
– *Glenn Gould's Solitude Trilogy: Three Sound Documentaries*. Sound recording. Toronto: CBC Records, 1992.
– and Jonathan Cott. *Conversations with Glenn Gould*. Boston: Little, Brown, 1984.
Haldas, Georges. *Passion et mort de Michel Servet*. Lausanne: L'Âge d'homme, 1975.
Hall, Charles Francis. *Narrative of the Second Arctic Expedition Made by Charles F. Hall: His Voyages to Repulse Bay, Sled Journeys to the Straits of Fury and Hecla and to King William's Land, and Residence among the Eskimos, during the Years 1864–'69*. Ed. J.E. Nourse. Washington: Published for US Naval Observatory by Government Printing Office, 1879.
Hampaté Bâ, Amadou. *The Fortunes of Wangrin*. Trans. Aina Pavollini Taylor. Ibadan: New Horn Press, 1987.
Hanke, Lewis. *All Mankind Is One: A Study of the Disputation Between Bartolomé de Las Casas and Juan Ginés de Sepúlveda in 1550 on the Intellectual and Religious Capacity of the American Indians*. DeKalb: Northern Illinois University Press, [1974].
Harrington, Richard. *The Face of the Arctic*. New York: Henry Shuman, 1952.
Huctin, Jean-Michel. "Eskimooq Imminorneq." *Atuagagdliutit/Grønlandsposten*, 2 March 2006, 12–13.
– "Jean Malaurie: nen eskimo begar ikke slvmord." *Atuagagdliutit/Grønlandsposten*, 3 March 2006, 14–15.
Huish, Robert. *The Last Voyage of Capt. Sir John Ross, R.N. Knt. to the Arctic Regions: for the Discovery of a North West Passage; Performed in the Years 1829–30–31–32 and 33: to which is Prefixed an Abridgement of the Former Voyages of Captns. Ross, Parry, & Other Celebrated Navigators to the Northern Latitudes: Compiled from Authentic Information and Original Documents. Transmitted by William Light, Purser's Steward to the Expedition: Illustrated by Engravings from Drawings Taken on the Spot*. London: J. Saunders, 1835.
Jacqueline, Bernard. "Les instructions de la S.C. 'de propaganda fide' aux vicaires apostoliques des royaumes du Tonkin et de Cochinchine (1659)." *Nouvelle Revue Historique de Droit Français et Étranger* 48 (1970): 624–31.
"Jean Malaurie: 50 ans de recherches au Groenland et dans l'Arctique." *Atuagagdliutit/Grønlandsposten*, February 2006.
Jenness, Diamond. *Eskimo Administration*. 5 vols. Montreal: Arctic Institute of North America, 1962–68.
Kardiner, Abram. *The Individual and His Society: The Psychodynamics of Primitive Social Organization*. New York: Columbia University Press, 1939.
Lamarck, Jean Baptiste. *Zoological Philosophy: An Exposition with Regard to the Natural History of Animals*. Trans. Hugh Elliott. Chicago: University of Chicago Press, 1984.
Lamarck, Jean-Baptiste. *Arcticles d'histoire naturelle*. Paris: Belin, 1991.

Leprieur, François. *Quand Rome condamne: Dominicains et prêtres-ouvriers.* Paris: Plon/Terre Humaine, 1989.

Luther, Martin. *Luther's Works.* Vol. 44, *The Christian in Society.* Saint Louis, MS: Concordia, [1955–86].

Lyall, Ernie. *An Arctic Man.* Edmonton: Hurtig, 1979.

Mackenzie Valley Pipeline Inquiry. *Northern Frontier, Northern Homeland: The Report of the Mackenzie Valley Pipeline Inquiry.* 2 vols. Ottawa: Supply and Services, 1977.

Maeterlinck, Maurice. *The Life of the Bee.* Trans. Alfred Sutro. New York: Dodd, Mead, 1967.

Maguire, Rochfort. *The Journal of Rochfort Maguire, 1852–1854: Two Years at Point Barrow, Alaska, aboard HMS Plover in the Search for Sir John Franklin.* Ed. John Bockstoce. London: Hakluyt Society, 1988.

Malaurie, Jean. *Call of the North: An Explorer's Journey to the North Pole.* Trans. Molly Stevens. New York: Harry N. Abrams, 2001.

– *Chants et tambours inuit: De Thulé au détroit de Béring.* Sound recording. Paris: Ocora (Radio France), 1988.

– "Du droit des minorités esquimaudes nord-américaines et des notions implicites au diagnostic de sous-développement." *Inter-Nord* 11 (1970): 296–309.

– "A French Homage to Dr. Diamond Jenness." *Inter-Nord* 19 (1990): 185–7.

– *Hummocks: Relief de mémoire.* Vol. 1, *Nord Groenland: Arctique centrale canadienne.* Paris: Plon/Terre Humaine, 1999.

– *Hummocks: Relief de mémoire.* Vol. 2, *Alaska: Tchoukotka sibérienne.* Paris: Plon/Terre Humaine, 1999.

– *Hummocks.* Pocket ed., revised and augmented. Vol. 1, bk 1, *De la pierre à l'homme: Avec les Inuit de Thule.* Paris: Plon/Terre Humaine, 2004.

– *Hummocks.* Pocket ed., revised and augmented. Vol. 2, bk 1, *Alaska, avec les chasseurs de baleine, mer de Bering.* Paris: Plon/Terre Humaine, 2004.

– "Igloolik Report." Ottawa: Northern Co-ordination and Research Centre, Department of Northern Affairs and National Resources, 1970.

– "Jésus-Christ indianisé." Preface to Joëlle Rostkowski, *La Conversion inachevée,* 11–19. Paris: Albin Michel, 1998.

– "Knud Rasmussen, 1879–1933: L'ethnologie au pouvoir." *Inter-Nord* 17 (1983): 153–65.

– "Kuujjuak (Fort-Chimo) 1970." *Inter-Nord* 20 (2003): 305–28.

– *The Last Kings of Thule: With the Polar Eskimos as They Face Their Destiny.* Trans. Adrienne Foulke. New York: Dutton, 1982.

– "Le développement industriel permettra-t-il au Groenland de rester groenlandais?" *Inter-Nord* 10 (1968): 105–18.

– *Les derniers rois de Thulé: Avec les Esquimaux polaires, face à leur destin.* 5th ed. Paris: Plon/Terre Humaine, 1989.

– *Les Esquimaux canadiens et le Canada: L'incommunicabilité.* Documentary film. 52 min. Paris: INA, 1980.

– *Les Esquimaux d'Asie et l'Union sovietique: Aux sources de la pensée inuit.* Documentary film. 52 min. Paris: INA, 1980.

- "Les Esquimaux du Keewatin intérieur: Un tragique bilan et un obscur destin." *Inter-Nord* 10 (1968): 258–64.
- "Les peuples arctiques: Six études historiques de politique administrative." *Inter-Nord* 16 (1982): 383–4.
- "Pas à pas vers les Inuit." In Jean Malaurie and Dominique Sewane, eds, *De la vérité en ethnologie: Séminaire de Jean Malaurie, 2000–2001*, 107–48. Paris: Economica, 2002.
- "Promotion indigène au Nouveau-Québec." *Inter-Nord* 10 (1968): 119–21.
- *The Siberian Eskimos and the Soviet Union*. Documentary film. 52 min. Paris: INA, 1980.
- "Sur l'asymétrie des versants dans l'île de Disko, Greenland." *Comptes rendus hebdomadaires des séances de l'Académie des Sciences* 234 (1952): 1461–2.
- *Ultima Thule: Explorers and Natives in the Polar North*. Trans. Willard Wood and Anthony Roberts. New York and London: Norton, 2003.

–, Léon Tabah, and Jean Sutter. "L'isolat des Esquimaux de Thulé (Groenland)." *Population* 7, no. 4 (1952): 675–92.

- and Jan Borm. "My Hummocks: An Interview with Jean Malaurie." *Studies in Travel Writing* 5 (2001): 106–29.
- and Jacques Rousseau, eds. *Du Nouveau-Québec au Nunavik, 1964–2004: Une fragile autonomie*. Paris: Economica, 2005.
- and Jacques Rousseau, eds. *Le Nouveau-Québec: Contribution à l'étude de l'occupation humaine*. Paris: Mouton, 1964.

Marsh, Winifred Petchey. *People of the Willow: The Padlimiut Tribe of the Caribou Eskimos*. Toronto: Oxford University Press, 1976.

McGoogan, Kenneth. *Fatal Passage: The Untold Story of John Rae, the Arctic Adventurer Who Discovered the Fate of Franklin*. Toronto: HarperFlamingo, 2001.

McKinlay, William L. *Karluk: The Great Untold Story of Arctic Exploration*. London: Weidenfeld and Nicolson, 1976.

M'Clintock, Francis Leopold. *The Voyages of the 'Fox' in the Arctic Seas: A Narrative of the Discovery of the Fate of Sir John Franklin and His Companions*. Boston: Ticknor and Fields, 1860.

Michelet, Jules. *The People*. Trans. John P. McKay. Urbana: University of Illinois Press, [1973].

Monsaingeon, Bruno. "Introduction." In Glenn Gould, *Écrits*, vol. 1, *Le dernier puritain*, ed., trans., and comp. Bruno Monsaingeon, 9-20. Paris: Fayard, 1983.

Morice, Adrian G. *Thawing Out the Eskimo*. 2nd ed. Trans. Mary T. Loughlin. Boston: Society for the Propagation of the Faith, 1943.

Muir, John. *Travels in Alaska*. Boston and New York: Houghton Mifflin, 1915.

Newman, John Henry. *The Arians of the Fourth Century*. London: Longmans, 1919.

Nietzsche, Friedrich Wilhelm. *On the Genealogy of Morals*. Trans. Walter Kaufmann and R.J. Hollingdale. *Ecce homo*, ed. and trans. Walter Kaufmann. New York: Vintage Books, 1989.

Pallu, Francis, and Pierre Lambert de la Motte. *Monita ad Missionarios: Instructions aux Missionnaires de la S. Congrégation de la Propagande*. Paris: Archives des Missions Etrangères de Paris, 2000.

Pascal, Blaise. *Pensées and the Provincial Letters*. Trans. W.F. Trotter. New York: Modern Library, 1941.

Péguy, Charles. *Basic Verities: Prose and Poetry*. Trans. Ann and Julian Green. New York: Pantheon Books, 1943.

– *Notre jeunesse*. Paris: Gallimard, 1967.

– *Pensées*. Paris: Gallimard, [1934].

Pelly, David. "Footprints in New Snow: The March toward Nunavut." *Above and Beyond* 7, no. 3 (Summer 1995): 7–10.

Phillips, R.A.J. *Canada's North*. Toronto: MacMillan, 1967.

Piaget, Jean. *The Science of Education and the Psychology of the Child*. Trans. Derek Coltman. New York: Orion Press, 1970.

Rasmussen, Knud. *Report of the Fifth Thule Expedition, 1921–1924: The Danish Expedition to Arctic North America in Charge of Knud Rasmussen*. Vol. 7, *Observations on the Intellectual Culture of the Caribou Eskimos*. New York: AMS Press, 1976.

– *Report of the Fifth Thule Expedition, 1921–1924: The Danish Expedition to Arctic North America in Charge of Knud Rasmussen*. Vol. 8, *The Netsilik Eskimos: Social Life and Spiritual Culture*. New York: AMS Press, 1976.

Ribeiro, Darcy. *Carnets indiens: Avec les indiens Urubus-Kaapor, Brésil*. Trans. Jacques Thiériot. Paris: Plon/Terre Humaine, 2002.

Richard E. Lee, Jr, and David Denlinger. *Insects at Low Temperature*. New York: Chapman and Hall, 1991.

Rostkowski, Joëlle. *La Conversion inachevée*. Paris: Albin Michel, 1998.

Ross, John, Sir. *Narrative of a Second Voyage in Search of a North-West Passage and of a Residence in the Arctic Regions during the Years 1829, 1830, 1831, 1832, 1833*. Paris: Baudry's European Library, 1835.

– *Observations on a Work, Entitled "Voyages of Discovery and Research within the Arctic Regions," by Sir John Barrow, Bart. Aetat. 82, Being a Refutation of the Numerous Misrepresentations Contained in That Volume*. London and Edinburgh: Blackwood, 1846.

Ross, M.J. *Polar Pioneers: John Ross and James Clark Ross*. Montreal and Kingston: McGill-Queen's University Press, 1994.

Ross, W. Gillies. *This Distant and Unsurveyed Country: A Woman's Winter at Baffin Island, 1857–1858*. Montreal and Kingston: McGill-Queen's University Press, 1997.

Rousseau, Jean-Jacques. *On the Social Contract, with Geneva Manuscript and Political Economy*. Ed. Roger D. Masters. Trans. Judith R. Masters. New York: St Martin's, 1978.

– *Social Contract and Discourses*. Trans. G.D.H. Cole. New York: E.P. Dutton, 1950.

– *The Social Contract, and the First and Second Discourses*. Ed. Susan Dunn. New Haven, CT, and London: Yale University Press, 2002.

Royal Commission on Aboriginal Peoples. *Report*. 5 vols. Ottawa: 1996.

Schneider, Michel. *Glenn Gould, piano solo*. Paris: Gallimard, 1988.

Schwatka, Frederick. *The Long Arctic Search: The Narrative of Lieutenant Frederick Schwatka, U.S.A., 1878–1880, Seeking the Records of the Lost Franklin Expedition*. Ed. Edouard A. Stackpole. Mystic, CT: Marine Historical Association, 1965.

Servetus, Michael. *Christianismi restitutio: Totius ecclesiae apostolicae est ad sua limina vocatio, in integrum restituta cognitione Dei, fidei Christi, iustificationis nostrae, regenerationis baptismi, et caenae domini manducationis; restitutio denique nobis regno caelesti, Babylonis impiae captivitate soluta, et Antichristo cum finis penitus destructo.* 1553. Reprint, Nuremberg: N.p., 1790.

Søby, Regitze Margrethe. "Rink, un visionnaire: Son action pour un Greenland groenlandais." *Inter-Nord* 18 (1987): 121–30.

Special Representative for Constitutional Development in the Northwest Territories. *Report.* Ottawa: 1980.

Starobinski, Jean. *Jean-Jacques Rousseau: Transparency and Obstruction.* Trans. Arthur Goldhammer. Chicago: University of Chicago Press, 1988.

Stonehouse, Bernard. *Animals of the Arctic: The Ecology of the Far North.* London, Ward Lock, 1971.

Tadié, Marc. "Perceptions extra-sensorielles des populations primitives." In Jean Malaurie and Dominique Sewane, eds, *De la vérité en ethnologie: Séminaire de Jean Malaurie, 2000–2001*, 31–54. Paris: Economica, 2002.

Talayesva, Don C. *Sun Chief: The Autobiography of a Hopi Indian.* Ed. Leo W. Simmons. New Haven: Yale University Press, 1942.

Tester, Frank James and Peter Kulchyski. *Tammarniit (Mistakes): Inuit Relocation in the Eastern Arctic, 1939–63.* Vancouver: University of British Columbia Press, 1994.

Turnbull, Colin. *The Mountain People.* New York: Simon and Schuster, [1972].

Turquetil, Arsène, Mgr. "Au Pays des Esquimaux." *Les Cloches de Saint-Boniface* 25, no. 6 (1926): 128.

Ulloriaq, Inuterssuaq. *Beretningen om Qillarsuaq, og hans lange rejse fra Canada til Nordgrønland i 1860'erne.* Copenhagen: N.p., 1985.

von Goethe, Johann Wolfgang. *Conversations of Goethe with Eckermann and Soret.* Trans. J. Oxenford. London: G. Bell, 1883.

– *Goethe's Theory of Colours.* Trans. Charles Lock Eastlake. London: Cass, 1967.

Watt, Charlie. "Message du sénateur Charlie Watt à l'occasion de l'édition de ce numéro d'*Inter-Nord* relatif au Nunavik." *Inter-Nord* 20 (2003): 304.

Weil, Simone. *Gravity and Grace.* Trans. Arthur Wills. New York: Putnam, 1952.

index